Die Twice

Die Twice

TWO CRIME NOVELS IN ONE

THE BUSINESS OF DYING

AND

THE MURDER EXCHANGE

SIMON KERNICK

ST. MARTIN'S MINOTAUR

NEW YORK

www.minotaurbooks.com

ISBN 0-312-35981-0
EAN 978-0-312-35981-2

The Business of Dying was originally published in Great Britain by Bantam Press, a division of Transworld Publishers, in 2002

The Murder Exchange was originally published in Great Britain by Bantam Press, a division of Transworld Publishers, in 2003

First St. Martin's Griffin Edition: May 2006

10 9 8 7 6 5 4 3 2 1

FOREWORD

by Lee Child

What's up with English crime fiction?

It's a question that gets asked with some regularity, and right now—early 2006—it's a newly relevant question, because our genre's Third Age is drawing inexorably to a close. A century ago the First Age was all about Arthur Conan Doyle and Sherlock Holmes. In hindsight we see that the Second Age—in full flower seventy years ago—was codominated by Agatha Christie and Dorothy Sayers. Then, perhaps thirty years later, the Third Age took over, with Ruth Rendell and P. D. James hitting their magisterial strides. For a hundred years, very little was published in the genre that didn't owe practically everything to one of those five authors. Sleuths that were amateur, or brainy, or aristocratic, or "more than" mere policemen, or eccentric, or unlikely, or who had arcane hobbies and enthusiasms . . . we've been there and done that. And what a ride it was. But now, with the grand dames—literally—Rendell and James on their last lap, what comes next?

Or, what's up with English crime fiction?

The same things that are up with England itself, really. Three factors are becoming increasingly massive over there—the nation is more than ever metrocentric, more than ever multicultural, and less than ever dominated by class.

England has in fact always been completely dominated by London. It's a small country with a huge capital city. It's a fact of life inside the country and out. People in the United States hear that I'm from England, and their next question is usually, "Which part of London did you live in?" But now the phenomenon is even greater than ever.

And London (and therefore England, remember) is now a huge ethnic mosaic, in my experience easily rivaling New York City for diversity. It's another fact of life, so well accepted now that it's no longer even worthy of notice or comment.

London is now an overwhelmingly middle-class city, which in traditional English terms means no class at all. Birth and accent mean very little there anymore. When I opened my first bank account—too many years ago to happily contemplate—you could pretty much guarantee that a bank manager would be white, from sturdy English stock, and educated at one of a narrow band of schools. Now you could pretty much guarantee that she wouldn't be any of those things.

The Fourth Age of English crime fiction writers grew up with these changes. They've internalized them. To their elders, class was always an issue. Stock, semicomic stereotypes were plucked from the lower orders and paraded for our smug amusement. Lord Peter Wimsey could quell a street riot with his accent alone. And wasn't he wonderful to accept a middle-class Scotland Yard Inspector as his brother-in-law! Faint but clear echoes of the same attitudes are clearly audible in the bucolic fantasy that is Kingsmarkham.

Fourth Age writers are past all that. That class is a dead issue is beyond taken for granted by them.

Their elders put people of color and non-English ethnicity into crime fiction from the start, but mostly as curiosities, often as villains, and never quite to be trusted. Fourth Age writers are past all that. Their casts of characters are as instinctively multicultural as the London phone book.

And their elders usually glamorized London itself: Scotland Yard was presented as an effortless center of excellence in comparison to dull provincial capabilities. "They've called in Scotland Yard" was as great an accolade as a rural crime could ever earn. Addresses in London were chosen for their glitter: Piccadilly and Belgravia—or maybe Bloomsbury, if some real sense of edge was required.

Fourth Age writers are past all that. London is where life happens, nothing more, nothing less, on the outskirts, near the M25 Beltway, out at Heathrow, in parts we've never heard of, but should have.

Fourth Age writers have moved on. And we should move on with them. Perhaps with Simon Kernick in particular, because he might just be the best of them. I've read all his books, purely as a fan. They've got great plots, great dialogue, great action, and some spectacular violence. But what strikes me most is how they're rooted in a kind of effortless modern authenticity. They're real. They're what England is today. In fact, all the above musing was generated by one simple question I asked myself: "How does he *do* that?"

So, what's up with English crime fiction? Simon Kernick is, that's what.

The Business of Dying
SIMON KERNICK

 St. Martin's Minotaur ⚏ New York

For Sally

Thanks to all those who helped in both the writing
and the publication of this book.

You know who you are.

Part One

INTRODUCING THE DEAD

1

There's a true story that goes like this. A few years back a thirty-two-year-old man abducts a ten-year-old girl from the street near her house. He takes her back to his dingy bedsit, ties her to a bed, and subjects her to a brutal hour-long sex ordeal. It might have been a lot worse had the walls not been paper thin. One of the neighbours hears the screams, phones the police, and they come and knock the door down. The girl is rescued, although apparently she still bears the scars, and the perpetrator is arrested. Seven months later he goes on trial and his lawyer gets him off on a technicality. Apparently she takes the legal view that it's better that ten guilty men go free than one innocent one's imprisoned. He returns to the area where he committed the crime and lives the life of a free man. The lawyer gets her money, courtesy of the tax-payer, as well as the congratulations of her partners on a worthy performance. They probably even take her out for a celebration drink. Meanwhile, every parent in a two-mile radius of this guy is living in fear. The police try to defuse the situation by saying they'll keep a good watch on him, but admit there's nothing else they can do. As always, they appeal for calm.

Three months later, the girl's dad gets caught pouring petrol through the guy's letterbox. The police, for once, have been true to their word and are actually watching the place. He's arrested, charged with arson and attempted murder, and remanded in custody. The local newspaper sets up a campaign to free him and starts a petition that gets something like twenty thousand signatures. Predictably the powers-that-be ignore it, interest fades, and then, before his case comes to trial, the dad hangs himself in his cell. Is this the tale of a progressive, forward-looking society, or one that's about to go down the pan? You tell me.

But the moral of the story, that's easier. If you're going to kill someone, plan it.

9.01 p.m. We were sitting in the rear car park of the Traveller's Rest Hotel. It was a typical English November night: dark, cold and wet. Not the best time to be out working, but who can choose their hours these days? The Traveller's Rest didn't look very restful at all. It was one of those modern redbrick structures with loud lighting, revolving doors, and that curse of modern times, a weekly karaoke night. The one thing going for it was the fact that the front car park had been shut for resurfacing. This meant our quarry would have to come round the back, away from the main entrance, and hopefully away from any stray civilians. Would they smell a rat? I doubted it. Not until it was too late anyway.

I hate the waiting. It's the worst part. It gives you too much time to think. So I lit a cigarette and took a long but guilty drag. Danny wrinkled his nose but he didn't say anything. He doesn't like smoking but he's not the kind to make a big deal about it. He's a tolerant sort. We'd been talking earlier about this case of the 'alleged' paedophile and Danny had been the one supporting the lawyer's ten guilty-men argument, which was typical of him. And bullshit too. Why the suffering of many is seen as being preferable to the suffering of one is beyond me. It's like running a TV station where twenty million viewers want to see gameshows and two million want to see operas, and only showing operas. If the people who believed it ever ran a business, it'd go bust in a day.

But I like Danny. And I trust him. We've worked together a long time and we know each other's capabilities. And that, in our line of business, is the key.

He opened the driver's side window to let some air in and I shivered against the cold. It really was a shitty night.

'Personally, I'd have gone after the lawyer,' I said.

'What?'

'If I was that girl's dad, I would have gone for the lawyer rather than the rapist.'

'Why? What good would that have done?'

'Because there's an argument that the rapist couldn't help what he did, that his urges were just too much to handle. I'd still cut his balls off, but that's not the point. The point is, the lawyer had the choice not to defend him. She was an intelligent, rational woman. She knew what he'd done and still she did all in her power to put him back on the streets. Hers was therefore the greatest crime.'

'I don't understand that argument at all.'

'The greatest evil in the world comes not from those who perpetrate it, but from those who excuse it.'

Danny shook his head like he couldn't believe what he was hearing. 'Jesus, Dennis, you're beginning to sound like some sort of Angel of Death. You want to calm down a little. It's not as if you're whiter than white yourself.'

Which was true. I wasn't. But I consider myself to have principles – codes of conduct to which I strictly adhere –

and that, I felt, gave me the justification to say my piece.

I was about to tell Danny this when the radio crackled into life.

'All right, they're here,' hissed the disembodied voice. 'Black Cherokee, three occupants. It's them.'

Danny started the engine while I slid silently out of the car, flicked the cigarette away, and walked towards the spot where the Cherokee would appear, knowing that this was going to be the one and only chance I was going to get.

There was a clank as it hit the speed ramp, then it came round the side of the main building and drove slowly into the car park, looking for a place to stop. I broke into a jog, waving my hands to get the driver's attention. In my Barbour jacket and shirt and tie, I looked every inch the harassed businessman.

The Cherokee continued moving but came to a halt as I reached the driver's side window and banged on it. 'Excuse me, excuse me.' My voice was different now. Higher pitched, less confident.

The window came down and a hard-looking sod with a square jaw that looked like it was made of cast iron glared out at me. I put him at about thirty-five. My face dissolved into nerves. Both the driver and his front- seat passenger, a smaller, older guy with Brylcreemed hair and a greasy face, were already relaxing. They saw me as no threat. Just a man who pays his taxes and does what he's told for a living. I heard the one in the back mumble something but I didn't even look at him.

'What do you want?' demanded the driver impatiently.

'Er, I was wondering . . .'

I brought the gun up from my pocket, had this momentary paranoia that I might not have released the safety, and shot him twice in the right eye. He made no sound, simply fell back into his seat, head tilted to one side, and shivered out the final ounces of his life.

The front passenger swore loudly and immediately flung up his arms in a futile effort to protect himself. I leaned down slightly to get a better view of him and pumped out a further two rounds. One hit him in the elbow, the other in the jaw. I heard it crack. He shrieked in pain and then coughed violently as his mouth filled with blood. He tried to retreat in his seat, scrabbling about like a madman, unable to accept the fact that it was all over. I steadied myself and fired again, hitting him square in the forehead. The window behind him bloomed with red and his greasy features immediately relaxed. So far the whole thing had taken about three seconds.

But the one in the back was quick. He was already swinging open the door and coming out with what looked like a gun in his hand. I didn't have time to take a closer look. Instead I retreated three steps and squeezed the trigger as he came into view. I got him somewhere in the upper body but still he kept coming, and fast. I continued firing, holding the gun two-handed, teeth clenched against the noise that was exploding in my ears. The momentum of the bullets forced him backwards, driving him into the door. He did a manic, confused dance to the tune of the gunfire, his arms and legs flailing, and angry red spots appeared like pox on his crisp, white shirt.

And then the magazine was empty and everything stopped as suddenly and dramatically as it had begun.

For a second he remained upright, holding onto the door for support, the energy almost visibly leaking out of him. Then he sort of half fell, half sat down, losing his grip on it in the process. He looked down at the blood on his shirt, and then at me, and I got a good look at his face, which I didn't want at all, because it was young, maybe late twenties, and his expression was all wrong. What I mean is, it wasn't the expression of a sinner. There was no defiance there, no rage. Just shock. Shock that his life was being stolen from him. He looked like a man who didn't think he deserved it, and that was the moment when I should have known I'd made a terrible mistake.

Instead, I turned away from his stare and reloaded. Then I stepped forward and shot him three times in the top of the head. The mobile phone he was carrying clattered noisily to the ground.

I dropped the gun into my jacket pocket and turned towards Danny, who was now bringing the car round.

Which was when I saw her, maybe fifteen yards away, standing in the light of the rear firedoor, a bag of rubbish in each hand. No more than eighteen and looking right at me, still too shocked to realize that what she was witnessing was real. What do you do? A movie pro would have taken her out with a single shot to the head, although there was no guarantee I'd even have hit her from where I was standing. And anyway, I'm not interested in hurting civilians.

Her hand went to her mouth as she saw I'd seen her, and I knew that any moment she was going to let out a scream that would probably wake the dead, which, with the dead only just being dead, I didn't want at all. So I lowered my gaze and hurried round to the passenger door, hoping that the gloom and wet had obscured my features enough to make any description she gave worthless.

I jumped in and kept my head down. Danny didn't say a word. He just hit the pedal and we were out of there.

It was 9.04.

The journey to our first change of transport took exactly four minutes and covered a distance of approximately two and a half miles. We'd parked a Mondeo in a quiet piece of Forestry Commission land earlier that day. Danny now pulled up behind it, cut the engine, and got out. I leaned under the passenger seat and removed a full five-litre can of petrol which I liberally sprinkled over the car's interior. When it was empty, I got out, lit a book of matches, stepped back so I was well out of the way, and flung them in, followed by the murder weapon and the two-way radio I'd been using. There was a satisfying whoosh as the petrol ignited, followed by a wave of heat.

When they came across the mangled wreckage it wouldn't tell them anything. We hadn't left any fingerprints and the car itself would be almost impossible to trace. It had been stolen in Birmingham six months ago, given new plates and a respray, and stored in a lock-up in Cardiff ever since. In this line of business, you can never be too careful. Contrary to popular belief, most detectives couldn't detect a heartbeat on a speed addict, but you never know when you might be up against the next Ellery Queen.

We now followed a pre-arranged route for four miles through a mixture of B and single-track roads and it was 9.16 when we pulled into the car park of Ye Olde Bell, a busy country pub on the edge of an affluent looking commuter village. Danny drove up to the far end and stopped behind a burgundy Rover 600.

This was where we parted.

'Did that girl get a good look at you?' he asked as I opened the door. They were the first words he'd spoken since the shootings.

'No, we'll be all right. It was too dark.'

He sighed. 'I don't like it, you know. Three murders, and now we've got a witness.'

Admittedly it didn't sound too good when he put it like that, but at the time there was no reason to think that we weren't in the clear.

'Don't worry. We've covered our tracks well enough.'

'There's going to be a lot of heat over this one, Dennis.'

'We both knew that when we took the job. As long as we keep calm, and keep our mouths shut, we won't feel any of it.'

I gave him a friendly pat on the shoulder, and told him I'd call him the next day.

The Rover's keys were behind the front driver's side wheel. I got in, started the engine and followed Danny out of the car park. He turned south and I turned north.

And that should have been that, but tonight was not my lucky night. I'd barely gone three miles and was just short of the turning that would take me back to London when I hit an improvised road-block. There were two Pandas with flashing lights at the side of the road: officers in fluorescent safety jackets were milling about a BMW they'd already stopped. My heart gave an initial jump but I quickly recovered myself. No reason to worry. I was a man on my own, unarmed, driving a car that had never been within five miles of the Traveller's Rest, and they wouldn't even have the vaguest description of me yet. The clock on the dashboard said 9.22.

One of them saw my approach and stepped out into the road, flashing his torch and motioning for me to pull up behind the other car. I did as I was told and wound down the window as he approached the driver's side. He was young, no more than twenty-three, and very fresh-faced. They say you can tell you're getting old when the coppers look young. I could just about have been this kid's dad. He looked really enthusiastic as well. That wouldn't last. A second officer stood a few feet behind him, watching, but the other two were preoccupied with the driver of the other car. None of them appeared to be armed, which I thought was a bit foolish under the circumstances. I could have run this roadblock and they wouldn't have had a chance.

'Good evening, sir.' He leaned down into the window and gave me and the car a gentle once-over.

It always pays to be polite. 'Evening, officer. How can I help?'

'There's been an incident at a hotel called the Traveller's Rest on the A10. About fifteen minutes ago. You haven't come that way, have you?'

'No, I haven't,' I told him. 'I've come from Clavering. I'm on my way to London.'

He nodded understandingly, and then looked at me again. You could tell that for some reason he wasn't entirely convinced, although I don't know why. I'm not the type who arouses suspicions. I genuinely look like a nice guy. There shouldn't have been any alarm bells.

But there were. Maybe I'd just met the new Ellery Queen.

'Have you got any identification, sir? Just for the record.'

I sighed. I didn't want to have to do this because it could well cause me a lot of long-term problems, but I didn't see that I had much choice.

For a split second I baulked.

Then I reached into my pocket and removed the warrant card.

He took it, inspected it carefully, looked back at me, then back at the warrant card, just to double check, probably wondering why his instincts were so wrong. When he looked back again, he had an embarrassed expression on his face.

'Detective Sergeant Milne. I'm sorry, sir. I didn't realize.'

I shrugged my shoulders. 'Course you didn't. You're just doing your job. But if you don't mind, I'm in a bit of a hurry.'

'Of course, sir, no problem.' He stepped back from the car. 'Have a nice evening.'

I said goodnight, and put the car in reverse. Poor sod. I remembered only too well what it was like to be out on nights like these, being paid a pittance to stand around for hours on end with the rain pissing down on your head. Knowing that the people you were meant to be looking for were probably miles away. Oh, the joys of being a uniformed copper.

I waved as I drove past, and he waved back. I wondered how long it would take him to lose the enthusiasm; how long before he, too, realized that by playing by the rules he was just banging his head against a brick wall.

I gave him two years.

2

I used to know a guy called Tom Darke. Tomboy, as he was known, was a buyer and seller of stolen goods. If you'd nicked something – whatever it was – Tomboy would give you a price for it, and you could be sure that somewhere down the line he'd have a customer who'd take it off him. He was also an informant, and a good one too if you measure such things by how many people his information convicted. The secret of his success lay in the fact that he was a likeable character who was good company. He used to say that he listened well rather than listened hard, and he never asked too many questions. Consequently, there wasn't a lot that went on among the North London criminal fraternity that he didn't know about, and such was his affability that even as the local lowlifes were going down like overweight skydivers no-one ever suspected old Tomboy of being involved.

I once asked him why he did it. Why, as the Aussies would say, did he dob in blokes who were meant to be his mates? Because the thing was he didn't really strike me as the grassing sort. He came across as being a decent bloke who was above such petty deceptions. Tomboy had two answers to this question.

The first answer was the obvious one. Money. There were good rewards on offer for information on criminals and Tomboy needed the cash. He wanted to retire from the game with his freedom intact because he believed that with the onset of technology, and its availability to the police for fighting crime, the writing was on the wall for middle-ranking career criminals such as himself. So it was a case of making hay while the sun shone, building up a nice little nest egg (he'd set a target limit of £50,000), and then getting the fuck out.

The second answer was that if he didn't dob them in, someone else would do it anyway. Criminals are usually notorious braggarts. Since they can't tell the whole world what they've done for fear of retribution, they like to boast about their exploits to one another. And since by definition they're a dishonest lot – as Tomboy once said, 'Whoever heard of such a thing as honour among thieves?' – sooner or later someone's going to inform on them if the money's right. All he did, if you believed his rationale, was get in there first.

So that was Tomboy's philosophy. There's no point in not doing the deed because one way or another it's going to get done, and if you're going to get paid to do it, all the better. I thought about that as I drove home through the rain that night. If I hadn't killed those men, someone else would have shot them. Either way they ended up dead. If you're in the line of business where you make enemies of people who'll pay to have you killed, you've got to be prepared to accept the consequences. That was how I justified it to myself, and that was how Tomboy had always justified it to me, and it had never done him any harm. In fact, it appeared to have done him a lot of good. The last I'd heard he was living out in the Philippines. He'd made his fifty grand, probably a lot more knowing him, and had invested it in a beach bar and guesthouse on one of the more far-flung islands.

He'd sent me a postcard from there a couple of years back in which he'd extolled the virtues of the laid-back tropical lifestyle. It had ended with him saying that if ever I fancied a job working at his place, I should let him know.

More than once I'd felt like taking him up on the offer.

It was getting close to eleven o'clock when I got home that night, home being a rented one bedroom flat at the southern end of Islington, not too far from City Road. The first thing I did was take a long hot shower to wash the cold out of my bones, before pouring myself a decent-sized glass of red wine and settling down on the lounge sofa.

I turned on the TV and lit a cigarette relaxing properly for the first time that day. I took a long slow drag, enjoying the fact that a potentially hazardous job had been completed successfully, and flicked through the channels until I found a report on the killings. It didn't take long. Murder's a numbers game. Kill one person and you barely make the inside pages. Kill three, especially in a public place, and it's big news. It adds a bit of excitement to the mundane grind of people's lives, even more so when it bears all the hallmarks of a so-called gangland shooting. Shootings are entertaining because they're not too personal. They make good conversation points.

Understandably, details were still very sketchy. The programme I was watching had a young female reporter on the scene. She looked cold but excited to be involved in what was potentially a meaty, career-enhancing story. It was still raining, only now it had turned into that light stuff that always seems to soak you more. She'd positioned herself in the rear car park and you could make out the Cherokee in the background about twenty yards away, behind reams of brightly coloured scene-of-crime tape. There were a lot of police and forensic staff in lab coats swarming all over it.

The report didn't last long. The girl confirmed that three people had been murdered – no idea as to identities – and speculated that they'd been shot. She then wheeled over the hotel's deputy manager, a tall, spotty young man who looked like he'd just got out of school, for his comments. They weren't, it has to be said, very enlightening. Squinting through his spectacles, he explained that he'd been working in the reception area when he'd heard a number of faint popping sounds (they all say that) coming from the rear car park. He'd thought nothing more of it but then one of the kitchen workers had come running in screaming and shouting that there'd been a murder. He, the deputy manager, had bravely gone out to investigate and had immediately discovered my handiwork, which was when he'd called the police. 'It was very shocking for all of us,' he told the reporter. 'You don't expect this sort of thing in a quiet area like this.' They all seem to say that as well.

The reporter thanked him before turning back to the camera and breathlessly promising further information as and when she received it. She then signed off, and it was back to the studio. It seemed I'd made her night anyway.

I took a drink of wine, taking my time swallowing it, and switched over. There was a programme about great white sharks on the Discovery Channel, and I sat watching that for a while, not really paying too much attention. Although I tried to empty my mind of the day's events, it was difficult not to think about the murders. I suppose it was only now that the full enormity of what I'd done was beginning to sink in. Three lives snuffed out, just like that. It felt like I'd crossed a threshold. I've killed before, I suppose that's obvious by now, but only twice, and in vastly different circumstances.

The first time was twelve years ago. I'd been one of a number of armed officers who'd turned up to a domestic incident at a house in Haringey. A man was threatening his common-law wife and their two young children with a gun and a carving knife. They'd got people trying to negotiate with him over the phone but the guy was drugged up to the eyeballs, shouting incoherently, and they weren't really getting anywhere.

Siege situations are the most frustrating a police officer can get involved in. You've got very little control over events so you can never really relax an inch, just in case something happens. But more often than not, nothing does. The suspect mulls over his actions, finally works out that he's trapped and that he's not going to get out of there except in handcuffs or a box, and eventually releases his hostages and simply walks out the door. It's frustrating because you want to be doing something to help end the situation, yet in most ways you're pretty much irrelevant to it.

On the day of the Haringey siege I remember it was hot. Stiflingly hot. We'd been on the scene about an hour and had the place completely surrounded when, without warning, our hostage taker had suddenly appeared in the front window, naked from the waist up, holding his gun. He was a big guy with the beginnings of a pot belly and a tattoo of an eagle straddling his chest. He'd shouted something from behind the glass, then opened the top part of the window and stuck his head out, shouting something else unintelligible. I was ten yards away behind a car on the street. Another officer was crouched down beside me. He was about fifteen years older than me and his name was Renfrew. I remember he got pensioned off a couple of years later after he got a glass in the face trying to break up a pub fight. Renfrew cursed the guy under his breath. You could tell he wanted to shoot him. Why not? The guy was just a waste-of-space dopehead who caused a lot more harm to the world than good. But Renfrew was a pro and, like a lot of coppers, he had one eye on the pension, so he was never going to do anything that might jeopardize his career. I was still a bit idealistic in those days. I didn't think about the pension. I thought about the wife and kids stuck in there with an unpredictable maniac.

I'd had an earpiece on. The chief superintendent spoke into it. Don't fire, he said. We're still negotiating. Keep him in your sights, but don't fire.

Then, just like that, our target had brought the gun up and pointed it wildly towards us. The chief superintendeant hissed something else into my earpiece, but I didn't hear it. It looked like the suspect was going to pull the trigger. I knew he wouldn't hit me from where he was standing. I had good cover, and he looked too stoned to aim straight, but I was still nervous. And angry. This bastard was just showing off his power, knowing we'd have to stand there like lemons, hamstrung by our limited rules of engagement. That got me, it really did.

So I'd fired. Two shots from the Browning. Straight through the window and into his upper body. One of them got him in the heart, but the autopsy confirmed that either of the bullets would have been fatal on its own. He died instantly, I think. Certainly before anyone could administer first aid.

I was offered psychological counselling and I took it because I was told that if I didn't, it would look like I didn't care that I'd killed a man. It didn't do me much good, mainly because I genuinely didn't care that I'd killed him. In fact, I was quite pleased. He'd wanted to kill me and I'd got in there first. But of course I didn't tell the counsellor that. I told him I deeply regretted having to take a life, even if it was in the line of duty. I guessed that was what he wanted to hear.

There was an inquest, and I was forced to give evidence. There was even talk about a criminal trial, especially when it was discovered that the gun he'd been holding was a replica, and I was suspended for close to two months, although that at least was on full pay. On the second day of the inquest, I was leaving the building by a side door when I ran into the common-law wife and her brother. She spat in my face and called me a murderer while the brother punched me in the side of the head. A uniformed officer intervened before things went any further, but the incident taught me two things. One, never rely on the support of people you're trying to help. As politicians have often found out to their cost over the years, the hand that pats you on the back one day can just as easily grab you by the balls the next. And two, never rely on anyone else for support either. In this world, you've got to get used to the fact that, in the end, you're always on your own.

No blame was ever officially attached to me over the killing of thirty-three-year-old Darren John Reid (who, it turned out, had a grand total of twenty-nine convictions, including eleven for violence, four of which related to his missus), but it might as well have been. I was taken off any further firearms duties (and have been to this day); banned from keeping guns privately; and my path up the career ladder slowed down one hell of a lot over the next few years. Crime, it seems, only pays when you're a criminal.

I'm not a bad man, whatever those who like to sit in judgement may think. When I started out I really did believe I could make a difference. My sole motivation was to take the bad guys off the street and bring them to account for the crimes they'd committed. After the Reid shooting, I slowly stopped caring. I suppose I finally realized what all defence lawyers know: however well intentioned its designers may have been, the law in practice only serves to help the criminal, hinder the police, and ignore the victim.

Having got to a point when I was as cynical as that it was only a matter of time before I fell in with the wrong company. The wrong company being, in my case, about as wrong as you can get, although when I first started doing business with Raymond Keen, one of North London's more colourful entrepreneurs, I wasn't to know quite how far it would go.

I've had a business relationship with Raymond for about seven years now. At first it wasn't too serious; nothing like that ever is. Just a few tips here and there, a helpful advance warning of impending police action, a sale of the odd bit of dope that went missing from police custody. Small things, but like cancerous lumps, small things that inevitably grow bigger. I wasn't even that surprised when two years ago he asked me to kill a bent businessman who was refusing point blank to pay him the twenty-two grand he owed him. The businessman was a nasty piece of work. One of his sidelines was importing kiddie porn. Raymond offered me ten grand to get rid of him. 'It'll strike a blow for creditors everywhere,' he'd said, although I wasn't quite sure how many creditors would follow his example and write off their debts with that degree of permanence. But ten grand's a lot of money, especially when you're on a copper's wage and, once again, he wasn't the sort of bloke anyone was going to miss. So one night I waited for him outside the lock-up he used. When he came out and walked over to his car, I emerged from the shadows and followed. As he opened the door, I pushed the silencer against the back of his hairless head and pulled the trigger. One shot was all it needed, but I added a second for good measure. Pop pop. All over. And I was ten grand richer. It was very easy.

But three men dead in one go? Danny was right, there was going to be a lot of heat over this one, although Raymond, who was the instigator of the whole thing, didn't appear too worried that any of it would get back to him. But then Raymond wasn't really the worrying type – which, I suppose, in his line of business, is something of a plus.

It was getting late. I drained my wine, drank a glass of water from the tap so that I didn't dehydrate myself, and made my way to bed. Looking back now, I already had a bad feeling about the whole thing but I was trying hard not to admit it to myself. Raymond Keen had paid me forty grand for killing those men. It was a lot of money, even after Danny had got his 20 per cent cut. Enough to justify a lot of things.

But nothing like enough to justify what was to follow.

3

Things started going downhill at exactly ten past eight the next morning. I'd been up for about twenty minutes and was in the kitchen making myself some toast for breakfast when the land-line rang. It was Danny, which was a bit of a surprise. I hadn't expected to hear from him today. He sounded agitated.

'Dennis, what the fuck's going on?'

'What the fuck's going on what?'

'Have you not seen the news this morning?'

I experienced the first stirrings of fear in my gut. 'No. No, I haven't. What's the problem?'

'The targets, that's the problem.'

'What do you mean?'

'They weren't who you said they were, Dennis. Just switch the TV on and you'll find out.'

I paused for a moment, trying to collect my thoughts. This wasn't what I wanted to hear. The most important thing, though, was not to say too much over the phone. 'All right, listen. Sit tight, don't worry about anything. I'll check things out and call you back later.'

'This is bad, Dennis. Very bad.'

'I'll call you back later, OK? Just stay calm and carry on as normal.'

I rang off and immediately looked around for my cigarettes. I needed to think things through, to try to locate what the fuck had gone wrong.

When I'd found them, I lit one, went through to the sitting room and flicked on the TV. I didn't hang about, I went straight to the news channel, but they were already on to something else. So I flicked on Ceefax, unable to suppress the feeling of dread at what I was going to see. I knew it was going to be bad, it was just a case of how bad.

It was the top story. Unlike the other stories, the headline was in bold block capitals, telling even the most shortsighted viewer that this was big news.

I had committed these three murders for Raymond Keen. Raymond had told me that the men were drug dealers, violent drug dealers, who were causing some associates of his serious trouble. But the headline staring back at me wasn't saying that at all. It was saying, TWO CUSTOMS OFFICERS AND ONE CIVILIAN GUNNED DOWN OUTSIDE HOTEL.

For a couple of seconds, I had this irrational idea that I'd opened fire on the occupants of the wrong Cherokee, but a couple of seconds was all I needed to scupper that particular one. I'd shot the people I was meant to shoot all right. Raymond Keen had set me up. For whatever reason, he'd wanted these men out of the way and had duped me into killing them. He knew that if he told me they were violent criminals whose business was supplying the masses with hard drugs, I'd have no problem pulling the trigger.

I sighed loudly and sat back on the sofa, willing myself to calm down. A serious mistake had been made, there was no denying that. But it had been Raymond who had orchestrated it. What mattered now was that I kept my nerve. There'd be a far bigger police operation to find the killers of two hard-working customs officers than there would have been to find the people who'd put away three low-level gangsters, which meant I was going to have to be extremely careful. I needed to know what it was these customs officers were doing, and who the hell the civilian was who was with them. Armed with that knowledge I could at least work out how how likely it was that the police could get on to Raymond. The whole thing was odd because I didn't think Raymond would ever get himself involved in the type of situation that put him and his business empire at risk. You don't get to his position and stay there by executing representatives of the forces of law and order.

I possess a mobile phone that's registered in the name of a man I've never met before, and that man always pays the bills. Whenever I need to make contact with Raymond I use that phone, and I used it now.

Unfortunately, it was Luke who answered. Luke is Raymond's personal assistant and bodyguard. He's the strong, silent type who tends to look at you as if you've just patted his bottom and blown him a kiss; all simmering rage and barely suppressed violence. Legend has it he once broke a love rival's legs with his bare hands, and he's supposedly an expert at some highfalutin martial art whose name I forget. Useful to have around in bar-room brawls, but that's about it.

'Yeah,' he grunted, by way of a greeting.

'It's Dennis, I need to speak to Raymond.'

'Mr Keen's not available.'

'When's he going to be available?'

'I can't tell you that.'

Conversations with Luke can be frustrating. He always acts like he's the heavy in a very cheap gangster flick.

'Give him a message. Tell him I need to speak to him urgently. Very urgently. He'll know what it's about.'

'I'll let him know you called.'

'Do that. And if I don't hear from him by the end of the morning, then I'll come looking for him.'

'Mr Keen doesn't like threats.'

'I'm not threatening him. I'm just telling you what'll happen if I don't hear from him.'

He started to say something else but I didn't bother waiting around to find out what it was. I rang off and put the phone in the pocket of my dressing gown. What a start to the fucking day.

I'm not a panicker by nature. I can sometimes be thrown off course by a shock, especially a big one, but I can generally pull myself together without too much difficulty. This, though, was different. Not only had I jeopardized my livelihood and freedom, I'd broken every moral rule I've ever made. I'd killed men who, on the surface of it at least, didn't deserve it.

I went back into the sitting room, located another cigarette and lit it, coughing violently as the smoke charged down my throat. I switched off the Ceefax and aimlessly flicked through the channels.

The phone rang again. The landline, not the mobile. I let it ring. It wouldn't be Raymond, and if it was Danny, I didn't want to talk to him for a while. Not until I had a better idea of what I was going to do. After five rings the answerphone kicked in. My bored voice told the caller I wasn't in but if he left a message with a number and the reason why he was calling me, I'd get back to him. Or her, I suppose. If my luck was in.

The beep went, then my immediate boss's voice came on the

line. I nearly jumped out of the seat. What the fuck did he want? Surely the trap hadn't closed that quickly?

'Dennis, it's Karl.' His voice sounded weary. 'I need you in now.' There was a short pause before he continued. 'I'm down at the canal just behind All Saints Street. It's eight twenty-five a.m. and we've got a body down here. If you get this message within the next two hours, make your way over. Otherwise just get down to the station. Cheers.'

He hung up.

As if I didn't have enough work on my plate without a murder to add to it. I was already investigating two rapes, an armed robbery, a missing housewife, a motiveless stabbing, and Christ knows how many muggings. All of which had occurred in the last month. In the last seven days I'd put in a grand total of fifty-nine hours' work on the job, as well as organizing last night's little foray, and I was exhausted. The problem these days was twofold: one, we didn't have anything like the manpower we used to have, or that our colleagues have abroad, because no-one wants to be a copper any more; and two, we have far more crime, especially crimes of violence. I suppose the one is caused by the other, at least in part. There's something about criminals these days too – and I'm not counting myself here – they tend to use violence a lot more casually. They take more pleasure in it too. Hurting or killing someone is no longer simply a by-product of committing a crime. To a lot of people it's part and parcel of the buzz they get out of it. At least when I'd put people down, I thought I was doing the world a favour. I might have made mistakes, but they were mistakes made in good faith.

I continued smoking the cigarette until it was down to the butt, then I used it to light another one. When that one was halfway down, I knew I could hold back no longer. The thing is, I can never sit still when there's a new investigation starting,

32

particularly a murder. I get a kick out of catching killers – maybe for the wrong reasons, I don't know, but it makes me feel good letting them know it's me who put them down, and fucked up their whole lives.

And, if nothing else, getting involved in this one would at least stop me mulling over matters I could do nothing about.

So I stubbed out the cigarette in the already overflowing ashtray and headed down to Regent's Canal, the grimy scene of many a heinous crime.

4

It was twenty to ten and raining when I arrived at the murder site. A uniformed officer stood at the entrance to the towpath talking to a guy in a trenchcoat who looked like a journalist. It's amazing how quick these people sniff out a story; it's like they've got an extra sense that can detect a fresh kill from miles away. I pushed my way past the journo, who gave me a dirty look but thought better of saying anything, and nodded to the uniform. I recognized him from the station, although I couldn't put a name to him, and he evidently recognized me because he stepped aside and let me through.

This part of the canal was fairly well looked after. The old warehouses had been knocked down to be replaced by office blocks that were built a few yards further back from the waters edge. A well-trimmed lawn had been laid down in the extra space with a couple of benches to add to the park-like feel.

The painstaking, monotonous hunt for clues was already in

full flow. There were about two dozen people widely scattered across the scene as they picked, probed and photographed every patch of earth. At the canal's edge stood four police divers, fully kitted up, ready to enter the treacle-like water. One of them was talking to DCI Knox, my boss's boss. He would be the senior investigating officer on a case like this, responsible for making sure that the investigation ran smoothly and nothing was missed. Almost certainly the key to a conviction lay in these few square yards.

A tent had been erected at the entrance to a narrow gap between two of the buildings. This was where the body would be and where it would remain until it had been examined and photographed in minute detail. I could see my boss standing next to the tent, talking to one of the forensic team. I made my way over, nodding to two CID men I recognized: Hunsdon and Smith. They were standing by one of the benches taking a statement from an old guy who had a Jack Russell on a lead. I guessed the old guy had discovered the body. His face was pale and troubled, and he kept shaking his head, as if he couldn't believe what he'd seen, which he probably couldn't. It's always difficult for people when they come into contact with the handiwork of murderers for the first time.

My boss turned round and nodded a curt greeting as I approached. It was a cold day, but DI Karl Welland was sweating. I thought he didn't look well. This was nothing new. He was overweight, red in the face, highly stressed, and, if my memory served me right, the wrong side of fifty. Hardly a candidate for a ripe old age. He looked worse today than usual, though, and his pale skin was covered in vivid red blotches. I felt like telling him he needed a holiday, but I didn't. It's not my business to offer lifestyle advice to my superiors.

He excused himself from the conversation he was having and

led me into the tent. 'It never gets easier, you know,' he said.

'The dead'll always keep dying, sir,' I told him.

'Perhaps, but do they have to die like this?'

I stopped and looked where he was facing. The girl couldn't have been more than eighteen. She was lying on her back in the paved alleyway between the two buildings, legs and arms splayed open in a rough star shape. Her throat had been cut so deeply that the wound had come close to severing her head, which was tilted at an odd angle to the rest of her; thick dried blood had splattered across her face and formed in irregular pools on either side of the body. Her black cocktail dress had been ripped badly around the chest area, exposing a small pointed breast. It had also been pulled up round her waist. She hadn't been wearing any underwear, or, if she had, she wasn't any longer. There was also a lot of congealed blood around the vaginal area, suggesting that her killer had stabbed her there as well, although I thought immediately that this would have been done after death as there didn't appear to be any defensive wounds on her hands or lower arms. She had died quite quickly, I was sure of that. Her face was screwed up in pain and her dark eyes bulged out, but there was no fear in them. Surprise maybe, shock even, but no fear. She was still wearing one of her shoes, a black stiletto. The other lay on its side a few feet away.

'She must have been freezing dressed like that,' I said, noting that she wasn't wearing any stockings or tights, nor were there any in the vicinity of the body.

'Looks that way,' said Welland. 'She was partially covered with an old rug when we found her. It's already gone off to the lab.'

'What do we know so far?' I asked, still looking down at the corpse.

'Not a lot. She was found just before eight o'clock this

morning by a bloke walking his dog. There hasn't been a great deal of effort to conceal her, and it doesn't look like she's been here that long.'

'I'd say by the way she was dressed, she was a Tom.'

'I think that's probably a fair assumption.'

'Goes off with a punter to a nice secluded spot, he pulls the knife out, puts a hand over her mouth, and the rest is history.'

'Looks that way, but we can't tell for sure. A lot of girls go out scantily clad these days. Even in weather like this. The first thing we need to do is identify her. You're on the squad for this one, Dennis. DC Malik'll be working alongside you, and you'll be reporting to me. DCI Knox is the SIO.'

'I've got a lot on at the moment, sir.'

'You're going to have a busy week, then. I'm sorry, Dennis, but we're short on bodies, if you'll excuse the pun. Very short. And it seems the world's lowlifes are all busy at the moment. What can I do?'

What could he do? He was right, of course. We were snowed under, and in those circumstances it's a case of all hands to the pumps. I was already losing my initial enthusiasm, though. It just didn't look at first glance like it was going to be an easy case. If this girl was a prostitute, it was highly likely we had a sex killer on our hands. If he'd been a clever boy and had worn gloves and avoided leaving any liquid evidence at the scene of the crime, then finding him was going to be an uphill battle. Whichever way you looked at it there was going to be a lot of legwork.

I looked back at the pathetic corpse of the girl. Some mother's daughter. It was a lonely way to say your goodbyes to the world.

'I want to get this one solved, Dennis. Whoever did this . . .' He paused momentarily, choosing his words. 'Whoever did this is a fucking animal, and I want him in a cage where he belongs.'

'I'll get on to it,' I told Welland.

He nodded, wiping his brow again. 'You do that.'

5

At 1.05 that afternoon, I was sitting on a bench in Regent's Park smoking yet another cigarette and waiting for my rendezvous. The rain had long since cleared and it was even threatening to be quite a nice day. I'd already attended the briefing session back at the station where Knox had worked hard to instil some enthusiasm and grit into the inquiry, not an easy task as no-one felt there was much hope of intercepting the perpetrator quickly. I'd now got Malik on to the task of identifying her, which, if she was a Tom, wouldn't take too long.

I liked Malik. He wasn't a bad copper and he was efficient. If you asked him to do something, he did it properly, which doesn't seem to be a common trait with a lot of people these days. And he wasn't idealistic either, even though he'd only been in the Force for five years and was university educated, which is usually a pretty dire combination. So many of the fast-track graduates who go shooting up through the ranks have all these big ideas about trying to understand the psychology and economics of crime. They want to find out what motivates and drives criminals rather than simply doing what they're paid to do, which is catch them.

I looked at my watch again, which is something I do constantly when I'm early for a meeting or the other person's late. In this case, the other person was late, but then Raymond was never the most punctual of people. I was hungry. Apart from the toast I'd forced down myself earlier that morning, I hadn't eaten in close to twenty-four hours and my stomach was beginning to make strange growling noises. I was, I decided, going to have to improve my diet and start eating more regularly. One of the DCs had told me that sushi was very good for you. The Japanese eat it all the time and, according to him, they have the lowest incidence of lung cancer in the industrialized world, even though they're the heaviest smokers. Raw fish, though. It was a high price to pay for a life of rude health.

'Care to join me for a walk, Dennis?' said Raymond, interrupting my thoughts. 'Or would you prefer to continue your meditation?'

There he was, bright as a bell, a wide smile on his big round face, as if the whole world were his playground and all was fair within it. That was Raymond Keen for you. He was one of those big, bouncy guys who simply oozed *joie de vivre*. Even his haircut, a magnificent silver bouffant of the kind so beloved of middle-aged men who want to put one over on their balding contemporaries, and which sat on the top of his head like a curled up Cheshire cat, seemed designed to tell the world what a jolly character he was, which was a little odd when you considered that one of his more active and lucrative sidelines was running a funeral parlour. But Raymond, as became clear when you got to know him, was a man with a deeply ironic sense of humour.

'I'll join you, I think,' I told him.

I got up and we started to walk across the grass in the direction of the boating lake. Some kids who should have been in school were playing football and a few mothers were out strolling with prams, but other than that the park was quiet.

I didn't beat about the bush. 'What the fuck happened, Raymond? You told me I was shooting drug dealers.'

Raymond attempted a rueful smile but he didn't look overly guilty. 'Give me a break, Dennis. I could hardly have told you the real targets, could I? You wouldn't have shot them.'

'I know I wouldn't have shot them! That's the point. You got me involved in something that's against everything I stand for.'

Raymond stopped and looked at me, a smile playing on his lips. Angry or not, it was obvious he knew there was nothing I could do about the situation. He had me pinned, and he knew I knew it.

'No, Dennis. That's where you're wrong. You got yourself involved. Admittedly, I embellished the truth a little bit—'

'You mean you lied.'

'But I needed them out of the way, and knowing – and all credit to you for this, Dennis – knowing your moral standpoint on this sort of thing, I thought I'd withhold some of the details. But I don't want you to lose sleep over it. These blokes were pondscum. They were blackmailing some associates of mine and the associates wanted them out of the way.' He sighed meaningfully. 'They were corrupt men, Dennis.'

'And that's meant to make me feel better, is it?'

'If it's any consolation to you, it makes me feel bad as well. I don't like the idea of men dying. Human life is a very precious thing, not to be taken away lightly. If there was any other way, any other way at all, you can claim a bet that I would have tried it.'

The phrase 'claim a bet' was one of Raymond's favourites, even though it meant absolutely nothing, and I'd never in my life heard a single other person utter it. Hearing it now annoyed me.

'Raymond, you have fucked me up. Do you have any idea the sort of pressure the murder of customs officers is going to generate? It's not like shooting three dealers who no-one's going to miss. These were family men who died doing the job they loved.'

'They were blackmailers who died because they were trying to blackmail the wrong sort of people. That's what they were.'

'But that's not what the media are going to say, is it? To them, these guys are the thin blue line, brutally murdered in the line of duty. They're going to be clamouring for a result on this. And you can claim a fucking bet on that.'

'Don't be facetious, Dennis.'

'I'm being serious. Deadly serious. The pressure to get a result on this one is going to be massive.'

'But they're not going to get a result, are they? We've done everything needed to cover our tracks. It was a well-planned operation. All credit to you for that, Dennis. It was a professional job.'

He started to walk again, and I followed. To him, the conversation was effectively over. He'd said his piece, tried to smooth the ruffled feathers of his part-time employee, and now it was time to move on.

I then did a stupid thing, a very stupid thing, that was to cause me and plenty of other people a lot of grief. I told him I'd been seen.

That stopped him dead. Which, of course, I knew it would.

'What do you mean?' There was an edge to his voice now and I wasn't sure if it was anger or nervousness. Probably both. Immediately I regretted opening my mouth. I'd just wanted to punch a hole in the smug air of confidence he was exuding, and it looked like I'd been only too successful.

'I mean, I was seen. One of the staff, a kitchen girl or something.'

'Did she get a good look?'

'No. It was dark and raining, and she was a fair way away.'

'How far?'

'Fifteen, maybe twenty yards. And I had my head down.

I doubt if she could give much of a description.'

'Good.' He seemed mollified. 'Why didn't they say anything about that on the news?'

'On something like this, where there's evidence that it was a planned killing, they won't want to risk putting the witness in any danger. Also, they'll still be questioning her.'

'How come you didn't shoot her?'

'Would you have wanted me to?'

'Well, it mightn't have been a bad idea.'

'What? Four killings? Come on, Raymond, this is England, not Cambodia.'

'Well, if you didn't think she saw anything, then I suppose there'd have been no point.'

'I *don't* think she saw anything.'

'Maybe not, then. There's no point killing anyone unnecessarily.'

'Especially when human life's such a precious thing.'

Raymond glared at me. He wasn't the sort of man who liked having the piss taken out of him. 'I don't really think you're in a position to get on your high horse, Dennis, do you?'

'So what were these customs men doing, Raymond, that was so bad they had to die?'

'As I said, they were blackmailing some associates of mine. Associates who are very important to the smooth running of my business.'

'That doesn't really answer my question.'

'Well, my apologies, Dennis, but that's all the details available at present.'

'It said only two of them were customs. Who was the other one?'

'Why so interested? You can't bring them back.'

'I want to know who I killed, and why.'

Raymond sighed theatrically. 'He was another piece of pond-scum. He thought he was setting the other two up. In that, he was wrong. Now that's all I'm going to say on the matter.'

I took a last drag on my cigarette and stubbed it underfoot, still feeling pissed off.

'Look, think of it from my perspective,' he continued. 'Just for a moment. I needed the job done and you're the best man I've got for that sort of work. It's unfortunate that your main talent lies in that direction; it's a particularly barbaric skill to possess, but there you go.'

'You didn't have to use me. A man like you's got other contacts.'

'What did you expect me to do? Ring round and get quotes in? I had no choice, Dennis. That's the long and the short of it. I had no choice.'

'Don't ever ask me to do anything like that again.'

Raymond shrugged, seemingly none too concerned. 'Last night was a one-off. It won't happen again.' He looked at his watch, then back at me. 'I'm going to have to go. I've got a punter at two o'clock.'

'A dead one or a live one?'

'She's deceased,' he said sternly. 'A car accident. Beautiful-looking girl, and only twenty-three . . . her whole life in front of her.' He crossed his hands in front of him and was silent for a moment, I assumed out of respect for the dead. Then it was back to business. 'Anyway, I've got to prepare and time's getting on. I don't want the poor thing to be late for her own funeral.'

'That's very thoughtful of you.'

'Thoughtfulness costs nothing, Dennis.'

'Which reminds me. There's the small matter of my remuneration.'

'As if I'd forget.' He fished a key out of the breast pocket of his expensive-looking suit and chucked it over to me. 'The money's in a locker at King's Cross. The same place as last time.'

I put the key in the inside pocket of my suit, resisting the urge to thank him. There wasn't, I concluded, a great deal to thank him for.

Sensing my continued annoyance, he flashed me a salesman's smile. 'You did a good job, Dennis. It won't be forgotten.'

'No,' I said. 'Somehow, I don't think it will.'

After we'd parted company I grabbed a sandwich at a café just off the Marylebone Road. They didn't do anything with sushi in it so I ordered smoked salmon, thinking it was probably the next best thing. The sandwich tasted like cardboard, but I wasn't sure whether that was as a result of the poor-quality bread or my own numbed tastebuds. I ate about three quarters of it, washing it down with a bottle of overpriced mineral water, then smoked two cigarettes in quick succession.

On my way back to the station I called in on Len Runnion at his pawn shop just off the Gray's Inn Road. In some ways, Runnion was one of Tomboy's successors. He dealt in stolen goods of pretty much every description, using the pawn shop as a cover. He had none of the class of Tomboy, though. A very short man with a leering smile that made Raymond's look genuine, Runnion had cunning, ratlike eyes that darted about when he talked. And he never looked anyone in the eyes, which is something I can't stand. To me, it means they've got skeletons in the closet. From what I knew of Runnion and from what I could guess from his general demeanour, I expect he had a whole graveyard in his.

In the armed robbery I was still effectively investigating, the two robbers had held up a post office and, after stabbing the postmaster's wife and one of the customers, had got away with several hundred vehicle tax discs as well as a small sum of cash. I strongly suspected that they were amateurs who wouldn't really know what to do with the discs other than sell them on to other criminals. Professionals don't knife two people for that sort of return. It was a fair assumption then that they'd try someone like Runnion as a possible conduit for the goods, and if they had I wanted to know about it.

Runnion claimed ignorance of any tax discs. 'What would I do with them?' he asked me as he polished some garish-looking costume jewellery. I stated the obvious and he told me that he wouldn't have a clue where to sell such things. I didn't believe him, of course. Men in his line of business always know where to unload contraband. I told him that the perpetrators had stabbed the postmaster's wife and one of the customers during the course of the robbery, and that the customer had been lucky not to bleed to death. 'He was sixty-one years old, trying to protect the members of staff.'

Runnion shook his head in mock disbelief. 'There's no need for that,' he said. 'Never any need for violence. It's all about forward planning, isn't it? If you use forward planning, no-one gets hurt. The kids these days, they just don't have any. It's the education system, you know. They don't teach them anything any more.'

This was probably true, but you don't need to hear it from a toe-rag like Len Runnion. I told him firmly that if he was approached by anyone offering stolen tax discs he should play them along a bit, get them to come back again, and inform me straight away.

He nodded. 'Yeah, yeah, no problem. Goes without saying. I don't have no truck with bastards like that.' Which, of course, he did. Among other things, Runnion was wel known for supplying firearms, usually on a rental basis, to whoever needed them. We

might never have caught him for it, but that didn't mean anything. We knew he did it. 'If I hear anything, I'll make sure
you're the first to know, Sargeant.'

'You'd better do, Leonard. You'd better do.'

'And will there, shall we say, be a little drink in it for me if I
come good?' The eyes darted about like flies in a field of shit.

'I'm sure we'll be able to come up with something,' I told him,
knowing that bribery was usually more effective than threats.
After all, as a police officer, what could I threaten him with?
That we'd look into his business affairs more closely when we
had the time? It would hardly have got him quaking in his boots.

It was five to two by the time I got out of Runnion's shop.
Rather than continue my journey to the station, I thought I'd
phone Malik to see how everything was going.

He picked up after one ring. 'Miriam Fox.'

'Miriam?'

'That's our victim,' he said. 'Eighteen years old, just turned.
Ran away from home three years ago. She's been on the streets
ever since.'

'Miriam. It seems a funny name for a Tom. I assume she was
a Tom.'

'She was. Six convictions for soliciting. The last was two
months ago. Apparently she came from a good home. Parents
live out in Oxfordshire, father's something big in computers.
Plenty of money.'

'The sort of people who call their kid Miriam.'

'It's a rich girl's name,' Malik agreed.

'A runaway, then.'

'That's what I can't understand. All over the world you've got
people struggling to get out of poverty and make a better life for
themselves, and this girl was trying to do exactly the opposite.'

'Don't ever try to understand people,' I told him. 'You'll just be disappointed. Have the family been informed?'

'The local boys are round there now.'

'Good.'

'I've got her last known address here. A flat in Somerstown, not far from the station.'

I had to hand it to Malik, he didn't hang about. 'Has it been sealed yet?' I asked him.

'Yeah. According to the DI, they've got a uniform down there at the moment.'

'Keys?' It was always worth asking this sort of thing. You'd be amazed how many times simple things like means of entrance to an abode got overlooked.

'I had to pick them up myself. The landlord was one cheap bastard. It turned out she was late with the rent. He asked me what he could do to get hold of the money she owed him.'

'I hope you told him where to get off.'

'I told him he'd have to talk to her pimp. I said as soon as I got his address, I'd give it to him.'

I managed my first smile of the day. 'I bet that pleased him.'

'I don't think there was much that was going to please him today.' Anyway, the DI wants us to check out the address. See what we can find.'

I told Malik where I was and he said he'd come by and pick me up en route. He rang off and I lit a cigarette, sheltering the lighter from the cold November wind.

As I stood there breathing in the polluted city air, it struck me that maybe Malik was right. What the fuck had Miriam Fox been thinking about, coming here?

6

For me, one of the worst jobs in policing is looking through the possessions of a murder victim. A lot of the time when a murder's an open-and-shut case, which mostly they are, it's not necessary to have to do it, but sometimes there's no choice, and it's a painful process, the reason being that it puts flesh and bones on people, gives you insights into what made them tick, and this only serves to make them more human. When you're trying to be rational and objective, this is something you could really do without.

Miriam Fox's flat was on the third floor of a tatty-looking townhouse that could have been improved dramatically by a simple lick of paint. The front door was on the latch so we walked right in. Bags of festering rubbish sat just inside the entrance and the interior hallway was cold and smelled of damp. Thumping techno music blared from behind one of the doors. It annoyed me that people lived like this. I was all for minimalism, but this was just letting things go. It had nothing to do with poverty. It was all about self-respect. You didn't need money to clear away rubbish, and a can of paint didn't cost much. You could get a lot of paint, plus brushes for everyone, for the price of a few extra-strength lagers or a gram of smack. It's all about priorities.

A uniformed officer stood outside the door of flat number 5. Someone in flat number 4, which was just down the hall, was also playing music but thankfully not as loud as the guy downstairs. It also sounded quite a lot better – hippy stuff, with a woman singing earnestly about something or other that was obviously important to her. The uniform looked pleased to be relieved of his guard duty and made a rapid exit.

I checked the lock quickly for signs of tampering and, seeing none, opened the door.

The interior was a mess, which I suppose I expected. At least it was in keeping with the rest of the building. But it wasn't the mess of someone who'd gone completely to pot and no longer cared about her surroundings, which is a lot of people's image of the desperate prostitute. It was a teenage girl's mess. An unmade sofa bed took up close to half the floor space of the none too spacious living room. It was liberally sprinkled with clothes, not the sexy ones a Tom wears to attract her customers, but leggings and sweaters, stuff like that. Normal stuff. There were two threadbare chairs on either side of the bed and all three items of furniture faced an old portable TV that sat on a chest of drawers. There were pictures on the wall: a couple of impressionist prints; a colourful fantasy poster of a female warrior on a black stallion, sword in hand, blonde hair waving in the imaginary wind; a moody-looking band I didn't recognize; and a few photographs.

I stopped where I was and gave the place a quick once-over. A door on the left led to a bathroom while one on the right led into a kitchen that didn't look to be much bigger than a standard-sized wardrobe. There was only one window in the whole flat as far as I could see, though thankfully it was large

48

enough to throw a bit of light into the place. The view it offered was of a brick wall.

On the floor in front of me, amid the teen magazines, empty KFC boxes, Rizla packets and other odds and ends, was a huge round ashtray the size of a serving plate. There were maybe ten or fifteen cigarette butts in it, plus the remains of a few joints, but what caught my eye were the pieces of screwed-up tin foil, the small brown pipe, and the dark patches of crystallized liquid, splattered like paint drops inside.

It didn't surprise me that she was a crack addict. Most of the girls are, especially the young ones. It's either that or heroin. It's what keeps them tied to their pimps, and it's why the money they earn is never quite enough.

I lit a cigarette, figuring it wasn't going to make any difference. Malik gave me the briefest of disapproving glances as he put on his gloves but, like Danny the previous night, he didn't say anything.

We got to work without speaking. Malik started on the chest of drawers on which the TV sat. We both knew what we were looking for: little clues, things that in themselves might seem irrelevant to the untrained eye but which, taken together with what else the investigation threw up, could be used to build up a basic picture of the life and ultimately the death of Ms Miriam Fox.

She must have been quite a pretty girl once. There was a photograph of her pinned to the wall at a slightly uneven angle. In the picture, she was standing in the room we were in now, dressed in a pair of jeans and a sky-blue halter top that exposed a pale midriff. She didn't have any shoes on and her bare feet were long and thin. One hand was on her hip while she ran the other through her thick black hair. She was pouting mockingly at the cameraman. I think the pose was supposed to be sexy, but

49

the overall impression was that of a young girl trying hard to be a woman. I didn't know her, and would never know her, but at that moment I felt sorry for her.

The drugs had taken their toll. Her face was gaunt and bony, the eyes sunken and tired. It looked like it had been months since a decent meal passed her lips, which was probably true. But there was hope in the photograph too, or should have been. The damage didn't look permanent. Given time, some sleep and a healthy diet, she could have turned things around and become pretty again. Youth, if not luck, had been on her side.

There was a mirror shaped like a smiling moon next to the photograph. I saw my reflection in it and I couldn't help feeling that I was also beginning to look ravaged by the wrong sort of living. My cheekbones were protruding too much. So pronounced were they that it looked as if they were trying to escape from the rest of my face. To add to my misery, tiny webs of burst blood vessels I hadn't noticed before had popped up on either side of my nose. They were still pretty small, three of them altogether the size and shape of money spiders, but they worried me because now they were there, they were going to be there for ever. Youth, unfortunately, was not on my side.

There's nothing worse for a vain man than seeing reality catch up and hit him. I've always thought of myself as quite a good-looking guy and, to be honest, that's what more than a few women have told me over the years. No-one looking at the face I was looking at would have said that now.

There were two passport-type photos, still attached to each other, tucked into the mirror between the plastic coating and the glass. I removed them as carefully as I could and took a closer look. They'd obviously been taken one after another in one of those photo-me booths you get in railway stations and the occasional department store, because they were essentially the same picture. Two laughing girls, arms round each other, faces pressed together. One of the girls was Miriam Fox, the other was younger and prettier. The younger girl had blonde curly hair cut into a bob and, in contrast to Miriam, a round cherubic face with a cute smattering of freckles. Only the eyes, nothing like as bright as the rest of her, trying to look happy but not quite making it, told you that maybe she too was a street girl. I put her at about fourteen, but she could have been as young as twelve. They were both dressed in thick coats and the girl had a winter scarf round her neck, so I guessed the photo was fairly recent.

They looked like good friends. Maybe this girl, whoever she was, could fill in some of the gaps in Miriam Fox's life. We'd have to try to locate her, if she was still around. I put the photos in my notebook and moved over to a battered-looking wardrobe next to the bathroom door.

We went over everything bit by bit. Malik discovered a wad of notes: eight twenties, a fifty (how often do you see one of those?) and a ten. He appeared quite pleased with the find, although I wasn't sure why. A prostitute keeping cash in her flat was hardly a revelation.

'It means she definitely planned on coming back here,' he told me.

I told him that that's what I would have assumed anyway. 'If she picked up a punter and he just turned out to be the wrong sort of guy, then there's no question that she went out intending to come back here. Why wouldn't she?'

Malik nodded in agreement. 'But we're still trying to discover a motive, aren't we?' he said evenly. 'And at least this provides evidence that she wasn't running away from something and got caught before she could escape. It gives more credence to our theory of a dodgy punter.'

Credence. That was an interesting word. Malik was right of course. It did help to close off alternative theories, leaving us scope to focus our enquiries on certain areas, but I thought that maybe he was unnecessarily complicating matters. Malik was trying to look at it from the angle of Sherlock Holmes, and you didn't need to do that. If a prostitute gets her throat slashed and her genitalia mutilated, and her body's discovered on the edge of a notorious red light district with the clothing interfered with, it's fairly obvious what's happened.

Or so I thought.

There was nothing in the wardrobe that told us anything. There were a couple of drawers in there containing various kncik-knacks; some books, including two by Jane Austen, which caused me to raise my eyebrows (how many whores read Jane Austen?); a bag of dope; an unopened carton of Marlboro Lights; a jewellery box filled with costume jewellery. Nothing unusual, but no address book or anything like that, which might have thrown up a few clues. The man who'd killed her may well have been one of her regulars, someone who could have been in love with her but whose love was not being reciprocated. Out of frustration, he kills her. Out of rage, he mutilates the corpse. An address book might have contained the details of this man, if he existed. But of course, these days things are a bit different. She might have kept details of her clients in a palmtop PC or on a mobile, rather than writing it down on paper. Obviously, in a block of flats like this you weren't going to keep readily saleable items such as electronic goods on display for your neighbours to pinch, so I presumed if she owned anything like that, and it seemed highly likely that she had, she would have hidden it somewhere in the flat.

'Did she have a mobile on her when they found her body?' I asked Malik.

'I don't think so,' he said, shrugging. 'But I'm not sure.'

I thought about phoning and asking Welland, then decided it would probably be easier just to look for it. I couldn't recall him saying anything about a mobile in the briefing. 'Give me a hand lifting up this bed, will you?'

Malik lifted it up while I peered underneath. Apart from a lot of dust, another book (which turned out to be another Jane Austen), and a pair of knickers, there was nothing there. I stood back up and Malik put the bed down again.

I was wondering where to look next when there was a loud knock on the door. We both stopped and looked at each other. The knocking came again. Whoever was on the other side wasn't particularly patient. I was keen to find out who it was, so I stepped over and opened it before he could knock again.

A stocky black guy, late twenties, was glaring at me. He didn't hang around. 'Who the fuck are you?' he demanded, pushing past me into the flat. He stopped when he saw Malik in his rubber gloves standing by the bed, and immediately twigged. I closed the door to prevent any quick escape. 'You're Old Bill, aren't you?' he added, somewhat unnecessarily.

'While you're here, sir,' I said, walking up behind him, ' we'd just like to ask you a few questions.'

'What's going on?' he asked, whirling round to face me.

I could see him calculating the possible reasons why we were there and whether it was worth him hanging about. It didn't take him long to decide that it wasn't. He shoved me once, very hard, in the chest and made for the door. I stumbled but somehow managed to stay upright. He grabbed the handle, pulled the door open and tried to slam it in my face. He almost got me as well but my reflexes didn't let me down and I managed to dodge it and run out after him, Malik hot on my heels.

I used to be a sprinter when I was at school, and at the age of thirteen I did the hundred metres in 12.8 seconds, but thirteen was a long time and a lot of cigarettes ago.

But I was still quick over short distances and as he rounded the corner and charged down the stairs, two at a time, I was only a few feet behind him. The door was slightly ajar and he pulled it open and kept running pretty much in one movement. But I was closing. As I reached the top of the steps I dived onto his back and grabbed him in a desperate bearhug. 'All right, come on!' I panted in as authoritative a voice as I could muster. But it didn't seem to work. He kept running, at the same time shaking himself out of my grip, and managed to plant an elbow in my face. I yelped but continued chasing, one hand stretched out trying to grab him by the collar, wondering amid the pain in my lungs exactly how I was going to bring this guy to heel.

Suddenly he slowed abruptly, half turned so he was sideways on to me, and brought back his fist ready to throw an almighty punch. Momentum kept me going and, even though I knew exactly what was going to happen, I had no way of stopping it. His fist connected perfectly with my right cheek, sending me completely off balance. My head pounded with the shock of the blow and I bit my tongue as I fell against a wall. My legs wobbled precariously and then went from under me, and I fell backwards onto the pavement, hitting it arse first.

Malik immediately screeched to a halt beside me. 'Are you all right, Sarge?' he yelled with more concern than I would have expected from him.

'Get after him!' I panted, waving him away. 'Go on, I'm fine.'

Which was bullshit, of course. I felt like death. My lungs were bursting and the whole right side of my face throbbed. I opened my eyes and my vision was partly blurred. Still sitting where I'd fallen, I watched as Malik disappeared up the street, all five feet eight of him, armed with nothing more than harsh words. Somehow I didn't think an arrest was imminent.

I was going to have to give up smoking. I couldn't have run much over thirty yards all told and it felt like I'd done a mile at a sprint. The problem with not taking regular exercise, especially when you combine it with a shit lifestyle, is you don't realize quite how unfit you really are. I was going to have start going back to the gym, even though my membership had lapsed close to two years ago. I couldn't embarrass myself like that again. That cheap piece of dirt, who from the way he acted was no doubt Miriam Fox's pimp, could have kicked the shit out of me if he'd wanted to, the contest was that one-sided.

Across the street I could see a middle-aged woman staring out of her window in my direction. She looked like she felt sorry for me. When I caught her eye, though, she turned away and was gone.

As I gingerly got to my feet, I found myself experiencing an impotent rage. He'd made me look a fool. I wished I'd had the gun I'd been using the previous night on me. I could have blown that fuck apart. I wouldn't even have needed to tire myself out. I could have just strolled down the steps, taken aim at the middle of his back, and fired at leisure. He might have been a solid boy, but I'd yet to come across anyone whose skin deflected lead.

Malik came back into view, walking without urgency, and the rage passed. We'd get him. It was just a matter of being patient. Maybe, just maybe, once he'd been released again, I'd track him down one evening and put him to sleep. The thought made me feel better.

Malik looked pissed off. 'I lost him,' he said, stopping in front of me. 'He was too fast.'

'I know I shouldn't say this, but I'm sort of glad you didn't corner him.'

'I can handle myself, Sergeant. Anyway, you're the one who took the pasting. Are you all right?'

I rubbed my cheek and blinked a few times. My vision was still a little blurred but it seemed to be moving back towards normal. 'Yeah, I think so. That bastard had a good punch on him, though.'

'I saw. So who do you think he was?'

I told him, and he nodded in agreement. 'Yeah, I'd have thought so too. So what do we do about him?'

'It won't take long to find out his name. There'll be plenty of uniforms on the streets tonight, talking to the other Toms. They'll find out who he is. Then we'll just reel him in.'

It dawned on me that he might also be the pimp for the blonde girl in the photo with Miriam, and I suddenly felt protective towards her. She was too young to be selling herself on the street and too vulnerable to be under the thumb of someone like him. The sooner we picked him up the better.

We went back to searching the flat but, though we spent close to another half an hour in there, we didn't find anything else of note. I checked in with Welland and he told us to speak to the other occupants of the block, which turned out to be something of a fruitless exercise. Number 1, the one playing the techno music, steadfastly refused to answer the door, which was probably because he couldn't hear us. A few more hours of that and he wouldn't be able to hear anything. Number 2 wasn't in. Number 3, a colourfully dressed Somalian lady with a young baby in her arms, couldn't speak English. She recognized Miriam's picture but I think she thought we were looking for her because she kept pointing upstairs. Without a Somali translator, there wasn't a lot more we could do, so we thanked her and left.

Number 4 eventually answered the door after we'd knocked at least three times. He was a tall, gangly bloke with John Lennon glasses and a badly trimmed goatee. He took one look at us and immediately clicked that we were police. In our trenchcoats and inexpensive suits, we were never going to be anything else. He didn't look too pleased to see us, which was no great surprise since the unmistakable aroma of freshly exhaled dope smoke was easing out of the gap in the door.

I did the introductions and asked if we could come in. He started to say that it wasn't a good time right now, which is what they all say when they've got something to hide, but I wasn't going to let this one go, not after drawing blanks everywhere else in the place. I told him that it was a murder inquiry, and that we weren't interested if he'd been smoking blow in the privacy of his own home. Malik, who came more from the zero-tolerance school of policing (where it suited him, of course) gave me the standard disapproving look I was beginning to get used to from my subordinates, but I ignored him.

The guy really didn't have much choice so he let us in and turned the music down. He sat down on a large beanbag and, waving in the general direction of the other beanbags assembled around the cluttered room, let us know that we too could sit down.

I told him we'd remain standing. He looked a mixture of nervous and confused, which was fine by me. I wanted to make him take this discussion seriously, to get him to rack his brains for information that could be of help.

As it happens, I didn't get a lot. His name was Drayer. He added that his first name was Zeke, but I told him I didn't believe anyone would have called their kid Zeke, not at the time he was born, which had to have been at least forty years earlier. He insisted that it was. I asked him if that was the name on his birth certificate. He admitted it wasn't. 'And have you changed it by deed poll?' He reluctantly conceded that he hadn't.

Eventually, I got it out of him that his real first name was Norman. 'Norman's an all right name,' I told him. 'It's no worse than Dennis, which is mine.'

'I know it's no worse,' he said, and left it at that. Cheeky bastard.

It turned out that Norman was a poet by trade. He performed his poetry in some of the local pubs and clubs and had also had a few bits and pieces published in various anthologies. 'It doesn't pay much,' he confided, 'but it's a clean life.' Looking round his worn-out living room, I wasn't sure I'd have used that description for it, but there you go. Everyone's entitled to their own illusions.

Norman appeared genuinely upset when he found out it was Miriam who'd been murdered. He hadn't really known her, he said, as she'd tended to keep herself to herself, but whenever he'd run into her in the hallway she had always smiled and said hello. 'She was a nice girl, you know. Made the effort. There aren't many like that in this city.'

We both nodded in agreement. 'It can be an unfriendly place,' I said, stating the obvious. 'Did Miss Fox have many visitors? Particularly male ones?'

'Er no, I don't think so,' he said, thinking about it. 'I saw one man go up there a couple of times.'

'What did he look like?' Malik asked.

'He was muscular, well formed. Attractive, I would think, to women. And there was a fire about him, a passion. An anger almost. As if somewhere inside him was a volcano waiting to erupt.'

'That's a truly terrible description,' I told him. 'Try again. Was he tall, short? Black, white?'

'He was black.'

I described the guy who'd just clouted me and it quickly

58

transpired that they were one and the same. Well, at least he'd been right about one thing. There'd certainly been an anger there.

'How often did he come and go?'

'I saw him maybe two or three times in the hall or on the stairs. He never spoke to me.'

'Over how long a period?'

He shrugged. I think he was pissed off that I'd mocked his descriptive skills. 'I don't know, maybe three months.'

'And when was the last time you saw him?'

'A couple of weeks ago. Something like that.'

'Not within the last two or three days?'

'No.'

'How long have you been here?' Malik asked.

'About a year now.'

'And was Miss Fox already here when you moved in?'

'No, she wasn't. She came . . . I don't know, about six months ago.'

'And you can't remember any other male visitors?'

He shook his head. 'No, I don't think so. Should I have done?'

'I thought poets were meant to be observant,' I told him. 'You know, viewing their surroundings and commenting on what they see.'

'What do you mean? What are you talking about?'

'She was a prostitute, Mr Drayer. Didn't you know that?'

It turned out he didn't, which was probably because there hadn't been any other male visitors that he recalled. She'd clearly kept her business and personal life separate. I showed him the photo-me images and asked him if he recognized the blonde girl. He said he did. He'd seen her a number of times coming and going with Miriam. 'They seemed like good friends. They used to laugh together a lot. Like schoolgirls.'

'That's what they should have been,' I said.

We asked him a few more questions about his own back-ground and what he knew about the other people in the flats, but didn't get any information of significance. If anything, Norman knew even less about his other neighbours than he'd known about Miriam.

It was just after a quarter to six when we finally got back to the station and reported to Welland, who'd taken up residence in a small office next to the incident room, from where he could control his end of the inquiry. He was pissed off because one of his witnesses in another case, a girl testifying against her ex-boyfriend who'd knifed someone in a pub fight, had decided to pull the plug and keep her mouth shut. Apparently someone had persuaded her to change her mind with a small threat of violence, leaving Welland's case in tatters.

'I've had the CPS on the phone all afternoon,' he moaned between vacuum-cleaner-like drags on his cigarette. 'Making a fucking fuss like they're fucking whiter than white.'

Malik made the mistake of asking if she'd had protection.

Welland glared at him. 'That fucking knifing happened three months ago and the trial doesn't start until February. I can't have a man with her all that time. Where the fuck am I going to get him from? Magic him up out of thin air?'

Malik backed off, knowing better than to get involved in one of Welland's rants. Welland finished his cigarette in three angry drags and used the butt to light another one. 'Anyway, what happened to your face?' he asked me eventually. I told him, and he shook his head angrily. 'We'll put a warrant out on him as soon as we've got his name. He might be able to throw some light on this. Did you find anything of interest there?'

I shook my head. 'Not a lot. There was no address book or mobile phone or anything, nothing that would give us any idea of her client list.'

'We're just going to have to ask around among the King's Cross girls tonight. See if they can throw up any names.'

'She's bound to have had a mobile,' I said. 'Have we got anyone checking whether there was one registered in her name?'

'Yeah, I've got Hunsdon on it at the moment, but it'll take time.'

I told him about the girl in the photographs and suggested it would be a good idea to try to trace her.

'Yeah, you're right. She might be able to help. There's a meeting tomorrow at eight thirty sharp. We'll be getting the preliminary autopsy findings, so make sure you're there. No fucking oversleeping. It's important we get momentum on this one,' he said by way of conclusion. 'You know what they say about the first forty-eight hours.'

I did indeed, but my momentum had gone for the day. The right side of my face still ached, and since I was going to have to be in early again, I decided it was time to knock off. I asked Malik if he fancied joining me for a drink, more out of politeness than anything else, since I didn't think he'd say yes. He looked at his watch for at least two seconds too long, then smiled and said why not, which was unusual for him. He generally liked to get away at the end of the shift back to his family, which was fair enough, although he wasn't averse to socializing with the bosses if he thought it would do him some good.

We adjourned to a pub called the Roving Wolf, which was a haunt for CID and some of the uniforms. It was busy with the after-work office crowd, a few of whom I knew by sight, and I said hello to a couple of people as I pushed my way to the bar and ordered the drinks – a pint of Pride for me, a large orange juice for Malik. We found a table in the corner away from the scrum, and I lit a cigarette.

'So, who killed Miriam Fox, then?' he asked, sipping his drink.

'Good question.'

'What do you think?'

'Well, it's early days yet, and a lot depends on the result of the autopsy, but I suppose my first thought's the obvious one, and that's because the obvious one's usually the right one.'

'A pervert?'

'I think so. You've got to say, it points that way. She died at the scene, there's no doubt about that. The area round the body was too bloodstained for her to have been taken there after death. And the location suggests she wasn't killed by someone who knew her. It's the sort of place she might well have gone for privacy with a punter, and the sort of place a killer might have gone for privacy with his victim.'

'So what do you reckon our chances of a result are, then?'

'Too early to say. If the killer's been careless like a lot of these guys can be, then we're sorted. Forensics'll have him in no time.'

'Unless, of course, he's not known to us.'

I didn't like to think of that scenario. 'True. But someone who can do that ... you know, grab a young girl from behind and cut her throat from ear to ear. Even in this day and age, I don't think there are many who could. Someone like that is likely to have done something that's brought him to the attention of the police before. But if he's planned it, and he's been careful, and he's picked someone who doesn't know him from Adam—'

'Like a prostitute.'

'Like a prostitute, then he could be miles away by now.'

'And what do you think? Do you think he's a planner or someone who just can't control his urges?'

'Well, my gut feeling is that he's a planner. But I haven't really got anything to back that up with, except for the fact that he picked a good spot to take her out, and he obviously knew what he was doing. What about you? What's your take on it?'

Malik smiled wearily. 'I think it's depressing that we learn all these investigative skills, yet how much do we actually ever need them?'

'What do you mean?'

'Well, unless the guy's an idiot or we get a lucky break, then we're not going to catch him, are we? No matter how clever we are.'

'Policework's all about lucky breaks, but you know what they say: in the end, you make your own luck.'

'Well, I hope we get lucky, then, because otherwise it's just a matter of waiting, isn't it?'

'He may not kill again,' I said. 'Sometimes they don't.'

'And if he doesn't, then he may never be brought to justice.'

'That's the trade-off. Let's just hope it doesn't come to that. To successful forensics,' I said, raising my glass.

'To successful forensics,' Malik intoned, not looking completely convinced.

For a few moments we both sat in silence, mulling things over. I took a long sip of my drink, thinking that I was glad the day was over.

'Did you hear about that shooting in Hertfordshire last night?'

My mind immediately snapped to attention. To be honest, I hadn't thought about last night's activity since my meet with Raymond. It might sound callous, but I'd been too busy. I felt a short rush of regret when Malik mentioned it, but it was a lot weaker than it had been earlier. I felt bad at what had happened, but what was done was done. Time can sometimes be a rapid as well as a great healer.

'Yeah, I did. I reckon there's more to that one than meets the eye.'

'So do I. I've got a friend, a guy I used to go to college with. He's a DC up in Hertford. They're handling the case. For the moment anyway.'

'Yeah, I heard. What's he got to say about it so far?'

'I haven't spoken to him yet. I expect he's under the cosh a bit. Same as us. I thought I might try him this evening, that's if they're letting him home for the night.'

I took an easy gulp of my pint, knowing that I was going to have to approach this carefully. 'When you do speak to your mate, find out a bit more about this case. It intrigues me.'

'And me. It's an interesting one. Looks like a gangland hit. It makes you wonder what those customs men were investigating.'

It did that, all right. 'Whatever it was, it must have been pretty big.'

'Well, you'd think so, wouldn't you? I think the key lies in finding out whoever the guy with them was. The civilian. When you know what his involvement was, I think you'll have the motive, and with something like this, once you've got the motive, you're two thirds of the way there.'

'It's proving it, though, isn't it? This was obviously well planned so you'd assume whoever was behind it has covered their tracks pretty well. You might find out who they are, but it's building a case against them that matters.'

Malik nodded. 'You've got to get someone to talk, that's always the key. Something like this, there's got to be a fair few people involved, and one or two of them are bound to get cold feet.'

I thought of Danny. Would he break? I doubted it. He'd known what we were going to do and had been happy enough to get involved. But Malik was right. There were a fair few people involved, some of whom I didn't know from Adam. Any one of them could end up talking, although it was a bit late to worry about that now. I was glad that, through Malik, I at least had a means of finding out how well the investigation was going.

'One way or another, it's going to be a difficult one to crack,' I added. 'Time consuming.'

'Perhaps. But definitely interesting. I'd love to talk to the man who did it. You know, the one who actually pulled the trigger.'

'Why? What'll he tell you? I expect he did it for money; something nice and mundane like that.'

Malik smiled. 'I'm sure he did – it's almost certainly a professional hit – but it takes a special kind of man to shoot dead three people without a second's thought. Just like that.' He clicked his fingers to signify his point. 'People he's almost certainly never met before. People who've never done him any harm.'

'You'd probably find that whoever did it was pretty normal underneath it all.'

'Normal people don't murder each other.'

This time it was my turn to smile. 'Normal people murder each other all the time.'

'I don't agree with that. Most murderers might look normal, but there's always something rotten inside that makes them do what they do.'

'I don't know. It's not always as cut and dried as that.'

Malik stared at me intensely. 'It *is* always that cut and dried. Murder's murder, and the people who commit it are bad people. There's no two ways about it. It's a black-and-white issue. Some murders aren't quite as horrific as others, but none of them are justifiable. Under any circumstances. They're just different shades of black.'

I could tell he felt passionately about what he was saying and thought it best not to say too much more on the matter. You never know when such conversations can be regurgitated and used against you somewhere down the line. So I conceded the point and the conversation drifted on through the awkward avenues of small talk before inevitably coming back to the case. After all, what else was there to talk about?

We both concluded that Welland was right about momentum. If we didn't turn up clues in the next few days, and it really did turn out to be someone unknown to the victim – which I have to say is what everything seemed to point to – then the bottom would fall out of this case very quickly and we'd be left with nothing. Either waiting for our mystery perpetrator to strike again (a worrying enough scenario in itself) or losing him for ever amid the vast ranks of the unsolveds, which somehow I felt would be even worse.

Malik stayed for two drinks to give him the opportunity to buy me a brew back, then it was time for him to return to the family seat in Highgate where his pretty wife and two young children awaited him. He offered to share a taxi with me but I decided to stay put for a while. I was hungry, but I fancied one more drink before I headed back to the flat. I'd got the taste of beer now.

One of the regulars, an old guy with a raspy voice whom I knew vaguely, came and joined me and we chatted about this and that for a while. Normal shit: football results, the price of beer, what a fuck-up the government was making of everything. Sometimes it's nice to talk to civilians. It doesn't require you to rack your brains in case you missed something. Things just flow along nice and easy. But when the guy started going on about his wife's pickled-onion-sized bunions, and I started thinking that I hoped I'd be dead by the time I got to his age, I knew it was time to go.

It was eight o'clock when the cab dropped me off outside my front door. The iron-grey cloud cover that had sat above the city most of the morning had now broken up completely, you could even make out the odd star. The temperature had dropped accordingly and the night had a pleasant wintery feel about it.

The first thing I did when I got inside was phone Danny, but he wasn't at home. I tried him on his mobile but got diverted to the message service, so I left one telling him to be in at five p.m. the next day so that I could drop the money round to him. Then I showered, washing off the dirt of the day, and thought about food.

I found a carton of something called creamy prawn risotto in the freezer. It said 'ready in twenty minutes' on the sleeve and the photo didn't look too unappetizing so I defrosted it in the microwave. While it was cooking, I took my usual seat on the sofa and switched on the TV, turning straight to the news channel.

Two passport-type photographs dominated the screen. They were of the Cherokee driver and his front-seat passenger. The driver looked different from the previous night. In the photo he was smiling broadly and there were laughter lines around his eyes. It gave you the impression that he'd probably been quite a nice bloke when he was alive. Old greasy face next to him looked better as well. He was still staring moodily at the camera, like he'd just been told off by someone twenty years his junior, but he'd lost the shiftiness he'd been exuding the previous night, and it looked like he'd washed his hair and given it a decent comb, which had improved his appearance no end.

The report named the driver as Paul Furlong, a thirty-six-year-old father of two young children, and his passenger as forty-nine-year-old Terry Bayden-Smith, who'd been with customs since leaving school. Bayden-Smith was divorced and presumably had no kids because none were mentioned.

Their faces disappeared from the screen to be replaced by a male reporter in a fleece coat standing outside the Traveller's Rest. There was still police tape everywhere and the Cherokee remained where it had stopped beside me, but activity had dwindled. A uniformed officer stood in the background guarding the scene, but he was the only person I could see. The reporter said that there'd been more than sixty detectives assigned to this case and that the police were confident of finding the killer. There were apparently a number of ongoing lines of inquiry but the reporter quoted a senior police source as saying that a quick result was unlikely.

I wondered if Raymond had been telling the truth when he'd said they'd been corrupt. Would it make what I'd done any better? Probably not. Once again I found myself wishing I hadn't got involved. Corrupt or not, there was going to be a huge amount of pressure on the investigating officers. Unlike us, they'd get all the resources they needed as well, always the way in high-profile cases where the public are clamouring for arrests. Again, very little mention was made of the third victim of the shooting, and they still weren't naming him, which surprised me. I was going to have to press Raymond to find out who he was. By now I was fairly certain he was more than just another piece of pondscum.

The murder of Miriam Fox didn't get a look-in, not even on Ceefax. I suppose a dead prostitute just doesn't carry the same kind of glamour, although that would certainly change if another Tom went the same way. There's nothing the public likes more than a serial killer, especially when he's not targeting them.

I ate my food while watching *Family Fortunes*. As always, Les Dennis did his best with only limited resources, kind of like the Metropolitan Police. Neither family was over-bright and the Dobbles from Glasgow had accents so thick that you had to wonder how they'd made it through the auditions. Les made a few jokes about needing a translator and laughed heartily as he tried to keep things going, but you could tell he was getting a bit tired of it. In the end they lost to the English family whose name I forget, and who went on to win the car.

After that I watched a film. It was a romantic comedy and it would have been quite entertaining but I had difficulty concentrating. I kept imagining the family of Paul Furlong huddled together in their living room, their faces red and tearstained. In my mind, the kids were a boy and a girl and they had blond hair. The boy was the older, maybe five, and the girl was a pretty little thing, about three. The boy kept turning to his mother who had her arms round both of them and asking why their dad was gone and where he had gone to. The mother, her voice breaking with emotion, said that he'd gone to heaven because sometimes that's where you have to go if God wants you for a particular reason. I thought of myself as a young kid and wondered how I would have felt if someone had snatched away my dad. My dad was dead now. He'd died five years ago, and it had been a blow even then, because I'd always held him in high esteem. When I was five, he'd been king of the world because he'd known everything there was to know about anything. It would have torn me apart if someone had taken him away then.

In the end, I could torture myself no more. Sitting alone in a poky flat, wallowing in the guilt of depriving kids of their father, was always going to be a recipe for disaster. So when the film finished, and the couple who hadn't been able to stand the sight of each other at first predictably got together and disappeared off into the sunset, I went to bed.

It was a measure of my exhaustion that I was asleep almost before my head hit the pillow.

7

Most nights my sleep is a blank space where nothing happens but that night was different. I dreamed of many vague things and woke up time and time again. Everything was a jumble, a messy kaleidoscope of images and thoughts and memories that for split seconds were ice cold in their clarity, but just as quickly faded like dying film heroes as I moved on to the next one.

Only one dream stayed in the mind. It came in the grey time just before dawn. In this dream, I was in a television studio watching an edition of *Family Fortunes*. I was up in the audience, but the audience was just a blur. The studio was very dark but there was a light that shone on Les Dennis, so you could see him well enough, and I remember that he was wearing a pink suit with a lime green shirt. Les was introducing one of the families but I couldn't make out their name because everything was too dark. He spoke to each of them in turn, and as he stopped in front of an individual player a light shone down on that person so you could see who was who.

First there was the driver of the Cherokee, Paul Furlong. He only had one eye, the other was just a bloody mess where I'd shot him, but he looked happy enough, and he laughed when Les told a joke. Then there was the front-seat passenger, Bayden-Smith. He still looked morose and most of the top of his head was missing. When he spoke, his voice sounded slow and drawling like a record on the wrong speed, and it took me a couple of seconds to work out that this was because his jaw was hanging off his face at an odd angle. I remember thinking that I was glad he didn't have kids. Then there was the back-seat passenger, but I couldn't really see his face very well and he kept looking away. Les tried to put him at ease by saying that he'd heard he was a very good skateboarder and inviting him to elaborate. But still he wouldn't look at us. Miriam Fox, who was standing next to him in a slinky black dress, her throat sliced from ear to ear, put a protective arm around his shoulders.

'You're Miriam,' said Les.

'That's right,' said Miriam in a pleasant voice.

'And what brings you here, Miriam?'

'I'm here with the dead.'

'Here with the dead!' laughed Les. 'That sounds good!' And he looked at the audience, and they all laughed too. 'And who's this?' he added, looking towards the person on the other side of Miriam. I couldn't see who it was because the light wouldn't shine on her and she was silhouetted in the darkness, but I had a dread feeling of familiarity. She was small, smaller than Miriam, and I thought I could make out curly hair.

'Is it your sister?' asked Les, still smiling, and Miriam suddenly looked very sad, as if Les had touched upon some secret tragedy. She started to say something but the words didn't come out or, if they did, I didn't hear them.

There was a long pause, and the audience fell silent.

Then Les turned back towards us, and he too looked troubled.

'These are the dead,' he said.

And then I woke up, sweating and frightened.

Part Two

HUNTING THE LIVING

PART TWO

Inspiration and Discipline

8

'Miriam Ann Fox, aged eighteen, died from a single stab wound to the neck delivered from behind. The wound was almost two inches deep, suggesting that it was a) a very sharp bladed knife, and b) a very strong person delivering the fatal blow. From the angle of the wound we can surmise that the perpetrator was considerably taller than her. She was five feet three; he, and I think we can safely assume it was a he in this case, is almost certainly between five feet ten inches and six feet two. The victim either bled or choked to death as a result of this one wound. The pathologist thinks that the perpetrator held her up while she choked and died, then laid her out on the ground on her back, before stabbing her four times in the vaginal area.'

'So he didn't have sex with her then?' asked one of the assembled group.

It was 8.35 the following morning and Malik, me, and the fourteen other detectives assigned to the Miriam Fox murder hunt were sitting in the incident room while DCI Knox, the official head of the investigation, stood next to a whiteboard giving his summary of what we knew so far. Welland sat next to him, but was once again not looking himself. If someone had asked me for a diagnosis of his condition I would have said his batteries had gone flat, which seems to happen more and more to coppers of a certain age, and I wondered briefly how much longer he was going to last on the Force.

No such concerns about Knox, who was a big charismatic guy with a deep, resonant voice that swept across the room. 'There's no evidence that she had sex either immediately prior to or immediately after her death,' he continued. 'According to the pathologist she died at some point between eight and ten on Sunday night. Now we've spoken to a number of the girls who work the area and she was seen by at least two of them at about eight p.m., which was when she generally started her shift. She spoke briefly to one of the girls, and the girl said that there was nothing untoward about her. She then moved down the street to her usual spot, which is the corner of Northdown and Collier Street, and from there she was picked up by a car – a dark blue saloon, we haven't got the make yet – and driven away. Usually the girls try to get the number of the cars but, sod's law, no-one did this time.'

There was a resigned murmur from the assembled men, including me. You don't expect to get too many lucky breaks in the course of your work, but on a case like this you need a few.

Knox paused to take a sip from his tea. 'They didn't drive very far though, as we know. The victim was killed at the spot where she was found. As the crow flies that's no more than a few hundred yards from where she was picked up. It's important we trace this car. We've got a dozen uniforms who are going to be doing house-to-house in the vicinity to see if anyone can remember seeing a vehicle fitting the description near the scene. If we're lucky' – more groans –'somebody might even have got a look at him. He would have been heavily bloodstained after the killing.

We're checking CCTV on every possible site from where she was picked up to where she was discovered, but so far nothing's turned up.'

'None of the Toms recognized the car, then?' asked Capper, who was a DS, the same as me. I didn't like Capper; never had. He had an unpleasant haircut and constant bad breath, but I wouldn't have held those things against him particularly, not on their own. It was the way he sucked up to senior management I didn't like.

Knox shrugged. 'They see a lot of dark-coloured saloons in their line of business so no-one remembers this one.'

'You said that the Toms tended to make notes of punters' registration plates.' It was me speaking this time.

'That's right.'

'Do they ever keep records of them?'

He shook his head. 'No, it doesn't appear so, not according to any of the girls who were spoken to last night. We still might get the number, though. We'll be appealing for information on *Crimestoppers* and in the area itself. Boards'll be going up round there this morning, so someone's memory might get jogged. We need to find out if she had any punters who she went with on a regular basis. Most of them usually do. We've got two statements from girls testifying that she was picked up on more than one occasion by someone in a red TVR, although no-one ever saw his face. Apparently she had a friend, a girl by the name of Molly Hagger, who used to work the streets with her, I believe you've got a photo of her, Dennis, but she hasn't been seen for several weeks.'

I felt a brief stab of fear. So that was her name. Molly. And now she was missing. 'There was a photograph of her with the victim at the victim's flat,' I said. 'It looked recent, so I think it would be useful to talk to this Molly.'

'If we can find her.'

'Have we got an address for her?' I asked.

Knox nodded. 'We think so. One of the girls said she thought she was staying at Coleman House. It's a council-run children's home over towards Camden. We haven't contacted anyone down there yet so I want you and Malik to pay the place a visit and see if you can find out where she is, and if any of the other people there have any information on the victim.'

I nodded. 'Sure.'

'We've also got to bring in the victim's pimp, who we've now identified as Mark Wells. Dennis met him briefly yesterday.' He looked across at me and winked, much to the amusement of everyone else. 'Wells has a long record of violence, including attacks on women, and at the very least we can bring him in for taking out DS Milne.'

Again there was more laughter. I managed a strained smile to show that I could take a joke, just like the next man, not that I felt much like laughing. My face still hurt and a darkening bruise had appeared under my right cheekbone overnight.

'We're applying for a search warrant for his house and a warrant for his arrest, both of which should be with us by mid-morning. We're going to lean on him hard. He's a cocky bastard by all accounts, but he's going to have useful information about the victim, and it's essential we extract it from him. He's also a suspect. So far, our only evidence of sexual assault is the stab wounds around the vagina, so it's quite possible that the killer's attempting to make it look like a sexual assault when, in reality, it wasn't his prime motivation. Now I don't want to put too much stock on that theory, because at the moment it is just a theory, but we've got to bear it in mind. And that means taking a close look at Mark Wells.'

He paused again, took another sip of his tea. 'We also need

the names of everyone in a three-mile radius of here who's been picked up for soliciting at any time in the last two years, giving particular preference to anyone with convictions for violence or sex offences. And we're going to need to interview them all.' Several people groaned, and Knox managed an understanding smile. 'Look, it's not going to be easy – it never is – but we've got to explore every possible avenue, and that means talking to the sort of people who could have done this, i.e. men who are known to be violent to women. This murder hunt is twenty-four hours old, ladies and gentlemen. At the moment the body's still warm but it's going to cool down fast, so we've got a lot of work to do. One hell of a lot. I want this killer brought to justice and I know you're the people to do it.' He accompanied this last sentence by enthusiastically whacking one of the desks with the palm of his hand, which was a very Knox-like gesture. I'm sure sometimes he thought he was working on Wall Street.

Brave words, too. Whether they'd be matched by deeds or not, though, remained to be seen.

The remainder of the meeting was spent organizing who was going to be doing what, and took about ten minutes, including questions. Welland was going to be leading the raid on Mark Wells's place as soon as the paperwork came through, which annoyed me a little bit. Since it had been me the bastard had hit, I wanted to be on the team which brought him in, but I suppose at the same time I also wanted to find out more about Molly, and it was going to be difficult to do both.

It was 9.20 when Malik and I left to go round to the Coleman House care home. Times were hard in our division of the Metropolitan Police and budgets tight, so we decided to save the taxpayers some money by taking the bus. In the end, though, it would probably have been quicker to walk. An accident on the Holloway Road had snarled up the traffic and we were stuck in it, stopping and starting, for what seemed like hours.

I told Malik about my dream as we sat there watching the world go by, or not as the case might be. It had genuinely rattled me. 'You know, I know it sounds stupid, but it was almost like some sort of premonition.'

He couldn't resist a grin. 'What? You think Les Dennis might be in danger?'

'I'm serious, Asif. This wasn't like any dream I've ever had. You know me. I'm not superstitious, and I'm not spiritual or anything like that. I'm not even a Christian. So it's nothing to do with my state of mind. It was just it was so vivid that when I woke up I was absolutely positive this Molly girl was dead.'

'Explain the dream to me again.'

I went through it all with him, missing out the details of the dead customs men, and whispering so that none of the other passengers, a mixture of old grannies and foreign students, could hear what I was saying. I didn't want them thinking I was some sort of nutter.

By the time I'd finished, we'd travelled the sum total of about thirty yards.

Malik shook his head and gave me the sort of look that suggested he thought it was grossly unfair that he should be taking orders from someone with such a tenuous grip on reality. 'Look, Sarge, I wouldn't worry about it. You know, a dream's just a dream. The chances are this girl's all right.'

'I hope so. I didn't like the sound of the fact that she hasn't been seen for a couple of weeks.'

'Only by the local streetwalkers. Maybe she's changed. Maybe she's realized that prostitution and drug addiction is no way to lead a life.'

I laughed. 'Do you really believe that?'

'Well, it's unlikely . . .'

'Dead right it is.'

'But it's possible. And anyway, maybe she's just plying her trade somewhere else. There's got to be more chance of that than of her being dead in a ditch somewhere.'

Malik said these last few words a bit too loudly and a couple of people turned round and gave us funny looks.

'Yeah, you're right,' I said. 'You've convinced me.'

But he hadn't.

We exited the bus on Junction Road when it became obvious that we weren't getting anywhere and took the tube, which thankfully was still running pretty much as normal. It was 10.20 when we got out of Camden station. It was slowly turning into a sunny winter's day, so we walked the rest of the way.

Coleman House was a large redbrick Victorian building on a road just off the high street. One of the third-floor windows was boarded up, but other than that it looked quite well kept. A couple of kids, a boy and a girl, sat on the wall in front of the entrance, smoking and looking shifty. The girl was wearing a very short skirt and a huge pair of black platform-soled trainers that, set against her spindly legs, made her look mutated. They both looked at us as we approached and the boy sneered. 'Are you coppers?' he said.

'That's right,' I told him, stopping in front of them. 'We're investigating a murder.'

'Oh yeah? Whose, then?' he asked, looking interested. Morbid little bastard.

'Well, why don't we start with you telling me your name?'

'What's it got to do with me? I haven't done nothing.'

'You can't make him give you his name,' said the girl confidently, looking me in the eye. I put her at about thirteen, and she would have been quite pretty except for the angry cluster of whiteheads around her mouth and the excessive use of cheap make-up. Thirteen, and she was already a barrack-room lawyer. I had a feeling they were all going to be like that in a place like this.

'I'm not trying to,' I told her. 'I'm just interested in knowing who I'm talking to.'

'If you want to talk to him, you need an appropriate adult present.'

'So, when did you graduate from law school then, young lady?'

She was about to come up with some other smart-alec answer but we were interrupted before she could get it out.

'Can I help you, gentlemen?'

The speaker was an attractive white female, early forties. Quite tall – about five feet nine – and, from the sound of her voice, someone in authority.

I turned in her direction and smiled, opening fire with the charm. 'I hope so. My name's DS Milne and this is my colleague, DC Malik. We're here as part of an ongoing inquiry.'

She managed a weak smile. 'Really, what now?'

'It's a murder investigation.'

'Oh.' She looked taken aback. 'Was there any reason why you were talking to the children?'

'I was just introducing myself.'

'No you weren't,' said the girl. 'He was trying to find out who we were.'

'Well, I'll take over from here, Anne. Aren't you and John meant to be with Amelia?'

'We're just having a quick smoke,' said the girl, not bothering to look up.

'Perhaps you'd better come inside, gentlemen, and we'll talk in there.'

I nodded. 'Of course. And you are?'

'Carla Graham. I manage Coleman House.'

'Well, then, please lead the way,' I said, and we followed her through the double doors and into the building.

The place had the unwelcoming feel of a hospital: high ceilings; linoleum floors; health-related posters on the walls warning against shared needles, unwanted pregnancy, and a whole host of other obstacles to a happy and fulfilling life. And there was a nasty reek of disinfectant in the air. Dr Barnardo's this wasn't.

Carla Graham had a spacious office at the other end of the building. She ushered us in and we took seats facing her across her sizeable desk. There were more doom-mongering posters in here as well. One showed a huge photograph of a young child, no more than five, covered in bruises. The caption above it read: Stamp on Child Abuse. Below the photograph it added: Not on Children.

'So, what's happened?' Carla asked. 'I hope none of our clients are involved.'

'Clients, meaning children?' It was Malik asking the question.

'That's right.'

'We don't really know, which is why we're here.' I then told her about the discovery of the body the previous day.

'I didn't hear anything about that,' she said. 'Who was the poor girl?'

'Her name was Miriam Fox.' Carla's expression didn't hint at recognition, so I continued. 'She was an eighteen-year-old prostitute, a runaway.'

She shook her head and sighed. 'What a waste. Not a shock, because the potential for this sort of thing to happen's there all the time. But a terrible waste, all the same.'

Malik leaned forward in his seat and I immediately got the feeling that he didn't much like Carla Graham. 'I assume you didn't know her?'

'I don't know the name, no.'

I took the photo of Miriam posing for the camera out of my suit pocket and passed it over to her. 'This is her. We think it's a recent picture.'

She studied it for a long moment before handing it back to me. As I took it back I noticed she had graceful hands with well-kept, unvarnished nails.

'She looks vaguely familiar. I may have seen her before with one of the clients, but I couldn't say for sure.'

'We've been talking to some of the other girls who work the same area as Miriam did and they say she was particularly friendly with a girl called Molly Hagger. They said that Molly lived here at Coleman House.'

'Lived is the right word. Molly was a client of ours for some months but she walked out about three weeks ago now and we haven't seen her since.'

'You don't seem too worried about that, Ms Graham,' Malik said, only just about concealing his dismay that she should take the loss of one of her 'clients' so lightly.

'Mr Malik,' she said, turning towards him, 'Coleman House is home to twenty-one children aged between twelve and sixteen, all of whom come from disadvantaged backgrounds and all of whom have behavioural problems of varying degrees of seriousness. They are placed here by the council, and we try to do our best for them but the law is not on our side. If they want to go out at night, they go out. If I or any of my staff lay a hand on them to try to stop them leaving, they can have assault charges laid against us just like that, and believe me they'd do it. Put bluntly, these kids do what they like because they know they can do what they like. Half of them can't write their names, but they all know their rights inside out. And often, I'm afraid, they simply decide they've had enough of us and walk out the door. Sometimes they come back; sometimes they don't.'

'Don't you try to look for them?' Malik persisted.

She looked at him in the way a teacher looks at a particularly foolish pupil. 'We're extremely understaffed. It's hard enough keeping control of the ones who want to be here without worrying about the ones who don't. And where would we look for her? She could be anywhere.'

'Did you report her missing?' I asked.

'I informed Camden Social Services and they will have informed the police, but I didn't report it myself. I didn't see much point.'

'How old is Molly Hagger?'

'Thirteen.'

I shook my head. 'It's a young age to be out on the streets.' It was. Far too young.

She turned to me now. 'Mr . . . ?'

'Milne.'

'Mr Milne, I can understand if you think I'm not taking Molly's leaving seriously enough, I can understand both of your concerns, but try to look at it from my point of view. I've been a careworker for a long time now, and I've tried to help a lot of kids make a better life for themselves. But the older I get, the harder it becomes. You see, a lot of the time these kids don't want to be helped. They get plenty of offers, I can promise you, but most of them just want to live fast, take drugs, drink. They're independent, but independent in all the wrong ways. They can't stand any form of authority but often they aren't capable of looking after themselves. They're not all like that of course, some do actually want to listen and learn, and they're the ones I find myself gravitating to. If I've tried to help someone, and they keep turning their noses up at that help, then eventually I have to stop.'

'And was Molly Hagger like that? Was she one of the ones who turned her nose up?'

'Molly came from a very difficult background. She was sexually abused from the age of four by both her mother and her mother's boyfriend. She was taken into care at the age of eight and she's been in it ever since.'

I thought of the girl in the photograph and felt mildly sick. 'Jesus . . .'

'It's far more common than most people think. You should know that, Mr Milne.'

'It doesn't make it any easier.'

'No, you're right, it doesn't. But, to answer your question, Molly wasn't one of our more difficult girls. She didn't resent her carers in the way some clients do, but she had a very different outlook on life that was a direct result of the experiences she'd suffered.'

'What do you mean?'

'Well, she had a very casual and very adult view of sex. She had male and female sexual partners from a very young age, and from the age of ten she was charging for her services to certain individuals.'

'Has she run away before?'

'She's walked out on a number of occasions and not been seen for some time. The last time of any significance was about a year ago when she took up with an older man. She ended up living with him for several months before he got tired of her and threw her out. That's when she came back here.'

'So you think that might have happened this time?'

'I would think, knowing Molly, that that's a very likely scenario.'

I nodded, more optimistic now that she was still alive. 'We're going to need to speak to all your other, er, clients, and the rest of the staff to see if anyone else knew Miriam Fox and might be able to give us any relevant information.'

'The majority of the clients aren't here at the moment. Most of them attend local schools, or are supposed to anyway. Those who are in the building now are the ones who have special learning needs, and require one-to-one tuition. They might not be too helpful.'

They weren't. There were seven of them altogether and we interviewed them one at a time in Carla Graham's office, with her present. Two refused to answer any questions at all with anything more than yes or no, and of the rest only one claimed to have heard of Miriam Fox, and that was Anne Taylor, the youthful legal expert I'd met earlier. She said that she'd known Molly 'a bit' and that Molly and Miriam had been friends, even though Miriam was older. Anne had seen Molly with Miriam a couple of times while out in the evenings (she denied knowing that either of them had been prostitutes), but claimed she'd never really spoken to Miriam beyond the usual pleasantries. 'She seemed a bit stuck up,' she told us. 'She thought she was better than anyone else.'

And that was it. Carla made some effort to get her charges to speak, but it was a losing battle. They weren't going to tell the police anything, not if they could help it.

After that we interviewed the other members of staff present, four of them altogether. Two of them recognized the photo of Miriam and identified her as a friend of Molly's, but once again, neither had had any meaningful contact with her so couldn't, or wouldn't, add any further information.

'I don't know how much help that was,' said Carla when we were finished.

'It's difficult to tell,' I said. 'That's the thing with murder inquiries. It can often be a long, slow process and it always involves talking to a lot of people. Most of the time you don't hear anything significant, but just occasionally you do, even if you don't notice it at the time.'

'Well, I hope you're successful. It's worrying thinking that there's some maniac out there who could easily kill again.'

'We'll catch the perpetrator. I'm sure of that.' I stood up, and Malik followed suit. 'Anyway, thanks for your assistance this morning. It's appreciated.'

'I'll show you out,' she said, getting to her feet and leading us out of the office.

At the double doors, I shook hands with her while Malik nodded briefly and walked out. 'We'll need to come back and speak to the other clients at some point,' I told her.

'Of course. It would help if you could phone ahead, though. I'd like to be here when you come.'

She had nice eyes. They were a deep brown colour, with laughter lines round their edges. I would make sure she was there when I came back. 'I'll do that. It'll probably be sooner rather than later. It's important to close every avenue of inquiry.'

There was a sound of hysterical yelling and shouting from one of the rooms down the hall. It sounded like one of the female clients was experiencing a lack of customer satisfaction. In reply, we could just about make out the calm, measured tones of one of the social workers. It was greeted with another blast of abuse. Talk about a hiding to nothing.

Carla Graham sighed resignedly. 'I'd better go and see what all that's about.'

'You certainly have a difficult job to do here,' I told her.

'We've all got difficult jobs to do,' she answered, a rueful smile playing about her lips, and turned to go.

'I think you had a bit of a thing for her,' Malik said, when I joined him outside.

I grinned. 'She's an attractive woman.'

'A little bit old.'

'For you maybe. Not for me.'

'A social worker, though, Sarge? It would hardly be a match made in heaven, not with your views.'

'Yeah. Somehow I don't think it's a goer.' But in an odd way I wished it could be. I needed some romance in my life.

It was getting on for one o'clock, so we grabbed some lunch at a nearby McDonald's. Malik plumped for Chicken McNuggets while I took the traditional route of Big Mac, fries, and a hot apple pie for pudding, washed down with a regular Coke. Not exactly the ideal start to my new diet.

'I didn't like her,' Malik said as he slowly chewed on a McNugget.

'I know you didn't.'

He swallowed. 'She was too cynical, you know? Like nothing would faze her.'

'It's no different to the way it is in our game. You build up a shell so that things don't affect you. You have to. I mean, let's face it, how would you like to work with those little fuckers?'

'No discipline. That's the problem.' He picked up another McNugget with his fork. 'Do you think any of them knew any-thing?'

'Anything of interest? I doubt it. I think we'd have known if any of them were lying through their teeth. They're not that good actors.'

'So it was a bit of a waste of time going down there, really.'

I smiled. 'Well, in some ways maybe.'

He ignored my comment, and changed the subject. 'I was surprised this morning by the preliminary findings.'

'That there was no sign of sexual assault?' He nodded. 'So was I. It sort of begs the question, what was she killed for?'

Malik hunted down and pinned his last McNugget. 'That's why we need to talk to the pimp.'

But talking to the pimp had not proved any easier for our colleagues than it had for us the previous day. When we got back to the station we heard that he hadn't been at home when DS Capper and three others had called there several hours earlier. Apparently, he had a girlfriend who lived in Highbury, and he was supposed to spend quite a lot of his time with her, but he hadn't been at her place either. Nor was she in residence. Both properties were now under surveillance and all patrols had been advised to bring him in for questioning should they come across him. So far no-one had.

When I left that afternoon at 4.20, citing a non-existent doctor's appointment as the reason for my departure (Malik made me feel guilty by looking concerned and asking if it was anything serious), the inquiry was heading towards thirty-six hours old with few substantial leads and a suspect against whom there was pretty much no evidence and who, so far, hadn't even got a viable motive.

There was, of course, still a lot of the race left to be run, as a sports commentator might say, but whichever way you looked at it the start hadn't been particularly inspiring.

9

After picking up the suitcase at King's Cross, I took it home, counted the contents (it was all there), and stuffed a jiffy bag with Danny's cut. I sealed the bag and placed the rest of the money, bar a couple of hundred spending, in a safe in my bedroom. It wouldn't stay there for long. I have a personal deposit box at a hotel in Bayswater where I stash my ill-gotten gains. One day I'm going to have a hefty lump sum. It doesn't pay interest, but it keeps growing.

I've known Danny for about eight years now. He was the brother of a girl I used to go out with. Her name was Jean Ashcroft and she was the only non-Force girl I've ever had a relationship with since joining up. We were together about a year, and for a while it looked like it was going to get serious. We'd even started looking at places to rent together, which is the closest I've ever been to any sort of real commitment, and I think it's probably fair to say that I loved her, as much as I've loved anybody in the sexual sense. But then Danny fouled things up. Not intentionally, mind, but a foul-up all the same. You see, in those days he was a bit of a rascal. Although he was intelligent and came from a respectable family, he didn't have a job, nor did he want one. He preferred dope dealing. It was easier, and it was more profitable. Somehow he managed to keep his illicit activities hidden from the rest of his family, including his sister, and so it turned out to be a terrible shock for them when one of his pathetically small-time deals went pear-shaped, and he ended up on the wrong end of a savage beating.

It was a typical piece of middle-class naivety, really. He was holding half a pound of speed he was meant to be selling to a contact of his, but the contact, deciding it was easier to steal the goods rather than buy them, set him up. On his way over to the contact's flat, three of the guy's mates ambushed him in the stairwell. However, since Danny hadn't yet paid for the stuff, he was loath to give it up. A very one-sided battle ensued and Danny ended up with a fractured jaw, smashed cheekbone, severe concussion, and God knows how many busted ribs. And he still lost the speed, which, by all accounts, had to be prised from between his broken fingers.

He was in hospital three weeks altogether, which, when you consider it was on the NHS, gives you some idea of the extent of his injuries. It really threw the cat among the pigeons as well. His dad seemed to think that, because it had happened on our patch, I should have known something about his activities and put a stop to them, or at least told him about them. So he turned against me. Danny's mum followed suit, being one of those people who are incapable of their own opinion. The thing was, I could have lived with that, no problem. I'd never liked either of them much anyway. The problem was Danny. Once he got out of hospital he wanted revenge on the man who'd set him up. He was also worried because the guy he'd bought the stuff from now wanted paying as well. In fact, he wanted a lot of favours and the only person he knew who was in a position to grant him any was me. I'd always got on well with Danny, even though he'd never been able to hide his dope dealing activities from me. In fact, I genuinely liked him.

So when he came to me begging for help, I said I'd do what I could. The guy who'd sold him the speed was a pretty low-level player, so a quick threat of prosecution and the possibility of worse got him out of the picture. It was the revenge thing that represented a problem. Danny wanted me to help him take the guy out, though help wasn't exactly the operative word since it looked like I would be the one doing most of the work. Danny was only five feet six and of proportionate build, so he wasn't what you'd call a useful ally. He wanted to ambush the guy in the same way he'd been ambushed, and return the kicking, but I talked him out of that one. I don't even know why I agreed to get involved at all. I could have just told him to cut his losses and be thankful that he no longer owed the other guy money, but

I didn't. Maybe it was a pride thing. Maybe I wanted him to look up to me. I don't know.

Anyway, I devised a compromise. A couple of months earlier I'd uncovered about fifty ecstasy pills in an unrelated search of a suspect's premises. Because we already had the suspect bang to rights on about a dozen other charges, I'd put the pills in my pocket, thinking they might come in useful at a later date, not so much as a commodity – even in those days there was a lot of controversy over the effects of E, and I didn't want anyone dropping dead of anything I sold them – but of course they had another use, and that was helping put away criminals who were proving particularly hard to pin down for their crimes. I'd never planted anything on anyone before, but I'd heard about enough cases to know that it usually worked. If it was carried out properly.

Which was the difficult part. The guy, whose name was Darren Frennick, didn't tend to leave his flat very much, apart from to do the odd deal, and we needed uninterrupted access. We thought about it for weeks, racking our brains for a way to get in there, before we came up with a simple yet foolproof solution. Frennick was an ugly bastard but, like all young men, he had a healthy sex drive. I knew a girl at the time who was a professional escort and who could be trusted with difficult jobs. So what we did was this. Having paid her a substantial amount, funded by Danny, and given her the tablets, we sent her round to the flat. She knocked on the door, and when Frennick answered she told him she was his escort for the evening. He started to claim ignorance, but she was a good-looking girl and he didn't want to look a gifthorse in the mouth, so he invited her in and kicked out the couple of mates he'd had round there at the time.

As we'd guessed, he didn't want to escort her anywhere, preferring instead to get straight down to business. But within seconds of his amorous advances she was claiming she wasn't that sort of girl and an escort meant just that. He asked her what the hell she was on about and continued with his pawing, which was when she showed him some of her kjung fu moves. One series of ferocious blows and kicks later and he was out cold on the floor. Quick as a flash, she used a pair of tweezers to remove the packet of pills from her handbag. Shebrushed them briefly against his fingers, then threw them under his bed. He was coming round by that time so she ran out of there, shouting and scream- ing, and immediately phoned the police on her mobile phone, saying that this man had tried to give her some pills and rape her. She gave the address and his first name, and the cops, knowing who he was, were round there like a shot. By which time, of course, she'd made herself scarce.

Five minutes later she called the police again, saying that she was sorry, she didn't want to get involved in pressing charges against the guy, but she had seen him put the pills back under his bed. Dispatch passed this information on to the officers on the scene, who'd entered the flat through the open door. A dazed and bloodied Darren Frennick was arrested and remanded in custody. He ended up serving nine months for supplying Class A drugs, which Danny didn't feel was revenge enough, but which I assured him was the best he was going to get.

And that should have been that. Except that it wasn't. I don't think Jean ever found out the full story, but somehow she got wind of the fact that I'd used an escort girl to set Frennick up, and worked out that this was a side of me she'd never seen before and one that she didn't particularly like. Things became strained after that, Jean repeatedly asking me if I'd ever slept with pros- titutes, and not believing me every time I said no. First, the living-together lark went on hold; a couple of months later, the relationship followed suit.

By rights, I should never have forgiven Danny for fucking up what will in all probability turn out to be my one chance of getting hitched, but he was so grateful for what I'd done, and felt so guilty for the problems he'd caused, that I found it difficult to hold it against him. Jean and I never really saw each other again after that. She met this chartered surveyor from up north and moved to Leeds with him, but Danny and I continued to keep in touch. Occasionally we did business together. One time I sold him a couple of kilos of dope I'd liberated from its wrongful owner. He tried to move it on but ended up selling it to under-cover Drugs Squad officers and getting nicked instead. They leaned on him hard, trying to get him to name his source, but his experience with Darren Frennick had hardened him. He feared prison – who doesn't? – but he kept quiet, even though they told him that co-operation would surely mean a lighter sentence. He ended up doing eighteen months.

Danny was not the luckiest man in the world; nor was he, in criminal terms, one of the best at his profession, but I trusted him absolutely, and there are very few people I can say that about. That's why I took him with me when I wen off to kill three men. Because I knew he'd keep his mouth shut.

He rented a basement flat up in Highgate, not too far from the cemetery, and it was twenty to six when I finally rang his door-bell. He opened the door slowly, keeping the chain on the latch, and poked his head round. His face was pale and there were bags under his eyes. He looked like a man with a lot on his mind.

'You're late, Dennis.'

'It's the pressures of policework. It makes punctuality close to impossible. Blame the government. They're the ones letting all the criminals out.'

He released the chain and let me in. I followed him into the kitchen, noticing that his feet were bare, and his shirt was hanging out the back of his trousers. A very slovenly state. It looked like he hadn't set foot outside the flat all day.

'D'you want a cup of tea, or something?' he asked, putting the kettle on.

'Yeah, thanks, a tea'd be nice.' I put the bag containing his share on one of the worktops and leaned back against the cooker. 'I've got your money here.'

He nodded, getting a couple of cups down from one of the shelves. 'Cheers.'

'Do you mind if I smoke?'

'You don't usually ask.'

'Well, I can see you're in a sensitive mood, so I thought I'd be polite.'

He turned to me, his face registering a vague disgust. 'This whole thing doesn't faze you at all, does it?'

I lit the cigarette. 'Of course it does. But it's been done now. We'll know to be more careful next time, but regrets don't change a thing.'

'It's not about regrets. This was a huge fuck-up, Dennis, and the cops aren't going to let go of it. Not until they've caught someone. And that means us.'

I took a drag on the cigarette, feeling tired of all the verbal sparring in my life. I'd once had the chance to become an apprentice plumber, which would have paid a lot more money for a lot less hassle. At this moment, I wished I'd gone that route.

'Danny, there's one thing about policework you ought to know. It's all about trails. If you leave a trail when you commit your crime, which most people do, then the police will follow it until they find you.'

'Don't patronize me, Dennis. I don't fucking need it.'

'But if you don't leave a trail then there's nothing to follow. The police just run into a brick wall.'

He sighed, then turned to pour the teas. I watched him as he beat the teabags with his spoon. He was agitated, badly so, I felt I might have overestimated his nerve. I took another long, thoughtful drag on the cigarette. Most cigarettes I smoke I don't enjoy. I think that's the case with the majority of smokers. You only put one in your mouth because you know that if you don't, you'll only be thinking about smoking and wondering when you're going to have your next one until you do. But this cigarette was different. It tasted really good.

'You know, looking at you with that makes me wish I'd started
smoking.'

'Do you want one?'

'You'd give me one as well, wouldn't you? Christ, Dennis, the things you get me involved in. And you a fucking copper . . .'

He passed me my cup of tea. It didn't taste very nice. Underbrewed and too much milk.

'I'm sorry about the job, Danny, I really am. I didn't know it was going to turn out to be customs men. If I had, I'd never have touched the thing with a bargepole.'

'So what were you told? Originally.'

'I was told it was three drug dealers. According to my contact, they were trying to muscle in on some friends of his.'

'And who was your contact?'

Danny had never met Raymond nor, as far as I knew, had he ever heard of him. I liked to make Raymond Keen, and my association with him, as quiet as possible. For obvious reasons. 'You don't want to know,' I told him. 'Seriously. There's no point.'

He thought about that for a couple of seconds, then let it go. 'So how did you know they were going to be there? At the Traveller's Rest?'

'Those blokes? Apparently my contact had set it up so that they were going there for a clear the air meeting with his associates. All I had to do was pick them off when they arrived.'

He shook his head and sighed. 'You know, I've been thinking about this shit all day. Ever since it happened. And if they were customs . . . Think about it. If they were customs, then how the fuck did your associate know they were going to be there?'

'He says they were corrupt. It was a blackmail job, that's all I know. They were crooked, they were obviously involved in something they shouldn't have been.'

'So, if that's the case, how do we know the police can't find a trail?'

'They can't find a trail through us.'

'But what if they can find a trail that leads to your contact? If those blokes were corrupt, then the cops are going to find out, aren't they? And if they were involved with the man who hired you in some way, then they'll be able to follow the trail back to him.'

'They won't. Everything was very carefully planned.'

'But that's not the worst of it,' he continued, ignoring my comment.

I looked at him. 'Really?'

'What if they weren't corrupt, Dennis?'

I was beginning to get tired of this. 'Look, Danny. My contact's a middle-aged businessman who's made a fair bit of money over the years. What I'm trying to tell you is that he's an intelligent man. He's not going to do anything that's going to get him in a load of shit.' I finished the cigarette and tea at the same time and threw the one in the other.

Danny signed. 'So what I've been thinking all day is this: Maybe there's more to this whole thing than meets the eye. This thing could be a lot bigger than we think. If those customs officers weren't corrupt then they were involved in something so sensitive that they had to die for it.' He emphasized the last words like a paperback detective making a speech to his assembled suspects. 'And if that's the case, then not only is your contact heavily involved, he's also got some fucking good contacts of his own to set this sort of thing up.'

'Well, if that's the case, then you shouldn't be worried. Because there's not much chance of us getting caught, is there?'

'Maybe not, but, well . . . you've got to think . . .'

'What? What have you got to think?'

He sighed again, choosing his words carefully. It took a long time to get what he wanted to say out. 'That what's the point in keeping us alive? We're loose ends, Dennis. Loose ends involved in something very, very major. And now we've done what we were meant to do, then, you know . . .' He let the sentence trail off into the distance.

'Jesus, Danny, you've got to get yourself into some gainful employment. You've been watching far too much TV. This isn't a fucking mafia film. If we keep our mouths shut and go about our daily business as if nothing's happened, then we'll be all right. I told you that on the night. Nothing that's happened since changes anything.'

'I hope you're right,' he said, but he didn't sound convinced.

I felt paternal towards him then. 'I am. Don't worry.' I stepped forward and patted him on the shoulder, not in a patronizing way, more of a man-to-man way. 'Just try not to think about it, and remember, in a few days' time it'll all have blown over.'

'Yeah, I know, I know. It's difficult, though. Sitting here all day.'

'Do you want to come to a pub quiz?'

'Eh?'

'A pub quiz. There's one I go to on Tuesday nights when I've got the time. It's teams of four. There's a couple of blokes I normally play with, but we're often short of a fourth.'

Danny looked at me aghast, his usually thin blue eyes bugging out like they were on mini springs. 'Are you serious? Fuck me, Dennis, I don't know how you can live with yourself.'

'What? Going to pub quizzes?'

'You know what I mean.'

'Like I said, we've just got to carry on as normal. And what's more normal than a pub quiz?'

'And to think my sister was going to marry you.'

'Lucky you came along and fucked it all up really, wasn't it?'

He shot me a guilty look then, which I knew he would. It was cruel really, making him pay again for something that happened all that time ago.

I grinned at him to show I was only joking, and clapped him on the shoulder again. Still very much man-to-man. 'Come on, it'll be a laugh. Shit, it's got to be better than sitting here biting your nails and gawking at the TV, waiting for your mugshot to appear.'

'I can't go back inside again, Dennis. Not after last time.'

'You won't have to,' I told him. 'I promise.' We looked at each other for a long moment. 'So, are you coming then?'

'Where is it?'

'Pub called the Chinaman. Just off City Road.'

Danny thought about it for a moment. It looked as though he was trying to work out whether he could afford to do something so frivolous when, by rights, he ought to be putting all his concentration into shitting himself. In the end it seemed he could afford to let his concentration slip for a few hours.

'Fuck it. Why not?' He picked up the jiffy bag. 'At least I won't be short of cash for a drink.'

10

'He was an accountant.' Malik chewed on his sandwich as he
spoke.

'You spoke to your mate, then?'

He nodded, finishing his mouthful. 'Yeah, last night. He's been
working round the clock.'

'I can imagine.'

It was twenty past two the following afternoon, and we were in
the station canteen. A fairly unproductive morning had been spent
helping to collate all the statements we and the other officers had
taken so far in an effort to make some sort of sense of them. So
far nothing was leaping out at us, and the one possible suspect, the
pimp, had still not been found. Nor was anyone sure where else to
look for him.

'How are they coming along with everything?'

'You know what it's like, Sarge. It was difficult for him to say
too much but it seems they're working on a lot of leads. From
what I can gather, they're concentrating on the accountant and
trying to establish what he was doing with those customs
officers.'

'Two customs officers and an accountant. It sounds like the name of a bad film.'

'It's an interesting combination, I'll give you that.'

I finished picking at the Caesar salad I'd ordered and pushed the plate away, thinking about the inevitable cigarette. 'What does your mate make of it all?'

'He said they'd already dug up a lot of info on the accountant and there was nothing to suggest he wasn't a sound guy. He didn't have a record or anything.'

I remembered the accountant's face, the shock on it as he looked down the barrel of my gun. I lit the cigarette. 'So what was he doing with them?'

'That's the million-dollar question. My friend says there was an official reason why they were together. He wouldn't say exactly what it was, but from what I can gather the accountant had information on something that was very useful to the customs men.'

'So they're pretty sure the customs men were part of some sort of investigation?'

Malik nodded slowly. 'That's my impression. He didn't say for sure, but I think that's the angle they're looking at it from.'

'So the only way the murderer would know they were there at that time—'

'Was if it was an inside job. It's a worrying thought. You don't like to think of the forces of law and order as being corrupt.'

'You think someone tipped the killer off?'

He shrugged. 'That's what it looks like. What else could it be?'

I hoped Malik's information was wrong – which, of course, it could have been. A lot of the time on big cases involving a lot of detectives, contradictory stories get thrown up. From my point of view, it would be a lot easier to believe that the three victims were the pondscum Raymond had labelled them. Not only did it make what I'd done a lot more palatable – at least to me – I also felt it would make it much more difficult for the investigating officers to come up with a result. If it was an inside job, then the list of people who would have been in a position to know where those men were going to be and when they were going to be there would be pretty short.

But at the moment, it was still conjecture. I knew I was going to have to find out more information from Raymond, but at the same time I was going to have to be careful about how I did it. I'd never looked at him as a threat before, but suddenly I didn't want to give him a reason for wanting me out of the way as well. Maybe there'd been more truth in Danny's words than I'd initially given him credit for.

'You look very thoughtful, Sarge. Everything was all right at the doctor's yesterday, wasn't it?'

'Oh, yeah, yeah. No problem. Nothing serious anyway. I'm just not looking forward to chasing around questioning the rest of those kids at the childrens home. It just seems like a hiding to nothing.'

We still had close to two thirds of the kids to take statements from, and, although I quite fancied the idea of seeing the alluring Carla Graham again, I didn't want to waste any more time talking to snotty little bastards who wouldn't help you if their lives depended on it. I'd already told Knox I didn't think we'd get anything helpful out of it, but he'd insisted. He wanted to make sure he covered every angle of the case, if for no other reason than to cover his arse from any future kicking by superiors frustrated by a perceived lack of results.

'Wasn't it you who told me when I started out that only five per cent of policework gets you anywhere, and it's always spread right across the one hundred per cent you have to do?'

I grinned. 'Did I really say that? Shit, that must have been a long time ago.'

'Two years. That's all.'

'I must have been lying.'

'So, what is the answer then? The secret of policework?'

I was about to tell him that it was not to give a fuck about it and make sure you earned an alternative income, when DC Hunsdon walked in. He looked pleased. There were only about a dozen of us scattered about the canteen and most were uniform. Since CID always like to stick together, he made his way over to us.

He stopped when he got to the table and leaned forward, smiling, hands on the top.

'I can see you're dying to tell us something,' I told him.

'We've got the pimp.' He spoke these words in the manner of someone saying, 'We've solved the case.' Somewhat optimistic, I thought.

'Oh yeah? Where was he?'

Hunsdon sat down and lit a cigarette. 'He came in here. Walked in with his brief about ten minutes ago.'

'Who's going to question him?' Malik asked.

'Knox is going to do it with Capper. They're going to lean on him hard.'

He didn't look at Malik as he spoke. Like a lot of the younger detectives, Hunsdon didn't like Malik. This was partly to do with the fact that he was a graduate, but also because he was Asian. There was a feeling that he got special treatment because of his ethnic background, a situation not helped by the way senior management tended to treat him as some sort of teacher's pet. The resentment was unjustified and stupid, but it was difficult to squash. It was a testimony to Malik that he never once acknowledged it.

'Do you think he did it?' I asked him.

Hunsdon shrugged. 'What else have we got?'

'Hardly a reason for pinning it on him,' I said.

'Yeah, but it's not just that, is it? The victim wasn't sexually assaulted but she was attacked in a way that was meant to make it look like a sexual assault, so it's probably not going to be a pervert. Plus, he was seen round the victim's flat just after the murder and attacked you when you tried to question him. And, if that isn't enough, he's got a history of violence, and he'd attacked the victim before. Put her in hospital a couple of months back with cracked ribs and concussion.'

'Yeah, but that's not the same as cutting her throat from ear to ear and hacking great holes in her genitals.'

'He fits, Sarge. Whatever way you look at it, he fits.' He said these last words firmly, and in a way that suggested there was no point continuing to argue with him.

Which there wasn't. Right or wrong, at least it meant that there was less work for the rest of us.

'How are you getting on with the mobile phone records? Did Miriam have one registered in her name?'

He nodded. 'Yeah, she did. And I tell you something, it took a fuck of a lot of phoning round to find out. The company's going to send us a list of calls she made and received over the past month.'

'Maybe it'll throw up something.'

'You never know,' he said, but he didn't sound that interested. In his mind, we'd already got our man.

11

As predicted, we ended up spending several fruitless hours at the children's home that afternoon trying to track down the various 'clients' we hadn't yet spoken to. We managed to pin down a few but no-one who could help us much. To be honest, it did prove to be a bit of a waste of time. Carla wasn't there either, which disappointed me. She had a meeting out in Essex and hadn't returned by five o'clock, which was the time we'd decided that we'd had enough. I phoned through to Welland and told him that he might as well send uniforms down for the rest of the statements because it simply wasn't worth using us for it, and he agreed without much resistance.

That evening it was Malik's turn to take off early. He had to pick his kids up from his mother-in-law's as his missus, who was some high-flying accountant, was off on a seminar in Monte Carlo or some other such exotic destination. It made me think. The last seminar I'd attended had been in Swindon. 'The Role of the Police Force in 21st-Century Britain' it had been called – about as interesting and informative as watching a car rust. I was definitely in the wrong job.

We left together and I took the tube down to King's Cross. I thought about heading back to the station and seeing what needed doing but decided a drink might be better instead. Welland had told me they were still questioning the pimp, and so far there was nothing of note to report, which didn't surprise me. You only turn up with your lawyer in tow if you don't want to say too much.

I found a pub on the Marylebone Road near the station which didn't look too shitty and took a seat at the bar. The barman was a young Australian guy with a ponytail and a silver ring through his eyebrow. There were only a few people in the place so we had a bit of a chat about this and that. He was a friendly sort, which is often the way with Aussies. I think it must be something to do with the fact that they're brought up in a nice sunny climate. I asked him what the crime situation was like over there. He told me it was pretty bad.

'It's getting worse too, y'know,' he said. 'A lot of guns around the place, and people more willing to use them.' I told him that that was the case everywhere. 'Don't I know it,' he said. 'Especially here. I always thought London was supposed to be a safe place.'

'I think you're about fifty years too late,' I told him, and we left it at that.

When I left the pub, shortly after seven o'clock, I decided to walk home and take in some of the sights of the red light district where Miriam Fox and her young friend, Molly Hagger, had plied their trade.

King's Cross isn't a lot like people expect a red light district to be. On the main drag there are the two railway stations on one side of the road, almost next to each other – King's Cross and St Pancras – while a few dodgy-looking fast-food outlets and amusement arcades cluster together on the other. A couple of ageing sex shops with their trademark blackened windows and garish lighting are the only sign that people come to the area with sex in mind, but even they look lonely and a little out of place. King's Cross is no Amsterdam or Hamburg. There's no obvious prostitution activity on the main roads, even after dark. The prostitutes might be there, but you wouldn't particularly notice them. The area tends to be fairly busy as the Marylebone Road links the west and east of the city, and there are always plenty of people about, which deprives the punters of their one great desire: anonymity.

But step away from the bright lights and into the dark, dimly lit backstreets and a new world awaits. Drifting in and out of view like ghosts are the whores and the crack dealers. Sometimes you don't even see them. Their disembodied voices reach out from the doorways and alleys and the questions they ask are always the same: 'Need any gear?' 'Looking for a good time?' Sometimes you can feel their eyes boring into you, trying to work you out, looking for your weaknesses, maybe deciding whether or not you're worth robbing. Cars ease idly by, sizing up the scene. If you look at them, you'll see that most of the time the occupant is a single, middle-aged man and they never return the look. They always turn away. These are the businessmen searching for their illicit thrill. Some of them are just frustrated, and need a quick fuck to bring them fleeting satisfaction. Others are perverts, people who want to do things to a woman their wives and girlfriends would never countenance. People who want things done to them that you and I couldn't countenance. And somewhere among them are the psychopaths, rapists and killers sweeping the area in their constant hunt for prey. This other world exists fifty yards from King's Cross station, but unless you look for it you'll never see it, and unless you see it you'll never understand the sickness that keeps it going.

It was a mild night with a strong wind. In my raincoat pocket I clutched a small cosh I occasionally carry about with me, purely for emergencies. It's less than a foot long and easily concealable on a winter's day. I've never used it in anger before and I'd never think about wielding it while on duty – it's more than my job's worth – but I was glad I had it now.

Two ageing prostitutes, their faces cracked and wrinkled like old leather, stepped out of the darkness and into my path. They wore ridiculously short skirts and pantomime make-up. 'How about some, love?' said one, forcing a leering smile. 'With a real woman.'

'I'm a police officer,' I said, pushing past her as politely as possible.

'So? Even coppers need a bit of fun,' she shouted after me. But her enthusiasm had faltered.

I didn't say anything. What was there to say to that?

I felt sorry for her. I felt sorry for them both. According to some of the other guys on the case these older girls were bitter about the competition provided by their more youthful counterparts like Miriam Fox and her friends, which was no great surprise. It's difficult enough to compete with newer, better, different models, and even worse when they undercut you. This rivalry had resulted in a number of incidents where older prostitutes had attacked the young ones, and several where they'd actually called the police to tell them about underage activity in an effort to get the girls off the street. Now the two competing groups tended to keep apart, but it was youth that had the most success.

It was quiet tonight, a result no doubt of the investigation, but business would soon return to normal. In the end, nothing gets in the way of capitalism. That's what's always annoyed me about the British attitude to paying for sex. It's all well and good having a big moral stance against prostitution, but that doesn't stop it happening. It doesn't even curtail it. Far better just to regulate the trade so that the girls are clean, pimp-free and safe, and the red light districts become tourist attractions, not drug-infested no-go areas like the one I was walking through now. Girls like Miriam Fox would almost certainly still be alive if they'd worked in Amsterdam or Barcelona, or wherever they were sensible enough not to attempt to change the laws of nature.

The scream came from somewhere behind me.

I didn't even register it the first time. You expect a scream on a street like this. Then it came again, louder and more desperate. It sounded like a young girl – a teenager – but whoever it was was pleading for help, the voice growing increasingly hysterical, and I knew straight away that something was badly wrong.

I swung round fast. A car was in the middle of the road about thirty yards away with its lights on and engine running. The driver, who I couldn't see very well, was leaning out of the passenger side and holding onto a girl who was struggling violently with him. There didn't seem to be anyone else around.

A part of me didn't want to get involved. Ahead of me were the bright lights and security of the Gray's Inn Road. I might have been a copper but I was off duty, in my own time, and I could be taking a big risk coming between those two. If it was a domestic she wouldn't thank me, they never do. I could end up with a knife in my gut or a gun in my ribs, all for being charitable.

But that part of me's still in a minority, thank God. I pulled the cosh from my pocket, ran into the road, and sprinted towards the car. The girl was now half in and the screaming was getting louder and louder as she realized how close she was to being abducted. Her thin, bare legs flapped wildly as inch by inch they disappeared inside the vehicle, which was now slowly moving forward.

I don't know if he heard me coming or not. I didn't make any noise – there's never any point advertising your presence if you don't have to – but my footfalls on the concrete were loud enough. As I got there, the car shot forward, but not before I'd grabbed the girl round the legs and pulled. For a moment the driver held on and I had this terrible fear that he was going to drag me along the tarmac. I stumbled and half fell but held on for dear life, somehow managing to keep my feet. That was it for him. The game was over, he wasn't going to get his prey, so he let go and she flew out the door, landing in a heap on the road. The momentum knocked me over too and all I could do was watch while he made his rapid getaway with a screech of tyres, turning a corner before I could even focus on his number-plate.

I got to my feet, putting the cosh away, then helped her up. 'Are you all right?'

She looked at me for the first time and I recognized her instantly as Anne Taylor, the girl who'd been outside Coleman House when we'd arrived there the previous day. She looked a lot less full of herself now, though. Her eyes were tear stained and her make-up was running. The shock on her face was clear.

She nodded slowly, checking her skirt and top for any damage. 'I think so . . . Yeah, yeah, I'm all right.'

I took her by the arm and moved her onto the pavement. 'Did you know him?' I asked.

'Probably just some pervert,' she answered, without looking up. 'I've never seen him before.'

'What did he look like?'

This time she did look up. 'Look, I'm not interested in pressing charges or nothing like that.' She shook herself free of my arm.

'You know, a thanks might not go amiss. I mean, I have just

helped you out of a difficult situation. Anything could have happened to you then.'

'I know how to look after myself.'

'Yeah, sure.' I took out my cigarettes and offered her one. She took it and I lit it for her, lighting one for myself at the same time.

'Look, thanks. It was good of you.' It was given grudgingly, but I suppose it was better than nothing. What is it with kids these days? The little bastards have never got any manners.

'Do you want to grab a quick coffee somewhere? Calm yourself down a bit?'

'No, I'm all right. I'm fine.'

'Come on. I'm buying.'

I could tell she was thinking that a sit-down and a hot drink might be quite nice. The problem was the company. 'I don't want to sit there with you going on at me about this and that, and questioning me. I ain't got time for that.'

'Look, just a coffee and a cigarette. I could do with one myself. I'm not used to that sort of exercise.'

She gave me a dismissive look. 'Yeah, I can tell.'

We found a café on the Gray's Inn Road not peopled entirely with lowlifes. I bought two coffees and we found a booth at the back.

'I'm surprised you're out on the streets so soon after what's happened.'

'I thought you weren't going to go on at me. If you're going to fucking lecture me, I ain't interested. I could be out earning money, you know.'

'Or you could be in the back of that bloke's car, bound and gagged—'

'Look, I don't need this fucking shit . . .' She started to get up from her seat.

'All right, all right, I won't lecture you. I'm just worried about your safety, that's all.' She sat down again. 'You had a narrow escape out there tonight. Remember that.'

'Don't worry about me. I can look after myself.'

'Yeah, you said that. I expect Miriam Fox thought the same thing.'

'There's perverts out there all the time. It's one of the risks, isn't it?'

'I suppose if you put it like that, yes it is. When we spoke yesterday, you said you didn't know Miriam Fox was a prostitute. That wasn't true, was it? You knew.'

'You coppers are all the fucking same, aren't you? You never stop asking questions.'

I laughed. 'Look, this is purely off-the-record talk. Anything you say here can never be repeated in a court of law. You ought to know that. All I'm trying to do is find the person who murdered Miriam and take him off the streets. So he can't do it again.' I pulled out two more cigarettes, again lighting hers. 'It's in your interests, probably more than mine, to make sure that happens.'

She thought about it for a moment, her self-interest clearly wrestling with her innate distrust of the forces of law and order. I took a drag on my cigarette and waited for her. I was in no hurry.

'Yeah, I knew she was on the game,' she said eventually. 'Course I did, but I didn't have much to do with her. She was a real bitch.'

'In what way?'

'Well, she just rated herself, you know? She looked down on the rest of us like we was some sort of fucking scum. And she was a scheming cow too. Always talking behind people's backs, turning them against each other. I never liked her, so I kept out of her way.'

'She was with Mark Wells, wasn't she?'

Anne nodded. 'Yeah, and I don't have nothing to do with him.'

'Why not?'

'He's a nutter. You get on the wrong side of him and he tears you a-fucking-part.'

'Do you think he might have had something to do with what happened to Miriam?'

'I thought it was a pervert that did it.'

'It might have been, but we don't know at this stage. It might have been someone else. Someone who knew her. Someone like Mark Wells.'

She shrugged. 'I don't know.'

'Do you think he'd be capable of it?'

'Look, you shouldn't be asking me that. I don't want to start answering those sorts of questions.'

'Anne, whatever you say to me here won't go any further than this table, and your name'll never be mentioned. I'm just trying to build up a picture, that's all.'

'If Mark Wells ever heard I'd mentioned his name to you, he'd fucking kill me.'

I thought about telling her he was already in custody, but held back. I didn't want to prejudice her answers, no more than I had done already, anyway. 'He won't hear it. I promise. No-one will.'

'He's a vicious bloke. I've heard some nasty stories about him kicking the shit out of people if they piss him off, and I heard he knifed this geezer once because he owed him some money for something. But what would he want to kill Miriam for? She was earning him cash.'

Which was a good point, and one that was going to need answering.

'Anyway,' she continued, 'he's already short of girls.'

114

'What do you mean?'

'Well, Molly was one of his girls and she's gone now.'

I thought about my dream again. 'Where do you reckon Molly's got to? I'd like to find her and ask her a few questions about Miriam. They were good mates, weren't they?'

She nodded. 'Yeah, they were. Fuck knows why. She was about the only one who liked Miriam.'

'Can you think where she's gone to?'

She looked down at the table top, dragging constantly at the dying remnants of the fag. We'd had quite an adult discussion, and it was fair to say that in some ways she was older than her years, but at that moment, she looked her age. A kid trapped in an adult's world.

She sat like that for what felt like a long time, not saying anything. I sat back in my seat, thinking that maybe I'd annoyed her in some way. It was difficult to tell. When she spoke, it was without looking up, and her words were quiet.

'I don't think she's gone anywhere.'

I wasn't sure I'd heard her right. 'What? What was that?'

This time Anne looked me right in the eyes, and I thought I saw the beginnings of tears in them. 'I said, I don't think she's gone anywhere.'

12

'What do you think's happened to her, then?' I asked quietly.

'I don't know,' she said, looking away.

'Well, you must have a reason for thinking that way.'

'Look, stop hassling me with all these fucking questions.'

I paused for a long moment, thinking that I was glad I didn't work with kids. Especially teenagers.

'I just don't reckon she's gone anywhere, that's all. In fact, I'm fucking positive.' This time I didn't say a word, but I was intrigued. 'She wouldn't have left Mark. I know that.'

'Mark Wells?'

'Yeah. She loved him, you know? She'd have done anything for him, even though he didn't give a fuck about her. He's already got a couple of girls so he didn't need Molly. I mean, he fucked her, but that was it. She was just an earner to him.'

I thought of the smiling face in the photo-me images. She was too young for those sorts of complications. 'You don't reckon she may have just got pissed off with Wells and decided to sling her hook? From what we've heard, she's walked out and disappeared before.'

'No, I don't reckon that. The last time she left it was with her old boyfriend, but she hasn't been with him for ages. She wouldn't have gone away on her own. Not without Mark. She was well into him. Talked about him all the time.'

'Were you and her close?' I'd asked Anne this yesterday and got a negative response, but this time I thought she might tell me the truth.

'Sort of. She talked to me a fair bit. You know, about this and that. But mainly Mark. She was always talking about Mark.'

'What did Miriam think about Mark? Do you know?'

She shrugged. 'She used to fuck him, but that was it. She weren't in love with him. Not like Molly.'

'And when you saw Molly last . . . when was that? About three weeks ago?'

She shrugged again. 'Something like that, yeah.'

'Was that about the time she disappeared?'

'I saw her one day in the home and then she went out that night and no-one ever saw her again.'

'How did she seem when you saw her? Was she in good spirits or was she pissed off about things?'

'She was normal, you know. Just like she always is.'

'She didn't say anything about leaving, or anything?'

'No. Nothing.'

So where did that leave us? I wasn't even investigating Molly Hagger's disappearance and yet here was a girl who knew her, and who knew Miriam Fox, telling me that there was something very suspicious about the whole thing. Once again, I was reminded of my dream. It was as vivid now as it had been when I'd woken up in the darkness, sweating and fearful, but it had lost its power as a premonition. Was there something in what Anne was saying, or was it the imagination of a teenager at work? Molly could easily have taken off somewhere without telling Anne, who admitted she wasn't that close to her. It was also quite feasible that Molly hadn't been as obsessed with Mark Wells as Anne was making out. After all, she was only thirteen years old, and even I knew that thirteen-year-old girls are pretty fickle when it comes to love.

'You don't believe me, do you?'

'Yeah, I believe you, but if she hasn't gone anywhere, then where is she?'

'I don't know.' She shrugged her shoulders and looked at me with eyes that didn't belong to a kid. 'Maybe she's dead.'

'Do you think that? That she's dead?'

She nodded slowly and with worrying confidence. 'Yeah. I think so.'

I cleared my throat, not liking the feeling I was getting. 'Do you think the person who killed Miriam might have killed her too?'

'Could be.'

'The man who attacked you tonight . . . what happened?'

'I was standing in my normal spot when he pulls up in this car. I should have been with Charlene, but she didn't turn up tonight so I was on my own. He just beckons me over like a lot of them do, then when I get over there, I take a look and I don't like the look of him.'

'What was wrong with him?'

'He just didn't look right, you know? He had this horrible smile and there was something about him. He gave me the creeps.'

'Go on.'

'Well, he opens the passenger door and pats the seat, and he's sort of leering at me like some sort of fucking perv, and telling me to get in. But I reckon he's kinky; he looks the type. The type who'll take you out somewhere quiet and really give you a going over, so I say no thanks and start to go. But he just grabs me and starts pulling me in, telling me it'll be all right, that he's not going to hurt me, but he's fucking rough and he's pulling me by the hair as hard as he can, the bastard . . .' She paused. 'And then you turned up.'

'What did he look like?'

'Biggish guy. Fat. Bald. Fat face.'

'What sort of age?'

'I don't know. About fifty or something.' Which probably meant thirty.

'And you've never seen him before?'

She shook her head. 'There was just something about him, you know? I don't normally feel that way about punters. I mean, they're all fucking old and ugly, most of them anyway. But this one was different. I just knew he was dodgy.'

I tried to remember the make of car he was driving. It was a

Mercedes saloon, not particularly new, and I think the colour was light brown or beige. Not dark-coloured like the one that had picked up Miriam. Other than that I had nothing.

'It'd be good if you could make a statement.'

'Why? I've just told you what he looked like. Do you think he could have been the one who killed Miriam?' It looked as if the thought had only just occurred to her.

'I don't know. I really don't. Maybe.'

She shuddered. 'Fucking hell.'

'You'd do a lot better not working the streets, Anne.'

'I need the money.'

I thought about sitting there trying to persuade her as to the error of her ways, but I'm almost certain it wouldn't have done any good. Change comes from within. You've got to believe that what you do is wrong and needs to stop, and I was pretty sure Anne didn't feel like that.

'Come on, let's take you back to Coleman House.'

She snorted. 'Fuck that. I'd only been out there ten minutes when you came. I haven't earned any money yet.'

'Call it a night off.'

'My man don't believe in nights off.'

'And who's your man?'

'Come on, you're a copper. I ain't telling you that.'

'Well, I hope he's an improvement on Mark Wells.' As if.

'Yeah, course he is.'

'Then he'll understand, won't he?'

She laughed, much too cynically for a thirteen-year-old. 'He won't be happy if I don't earn him some cash.'

What a gentleman. 'All right, let me do you a deal. I'll give you forty quid if you go back to the home tonight.' It was a stupid gesture. The money would end up in the hands of her pimp or the local crack dealer, who were probably one and the same. And if Anne chose to put herself in danger, it was hardly my concern. Especially as whatever happened tonight, she'd be back on the streets tomorrow anyway. But I didn't want to be responsible for leaving her out there tonight.

'Forty quid. And what do you want for that?'

'Nothing from you. All you have to do is go back home for the night and stay there.'

'That ain't a lot. Forty quid's fuck all. I could earn ten times that.'

'It's all you're going to get. And you don't have to do anything for it.'

She thought about it for a moment. 'Make it fifty, and I'll do it.'

'You're in the wrong job. You ought to be a trained negotiator.'

I insisted on going back to Coleman House with her as I didn't trust her to go alone. We got a black cab and the driver gave me a dirty look when he saw her in tow. In the end, I felt dutybound to show him my warrant card so he'd know I wasn't some perverted punter who'd forgotten his transport for the night.

We didn't say much in the cab, and when we arrived she jumped out without a word along with her fifty quid, and disappeared inside. I could have just gone back home, but while I was there I thought I'd check to see if Carla Graham was around. Malik was right, she wasn't my type, but there was not exactly a wealth of good-looking women in my life, so I liked to make the best of any opportunities I got in that department. Even if it was just talking.

I had to ring the buzzer to get in. A woman's voice came over the intercom. She couldn't say her 'r's, and I recognized her as one of the staff members we'd interviewed yesterday. I think she'd called herself Katia, or something equally bizarre beginning with a K. A youngish girl with a revolutionary's stare who'd come across as the sort who thinks all coppers are Nazi stormtroopers just itching to truncheon a few minorities. I told her who I was and asked if it was possible to speak with Ms Graham.

'I think she's with Dr Woberts,' she told me. 'I'll just see if she can be made available.'

'Tell her I'll come back first thing tomorrow morning if it's more convenient,' I said, thinking that that would probably be less preferable to seeing me now.

About thirty seconds passed, then the door opened. 'Katia' stood there, looking overweight and tired. 'She's in her office,' she said, glaring at me as if I'd just pinched one of her nipples.

I nodded and walked past her. The place was quiet, making me wonder where everyone was. Up to no good probably. Anne would surely be out again in ten minutes making my cash gift to her an even bigger waste of time than I'd already thought.

I knocked on the door of her office but walked in without waiting for an answer. Carla Graham was standing by her desk talking to a short middle-aged man in a three-piece suit. She was wearing a light grey trouser suit with a white blouse. A simple string of pearls adorned her neck.

She smiled at me, but I thought there was a hint of effort in it which I've learned to get used to – you have to when you're a copper – but which still disappointed me, coming from her. 'Sergeant Milne. You must be working overtime tonight.'

I smiled back, stepping up to the desk. 'Unfortunately in our job it's difficult to keep to office hours. Thanks for taking the time to see me.'

'You only just caught me. This is one of my colleagues, Dr Roberts. He's a child psychologist.'

We shook hands.

'I'm not actually based here,' he said in a pleasant, almost feminine, sing-song voice. 'I do work at sites all over the borough.'

'I expect you're kept fairly busy, then.'

'We have a lot of children with special needs, but it's very satisfying work.'

'I'm sure it is,' I said, not meaning it at all.

'I understand you're investigating a murder,' he said, looking at me with undisguised interest. He had quite a jolly face, which struck me as unusual for his line of business. Most psychologists spend their whole lives with their heads up their arses. For a profession with such a huge and constant failure rate, they take what they do remarkably seriously.

'That's right,' I said. 'A girl not much older than some of the people you deal with. Her name was Miriam Fox. She was a runaway.'

He shook his head. 'It's a tragedy, Sergeant. I always feel if we can influence them while they're young, we can help prevent them taking the path that leads to this sort of thing.'

I felt like telling him that he and his colleagues had always had ample opportunity to do just that, but had clearly failed. But I didn't. The doctor looked a sensitive sort and I didn't want to upset him. For some reason, I actually thought he seemed quite a nice bloke. He reminded me of an eccentric music teacher I'd had in school who used to wear brightly coloured bowties and who was truly enthusiastic about what he did. I'd never liked music at school, it was one of those subjects that seemed to glory in its irrelevance, but I'd always liked classes with him.

'It must be a frustrating task,' I said.

'And how is the investigation going?'

'These things take time, but we're confident of a result.'

'I understand there's been an arrest.'

I eyed him curiously. 'That's right. How did you know?'

He smiled. 'I'm addicted to the news, I'm afraid, and now I have the internet on my laptop, I'm always checking what's happening. The local news said a man surrendered himself to the police today.'

'That's correct, but I can't comment any further on it, as you can appreciate.'

'Of course, of course, I understand. Forgive my inquisitiveness, Sergeant, I just always like to know what's going on.'

'Don't we all?' I told him.

A pregnant pause followed as Roberts presumably tried to think of something else to ask, but I guess he must have realized that he wasn't going to get much information out of me because he called it a day. 'Well, I mustn't hold you up. Good luck with the case.' He put out his hand and I shook it.

He said his goodbyes, excused himself, and I turned to Carla. She was looking even better than she had done yesterday and I had no choice but to try and picture her naked.

'I was just about to finish for the night, Mr Milne. It's been a very long day.'

'And I appreciate you seeing me, Ms Graham. Look, is there a pub near here? Maybe we can talk in less formal surroundings, if that would make things easier?' Christ, that came out easily.

She raised one of her eyebrows and gave me a funny look. Maybe I'd overstepped the mark, but you don't win prizes without buying tickets. 'Are you suggesting we go out for a drink?' There was enough of a hint of playfulness in her voice to tell me she wasn't offended.

I smiled. 'Well, technically, I suppose. But please don't feel it's your civic duty. We can talk here if you'd prefer.'

She sighed. 'There's a pub round the corner that's not too bad.

We can talk there if you want, but I can't stay too long. I'm exhausted, and I've got another long day tomorrow.'

The pub was a two-hundred-yard walk from Coleman House, far enough away to avoid seeing any of the home's clients. It was a huge place, built on two storeys, and was clearly popular with the student crowd. Although busy, it was spacious enough to accommodate everyone amply and there were still a few tables spare.

As we walked to the bar, Carla said hello to two people she knew – both men, both younger than me – and I found myself feeling mildly jealous. I ordered a vodka orange in a superficial attempt to appear sophisticated, and a vodka tonic for her.

'I thought police officers weren't meant to drink on duty,' she said when we'd found a corner table a respectful distance from anyone else.

'Well, I'm not officially on duty.'

She raised both her eyebrows this time. 'Oh. I was under the impression you wanted to see me regarding the investigation.'

'I do. That's the reason I'm here, but what I want to talk to you about is off the record. I'm here in an unofficial capacity.'

She looked interested, and now I had a bit of a problem. If I was honest with myself, the only reason I was there was to see her; everything else was somewhat peripheral. I was concerned about what Anne had told me but I wasn't quite sure how I was going to explain that.

'Go on.'

She was watching me closely, and I found myself watching her back. She had beautiful brown eyes that seemed to swallow you up. Not for the first time, I found myself wondering what the fuck she was doing managing a children's home.

'I ran into one of your clients this evening. Anne. She was in the middle of being abducted by one of her prospective customers.'

She looked genuinely concerned. 'Is she all right?'

'Yeah, she's all right. But she was lucky, Ms Graham. If I hadn't been there, I don't know what would have happened. Somehow I don't think it would have been a happy ending.'

'These girls . . .' She shook her head slowly. 'There's no telling them. It's as if they've got a death wish.'

'Well, it could be a wish that ends up being fulfilled.'

'I know, I know. What's so tragic about the whole thing is that Anne's got so much intelligence. She could really do something with her life if only she'd listen to people. Where is she now?'

'I took her back to your place. That's when I came in to see you.'

'You should have told me.'

'Don't worry. She's okay. She took it remarkably well. We talked for a while afterwards and she seemed concerned, particularly about Molly Hagger's disappearance. She seemed to think that Molly didn't just walk out—'

'What did she think had happened to her?'

'She wouldn't say for sure, but I think she felt something untoward had happened.' I briefly explained the reasons Anne had given me, without mentioning Mark Wells by name. When I'd finished I had to admit to myself that they sounded pretty flimsy.

Carla took a packet of Silk Cut out of her handbag and put one in her mouth, before realizing that she hadn't offered me one, and hastily pointing the pack in my direction.

I declined. 'My throat demands something stronger,' I said, taking a pack of Benson & Hedges out of my shirt pocket.

She lit my cigarette for me and I got a vague but pleasant smell of her perfume as I leaned forward.

'I thought you said you'd arrested someone for the girl's murder.'

'We have, and we're questioning him very closely, but we have to keep our options open. It might be that he's also responsible for murdering Molly Hagger. It might be that he's not responsible for anything.'

She took an elegant draw on her cigarette. 'Do you think she's dead?' she asked.

'I don't know. Anne was adamant that Molly Hagger would never have gone away of her own accord, but she could well be wrong.' I paused, then decided to jump in at the deep end. 'You can't think of any other girls who've left the home in the last few months who, perhaps, you didn't expect to lose?'

Carla gave me a reproachful look. 'Mr Milne, I understand your concerns, and I sympathize with them. If anything's happening to young girls it's essential it gets uncovered, but, with due respect, not every female client at Coleman House is a teenage prostitute. Some get involved in that sort of thing, I won't deny that, but they're in a minority, and we certainly don't keep the streets of King's Cross stocked up with underage girls. There are dozens of care homes in a three-mile radius of here who have exactly the same problems as we do. Do you really think it's likely that our clients are being picked off one by one by some unknown murderer?'

'No, no, of course not. I'm sorry if it came across like that. I'm just trying to look at every avenue.' I took a sip of my drink, noting that hers was getting dangerously near to the bottom of the glass. I didn't want her to go – not yet – but I wasn't doing too well at charming her into staying. 'Will you do me a favour, though? Just to indulge me.'

'What?'

'Will you just let me know if any of your clients absconds, or goes missing under suspicious circumstances? Please. Anything you say will be treated with the utmost confidentiality.'

She nodded. 'All right, but we get that happening a lot of the time, as I said to you and your colleague yesterday. Most of the time, it's just that. Them absconding. Looking for greener pastures. It's the same for all the homes, especially in a city the size of this one.'

'Yeah, I know. That's the problem. If you were, say, a killer, and you didn't want to get caught, they're just the type of girls you'd go for. Ones who can disappear without a trace and no-one's too worried.'

'But I do worry – we all worry – for our clients because we know the pitfalls that await them round every corner. But without resources, and without authority . . .'

'Yeah, I know. What can you do?'

'Exactly. But if any of the girls goes missing, I will let you know.'

'Thanks. I appreciate it.' I took a drag on my cigarette, knowing I had to do something to keep the conversation alive if I was going to keep her here. 'It seems ridiculous that these kids can just do exactly what they want when they're so, you know, unequipped for life.'

'It's a debate we have constantly within the profession,' she said. 'It goes against the grain for many of us to take authoritarian measures, but sometimes I genuinely feel there's no alternative. These children are vulnerable, they just don't know it.'

'It's funny,' I said, not wanting to lose the moment, 'but when I was a kid, my mum used to tell me what a cruel world we lived in. She always said enjoy everything while you're young, but be prepared, because when you get older you'll see that there are a lot of bad people out there. And you know what? I never believed her.'

'But you do now?'

'Yeah, I do now. If anything, she was more right than she could have known.'

'You're beginning to strike me as the sensitive type, Mr Milne.'

'I'm not quite sure whether I should take that as a compliment or not.'

She thought about that for a moment, looking at me over her glass. 'Take it as a compliment. It's how it was intended.'

'We're not all fascist bullyboys, you know. Some of us are actually quite nice people – especially when we're not at work.'

'I don't doubt it. And just because I'm in the profession I'm in, it doesn't mean I'd automatically think you were all fascist bullyboys.'

'But some of your colleagues do.'

'Some of the younger ones do, yes. When I first joined social services, I was probably a lot more black and white in my view of the forces of law and order too. But that was a long time ago.'

'Not that long, I'm sure,' I said with mock chivalry.

She smiled. 'Now that I will definitely take as a compliment.'

'It's how it was intended.'

She looked at her watch, then back at me. 'I really ought to be going, Mr Milne. Time's getting on, and I'm driving.'

'Well, have one last drink with me. It's a rule I've got that I always have to have a minimum of two drinks in every pub I go into. One drink means you're in too much of a hurry.'

'It's an interesting theory. All right, then, I'll have one more. But let me buy.' She stood up. 'Same again?'

'Please.'

I watched her as she walked across to the bar. She was wearing black high-heeled boots and she carried herself extremely well, moving with a grace I would normally associate with a model. Or maybe it was just me. I was already fully aware that I had the hots for her. I expect she knew it too, but it was only watching her then that I realized quite how much I wanted to rip her clothes off and make love to her on the spot. It had been close to six months since I'd last had sex so it wasn't going to take a lot to get me going, and the last time had been no great success either. On that occasion it had been a woman DC from the station who'd been as drunk as me, so it was never going to be a match made in heaven. She'd been engaged to a lawyer from the CPS and I'd got so worn out that I'd had to fake an orgasm. Twice. Although I must have done something right because she'd wanted to see me again afterwards.

This time, there was more than just a desire to have sex, although this came high on the list. I was attracted to Carla in a way I'm not used to. The last time I'd had a feeling like this was when I'd started going out with Danny's sister, and that had been a long time back.

She stayed for about another twenty minutes. I was desperate to go to the toilet for most of the conversation but held back, not wanting to give her an excuse to realize that she ought to be on her way home. We chatted about this and that, mainly to do with our respective jobs, and I found her an interesting and intelligent talker. She was single as well, which helped. Divorced with no kids, she said that most of the time she was married to her work. I told her I knew the feeling.

I kept looking for an opportune moment to ask her out but one never came, or maybe it's more accurate to say that my nerve let me down. I mean, she was a serious career woman with an air of authority about her more suited to a politician than to social services, and I was like a schoolboy in love for the first time with feelings that were more seventeen than thirty-seven.

When she'd finished her drink, she stood up and offered me a hand to shake. 'I really must be going, Mr Milne. It's been very pleasant. It's just a pity that the reason we've been brought together is so tragic.'

I stood up and shook, squeezing her hand tightly. 'Unfortunately, that's the way it goes sometimes. Well, it was nice to talk to you, Ms Graham.'

'You may as well call me Carla.'

'Well then, I insist you call me Dennis.' It sounded a really shite name when I said it like that. Really unsophisticated. Like Wayne, or Eric. For a moment I wondered why I'd never changed it to something better. Even Zeke would have been an improvement.

She smiled. 'Well, Dennis, I hope the investigation goes well.'

That was my opportune moment, but I bottled it. 'I'm sure it will. I'll be in touch if there's anything else we need. And obviously, as I said earlier–'

'I'll definitely let you know if any of the girls goes missing, but, as I told you, it does happen a lot, and there's usually an innocent explanation, if I can use a word like that.'

'Sure, I understand.' I finished my drink. 'Let me walk you to your car.'

'There's no need. It's only parked round the corner. I'd offer you a lift but I've got a very early start.'

'No problem, I understand.' At least my bladder would thank me.

I sat back down and she turned to go, then turned back again. 'Oh, one last thing. Tell me, how did you get Anne to go back to the hostel?'

'I bribed her.'

'With what?'

I felt a bit sheepish admitting what I'd done, but did it anyway. 'I paid her to go back. I gave her some money in lieu of any earnings she would have got by staying out there.'

I wasn't sure if this would please her or not. Probably not. But, surprisingly, she looked at me with what I thought was a measure of respect. 'You *are* a sensitive soul, Dennis.' She smiled. 'I'm almost certain it was a futile gesture. Girls like Anne aren't going to be redeemed suddenly, but I appreciate your concern.'

'Thanks,' I said, and watched her as she disappeared out of the door.

It was ten past nine and I was tired, a long way from home, and desperate for a piss. The evening's events had at least given me some insight into the type of world these girls inhabited, and the type of people out there preying on them. But whether it helped move the case on or not, I wasn't sure.

13

'We're going to charge the pimp,' Malik said excitedly as I walked into the incident room at a quarter to nine the next morning.

The place was buzzing, as is always the case when you've had a result, and most of the detectives who'd been involved were sitting about looking pretty pleased with themselves, although I couldn't see Welland anywhere, and Knox wasn't in his office. Charging Mark Wells and convicting him were two different things, of course, but it sounded like there was definitely room for a lot of optimism. Clearly there'd been some sort of significant breakthrough in the past few hours.

'You missed all the action, Dennis,' DS Capper said loudly. 'Where were you?' Capper was at his desk along with two of his

DC cronies, one of whom was my last sexual conquest – if you can count two faked orgasms as a conquest.

I stopped in front of them. 'What happened, then? Did he confess?'

'He will do. Now that we've got the shirt he was wearing when he killed her. Covered in her blood.'

Capper looked far too self-satisfied for my liking. It was hard enough speaking to him when he was having a bad day, well nigh impossible when he was having a good one. I said to the room in general that it was a piece of very good news, smiled as if I'd just been told I had a really big cock, and sat down at my desk. Malik followed me and seated himself on the other side.

I looked at him with surprise. 'Shit, that all happened fast. When did you hear about it?'

'I saw it on Teletext first thing this morning and came straight in. That was a couple of hours ago.'

'Who found the shirt, then?'

'We got a tip-off. Apparently one of Wells's girls called in last night and said that Wells had admitted to her that he'd killed Miriam Fox and dumped the clothes nearby. They did another search of the area and found the shirt. It went off to forensics in the early hours of this morning. The preliminary tests show an exact match between the blood on the shirt and Miriam Fox's blood.'

'That was quick.'

'Time's of the essence, isn't it? By lunchtime we'll have already had him for twenty-four hours.'

'So it's not a done thing yet?'

'No, but it looks like it's going to go that way. It's definitely the murderer's shirt and we've got a good link between it and Wells.'

'Who was the caller? Did she give a name?'

Malik shook his head. 'No, but you can't blame her, can you? She's not going to want any publicity.'

I nodded slowly and lit a cigarette. It was a fair point.

'What's up, Sarge? You don't look totally convinced.'

I yawned. 'Nah, I'm just tired. I didn't sleep too well last night.' I had a bit of a hangover as well. I'd left the pub shortly after Carla had gone but had stopped off at the Chinaman on the way home for a quick one. Unfortunately it had turned into a slow three. 'You wouldn't do an old man a favour, would you?'

'That old man being you?'

'That's right.'

'What is it you want?'

'A bacon sandwich and a nice cup of tea.' He gave me a dirty look. 'Please, Asif, I wouldn't ask if it wasn't an emergency.'

'You've got to change your diet, Sarge. You eat nothing but crap.'

'Well, get me an apple as well.' I fished into the pocket of my suit and brought out two pound coins. 'Please. Call it a personal favour. I won't ask again, I promise.'

He took the money reluctantly, checking that no-one was watching, and got up. 'This is a one-off, Sarge. Remember that. It's only because you look so bloody rough that I'm agreeing.'

'Your pity will be rewarded,' I told him piously.

When he'd gone, I started to think about this new development. I hadn't slept well because I'd been thinking about my conversation with Anne and the possibility that there was some sort of serial killer on the loose targeting underage prostitutes. It was a flight-of-fancy theory, really. Though they make ideal fictional villains and endless fodder for real-life documentaries, in reality serial killers are as rare as dinosaur turds. If there were more than two operating in this whole country of close to sixty million people at any one time, I'd be extremely surprised. But I suppose these things do occasionally happen, and if such a man was at work he'd picked the right sort of place and the right sort of victims to keep himself concealed. The only thing was, if Molly Hagger and any other girls had fallen victim to this man, where were the bodies? And why was Miriam Fox's left in such an obvious location?

These were the questions that had prevented me getting anywhere near the seven hours' slumber I need to function at what passes for optimum efficiency. I'd even managed to incorporate Carla Graham into the various theories and trains of thought I'd tossed about my brain. In the better ones, I'd solve the case, find the killer (even going so far as catching him as he prepared to despatch his latest victim), get a promotion, and end up fucking Carla's brains out.

Fat chance. But at least a man can dream.

The bacon sandwich tasted good anyway, and I was so hungry I even ate the apple down to the core.

At 9.15, Knox came into the incident room with a very tired-looking Welland. Welland sat down immediately and it looked like he needed to. Knox, meanwhile, addressed the rest of us. 'We've just told Mark Wells about the latest developments and once again he categorically denies any involvement, but, to use the old phrase, he would say that, wouldn't he? He certainly looks far more worried than he has been. As we all know, he's a cocky bastard, and he's lost a lot of that now. We should get the rest of the results on the shirt later this morning and they'll tell us whether it belongs to Wells or not, although from the way he's behaving, I feel fairly certain it's his.'

'So we're going to be knocking out the champers later, then?' This was Capper.

Knox smiled. 'It's far too early even to think about a celebration drink yet. We've done well, very well, and it's been a team effort, but until you hear otherwise, it's still business as usual.'

He strode into his office, leaving Welland where he'd sat down. One of the women DCs asked Welland if he was all right. 'Yeah, yeah, I'm fine,' he replied. 'Just a bit under the weather.' Someone suggested that he go home for the day, but he said he'd stick around and wait for Wells to be charged. 'I want to see that bastard squirm,' he said, with more vigour than I'd have thought his body would allow.

'He looks terrible,' said Malik quietly, turning to me.

'Yeah, I know. He should take a few days off. He needs it. And the taxpayer owes him a break. He's done a good job on behalf of society.'

Not that anyone had ever thanked him for it; or any of us, for that matter. It may be that it's not accurate to describe all coppers as unsung heroes, but neither is it fair to view them as the constant villains of the piece, which is usually the way we're portrayed whenever we get a mention on the box. And Welland, more than most, was one of the good guys. He'd put his all into policework, so now he might as well take something back.

'If I was him, I'd go for early retirement,' said Malik.

'If I was him, I'd have gone for it ten years ago.'

He gave me a disbelieving smile. 'No you wouldn't. You enjoy the whole thing too much.'

'Bullshit I do.'

My phone rang and I had a sudden rush of adrenalin, hoping it was Carla. But if she was the person I most wanted to speak to, then the person on the other end of the line had to be one of those whose voice I least wanted to hear.

'It's a Jean Ashcroft for you, Mr Milne,' said the civilian receptionist.

Christ, what the hell did she want? 'Thanks, can you put her through?' There was a pause as she came on the line. 'Hello, Jean. Long time no speak.'

'Hello, Dennis. Look, I'm sorry to bother you . . .' Her tone was strained, formal.

'It's no problem. No problem at all. What can I do?'

'It's Danny,' she said. 'I think he might be in trouble.'

'What makes you say that?'

'Well he phoned me last night and, you know, he never normally phones me, so I knew something wasn't right. He didn't sound himself, Dennis. It was all very strange. I think he'd been drinking, or smoking something, and he was rambling, going on about changing his life, doing something different, saying that it was definitely time to make the break and go . . . and he said something about having saved up some money, a lot of money.'

'Maybe he has.'

'He doesn't have a job, Dennis. He would never have been able to raise a lot of money,' she stopped for a quick sniff, 'unless he's involved in something. You know, something criminal. That's what I'm worried about. You know what he's like. It would break my mum's heart if anything happened to him again, especially after all that stuff before. And now with Dad gone.'

'Look, I understand you're worried about him. It's only natural. And I know he's had his brushes with the law, but he hasn't been in trouble for a long time now.' Malik was looking at me quizzically now, but I waved him away, intimating that it wasn't business. Not police business, anyway. He stood up and walked off. 'I don't think you should let one drunken phone call get you too concerned. Seriously, Jean.'

'You still see him sometimes, don't you?'

'Yeah, occasionally, but not as often as I'd like.'

'You know, whenever we speak, which I know isn't that often, but whenever we do, he always talks about you. I think he looks up to you. Would you do me a favour? Please. I understand what you're saying about not getting too worried, but would you go round and see him, just to check things out? See that he's OK.'

This was all I needed. 'I really think you're worrying unduly. Danny's no fool. He's done his time. He won't make the same mistake again.'

'Please, Dennis. I'm sure you're busy, but it would mean a lot if you could just check up on him.'

'OK, I'll see what I can do, but I'm sure it's nothing.'

'Thanks. I really appreciate it.' And it sounded like she did.

I took her number in Leeds and said I'd get back to her one way or another in the next few days. We talked for a few moments longer, but the conversation was stilted and uncomfortable. Far too much water had passed under the bridge, and I was happy to hang up. Jean Ashcroft had been a good-looking girl once upon a time, and good company too, but now she was nothing more than a half-forgotten part of my past. Danny had really fucked up by talking to her. He'd seemed fine the other night at the pub quiz. We'd had a few drinks, a few laughs, and had even come a close second to the winners, and when I'd left him he'd been OK. Not exactly full of the joys of spring, but OK nevertheless. It was clear, however, that being cooped up at home for much of the time, with just himself for company, was making him seriously paranoid, and that was dangerous. Fuck knows what he'd do if they ever really got close. I was going to have to give him a good talking to. Knock some sense into him. Get him to calm down.

What was it that American president once said? The only thing we have to fear is fear. Well, Danny feared fear, and it was beginning to make him a liability.

14

At 11.55 that morning the results from the lab came back confirming that hair samples found on the shirt belonged to Mark Wells, and that it could safely be surmised that the shirt belonged to him.

At 12.10, the questioning of Mark Wells by DCI Knox and DI Welland recommenced. The suspect still denied any involvement in the crime and became hysterical when told of the new evidence against him, at one point attempting to assault both the officers present. He had to be physically restrained before questioning could continue. His solicitor then requested some time alone with his client to discuss these new developments, and this was granted.

At 12.35, the questioning once again resumed, Wells's solicitor sticking to the position that his client had had nothing to do with the murder of Miriam Fox. However, neither he nor Wells could offer any realistic explanation as to why the shirt had been found so close to the murder scene covered in the victim's blood. Wells suggested that it must have been stolen.

At 1.05, twenty-seven-year-old Mark Jason Wells was formally charged with the murder of eighteen-year-old Miriam Ann Fox. For the second time that day, he had to be physically restrained from attacking his interrogators. During the ensuing altercation, his solicitor was accidentally struck in the face by Wells and required medical treatment for a bloody nose. In a rare moment of wit, DS Capper later claimed this to be a double result for the Metropolitan Police.

At 2.25, still a little sleepy from my canteen lunch of lasagne and garden vegetables, I was called into Knox's office.

Knox was sitting behind his spotless desk looking serious, which surprised me a little under the circumstances. 'Hello, Dennis. Thanks for coming in. Sit down.' He waved to a seat. 'You've heard the news, then?'

'About charging Wells? Yes, sir, DI Welland told me.'

'DI Welland's had to go home, I'm afraid.'

'He didn't look too good, sir, I have to admit.'

'He isn't, I'm afraid. In fact, he hasn't been his best for some time.' I didn't say anything, so he continued. 'He went for some tests a couple of weeks ago and he received the results this morning.' I felt a mild sense of dread. Knox sighed loudly. 'He only told me after we'd charged Wells. I'm afraid DI Welland has prostate cancer. There's going to be an official announcement this afternoon.'

'Jesus.' What a day. 'I knew something was wrong but I didn't think it would be anything like that. How bad is it?'

'Well, it's cancer, so it's bad. As to whether it's terminal or not, I don't know. Neither do the doctors. A lot depends on how he responds to treatment and his overall attitude.'

'There won't be anything wrong with that. The DI's a fighter.'

I suddenly felt like crying, which is something I haven't done in a long, long time. It was the injustice of it all. Here was a man who for thirty years had been trying to do the right thing and he was repaid with a life-threatening illness, while there were criminals and politicians out there who'd spent just as much time trying to line their own pockets and were as healthy as a new heart. The moment passed, and I asked Knox if he minded if I smoked.

'No-one should really be smoking in here, especially under the circumstances, but go on then.' He watched me light it and told me that I ought to give up. 'It won't do you any good, you know,' he told me sternly, which was a statement of the obvious if ever I'd heard one. That's the problem with health fascists. They never understand that you know as much about the facts as they do.

'A man's got to have some pleasures,' I said, which is my standard defence in these sorts of matters.

'Perhaps. But anyway, I digress. I didn't bring you in here to discuss any bad habits you might have. I wanted to speak to you because, at the very minimum, DI Welland's going to be on sick leave for three months, and I suspect it will be considerably longer. It might even be the case that he never comes back. So we have a temporary vacancy.'

I felt as though I ought to say something at this juncture but, because I couldn't think what, I kept my mouth shut. I was beginning to get the first stirrings of interest, though. The DI's position. I could handle that, even if it was only temporary.

'Obviously we want to promote from within the CID at this station, as that'll give us the continuity we need, and it'll give DI Welland the chance to slot back in, when and if he's able to return to duty.'

'I understand.'

'And it's for that reason we've decided to go with DS Capper as the acting DI.'

And to think I'd been getting optimistic. I fought hard not to show my disappointment at being passed over in favour of an idiot like Capper, but it was difficult.

'I wanted to tell you first before we announced it so that I could explain our reasons.'

'Which are?'

He gave me the usual management waffle about how Capper had more experience at plainclothes level (there was about two months in it); was better qualified (he'd been on more training and awareness courses than I had, most of which were about as useful as suntan lotion in a snowstorm); and had a more positive attitude towards certain aspects of the job (such as kissing arse).

What can you say to that?

'That's not to say that you're in any way a bad copper, Dennis. Because you're not. You're an extremely valued member of the team. I want you to understand that.'

'I understand, sir,' I said, hoping that we could bring this bout of making me feel better to a swift end.

'You've done a great job over the years.'

'Thanks.'

'I know you're disappointed.'

'I'm all right, sir.'

'That's understandable, but try to take some positives from it.'

'I will, sir.'

'Now, to wrap this Miriam Fox case up we have a task that requires experience and tact.'

'I'm all ears.'

'I want you to go down to see her mother and father and talk them through the progress we've made on the case. It'll be good public relations and it'll give them an opportunity to bring themselves up to date with what's been happening. They've been told by local police that charges have been laid against the man in custody, but that's all.'

'What else do they need to know?'

'It's felt both by the Chief Super and myself that they'd benefit from a personal visit by one of our more senior officers. I'd like you to go down there tomorrow morning and take DC Malik with you.' I think I must have made a face because Knox fixed me with a stern look. 'Look, Dennis, the Metropolitan Police has one hell of a lot of critics, as you know. Miriam Fox's father is an influential man and a local Labour councillor. We need to get people like him on our side.'

There was no point arguing. The decision had been made, so nothing was going to change it. I nodded to show that I understood. 'Is that all, sir?'

'Yes, that's it. Thanks for your understanding., Dennis. I knew you wouldn't let us down.'

I stood up. 'I'm sorry about the DI. I'd like to visit him, if it's possible. When does he begin his treatment?'

'Monday. I'll let you have the hospital details when I get them.'

'Yeah, that would be good. Thanks.' I took a last drag on the cigarette and looked about for an ashtray. There wasn't one, so Knox passed me a three-quarters-empty coffee cup with the legend World's Best Dad scrawled on the side. Better parent than man manager, then. I chucked the butt in and he put the cup back on his desk. 'It's good news about Wells, anyway.'

Knox nodded. 'Yes it is. It's always good to get a result this quickly.'

'Did we locate the car he was driving when he picked her up?'

'Forensics are doing tests on his car at the moment.'

'And is it a dark-coloured saloon?'

'It's a maroon BMW, so I think that counts. It would look dark-coloured at night on a dimly lit street. Why? Do you think there's a problem?'

I shrugged. 'Not necessarily. It's just that when Malik and I ran into him at Miriam Fox's flat he looked totally shocked to see us, and it was instinctive shock too, not put on. If he'd killed her he'd expect to see coppers at her place. Also, what would he be doing going back there?'

'Maybe there was some incriminating evidence he wanted to recover.'

'There wasn't. We checked the place thoroughly, remember.'

Knox sighed. 'Dennis, just what do you want us to do? We've got a violent pimp with plenty of convictions for assaults against women who's known to have attacked the victim within the last few weeks and whose shirt was found covered in her blood less than a hundred yards from where she was killed, and who's so far failed to provide us with any sort of alibi. We can hardly let him go, can we?'

'But it doesn't necessarily mean he's the one, does it? You only found the shirt because of a tip-off. And that's the only thing that really connects him to the murder, isn't it?'

'Well, it's a pretty big thing, don't you agree? It's definitely his shirt, it's got his hair fibres all over it, for Christ's sake.' He was beginning to get annoyed now. Knox was a man who liked to feel he was in control, he didn't like it when people started knocking holes in his theories.

I nodded slowly. 'True, but it's still the only connection. And there's still the little problem of motive. I mean, why did he kill her?'.

'Dennis, what's your fucking problem? Have you got some alternative theory you'd like to share with us all? Because if not, stop trying to undermine all the work we've done.'

I thought about telling him about Molly Hagger's disappearance and the possibility that there was something more to all this than a simple dispute between a pimp and his whore, but

I held back. In a way I was too embarrassed to say something. I had nothing concrete at all, just a few flimsy ideas and that old classic: the instinctive feeling that something wasn't quite right.

'No, I don't have anything else, I'm just concerned we get the right man. The last thing we need is an acquittal and allegations of a frame-up.'

'I'm glad you're concerned. It shows you care. But believe me, Mark Wells is our man. If I wasn't damned sure, I wouldn't be charging him. OK?'

'OK.'

'And, Dennis, bear this in mind.'

'What, sir?'

'There hasn't been a single killing of a prostitute in the whole of the south-east with an MO like Miriam Fox's, so it's almost certain it was a one-off. Do you see what I'm saying?'

'Yes, sir.'

'Don't complicate matters, because a lot of the time they don't need complicating. Now, can you do me a favour and send DS Capper in?'

And that was that. I left the room without saying another word, wondering just how much worse things could get.

I found Capper over at the photocopier talking to Hunsdon. I told him Knox wanted to see him, and he went off with a sly smile. When he'd gone, I turned to Hunsdon.

'Have you got those phone records yet?' I asked him.

'Yeah, they faxed them through this morning. I've got them here somewhere.' He picked up a pile of papers from the in-tray and went through them quickly.

'Were they any use?' I asked him as he searched.

'Not really,' he said, handing me two sheets of A4 paper.

I took them off him and glanced down the first page, which detailed outgoing calls. There was a total of ninety-seven listed,

144

all made in the twenty-eight days up until the date of the murder. The left-hand column gave the date and time of each one, the right-hand column identified the numbers called. The second sheet detailed the incoming ones, of which there were fifty-six.

'These numbers have got no names with them,' I said, looking up at him.

'That's right. That's why they're not much use.'

'Can't they identify the person each number's registered to?'

'Yeah, but apparently that takes a lot longer because it involves more than one company. There's a lot of cross-checking databases, that sort of thing, but they're on the case at the moment. I should be getting a list any time now.'

I put the sheets in the copier and ran a copy, giving the originals back to him. 'Look, can you give me the names of the people you're dealing with? I don't mind chasing it.'

He looked at me uncertainly. 'What's the point? They're not going to tell us anything. So she made calls to Wells and he made calls to her. That stands to reason.'

'Humour me.'

'The bloke I've been dealing with is called John Claire. I've got his number back at my desk.'

'Well, let's go back and get it, then.'

Reluctantly he returned to his desk with me in tow and dug out the number. I got the feeling he hadn't exactly been pushing himself to get the information on Miriam's records, but that was Hunsdon for you. He wasn't a bad copper in many ways, but he was a lazy bastard, and not the best at performing routine tasks, especially when he thought the tasks themselves were a bit pointless.

I wrote the number down and he asked me again what the point of chasing it up was.

It was, I suppose, a good question. I think at that precise

moment my interest stemmed from a real desire to put one over on Knox and Capper and wipe the smiles off their faces. Maybe Wells was the man responsible for Miriam's murder, but it just didn't seem to me to be as cut and dried as they all thought. For the sake of a couple of phone calls, I was more than happy to be the one who proved them wrong.

15

There were seven numbers which came up more than three times among the phone calls to and from Miriam Fox's mobile, and I decided to concentrate on finding out who they belonged to, as well as all the numbers she'd either called or received calls from during the last three days of her life. It was quite possible that they wouldn't tell me anything; even if they did, it was still going to be extremely difficult to get Knox to authorize any further investigation, particularly now that he'd charged Wells. But I still felt it was worth a try.

I called John Claire from my desk, but his line was busy. I lit and smoked a cigarette down to the butt and called him again, but it was still engaged. He was obviously a hard-working boy. I was going to give it five minutes and try him again but I never got the chance. A knifepoint robbery had occurred at a back-street newsagent's less than half a mile from the station and I was ordered to attend with Malik to take statements from the proprietor and any witnesses. We were there for about an hour, trying to calm down the proprietor's wife, who'd had a knife held against her throat by a kid of no more than thirteen while his five laughing mates had ransacked the place. The husband, who'd been out at the wholesaler's, was distraught. He harangued us and society in general for turning out kids who thought so little of using violence. We didn't try to argue with him. He was right. I told them we'd do what we could to apprehend the perpetrators and thanked them for their help. We then got a squad car to take the wife to hospital for a check-up and returned to the station to file our report.

At ten past five, I tried John Claire's number again. This time he answered immediately. I explained who I was and why I was phoning.

'Yeah, I was dealing with one of your colleagues, DC...?'

'Hunsdon.'

'That's right. I was trying to get together some information for him. Telephone records.'

'Yeah, I know. How far are you down the line? It's just I need them pretty quickly.'

'I've already sent them,' he said, sounding surprised. 'I emailed them to him this morning.'

'No, we've got the actual numbers, it's the people they belong to we need to know. Who the phones are registered to.'

'Yeah, I know. That's what I sent him. I sent him a list with the numbers on it yesterday. I had to chase down the names of the people and it took a bit of time. I said as soon as I got the information I'd get it across to him. And I did. This morning.'

Clearly, Hunsdon hadn't been checking his mail. I lit a cigarette. 'Maybe the network's down here today or something. Can you send it again?'

'Yeah, no problem.'

'I'll give you two places to send it to, just to make sure it goes through.' I reeled off my work and home addresses, and waited while he wrote them down. 'And can you do it immediately, please?'

'Yeah, of course,' he said, sounding a little nervous. 'No problem, officer.'

I thanked him, and hung up.

The mail hadn't arrived when, ten minutes later, Capper phoned through and asked to see me in Welland's office for a quick chat. He was sitting behind Welland's desk looking far too comfortable when I went in.

'I understand you've been told the news,' he said, making only a cursory attempt to contain his pleasure.

'That's right. Congratulations.'

He swung round slowly in Welland's mock leather seat. 'Thank you. Now, I want us to work together, Dennis. I know we haven't always seen eye to eye in the past, had our ups and downs, but it's important we all pull in the same direction.'

'I agree,' I said, avoiding calling him sir.

'How did it go this afternoon at the newsagent's? Do we know who did it?'

'I can't say for sure, but I think the one with the knife's Jamie Delly.'

Delly was the fourth and youngest boy in a family of petty criminals, all of whom possessed a nasty streak. He'd first been nicked at the age of eight for trying to set his school on fire; ten years earlier his mum had assaulted me with a frozen leg of New Zealand lamb when I'd tried to arrest her for shoplifting.

'That little toe-rag. Bit out of his league, isn't it?'

'Well, he's growing up now. Time to move on from nicking kids' dinner money and shoplifting.'

'Didn't his mother—?'

'Yeah, yeah. Leg of lamb . . .'

'You're lucky you didn't get the chop.' Capper grinned at his wit, showing an unruly set of stained teeth. I would have grinned too if I hadn't heard the joke at least a hundred times before.

148

'Can we get him for this?' he asked, becoming serious again.

'I should think so, if the proprietor's missus can pick him out in an ID.'

'Get one organized, will you?' he said in a tone that almost begged him to round off the sentence with a 'there's a good lad'. I nodded, and said that I would, keen not to rise to the bait, although wondering how long I was going to be able to put up with this man as my boss. 'Another thing, Dennis, before you go. I understand you were trying to take over Hunsdon's end of the Fox inquiry, telling him you'd chase up the information on the phone records. Is that right?'

'I thought there might be something in there somewhere that could be of use.'

'And you didn't think DC Hunsdon was capable of finding it?' He eyed me closely.

'I was just interested in seeing what I could find. Hunsdon had to make a couple of phone calls, I offered to make them for him.'

'We've charged someone, Dennis, all right? That's it, end of story. I can't have officers of mine going over old ground. We haven't got time. And if for some reason you're not busy enough, I can always assign you some more cases. Because we've got plenty of them.'

'OK, point taken.'

'Have you chased up these records?'

Instinctively I decided not to tell him. 'No. No, I haven't.'

'Good. Don't bother. Concentrate on the stuff that's assigned to you, OK? And if there's anything I can do to help, let me know. Like I say, I want us to work together.'

I asked him if that was all. He said it was.

'I'll get back to work, then,' I said, but I didn't. I got my coat, told

Malik I'd see him in the morning, and headed out of there.

16

I stopped at the Roving Wolf for a quick pint, then caught the bus home through the rush-hour traffic. It was half past six when I walked in the door, and I rang Danny's home number as soon as I'd shut it behind me.

He answered after three rings. 'Right,' I said, without preamble. 'Do as I say. Go to the nearest phone box, get its number, then phone me with it. Stay where you are and I'll phone you back.' He started to ask what it was all about, but I cut him off.

Five minutes later he called back and gave me the number. I wrote it down, then called it using Raymond's mobile.

'Christ, what the hell's this all about?' he asked, picking up the phone. 'What's all this cloak-and-dagger stuff?'

'I wanted to be able to speak freely,' I said. 'I got a call this morning, Danny. From your sister.'

'Oh, shit.'

'Yeah, that's what I thought. Now, tell me something. What the fuck are you phoning her for? I told you to just keep calm and let everything blow over.'

'I know, I know. It's just that it's fucking difficult, Dennis.

You know, I can't stop thinking about what happened. I'm even dreaming about it. I was in the pub last night and there was even talk that it had something to do with the Adamses. Do you know anything about that?'

The Adamses, for those who've not heard of them, are the shadowy North London crime family few people tend to know anything about, but whose name is usually linked to any so-called gangland crime where there are no immediate suspects. I'd have bet my life that Raymond had never even met one of the Adams family, let alone agreed to commit murder for them.

'Don't be fucking daft, Danny,' I told him. 'Do you really think I'd get involved with people like that? And do you genuinely believe that people like the Adamses sub out this sort of thing to blokes they don't even know. They've got plenty of resources of their own. So, who was saying all this shit, then?'

'There was a bloke called Steve Fairley in there. He was saying it. I wouldn't have taken much notice if it had been anyone else, but he's a bit of a player. Knows about these things. That's what worried me.'

I knew Steve Fairley. Tomboy had told me about him. If he was a player, then he was very much Vauxhall Conference. 'And you reckon the Adamses decided to tell him all about it, do you? You know, make sure as many people know about it as possible?'

'Look, I know it sounds stupid—'

'You're right. It does.'

He sighed. 'It's just getting to me, that's all.'

'But telling your sister, Danny, of all people. I mean, what the hell's she going to do to help you out of your predicament? Give you a character reference? Now she's been on to me saying she thinks you're in trouble, and can I go and visit you and find out what's wrong, and then get back to her. I don't need this, Danny.'

'I'm sorry, I really am. It won't happen again.'

'It better not.' I almost told him it was that sort of talk that could get us all killed, but held back. There was no point making him even more jittery than he already was.

'I didn't tell her anything important, I promise.'

'You told her you'd saved up some money, that got her suspicions going straight away.'

'Yeah, but there's no way she can link that to anything that's happened.'

'No, that's right, but if you start pouring out your heart every time you've had a few drinks then sooner or later something might slip out, something that could incriminate you and me, and that'd be a truly fucking stupid way to get caught. Now, let me tell you something. Every day that passes means they're less likely to catch us. The trail gets that little bit colder. Like I've said all along, all you need to do is keep calm and everything'll be fine. If it's any consolation, the only person who's got any idea of your involvement is me, and I'm not going to say a word to anyone. So you're OK, understand?'

'Yeah, yeah, I understand. I'll make sure I keep shtum. It was just one of those things.'

'Look, now you've got some money, why don't you take a little holiday? Get away for a few weeks. It's got to be better than sitting around trying to think of all the things that could possibly go wrong.'

'Yeah, maybe you're right.'

'When was the last time you had a holiday?'

'Shit, I don't know. Ages ago.'

'Well, fuck it. Treat yourself. It's dogshit weather. You're not going to be missing much. And by the time you come back all this will have died down and everyone'll be talking about some other heinous crime.'

'You've got a point. Maybe I will.' There was a long pause. Eventually he spoke again. 'I'm sorry, Dennis. I really am. I won't fuck up like that again.'

'I know you won't,' I told him. 'I know you're not that fucking stupid.'

'What are you going to tell Jean?'

I thought about it for a minute. 'I'll tell her I talked to you and that you've turned over a new leaf. Rather than aid and abet criminals in their criminal ways, you now try to put them behind bars where they belong. I'll tell her you're a police informant and that's how you've made some money, but that it's all very hush hush and she can't talk about it to anyone for fear of blowing your cover. Hopefully that way she'll leave you alone. What do you think?'

'I think you're a cunning bastard, Dennis.'

'Take that holiday, Danny. OK?'

'Yeah. Yeah, I think I will.'

'I'll talk to you soon.'

I hung up and walked into the lounge, sitting down on the sofa with my cigarette. Had I managed to calm him down enough to cross him off my list of worries? It was a good question. What I'd said was eminently sensible, if not altogether true. I wasn't the only person who knew of his involvement in the killings. I'd been forced to give some details about him to Raymond before he'd allowed me to take him on the Traveller's Rest job. Armed with those details, if Raymond really wanted to find Danny, he'd probably be able to. There was no point telling Danny that, though. Hopefully, he would take my advice and leave the country for a while. It would certainly make my life easier. If the truth be told, he was rapidly becoming a thorn in my side. For the first time I thought maybe it would be better for everyone involved if I simply took him out, and quietened his fears for ever. Not that I seriously thought I could ever pull the trigger on Danny. I'd known the little bastard too long. But if I'd been a more ruthless man maybe I'd have done more than let the thought rumble through my mind. That was a measure of how concerned I was.

I finished the cigarette and stubbed it out in the overflowing ashtray, remembering the mail John Claire was meant to have sent me. I got up, went through to the bedroom, and switched the PC on. While it booted up I went and got myself a beer from the fridge, feeling pleased that I was home for the night and cocooned for a few hours at least from the problems of the world.

Claire's email had arrived at 5.31, so at least he'd been true to his word. I opened up the attachment and saw that what he'd sent was a copy of the original document but with a third column tagged on containing the names of those to whom each individual number was registered.

I didn't recognize the first name on the list. It was a man, most likely a punter. The second name was a man's as well, again one I didn't recognise. The next number wasn't registered to a particular individual, which probably meant it was a pay-as-you-go mobile. Maybe it belonged to Molly Hagger. I thought maybe it would be a good idea to phone it and find out. The third name was Coleman House, which stood to reason.

I didn't read the fourth name. Or the fifth.

I was too busy looking at the sixth.

And wondering why Carla Graham had lied to me when she said she hadn't known Miriam.

17

I really didn't know what to expect as I turned the car into the short gravel driveway that led up to the Fox residence. The house itself was an attractive and spacious two-storey building constructed in an L-shape with a thatched roof and lattice windows, set in enclosed gardens. It was on the edge of a small village a few miles west of Oxford towards the Gloucestershire border, so a fair drive for Malik and me. It had taken us about two and a quarter hours through the usual heavy traffic, and it was now just after eleven.

'Just in time for a nice cup of tea,' I said, pulling up in front of the house.

Malik looked a little nervous. I guess he too didn't know what to expect from this sort of visit. It was never going to be easy. These people had found out only four days ago that their daughter had been murdered. They may not have seen her for close on three years, but they were still going to be in a state of shock. It would take years for their lives to return to normal, if they ever did.

To be honest, my mind was elsewhere. I wanted to know why

Miriam Fox had phoned Carla Graham three times during the last fortnight of her life, twice to Carla's mobile, and why Carla herself had made two calls to Miriam's number, the last of them just four days before she was murdered. That many calls was no accident. Those two had known each other, and the only conceivable reason why Carla hadn't said anything to us about their relationship was that she had something to hide, although what that something could be I had no idea. I'd phoned Coleman House straight away, ostensibly to let her know that we'd charged Mark Wells, but also to arrange another meeting so I could ask her about it, but she'd left for the night. I'd tried her again before we'd left this morning but she was in a meeting. I hadn't bothered to leave a message. There was no point alerting her to the fact that I was trying to track her down. For the moment it could wait.

I straightened my tie and banged on the huge brass doorknocker.

The door was opened almost immediately by a largish middle-aged lady in a sweater and long skirt. Although she looked tired, with large bags under her eyes, she appeared to be bearing up reasonably well. She had a light covering of make-up on and she even managed a smile of greeting. 'Detective Milne?'

'Mrs Fox.' We shook hands. 'This is my colleague, Detective Constable Malik.'

They shook hands as well, and then she stood aside for us. 'Please, come in.'

We followed her through the hallway and into a large, very dark sitting room. A fire blazed in the grate, and sitting in one of the seats facing it was a shortish bearded man with glasses. He stood up slowly on seeing us and introduced himself as Martin Fox. If Mrs Fox appeared to be bearing up well, then Mr Fox was the exact opposite. His whole body appeared slumped as if the guts had been knocked out of him, and even his speech was slow and forced.

The gloom seemed to spread from him like an infectious cloud. I got depressed just being within five feet of the bloke.

We sat down on the sofa and Mrs Fox asked us if we'd like anything to drink. We both opted for tea, and she went off to make a pot.

While she was gone, Malik told Fox that he was very sorry about his loss. He sounded like he truly meant it as well.

Fox sat back with his head against the seat, not looking at us. 'Did she suffer?' he asked, speaking slowly as if carefully choosing his words. 'When she died, did she suffer? Please be honest with me.'

Malik looked at me for a bit of help on this one.

'She would have died very quickly, Mr Fox,' I said. 'She didn't suffer. I can assure you of that.'

'The newspapers said only that she was stabbed.'

'That's the only details we released to the media,' I said. 'They don't need to know anything more than that.'

'Was she stabbed many times?' he asked.

'She died from a single wound,' I said, not mentioning anything about the mutilation.

'Why?' The question hung in the air for what seemed like a long time. 'Do they know, these people who commit these terrible crimes? Do they know the hurt they cause? To the ones who are left behind?'

I ached for a cigarette but knew without asking that this would be a non-smoking household. 'I think,' I said, 'that most really don't have a clue of the suffering they inflict. If they did, I'm sure a lot of them would think twice before doing what they do.'

'And do you think that this man . . . the one who killed my Miriam . . . do you think he knew what he was doing?'

I thought suddenly about the families of the customs officers and the accountant. I knew what I'd been doing. Had always known. 'I'm not sure, Mr Fox. It could well have been a spur-of-the-moment thing.'

'It doesn't matter. People like that should be put down. Like dogs.' Maybe he had a point. 'I never believed in the death penalty. I thought it was barbaric for a society to put to death its citizens, whatever their crimes. But now ... now ...' His face, still only visible in profile, was contorted with a terrible frustration. 'I'd pull the trigger myself. I really would.'

Before I could give him my standard police spiel that these feelings were understandable but ultimately counter-productive, Mrs Fox thankfully returned with the tea. Fox slipped into a sullen silence. Doubtless he'd been venting his spleen to her in similar vein all week. She sat down at the opposite end of the room to her husband so that we were between them, and poured the tea from a china teapot.

'The reason we're here,' I said, thinking that I really didn't have a clue what it was, 'is to update you on what's happening with the inquiry, and let you know what'll happen now that we've arrested someone.'

'Who is the man who's been charged?' asked Mrs Fox.

I told her who he was and what his relationship was to their daughter, careful not to give away too many details. Pre-trial, police officers have got to watch what they say in case they blurt out anything that might prejudice a fair hearing for the suspect.

'You think he's the one, then?' she said, when I'd finished.

'Bastard,' Fox added, with a violent snarl. Mrs Fox gave him a reproachful look, though she must have felt the same.

It was a good question. I was 50 per cent certain at best. Malik, from the conversation we'd had on the way down, was closer to 80 per cent. Like Knox, he couldn't see any viable alternative, which made drawing conclusions easier for him.

It was Malik who answered. 'We're very sure it's him, Mrs

Fox. As sure as we can be. There's substantial physical evidence linking him to the scene of the crime.'

'Good. I don't think I could stand an acquittal. Not on top of everything else.'

'We can't predict the future, Mrs Fox,' I said, 'or juries. We can only do our best. But I think the case is very strong.'

'Bastard,' said Fox again, still not looking at us. I think he meant Wells, but it was difficult to tell.

'Mark Wells will spend a considerable part of the rest of his life in prison if he's found guilty, Mr Fox,' Malik told him. 'And we're going to do everything in our power to make sure that happens.'

'It's not enough. No prison sentence is good enough for him. Not after what he's done.'

It was, I thought, amazing how socially liberal people like Labour councillors soon changed their tune on crime when it actually had an effect on them. At that moment, Fox looked to be only a couple of steps away from becoming a Charles-Bronson-type vigilante, although without the guns or the menace. Or, it seemed, the energy.

Mrs Fox looked across at her husband and gave him a brave smile. 'Come on, Martin. We've got to stop trying to be so bitter. It doesn't help.'

Fox didn't say anything. I took a sip of my tea and decided to try to finish this interview as swiftly as possible. But before I could continue my spiel about how there was going to be a long wait for the trial and how we would keep in touch regularly in the meantime, Mrs Fox suddenly burst into tears.

Malik and I sat there respectfully. Fox continued to sit in exactly the same position he had been in for the previous ten minutes, staring at an ill-defined point somewhere in the middle distance. I thought he was being ignorant. I know he'd had an immense trauma, but sometimes you've just got to be strong.

'I'm sorry,' she said, dabbing her eyes with a handkerchief. 'It's just . . .'

I put on a stoic smile. 'We understand. You've had a terrible loss. You've got to let it out.'

'I know. That's what the counsellors have been saying.'

'Don't worry about us,' said Malik.

'You know,' she said, looking at both of us with an expression of disbelief, 'it's such an awful, awful waste. That's the hardest part. When you think what she could have been. What she could have achieved if only she'd stayed here with us . . . people who loved her. Instead she ended up dying such a lonely and degrading death. Why?' This was the second time that question had been asked this morning. 'Why did she have to run away and leave us like she did?'

'Leave it, Diane!' snapped Fox, swinging round in his seat and fixing her with a rage-filled stare. Malik and I looked at him, surprised at the violence of his outburst, and his features relaxed a little. 'Just leave it. There's no point going over this again.'

But Mrs Fox clearly had matters to get off her chest. 'Do you know, in the three years she's been gone she never once tried to make contact with us? Not once. Not even a call to let us know she was all right. Nothing. Do you have any idea how that made me feel?'

'We have evidence to suggest that Miriam was taking quite a lot of hard drugs,' I said. 'Sometimes that can take over a person's life to such an extent that they lose track of what their priorities should be. Maybe that's what it was like for her. It doesn't mean she didn't care. It's just that the lure of the drugs may have been stronger.'

'She could have called, Mr Milne. Just once. If not for our sake then for her sister's. Chloe was only twelve years old when Miriam left. She could have contacted her.'

'Leave it, Diane. Please.'

'No, Martin. I've suffered as much as you. I should be allowed to say my piece.' She turned to us again. 'I miss Miriam terribly. I have done since the day she walked out of this door. I loved her more than anything I can describe, but that doesn't detract from the fact that what she did was unforgivable. To put us all, the whole family, through three years of living hell. That was . . . it was so selfish. I loved Miriam, I really did. But she was not a nice person. I'm sorry to have to say it, I really am, but it's true. It is, Martin. It's true. She was not a nice person.'

'Shut up! Just shut up!' His voice reverberated around the room, the slack, hollow face now fiery red with emotion.

'Calm down, Mr Fox,' I said firmly. 'Your wife's just trying to speak.'

'She doesn't need to say that. She doesn't know what she's say-ing. It's our daughter you're talking about, you know . . .' He faltered, slapped his head in his hands, and began sobbing loudly.

Mrs Fox stared at him for some time, her bottom lip quiver-ing as she fought for control over her emotions. For a moment, I thought I saw a hint of contempt in her eyes, but I couldn't be sure. The atmosphere was thick with tension and I could see that Malik had sweat forming on his brow. It had been a difficult few minutes, but this was what the job was all about. This was what we were paid less than double-glazing salesmen for.

I broke the silence by briefly explaining the process for the next few months: the magistrates appearance today, the pre-trial preparations, the possibility of adjournment, et cetera, but I didn't think either of them was really listening. They looked lost; beaten by the whole thing. Fox had taken his head out of his hands, but once again he declined to look in our direction.

Finally, I put my empty teacup on the table and asked them if they had any further questions.

There was a long pause.

'I don't think so, Detective Milne,' Mrs Fox said finally. 'Thank you both for coming.'

We all stood up, including Fox, who looked as though he might fall back down at any time.

'Is there anything else you need?' I asked them both.

'No, we're receiving plenty of support from family and friends, and we've had some counselling.'

'Good. It's important you talk to people about your feelings.' I looked at Fox when I said this, but he looked away. 'It helps.' This was bollocks, of course. It didn't. Recovery comes from within, not from people who don't know you.

They both nodded, and we all shook hands again. Mrs Fox turned towards the door, then suddenly turned back towards us.

'One thing,' she said. 'You never mentioned the reason why this man . . . why he killed Miriam.'

Malik got the answer in first, which was probably for the best. 'As DS Milne mentioned, the suspect hasn't admitted his guilt yet, so we're not entirely sure. However, since there were no signs of sexual assault, we believe it was the result of an argument between the two of them. Probably about money or drugs.'

She shook her head. 'It seems such a petty reason to end someone's life; to destroy every dream they've ever had.'

'There are no good reasons for murder,' said Malik. 'They all leave the same amount of pain.'

She managed a weak smile. 'I think you're probably right.' She led us out to the front door and stopped in front of it. 'Thank you both for coming. It's very much appreciated, I promise you. Even if it's not that obvious. And I do apologize for getting so emotional. It's very difficult . . .'

We both told her once again that we understood entirely. With that, the door opened and we were out of there.

There was a pub a few miles down the road and we stopped for a drink and an early lunch. It was empty. We ordered our drinks from the bored-looking landlord and took a table in the corner.

'What did you think of it in there?' Malik asked, sipping his orange juice.

I knew what he was getting at. 'I detected a bit of an atmosphere and I got the feeling that maybe Mr Fox felt a little guilty about something.'

'Yeah, that crossed my mind. Do you think, you know, anything ever went on between him and Miriam?'

'It happens. It happens in a lot of families, rich and poor. And I suppose it would explain a lot: like why she went away in the first place, why she put up with a life as an underage prostitute, why she never made contact with them. But we might be completely wrong. I get the impression she was a difficult kid anyway. Anne Taylor called her a real bitch when she was talking about her, and not even to phone your mum or your sister through all that time . . .'

'It makes me think that maybe now we've got a motive for Wells. If she had that sort of difficult personality, and it looks like she did, then she could easily have had a major falling-out with him.'

'It's possible.'

'Maybe he thought he was being clever by making it look like a sex crime.'

'It's certainly a viable theory.'

'But you're still not convinced?'

I sighed. 'Not entirely, no.'

'There's a lot of evidence building up, Sarge.'

'Yeah, there is, but there are unanswered questions too. Stuff that puzzles me. Like why Wells came back to the flat.'

'Maybe he's just thick. Plenty of criminals are.'

I told him about the phone records. 'It looks like she and Carla had at least five conversations in the last weeks of Miriam's life. What I can't understand for the life of me is why Carla would pretend not to know her, when it's clear she did. Not unless she had something to hide.'

'And you think it might have something to do with the murder?'

I shrugged. 'I don't know. All I know is that I don't like unanswered questions, and I don't think there's an innocent explanation for it.'

'I told you there was something dodgy about her. I could see it right from the first minute. So, what do you intend to do about it? There's no way Knox is going to want any extension of the inquiry. Not now he's got Wells.'

'I'm going to go and see her, Asif. Make some excuse why we need to talk, then spring it on her.'

'Are you sure that's the reason why you want to see her?'

I gave him a withering look. 'It's definitely the most important reason.'

'Well, let me know what you find out. Although, I still think it was Wells who did it.'

Our food arrived. A tired-looking ploughman's lunch for me, a chilli con carne that bore more than a passing resemblance to dog food for Malik. The landlord gruffly ordered us to enjoy our meals, although I didn't think there was much danger of that.

'Don't say anything about this thing with Carla Graham to anyone else,' I told him, taking a bite of stale bread. 'Capper got wind that I was getting the phone records off Hunsdon and he told me to leave it alone. I don't want to give him any more ammo to fire at me. Not now he's the boss.'

'Don't worry, I won't say anything.' He spooned down a few dollops of chilli, then looked at me seriously. 'You know, I thought it was bad them making him acting DI instead of you. You could do that job one hell of a lot better.'

'It's all politics, Asif. If you play the game, you go places.'

'Then why don't you play the game, Sarge? Forgive me if I'm speaking out of turn, but you're wasted at DS level. You should be running murder investigations, not just being a little cog in them.'

I forced down a fatty lump of ham, then pushed the plate away. I wouldn't have enjoyed that meal if I hadn't eaten for a week. 'I play it,' I said, lighting a cigarette, 'I just don't play it with the same enthusiasm any more, now that the rules are always changing.'

'You can't live in the past, Sarge. The world changes. Even the Met changes. The secret's to adapt. Change with it. Learn the rules. You could still go places.'

'They made you DS, didn't they? Put you in Capper's role.'

He looked surprised. 'How did you know? Knox only phoned me last night. He said he wasn't going to announce it until this afternoon.'

'He hasn't said a word. Not to me, anyway. I guessed. There was something on your mind this morning when we drove down here. You were quieter than usual. Also, you were the obvious choice.'

'You think so?'

'Yeah, I do. You're a fuck sight more talented than any of the other DCs we've got. You'll make a good DS. When's it effective from?'

'Monday, if it all gets sorted out.' I took a drag on my

cigarette but didn't say anything. 'You're not pissed off are you, Sarge?'

I turned to him and smiled. 'No. I'm glad it's you and not anyone else. Congratulations. You deserve it. Unlike Capper.'

'You know, I don't want to sound clichéd or anything, but I've learned a lot working with you. It's been a real education.'

'Don't overdo it. It's me you're talking to, not the DCI.' But I was secretly pleased. I'm just like anyone else. I like compliments, even if they're not entirely truthful.

'Well, I mean it, anyway.'

He went back to eating and I went back to smoking, blowing my cancerous fumes up at the olde worlde beamed ceilings.

'Thanks,' I said. 'It's appreciated.'

Ten minutes later we were back in the car, heading home.

18

We weren't back in Islington until close to five o'clock. An accident on the M40 had caused massive tailbacks, and since neither of us had any idea of alternative routes, we were forced to crawl along at ludicrously slow speeds for hours along with thousands of other irate drivers.

I got Malik to drop me off near home. Somehow I couldn't face going back to the station where the talk would doubtless be of promotions and terminal illnesses, and where I suddenly felt as much an outsider as I ever had. Welland had been an ally, a man who'd often stood up for me in the past. Now he was gone. As a replacement, Capper had to be what a media commentator would call 'the nightmare scenario'.

When I got in I checked my messages. There were none on my home phone, but Raymond had left one on his mobile. He wanted to see me as soon as possible and gave me a number to call back on. He signed off by saying it was urgent, but nothing to worry about too much, whatever that was meant to mean. It was unlike Raymond to leave messages for me, unless it was important. I phoned the number he'd left but it too was on answerphone service, so I left a message for him saying I'd meet him at our usual spot at two the following afternoon unless I heard otherwise. I wanted to see him anyway. There was, it was fair to say, a lot to discuss.

After that, I tried Carla Graham, but she'd left Coleman House for the day and I didn't want to risk calling her on her mobile. She might wonder where I'd got the number from. I told the woman on the other end of the phone that it was the police and asked when Carla was expected back. I was told she was on weekend day shifts and would be in the following morning. I said I'd call her then.

Outside it was raining, but I fancied a walk, and maybe a drink somewhere, so I strolled round the corner to the Hind's Head, a quiet little place I frequent occasionally.

There was no-one in there and I didn't recognize the lone barman. He was reading the paper when I came in. I took a seat at the bar and ordered a pint of Fosters, lighting a cigarette and removing my damp coat.

There was a slightly crumpled copy of the *Standard* next to me on the bar. Since the barman didn't look too chatty and there was no-one else to talk to, I leaned over and picked it up.

The shock hit me right between the eyes like an express train.

The headline was in huge block capitals covering half the page: E-fit of Customs Killer. Facing it on the opposite side of the page was a detailed photofit picture of a thin-faced man, thirty-five to forty, with short dark hair and eyes that were just slightly too close together.

If I'd asked an artist to paint a quick picture of my face, he couldn't have done a better job. The likeness was uncanny.

The whole world seemed to cave in on me as the full implications of what I was looking at flooded into my brain like water surging through a burst dam.

Now I knew that more than at any other time in my entire life, I was in real danger. Not just from the cops but from people whose faces I didn't even know.

But who knew me. And who now realized that I was a lot better off to them dead than alive.

Raymond was right. I should have fucking shot her.

Part Three

UNRAVELLING

19

At exactly 12.55 p.m. the next day, I arrived at R.M. Keen's Funeral Home for the Recently Bereaved, a mouthful if ever there was one. Set slightly back from the road in the attractive, leafy setting of Muswell Hill, it was definitely the sort of place you'd like your corpse to be stored before it went up in smoke. The building itself, hidden from the road by a gentle canopy of beech trees, was a converted nineteenth-century chapel with old-fashioned lattice windows which looked to have kept much of its original character. Fresh flowers sprouted from stone vases on either side of the oak door. I half expected to be greeted by the vicar's wife. There was a gravel car park out front containing a couple of hearses, a sprinkling of other cars, and Raymond's royal blue Bentley. So at least I knew he was there.

The door was locked. A sign on it asked prospective customers to use the intercom and kindly wait for assistance, so I did just that. A few seconds later a grave, middle-aged voice, sounding not unlike Vincent Price, bade me good afternoon and asked how he could be of assistance. I'm all for creating the right atmosphere, but I think this bloke was taking it a bit far.

'I'm here to see Mr Raymond Keen,' I said as gravely as I could.

'Is Mr Keen expecting you?'

'Yes, he is.'

'And your name is?'

'Mr Milne. Mr Dennis Milne.'

'I'll just see if Mr Keen is available.'

Raymond, of course, wasn't expecting to see me for another hour, and in a completely different location, but I was no longer taking any chances. The e-fit had spooked me sufficiently to start distrusting everyone. Raymond was not going to want me falling into the hands of the police, and if he had to I knew he'd have no qualms about guaranteeing that I didn't. The only thing going in my favour was the fact that he didn't know I'd been stopped at a roadblock that night, and had given the police my true identity. At least I hoped he didn't know. At this point it wouldn't have surprised me that much if it turned out he had someone on the inside of the police investigation as well.

Vincent Price came back over the intercom. 'Mr Keen will see you now. Please come in.'

I opened the door and walked into the foyer, which was done out in oak panelling. Vincent was sitting behind a large, very tidy desk, although in the flesh he looked more Vince Hill than Price.

He gave me the standard gloomy look. 'If you go down the hall, Mr Keen's office is the last door on the right.' He pointed to a poorly lit corridor leading to the back of the building, and I followed it down, not bothering to knock when I reached the last door on the right.

Raymond was smoking a fat cigar and poring through a number of open files spread out in front of him. God knows what they contained. It could have been anything. VAT receipts, profit and loss accounts, information so valuable people had to die for it . . .

He looked up and smiled broadly as I came in. 'Dennis, this is a rare honour, and most unexpected too. Please, take a seat.'

I sat down in a comfortable, high-backed leather chair that probably cost what I got paid in a month. 'Yeah, sorry about the intrusion, Raymond. I thought it might be easier if we met here.'

He continued smiling. 'Really? And why's that?'

I met his stare and held it. 'Suffice it to say I'm a little bit nervous at the moment.'

'Yes, I'm sure you must be. That photofit of you was a remarkable likeness. Frighteningly so. The question is, what do we do about it?'

'There's nothing we can do. We'll just have to sit tight. It's highly unlikely anyone who knows me'll think I did it.'

'I should hope not. If they did, it wouldn't say much about you, would it?'

I lit a cigarette, thinking that Raymond almost certainly didn't know about the police questioning me near the scene.

'Well, you asked to meet me, Raymond. So what can I do for you?'

'Too many people know about what happened. Your mate, the one who drove you, he's one of them . . .'

'He's all right. He won't say anything.'

'How can you be sure of that?'

It was a very good question. Hopefully, because he'd left the country. I hadn't heard from Danny the previous night after my e-fit had appeared, so I assumed, or hoped at least, that he'd taken my advice.

'The reason I took him was because I knew I could trust him not to start panicking.'

'Have you spoken to him since?'

'Yeah, when I gave him his share. He was pissed off he'd been lied to about the targets, but then so was I . . . but it wasn't a major problem for him. He'll be all right.'

'You've not spoken to him since the photofit came out, then?'

'No, but he told me the other day he was off down the Caribbean for a couple of weeks. To spend a bit of his money.'

'A wise move,' he said, shuffling some of his paperwork around the desk. 'And you're sure that's where he's gone?'

'Well, as far as I'm aware, yeah. What are you getting at exactly?'

'Just making sure. I wouldn't want to think he's got all worried and gone to the police.'

'He wouldn't do that.'

Raymond eyed me closely. 'So you'll vouch for him, then?'

'He won't cause any problems. Like I said, that's why I took him.'

'Good, good.' He nodded his head slowly. 'I only wish I could say the same about the other guy.'

'Which other guy?'

'Our man. The one there on the night, out the front. Waiting for them to arrive. That's what I wanted to see you about.'

'What do you mean?' As if I didn't know.

'He's a nice lad, don't get me wrong, and it's a hard decision to have to make, especially as I know his mother so well, but . . .' He sighed, then looked at me as if inviting some sympathetic understanding. 'He's a liability too. I think we're going to have to deal with him.'

I'd never actually met Raymond's man, the one who'd radioed in the victims' arrival, but I remembered he'd sounded youngish, no more than twenty-five, and although he'd put on the tough-guy act when talking to me I knew he'd been shitting himself on the night. You can always tell. There's always something just that little bit shaky in the voice of someone who's battling unsuccessfully to control fear. Not that he'd had much to worry about. All he'd had to do was watch out for the Cherokee and inform me when it turned up. I'd had the hard part. I assumed I was going to have the hard part now.

'So, what are you telling me for?'

'You know exactly why. You're my most reliable man, Dennis. A difficult job like this requires the touch of an expert touch, not some rank amateur.'

I dragged hard on what was left of my cigarette and shook my head. 'Jesus, Raymond. This is getting out of hand. We can't just keep on fucking killing people.'

'He's the last one, Dennis. You can claim a bet on it.'

'You said that to me five days ago. Your exact words were: "It won't happen again." That was Monday. Today's Saturday. What are you going to want me to do next week? Assassinate the fucking Pope?'

'Look, I wasn't to know that the little bitch who saw you'd have a photographic memory, was I? I told you you should have shot her. The fact is, this fucking photofit's got everybody nervous. Very nervous.'

'And that's another thing, Raymond. Who exactly is this *everybody* you're working with? I hear on the news that I've killed an accountant who, as far as anyone knows, had an unblemished record. So, tell me, who are your associates, and what did they want this guy dead for?'

'The more you know, Dennis, the worse it'll be for you. You know that. Think about it.'

I sighed. 'If I take out this other guy, then what's to stop me being the next on the list?'

'Dennis. At the moment, you're all right. I know you can't go to the police and make any sort of deal. Everybody knows that.

You're too heavily involved. There's so much blood on your hands, it's dripping onto the carpet.'

'Thanks.'

'I'm just trying to make you feel better, that's all.' He shot me a smile that I think was meant to show he knew how I felt, and pointed his cigar in my direction. 'And if you don't know anything about the reasons behind what happened then, again, you're no threat to anyone. No threat means there's no point in taking you out, so you stay alive. Which is what you want.'

'And Danny?'

'Your mate? Well, if you say he's all right, he's all right.'

I sighed. 'I just don't like the way things are going, that's all. It's getting out of hand, and in my experience that's when things start to go wrong.'

'Look, Dennis, I don't need it either, but it's what's got to happen. The bloke's name is Barry Finn. He's been walking round the last few days like someone's got a pair of shears wrapped round his bollocks. He's jittery, and it's noticeable. It's not a situation we can allow to continue.'

'And how much are you offering in payment?'

He raised his eyebrows. 'Dennis, this is all about making sure we all stay at liberty, not about making a quick profit. Be serious.'

'Fuck that, Raymond. This whole thing's about profit, and don't pretend otherwise. You want me to kill him, you're going to have to pay up. I'm taking a risk here.'

'You're taking a bigger risk by not doing it, I promise you.' There was the first hint of a threat in his voice.

I looked up at the nicotine-stained ceiling, focusing on a flimsy, dust-covered spider's web that hung forlornly there. I looked for the spider, but guessed he was long gone.

'When do you want him taken care of?' I asked wearily, knowing full well that I had no choice.

'As soon as. Preferably before the end of the weekend. Definitely by Monday.'

'It's not going to be easy. If he's as paranoid as you say he is, he's going to expect someone to take a pop at him.'

'Did he see you on the night?'

I shook my head. 'No. We just talked on the radio. I couldn't even tell you what he looked like.'

'That's another reason to use you. He's worked for me for a long time so he knows what most of my people look like.'

'And if I do it, I want it to be the end of it. Understand?'

Raymond nodded. 'Yeah, I understand. It will be.'

His mobile rang. He looked as though he was going to ignore it, then decided it might be important, and took the call.

I took the opportunity to light another cigarette. Raymond listened to whoever was talking on the other end for what seemed like quite a long time, told the caller to get over to the funeral home straight away so they could discuss whatever it was that needed discussing, and pocketed the mobile. It sounded like our meeting was over.

'You're going to need to give me all the details on this guy,' I told him. 'Photograph, address, any other relevant information.'

He smiled. 'No need.'

'What do you mean?'

He patted his jacket where he'd replaced the mobile. 'That was him. He's on his way over here now.'

20

'This is what I call a stroke of good fortune,' Raymond said, rubbing his hands together.

'Don't tell me you want it done here?'

'Why not? It's as good a place as any. In fact, better. Are you carrying?'

I was. A six-shot 2.2 I'd bought from Tomboy years back which I kept for emergencies only. I considered my current plight to be as close to an emergency as I was likely to get and I was fully prepared to use it to defend my liberty and maybe my life, although I didn't like the idea of turning it on someone who presented no direct threat.

'I am, but I don't want to get it dirty. I need it for protection, and if I have to fire it again down the line I don't want to have to worry about this thing getting back to me. '

'Don't worry about that. No-one's ever going to find the body.'

'How can you be sure?'

'Just take my word for it. It's not going to be found.' Have you got a silencer?'

'Of course not. I wasn't planning on carrying out any assassinations today, believe it or not.'

He shrugged. 'No matter. The walls are thick in this place. It was built when things were made to last. No-one'll hear anything.'

'Raymond, for fuck's sake. This sort of thing needs planning. I can't just take someone out off the cuff. Not with ten minutes' notice.'

He stood up and fixed me with a hard stare. 'Of course you can. Think positive, Dennis. The problem with you is you're too fucking negative about everything.' He looked at his watch quickly. It was a Cartier or Rolex. Flash bastard. 'Now we've got to get things sorted out. He doesn't live too far away so he'll be here soon.'

I started to say something but he shifted his bulk out of the chair and walked past me towards the door, leaving me no option but to follow. He strode purposefully down the hall and up to the front desk. Vincent was still there.

'I've got some business that needs sorting, Frank, so I'm going to have to shut up shop. We're not expecting any deliveries, are we?'

'No, not today, Mr Keen,' he answered in that funereal drawl of his.

'Well, do me a favour and make yourself scarce, there's a good man.'

He didn't need asking twice. He'd obviously had to piss off at short notice before. I didn't like the way he looked at Raymond either. There was fear in his expression. He knew things about Raymond he'd rather not know, that was my impression. He nodded, got his coat, and went out the door without another word.

'So, how are we going to do this?' Raymond said, looking

about him for pointers. One word described his overall attitude: excited. He seemed genuinely excited at the prospect of committing murder. 'Come on, Dennis. Help me out here.'

I thought about trying to reason with him but knew there was no point. I could have walked out and left him to it, but it wouldn't have done me any good. One way or another, Raymond's man was going to die, and at that moment I guessed that if I co-operated in his demise I might be helping myself at the same time.

'The best thing is to put me on reception. When he arrives, I'll let him in and tell him to go down to your office. He'll go down, you'll start talking, then I'll come down and knock on the door. You'll ask me to come in, so in I come. I'll have a couple of coffees ready. I'll put them down, you carry on talking to him, and when his back's turned to me, I'll shoot him.'

'I don't know, Dennis. I don't really want it done in my office. Can't you just do it in here?'

'How?'

'Well, either when he opens the door, or when you've directed him down the hall. Maybe you can just walk up behind him and pop him while he's en route.'

I shook my head. 'It wouldn't work.'

'Why not?'

'Too risky. If he's as nervous as you say he is, he'll probably suspect something like that. He'll be watching his back on the walk down to your office, and if I try anything, chances are it'll fuck up. Same with shooting him when he walks in the door. There's too much scope for failure. It's got to be done in an enclosed place where he can't escape.'

He nodded slowly, digesting my words. 'All right, fair enough. But we're going to have to do something about your clothes. You look far too casual to be working in a place of rest, even on a

Saturday.' He disappeared into one of the rooms off the hall and reappeared a few seconds later with a shirt and black tie. 'That should fit,' he said. 'There's nothing I can do about the jeans. Hopefully by the time Barry notices them he'll be half a second away from a fully ventilated head.'

I took the gun out of my leather jacket pocket, removed the jacket and the sweatshirt I was wearing underneath, and chucked them down behind the reception desk, out of sight. I then hurriedly pulled on the shirt and tie and stuffed the gun down the back of my waistband. The shirt was a bit small and I couldn't do the top button up – not without choking myself, anyway – but I didn't suppose Barry would be paying too much attention.

'You've got to sound very respectful when you speak as well. We're very customer-orientated in this business. Try to talk slowly, and sound like you're thinking about what you're saying.'

'I'll see what I can do.'

I sat down behind the desk and lit a cigarette.

'Blimey, Dennis, you can't just sit there with a fag in your mouth. It doesn't set the right fucking tone. Respectful, remember.'

'It's Saturday, and we're not expecting punters. Call it a perk for having to work odd hours.'

He shook his head in an annoyed fashion, but let it go. 'Right, let's get this straight. You send him down to my office, we start talking—'

'You offer him a cup of coffee because you're having one yourself. You phone through to me in reception, and I go and make it. Now, where's your coffeemaking equipment?'

'That door behind you goes into a kitchen. All the stuff you need's in there.'

'Fine. I'll bring it down, and we'll take it from there.'

I couldn't help thinking what a mistake I was making getting involved in such a hastily planned murder. Some time soon my luck was inevitably going to run out.

Raymond appeared to read my thoughts. 'All this'll be over soon, Dennis. Then we can get back to making money, pure and simple.'

I nodded, taking a drag on the cigarette. 'I'm thinking . . . after this I might do what my driver's doing – you know, take a long holiday somewhere. Maybe even permanent.'

'The crime figures'll go up without you, Dennis.'

I managed a humourless smile. 'Somehow, I don't think so.'

The sound of wheels on gravel outside stirred me from my thoughts.

'He's here,' Raymond said, looking out of one of the lattice windows. 'I'll get down to my office.'

I straightened my tie, feeling almost like a new guy on his first day in the office, and put out the cigarette.

A few seconds later the buzzer went and I leaned down to the intercom speaker and asked, in as grave a voice as I could muster, who was there. I'm not a bad mimic, and it came out pretty well.

A flustered voice asked for Raymond. 'We are closed at the moment, sir,' I told him.

'He's expecting me. My name's Barry Finn.'

I told him to hang on while I checked with Mr Keen, sat there for a few seconds, then came back on the line. 'Please come in.' I pushed the small red button on the intercom, which I assumed released the lock and was pleased to find out that it did. That could have fucked things up, if I couldn't even open the door.

Barry Finn was slightly older than I'd expected, about thirty, no more than five feet seven tall with a mop of dirty blond hair. He had the pinched, wary features of a small-time villain and his eyes were darting about in overdrive. Just like Len Runnion's always did. This was a man carrying a lot of weight on flimsy shoulders. Immediately I knew Raymond was right to want him out of the way, although it didn't say much about his judgement that he'd used him in the first place. Still, maybe you could have said the same about mine.

I gave him a stern, headmasterly look and pointed him in the direction of Mr Keen's office. He didn't say a word and took off down the hall. It felt strange knowing that he only had a few more minutes of life left in him, and a bit sad to think it was going to be spent worrying about something he could do nothing about.

Now it was time to wait. Raymond, however, was not hanging about. Within two minutes he phoned through, gruffly telling me to get him a coffee, not bothering to say please. I was glad then that I wasn't a full-time employee of his. He had the sort of brash attitude with his staff that gives capitalism a bad name.

I checked the gun for the second time since sitting down and took the safety off before replacing it in the waistband of my jeans. Then I went into the kitchen and put the kettle on. While I was waiting for it to boil, I gave the place the once-over. I've never been in an undertakers' kitchen before, and wasn't sure what to expect. Maybe a few jokey pictures of the employees posing with the corpses, or some coffin-shaped fridge magnets. But there was none of that. Everything looked depressingly normal. Clean and tidy as well. Scattered about the walls were postcards from various far-flung destinations. One was even from Dhaka in Bangladesh, which struck me as an odd destination to spend your holidays. The photograph was of a toothless, bare-footed rickshaw driver smiling at the camera. I took it off the wall and saw that it was from Raymond. He said that the weather was too hot and he was looking forward to getting back. If the photo on the front was the best the Bangladeshi tourist industry could do, I couldn't blame him.

The kettle boiled and I poured Raymond's coffee, substituting the two sugars he'd ordered for salt, just so he'd know I wasn't his skivvy. I found a battered Princess Diana memorial tea tray, put the cup on that, and headed off down the hall.

To keep up the ruse, I knocked on the door and waited until I was called in, which took all of about a second.

Raymond beamed at me as I stepped inside and Barry looked round quickly, just to check that everything was all right. 'Ah, thank you, Dennis. Just what the doctor ordered. Are you sure you don't want one, Barry?'

Barry shook his head, but didn't say anything.

I walked over and Raymond took the cup from the tray, managing a brief thanks. He turned back to Barry. 'So don't worry about it,' he told him. 'It's not going to be a problem.'

Still holding the Princess Diana commemorative tea tray, I reached down and pulled the gun from my waistband.

Barry must have sensed I was still in the room. As Raymond continued to gabble, he turned round at the exact moment I raised the gun. The wrong end of the barrel was only three feet from his head.

His eyes widened and his mouth opened. Before he could say anything, I pulled the trigger, wanting to get this over with as soon as possible.

But nothing happened. The trigger didn't move. I squeezed harder. Still nothing. The fucking thing was jammed.

'Don't kill me! For fuck's sake, don't kill me!'

The words were a frightened howl, and it struck me then that it was the first time anyone had ever had the chance to ask me for mercy. It hurt, because it made me feel doubt. Doubt that I had the strength to kill a man face to face in cold blood. He raised his arms in surrender, the mouth opening and shutting ever so slightly like a tropical fish, unintelligible pleas for mercy

184

trembling out. I felt like I was frozen to the spot, like I was completely and utterly incapacitated. What did I do now? What could I do now?

'For the love of God, Dennis! Shoot the bastard!'

Reflexively I pulled the trigger. Again, nothing happened. I knew then that the weapon was useless. It was never going to unjam in the next five seconds.

'Come on!' yelled Raymond, his face red with frustration.

Barry half turned to his boss, still keeping one eye on the gun. 'Mr Keen ... Raymond ... what are you doing? I won't say nothing—'

'Finish it!'

'The gun's fucking jammed, Raymond!'

'Oh, for Christ's sake!'

In a surprisingly deft movement, he reached over, grabbed a medium-sized statuette of a golfer taking a swing from the side of his desk, and whacked Barry over the head with it. It broke immediately, the golfer's head and torso flying across the room. Barry yelped in pain, but that was about it. He was hardly incapacitated.

This seemed to galvanize Barry into action. Seeing that he was dealing with people who'd have difficulty killing a rumour, he jumped to his feet in an attempt to escape, whereupon I slammed the tea tray into his face, knocking him back down again. He lashed out with his legs, but I jumped aside and tried to hit him with the butt of the gun. It caught him on the arm as he raised it to protect himself, and with his other hand he punched me in the kidneys. This time it was my turn to yelp in pain. I staggered backwards, creating an opening between him and the door. He was off the seat like a greyhound out of a trap and heading towards salvation.

I suddenly had a vision of spending the rest of my days behind

bars, stuck in segregation along with the paedophiles and informants, and it was that which stopped me from letting Barry Finn
go. Raymond was yelling something, but I couldn't hear it. I
jumped on Barry as he reached the door and tried to pull him
backwards, dropping the gun in the process.

But Barry had a lot of incentive to get out of there and he
wasn't going to give up easily. Despite my best efforts, which
included trying to gouge his eyes, he managed to open the door
and stagger unsteadily down the hall with me on his back. He
managed about four paces before Raymond came running round
the front of him, his face a panting mask of adrenalin and
rage.

'All right, Barry boy, let's go quietly now.'

But Barry wasn't going to go quietly, not if he could avoid it.
He desperately tried to dodge round Raymond with all the agility
of a pantomime horse.

Raymond stood his ground, and punched him hard in the
stomach.

Barry gasped as the wind was taken out of him. He fell to his
knees and held that position for maybe a second, before toppling
over onto his side. I jumped off his back, thinking that Raymond
must have one hell of a punch on him. Which was when I saw
the bloodied knife in his right hand.

'Pick him up, hold him,' he demanded excitedly.

Barry was crawling along the floor on his stomach, blood oozing out from under his body. Raymond kicked him viciously in
the side, which I thought was a bit unnecessary, but he had the
look of the sadist about him that day. I've seen it plenty of times
before. Sometimes they just get carried away.

'Go on, pick him up, Dennis. Now.'

Barry coughed and tried to say something, but it just came out
like a splutter. I felt sick. This was different from a shooting. It

was so much more messy and, in a bizarre way, so much more personal.

I stood behind him and pulled him up by the arms. His body made a horrible squelching sound as it disengaged from the pool of blood forming below him, and I had to fight to stop myself from puking.

Raymond's face split open in a wild, maniacal grin and his eyes widened dramatically, as if they were trying to drink in as much of the scene as possible. Again Barry tried to get words out, but it was too late. The hand containing the knife darted out and there was a splitting sound as the blade peeled through soft flesh. Barry gasped. Raymond stabbed again. And again, his face beaming savagely, lost in the joy of murder, his right arm pumping like a demented piston. Barry tried to struggle but his movements were weak and drawn, and every thrust of the knife took just that little bit more out of him. The blood dripped heavily onto the floor and I struggled to hold him upright, slipping slightly in the mess below.

'Please,' I heard him whisper through clenched teeth, or maybe it was just air escaping, I don't know.

Either way it was over, and finally his resistance went altogether and he slumped in my arms. Raymond had stabbed him at least a dozen times.

Raymond stood back, panting with exertion, and admired his handiwork. His crisp white shirt was spattered with gobs of blood. 'All right, he's gone. You can put him down now.'

I laid him gently on the floor and stepped away. There was blood everywhere, although thankfully the dark hardwood flooring served to disguise the worst of it.

Raymond, still holding the knife, wiped sweat from his brow. 'It's a shame he had to go like that. I always quite liked old Barry. What the fuck happened with your gun?'

'It jammed,' I said. 'It happens sometimes.'

'This is a fucking mess, Dennis. By rights you ought to clean it up as it was your gun that caused it.'

'What are we going to do with him?' I asked, still partially numbed by what had just happened. I'd never seen so much blood in my life. It seemed every drop Barry had owned was now spread out between me and Raymond. Every now and again his body twitched malevolently. A faint but growing odour of shit drifted silently through the still air.

'Well, he's already beginning to go a bit ripe, so we'd better get him packaged up. We'll stick him in one of the coffins for now.'

He put the knife down next to the body and motioned for me to follow him. We walked back down the hall and he opened up a door a little bit further down on the opposite side from his office. A number of coffins were stacked up in lines on shelves against one wall. They all looked to be much of a muchness, although some were bigger than others.

Raymond took a quick look at them, then selected the one he wanted and pulled it down. It was a cream colour – almost white – with iron handles, and it looked quite cheap – which, I suppose, stood to reason, since he wasn't going to be making any money out of Barry's disposal. I got one end of it and we took it outside and put it down on one of the few dry spaces on the floor, before lifting Barry's bloodsoaked corpse up and chucking it in. Although I worked hard to avoid it, a few splashes of blood got on my jeans, which basically spelled the end for them. Raymond put the lid down, and after that we cleared up the rest of the mess as best we could, which took a good twenty minutes and involved me doing most of the mopping up while Raymond acted in something of a supervisory role.

When we'd finished, I went and got myself a glass of water

from the kitchen. I drank it down fast, then poured myself another and drank that down as well. I was still feeling nauseous so I took some slow, deep breaths and focused on one of the postcards. This one was from India, from somewhere called Mumbai, which I hadn't heard of. I wondered briefly who'd gone there for their holidays, but didn't bother to look.

When I felt a little bit better I walked back into the hallway. 'Are you all right?' Raymond asked. He was kneeling down beside the coffin hammering in nails while chewing on a cigar. He looked a bit knackered, but that was about it. You wouldn't have guessed he'd just stabbed an employee of his to death.

'I don't ever want to have to do that again,' I told him.

'You know how it is, Dennis. Sometimes you've just got to do these things.'

I snorted. 'There've got to be better ways to earn a living.'

'Too right, and after this I'm going back to concentrating on my core business. There's big money to be made in undertaking. And it's a steady market. You see this?' He banged the coffin with his hammer. 'One of these costs thirty-seven quid from the manufacturers. Thirty-seven quid. But you know what? The cheapest one I sell'll cost a punter four hundred. That's a one thousand per cent mark-up. And the beauty of it is that no-one argues. I mean, who the fuck's going to negotiate over the price of their nearest and dearest's funeral costs? Only a right heartless bastard'd think about doing that. And thankfully there aren't too many of them about.'

There wasn't a lot you could say to that. 'So what are you going to do with the body?'

'I'll put it in the back of one of the hearses and drive it up to some associates of mine.' I raised my eyebrows. 'They're professionals, Dennis. Don't worry. They know how to make people disappear.'

'Are you sure you can trust them? This is a body we're talking about here, not a caseload of porno videos.'

'Let's just say I've worked with them before and they've proved reliable.'

'And they can be trusted to get rid of him?'

He stood up and smiled at me. 'Dennis, you of all people should know that if you want to make someone disappear, and you know what you're doing, then, bang' – he clicked his fingers – 'they'll just vanish into thin air. Never to be seen again.'

I thought of Molly Hagger then and shuddered.

'Grab the other end, will you?' he said.

I did as I was told, and together we loaded the coffin into one of the hearses so that it could begin its final journey to an anonymous resting place.

21

It was twenty past three when I picked up the phone and called Coleman House. I was back at home, sitting on the sofa with a cup of coffee and a cigarette.

Someone whose voice I didn't recognize answered, and I asked to be put through to Ms Graham. I could hear my heart thumping. I wasn't sure whether it was because of the shock of what I'd been a part of earlier, or simply nerves at the prospect of speaking to a woman I fancied, and trying to get her to see me.

I pictured Barry Finn. I could hear the gruesome gasping noises he made as Raymond stabbed him, like an old man with emphysema.

'Hello, Mr Milne. Dennis.'

'Hi, Carla, sorry to bother you.' My heart was beating louder than ever. For a second I wanted to put the phone down and get the hell out of my flat. Go for a run or something. 'You heard about the charges being laid for the Miriam Fox murder?'

'Against the pimp? Yes, I saw it in the paper.'

'I tried to reach you to tell you yesterday but you were out, and I didn't really want to leave a message.'

'Thanks for letting me know. I suppose that means you won't have to come back here again.'

'That's right.' I paused for a moment, wondering how best to put this. 'There were a couple of things I wanted to run by you, though.'

Her tone didn't change. 'What sort of things?'

'Nothing to worry about, just some background information I need. I'd rather not discuss it over the phone. Is it possible we could meet somewhere?'

'Is it very urgent?'

I didn't want to alarm her. 'Not particularly, but it would be nice to get it out of the way.'

'I'm trying to think when I'm around . . .' She didn't sound unduly worried. 'I've got a lot on this afternoon.'

'This evening?' I ventured.

She thought about it. 'How about tomorrow evening? That'd be easier. Why don't you come round to my flat? It's up in Kentish Town.'

This was an invitation if ever I'd heard one. 'Yeah, of course. I could do that. What's the address?'

She told me, and I wrote it down in my notebook. 'I'll find it. What sort of time?'

'I normally eat at about seven. Come round after that. About eight?'

It sounded as though we were arranging a date, and I suppose in a way we were. 'Eight o'clock's fine. I'll see you then.'

We said our goodbyes and I hung up, not knowing whether to feel pleased with myself or not. I was glad that I was going to get the chance to see her again, even if what I had to say wasn't exactly going to endear her to me. I was interested too in what her answers were going to be. I didn't at that point think that she'd had anything to do with the murder, but something had definitely been up between her and Miriam Fox and I wanted to know what it was.

I sat there for a few seconds mulling over the possibilities, but I found it difficult to concentrate. The problem was, I couldn't help thinking about Barry Finn. Usually I can rid my mind of inconvenient thoughts – its something you've got to be able to do if part of your life involves ending the lives of fellow human beings – but this killing had hit me a lot harder than any of the others. It was the indignity of it. Right now, he was probably laid out on tarpaulin in someone's garage being slowly and carefully dismembered like a piece of rancid meat.

Knifing a man to death in cold blood while he struggled to understand what the hell was going on, then sentencing his relatives to years of torment by removing all traces of his existence; making him vanish into thin air, like Molly Hagger and who knows how many other lost souls. Whichever way you chose to look at it, it was a shameful way to make a living.

I picked up my coffee, went to take a drink, then decided I needed something stronger. A lot stronger. Outside, the day had become grey and cloudy, and it had begun to spit with rain. There was a half bottle of Remy in the cupboard so I poured myself a couple of fingers, and filled a pint glass with the contents of a can of Heineken from the fridge. There didn't seem any point doing things by half measures, and I had nowhere to go for the rest of the day.

I drank the brandy down in one, lit a cigarette, and took a good draw of the beer. I smoked the cigarette down to the butt, finishing it at about the same time I finished the beer. I poured myself some more brandy, drank it down, lit another cigarette. I didn't feel any better. I could still picture Barry Finn. I could hear the noises he made as he died: that horrible gasping as he fought for breath through punctured lungs. Futile. All futile. I thought of the pleasure Raymond had taken in the murder, like a kid playing his first ever Playstation game. I'd never really taken him for a sadist before, but I wouldn't underestimate his potential for cruelty again. Would he have worn that same smile had he been killing me? Somehow I felt sure the answer was yes. Maybe, he was even now planning my demise with his mysterious associates, men adept at making bodies disappear.

And how close were the coppers to me? Had the young cop at the roadblock talked to the investigating officers? Were they checking my background, viewing me now as a possible suspect? Had they gone further? Was I under surveillance even as I sat here getting drunker and drunker?

Paranoid thoughts were suddenly swarming through my brain like steamers on a tube train. There seemed no end to them, and no way to escape the strength-sapping fear they generated. I'd never had a panic attack before, but I could feel one coming on.

I filled the brandy glass again and found another can of Heineken in the fridge. I drank the one, then took a long gulp from the other. I tried to imagine what it felt like to take a knife in the gut. I'd read somewhere once that it was like being hit with a cricket bat, except twice as bad. I got the feeling it was plenty worse than that, especially when you were being held in a vice-like grip by someone you'd never met before and the one doing the knifing was your employer, someone you knew and trusted. Christ, I hated myself; for just a few seconds, I truly hated myself. I was no amoral bastard who didn't give a fuck about his actions. I felt guilty. I knew I'd done wrong, I really did, and that was what was getting to me.

At some point the drink hit me hard. Cricket bat hard. I came over very tired and knew I was going to have to lie down. In a way, it was a relief. I lay back on the sofa and let the weariness wash over me, finally ridding my mind of its demons.

I don't know for how long I slept. Maybe a couple of hours, something like that. I needed it anyway, however long it was.

I was woken by the sound of the phone ringing. It was pitch black in the room and I could hear the rain coming down outside. My mouth was desert-scrub dry and I had a headache, a result of the fact that I'm not used to drinking brandy during the day. I closed my eyes again and waited for the call to go to answerphone.

It was Malik. I picked up as he was starting to leave a message.

'You sound in a bad way, Sarge,' he told me in a manner that was far too cheery for my liking.

'I've been asleep. You woke me up.'

He started to apologize but I told him not to worry. 'I needed to wake up anyway.' I yawned. 'Where are you phoning from?'

'The station.'

'What are you doing down there? It's your day off.'

'Just doing a little bit of overtime.'

'Very conscientious.' And sensible too, now that he was on the verge of promotion. It was important to show enthusiasm while you could still manage it. 'So, what can I do for you on this shitty, wet evening?'

'We've found the murder weapon in the Mark Wells case.'

I was suddenly more interested. 'Oh yeah? Where was it?'

194

'In a park not far from Wells's flat. It was in some bushes. A kid looking for his football found it.'

'Prints?'

'No, but you can't have everything, can you? It's definitely the weapon that killed her. A butcher's knife with a ten-inch blade. It's got her blood all over it.'

'How do we know it belongs to him?'

'He threatened people with a very similar knife on two separate occasions in the weeks before the murder. It's his knife, Sarge. It's definitely his.'

'Shit. And, you know, I still wasn't convinced.'

'They're doing a load of other tests on it as well. Just in case he left any DNA traces.'

'I'm glad that bastard's going down. That'll teach him to hit me.'

'And that's not the only thing. Wells's brief came in today.'

'He's recovered from his injuries, has he?'

'No, it's a different one now. He sacked the other guy. Anyway, he comes in and says that Wells has been thinking about this business of the shirt and he reckons he did own a shirt like the one we found once, but that he gave it away a long time back.'

'He gave away his shirt? Who the hell does that?'

'Yeah, and get this. He reckons he gave it to one of his girls.'

'Which one?'

'Well, that's the thing. He said he gave it to Molly Hagger.'

22

We both agreed that this sort of story wasn't going to get Mark Wells very far in court, especially as, conveniently, the person he'd supposedly given it to had disappeared into thin air. I wasn't entirely sure whether this new information cemented the case against him or not. The fact that I'd only just woken up, having not long consumed nearly half a bottle of brandy mixed with beer, didn't make matters any easier.

'Have you seen Carla Graham yet?' he asked.

'No, not yet.' I resisted the urge to tell him I'd made an appointment with her. 'I don't suppose I'll bother now. It doesn't look like there's much doubt it's Wells, and there's no point raking up stuff that's got nothing to do with the murder.'

'It'd be interesting to see why she lied.'

'Yeah. Maybe I'll ask her if I ever run into her again.'

The conversation moved on to other things, all of them brutal. Malik told me that we had another possible murder inquiry on our hands. An eighty-one-year-old lady had held onto her handbag after a gang of young muggers had decided to relieve her of it, and had fallen on her head during the struggle. She was now in intensive care and the doctors were doubtful she'd pull through. Two people had been glassed the previous night in a pub fight, and one was going to lose his eye. One arrest: a nineteen-year-old who was already on bail for another assault. I recognized the name but couldn't picture his face. Three more suspects were still at large.

I asked Malik about the Traveller's Rest case. Had he spoken to his mate about it again? He said he hadn't, and laughingly told me that the e-fit and my face bore a startling resemblance.

'Do you think so?' I asked him.

'What? Don't you?' He said it in a manner that suggested he couldn't believe I couldn't see it.

I reluctantly agreed that there were similarities, but assured him I'd had nothing to do with it. 'But if you don't see me Monday, it means I've fled the country.'

'Somehow I think I'll be seeing you Monday, Sarge.'

I told him he didn't have to call me that any more, not now he was DS.

'Oh yeah, I suppose I don't. See you Monday then, Dennis.'

I think I preferred Sarge.

I said my goodbyes and rang off. It was almost six o'clock, and I had nothing to do. I don't really have many friends, as such. It doesn't usually bother me. I'm not the sort to get bored. I work fairly long hours and I don't mind my own company. But tonight I didn't feel right. I wished there was someone I could talk to about my predicament, though Christ knows what I'd say. That I was a part-time professional killer as well as a copper, that I'd murdered more people in the past week than some self-respecting serial killers manage in the whole of their wicked careers; and how things were now spiralling out of control and my life was in danger. I'm not sure I'd have got much in the way of sympathy. I certainly didn't deserve any.

I'd bought myself some more of that creamy prawn risotto, so I made that for my supper, and washed it down with a couple of glasses of sparkling mineral water. Then I had a long shower, cleaned my teeth, and put some fresh clothes on.

In the end, I didn't bother going anywhere. It was raining too hard, although on the weather forecast they said it wouldn't last. Apparently a cold spell from Siberia was on the way. Nice. *Die Hard 2* was on one of the Sky movie channels so I watched that for a while, glugging steadily on a bottle of red wine until I finally fell asleep at about the time the evil South American dictator murders his guards.

I'd seen it twice before, so I wasn't worried. I knew he'd get his comeuppance and Bruce Willis would see that justice was done, just like a true copper should, not by following a load of bureaucratic rules and resigning himself to remaining a shitty little cog in a large and inefficient machine, but by bypassing the courts, the probation service and the prisons – those eternal obstacles to true punishment – and just blowing the heads off the baddies instead.

Which, if you're honest with yourself, is much the best way.

23

Danny phoned just after midnight, as I was emptying the ashtray into the bin in the kitchen. I thought about letting it go to answerphone but, given the circumstances, anyone phoning was probably worth talking to, and I picked up after the third ring.

I was disappointed to hear his voice, and the obvious fear in it. 'Dennis?'

'Danny. What is it? I thought you'd taken my advice and taken off for a bit.'

'Look, I saw the picture—'

'Careful what you say, Danny,' I said firmly. 'If you want to talk, do what we did last time, OK.'

'I'm scared, Dennis. Really fucking scared. And this time I'm not exaggerating. I've booked a flight, right, like you said. I'm off to Montego Bay tomorrow on the eleven thirty flight out of Gatwick . . .' His words were tumbling out. I stepped in to interrupt him again, fearful he was going to say something stupid, but he was determined to speak. 'But I was out tonight, down the pub for a quick drink, and I was on the way home just now and this car pulls up outside my flat with these two blokes in it. They slow right down, and clock me, and then one of them reaches down to pick something up.'

'All right, all right. Where are you now?'

'I'm at home. As soon as I saw them I was down the steps like shit off a stick. I got the key in the lock just as one of the blokes appeared at the top of the steps. He had something in his hand. I think it was a gun or something. I just turned the key, ran inside and double-locked the door behind me.'

'Has he gone, this bloke?'

'Yeah, yeah. I think so.'

'And you're pretty sure it was a gun he was carrying?' I was conscious that someone could be listening into this call, but I knew I was never going to get him to a payphone now.

'It looked like it, yeah. He had a long coat on and he had one hand in his pocket. He was pulling something out of it. I thought it was a gun.'

'But you didn't see for sure?'

'No, but I'm not fucking around, Dennis. This bloke was after me. I'd bet my fucking life on it.'

'OK. Calm down. What did he look like?'

'I didn't get much of a look. It was dark and I was trying to get away. He was dark-skinned—'

'Asian?'

'No, more Mediterranean or Arab.'

'And you'd never seen him before?'

'No, never.'

'How old?'

'I don't know. Maybe thirty.'

I tried to collect my thoughts for a moment. 'All right. Stay put. Make sure all the locks are shut on the doors and windows.'

'They are. I've done all that.'

'Good. I doubt if they'll hang around, whoever they are. No point getting people's suspicions up. All you need to do is stay put tonight, and catch that plane tomorrow. Just keep your wits about you when you leave the flat.'

'Who do you think they were, Dennis? Anything to do—'

'I told you,' I snapped, 'careful what you say. To be honest with you, they could be anyone. There are enough fucking criminals about. I can vouch for that. They may just have been opportunistic robbers.'

'No. They were definitely after me.'

'Well whoever they are they didn't get you, so keep calm. And remember, tomorrow night you'll be sitting on a beach sipping cocktails, away from all this shit and knowing that everyone'll have forgotten about it by the time you get back.'

'Look, Dennis. Can you come over? Just to check things are all right. You know, I'd appreciate it. It's just that I'm on my fucking own here.'

I sighed. 'Danny, it's gone midnight and I've drunk enough to sink a fucking battleship. I doubt if I'd be in a position even to find your place—'

'I'll pay for a taxi, don't worry about that.'

'Come on, what is this? You'll be all right. They'll be gone now, I guarantee it. And if you hear anything later, anyone trying to break in, just dial nine-nine-nine. Seriously, it'll be OK.'

Now it was Danny's turn to sigh. 'OK. OK, I'll do that. I just wanted to run it by you, that's all. If I'm in danger, then you're going to be too. Maybe you ought to think about a holiday as well.'

'Maybe I will. Perhaps I'll join you on the beach at Montego Bay in a few days. Look, take care, eh? And call me when you get back.'

'No problem,' he said, which were the last words he ever uttered to me. For all I know, they could have been the last words he ever uttered, full stop.

I hung up and walked over to the window, looking out across the quiet, rain-swept street. Nothing and no-one moved down there. Part of me felt guilty that I hadn't gone over to see him, but what could I have done? The advice I'd given him was as good as he was going to get, and I genuinely didn't believe he was in any danger, not now that he was safely inside his flat.

At the same time, however, I think I already knew his experience had been more than a simple street robbery. It was just that I didn't want to admit it to myself. Because, as he pointed out, if they were after him then, for all Raymond's protestations to the contrary, it meant they were almost certainly coming for me next.

24

At half past ten the following morning, I phoned Danny and got his answerphone. I didn't leave a message. I tried him on his mobile but it was switched off. I tried both numbers again an hour later, and again got no answer. In the cold light of day, I decided that he'd got off all right and was now thirty thousand feet above the Atlantic heading for the sunny Caribbean.

At a quarter to twelve, I went out and got some breakfast at a café I know on Caledonian Road, trying hard to forget my many troubles.

Carla Graham lived on the top floor of an attractive white-brick Edwardian townhouse set in a narrow cul-de-sac that had too many cars parked along it. I paid the sullen-faced cab driver a twenty and wasn't offered any change so, rather than argue, I left it at that and walked up the steps to the front door.

It was five to eight, and the night was cold and clear with an icy wind that found its way right through to the bones. There was a flashy-looking video entry system and I rang the buzzer for number 24C. After a few seconds, Carla's voice came over the intercom.

'Hello, Dennis,' she said, sounding not too displeased that I'd made it.

I smiled up at the camera and said hello, and she told me to come straight up the stairs to the third floor. The imposing-looking front door clicked open and I stepped gratefully inside. It locked automatically behind me.

She was waiting for me at the top of the stairs with the door open behind her. Although only casually dressed in a black sweatshirt and trackpants, she still looked close to stunning. It was something in the way she carried herself. Hers was a natural beauty, the sort you can tell looks just as good at six a.m. as it does at six p.m. Her hair looked recently washed, and once again I noticed a light aroma of perfume as we shook hands. What she was doing in the grim and worthy world of social work remained as much a mystery as ever.

'Please come in,' she said with a smile, and led me inside, through the hallway and into the lounge. 'Take a seat.' She waved her arm, indicating that I could park myself anywhere.

It was a sumptuous room with high ceilings and big bay win-dows that gave it an airy feel, even on a cold winter's night like this one. The floor was polished wood and partially covered with thick Persian rugs. All the furnishings were obviously expensive yet tasteful, and the walls were painted in a light, pastelly green that shouldn't have suited it but somehow did. Normally I wouldn't have noticed any of this, or very little of it anyway, but this was the type of room that demanded attention.

'This is very nice,' I said. 'Maybe you should have been an interior designer.'

'It's one of my hobbies,' she said. 'It's a lot of work, and it costs a bit of money, but it's worth it. Now, what do you want to drink?'

There was a half-full glass of red wine on the coffee table next to an expensive-looking bottle. A cigarette burned in the ashtray.

'Well, if it's not imposing, I wouldn't say no to a drop of that wine.'

'I'll get you a glass,' she said, and stepped out of the room.

I removed my coat and sat down on a comfortable chair, feeling more than a little awkward. It was an odd situation. On the one hand, I was intensely attracted to Carla Graham, while on the other, I saw her as someone who at the very least was withholding information in a murder inquiry and who, at worst, was a suspect. In the end, I found it difficult to decide whether I'd rather fuck her or nick her. I knew I wanted to do one of the two.

She came back and poured the wine before handing me the glass. Once again I caught the smell of her perfume. I realized, with some horror, that it was giving me the beginnings of a hard-on.

She sat down on the sofa opposite me, picked up her cigarette out of the ashtray, and looked earnestly in my direction, as if she had no idea why I might be there.

'So, what can I do for you, Dennis? You said there were some things that needed clearing up.'

I cleared my throat. 'Yeah, there are. Mark Wells, the pimp we've charged, suggested that he once gave one of his shirts – a dark green one with medium-size collars – to Molly Hagger. This would have been a few months ago, and it would have been far too big for her. Did you ever see a shirt like that in Molly's possession?'

She furrowed her brow, thinking about it for a couple of seconds. 'No, I don't recall anything like that. Why would he have given her a shirt?'

'I don't know. He just said he gave it to her. I expect he was lying.'

'Why's it relevant to the case?'

'It probably isn't. Just something I wanted to check.' She gave me a puzzled look. 'What might be more relevant, though,' I continued, lighting a cigarette, 'is why you told me at our first meeting that you didn't know Miriam Fox when I know you do.'

If my statement had shocked her, she didn't show it. She just looked put out that I'd effectively accused her of lying, especially as I was sitting in her comfortable chair enjoying a glass of her good wine. And it was good, too.

'I don't know what you're talking about, Detective Milne.' No Dennis now. 'I never knew Miriam Fox.'

I locked eyes with her, trying to stare her down, but she held my gaze. 'Look, Carla . . . Miss Graham. There's no point denying it. I've seen Miriam Fox's phone records. There are five calls logged. Three were made by her, two by you.'

Carla shook her head, her face a picture of innocence. 'There must be some mistake.'

'There's no mistake. I checked. And I double-checked. You had five conversations with Miriam in the last few weeks of her life, and God knows how many before that. Now, I want to know what those conversations were about, and why you wanted them kept hidden.'

'Look, I don't have to answer questions like this. I want my lawyer present if you're going to carry on.'

'Do you? Are you sure about that?'

'Yes, I'm very sure. Here you are, near enough accusing me of murder in my home—'

'I'm not accusing you of anything. I'm just trying to tie up any loose ends. At the moment, we're simply two people having a conversation. None of what you say's admissible in a court of law.'

'So why the hell should I talk about it?'

'Because if you don't, I'm going to have to go back to my superior and tell him about the phone records. At the moment, I'm the only person who knows anything about them. If your explanation satisfies me that you know nothing about the murder, I'm prepared to keep it that way; if it doesn't, I'm going to tell him anyway. At least this way you get your chance to tell me your side of the story without anyone else being involved.'

'So you're here unofficially? Like the last time we met?'

'I'm here in a semi-official capacity. It could go either way. Now, what were those conversations with Miriam Fox about?'

She sighed, as if bowing to the inevitable. 'I suppose I half thought this was what you were coming round about.'

She finished her cigarette and immediately lit another one, taking a deep drag. I sat watching her impassively, wondering what I was going to hear, and what I was going to do when I'd heard it.

'Miriam Fox was blackmailing me.'

'What about?'

'About an area of my private life.'

'Go on.'

'She knew something about me that I would rather have kept secret and she was trying to exploit the situation to her advantage. She was like that.'

'So I keep hearing. And this area of your private life . . . what is it exactly?'

She looked me firmly in the eye. 'I'm what's colloquially called a lady of the night, Detective Milne. I escort middle-aged, usually middle-class, men for money. Sometimes I fuck them.' There was a defiant expression on her face as she spoke, as if she was daring me to criticize her.

I didn't bother rising to the bait. I've heard plenty of worse revelations than that in my time, although I have to say it did catch me off guard. 'Well, I suppose it stands to reason. You don't get these sorts of furnishings on civil servant's wages.'

'You're not shocked that a person in my position is involved in something like that?'

I smiled and took a decent-sized sip from my wine, thinking that this was something of a surreal moment. 'People in positions a lot higher than yours are involved in that type of thing, though usually as customers rather than suppliers, so, no, I'm not shocked. Is this a regular thing, this escort work?'

She nodded. 'Yes, I suppose it is. I tend to do a couple of nights a week, sometimes more.'

'Is that what you were doing last night?'

'None of your business.'

'So how did some low-level street girl like Miriam Fox find out about your extra-curricular activities? I presume you weren't . . . moving in the same circles.'

'Let's just say she found out.'

'How did she know who you were?'

'Two or three years ago, when she first ran away, she was arrested for soliciting and ended up at Coleman House. She didn't stop long, a couple of weeks at most. She was a very difficult girl to handle and she seemed to have a hatred of authority. I think there might have been problems at home that had helped to shape her personality, but she never talked about them. In fact, about the only time she did talk was to throw abuse. There were quite a few confrontations with staff, including myself, and then one day she decided she'd had enough and walked out. Like a lot of the girls do.'

'Wasn't it a bit dangerous to suggest to us when we first inter-viewed you that you didn't know her?'

She shifted in her seat and put one leg up on the sofa. It was a vaguely provocative pose, although she didn't seem to notice it.

'Not really. None of the current staff were there, when she was there, and originally she gave a false name when we took her in. It would have been difficult to check up on it, and why would you have bothered?'

Which was fair enough, I suppose. 'And when was the next time you saw her?'

'But you said she was blackmailing you.'

'She was. Look, I'd really rather not go into details, Mr Milne.'

'I'm sure you wouldn't. But it's important I know.'

'So you can calculate whether I'm telling the truth or not?'

I nodded. 'Basically, yes.'

She picked up her wine and took a large drink, as if fortifying herself. 'Look, I'll be honest with you. I don't actually know how she found out. I can guess, but that's about it.' I waited in silence for her to continue. 'Let me start with how it works. My clients tend to be businessmen, men with plenty of spare money. The usual procedure is for us to go somewhere for dinner, then back to a hotel, or their place, for the rest. That way, I keep control of the proceedings, and don't get myself into any situation where I'm unnecessarily vulnerable.'

'That stands to reason.'

'A few weeks ago, though, one of my regular clients – a high-powered lawyer, and someone I've been seeing for several years – was caught kerbcrawling in King's Cross. You might have heard about it.'

I nodded, remembering the case vaguely, though not the name of the punter concerned. Kerbcrawling wasn't big news these days, even when it involved such a richly deserving case as a wealthy lawyer.

'Apparently, it was the second time it had happened to him. He'd been caught doing the same thing a few years ago in

Paddington.' She shook her head, as if annoyed with herself for getting involved with someone so unreliable. 'I was worried, I didn't need that sort of hassle, not the sort that could easily compromise me. Afterwards, I went round to his place and confronted him. I asked how often he did it and he swore that both times had been one-offs. He was obviously ashamed about it. He was also obviously lying. No-one's that unlucky. So I asked some of the girls in the home if they knew anything about him, whether he'd ever propositioned any of them, more as a matter of conversation than anything else. It was easy enough to do. The case had made some headlines in the local paper, so people seemed quite happy to talk about it.'

'And?'

'And several of the older ones had had some involvement with him. One had even got to go back to his apartment in Hampstead Heath, the same place I'd visited on many occasions. Apparently, he also liked to do it without a condom, which might have been one of the attractions of using street girls. They don't tend to be so fussy. So I ended our arrangement with him straight away. I'm not interested in dealing with people who lie to me and who have such a dubious attitude to the sexual health of both themselves and others.'

'Then two, maybe three days after I'd confronted him, I got a telephone call at Coleman House. It was Miriam Fox. She told me she knew that I'd been seeing the lawyer, and that I'd been getting paid for my time.' She sighed. 'As I said, I couldn't honestly say exactly how she found out. I think he must have used her services a number of times, so she'd almost certainly been at his apartment at one time or another. Maybe she found some evidence that I'd been there.'

'Like what?'

'I told you, I don't know. Maybe she was leaving one night

when I was arriving; maybe she was watching the place and saw me there. You know what some of these street girls are like: they go to a place, then tell their pimp how many valuables the punter's got, then they plan to rob it. She could have been surveying the apartment for her pimp, and saw me.' She shrugged her shoulders hopelessly. 'The point is, she knew. That's all I can tell you."

'What did she want from you?' I asked.

'The same as most blackmailers. Money. She told me that if I didn't pay her five thousand pounds, she'd expose me to the local authority and the newspapers.'

'That must have given you a bit of a shock.'

'It did. I couldn't believe what I was hearing. It just seemed so . . . unfortunate.'

'What did you say to her?'

'There were other people in the room with me at the time so I couldn't really say a lot. I got a number off her and told her I'd phone her back. When I did call her back, she repeated her demand for the money. I told her I didn't have that sort of cash and we had a bit of an argument. Eventually she said she'd settle for two thousand. For the time being. Those were her words. For the time being. I repeated that it was going to take a while. She gave me a week.'

'Did you ever give her any money?'

'I never actually met up with her at all. A week later she phoned me on my mobile – I'd given her the number – and I stalled her again. I said I'd managed to get some of it, but not enough. I told her she'd have to give me another week. To be honest, I didn't know what to do. I knew it wouldn't stop with just one payment, that she'd come back to me for more and would keep coming back until she'd bled me dry. I mean, she was a drug addict and she wasn't going to beat her addiction suddenly. And she was the sort of girl who would have told the authorities anyway, just to spite me.'

'What happened after the other week was up?'

'I phoned her on her mobile and left a message. I told her I was no longer interested in giving her any money and she could go fuck herself as far as I was concerned."

'That was a bit of a brave move.'

She shrugged again. 'It was a calculated risk. I'd given it a lot of thought. I knew she'd probably report me, but I was hoping that neither the authorities nor the papers would take the word of some crack-addicted runaway. And even if they did investigate, I thought I'd probably be able to cover my tracks well enough so that they wouldn't discover anything. Anyway, she called back the next day and tried to persuade me that I was making a mistake. She was pissed off that I was calling her bluff, and she sounded pretty desperate as well. Perhaps she owed someone some money – her pimp, or somebody like that. In the end, I was almost feeling sorry for her.' She managed a slight smile when she said this, and took a sip of her wine, more confident, it seemed, now that she'd got this off her chest. 'We talked for a couple of minutes, she got quite hysterical, called me a bitch, said I'd regret messing her around, and then I just hung up.

'And that really was the end of it. It was the last time I spoke to her. A few days later she was dead.' She lit another cigarette, and I noticed her hands were shaking a little. 'That doesn't sound good, does it? Someone blackmailing me, and then they end up murdered?' Again, I didn't say anything, just sat there and let her speak. 'That's the reason, or one of the reasons anyway, I didn't say anything to you. So, now you know. What are you going to do about it? Are you going to tell your superior?"

'Well, it would be difficult to avoid the fact that you've got a motive for wanting her out of the way . . . but then so have a few other people. She was clearly the sort of girl who attracts enemies. Did you kill her?"

She looked me in the eye. 'No, I didn't. I had nothing to do with it. I might have had a motive, but not a strong enough one. Even if someone had believed her, I wouldn't really have been losing that much. I'm getting tired of the job at Coleman House anyway. It never seems to be doing anything to improve the lot of the people I'm meant to be helping, and I doubt if it accounts for more than a third of my earnings these days. I certainly wouldn't kill anyone over it.' She finished her wine and poured the last drops from the bottle in equal measures into her glass and mine. I doubt if there was more than a mouthful each. 'Do you believe me, Mr Milne?'

It was a good question. On balance, yes, I did. Her story sounded plausible. Coincidental, but still plausible. More so than any alternatives I might have thought up, and I was almost certain she hadn't delivered the fatal blow. She was tall and lithe, but it had been a man, and a strong one at that, who had killed Miriam Fox. That meant that for Carla to be guilty she would have needed to have got someone else involved in the plot, which, as far as I could see, would have defeated the object of it in the first place. And she was right too. All to defend a job managing a care home for delinquent kids? Somehow I didn't think so.

I sighed. 'I'm not going to take it any further, put it like that.'

'But you don't believe me?'

'I don't really know what to believe. It's a pretty strange story, you've got to admit that. One minute you're a high-powered social worker managing a kid's home, the next you're an escort girl with a nice line in kinky customers.'

'You certainly know how to make it sound degrading.'

I gulped my mouthful of wine. 'Well, isn't it? Getting fucked for money by middle-aged men who'll dip their wick with anyone who'll take the cash off them? It's hardly what you'd call satisfying and useful work.'

'I'm not going to apologize for what I do. I provide a service, nobody gets hurt, and sometimes, you know . . . sometimes it is quite satisfying. And if I get paid for it too . . . it's all the better, isn't it?'

'I don't know. Is it?'

'Have you ever paid for sex, Mr Milne? Dennis?'

I smiled. 'Why? Are you offering?'

She smiled back. 'I'm very choosy about who I sleep with.'

'Well, I guess that's me out then. A nosey, cynical copper's hardly a prime catch.'

She didn't say anything and we sat in silence for a few moments, both, I think, pondering our positions in the world and what we'd actually achieved. It struck me then that the two of us weren't really all that dissimilar. Both leading murky double lives we'd far rather keep deeply buried. The difference was, I'd kill to preserve the secrecy of mine. At least I hoped it was the difference.

'Do you want another drink?' she asked me eventually.

I looked at her, not sure whether she actually wanted me to stay or not. She gave a weary smile back, which I took to mean yes. 'Are you having one?'

She nodded. 'Why not?'

I watched her as she turned round in her seat and removed a bottle of brandy from a cupboard behind the sofa. Her bottom looked remarkably pert.

'Will this do?'

'Perfect,' I said as she put two fresh glasses down on the table and poured a hefty slug into each.

I offered her a cigarette from my pack, but she opted for a Silk

Cut. I lit mine and sat back in my seat, thinking that there was something about her story that turned me on. The prim, well-spoken manager who turns into the whore by night. I know it's the fantasy of a lot of men, and in that respect I was just like everyone else.

'So how did a respectable lady like yourself get into . . . escort work?'

She took a drink of the brandy and pulled the sort of face you pull when you're quaffing neat spirits. 'It's a long story.'

'That's just the way I like them.'

'I was married for a long time to a man I really cared about. He was a social worker, like me. We met at university, fell in love, and that was it really. Neither of us really believed in marriage, but I think we wanted a way of showing how committed we were to each other. We both totally believed in what we were doing; I suppose people do when they're young. We didn't have a lot of money, but it didn't really seem to matter. We rented a nice little two-bedroom flat in Camden, and things were good. You know what it's like when you're in love. You're happy with your lot.'

I nodded to show I understood, but I wasn't sure if I did.

'Then, one day, he told me he'd met someone else. A girl in the department. He didn't even seem that sorry about it. He talked about it as if it was one of those things; something that couldn't be helped. All our time together, eight years of marriage, the whole relationship . . . it ended just like that.' She gave me a look that demanded understanding, if not sympathy, her face a combination of sadness and anger. 'He moved out the next day and applied for a transfer to York, which was where she came from. Apparently she was pregnant and wanted to be closer to home. Sometimes I think that's why he went for her. Because she wanted kids, and I wanted to wait for a while.'

'It must have been very hard on you,' I said, stating the fucking obvious.

'It was. I was suddenly on my own for the first time in a long time, and what made it worse was that without Steve I couldn't pay the rent on the flat, so I had to move out of there too, and that part really hurt. I'd worked so hard to make it a home, spent hours and hours getting it just right, and in the end it was all for nothing.

'So, there I was, broke, single, and depressed. Even the job didn't seem to be going right. I was moving up the ladder, but not as fast as I'd have liked, and the work was providing a lot of frustrations. Kids who you put so much time into, who you really thought were going to make it, ended up overdosing on smack and barbiturates, or turning their back on you, and all that bureaucratic interfering. It was a real low point in my life, probably the lowest. At one time it even crossed my mind to, you know . . .' She trailed off.

'But eventually I pulled myself together and life went on. But I was a changed person, Dennis. I lost a lot of my idealism, I was harder, more focused. Then, one day, I read an article about a housewife who worked in the days as a part-time call girl. She didn't do it for the money. I think she was more interested in the adventure, and maybe the sex, but she seemed happy with the way it worked out and at the time money for me was still very, very tight, so I thought, I could do that. I'm attractive, I'm quite good company. And I'm certainly lonely enough to appreciate the attention, even if it was from people I wouldn't normally have associated with. So I decided to give it a go.'

'You've been doing it for a while, then?'

'I suppose I have. I've never really thought about it. It's a part of my life now.'

'I still can't believe it,' I said, taking a sip of the brandy. 'When

I first met you I'd never have guessed that, you know, you were involved in this sort of thing. I'm not condemning it. It's just a bit of a shock.'

Carla shrugged.

'And do you enjoy it?'

She appeared to think about it for a moment. 'Sometimes. Not all the time. Maybe not even much of the time. But sometimes. So, how about you? Did you always want to be a copper, or did you just fall into it?'

I took a long drag on my cigarette. 'I think I always wanted to be one. You know, when I was growing up, I had this real sense of justice. I hated bullies, and I hated it when people did something bad and got away with it. I thought it would be really good to do a job where you could stop that sort of thing from happening, and when it had already happened you could punish the perpetrators. I also thought it would be a bit of an adventure.'

'And has it been?'

I took a couple of seconds to answer. 'Well, I suppose it's had its moments, but, to be honest with you, they've been pretty few and far between. A lot of the time it's just endless paperwork and dealing with people who live shitty lives and do all these shitty things to each other for the most mundane reasons. And, you know, you can never seem to stop them.'

'That's human nature, Dennis. It's what a lot of people are like. They grow up without values, alienated from the society they live in. You can't just turn them into model citizens at the drop of a hat.'

'But everyone's taught right from wrong. Whether it's in the media, at school . . . It's just a lot of them aren't interested. They have no fear of doing wrong; that's the problem. I guess it's because they have no respect for us, the people who are meant to be stopping them. You should hear the shit we put up with every day.'

She smiled. 'It's probably exactly the same as the shit we put up with every day.'

'Why do we do it, eh?'

'Because we care,' she said, and I suppose that was as good a reason as any. Although the problem I had was that I'd stopped caring a long time ago, and perhaps, in a way, so had she.

I finished my brandy and she refilled the glasses. When they were full, she picked hers up and raised it for a toast.

'To the carers,' she said.

'To the carers,' I intoned.

We clinked glasses, and once again I got a smell of that wonderful perfume. I was feeling relaxed now, at ease with the world; the drink and the company removing the heavy loads of worry from my shoulders.

We talked for a long time. An hour ... two hours ... maybe more, I can't honestly remember. Pretty much a bottle of brandy's worth. Not really about anything in particular. Just things.

At some point I began stroking her smooth bare feet while we chatted, my head spinning with booze and lust and confidence as my words tumbled out. Her toes were painted a beautiful plum colour and I bent down to kiss them one by one, taking them into my mouth, revelling in the intimacy of the contact. She moaned faintly, and I knew then that I'd conquered her. That this was it. That I was going to make love to the woman I'd fantasized about these past few nights, who I'd thought was far too good for me, but who had now shown her true, vulnerable colours, and who I wanted with a desperation that even now I find impossible to describe.

25

When I woke up I had that feeling you sometimes get where you don't know where the hell you are. Well, where I was was in a beautiful king-sized bed in a darkened room. To my right, I could see the dull half-light of a winter morning peeping round the edges of long, crimson curtains. I was on my own in the bed, but there was a faint smell of perfume in the air and the noise of someone moving about coming from somewhere outside the door.

It took maybe three seconds to work everything out and remember the events of the night before. The sex had been surprisingly ferocious; either she was a very good actor (which I suppose a lot of women in her situation must be) or she'd really been enjoying herself. I preferred to think it was the latter, and was pleased with my own performance, which had been solid if very much second fiddle to that of the opposition. I guess she'd had a lot more practice than me.

I sat up in bed and looked at my watch. It was twenty past seven and my head hurt. Monday morning, the start of a new week. I wasn't looking forward to going back to the station, and once again thoughts of jacking it all in drifted into my mind. I had the money to make a move. It was just a question of whether I had the guts.

The door opened and Carla appeared, dressed in a thin black kimono-style dressing gown, carrying two cups of coffee. She was looking six a.m. good.

'Oh, you're awake, then?' she said, handing me one of the cups. 'I thought I was going to have to pour a bucket of water over you.'

'I'm usually a pretty heavy sleeper,' I said, 'and I had enough exercise yesterday to put me out until this afternoon.'

She smiled but didn't say anything as she put her cup down on top of a chest of drawers and switched on the main light. She slipped off the dressing gown to reveal a naked body that seemed to have aged perfectly. I watched her hungrily as she slowly dressed, starting with expensive-looking black underwear.

'It's a pity you've got an early meeting,' I told her.

'Don't I know it,' she said, without looking round. 'I've got a hangover from hell. Drinking at home always seems to do that to me.'

I bit the bullet. 'Are we going to see each other again?'

She pulled on a pair of tights. 'Look, Dennis, I don't want to hurry anything, you know. Last night was, well, a one-off.'

'Is that what you want it to be?'

She came over to the bed and sat down on it, facing me. 'Remember what you came over here for: to question me about a murder in which I was a suspect. You still haven't told me straight that I'm not one. Things happened, but that's because we were both pretty inebriated. It's not exactly the ideal way to start a relationship, is it?'

'I'm not proposing marriage, Carla. It'd just be nice to see you again, that's all.'

'Do you know what you're getting involved in, Dennis? I see other men. It's not something I'm going to stop overnight, and I don't know how easy you'll find it to deal with that.'

'I'm quite a liberal guy.'

'You're a copper.'

'I'm a liberal copper and I had a good time last night. I got the impression you did too. It's an experience I want to repeat, that's all. Shit, I'd even pay for it.' She shot me a bit of a dirty look. 'I'm joking,' I told her.

'Look, I'm not trying to give you the brush-off, Dennis, but my life's complicated. The last time I had a boyfriend, he tried to get me to change the way I live, and I'm not the sort of person who likes to be told what to do. I value my independence. And I know it sounds shallow, but after what I went through after the divorce, I value the money as well.'

I leaned over and patted her on the knee, letting my hand linger there for a moment. She didn't, it has to be said, seem desperately interested.

'I understand, but I'd appreciate it if we could at least pop out for a drink one night.'

She stood up and pecked me on the forehead. 'Yes. We can do that. Give me a call some time.'

Realizing that I wasn't going to tempt her back into bed, I got up and started putting on my crumpled clothes – clothes I was now going to have to turn up for work in.

By the time I'd located everything and put it on, Carla was at the dressing table applying the finishing touches to her face. I stopped beside her and bent down to kiss her on the head. She patted me on the hip in a way that reminded me of the way you pat a dog.

She must have seen the creases of disappointment on my face because she managed a weak smile. 'I'm sorry, Dennis. I'm not the best person in the mornings. I take a while to get going,. It's normally lunchtime before I can get enthusiastic about anything.'

'No problem. I understand. I'll call you, then.'

'Yes.'

'Have a nice day.' That one just slipped out, for want of something better.

I winked at her as I shut the bedroom door behind me and headed out, wondering if I'd done something wrong. Probably, although whatever it was I couldn't for the life of me work out. But that's women for you. Complicated and unpredictable.

Just like my days were becoming.

26

Work that day was mundane. There was a meeting first thing about the mugging of the old lady. Apparently she'd survived the weekend but had yet to regain consciousness, and Knox was pissed off. Things were not going well in our division crime-wise, and the clear-up rate on offences of violence was now hovering below the 20 per cent mark, which, as he told us, was utterly unacceptable and wouldn't look too clever in the performance league tables.

To remedy this, however, there was going to be a series of raids the following morning at the homes of a number of mugging suspects, aged between twelve and sixteen, one or more of whom could well have been involved in the attack on the old lady. There were nine homes in all to search, so it was going to involve all of us. 'It's time to take the battle to them,' he concluded loudly, but for me the message was muted. I remembered him saying exactly the same thing a few months back about crack dealers in the area. We'd simultaneously raided a total of fourteen premises in an operation Knox had cunningly codenamed 'Street Shock', had recovered drugs with a street value of more than twenty-five grand, and made a total of nine arrests. Five were later released without charge; one absconded while on bail and hadn't been seen since; one pleaded guilty and received a fine and suspended sentence; one was acquitted by a jury who believed his story that he hadn't known the stuff was in the house; and one was now in custody awaiting trial, having previously been released on bail and re-arrested twice in the space of three weeks for dealing. The only shock was the one the taxpayers would get if they ever discovered what a pathetically negligible effect such an expensive and time-consuming operation had had on both the criminals and the local crime figures. It was hardly a wonder our clear-up rate was so bad. Most of the time, it just wasn't worth the bother.

I had a brief chat with Malik after the meeting had concluded, but neither of us had time to cover much ground. He was now heavily involved in the mugging case and was keen to make a good impression.

After that, Knox had me writing up reports on all my current cases, which took all morning and a good part of the afternoon. He told me Capper wanted to take a look at what I was working on to see if there was any mileage in giving me additional resources; in other words, to see if there were any mistakes I was making. Apparently, the two of them were particularly keen for movement on the armed robbery case, which appeared to have ground to a complete halt. Which was true. It had. But I wasn't quite sure what more I or any of my colleagues could do to kickstart it. If no-one gives you information and the perpetrators haven't left any obvious clues, a detective's room for manoeuvre is somewhat limited. But it transpired that the Chief Superintendent had had a meeting with representatives of the Kurdish community (both the stabbing victims – the shop's proprietor and the customer – were Kurds) who'd told him they wouldn't rest until the culprits were caught. They had also raised that possibility, so dreaded of all senior Met officers, that racism might be playing a part in holding things up. Obviously, the Chief Super was keen to show his community bridge-building skills, and since much of the work on the case had been done by me, I was going to have to indulge in some serious arse-covering. Knox also suggested that at a later date I too might have to prostrate myself in front of these so-called representatives of the community so that they could have a go at me as well – another good reason to resign, if ever I needed one.

It was difficult to concentrate on the report writing. I kept thinking of the sex with Carla, and wishing that I could repeat the experience. I had to make a conscious effort not to call her number. I knew she wouldn't appreciate it. Not today. She was, as she said, a woman who liked her independence. Fair enough. I'm a man who likes mine – most of the time anyway – but I still harboured hopes that I could get something going with her.

Some time around lunchtime, Jean Ashcroft phoned again. She asked me if I'd been round to see Danny. I told her I hadn't but that I'd phoned him, and everything seemed all right. She said she'd tried to get hold of him but he wasn't answering his phones, and I mentioned that he'd gone away on holiday for a couple of weeks.

'Did you find out where he was getting his money from?' she asked. 'It's just not like him to have any, you know.'

I told her that I wasn't sure (I'd given up on the police informant story, thinking it might prompt her into further investigation), but said that I didn't think it was anything to be overly concerned about. 'Maybe he's got less money than you think,' I added. 'You can get these last-minute deals for hardly anything now, so I expect he just picked up something cheap. I checked with some colleagues up his way and they say he's not in the frame for anything they've got on the go.'

'But he didn't say anything about what was worrying him?'

'No. But I wouldn't read too much into it. He didn't sound like he had anything serious on his mind, and I can usually tell. It's my job.'

'Did you say it was yesterday he went on holiday?'

'That's what he told me he was doing when I called him.'

'Well, I've tried his mobile this morning and he's still not answering.'

I said that this was probably because he couldn't get a signal where he was, and I think I managed to convince her not to panic about it. 'He'll call back soon, I'm sure,' I said, but for the first time I began to get a bad feeling about it all. I made a mental note to call Raymond when I got the chance, just to confirm that neither he nor his jittery associates had tried to track Danny down. Finally, I said my goodbyes to Jean and got back to my report writing.

I left the station at five thirty that night, having got the feeling that under Capper I was going to be pushed to one side of things, and that my time at the station really was coming to an end. I fancied a drink, if only to get rid of the dry, sour taste in my mouth and the worries constantly surfacing in my head, but decided instead to go and visit DI Welland in hospital. It was duty, really. I don't like going to hospitals (who does?), but Welland needed some moral support. When I'd been put in one three years ago, having received an enthusiastic tap on the head with an iron bar when an arrest went wrong, he'd visited me three times in the six days I'd been in there. The least I could do now was return the favour.

He was being treated at St Thomas's, and it was five past six when I got there, armed with a jumbo box of wine gums, which were always his favourite, and a couple of American true crime magazines.

Hospitals always smell so uninviting and, in England at least, they usually look it too. Being a copper, I've had to spend more than my fair share of time in them. Aside from the many visits I'd made to interview victims and sometimes the perpetrators of crime, I'd ended up being on the receiving end of treatment on three separate occasions, all work-related. There'd been the iron bar incident; the time during my probationary period when a mob of rampaging Chelsea fans had used me for kicking practice; and an incident early on in the Poll Tax riot when a huge crop-headed dyke had whacked me over the back of the head with a four by four while I'd been trying to resuscitate some old granny who'd just fainted. In that case my assailant had been arrested on the spot and, ironically enough, had turned out to be a nurse.

Welland was in a ward at the back of the hospital and they'd got him a private room. He was sitting up in bed in his pyjamas reading the *Evening Standard* when I knocked and went in. He was much paler than usual, as if he was a bit seasick, but he didn't appear to have lost any weight, and all in all he didn't look quite as rough as I'd expected.

He looked up and managed a smile when he saw me. 'Hello, Dennis.'

'How are you, boss?'

'I'm sure I've been worse, but I can't honestly remember when.'

'Well, you look all right for it. Have they started the treatment yet?'

'No, it's been postponed until tomorrow. Lack of specialist staff, something like that.'

'That's the NHS for you. They make the Met look over-manned. Here, I brought you these.' I put the wine gums and magazines down by the side of the bed. He thanked me, and with a quick gesture offered me a seat.

I sat down in a threadbare chair next to him and said some-thing else to the effect that he looked remarkably healthy given the circumstances, which is the sort of inane bullshit you have to come out with at times like this, even though no-one ever believes it. I once remember telling a girl whose face had been partially melted by acid thrown at her by an ex-boyfriend that she'd be all right in time. Of course she wouldn't and neither would Welland.

'It's good of you to come, Dennis. Thanks.' He sat back further into the pillows, looking tired, and I noticed that he sounded short of breath when he spoke.

'Well I wouldn't say it was a pleasure, sir, because visiting a hospital never is, but I wanted you to know we hadn't forgotten about you or anything.'

'How is work? I miss it, you know. Never really thought I would, but I do.'

'It's the same as ever,' I told him. 'Too many criminals, not enough coppers. Plenty to keep us busy.'

He shook his head. 'It's a hiding to nothing sometimes, isn't it?'

'It sure is that,' I agreed, wondering where this conversation was going.

'You know something, Dennis. I've always thought you were a good copper. You know the job, you know what it's all about.'

He turned his head and looked at me just a little bit too closely for my liking. I had the feeling this was going to turn into one of those deep conversations about life and policework I could really do without.

'I've always done my best, sir.'

'We've known each other a long time, haven't we?'

'Yeah, we have. Eight years you've been my boss now.'

'Eight years ... Christ, is it that long? Time just goes, doesn't it? One minute you're a young copper with it all in front of you, and before you know it ... before you know it, you're this ... Sat in a hospital bed waiting to begin the treatment that could save your life.' He was no longer looking at me, but was staring up at the ceiling, seemingly lost in his thoughts. 'Funny how things go, isn't it?'

'Yeah, it is.' It was. 'Eight years.' I shook my head. 'Shit.'

'You know, these days they've got so many new faces. All these graduates who've come in with their new ideas. A lot of them are good blokes, don't get me wrong, and women ... but they don't really understand the fundamentals of policework. Not like you and me. We're old school, Dennis. That's what we are. Old school.'

'I think we're a dying breed, sir. In a few years' time we'll be gone altogether.'

'And you know what? They'll miss us. They don't like us, they think we're dinosaurs, but when we're gone they'll miss us.'

'People never get appreciated until they're gone,' I said.

'That's exactly it. These new people – these men and women with their degrees – they just don't understand policework. Not like you and me, Dennis. They don't know that sometimes you've got to bend the rules to get on.'

I felt a sudden sense of shock. I'd always been very careful not to involve Welland in any of my murkier dealings, and as far as I was aware he knew nothing about any wrongdoing I'd ever committed.

'I've always tried to play it fair, sir. Sometimes I've had to lean hard on people, but it's always been by the book.'

'Sometimes you've got to do these things,' he said, continuing as if I hadn't spoken, still staring up towards the ceiling. 'People don't realize the sort of job we have to do, the sort of scum we have to deal with the whole time. They just take the whole thing for granted. Do you remember when the Home Secretary visited that time?'

I remembered all right. Two years ago it had been. He'd marched in all smiles, pumping hands left, right and centre. Telling us how he was going to increase recruitment and how he and the government were going to introduce legislation to make it easier for the police to gain convictions and harder for the criminals to avoid the long arm of the law, which, needless to say, had never happened. Come to think of it, he'd used the phrase 'taking the war to the criminals' as well. Maybe that's where Knox had got it from.

'Who could forget?' I said.

'He talked about how he really empathized with us, how he knew how hard the job we had to do was. But he didn't. None of them do. If they did, they'd untie our hands and pay us more. Make it worthwhile upholding the law.' He sighed. 'Sometimes you've got to bend the rules a bit, make a few pennies here and there to supplement things. If a piece of evidence goes missing, who's going to notice? In the end, it's only going to get burned anyway. Why not make something out of it?'

Still he wouldn't look at me. I felt increasingly uncomfortable sitting there in that shitty little room listening to things I really didn't want to hear. In a way, he sounded as though he was rambling, but I knew he wasn't.

'What are you trying to say, sir?'

'You know what I'm trying to say, Dennis. I know you've bent the rules in the past—'

'I've always tried to play it fair,' I said, repeating the phrase

I'd used earlier, but it sounded lame now, and I knew it. 'I don't think I've—'

This time he turned and faced me. 'Dennis, I know you've done things in the past you shouldn't have. I know it. No question. Stuff's gone missing, sometimes bad stuff like dope, and you're the only person who could have taken it.' I tried to say something, but he put up a hand to stop me. He wanted to say his piece, and nothing was going to stop him. 'You're a good copper. You always have been. But I'm not blind. And I'm not stupid. I'm not saying you're bent, not by any means, but I know you've cut corners and made a bit of illicit cash here and there; done a few dodgy deals. Fair enough, I say. You've worked hard over the years. You've put away a lot of very nasty people, people who'd probably still be free if it wasn't for your efforts. I know that in a couple of cases you've had to use – how shall I put it? – unconventional means to put people down. And I understand that, I really do. The law's a straitjacket sometimes. I know it and you know it, because we're old school. These new people, they don't have a clue how it works . . .' He turned away again, presumably signifying that he'd got what he wanted off his chest.

For a moment I just sat there, not sure what to say. What could I say? He had me bang to rights, and the thing was, I'd never seen it coming. Maybe I'd just been far too cocky for my own good. I exhaled slowly and wished I could have a cigarette.

'You know what I like about you, sir? You never mince your words.'

'No point. Not when you're in my position.'

'What have the doctors said about the . . . the er . . . ?'

'The cancer? You can say the word, you know.'

'Do they think they've got it early?'

'It doesn't look too good, Dennis. It might be all right, but the odds aren't in my favour. I'm not sure how much they're in yours either.'

I felt an immediate spasm of fear. 'What do you mean, sir?'

He sighed, and there was a short silence before he continued. 'I want you to be careful, Dennis. I've always liked you, you know. A lot more than sometimes I've let on. I liked the way you never backed down. You've got guts, and that's something in very short supply these days.'

'What are you trying to say, sir?'

He turned to face me again. 'I'm saying, watch your back.'

'And what's making you say that?' I asked, my voice steady. 'What have you heard that I ought to know about?'

'I had visitors earlier.' There was a pause. I didn't say anything. He sighed. 'Two men from CIB.'

So they were on to me. In a way it had always been coming, ever since they'd issued the e-fit, but I still had difficulty containing my shock. 'What did they say?'

'They asked a lot of questions.'

'What kind of questions?'

'About your background, your attitude ... all sorts. They wanted to know whether you had more money than might be expected of a serving copper, whether there'd ever been any suggestion of ... corruption.' He emphasized the last word, taking his time to pronounce it.

'What did you tell them?'

'I told them you were a good copper, that I couldn't think of a bad word to say about you except that maybe sometimes you were too eager to get a conviction.'

'Thanks, sir.'

'Whatever it is you've done, Dennis, be careful. Because they're on to you.'

I sat there for a couple of seconds as the full magnitude of his words sank in. In a strange way, I felt relieved that Welland hadn't linked me with the e-fit. I don't think I could have handled receiving the odium of someone I respected. Not after everything else.

'Don't worry, sir. It's nothing serious. I promise.'

'Sure. I understand.'

Again there was a silence, this time broken by me suggesting it was time to leave. 'I need to think about things,' I told him.

'You've got to get yourself back on track,' he told me. 'Be a good boy for a while.'

'Yeah, I know.'

'You're a good copper, Dennis.'

'Maybe.'

'And it was nice of you to come and see me. I appreciate it. I really do.'

I stood up and patted him gently on the arm. 'It was no more than you deserve. Thanks for saying good things about me.'

He gave a nod of acknowledgement, and I turned to go.

'One thing that was funny,' he said as I reached the door.

I stopped and turned back. 'What was that, sir?'

'Just that for some reason they seemed really interested in your firearms training.'

I shrugged, not giving a thing away. 'You know how it is. They've got to ask these things. Maybe they want to fit me up for a few murders as well.'

He managed a weak smile. 'You never know with the lot they've got up at CIB.'

I turned away from his gaze, hoping I'd imagined the knowing look.

27

Unravelling. It was all unravelling, so fast that I couldn't keep up with it. With each passing hour, my room for manoeuvre was becoming more limited. The gates to freedom were closing, and unless I made the right decision, and made it quickly, my life was effectively finished and I could look forward to the rest of my days behind bars, segregated from the bulk of the prison population for my own protection. As for how long would that be? Thirty years? At least. Triple murder. Maybe even quadruple murder. Thirty years without a single taste of freedom.

Sitting alone that night at a corner table in the Chinaman, the drink doing little to calm my nerves, I tried to consider my options. They clearly had me down as a suspect, I could no longer doubt that. The copper at the roadblock had seen the e-fit and had put two and two together. Doubtless, by now they'd have got hold of a recent photo of me to show their main witness, the girl at the hotel, and presumably she'd picked me out as the killer. The question now was whether this, on its own, was enough evidence to secure a conviction. At the moment they clearly felt there was no point snatching me off the streets and charging me. There could have been several reasons for this, the most obvious being that they wanted me to lead them to whoever it was who had ordered the killing. Another would be that they wanted to gather further evidence against me without my knowing it, then spring their trap. Obviously, given my integral role in the saga, they would know there was no point offering up the carrot of a more lenient sentence for co-operating. I had no incentive whatsoever to tell them anything, however hard they leaned on me, and they'd know that.

It was a potentially embarrassing situation too. A serving police officer in a reasonably high position within the Force, and a background that included seventeen years' pretty much unblemished service, being arrested on suspicion of three counts of murder. No-one in authority wanted that scenario, not until they were truly convinced that I was the man they were looking for. This at least gave me a slight chance of escaping the fate that was otherwise in store. But the fact remained that I was almost certainly now under close surveillance. Even more embarrassing than having me arrested was not having me arrested with news leaking out that I'd been in the frame but had slipped through the net.

I finished the scotch and water I was drinking and casually surveyed the pub, looking for anyone who didn't belong. Police surveillance teams can be good, especially if they're using the best people they've got, but if you're aware that you're under their gaze it makes their job one hell of a lot more difficult. I clocked a middle-aged guy at the far end of the bar in a cheap-looking black suit with his tie askew and the top buttons of his shirt undone. He was talking animatedly to Joan, the landlady, and it looked like he was telling her a joke. I watched him for a couple of seconds, then scanned the rest of the bar. A few stools down from him were a couple of businessmen types I recognized, and down from them were a group of younger blokes, only just out of their teens, clustered around the jukebox. Two couples were at separate tables just in front of the bar, one of them I recognized, the other I'd never seen before. The second couple were sitting there looking bored and not really saying much to each other, so they were probably married. The woman looked up and caught my eye, but there was no momentary sense of concern there at being rumbled. She wasn't police. In fact, she actually appeared quite pleased I'd been looking at her and shot me the briefest of smiles. Her husband, or whoever he was, didn't seem to notice, so I smiled back before turning away.

There were maybe a dozen other people in the place all told, sprinkled across the tables, all seemingly involved in their own private conversations. I didn't concentrate my attention on any-one for very long. The last thing I needed was for the surveillance team – if, of course, there was one – to realize I was on to them. The moment that happened, I'd be straight into custody, and maybe they might even be able to trace my awareness of their operation back to Welland, and I didn't want that to happen. The DI had done me a favour by covering my arse and letting me know what was happening, particularly when you took into consideration the fact that they'd been asking about my firearms experience. A lot of people would have forgotten their loyalties at this point and blurted out everything they knew. But not Welland. He knew the score. Or thought he did, anyway. Thinking back, I was sure that I'd imagined the look of suspicion on his face. There was no doubt that had he realized the full extent of my crimes it would have been a different story. One of the things going in my favour was that few people were ever going to think me capable of mass murder, which probably wasn't something to brag about, but was at least useful.

I lit a cigarette, thinking there was nothing to hold me back from running. This whole thing wasn't just going to go away. Not now. The investigating officers were going to keep sniffing around until they had the information they wanted. Then, one way or another, they were going to pull me in. And if Jean Ashcroft heard about any of this, she was likely to tell the cops about Danny, and then the shit really would hit the fan.

Danny. I'd tried his mobile again when I'd left the hospital, hoping he'd pick it up and tell me he was sitting on the beach sipping a pina colada, but it had still been switched off. I tried it again now, dragging on my cigarette as I waited vainly for a response. The longer he didn't respond to calls, the more I was forced to conclude that something bad had happened, and this left another problem. Raymond and his associates didn't need to keep me alive either. If they too got wind of what was going on they would definitely come for me – if they weren't coming already. Either way, my future looked grim so long as I stayed put.

But running away from everything – my career, my life: it was a big step. And then there was Carla Graham. Maybe she didn't want anything serious, but it was just possible that I could change that. Amid all this, she was the only positive thing keeping me going.

I picked up my mobile and thought about calling her. I was aware I might piss her off, but events were moving too rapidly for me to sit back and be patient. If she rejected me now it wasn't actually going to make a great deal of difference. I stared at the phone for maybe ten seconds, then put it down. I'd wait until tomorrow.

I finished my cigarette, then went up to the bar to get another drink. Joan was still chatting to the middle-aged man, and they were laughing like old friends, though you could tell from the way she excused herself from the conversation that they didn't actually know each other.

'What can I get you, Dennis?' she asked, before turning back to the guy. 'You see this bloke here?' she said, meaning me. 'Changes his drink all the time. You can never tell what he's going to have. Isn't that right, Dennis?'

'A man should never be too predictable,' I told her, and ordered a bottle of Pils, as if to prove the point.

As she turned away to get it, I gave the guy a brief smile. He smiled back awkwardly, then looked away. I noticed he was drinking Coke. Suspicious in a place like this, but not unheard of.

Another youngish couple came in and I found myself eyeing them closely. She sat down at a table near the bar and removed her hat and scarf, appearing not to notice me. Her boyfriend/colleague approached the bar and I turned away and paid for my drink, careful not to draw attention to myself. Jean asked me if I was dealing with the case of the old lady who was mugged. She told me that the victim was the mother of one of her former regulars. I told her I wasn't, but that I thought there might be arrests soon. 'It was kids who did it, and kids always end up giving themselves away. They can never keep their mouths shut.'

'Little bastards,' she said. 'They should bloody hang 'em.'

Which were probably the sentiments of 80 per cent of the population, not that it would ever make any difference. Usually, at this point, I'd have put on my police hat and tried to convince both myself and my audience that the perpetrators would end up receiving their just punishments, but this time I didn't bother. They wouldn't.

'Don't ever rely on the courts for justice, Joan,' I told her. 'They're afraid of it.' I turned to Coke Drinker. 'Isn't that right?'

'I never talk politics,' he answered, without looking me in the eye. 'It's too easy to make enemies.'

'Well, someone should do something about it,' Joan grumbled, and went off to serve the guy who'd just come to the bar.

I didn't bother returning to my seat but drank my beer quickly and in silence. When I'd finished I looked for Joan but she'd disappeared out the back. I nodded to Coke Drinker, who nodded vaguely back in my direction, and walked out.

The cold spell from Siberia had well and truly arrived, and an icy wind ripped through the narrow street. I pulled my coat tight around me and started walking, occasionally looking back. The parked cars lining both sides were empty and no-one came out of the Chinaman behind me.

After about fifty yards I turned into a side street and waited in the shadows, shivering against the cold, telling myself I was a fool because if they were following me it would only confirm what I already suspected, and would make no difference to my predicament.

But still I stood there. Five minutes passed. Then ten. A car came by slowly with two men in it, but I couldn't make them out properly. It carried on and accelerated away at the end of the street.

An icy rain began to fall and I broke cover, heading for home, but keeping to the shadows, not knowing who was going to be waiting for me when I got there.

28

When I got near my flat, I surveyed the street carefully, looking for anyone or anything that might be out of place, but it seemed the cold had driven everyone indoors. Only when I was satisfied that the silence was genuine did I walk hurriedly up to my front door and ram the key in the lock, still half expecting some hidden assassin to emerge from the darkness, or a shouting posse of armed police to charge me, screaming staccato orders.

Nothing happened, and there was relief when the door closed behind me for the last time that night.

The first thing I did when I got upstairs was phone in sick. I didn't know how much they knew at the station about the investigation into me but I found it hard to imagine that Knox wouldn't have been informed of it by now. Next I rang Raymond's mobile, but he wasn't answering, and neither was Luke, his bodyguard, so I left a message asking for him to call me and telling him I wasn't going to be at home for the next couple of days. Just in case he was thinking about sending anyone round. Then I made a cup of coffee and told myself not to panic. Foresight, if not right, remained on my side.

I went to bed about ten o'clock and fell asleep surprisingly easily. I remained out like a light the whole night, and for once I actually felt partially refreshed when I awoke the following morning at just after eight.

It was now time to plan my next move. Each day I remained here the chances of my being arrested grew higher, which meant that I was going to have to take the plunge fast. I needed to shake off my surveillance, grab the money from the Bayswater deposit box, and go to ground for a bit. As soon as I started running and they realized that I was on to them, that was it; there'd be no turning back. I was going to have to keep running for the rest of my life.

I went round the corner to get a paper, acting as casually as possible and not spotting anything or anyone untoward, then returned to read it over a light breakfast of toast and coffee. There was no obvious mention of the Traveller's Rest investigation within its pages and nothing on the Miriam Fox case. Now that an arrest had been made and charges laid, there'd be no further mention of her murder until the trial, and probably not much coverage then. Instead, there were the usual tales of woe from Britain and abroad: a farming crisis; renewed famine in Africa; a couple of food scares; and a liberal sprinkling of murder, mayhem and fashion tips.

When I was on my sixth cigarette of the day, I decided I had nothing to lose by calling Carla Graham. I phoned her office from Raymond's mobile, concerned about the possibility that my own phones had been bugged. She picked up on the fourth ring and I was relieved to hear no meeting-type noises in the background.

'Hello, Carla.'

'Dennis?'

'Yeah, it's me. How are you?'

She sighed. 'Busy. Very busy.'

'Well, I won't keep you long.'

'I was going to call you today anyway,' she said.

'Oh yeah?'

'Look, I don't want you to take this too seriously, but you said to let you know if anyone else went missing.' An ominous sensation crept up my back as partially buried thoughts suddenly unearthed themselves like zombies in a graveyard. 'And someone has.'

'Who?'

'Anne Taylor.'

Anne. The girl I'd shared coffee with less than a week ago. The girl I'd saved from abduction.

'Jesus, Carla. When did this happen?'

'She was last seen on Sunday afternoon.' She seemed to sense my unease. 'She's done this before on several occasions so I don't think there's any real cause for alarm. And obviously, there is a man in custody for the murder.'

'I know, but it isn't as cut and dried as that. There are a lot of unanswered questions, and everyone's innocent until proven guilty. You of all people should know that.'

'I still don't think you should read too much into it. Anne is that type of girl.'

'And so was Molly Hagger, but you can't help getting concerned. When did Anne last go missing like this?'

'About a month ago.'

'How long was she gone for then?'

'A couple of nights. A similar length of time to this. That's why we haven't been too worried. The last time she went AWOL it was because she was off on a binge with an older woman. She got stoned, fell asleep, and when she woke up twenty-four hours later she came back here.'

'And before that? When did she last go missing before that?'

'I can't remember. A few months ago. Look, Dennis, no-one here thinks anything untoward's happened.'

'So why were you going to phone and tell me?'

'Because you asked me too. Personally, I think Anne's doing her usual thing, which is going out, taking drugs, and doing exactly what she fancies, regardless of what anyone tells her, because that's what she's like. But I felt I ought to tell you because you were worried and I suppose I'd never forgive myself if Anne did end up like Miriam Fox, dead in some back alley with her throat cut, and I hadn't bothered reporting it. Although I still think the chances of that happening are fairly remote.'

'OK, OK, I get your point. I don't like it, though.' And I didn't. Anne's disappearance had sown more doubts in my mind. Maybe somehow, defying all the odds, Mark Wells wasn't our man. Not that it should have mattered; I had far bigger fish to fry now. I sighed. 'Look, do me a favour and inform the police. Tell them what's happened.'

'Dennis, you *are* the police.'

'Not any more I'm not.'

'What are you talking about?'

'I resigned. Yesterday.' Not quite true, but it might as well have been.

'Are you playing games, Dennis? Because if you are, I'm not interested.'

'No, I'm not. Honestly. I handed my notice in. It's been a long time coming.'

'But what are you going to do? I mean, are you trained for anything else?'

Killing people, I thought.

'Not really, but I've got a bit of cash put aside. I thought I'd maybe head abroad for a while. Do some travelling. I've always wanted to do something like that.'

'Well . . . Good luck with it. I hope it works out for you. When are you hoping to go?'

'As soon as I can. Probably before the end of the week.'

'You know, I think I'm jealous.'

'You could always come with me.'

She laughed. 'I don't think so. Perhaps one day I'll come out and visit you.'

'You should do. What's keeping you here?'

'I can't believe I'm actually being encouraged to be more of a rebel by a policeman. I don't know, Dennis. At the moment I'm happy the way things are.'

'Are you? Really?'

There was a short silence on the other end of the line before she spoke again. 'It just wouldn't work. I don't know you well enough. I think we should leave it at that.'

'OK, but it'd be good to see you one last time before I go.' As soon as I said this, I knew that this was a risk I should not be taking, but I didn't seem able to help myself.

'Yes,' she said, 'it would, but I don't know when we're going to get the chance.'

'Look, I remember you saying the other night that you liked poetry. They're doing a reading by some contemporary poets tonight at a place called the Gallan Club, not far from me. Why don't we meet there for a drink? It's a nice spot.'

Carla ummed and aahed for a few minutes, but finally agreed to come over for an hour or so. I began to tell her where the club was but it turned out she knew the place vaguely anyway. 'And don't forget to tell the police about Anne,' I added. 'Report it formally. You never know what might have happened and it's better to be safe than sorry.' Again she told me that she thought there was nothing to worry about, but I insisted and she ended up agreeing to do it.

After I'd hung up, I made another cup of coffee and lit cigarette number seven. Anne Taylor was not my concern. Even if I'd stayed a copper and remained connected to the Miriam Fox murder case, she would still not have been my concern. Mark Wells was almost certainly Miriam's murderer. But I couldn't help wondering what had happened to Molly Hagger and where Anne had got to. I would certainly have expected really to have surfaced by now. Her best friend had been killed, and it was difficult to believe that she wouldn't have at least shown her face to find out what was going on, or contact the authorities if she believed Wells was responsible. And now Anne had disappeared only a few weeks after Molly. There might, as Carla clearly thought, be a perfectly logical explanation for it, but for me it was all too coincidental, particularly on top of the attempted assault the previous week. I couldn't help but feel that I was missing something, something neither I nor any of my erstwhile colleagues were aware of, but try as I might I couldn't put my finger on what it was. And, with everything else, it felt like it wasn't worth trying.

But sometimes, you know, it's difficult to let go. So I picked up my home phone, this time not caring who was listening in, and made a call to Malik's mobile.

It rang ten times before he answered, and when he heard my voice I couldn't tell whether he was happy that it was me or not. I wondered briefly if he knew that his superiors were on to me.

He asked me how I was feeling, having presumably heard that I'd phoned in sick, and I told him I was OK just a little under the weather.

'I haven't been sleeping too well. I think I need a holiday.'

'Why don't you take a couple of weeks? You're bound to be due it.'

'I am. Maybe I will.'

'Anyway, what can I do for you, Dennis?'

Dennis. I was never going to get used to that from him. 'How did the raids go this morning? Have we laid any charges yet?'

'We pulled in everyone we were meant to, but no charges yet. You know what it's like with these kids. It's like treading on egg shells. You're not even allowed to raise your voices with them in case they get upset.'

'I'm sure one or more of them did the old lady.'

'I think everyone's sure of that. It's proving it that's the problem, not that I have to tell you that.'

'How is she?'

'The old lady? Touch and go. What I think personally is that one way or another she's going to die as a result of what happened. It might take a few weeks – it might even take a few months- - but either way, those kids were responsible.'

I agreed with him. 'Look, the reason I'm calling is the Miriam Fox case.'

'Oh yeah?' He spoke the words without much enthusiasm. I told him what Carla had told me about Anne's disappearance while he listened at the other end. When I'd finished, he asked me what I was doing talking to Carla. 'I thought you weren't going to bother contacting her.'

'She contacted me. I told her to if anyone else went missing. And this one seems like one coincidence too many. Two young girls, both no more than fourteen, disappear within a month of each other from the same children's home. At the same time, a girl both of them have had some association with, and who was best friends with one of them, is murdered. All three were prostitutes working the same area of King's Cross. I know people disappear, and I know we've got Mark Wells in custody, and that the evidence against him's good, but something about this just isn't right.'

'Like you said, people disappear . . .'

'Yeah, I know. I know. People disappear all the time, especially teenage crackheads, but with this frequency? And we know one met a violent end, and one of the others was assaulted during an attempted abduction just a matter of days ago, something I was witness to. And now we've got this thing where the evidence against the suspect in the murder – the shirt – is linked to one of the missing girls.'

'I wouldn't read too much into that, Dennis. Giving the shirt away to someone who's not around to deny it is just an easy excuse for Wells to use.'

'Has anyone been trying to find her?'

'Who? Molly Hagger? Not that I'm aware of. But if you're concerned, you should be talking to Knox, not me. Why don't you see what he has to say about it?'

'Because I know what he'll say, Asif. That we've got a man in custody, that there's no evidence for extending the inquiry further . . .'

'And he'd have a point, wouldn't he? You're right, it all seems a bit coincidental, but what can we do about it? On Hagger and the other girl, there's no evidence that anything untoward's happened, and, as you say, they're not the sort of girls whose disappearance is going to cause anyone any surprises.'

'I just wanted to run it by you. See what you thought.'

'And I appreciate you thinking of me. What I'd say is this. It's strange, but strange is all. Maybe you ought to keep your ear to the ground and see how things pan out, maybe have a few words with some of the street girls, but I wouldn't worry about it too much yet. There's plenty of other things to concern yourself with, and you shouldn't be thinking about them anyway. You ought to be in bed resting and getting yourself well so you can come back here and help us out.'

But I'd never be going back to help them out. I'd miss Malik, even if he had started calling me Dennis and dispensing advice just a little bit too readily. He was a good copper, though, and the thought that perhaps I had played a small part in getting him that way felt good. I told him he'd be doing me a favour if he could keep his ears open for any relevant developments among the King's Cross whores, and he told me he would. I thanked him, said that I'd see him shortly, promised him t I'd get to bed straight away and take it easy, then rang off.

But I didn't go to bed. Instead, I spent the rest of the day mulling over my plans and making preparations; occasionally phoning Danny's mobile, always without success; sometimes stopping to look out of the window at the iron-grey sky and pondering the fates of Molly Hagger and Anne Taylor; wondering what secrets Miriam Fox had taken to her grave.

And all the time something was bothering me, and I couldn't put my finger on what it was. Something I'd missed; something that flickered and danced round the recesses of my memory like the shadows of a flame, irritating me because it was important in some ill-defined way but I was unable to coax it out, however hard I tried.

And as darkness fell on my last night as a serving police officer, and the rain the forecasters had warned us about finally swept in from the west, I realized I was still just as ignorant of what had happened in the Miriam Fox murder case as I had been on the morning I'd first stared down at her bloodstained body.

29

I phoned a minicab to take me down to the Gallan Club, and it got me there at about a quarter to eight. It was raining steadily and, though not as cold as the previous night, there was still a bite in the air.

I'd never been to the Gallan before, even though it was only about half a mile from where I lived. I'd walked past it plenty of times though, most notably the previous day when they'd had a blackboard outside saying that tonight was contemporary poets night. It wasn't really my cup of tea, but I suppose it made a change from sitting around in the pub. It was quiz night at the Chinaman as well, and it would be the first time I'd missed it for non-work reasons for as long as I could remember.

The interior of the Gallan was small and dimly lit. The stage, empty when I walked in, was at the end furthest from the door, while the rest of the floor space was taken up by evenly clustered round tables. A bar on the left-hand side ran the length of the room. All of the tables were occupied, and a small crowd milled about the bar. Most of those present were the type of people you'd expect at a poetry evening where the headline act was someone called Maiden Faith Ararngard: fresh-faced students in long coats, sipping delicately at their beers; a group of eco-warriors with an overabundance of piercings and pantomime clothes; and a few older intellectual types who looked as though they spent every waking hour in the hunt for hidden meanings to pointless questions.

I'd half expected this type of line-up and had dressed down as far as my wardrobe would allow so that I didn't look too much out of place. It hadn't worked. Faded jeans and a sweatshirt with a hole in the elbow were never going to blend me in with this crowd, although at least I was pretty much guaranteed there'd be no undercover coppers in here. Like me, they'd have stuck out a mile.

Carla hadn't arrived, so I went to the bar and ordered a pint of Pride from a guy with a bolt through his nose and a beard that was close to a foot long. He gave me a bit of a funny look like I'd come dressed as a Doctor Who villain, but he was efficient, and that's always the most important trait for any bar-man. I paid for my drink and stood close to the door so that I could see Carla when she made her entrance.

I didn't feel particularly comfortable in there, and in a way that said something about her and me. She knew we were never going to be an item; it was me who found it difficult to accept. But accept it I was going to have to do. From tomorrow I was on the run. I had a false passport in my possession which I'd got from one of Len Runnion's contacts a few months back. It had been an insurance policy after a CIB investigation into a couple of ex-colleagues at the station had given me a case of cold feet. It was a good one, too. I'd grown a ten-day beard and put on some glasses for the photograph and it looked very unlike me. But I wasn't going to be able to use it yet. There'd be an all-ports alert out for me as soon as I broke cover, which would mean me having to lie low for a couple of weeks until the fuss had died down. Maybe I'd drive down to Cornwall or up to Scotland, somewhere a bit isolated. Not for the first time that day, I experienced a strangely exhilarating feeling of apprehension.

I was vaguely amused to see that the first act up was Norman 'Zeke' Drayer, a.k.a., apparently, the 'Bard of Somerstown'. Norman was dressed in a lincoln green jacket with tassles that looked as though it was made of felt, a pair of cricket whites, and knee-length black boots. Thankfully, he didn't have a hat with a feather in it on his head, or he'd have been a dead ringer for Robin Hood.

He danced onto the stage to polite applause and immediately opened up with a bawdy ballad about a buxom country girl called Annie McSilk and the difficulties she had fending off the advances of amorous farmers. It was actually quite good, and I had a few laughs in spite of myself, even if it did go on a bit too long. Unfortunately, it was also the high point of his act. The next three poems in his stint veered off into the boring half-Wworld of social justice and had me looking at the door every twenty seconds for any sign of Carla. By the time he danced off the stage, with theatrical bows all round, the applause had been all but drowned out by the buzz of individual conversations.

I was jealous of the people in there, jealous because they had nothing to fear. I watched them as they talked among themselves, discussing their issues as if they were of real importance, safe in their cocooned little worlds.

I felt a tap on the shoulder and turned round to see Carla

standing there. Her face was more heavily made up than usual, but the effect seemed to add to rather than detract from her beauty. She was dressed in a long black coat, underneath which was a simple white blouse and a pair of tight-fitting jeans. She greeted me with a brief peck on the cheek and I told her she looked good.

'Why, thank you, kind sir,' she replied with a faint half smile.

'What do you want to drink?'

'I could murder a vodka and orange.'

I got the attention of a barmaid, who came over and took the order.

'So, you're really going then, Dennis?' she said, when the barmaid had gone. 'You know, I really didn't think you'd have the bottle.'

'Appearances can be deceptive,' I told her. 'Any news on Anne?'

'Nothing yet, but one of the other girls said that she'd been seeing a new man, and apparently she'd talked about going off with him.'

'Really? Well, let's hope it's that then. Did you report it to the police?'

She nodded. 'I did. They didn't seem that interested.'

'Did you tell them about Molly?' She nodded again. 'And they still weren't interested?'

'They're street girls, Dennis. They do this sort of thing. You know, I don't know how you're going to handle not being a copper. You're just too interested in whatever's happening around you.'

'It'll do me good to get out of this place. Perhaps when I'm away from it, I won't worry about everything so much.'

She smiled. 'We'll see. You'll probably be back inside a month.'

'Somehow I don't think so.'

'Well, keep in touch, won't you? Send me postcards from your various destinations.'

'Of course I will.' I eyed her closely. 'You know, I don't want to sound too sickly about this, but I'm going to miss you. I think we could have done OK together.'

'Do you?' She returned my look. 'Maybe, but like I said, Dennis, now's just not a good time.'

I nodded. 'Fair enough. I'd better make the best use of tonight, then.'

'Make sure you do,' she said with a smile. 'My time doesn't come cheap.'

There wasn't a lot you could say to that.

A table came free on the other side of the room from the bar and we took it as the next act, a plain-looking girl with spindly legs called Jeanie O'Brien, came on. She was carrying a stool, which she sat on to face the audience.

'I know her,' Carla said. 'I've seen her perform before. She's good.'

She was too, but I wasn't really listening. Unfortunately, Carla was, which meant that the conversation was strained and pretty one-sided, with me doing most of the talking. I finished my beer quickly, wondering why on earth I'd risked everything by sticking around for one more night.

'Do you want another drink?' I asked her eventually.

She looked at her watch. 'One more. Then I've got to go.'

I was coming back towards our table with the drinks when I ran into the Bard of Somerstown himself. Drayer acknowledged me straight away and immediately looked nervous.

'Er, hello officer. How are you?'

I stopped in front of him. 'Not bad, Norman. A most distinguished performance out there earlier.'

'Oh, you saw it, did you? I' afraid it wasn't one of my best. What are you doing here anyway? Not that I mind, of course, but it just doesn't seem to be your sort of gig.'

'It isn't. Not really. But the lady I'm with—'

'Oh yeah. I saw you with her earlier.'

'Well, she's into poetry.'

He nodded vaguely. 'Oh yeah, nice.'

I looked over at our table. Carla was elegantly puffing on a Silk Cut, staring into space. At that moment she really did look like a high-class escort girl, aloof from the world around her. And I wondered then whether she felt anything for me at all, or whether she'd just bedded me because I'd been there at the time.

'I heard you arrested someone for Miriam's murder.'

'That's right.'

'Do you think it's him?'

How many times had I been asked that? As if I was going to say no. 'The evidence points that way,' I replied, but I wasn't really thinking about what I was saying. I was looking over his shoulder at Carla, and I was thinking. Turning stuff over and over in my mind.

'Because, you know, I was thinking, when I saw you earlier, that it was odd.'

I looked back at him. 'Odd?'

'Well, when I saw the woman you're with, I thought she looked familiar. And I tried to remember where I'd seen her before.'

'And? When have you seen her before?'

'Well, that's the funny thing. I wouldn't have remembered if I hadn't seen her with you just then.'

'Where did you see her, Norman?'

'In the hall outside my pad.'

I tried to keep the desperation out of my voice. 'When? When was that?'

'A couple of weeks back.'

'Before Miriam's murder?'

'Yeah, yeah. It would have been.'

'Why didn't you tell us this when we came round to visit you last week?'

He sensed my displeasure. 'Because, you know, well, you only seemed interested in what male visitors she'd had, and I couldn't even have told you if she'd been at Miriam's place or not. I just saw her and I thought she looked nice. And then I sort of forgot about it until tonight, when I saw her with you. There's no problem, is there?'

I shook my head, focusing my mind elsewhere. Putting together the final pieces. It was a while before I spoke. 'No. There's no problem.'

'Is there anything wrong, man? Are you OK?'

I nodded slowly, and looked away from him. 'Yeah, I'm fine. Just a bit tired, that's all.'

So Carla had been lying again. I should have known her story was bullshit, but maybe I'd been concentrating on too many other things to have seen the holes in it. I looked at her once again, and this time she looked back. I think she must have seen something in my face that told her I knew, because her eyes widened. Drayer turned round to follow my gaze and started to say something, but I wasn't taking any notice. Then Carla's eyes widened even further – she must have recognized him too.

I pushed past Drayer and strode up to the table, slamming the drinks down on it.

Carla stood up, the concern etched across her face. 'Look, I can explain. I didn't want you to know that I'd paid her—'

I grabbed her tightly by the arm and pulled her towards me. 'Dennis. You're hurting me.'

'You're fucking right I am. You've played me for a fool, Carla.'

'Let go of me,' she hissed, eyes narrowing. 'I admit it, I lied. I did meet her, but—'

'You didn't just meet her, did you? You killed her. Either that or you know exactly who did.'

'What on earth are you talking about?' Her expression was one of utter astonishment, but I wasn't falling for that one again.

'When we were talking this morning, you said to me you didn't want Anne Taylor to end up like Miriam Fox. Dead in a back alley with her throat cut. Those were your exact words. Remember?'

She tried to shake her arm free. 'I told you to let go—'

'But the only people who could possibly know that Miriam Fox had her throat cut were us – the police – and the murderer.'

'No, no, no.' She shook her head wildly. 'I don't know what you're talking about. You . . . you're accusing me of killing that girl. You bastard!' She yelled out these last two words, and people started turning round to look at us. Then, with her free hand, she reached down, picked up her drink, and chucked the contents of it in my face.

The alcohol stung, and I blinked rapidly, momentarily releasing my grip on her arm. Before I could recover, she pushed me back into one of the chairs, turned and stormed out.

But I wasn't letting her go that easily, not until I'd found out what had really happened. I stood back up, rubbing the stinging alcohol out of my eyes, and started after her, but I'd made only five paces when a big guy with thick dreadlocks stepped in front of me and blocked my path.

'All right, mate, leave her alone.'

'Out of my way. I'm a police officer!' I snapped, realizing as soon as the words were out that this was not the sort of venue to be declaring your links with the oppressive capitalist system.

'Well, fuck you, then,' he said evenly, and punched me on the side of the head.

I stumbled back while his rake-thin girlfriend grabbed hold of him and told him not to get himself into any trouble. He started telling her to leave him be, but he never finished the sentence because I came forward with my trusty little truncheon in hand and smacked him round the face with it. He went down hard, hitting the floor with a satisfying thud, and his girlfriend screamed. I kept walking, keeping my head down, making for the door, once again caught completely unawares by the speed and direction of events.

30

It was raining even harder when I got outside. I looked up and down the street but could see no sign of Carla. It was quiet out there tonight. The traffic was running smoothly and there didn't seem to be many people about. About fifty yards away I could make out a black cab waiting to turn right into a side street, and I wondered if she was inside it. I didn't bother trying to find out, knowing it would be gone long before I got there, and instead lit another cigarette and stood where I was, trying to take in what I'd just heard. She'd stitched me up perfectly. I'd genuinely thought there'd been a shared attraction when all the time her sole purpose had been to throw me off track. And it had worked, too. Far too easily.

There was a bus shelter across the road and I jogged over to it, fiddling around in my pocket for the mobile. When I reached the shelter I dialled Malik's home number. His wife answered after a couple of rings. I'd met her once or twice in the past, and when I came on the line she asked me how I was. I told her I was fine, but that it was urgent I talked to him. 'It's about a case we were working on.'

'I don't like him getting too many calls at home, Dennis. He works hard enough as it is.'

'I know, I know. I wouldn't ask if it wasn't important.'

Reluctantly, she went off to get Malik and he came on the phone a few seconds later.

I didn't beat about the bush. 'Carla Graham. You were right about her. She's a conniving, cynical bitch and she was involved in the Miriam Fox murder. I don't know how or why, but she's definitely involved. I think it might be something to do with blackmail. Drayer, that poet guy we met when we went round to Miriam's flats, he remembers seeing her—'

'Whoa, Dennis, slow down. What is this? When did you see Drayer?'

Out of the corner of my eye I saw two figures walking towards the bus shelter. They both had their heads down, which I thought was strange. They were ten yards away and walking purposefully.

'Just now. Two minutes ago.'

Eight yards. Seven yards. They both had their hands in the pockets of their long coats. Malik was talking into my ear. Suddenly I wasn't listening any more.

Six yards. One of them raised his head, and our eyes met. I knew straight away that he was here to kill me.

There was no time even to freeze with the fear that shot through me.

Keeping as casual a face as possible, and still clutching the phone to my ear, I turned slowly on my heels and then, without warning, broke into a manic sprint, the adrenalin coursing through me. I dropped the phone in my pocket as I ran, sneaking a rapid peek over my shoulder. My movement had caught them by surprise, but only for a second. One pulled a sawn-off shotgun, the other a revolver. They lifted them in my direction, still walking purposefully, not even breaking stride. And still only a matter of yards away.

I didn't think. I just didn't have time. Reflexively, I veered sharply right and began running across the road. A car was forced to brake suddenly, its tyres skidding on the slick tarmac. I heard the driver shouting something angry but unintelligible.

An explosion shattered the night air and something whistled past my head. I kept running, keeping low, trying to move in a zig-zag pattern to make it more difficult for them to hit me. More shots, this time from the revolver. Close. Far too close. Any second now and I was going to get a bullet between the shoulder blades.

I could hear them right behind me, charging after me across the street. I hit the pavement on the other side and ran, crouching, using parked cars for cover. The shotgun blasted its load again and a shower of glass from a rear windscreen sprayed the ground. There was no way I was going to outrun these boys. They knew it. I knew it. All I could do was to keep going. With my head down and my body straining forward, I continued down the pavement as fast as my legs would carry me, knowing that all this effort was probably going to be in vain but too desperate to care.

From somewhere in the direction of the Gallan club I heard a woman scream in terror as she saw what was happening. For a split second I imagined her standing horrified above my bullet-riddled corpse. At that moment I was so frightened I could have pissed my pants.

Then, without warning, I caught a glimse of a man in a suit running across the street in an effort to get between me and my pursuers. He was holding something up in his right hand. A warrant card. He must have been a member of my surveillance team.

'Police, police! Drop your weapons!'

He'd got onto the pavement behind me and was standing in front of the gunmen. Ahead of me, on the other side of the street, I could see his partner – a shorter, fatter guy who looked a few years older. I recognized him straight away as the guy at the bar in the Chinaman the previous night. The Coke drinker who never liked to talk politics. He was waiting to cross the road to apprehend me, but a car speeding down the street was holding him up.

'Police! Drop your weapons now!'

It was the tall one again, but his voice betrayed his desperation as he suddenly realized he'd almost certainly bitten off more than he could chew. I kept running, but briefly turned round. He was ten yards behind me and the gunmen had stopped in front of him. One was looking round him at me, and I could sense his urgent desire not to let his quarry disappear.

There was a second's silence. instinctively I slowed down as the drama played itself out. On the street cars were stopping to get a look at what was happening, allowing the other copper to cross. He ran towards me, but he too was watching his colleague. It looked like the whole street was.

The shotgun barked again, and the man who'd tried to prevent my execution flew backwards through the air. He seemed to hover above the ground for an indeterminate but memorable period of time before hurtling downwards with a crash, as if an invisible hand had tipped him out of its palm. He lay there, not moving.

His colleague froze. Still in the middle of the road. And then he put a hand to his mouth as the shock of what he'd just seen hit him. He tried to shout something, something that could give him some control over a chaotic situation, but nothing came out.

And before he'd even moved, my pursuers came after me again, the shotgun guy reloading and running at the same time. His friend with the handgun was ferociously quick. He came at me in huge bounds, reminding me bizarrely of one of the two-legged hunting dinosaurs in *Jurassic Park*, and there was a fixed, maniacal smile on his face. For a moment I felt like I was in some sort of slow-motion nightmare, that whatever I did, how-ever fast I moved, he was going to catch me. But I kept running, knowing there was no choice, not daring to look back as the shots cracked around me. And as I ran, my lungs and throat filled up with phlegm and I couldn't breathe. I knew I was just seconds away from the end.

There was a yelp and the sound of someone slipping, and I looked over my shoulder to see handgun man falling onto the wet ground, holding the gun up in the air. Relief didn't even cross my mind. The one with the shotgun was right behind him, and by now he'd reloaded. He jumped over his colleague, then stopped, lifted the weapon to his shoulder, and prepared to fire. Eight yards separated us. Even though I was still running, he couldn't miss.

Coming up on my left was a Chinese takeaway. It was my only chance. I flung myself forward onto the pavement at just the moment he pulled the trigger, taking it at a roll. The shot flew shrieking over my head and into the distance, and I was im-mediately back on my feet and charging at the takeaway door like a runaway bull. He fired again, but I'd already hit the door at a dive. It flew open and I fell inside, hitting the tiled floor elbow first, ignoring the pain that shot right up my arm.

I wanted to lie where I was for a couple of seconds and get my breath back, and it took a huge effort of willpower to force myself to my feet. I heard footsteps on the pavement outside and I knew that they were only seconds behind me. The lone customer in the place – a middle-aged man with a checked shirt and an expression of sheer dismay – stood watching me silently. Behind the counter, the young Chinese server, who couldn't have been a day over eighteen, looked just as confused by the whole situation.

I turned round as shotgun man appeared at the door. He levelled the weapon, the customer swore and fell back onto one of the chairs, and I charged the counter. The Chinese guy shrieked and dived out the way as I rolled over it like it was an assault course obstacle, crashing down the other side. The shotgun barked again and the glass covering the menu board above my head exploded into a hundred pieces that fell about me like jagged snowflakes as I wriggled maggot-like across the floor.

The door marked 'Private – Staff Only' was my only means of escape. I headbutted it open, crawling on my hands and knees, and desperately pushed my body through. I was in a small corridor leading through to the kitchens. Back in the shop, I could hear shouting and the sound of someone else coming over the worktop. I ran forward into the kitchens where half a dozen Chinese in chef's whites were busy at work. They all turned round as I charged in, and one jumped in front of me.

'No, no. Not allowed. No customers!'

I looked round desperately for an exit door, knowing I had seconds.

The chef, who just about came up to my chest, grabbed me by the lapels of my jacket. 'No customers! You must leave!'

He began pushing me backwards, and another younger chef armed with a wicked-looking meat cleaver started coming round the main worktop. I spotted the back door behind them in the corner. It was held slightly ajar by a piece of cardboard. I felt a surge of relief and panic in roughly equal measure.

Hearing the rapid footfalls in the corridor behind me, I screamed something incoherent and pushed the chef aside. He fell into a load of pots and pans and cried out. The other chef, the one with the cleaver, went to raise it above his head, and I thought momentarily that this would be a very stupid way to die, cut down by an irate kitchen worker while fleeing a professional assassination team.

I ripped the warrant card from my pocket, the last time I would ever use it. 'Police! I only want to get out! Get out of my way!' I charged past him, and he actually did get out of the way. There was a load of panicked shouting from all around me, and I knew that my pursuers were in the room.

I kicked the door open without pausing and ran out into the litter-strewn back yard as it slammed shut, rattling, behind me. A few yards ahead was a wall piled up with rubbish, facing on to the backs of terraced houses. I could have run for it but I didn't think I'd make it over before they put a hole in me. It was a time for hard decisions.

Resisting the temptation to bend over and throw up, I side-stepped and positioned myself by the door on the opposite side to the direction it would open, knowing that if I fucked this up then they would have me. No question. But there was little time for fear. Within a second, there was a commotion from inside the kitchens, more shouting – most of it foreign and unintelligible – and then the door flew open again and shotgun man came charging into view, automatically looking towards the wall ahead.

With a speed I didn't think I was capable of, I threw myself into him, grabbing the gun in the process. I shoved it upwards, pushing all my weight against his body, the power and surprise of my attack forcing him back so he blocked the doorway. At the same time, instinctively, reflexively, whatever you want to call it, he pulled the trigger, not having had the time to realize that the barrel had just been thrust into position right beneath his chin.

The noise was louder than anything I think I've ever heard in my life. It ripped through my ears and shook my whole body right down to the toes. A huge splash of blood soaked my face like warm, vile treacle as the top of his head was ripped away, its contents scattered high up the door and across the windows. He fell backwards, and I tugged the weapon from his grasp.

His partner was right behind him and he was forced to get out of the way as the corpse hit the floor. He looked down at the bloody head, then back at me, his face a mask of rage.

'Bastard!'

He raised the gun and I threw myself backwards as he fired, landing on my back on the paving slabs. He fired again, missing my head by inches, the bullet ricocheting up off the concrete. But I'd swung the shotgun round now so it was facing him, and finally it was my turn to pull the trigger.

I tried to balance it and take aim, but time was too short. The weapon kicked in my hand and a huge meaty chunk of his left leg just above the knee disappeared. The leg collapsed uselessly, and he collapsed with it, dropping the gun as all his efforts were put into howling in agony. He was still sitting upright when I got his head in my sights and pulled the trigger again.

But the weapon was empty.

The Chinese had gathered around the door and were looking down at the carnage with a mixture of fear, shock and morbid excitement on their faces. I was panting heavily, I was exhausted, but this wasn't over yet. In the distance, above the ringing in my ears, I could hear the sound of sirens converging on the scene from all directions, but it sounded as though they were still some way distant.

I got to my feet and waved the weapon at my audience. They all scuttled out of the way and I stepped forward, grabbed the wounded would-be assassin by his hair and dragged him outside, before picking up his gun and putting it in my pocket. I shut the door and turned to face him. His howls had now subsided into heavy, desperate breathing interspersed with little shrieks of pain through clenched teeth. He was holding onto the huge wound with both hands in a vain attempt to stem the copious flow of blood.

I leaned down. 'Who sent you?' I hissed, between pants. 'Who sent you?'

He looked Mediterranean, Turkish perhaps, and I put him in his early thirties. He could easily have been the guy who'd spooked Danny. Probably was. He could even be the man who'd killed him. Because, by now, I was sure he was dead.

He didn't answer. He didn't even look at me. In the distance, the sirens were getting louder and more numerous. Time was running short. I hit his hands with the butt of the shotgun, forcing him to release his grip on the wound. As he did so, I thrust my hand into the torn flesh and scraped my fingernails along it. His scream would have deafened me under normal circumstances, but I was partially deaf anyway.

'Who sent you?'

'No speak English,' he whimpered, shaking his head. 'No speak English.'

This time I slammed the butt into the wound, and when he put his hands on it instinctively, I slammed it into them too. He was screaming, so now I cracked him in the face to shut him up, cutting his lips. Blood spewed down his chin.

'Who the fuck sent you? Tell me! Now! Who?' I grabbed him

by the hair again and snapped his head back so he was looking me right in the eye.

I think he saw the ruthlessness in my expression and realized there was no point delaying any further, even though the sirens were coming in from all sides. 'Mehmet Illan,' he whispered.

'Who?'

'Mehmet Illan.'

'Who the fuck is he?'

Before he could answer, there was the sound of footsteps from inside the kitchen and I heard someone running through. I took a step back and raised the butt so that it was level with my head. This time, as the door opened, Coke Drinker emerged, panting into the darkness and right into my line of fire. I heard one of the Chinese staff shout 'Look out!' in a high-pitched, dramatic voice, but it was way too late for that. I hit him full on in the face with the butt, demolishing his nose like soft fudge and scattering flecks of blood across both cheeks. He went down on both knees, hands covering his injured face, and I knew he was no longer any problem. There were other voices coming from the street, shouting, giving orders. Coppers' voices, doing what they do best: bringing situations under control.

Still packed with adrenalin, I dropped the shotgun, turned, and ran for the wall, vaulting up onto it in one less-than-graceful movement before manoeuvring myself over. I slid down the other side and landed in more sacks of rubbish. I was now in someone's ill-kept back garden. There was an alley running down the side of the adjoining house, so I clambered over the rickety wooden fence separating the two gardens and followed it, emerging on the next street. I crossed it straight away, then began jogging in the opposite direction to the Gallan, trying to wipe the blood from my face.

I heard a police car approaching behind me so I

darted into another sidestreet and kept running. The car continued on, missing me, and I kept going, trying to put as much distance between myself and the carnage as possible.

But exhaustion was taking hold. I had a stitch in my right side and I was having difficulty breathing. My legs felt as though they were going to go under me at any moment, and the only thing keeping me going was the fear of getting caught.

And the desire for revenge. One way or another the people who were trying to fuck me up and put me out of existence were going to pay for their crimes. I wasn't going to die that fucking easily.

Another hundred yards, another hundred and fifty, and then I could run no more. I half jogged, half staggered into a dingy-looking back alley by the side of a school and found a spot out of sight of the road. I sat down against the wall and panted my breath back to normal – a task that seemed to take for ever. Above my head, the clouds unloaded their rain on the city. Slowly, the sirens faded away.

The desire for revenge. It was the only thing I had left in the world.

Part Four

THE BUSINESS OF DYING

31

I could have walked away from the whole thing. Gone underground, waited a few months, then left the country. That was
basically what I'd intended to do, but, in the end, I felt that I
couldn't leave things as they were. Questions needed answering,
and scores needed settling. It was as simple as that. Everyone had
fucked me up: my bosses at work, Raymond Keen, and now even
Carla Graham.

Carla Graham. That she was somehow involved in the murder
of Miriam Fox was no longer in doubt. It was almost certainly
not her who'd pulled the knife across her throat, not given the
size and depth of the wound. But she definitely knew who'd done
it. And why. It was her motive for being involved that intrigued
me the most because for the life of me I couldn't understand
what it could be. She was right about the blackmail plot – it just
didn't seem enough to kill someone for. And what about the
evidence against Mark Wells? Were he and Carla in it together?
It was difficult to conclude otherwise, given the evidence against
him, and yet it made no sense. Neither could I understand why
he'd gone round to Miriam's flat after the murder and been

genuinely shocked to discover police officers there. If he'd been the killer, surely he'd have expected that and avoided the place?

I was still in the dark, and I didn't like it. I should have cut my losses, but I guess I'd simply hit the point where everything had gone so far downhill that I no longer cared what happened, as long as I got the chance to get even with the people who'd been pulling the wool over my eyes through all this.

That night, after getting my breath back and wiping the worst of the blood off my face, I hurried home through the back streets and threw on a single set of new clothes, before hailing a cab on City Road and getting it to take me to Liverpool Street station. From there, I got on the Underground and took the Central Line right back across town to Lancaster Gate, before making my way to Bayswater using a combination of walking and the bus.

It was five to eleven by the time I arrived at the hotel where I kept the safety deposit box. I knew the owner vaguely from my previous visits, and he was at the desk in the cramped foyer when I walked in, smoking a foul-smelling cigarette and watching football on a portable TV. He nodded as I approached, and I told him I wanted a room. Without taking his eyes off the TV he leaned over, removed a key from one of the numbered hooks on the wall behind him, and put it down on the desk.

'Twenty pounds per night,' he said, in a thick foreign accent. 'Plus twenty deposit.'

I told him I wanted to book for three nights and counted out four twenties. He took the money, again without taking his eyes from the TV. 'Up the stairs to the third floor. It's on the right.' One of the teams scored and the commentator shouted excitedly in Arabic or Turkish, or something like that, but the owner didn't bat an eyelid. I assumed he supported the other side.

The room was small and horrifically done out in 1970s style orange and purple, but it looked clean, and that was good enough for me. It was private, too. I wouldn't draw attention to myself staying here, where the remainder of the occupants were almost certainly going to be newly arrived illegal immigrants and asylum seekers, and where the owner probably wouldn't go voluntarily to the police about anything.

I threw off my clothes and lay down on the bed, lighting a cigarette and taking a deep breath. The chase was on now, but the police were still in a difficult position. They couldn't just print my photo in the next day's papers. It might have been pretty obvious that I had been involved in the Traveller's Rest killings, but they still couldn't be absolutely sure that I didn't have an alibi for the night in question. For all anyone knew, I could have had a mistress up in Clavering I'd been seeing on the sly; I could have been with her on the night in question. And maybe it was simply coincidence that the killer looked so much like me. For the first, and probably the last, time in my life I actually gave thanks to those who had drafted the laws of our great country for making them so obviously in favour of the criminal. They needed hard evidence against me, and maybe at the moment they just didn't have enough. They'd be pulling out all the stops to find me, but they'd still be doing it with one hand tied behind their backs. For that reason, and that reason alone, I still felt there was hope of evading capture.

I finished the cigarette and lay there for a long time, staring at the ceiling and wondering where I was going to be in a year's time. Or even a week's. Out in the hallway a door slammed and I heard a lot of shouting in a foreign language. A man and a woman were arguing. It lasted about two minutes, then there was the sound of someone running down the stairs. I picked up the mobile and wondered whether it was worth trying Danny again. I decided against it. Somehow I knew he wouldn't answer.

I sighed. Somewhere out there, Raymond Keen was relaxing,

enjoying the fruits of his success. Some time soon he'd find out that the attempt on my life had failed, which was going to be more than a little inconvenient.

And some time after that he'd find out that he'd made a big mistake trying to silence me.

32

I left the hotel at just after eight o'clock the following morning, dressed in the clothes I'd changed into the previous night, and took a walk in the direction of Hyde Park. It was a brisk morning and a watery sun was fighting to push its way through the thin cloud cover. I stopped for breakfast and coffee at a cafe on the Bayswater Road and took the opportunity to take a look at the papers.

The shooting incident at the Gallan was front-page news, as I'd expected. However, at the time of going to press, details were still fairly limited. They'd named the dead police officer as Detective Constable David Carrick, aged twenty-nine, but the man I'd despatched remained anonymous. I wondered if they'd ever find out who he was. The report confirmed that a third man had suffered gunshot wounds at the scene and was now under police guard in hospital, where his condition was described as serious but not life-threatening. For the most part, the story revolved around the drama of the shoot-out, with the inevitable witness reports, but it was clear its authors didn't have any real idea what it had been all about. There was a quote from one of the Met's assistant chief constables saying that gun crime, though on the rise, was under control in London, although I don't suppose many of the readers believed him. The paper's leader column assumed that drugs had been the motive behind the shooting and claimed that the government was going to have to do something radical to quell demand among the nation's youth. Which was a sensible enough viewpoint, even if it remained to be seen whether drugs had actually been the motive in this case. Whatever Raymond and his associate, Mehmet Illan, were involved in was still a mystery. The only thing I could say for sure was that it was both illegal and highly profitable, drugs, I suppose, was as good a guess as any.

When I'd finished eating and reading, I carried on down the Bayswater Road in the direction of Marble Arch and stopped when I found a phone box just off the main thoroughfare. I wasn't sure how Malik would react to my call – badly, probably – but he was in a better position than me to do something about the Miriam Fox case.

He answered his mobile after one ring. 'DS Malik.'

'Asif, it's me. Can you talk?'

There was a short silence.

'About my call last night—'

'Look, what the hell's going on, Sarge? The word is you're involved in a lot of very bad stuff, that you had something to do with the shooting last night. A police officer got killed—'

'I won't piss you about, Asif. I've had some problems. I've got into bed with a few of the wrong people—'

'Oh shit, Sarge. You of all people. Why the fuck did it have to be you?' He sounded genuinely hurt.

'It's not what you think.'

'Isn't it? They told us this morning that you're a strong suspect in the Traveller's Rest killings. Is that why you were so interested in how the investigation was going?'

'Oh, for Christ's sake, Asif. It's me you're talking to. The man you've worked with for four years. Do you really believe I'm a triple murderer?' I was conscious that there were probably people listening in to this call and they would be trying to trace its source urgently.

'So what were you doing up there that night? They said you were stopped at a roadblock near the scene.'

'I was stopped, but I was on the way back from Clavering. I've got a woman up there, someone I see occasionally.'

'You've never told me about her.'

'She's married. You wouldn't have approved. But that's not what I'm phoning about. Believe what you want to believe, there's nothing I can do about that. But I want you to investigate Carla Graham. She's definitely involved in the Miriam Fox killing and maybe those other disappearances I was telling you about as well.'

'How do you know?' He was trying to keep me talking, there was no doubt about that.

'I just do. She knew things only someone involved could know, and that's definite. All I'm asking is that you put some tabs on her, check her background. Maybe even lean on Wells some more.'

'We can't. He's been charged.'

I exhaled loudly. 'Just look into her background. That's all I'm asking.'

'All right, I'll see what I can do.' There was a short pause. 'What were those men after you for last night?'

'Because I made a mistake. I got involved in something I shouldn't have, and now they want to make me pay the price.'

'I never took you to be corrupt, Sarge . . . Dennis. hat the hell made you think you could get away with it?'

I ignored the question. 'I'm sorry. I truly am.' I wanted to say something else, but I didn't know what, and I didn't have the time anyway. He started to repeat the question but I hung up, sad that now even he was against me. But not really that surprised.

I jogged across the road and into Hyde Park, feeling like a pariah. I didn't think they'd had time to get a trace on me, but there was no point hanging around to get proved wrong, so I made my way slowly back to Bayswater, figuring that my next move was to buy some clothes and a toothbrush.

33

As the day wore on, I couldn't help thinking that Carla Graham was going to get away with her role in the murder of Miriam Fox. Malik hadn't seemed overly interested in what I had to say: even if he did believe me, there was no way Knox or Capper or anyone else was going to act on it. In the end, what was there to act on? Just the word of a disgraced police officer who was now on the run.

It bothered me that justice wouldn't be done. I suppose you could say that justice is rarely done in this world and that the vast majority of people don't get the fate they deserve, but that would be missing the point. I knew Carla Graham had done wrong and I wanted her to be called to account for it. I also wanted to find out whether she could shed any light on what had happened to Molly Hagger and Anne Taylor. I was pretty certain by now that Molly was dead and it was important to me to find out why and how. And who it was who'd killed her. It would, I thought, be a chance to atone for my many sins. Even if no-one ever realized that I'd solved the case and punished the perpetrators, at least I would have the satisfaction of having redeemed myself in my own eyes. Which was a lot better than nothing.

It wasn't going to be easy to get Carla to talk voluntarily. I knew that. Knowing her, she'd already have some story concocted as to how she'd found out about the manner of Miriam Fox's death – she was obviously pretty creative in that department – and would be fully aware that one verbal slip-up on her part to a man who'd just resigned from the police force was not exactly going to do a great deal to build a criminal case against her. But get her to talk I would. Carla Graham was a tough cookie who'd be able to withstand some pretty rigorous questioning, but this time it wouldn't do her any good. I would be visiting her in a very unofficial capacity. And with nothing to lose.

By four o'clock that afternoon, I'd decided on my strategy. At ten past, I found a callbox in Kensington, phoned the *North London Echo*, asking to speak to Roy Shelley. I went on hold to the sound of Marvin Gaye's 'Heard it Through the Grapevine', and it was about a minute before he finally came on the line.

'Dennis Milne. Fuck me, I haven't heard from you in a while. What do you want? Renew your subscription?'

'No, I might have something for you. Something that'll sell a lot of papers.'

'Oh yeah?'

'But I need something from you first.'

'You're not pissing me about are, you, Dennis? No disrespect, but I don't want to waste my time here. There's talk of redundancies at this place at the moment and I don't want to be first in the queue.'

'You'll be last in the queue if you run this story, Roy. It's big stuff, I promise you. The sort of stuff the nationals love.'

I could almost hear his interest cranking up at the other end. I'd known Roy Shelley a long time. He was what you'd call an old-school reporter. A pisshead who could sniff out information faster than any copper I knew.

'Can you give us a little snifter?' he asked. 'Just so I've got some sort of idea what to expect.'

'Not yet, but I promise you it'll be one hell of a lot better than you can imagine. It might even turn out to be the story of your career. But, like I said, I need something from you first.'

'What?' His tone was suspicious.

'Does the name Mehmet Illan mean anything to you?'

He thought about it for a moment. 'No. Should it?'

'I don't know. But can you do me a favour and find out anything you can about him. He's Turkish, I think.'

'Well, he would be with a name like that.'

'I would imagine he's based somewhere in North London, and he's definitely involved in a lot of dodgy dealing.'

'What kind of dodgy dealing?'

'I'm not a hundred per cent sure, but I think, if you ask around enough, you'll find people who know him. But try to be discreet.'

'And is this guy part of the story you've got?'

'He's a part of it, yes. But just a part. There's a lot more besides. How soon can you get me the info on him?'

'It could take a day or two.'

'Too long, Roy. I need it fast. The sooner I get it, the sooner you get your story.'

'Dennis, I don't even know who the bloke is.'

'Yeah, but you can find out. That's why I called you. I'm uncontactable at the moment, but I'll call you back at ten a.m.

tomorrow. If you can get me the gen by then, I'd appreciate it.'

'This'd better be a good story, Dennis.'

'It is. I promise you. And something else too.'

'What?'

'Whatever you do, don't tell anyone I called. And don't make any attempt to get hold of me either. I can't explain why at the moment, but all will be revealed very shortly.'

'Christ Almighty, you're sounding like a fucking Robert Ludlum book. At least give me a sniff of what's going on.'

'Roy, if I could, I would. But I can't. Not for a day or two anyway. Just be patient. It'll be worth it.'

He started to ask another question, but I said my goodbyes and hung up.

After that, I made another phone call, but the person I was after wasn't in. No matter. It could wait.

I stepped out of the phone box and hailed a passing black cab. I got him to drop me off halfway up Upper Street, paid him his money, and went to pick up my car, which was parked on an adjoining street a couple of hundred yards up from my flat. I knew they'd be looking out for me on the off chance that I was stupid enough to return home, but they'd only have a couple of people watching the place, and my car was parked far enough away to avoid getting spotted. I was relieved to see that it was exactly where I'd left it more than a week earlier, which for London isn't too bad. It started first time, too. Maybe my luck was changing.

My first port of call was Camden Town. After hunting around for what seemed like a long time, I found a free meter on a residential street and then made my way over to Camden High Street to get my bearings before heading in the direction of Coleman House. I passed the pub where I'd first had a drink with Carla only a week earlier and, after hesitating for a moment, went inside. At this time in the afternoon it was still quite quiet, with only a sprinkling of students, old codgers, and the unemployable dotted about the place. That would all change in half an hour when the after-work crowd started to pour in.

I ordered a pint of Pride from the bar and asked the barman where the payphone was. He told me it was in the corridor leading to the toilets. There was no-one around when I walked in, so I dialled Coleman House reception.

'Carla Graham, please,' I asked in as official a voice as I could muster.

'She's not here at the moment,' said the voice at the other end, a woman whose tones I didn't recognize. 'Can I ask who's calling, please?'

'Frank Black. Black's Office Supplies. I'm actually returning her call. She was interested in some prices.'

'Can I put you through to her assistant, Sara?'

'Well, it's actually Miss Graham I need to speak to. Do you know when she's back?'

'I'm afraid she won't be in until tomorrow now. She's at a seminar this afternoon.'

I said I'd phone back, and hung up. After that, I tried Len Runnion's number again, but there was still no answer.

I went back into the bar, took a stool facing the wall near the door, and drank my drink. A mirror stretched right around the wall at head height, and my reflection stared back at me mournfully. I looked a mess, mainly because I hadn't shaved that day, which was deliberate. I was growing a beard now, in keeping with my passport photo. I was also going to have to fatten up a bit. I'd been at least half a stone heavier in the photo, and to be on the safe side I wanted to add another half stone on top of that. I'd had a McDonald's for lunch, which had been a good start, but I was going to have to have a similarly fatty supper for it to have any effect. From now on I was on a diet of greasy, bad food in large quantities until further notice. And I'd probably be one of the first people in the world to actually benefit from it.

I felt like I needed Dutch courage for what I was about to do, so I ordered another pint and drank that with a couple of cigarettes and a bag of cheese and onion crisps I didn't want but felt sure I ought to have. By the time I'd finished it, the predicted after-work crowd had materialized and the bar was three deep with loud, suited individuals and young secretaries out for a good time. The clock above the bar told me it was twenty past five.

Outside, darkness had long since fallen and the streets were crowded with commuters and early Christmas shoppers. The day after tomorrow would be the first of December. The year had gone fast, as they always seem to do. This time, however, I'd be glad when it had been and gone. Memorable it might turn out to be, but for all the wrong reasons.

By the time I got back to the car it had started raining. I jumped in and fought my way through the crawling rush-hour traffic, hoping that I got to Carla's flat before she did. My plan was to wait outside until she arrived, then apprehend her at the door. I'd try to get inside through charm alone – I didn't want to cause a scene – but if she didn't want to play ball, I'd pull the gun I'd taken ownership of the previous night. I didn't think she'd argue with that. After that, I'd play it by ear.

But the traffic was a lot worse than I'd expected and I wasn't totally sure of my bearings, so it was well gone six when I pulled into Carla's cul-de-sac. I managed to squeeze into a parking space about twenty yards down from her building and cut the engine. I could make out her flat through the outstretched skeletal branches of a beech tree. There were several lights on. So she was home.

I cursed silently. I should have got there earlier rather than dawdled over my pints. Now it was going to be difficult to get inside. I lit a cigarette and weighed up my options. I didn't think she'd let me in if I rang on her buzzer. We'd hardly left on the best of terms, and she had no reason to talk to me. What was I going to say? That I wanted to come up and accuse her of murder for a second time? Breaking in was another option, but I remembered the building's security system being fairly elaborate. The door had been new and the lock was a five-bar. I didn't think my housebreaking skills stretched to that, not without equipment.

Which meant waiting for an opportunity to present itself. I finished the cigarette, took a swig from a bottle of Coke I'd brought with me, and lit another cigarette, wondering what I was going to do when and if she admitted her part in the whole thing. I could hardly make a citizen's arrest, not in my position, and I didn't think I had the stomach to kill her in cold blood. Which kind of cut down my options. Yet somehow I still felt that I was doing the right thing by coming here. I had to get to the bottom of this before I could continue with my life.

I think I'd been there about ten minutes, maybe a bit less, when a car drove into the cul-de-sac looking for a parking space. I slid down in my seat, not wanting to draw attention to myself, and the car continued past. When it got to the end it made a torturously slow U-turn in the limited space available and drove back out again. About a minute later, I saw the driver, a middle-aged businessman, walk past on Carla's side of the road. He stopped when he came to Carla's building and fished about in his coat pocket for his keys.

I stepped out of the car and crossed the street as casually as possible, coming up behind him as he was mounting the steps. He heard my footfalls and whirled round, his face etched with the automatic fear city dwellers always experience when someone approaches them from behind at night. His expression eased a bit when he saw it was a man in a shirt and tie, but remained suspicious nevertheless.

'Yes. Can I help you?'

I pulled out my warrant card and showed it to him. 'I'm here to see Miss Carla Graham,' I said authoritatively, looking him right in the eye. 'I understand she lives on the top floor.'

He put his key in the door. 'That's right. Well, you'd better buzz her—'

'I'd rather she didn't know who it was, sir. You see, I'm not one hundred per cent sure she'll want to speak to us.'

He looked at me curiously but decided in the end that I was probably who I said I was, and turned the key in the lock. 'I assume you know where to go,' he said, as I followed him inside.

'Yes, I do. Thanks.'

'Sorry to seem suspicious, but you know what it's like.'

'Dead right. You can never be too careful these days.'

He moved off down the hall and I made my way up the stairs, remembering back to that night just three days ago when I'd walked up them the first time. A lot had changed since then.

When I got up to the third floor, I stopped outside her door and listened carefully. The television was on with the volume turned up high. It sounded as though it was switched to the news. I pressed my ear against the door and tried to pick out any other sounds, but couldn't hear anything.

I reached down and tried the handle, but it wouldn't give. The door was locked, so I leaned down and checked the lock itself. It was an easy one. Reaching into my pocket, I pulled a credit card from my wallet and manoeuvred it into the tiny gap between the door and skirting. The lock gave without resistance, and slowly I turned the handle.

I stepped into the hallway and gently eased the door closed

behind me, putting the chain across it to delay her if she tried to make a getaway. There were no lights on in the hallway itself but the sitting-room door on my left was open, providing some light. I stopped and listened again. Nothing. Not a sound.

Making as little noise as possible, I slowly put my head round the sitting-room door.

The room was empty. In the corner, the TV blared as a news reporter in some dusty war-torn location gave a dramatic run-down on whatever conflict it was he was covering. A half-drunk cup of coffee sat on the teak coffee table, and next to it was an ashtray with two butts in it. I waited a moment, then, still hearing no sound from anywhere in the flat, walked inside. I leaned over and dipped my finger in the coffee. It was cool, but not cold. Maybe half an hour old. No more than that.

I retreated back into the hallway. Immediately to my right was the kitchen. The door was half closed but the light was on inside. I pushed it open and had a quick look but, like the sitting room, it too was empty. That only left two rooms, one of which was the bathroom, right opposite me at the end of the hall. Its door was wide open. I crept up, paused for a moment, then reached round and pulled on the light.

Empty.

Which left the bedroom.

I assumed she must have gone out for something; either that or she'd taken a very early night. It didn't matter. I could wait for her easily enough. I didn't suppose she was having a romantic tryst in there, otherwise I'd have been able to hear her. Carla was not a woman who could enjoy a quiet fuck.

I stepped forward and listened briefly at the door. Again, just silence.

Slowly, ever so slowly, I turned the handle. The door creaked open.

It was pitch black. Even without looking, I could tell the curtains were closed. I stepped inside, waited a moment, then reached for the light switch, trying to remember which side of the door it was on. Again, no sound. No sound at all.

I picked the right side, found the switch, and flicked it on. It seemed very bright and I blinked rapidly as my eyes refocused.

It took me two, maybe three seconds to see the huge dark stain that spread high up the wall behind her kingsize bed. Beneath it, lying face forward on the heavily bloodstained sheets at a slightly skewed angle from the wall and with its arms and legs spread wide, lay the fully clothed corpse of Carla Graham. She was wearing a white blouse, whole swathes of which were now crimson, black trousers and socks. One of her bedside lamps had fallen off its perch and now lay on its side on the floor, the only obvious sign of a struggle, and her hands were gripping onto great clumps of the sheets. There was a vague, airless smell in the room but nothing like as pungent as the stench in the funeral home after Raymond had murdered Barry Finn.

I stepped forward, still finding it difficult to believe what I was seeing, and gingerly approached the body. I didn't want to touch it, not without gloves on, but I wanted to check that she was actually dead, although with that much blood it was difficult to believe she could be anything but.

Her eyes were open. Wide. Terrified. But still beautiful some-how, even in death. We could have been something. We really could have. At that moment, I felt a bitter regret that it had come to this.

The gaping wound in her throat was partly obscured by her hair, but I could see that it was very deep and very wide ... similar to the one that had ended Miriam Fox's life. Out of the corner of my eye, I watched a droplet of blood ease slowly down the wall. I looked back down at Carla's throat. The blood was still oozing out of the wound, though its flow was now down to a trickle.

She had died only a short while before. A very short while. Ten, fifteen minutes. No longer than that. The blood hadn't even coagulated yet. I'd been outside for about ten minutes, sitting in the car. No-one had left the building in that time. It had taken me five minutes to get up the stairs, give the flat the once-over, and come into the room where I stood now. That was fifteen minutes in total. In my estimation, she'd almost certainly been alive fifteen minutes ago.

Which meant only one thing.

I heard the movement behind me and whirled round at just the second the knife came flashing through the air in a great arc, still dripping with Carla's blood. I jumped backwards and banged into the bedside table. The blade swished past perilously close to my skin, almost touching it, only an inch separating me from certain evisceration.

My attacker was a big man, well over six feet with a build to match. He had a black baseball cap pulled low over his face, but I could make out the look of steely determination beneath it. There was no way he was going to let me live. Not now I'd seen him.

He stumbled slightly with the momentum of his swing and I jumped forward, grabbing him by both wrists and kicking him as hard as I could in the shins. He flinched with pain but maintained his balance, and pushed me back against the table, at the same time twisting his way out of my grip.

Now he had both hands free again, and he brought the knife up in a rapid thrust aimed at my belly, but I leaped aside, landing on my back on the bed, my head resting on Carla's still warm corpse. I could feel the blood-drenched sheets wet against my body. I tried to kick out as he lifted the huge knife above his head but his legs were pressed up tight against mine, making movement next to impossible.

He brought the knife down hard, but I wriggled violently and grabbed his arm with both hands, pushing it to one side and banging it against the wall with all the strength I could muster. He didn't release his grip. Instead, with his free hand he punched me hard in the face and I felt a terrible pain shoot through my cheek. He punched me again, a triumphant look in his eyes, and my vision began to blur.

Then, suddenly changing tactics, he stopped punching me and reached over to grab the knife from his other hand, which I had pinned against the wall. In doing so, he relaxed the pressure on my legs, and before he had a chance to stab at me again I kicked out wildly, cracking him in the knee with the heel of my new brogues. He jumped backwards out of range of my feet and his cap flew off, revealing a thick head of unkempt hair. The loss of it appeared to distract him momentarily, like Samson losing his locks, and I took the opportunity to roll across the bed, forcing myself over Carla's slick, greasy body.

I seemed to roll for ages before finally crashing down the other side. I could hear my attacker coming round the front of the bed, and I desperately hunted through the pockets of my coat for the gun I'd taken the previous night. I got a grip on the handle and tried to tug it out, but it snagged on the material. He was coming into full view, replacing the black cap on his head, the knife held wickedly aloft. Only feet away. I felt the material around my pocket tear. I pulled again, desperately trying to get it out, panic threatening to fuck up everything.

Suddenly the handle came free and I whipped the gun out, pointing the barrel at my assailant. He saw it and stopped dead, then made a split-second decision turn and run for the door. I located the safety catch, flicked it round, then sat up and took aim. He was almost through the door but I managed to get off a shot. It went wide and high, hitting the upper door frame. He kept going, disappearing from view, and I jumped to my feet and started out after him.

When I came out into the hallway he was at the front door, fiddling with the chain. He turned, saw me, gave me one last defiant look, and pulled it open. I fired again as he started down the stairs, but again the bullet went wide and high. It was no wonder the Turk hadn't been able to hit me the previous night. The sights on this gun were so out of kilter I'd have had to aim at the ceiling to get any chance of actually putting a hole in my target.

I could hear his heavy footfalls on the stairs, taking them two at a time. There was no way I was going to catch him now. I stopped where I was, panting with exhaustion and shock. That had been close. Far too close for comfort. That made two attempts on my life in twenty-four hours, neither of which had been that far from success. So far I'd emerged unscathed, but it was only a matter of time before my luck ran out.

And now I was never going to get any answers from Carla Graham.

But her killer would know them. And luckily for me I knew him. Or knew his name, anyway.

There's a true story that goes like this. A thirty-two-year-old man once kidnapped and repeatedly raped a ten-year-old girl. He took her back to his dingy flat, tied her to a bed and subjected her to a prolonged and sickening sexual assault. He might have killed her too, apparently he'd boasted in the past of wanting to murder young girls for a thrill, but a neighbour heard the girl's screams and called the cops. They turned up, kicked the door down, and nicked him. Unfortunately, he later got off on a technicality and the girl's father ended up behind bars, and later under the ground, for trying to extract his own justice. I remembered the case because an ex-colleague of mine had worked on it. It had been two years ago now.

The rapist's name was Alan Kover, and he was the man who'd just tried to put a knife in me.

There were more footsteps on the stairs, this time coming up. I placed the gun back in my pocket and walked over to the front door. As I was shutting it behind me, the guy who'd let me in emerged from round the corner. He was carrying a heavy-looking torch that I think was his best effort at a weapon, and wearing a very concerned expression.

'What's going on?' he asked. 'I've just seen a man with a knife come charging down the stairs.'

I started down towards him. 'Call the police,' I said.

'But I thought *you* were the police.'

'Not any more I'm not.'

'Then who the hell are you?'

I pushed past him without stopping. 'Someone who hopes good luck comes in threes.'

34

'Mehmet Illan. Forty-five years old. Turkish national, he's been resident in this country for the last sixteen years. He's supposedly just a businessman, but apparently he's got previous convictions in Turkey and Germany for drugs offences, though no record here. He's got a number of companies on the go doing all sorts: import/export – mainly foodstuffs and carpets; a chain of pizza parlours; a PC wholesalers; a textile factory. You name it, he's got an interest in it somewhere down the line. But the word is that a lot of his companies are just fronts for money laundering, and that his real profits come from elsewhere.'

'Oh yeah? Where?'

'Apparently he used to import a lot of heroin overland from Turkey and Afghanistan, although no-one's got any hard evidence of that, but now he's in the people-smuggling business. You know, asylum seekers.'

'I hear there's big money to be made in that sort of thing.'

'Very big. These people come from all over the place and they'll sell everything they've got to get the money to pay the smugglers. The going rate can be as much as five grand per person, so one lorryload of twenty people can be worth a hundred K to the people doing the smuggling. If they only shift a hundred a week, they're still clearing half a million, and chances are they'll be shifting a lot more than that. It could be thousands.'

'And you think this guy Illan's involved in that?'

'That's what I'm hearing. My information says he's a major player, but he's done a good job of keeping himself as far away from the action as possible, so no-one's got anything concrete on him. What's your interest in him anyway?'

'I might have got something on him. You'll hear about it before the end of the week. You'll be the first to know.'

'Whatever it is, be careful, Dennis. This guy is not to be messed with. You know those three blokes shot dead the other week – the customs men and the accountant . . . ?'

'Yeah?'

'The accountant was something to do with one of his front companies, and the talk is that Illan was the guy behind the murders, although proving it's another matter. So, he doesn't fuck about. You piss him off, you die. If he's prepared to commit triple murder, he's prepared to kill a copper.'

'Don't worry, I'm not going to do anything stupid.'

'So if you didn't know anything about this guy – and I assume you didn't otherwise you wouldn't have been phoning me – what is it exactly you've got on him?'

'Be patient, Roy.'

'Patience doesn't sell newspapers, you know that.'

I put some more money in the phone, knowing that I was going to have to give him something.

'I think I can prove a link between him, some other criminals, and the deaths of those three blokes.'

I could hear his breathing change at the other end. He was excited, but nervous at the same time in case I was bullshitting.

'Are you serious?'

'Deadly.'

'So, why are you telling me? Why aren't you arresting these people?'

'It's a long story, Roy, but basically you're going to have to trust me.'

He sighed. 'I knew it was too good to be true.'

'I've resigned from the Force,' I told him. 'There were a couple of minor irregularities. It was with immediate effect. That's why I haven't arrested anyone yet.'

'Christ, Dennis. Really? What did you do?'

'Suffice to say I've had some involvement with people who know Mehmet Illan. Not major involvement, but enough to get me sacked. And enough for me to know a few things about them.'

'Tell me more.'

'Not now. I need you to do something else for me. It shouldn't take five minutes.'

'What is it?'

'Alan Kover. Remember him?'

'The name rings a bell.'

'He was that child rapist who got off on a technicality. The girl's father got arrested trying to burn his flat down and ended up committing suicide. It was about two years back, over in Hackney.'

'Yeah, yeah, I remember.'

'Kover's still walking the streets and I need to find him. Urgently.'

'Is he involved in this?'

I decided to lie. It was easier. 'He might be, I'm not sure. Can you get me his current address?'

'Dennis, you're asking me to do a lot here. This sort of stuff could get me in one fuck of a lot of trouble. What the hell are you going to do to him, anyway?'

Again, I lied. 'Nothing. I just need to speak to him. You do this for me, I promise no-one'll ever know it was you, and you'll get the exclusive on this story. After this, the whole of Fleet Street'll be beating a path to your door. I promise.'

'It might not be that easy. He might have changed his name.'

'He had previous convictions so it's unlikely he'll have been able to change his name. He should be on the Sex Offenders Register.'

Roy sighed. 'I'll see what I can do.'

'It's important, and I'm going to need the information quick.'

'Give me more of a snifter on this story. Something to really whet my appetite.'

'Get me Kover's current address by tonight and I'll tell you a bit more then.'

'This'd better be fucking good, Dennis.'

'I'll call you on this number at five tonight.'

'I've got a meeting. Make it six.'

'Six it is. And same thing applies. Don't tell anyone you've heard from me.'

The beeps went as he started to say something else, and I hung up without saying goodbye.

I stepped out of the phone box into the morning rush hour and made my way slowly back towards the hotel.

35

'With you in a minute,' came a voice from the back of the shop as I shut the door. I pushed the bolt across and switched the sign round from OPEN to CLOSED – not that I expected to be disturbed. Len Runnion's shop is hardly a mecca for retail activity. Still, always easier to err on the side of caution.

He appeared behind the counter wiping what looked like a Chinese ornamental vase with a cloth, presumably to get rid of fingerprints. When he saw me, he attempted a smile, but it wasn't a very good effort and his eyes started darting around alarmingly, always coming back to the vase in his hand.

'Oh, hello, Mr Milne,' he said as jovially as possible. He put the vase down under the counter. 'What can I do for you?'

'Guns,' I said, approaching him. 'I want some guns.'

His eyes seemed to go into overdrive, and he took a step back. I think there was a look on my face that scared him. 'I don't know where you'd get them sort of things from,' he said nervously. 'Sorry, I can't help on that one. I make it a point never to go near any sort of weapon.'

I stopped on the other side of the counter and eyed him carefully. 'I'm no longer a police officer,' I told him, 'so I'm not interested in nicking you for anything. Now, we can do this the easy way or the hard way.'

'Look, Mr Milne, I don't know what the fuck you're talking about so I think you'd better leave if that's the sort of thing you've come for.' He was more confident now that I'd told him I was no longer with the Force.

However, the confidence was shortlived. I pulled out the gun I'd taken from Illan's man and pointed it directly at his chest. 'I'm not fucking about, Leonard. I need at least two firearms other than the one I'm pointing at you, preferably ones that are magazine loading. Plus a reasonable quantiity of ammunition.'

'What the fuck is going on here, Mr Milne?' he asked unsteadily, his eyes for once very much focused as they stared at the gun. 'Is that thing real?'

'Very much so. Now, I know you deal in illegal firearms, everyone knows that.'

'I don't know what you're talking about—'

'Yes you do. You know exactly what I'm talking about. You're going to supply me the two weapons I've just asked for now – today – or I'm going to kill you. It's as simple as that.'

'I've got no guns. I promise.'

'You know something, Runnion, I've always disliked you. And I'll bet you shifted those tax discs from that Holloway robbery as well.'

'No, I didn't. I'm serious—'

'But you know what? That's nothing to do with me any more so I'm not even going to pursue it. I'll leave that to other people. But what I will tell you is this: if you don't get me these two guns this afternoon, you are a dead man. It's as simple as that.'

I moved the gun upwards so it was pointed directly between

his eyes. A bead of sweat rolled down his forehead and onto his nose. He blinked rapidly, but remained stock still. I think I'd convinced him I was serious.

'Please stop pointing that thing at me.'

'Are you going to get me what I want?'

'It's going to take some time.'

'Have you got the ones I want in stock?'

'I don't carry stock. Not of that—'

'Stop lying. I repeat: have you got the ones I want in stock?'

'I can get you two guns like that, yes.'

'Where are they?'

'I've got some gear over in a lock-up in Shoreditch. Guns. I should have what you're looking for. Now, please stop pointing that thing at me. It might go off.'

I doubted I'd have hit him if it had, but I wasn't going to tell him that. I lowered the gun and smiled. 'Let's go over there now. Have you got transport, or shall we go in my car?'

'I can't go now, Mr Milne. I've got things I've got to do.'

I laughed, but there was no humour in it. 'We're going now,' I told him. 'My car or yours?'

He sighed, then looked at me as if he still couldn't quite believe I was doing this. I looked back at him in a way that convinced him I was.

'We'll take mine, then,' he said. 'It's out the back.'

He went and locked up the front of the shop properly, then the two of us exited the rear door, fighting our way through the boxes of crap, unsafe electrical goods, and stolen property that made up the vast bulk of his inventory. The back door emerged into a tiny potholed car park containing two cars that looked like they were just about ready for the knacker's yard. We got into the slightly more respectable of the two – a rusty red Nissan which had probably looked quite flash and sporty back in the mid-1980's – and drove slowly out into the street.

The mid-afternoon traffic was heavier than usual due to an accident on Commercial Road backing things up and it took three quarters of an hour to make a journey that wasn't much the wrong side of a mile. We didn't speak a lot on the way. Runnion did ask a few probing questions about who it was who'd provoked my ire and whether I was going to kill or simply wound them, but I told him to keep his mouth shut and his eyes on the road, and after a while he got the message. I felt strangely detached from the whole thing. I was doing everything instinctively without any real thought as to the possible consequences. Nothing really seemed to matter. I had a plan, and if it succeeded I would be pleased, but if it failed, then so be it. I might even end up dead, yet, sitting there in the choking traffic, even that thought held no fear. And the funny thing was, it wasn't such a bad feeling to have. It felt almost liberating to know that this world, so often wrought with pressures and tensions, was no longer of real importance. Life for me had come down to a set of tasks that I would either complete or not complete. It was as simple as that.

The lock-up was one of a row on a narrow back road off Great Eastern Street. Runnion parked up on the pavement directly outside, and we got out together. There weren't many people about- a few City types taking shortcuts, the odd courier – and you wouldn't have thought you were only a couple of hundred yards from one of the largest financial districts in the world.

I stayed close to Runnion, keeping my hand in my coat pocket with the gun. 'Don't get any ideas about running,' I told him as he opened it up. He didn't say anything, and stepped inside. I followed him in, trying not to look too conspicuous, and pulled the shutter down behind me as he switched on the light.

Unlike his shop, the lock-up was remarkably tidy. There were boxes piled up on both sides but there was space to move about in the middle. At the far end, under a pile of tarpaulin, was a wooden strongbox which Runnion had to unlock. From inside it, he removed a large holdall which he put on the floor.

'Pick it up,' I told him. 'We're going back to your house.'

'What?' He looked at me, aghast. 'What for?'

'Because I want to take my time choosing and this isn't the place to do that.'

He started to argue, but I pulled the shutter back up and waited for him to walk out. He put the holdall in the back seat, secured the lock-up, and we were on our way again.

Runnion lived in a row of reasonably well-kept terraced houses in Holloway. I'd raided it once with Malik and a couple of uniforms looking for stolen property, which, predictably, we hadn't found, but I remembered it being quite a homely place. That had been about a year ago now and he'd been married at the time to a surprisingly pleasant wife who'd even offered us a cup of tea as we rummaged through their possessions, which is something of a rarity. She'd left him now and I kept enough tabs on him to know that he lived on his own.

Because we were moving away from Commercial Road, it took a lot less time to get to his house, even though the traffic was still heavy. We went inside in silence and sat down in his sitting room. There were a couple of dirty plates on the floor and various other bits and pieces of rubbish. Nothing like as tidy or as homely as I remembered it.

I motioned for him to sit down. He thanked me sarcastically, putting the holdall down on the floor between us. He was a lot cockier now than he had been, a result no doubt of the fact that he was getting used to the situation.

'Do you mind if I smoke?' I said, lighting a cigarette without offering him one. He shook his head and mumbled something, lighting one for himself. I sat back in my seat and took the gun out of my pocket. 'OK, show me what you've got in there.' He unzipped the bag and gingerly took out a shabby-looking .22 pistol. 'That's no use to me,' I told him. 'Keep going.' He put the .22 on the carpet and reached back into the bag like a miserable Santa, emerging this time with a sawn-off pump-action shotgun. I shook my head, and he carried on. Next up was more in tune with what I wanted: a newish-looking MAC 10 sub machine pistol. There was no magazine in it, but after a quick rummage around Runnion came up with two taped together. 'I'll have that one,' I told him, and he put it to one side.

He pulled out a further three weapons – all handguns – and told me that was all he'd got.

I smiled. 'Well, it's not bad for a man who likes to keep away from weapons.' Still holding onto my own gun, I gave each of them a brief inspection and settled for a short-barrelled Browning. 'Have you got ammo for this?' I asked him.

'Should have,' he said, and once again began a search of the bag, bringing out a couple of mint-condition boxes of 9mm bullets which he put with the MAC 10 and the revolver.

I took a long drag on my cigarette and watched him carefully as he put everything else back in the holdall. When he'd finished, I stood up and picked up my newly acquired weapons. I put the MAC 10 in the pocket of my raincoat, along with the magazines, and stubbed my cigarette out in an overflowing ashtray. I picked up the Browning and inspected it again, removing the magazine, checking the bullets.

'You haven't got a silencer for this, have you?' I asked.

'No, I fucking haven't,' he said, remaining seated.

'Well, I hope when it comes down to it, it works.'

'I'm sure it will.'

I released the safety and pulled the trigger.

It did.

36

'I've been hearing some funny rumours today, Dennis.'

'Oh yeah?' I leaned back against the phone-box glass and took a drink from the can of Coke I was holding. All part of the new diet. 'What sort of rumours?'

'That you're involved in a lot of serious shit. That the police are looking for you with a view to questioning you about some very nasty crimes indeed. Possibly even murder.'

I whistled through my teeth. 'Serious allegations. Where did you hear them from?'

'Are they true?'

'Behave. You've known me for close to ten years. Do you really think I'd be involved in murder?'

'And I've been in journalism for close to thirty years and one thing I've learned is that people are never what they seem. Everyone's got skeletons in their closets, even the vicar's wife. And some of them are pretty fucking grim.'

'I've got skeletons, Roy, but they don't include murder. Now, have you got the information we were talking about?'

'I'm concerned, Dennis. I don't want any of this coming back to me.'

'It won't. Don't worry.'

'That's easy for you to say.'

'What do you mean, easy? I'm the one who's on the run. Look,

I promise all you'll get out of it is a fucking decent story.'

'When? You keep telling me this, but so far I haven't got a thing to go on and I've put my neck on the line for you.'

I sighed and thought about it for a moment. 'It's Thursday now. You'll have your story by tomorrow.'

'I'd better do.'

'You will. So what's the address then?'

'What are you going to do to him?'

'I need to ask him some questions. That's all. He can solve a puzzle for me.'

'44b Kenford Terrace. It's in Hackney. That's all I know. And don't ever fucking tell anyone you heard it from me.'

37

I sat for a long time in the cold darkness waiting for Alan Kover.

His flat, not the one in which he'd committed the infamous rape, was stark in its minimalism. There was only one chair in the cramped little sitting room. It faced a cheap portable TV which had a small cactus plant on it, the only decoration of any kind in the whole room. I sat with my back to the door, watching the blank screen. Watching and waiting and thinking. Kover was the last key in the mystery surrounding Coleman House and its inhabitants. From the wound on Carla's throat, and the way she'd been attacked from behind, I felt sure that he had also been the man who'd murdered Miriam Fox. But such a scenario still threw up far more questions than answers. Presumably, Kover and Carla had been involved together in Miriam's killing. There was no other way she could have known the details of it. But how the hell had two such disparate personalities come together, and what on earth did they kill Miriam for? And what, if anything, did her death have to do with the disappearances? Kover and me, it seemed, had a lot to talk about.

I wanted to smoke. Badly. But I couldn't risk doing it in his flat so I opened my third can of Coke of the day and took a sip. What depressed me about this place was that there was nothing remotely homely, or even human, about it. It was like a bad attempt at a show home created by some very lazy people. I'd checked it over thoroughly, just to see if there were any clues as to what had been going on, but had found nothing. Nothing at all. Just kitchen cupboards with pots and pans in them, a wardrobe with some clothes, a bathroom with a toothbrush and soap. Not a thing that could tell you anything about his personality. For a few minutes I'd even thought I'd got the wrong address, but then I'd felt about under the bed and had pulled out a load of crumpled, dried-out tissues, and I knew then that this was where Kover resided. They'd said he had an unusually high sex drive, but he was sensible enough, having been on the receiving end of police attention, not to leave anything about that could get him into trouble. There were some unlabelled tapes piled up on the video recorder beneath the telly but I doubted if they contained anything incriminating.

I looked at my watch for the hundredth time since breaking in: 8.20 p.m. This time eleven days ago I'd been sitting outside the Traveller's Rest in the pouring rain with a man who was almost certainly now dead. I'd tried Danny's mobile three more times since the attempt on my life, and he still hadn't answered. The message kept saying that the phone I was trying to call was probably switched off and that I should try again later, but I knew there was no point. He would have answered by now. Even in Jamaica.

Behind me, I heard a key turn in the lock. Slipping out of the chair, I moved through the darkness until I was standing behind it as it slowly opened. A large figure emerged carrying a shopping bag and, though I couldn't make him out properly, I could tell it was Kover. The cosh came silently out of my pocket and, as he shut the door and turned to switch on the light, I cracked him hard over the back of the head.

He went down on his knees without a sound and stayed in that position for a second, so I hit him again. This time he toppled over on his side, and I knew he was out cold.

I worked fast. Grabbing him under the arms, I pulled him over to the chair I'd been sitting in, and flung him in it. He was already moaning and turning his head so I knew he wouldn't be under for long. I picked up the length of chain I'd brought with me and wrapped it three times round his upper body, securing it tightly to the back of the chair before padlocking it and chucking the key into my pocket. Next I produced some masking tape from my coat and used it to secure his legs and gag him.

By this time his eyes were fluttering and he was coming round. I lit a cigarette, savouring the first taste, and went round switching on all the lights before filling up the kettle and switching it on to boil. There was a four-pack of cheap lager among his shopping so I pulled off one of the cans and opened it, putting the rest in his sparsely populated fridge. I took a long drink – my first alcohol of the day – and stood watching him.

It took him a minute or two to realize where he was. He saw me, and his eyes widened. I smiled at him. He attempted to move, realizing then that he was helpless. I put my fingers to my lips to indicate that he should be quiet, then removed the tape from his mouth.

'What's going on?' he demanded. His voice was surprisingly high-pitched for a big guy and, though it sounded confident on the surface, there was a hint of nervousness which, under the circumstances, was no great surprise. 'I'm not saying nothing without my lawyer here.'

This was an interesting statement. It meant he knew exactly who I was. Maybe Carla had told him. I laughed and took a drag on the cigarette, stepping backwards. I had a perverse feeling that I was going to enjoy finding out.

'You tried to kill me last night,' I said.

'I don't know what you're talking about.' He struggled against his bonds. 'Now let me out of all this stuff. I could sue you for this.'

I pulled the tape back over his mouth and stubbed the cigarette out on his carpet. 'You know who I am, don't you?' I said. 'You know I'm a copper.' I paced slowly round the chair. 'Unfortunately, what you don't know is that I've left the Force. And what you also don't know is that I'm a killer, and that I've killed people who've deserved it a lot less than a piece of shit paedophile like you. So what I'm saying is this: I'm not like anyone who's ever questioned you before. I'm not here to put you behind bars. I'm not here to try to find out why you do the things you do. I'm here to find out some answers and if you don't give me those answers I'm going to blow your fucking brains all over this shitty wall, and that's after I've kneecapped you.' I stopped in front of him and pulled the Browning from my pocket, placing the barrel hard against his forehead. His eyes widened. 'OK? First question: why did you kill Carla Graham?' Once again, I removed the tape from his mouth.

'I don't know what you're talking about,' he blustered, looking down at his hands. 'Honestly.'

I pushed the tape back, then turned and walked into the kitchen, picking up the freshly boiled kettle.

He knew what was coming when he saw me emerge with it, but

there was nothing he could do. Desperately, he struggled in the seat as I stopped in front of him, stood there for a moment, then ever so gently tilted it until the boiling water dribbled slowly out and onto his upper left thigh. I increased the flow a little, moving to his other leg, watching as his face stretched tight and red with pain and his eyes bugged out of his head. I stopped, paused for maybe three seconds, then repeated the procedure, this time chucking a little on his groin for good measure. His wriggling became hysterical and a surprisingly loud moan came from behind the tape as he tried to cry out. His face was now beginning to go purple.

I stood back and watched him for a little while, a serene smile on my face. I felt that I was performing a worthwhile task, probably the most worthwhile task I'd performed in my whole career.

Without warning, I chucked a load more over his groin, waited while the pain racked through him in great agonized bursts, then put the kettle down and took a drink from the beer.

'Right. I hope we understand each other now. There's no limit to the pain I'll inflict on you if you don't answer my questions truthfully, so it's in your interests to just get it over with. And in case you think about crying out.' I reached down beside the chair to where the small jerry-can of petrol sat and poured its contents all over his body and head. 'If you thought hot water was painful, then nothing will prepare you for this.'

I put the can down and removed the tape. This time I crumpled it up and chucked it on the floor. I was confident I wouldn't need it again. He'd answer my questions now all right. Kover gritted his teeth, still fighting against the effects of the scalding, and turned uncomfortably in his seat.

'Now, let's start again. Carla Graham was involved in the murder of Miriam Fox. I know that for a fact. And I suspect you were too. What I'm missing is the reason. Whatever it was, you and her fell out about it, and you responded by butchering her on her own bed. Now, let me tell you something. There's no point in you not telling me the whole truth or protecting anyone else who may be involved or whatever, because if I get one word of a contradiction in your answers, then you'll burn. It's as simple as that. And I know you know that I'm serious.'

'Look, I didn't even know her! She was just—'

I pulled a lighter from my pocket and stepped forward, igniting the flame so it was only inches from his petrol-soaked face. Instinctively, he turned his head, but I followed it with the lighter and the flame remained right in his field of vision. He let out a fearful moan.

'You know, Kover, you're a very slow learner. I know you knew her. There's no way you got through the security door into her building without being let in, and there was no forced entry to her flat because I was there just after you, remember? You knew her and, for whatever reason, I think she was expecting you. So, I'm going to ask again: why did you and Carla murder Miriam Fox, and why did you then kill Carla?'

There was a long pause. The moment of truth. It was like opening a door, although even in my darkest nightmares I could never have been prepared for what I heard that night.

'I killed her. The one last night. But I didn't know her, I swear it.'

'Then what did you kill her for?'

He sighed, his face still reflecting the pain he must have been in. 'Because I was told to.'

'By who?' He didn't say anything. 'By who, Kover? There's no point protecting anybody here, you know. Not in the position you're in.'

'This bloke who worked with her. He was the one who told me to do it.'

'What's his name?'

'Dr Roberts.'

'Dr Roberts, the child psychologist? The guy from Coleman House?'

'Yeah, him. That's how I got in the flat. He had keys. I think he took duplicates.'

I was confused. 'What did he want her dead for?'

'She was on to him for something.'

'And what was that?'

'Look, it's all a bit complicated.'

'I don't care how complicated it is. Start talking.' I flicked on the lighter again, just to remind him that I wasn't fucking about. It had the desired effect.

'She knew he'd had something to do with the murder of the whore. The one you lot found last week down by the canal.'

'Miriam Fox?'

He nodded.

'You killed her, didn't you? Miriam Fox.'

'Yeah, I killed her,' he said eventually.

'So, Carla Graham had nothing to do with the murder?'

'No.'

I felt an overwhelming gloom then. Guilt sank slowly down onto my shoulders. Guilt that I had seen only the worst in her. That I'd misjudged her and that her anger at my false accusation had been genuine. And that, in the end, I'd done nothing to save her.

'How did Carla find out about Roberts's involvement?'

'I don't know for sure, but I think he told her something only the killer could have known, and for some reason she picked him up on it yesterday.'

So that was how she'd known the manner of Mirian's death. Roberts must have let it slip while talking to her. I felt another terrible pang as it became clear that, by confronting her in the Gallan, I'd effectively colluded in signing her death warrant.

'And so he called you to sort it out?'

He nodded again, not looking at me. 'Yeah, that's right.'

'So how did a respectable child psychologist know a convicted lowlife paedophile like you? How did he know you so intimately that he could call upon your help to commit murder? Twice.'

'He just knew me, all right?'

'No, it's not fucking all right. I'd tell me if I were you. And while you're about it, I'd also tell me why the two of you murdered Miriam Fox.'

'She was blackmailing Dr Roberts,' he said eventually.

'What about?'

'He was interested in little kids.' Was. That was interesting. I'd pick him up on that later. 'She found out about it.'

'How? I'd have thought she was a little bit old for a child molester.'

'She was. But he was diddling one of her mates from the home. Her mate must have told her about it and she started putting the squeeze on. Told Dr Roberts he'd have to pay her to keep quiet.'

'So she had to die?'

He nodded, looking away. I took a drink from my beer and watched him closely.

Roberts's number must have appeared on Miriam's phone record too, but in my shock at seeing Carla's name there I'd overlooked it. Perhaps if I'd been concentrating harder I could have wrapped this whole thing up a lot sooner. And Carla would still have been alive.

'And that's it, then?'

He looked up at me, his face asking to be believed. 'That's it. That's how it was. You know, I didn't mean to get involved. I wish I hadn't. I really do. I just want to be left alone now; you know, to get on with my life.'

I sighed. 'Two people dead just because some crack-addicted street girl threatens to make accusations.'

'That's how it was,' he said, an irritatingly earnest look on his face. 'I honestly wish I'd never got involved.'

'I bet you do.' I lit another cigarette. 'That Miriam Fox must have been some blackmailer.'

'She was. She really knew how to turn the screws.'

I sighed, then walked over to Kover. I leaned down close to his face and lit the flame on the lighter. He cowered back in the seat again. 'You're lying,' I told him. 'It was more than just a case of a doctor abusing his patient, wasn't it? Tell me the truth. What was going on between you and Roberts, and why did Miriam have to die?'

I kept the flame inches from his petrol-soaked face, determined that I would get the whole truth out of him. It wasn't that his story wasn't plausible, although it still didn't explain his relationship with Roberts; it was more that he was too keen to get me to swallow it. I've seen that sort of behaviour before from criminals. They want you to believe a certain series of events, even if it incriminates them. The reason's simple: they're usually hiding something worse.

'I'm telling you the truth,' he spluttered desperately. 'I swear it.'

I took a punt. 'What about those girls who went missing from Coleman House, Kover? What about them?'

'Look, I don't know—'

'You've got ten seconds to start talking. Otherwise you burn.'

'Look, please—'

'Ten, nine, eight, sev—'

'All right, all right, I'll tell you!'

I flicked off the lighter and stood up. 'It had better be the truth this time. Because otherwise I start the counting again at seven. Maybe even five. I'm tired of being fucked around.'

'All right, all right.' He paused for a moment to compose himself, then opened his mouth to say something. Then stopped. I think I knew then that it was going to be very bad. 'Me and Dr Roberts . . . we had a little business going.'

'What kind of business?'

'Girls. Young girls.'

I dragged hard on my cigarette, feeling full of dread. 'Tell me how this business worked.'

There was another pause while he thought about answering. In the end, though, he knew, like I knew, that he had no choice. 'I had a client, a bloke who wanted young girls. Except, the thing was . . . he wanted them permanently.'

'What do you mean?'

'He wanted girls who weren't going to be missed.'

'What was he doing with them?'

'Well, you know . . .'

'No, I don't know. Tell me.'

'I think he was killing them.'

'Why? For kicks?'

'I think so, yeah.'

In my time as a copper, I'd come across cases where paedophiles had murdered their victims. Sometimes to make sure they couldn't tell anyone what had happened, but more often than not because the act of murder served to heighten the pleasure of the sexual act. Killing while coming. There are some people in this world for whom that's the ultimate thrill.

'Jesus.' I shook my head, trying to take it all in. 'So how did it work?'

'Dr Roberts would pick the girls, the ones he thought could

disappear without it getting noticed, ones he was treating. He'd give me the rundown on their movements, tell me the best time and place to snatch them, then I'd do the rest.'

I stared at him, feeling sick. 'And how many times did you do this? How many girls disappeared?'

'We didn't do it much.'

'How many?'

'Four altogether.'

I dragged hard on the cigarette. 'Over how long a period?'

He thought about it for a moment. 'I don't know, about eighteen months. Something like that. The girl – the whore – she got a sniff of what was going on. Dr Roberts chose one of her mates for taking, and somehow she rumbled it. That's when she started blackmailing him, saying she'd expose him to the cops unless he paid her.'

'Did you know the name of Fox's friend? The girl Roberts . . . picked?' I found the last word difficult to say.

He shook his head. 'No, no. I never knew their names.'

'It was Molly Hagger.' He looked back at me blankly. 'Her name was Molly Hagger, and she was thirteen.' He looked down at his hands again, not saying anything. 'And Miriam Fox had to go because she was threatening to go to the cops?'

'Yeah. I picked her up pretending to be a punter. Then I did her.'

'I know. I saw the body.'

I stood there for a long moment, trying to digest what I'd heard, wanting at the same time to throw my guts up until there was nothing left. I have never felt so sick and depressed, so weary of it all, as I did standing there in that cramped little room with this fucking monster.

'And who was the last one you took? Was it a girl with black hair about the same age?'

'No. That girl, Fox's mate . . .'

'Molly. Her name was Molly.'

'She was the last one. The client didn't like us doing it too often. Otherwise it raised suspicions.'

Which left another mystery. What had happened to Anne Taylor? Although that one at least would have to wait for another day.

'And this client of yours, what's his name?'

Kover looked me right in the eye.

'Keen,' he said. 'Raymond Keen.'

38

I tried hard to hold in the shock that smacked me right between the eyes. Raymond Keen, a man I'd known for seven years, a man I'd killed for, involved in something so terrible that just the birefest thought of it made my skin crawl.

'I know Raymond Keen,' I told him. 'It doesn't seem his style to kill kids in some sort of sex game.'

'Why would I lie?' he answered, which at this juncture was a fair point. 'He's the client. I don't know if he's getting the girls on behalf of someone else.'

I thought about it for a moment. Raymond, after all, was a businessman. It was difficult to believe that he could be involved in a business quite so base and sick as the planned murder of children, but in the end no more difficult to believe than the involvement of Roberts, whose job it was to look after the mental welfare of children, and I had no doubt that Kover was telling the truth about his part in all this. There was, I suppose, a ruth-less logic in it all. Somewhere out there there were people – hopefully few, but who could tell – who got their sexual thrills from killing kids. Perhaps Kover was right, and Raymond was simply tapping into this vile market, using kids whose disappear-ance wasn't going to attract much attention. And like all his ventures he was keeping as far away from the action as possible. It was easy to see why and how he'd recruited someone like Kover, who was never going to have any sort of moral problem in sending kids to their deaths. But Roberts? That was far more difficult to swallow.

'So, where's Roberts now?'

'I had to tell Mr Keen about what happened with the other woman, that I'd had to kill her. He was worried about Dr Roberts letting stuff slip and giving the game away, so he got me to do Roberts as well. Just to stay on the safe side.'

'How did you kill him?'

'I asked to meet him last night to discuss things. I picked him up outside his flat. When he got in the car, I just leaned over and stuck a knife in his guts, then locked the doors. Then I drove up to Mr Keen's place. He said he'd take it from there.'

'You have been busy these past few days. So, Mark Wells—'

'Who?'

'The man who's been charged with the murder you committed. Or one of them, anyway.'

'Oh yeah, the pimp.'

'Was he involved in any way?'

Kover shook his head. 'No. He had nothing to do with it.'

'So how did you manage to set him up?'

'Dr Roberts did it. At first he wasn't going to bother, but he got cold feet when you lot came knocking. He said you came to Coleman House asking questions. I think it spooked him a bit.'

'How did he get hold of Wells's shirt?'

'It was in the girl . . . Molly's possessions. She told him once that the shirt reminded her of him. I think she was in love with the bloke or something. The possessions were still at the home, so Dr Roberts just took it out and planted it. He was cunning like that. Then he phoned, put on a woman's accent, and tipped off you lot.'

I remembered his pleasant sing-song voice. If anyone could have impersonated a female, it would have been him. Bastard.

'What about the knife?'

'He'd heard from girls at the home that this Wells liked to threaten people with a big butcher's knife, so that's what I . . . that's what I killed her with. I kept the weapon, and just to, you know, fix him up perfect, Dr Roberts planted it near his place.'

'And that was that.'

'That's how it happened.'

'Raymond supplies you with a mobile, right?'

He nodded. 'Yeah.'

'Where is it?'

'Why? What do you want it for?'

'Don't fuck me about, Kover. You're the one who's tied up and drenched with petrol. Where is it?'

'In my pocket.' He just about managed to pat the outer pocket of his coat.

I stepped over and removed it, switching it on. 'I'm going to dial Raymond's private number now. When he picks it up, you're going to tell him you want a meeting with him as soon as possible. Preferably tonight. I expect he'll be reluctant. Don't worry. Be aggressive. Insist. Get a time. Make sure you definitely get a time. And don't give a fucking thing away. Understand? You fuck this up and you'll burn like a piece of charcoal.'

'Look, please. Just let me go. I've told you what you wanted to know.'

I punched in the numbers and put the phone to his ear. Just to show I meant business, I flicked the lighter on again and waved it gently in front of his face.

A minute passed. It didn't look promising. Then Kover was talking.

'Raymond, it's Alan. I need a meet. It's urgent.' There was a pause, and I could just about make out Raymond's booming tones at the other end, although I couldn't hear what he was saying. 'Something's come up. Something I can't talk about over the phone.' I leaned forward so that my ear was close to the phone. I could smell Kover's dry, sour breath. Raymond said something about being unavailable for a while. Kover kept trying, saying that he desperately needed to talk. I think Raymond asked him why again, and he tried to explain that it was confidential, that it was something that had to be discussed face to face. He carried on in this vein for maybe another minute, then he began to listen. Then he said OK a couple of times and the line went dead.

I stood back up and lit yet another cigarette. 'Well?'

'He says he doesn't want to meet anyone, but if it's an emergency, then I should get up to his house tonight. Before midnight. He says it's at—'

'Yeah, I know where it is.' Raymond's main residence was a mansion on the Hertfordshire/Essex border. I'd never been there before, but I was aware of its location. I dragged on the cigarette. 'Did he say he was going anywhere? After midnight?'

'No, he didn't say anything.'

'One more question. How the hell did you and Roberts ever get involved with Keen?'

'Dr Roberts knew him from somewhere. And I knew Dr Roberts.'

I didn't bother asking how Kover and Roberts knew each other. Doubtless it was down to their shared interest.

Sighing, I turned and walked over to the window. The view was of a gloomy monolithic towerblock which was so close that it would have blocked out the sunlight, had there been any. Outside it was raining hard, and fog was obscuring the glow of the bright orange street lights. A man, his coat pulled up so it was almost completely covering his face, hurried past on the street below. He was half running, as if simply being outside was enough to put him in mortal danger.

As I stood there looking out, I remembered back to when I'd been a kid of thirteen. We'd had a field out the back of our house with a huge oak tree in it. We used to climb it during the summer. My dad used to come back from work every night at half past six, rarely earlier and never later, and me and him and my sister would go out into the field and play football. We did it every night, unless it was raining, and it was best in summer when the sun went down behind the tree and the neighbours' kids came out and joined in. They'd been good days, probably even the best days of my life. Life's good when you're a kid; it should be, anyway. I pictured Molly Hagger, the little blonde girl with the curly hair. Thirteen years old. Her last hours must have been a confused, terrifying hell. Abducted from the grey, bleak streets of a wet, cold city – a city that had put her on to drugs and stolen any last scrap of innocence she had – and taken away to be used, beaten, destroyed, for the pleasure of men who dripped with the sickness of absolute corruption. Men who would steal a life just to create a better, more satisfying orgasm. She should have been playing football and having fun with parents who cared. Instead, her remains lay anonymous and forgotten, somewhere they'd never be found. Forgotten by everyone, even by her best friend, who'd tried to use the situation for her own selfish advantage.

Forgotten by everyone except me.

'Look, can you let me out of here? I need a doctor for these fucking burns. I'm in a lot of pain.'

I continued to stare out of the window, puffing thoughtfully on my cigarette. I thought of Carla Graham and wondered if, had she lived, we'd have got anywhere together.

'You know, Kover,' I said, speaking without looking at him, 'I've done a lot of bad things in my life.'

'Look, I've answered your quest—'

'Some of them really bad.'

'Don't do anything stupid, please!.'

'This, however, is not one of them.'

I swung round, and before he could react the cigarette had left my hand. The funeral pyre began to burn, the roar of the flames drowned by his screams.

39

Raymond Keen. The instigator of it all. Like a fat, malevolent spider, he'd watched over this bloody web of murder, greed and corruption, unworried by who got caught up in it and how they met their ends. Only he could supply the final answers to my questions. And only by ending his life could I finally redeem myself in my own eyes, and the eyes of those who would sit and judge me.

I drove across the rain-soaked city, my mind a wasteland of torn images. Somewhere inside I felt fear, a fear that I might die in my pursuit of justice and revenge, that my time on this earth might be only hours from completion. But hatred conquered it.

It was a hatred that seemed to rise right up from the unmarked graves of not only the children Raymond had murdered, but from every victim of every injustice in the world. In the end, this consuming hatred would only subside when my revenge was complete.

I stopped at a phone box on a lonely back road in Enfield and put a call through to the number of a restaurant in Tottenham that Roy Shelley had given me. A foreign-sounding man answered and I asked to speak to Mehmet Illan. The man claimed not to know anyone of that name, which I'd half expected.

'Look, this is urgent. Very urgent. Tell him it's Dennis Milne and I must speak to him.'

'I told you, I don't know no Mehmet Illan.'

I reeled out the number I was calling from. 'He will want to speak to me, I promise you. Do you understand?' I repeated the number, and I got the impression that he was writing it down.

'I told you—'

'I'm only going to be on this number for the next fifteen minutes. It's a payphone. After fifteen minutes I'm gone, and he'll regret the fact that he missed me.'

I hung up, and lit a cigarette. Outside, the rain continued to tip down and the street was empty. There were lights on in the houses opposite and I watched them vaguely, looking for signs of life. But there was nothing. It was as if the whole world was asleep. Or dead.

The phone rang. It was barely a minute since my call to the restaurant. I picked up on the second ring.

'Dennis Milne.'

'What is it you want?' The voice was slow and confident, and the accent cultured. He sounded like he was from one of the higher social classes in his native land.

'I want you to do something for me. And in return I'll do something for you.'

'Is your line secure?'

'It's a payphone. I've never used it before.'

'What do you want me to do?'

'I want you, or some of your representatives, to get rid of Raymond Keen. Permanently.'

There was a deep but not unpleasant chuckle at the other end. 'I think you're making some sort of mistake. I don't even know a Raymond Keen.'

'Raymond Keen's going down. I've got evidence that's going to convict him of some pretty horrendous crimes.'

'I don't see what that's got to do with me.'

'If he goes down, he'll talk, and my understanding is you've got an interesting business relationship with him. One you'd rather keep secret.'

'What evidence, exactly, do you have on this Raymond Keen you're talking about?'

I took out the portable tape player on which I'd recorded the interrogation of Kover. 'This,' I said, pressing the play button and putting the machine next to the mouthpiece. I'd wound it forward to the most incriminating part and was pleased at how good the sound quality was. Kover detailed Raymond's role in the murder not only of Miriam Fox but of as many as four young girls as well. I switched it off before I got to the bit where I incinerated him.

'It sounds like a lot of that so-called confession was given under extreme duress. Surely, then, it would not be admissible in a court of law?'

'Maybe not, but if it fell into the hands of the police, I'm certain they would have to act on it. And I think you'd find they'd leave no stone unturned to put him away, and if they did that . . . well . . . I imagine they'd turn up a lot of stuff that would affect other people. And those people might get tarred with the same brush. And who wants to be closely associated with a child killer? Because I can assure you that's exactly what Raymond Keen is.' There was silence on the other end of the line. 'Raymond's at home at the moment. I think he's getting a little nervous about things. In fact, I think he might be preparing to fly the nest even as we speak, so you're going to have to be quick about things. If he's still alive in twenty-four hours the police are going to get that tape I've just played you plus all the other evidence I've unearthed on Raymond's nasty little sideline.'

'And after that? If Raymond Keen disappears, what guarantees are there that there will be no further repercussions?'

'I'll have got what I wanted. The tape'll be destroyed because, as you say, it incriminates me as well, and I'll disappear off the face of the earth.'

'You could be recording this conversation, What's to stop it being used against Mehmet Illan at a later date?'

'You're just going to have to trust me on that. Whatever happens, if Raymond's still alive tomorrow night, I'm going to the police. If he isn't, I won't. And to be honest, I'd prefer not to.'

'It would be useful if you disappeared sooner rather than later.'

'The moment Keen's gone, so am I.'

'OK. Well, thank you very much for your call.'

'One last question. My driver for the hit at the Traveller's Rest. Do you know what's happened to him?'

'I'm afraid I can't help you there.'

I didn't say anything. Maybe he was telling the truth, maybe he wasn't. He hung up without further preamble, and I slowly replaced the receiver in its cradle. Would he take the bait? I thought he had enough incentive, but I couldn't be sure, and I wasn't a hundred per cent certain he had the necessary fire-power to carry out an assault on Raymond's place. After all, the two men he'd sent against me had hardly been armed to the teeth. One had had a sawn-off, the other a revolver with a badly sighted barrel. And they hadn't exactly been accomplished assassins either. But he was going to want Raymond out of the way, and badly, which counted in my favour.

I got back in the car and thought about driving back to Bayswater, but decided against it. I hoped that I had just sentenced Raymond Keen to death, but maybe Illan would call my bluff and do nothing. I decided I had to go to Raymond's house, to check that he was there and what the level of his security was. I was armed, so if he was on his own I'd finish him off myself, but only after I'd found out who else, if anyone, was involved in the killing of the kids.

It was a quarter to ten and still raining when I pulled up just down the street from Raymond's residence. It was a big, modern house set behind high walls in two or three acres of land, part of a very plush new estate built on what was once farmland, a mile or so out of the nearest village. Only he and Luke lived there now. Raymond's wife had died ten years ago, supposedly the result of natural causes, but in the light of what I'd heard about Raymond these past few hours, even that diagnosis had to be taken with a pinch of salt. He had three kids, all girls, ironically enough, and all grown up and moved away, so it would just be him and whatever security cover he had.

I got out of the car, took my raincoat containing the MAC 10 and the Browning out of the back seat, and put it on. The street was empty, with not a single car parked on it, and the houses were far enough apart to give the area a real sense of privacy. I assumed the sort of people who lived here were City bankers and lawyers, high fliers who liked to think that they'd achieved something in life because their houses had eight bedrooms and walk-in wardrobes. They were going to get one hell of a shock when they found out what one of their neighbours had been up to, but, you never know, perhaps they'd enjoy the controversy. At least it would give them something to talk about.

The wall bordering Raymond's property was ten feet high and topped with short, vertical spikes to deter intruders. I walked up in the direction of the front gate, keeping an eye out just in case this place too was under surveillance. Not surprisingly, the imposing wooden gates were locked and access was via an intercom system. I walked back to the car and drove it slowly down until it was parallel to the wall. I then brought it up onto the kerb and as close to the wall as I could. Hoping that no-one was going to pay too much attention to my vehicle and its strange parking position, I listened for a moment and, hearing nothing, clambered up onto the roof. My head was now just below the top of the wall.

I took a deep breath and jumped up, grabbing hold of two of the railings, scrambling upwards until my feet were at the top of the wall and I was bent over almost double, my toes touching the railings only inches from my fingers. It was a painful position to hold. Below me I could see a thick, wiry hedge that looked as if it would provide an extremely painful landing. Gingerly I stepped over the railings and tried to turn myself round so that I was facing out on to the road, but started to lose my footing. As I slipped, I jumped at the same time, just managing to clear the hedge. I landed awkwardly on the grass, a sharp pain shooting up both legs, and rolled over in the wet, hoping I hadn't broken anything. I lay where I'd fallen for a few seconds, letting the pain in my ankles fade away, and then slowly got to my feet. I took the MAC 10 from my pocket and loaded the magazine into it, flicking off the safety at the same time.

The house was about fifty yards in front of me, a large

three-storey rectangular structure that looked like an attempt to recreate, with some success, one of those country houses of old. There was a drive that went right down to it before widening to encompass the whole façade of the building. Raymond's blue Bentley was parked outside, along with a Range Rover that I think belonged to Luke. What immediately caught my attention was the fact that Raymond's boot was open, as was the front door to the house. There were a lot of lights on inside and I got the feeling that something was going on.

The lawn leading up to the house was peppered with apple trees, giving enough cover for me to make a cautious approach. When I got to the edge of the driveway, about ten yards from the front door, I crouched behind one of them, shivering against the wet, pondering my next move. I didn't want a confrontation, not if I could help it. Far better to let Illan do the dirty work.

The sound of voices came from inside, and Raymond emerged with Luke in tow. Both were carrying suitcases. Raymond was complaining loudly about the inclement weather, though quite what he expected of England at the end of November was beyond me.

'I'll be glad to fucking get away,' he told his bodyguard as they placed the cases in the back of the Bentley. 'I'm not fucking bull-shitting you, I've had enough. It's no wonder our ancestors conquered the fucking world. Anything to have got out of this shithole.'

They turned to go back inside, Raymond still moaning, Luke still grunting in a weak effort to sound interested in what his boss was saying. So, my guess had been right. He was fleeing the coop. An intelligent move. The only problem from Raymond's point of view was that it wasn't going to happen.

I moved out from behind the tree and crept over the gravelled driveway until I was up at the house. Then, slowly, I made my way round towards the front door. Because of the way the porch jutted out a few feet from the rest of the house, I had good cover. So much so that neither Raymond nor Luke spotted me when, a few moments later, they came striding out to the Bentley with two more suitcases.

Without warning, I stepped out of the shadows, raised the MAC 10 and walked towards them, my feet crunching on the gravel. They both turned round at exactly the same time. Raymond looked momentarily shocked, but quickly regained his composure. Luke just glared and reached into the pocket of his leather jacket.

'Get your hands where I can see them. Now!' I pointed the weapon directly at him.

He continued to glare, but slowly raised his hands. Raymond did the same.

'What's the problem, Dennis?' he asked. 'What's all this?' His voice sounded genuinely surprised, but then Raymond had always been a good actor. At one time he'd even convinced me that he was nothing more than a loveable rogue.

'I think you know what the problem is, Raymond. Firstly, I'm not best pleased that you've tried to have me murdered—'

'Dennis, please. I don't know what—'

'Shut the fuck up, and stop playing me for an idiot. And secondly, and more importantly, I've unearthed some disturbing information about you which I want to discuss in more detail before I fill you with holes.'

His expression didn't change. It was all still hurt and shock, as if he truly couldn't understand why he was being held at gunpoint by someone he'd always trusted. 'Look, Dennis, I've always tried to—'

'Alan Kover.' This time a flicker of concern crossed his face. 'I've just finished having a chat with him. He filled me in on some interesting details regarding the work he did for you.'

'I've never heard of an Alan Kover,' he said loudly, but with a marked lack of conviction.

'Details about kidnapping young kids—'

I heard movement on the gravel behind me. Immediately I knew I'd made a mistake by addressing Raymond and Luke with my back to the front door. I started to turn round, but before I could fully react my head seemed to explode with pain as something hard struck it with a lot of force. I felt my legs buckle beneath me and I sank to my knees as I was hit again. I tried to hold onto the MAC 10, knowing that it was probably my only chance of survival, but it seemed to slip effortlessly from my grasp. My head spun and the whole world felt like it was floating away from me. All the time I cursed myself for being so stupid.

I fell forwards onto the gravel but managed to roll onto my side. Above me stood Luke's younger brother, Matthew, an iron bar in his hand and a less than Christian look on his face.

Raymond came into view and gave me a nasty little kick in the ribs. 'Fucking hell, Dennis, you're beginning to really annoy me now. You keep popping up like a fucking unwanted jack-in-the-box. Why can't you just get out of my face?' I wanted to tell him that I would have done if only he'd left me alone, but the act of speaking seemed one effort too far, and it would have been futile anyway. 'Get him inside, Matthew. Out of the fucking way.'

'What do you want me to do with him, Mr Keen?'

'Lock him in the cellar. I'll phone Illan. His boys can come and deal with him. It's their fucking fault he's still here in the first place. And make sure they don't do anything to him here. I don't want any mess in my house.'

'No problem, Mr Keen.' He leaned down and pulled me up roughly by the shoulders. Although conscious, I wasn't in much of a position to resist.

Raymond put his face up close to mine. 'Goodbye, Dennis. I'd say it's been a pleasure knowing you, but it hasn't been. Not at all. You were always a miserable cunt. You strike me as the sort of bloke who'd be a lot happier dead, so maybe I'm doing you a favour.' He gave me a patronizing slap on the cheek, enjoying my helplessness. 'Ta ta.'

He stood up and turned away. 'Have we got everything then, Luke?'

'Seems so, Mr Keen,' Luke mumbled in reply, slamming the boot shut.

'Then let's get out of here. I can't stand another fucking day of this rain.'

They both clambered into the car while Matthew picked up the MAC 10 and, with his free hand, dragged me backwards along the gravel and into the house. He hauled me through the porch and set me down in the large inner hallway by the rather grand-looking staircase that led up like some Hollywood film set to the main balcony. For some reason, I couldn't help thinking what a sumptuous place it was that Raymond owned.

He turned and went to open the door under the stairs, but it was locked. He fiddled in his pocket for a key and ended up producing a whole bunch of them. As he searched for the one he wanted, still holding both the gun and the iron bar, I felt my strength slowly coming back.

'Don't you fucking try anything, son,' said Matthew, seeing a flicker of movement in my legs.

'I wouldn't do this if I were you,' I told him in a strained voice. 'Getting involved in the murder of a police officer. You could go down for twenty years for this.'

'Shut up and don't fucking speak!' he snarled, but I could hear the nervousness in his voice.

'And what's your boss doing while you're organizing my murder? Running away, like he always does—'

'I told you to shut up!' he snapped, and turned back to his task, this time leaning the MAC 10 against the wall in front of him so that he could hunt through the keys more easily.

I remembered the gun in my other pocket. It struck me that in his hurry to get away, Raymond had been very slipshod, and Matthew was obviously no pro. Slowly, I started to reach down into the pocket. At the same time, Matthew found the key he wanted and placed it in the door. He turned round quickly to check what I was doing, and I think he saw that my hand had moved. He started to say something, but suddenly the angry crackle of gunfire came from somewhere outside. Another burst followed, then several individual shots, then through the open front door came the sound of a car reversing rapidly. It seemed Illan had taken my advice. And quickly, too.

Matthew turned and ran towards the door, shouting at me to stay where I was in tones laced with panic. Inexplicably, he left the MAC 10 where it was but continued to clutch the iron bar for dear life, as if the one offered him more protection than the other. I heard him curse as he reached the front entrance. More shots followed, and there was the sound of glass shattering.

Slowly, I forced myself to my feet, shaking my head to try to rid it of the grogginess I felt. I stumbled slightly but kept my balance. The back of my head felt as though it was on fire, but at least I was alive. For now.

I took the gun from my pocket. I'd already released the safety and it was cocked and ready to fire. The car screeched to a halt right outside the front door, kicking up gravel, then there was the sound of another car stopping right behind it. I heard Raymond's voice, panic-stricken now, then Matthew disappeared from view, screaming his brother's name. Raymond yelled at him to get back inside and there was the sound of running feet. There were more shots, and from somewhere a scream of pain.

I stopped and took aim at the hall door. A split second later, Matthew came running through it, followed immediately by Raymond. Raymond's face was covered in tiny cuts. There was no sign of Luke. I didn't hesitate but opened fire in rapid succession. My first bullet hit Matthew in the face and he flailed backwards, temporarily blocking Raymond as a target. I hit him again in the stomach and upper body, and he and Raymond fell to the floor together.

Almost immediately, a hooded gunman came charging through the doorway, holding a pistol. He turned and swung it in my direction so I kept firing, not knowing what else to do. I hit him in the shoulder, and I think the chest. He whirled round in a ferocious pirouette before banging into the doorframe then momentarily disappearing from view.

The gun was empty. On the floor, neither Raymond nor Matthew moved. I took a step backwards and suddenly a second gunman burst in. Knowing where my shots had come from, he crouched down and unloaded a volley of fire in my direction. Dropping the gun, I dived for cover and rolled round the other side of the staircase and temporarily out of range. I heard him running towards me and with every last bit of strength I had left I wriggled over to the MAC 10, grabbed it, and rolled round.

He was coming round the side of the staircase, gun outstretched in front of him. He fired as soon as he saw me, the first bullet ricocheting off the expensive cream carpet, not far from my head. Two more bullets flew past me, equally close, and I pulled the trigger of the MAC 10.

The whole world seemed to explode in noise. A hail of bullets ripped through my attacker, sending him dancing in a ferociously manic jig as his body seemed to burst open. Ornaments, furnishings, glass . . . everything seemed to shatter as the bullets tore apart their target and flew off in all directions, stitching an angry blood-splattered pattern right across the wall. A dozen small wounds blended together and became a gaping hole in his midriff, exposing pale lumps of fat and the first writhing coils of intestine.

The magazine emptied in the space of a couple of seconds, the spent shells forming a pile on the carpet. For a moment, the gunman kept his feet, stumbling awkwardly about like a blind man, both hands clasping his guts and trying to put them back where they belonged. But I think it must have dawned on him that it was a futile exercise, and he fell to the floor and lay there moaning weakly.

For a couple of seconds, I didn't move. My head was pounding and I felt an intense tiredness. But I knew it was nearly over. All I had to do now was make sure Raymond was beyond help and make my getaway. Then I would have done what I'd set out to do, and I could sleep for as long as I wanted.

I got to my feet and looked over at Raymond and Matthew. Both were lying motionless in a heap by the door, their faces red with blood. Out in the porch I could hear the sound of someone moaning, presumably the other gunman. At the same time, the other car – the one that had been carrying Illan's assassins – reversed and turned round in the drive, before pulling away.

I approached the door and gingerly put my head round it. The gunman was lying on his front and a pool of blood had spread out below him. He still had hold of the gun, but his grip looked weak. He was trying to crawl towards the front door but didn't seem to have the strength to make it. I stepped towards him, leaning down to pick up the gun.

And then, for the second time that night, I heard a noise behind me. I swung round, eager not to get caught out again, just as Raymond, bellowing like an angry bull, charged me. He threw a punch, but I managed to read his intentions and dodged it, although I was unable to get out of his way as he ran into me head on, and I toppled over backwards under his weight.

I landed heavily on the back of the gunman, who let out a weird high-pitched squeal as the air was forced out of him. The gun fell from his fingers with a clatter. Winded myself, I desperately tried to parry the blows Raymond rained down on me. I managed to catch him on the chin with a punch of my own, but it wasn't enough to cause any real damage. He hit me back in the the spot where Kover had caught me the previous night, my already tender right cheek, and I felt something break.

Sensing that I was fading, he reached across me and went for the gun. And that was when I thought of Molly Hagger and the anonymous, gruesome death she must have suffered. Only thirteen years old. Still a fucking kid. And I knew I couldn't die without making Raymond Keen pay for his crimes. With a strength born of pure rage, I shot upwards, knocking him off balance, and headbutted him bang on the bridge of the nose. I heard the bone snap with a hideous crack and he screamed in agony. Out of the corner of my eye, I saw him bring up the gun, but his grip had loosened with the shock of my blow and I ripped it out of his hand, smacking him on the side of the head with the butt at just the moment he punched me again, knocking me backwards.

But this time I kept hold of the gun, and swung it round so it was pointed straight at him. His eyes widened and he froze. I sat back up, and this time he made no effort to resist. With one hand, I grabbed him by his thick mane of hair; with the other, I pushed the barrel against his eye.

'Now, now, Raymond. Easy does it.'

I pushed him backwards and got to my feet, still holding the gun tight against him. When we were both standing up, I gave him a shove and walked back into the inner hallway with him retreating in front of me. Blood poured liberally out of his damaged nose.

'Look, Dennis, I've got money. Plenty of it. We can come to some arrangement.' This time there was no mistaking the fear in his voice.

I stopped in front of him, keeping the gun trained on his face. Five feet separated us. 'I know everything that's been happening with Kover and Roberts and those kids.'

Raymond shook his head, then looked at me. 'Shit, Dennis, I never meant to get involved in it all, I really didn't.'

'That's what Kover said. I didn't believe him, and I don't believe you. Now, while you're here, there are a few questions I need answering.'

'OK.' He was playing for time.

'Every time you give me a wrong answer, or one I don't believe, I'm going to shoot you in either a foot or a kneecap.'

'Easy, Dennis. Come on.'

'How the hell did you and Roberts ever get involved together?'

'I've known him for years.'

'How?'

'I met him at a charity function once.' I snorted at the irony, but didn't say anything. 'We got friendly. I found out he had something of a coke habit so I started supplying him with the stuff – for a nice low cost, of course, which he appreciated. I liked him, you know, even though it didn't take me too long to find out about his little perversions.'

'Go on.'

'He had money troubles. Big money troubles. And not a lot in the way of scruples. Like most of them kiddy fiddlers.' He sighed. 'You know how it is, Dennis. Sometimes you can just see the evil in people. I saw it in him.'

I wondered then if he'd ever seen it in me.

'And what happened to the kids? Where are they now?'

'Dead. All dead.'

'Why? What did you do with them?'

'If it's any consolation, Dennis, I didn't kill them. I had a client, a bloke who was very, very sick. He got off on torturing children. Liked to suffocate them while he was, you know, doing his thing.'

'Jesus.'

'I wouldn't have got involved, I really wouldn't have done, but he was – is – an important man. We needed him for the business. If there was any other way–'

'Raymond, there's always another way. And what the fuck did you get out of letting him do that sort of—' I couldn't say it. 'What did you get out of it anyway?'

'We filmed him. He used to do the deed in this house I rent up near Ipswich, and we put a hidden camera in there to record him at it. We kept the tapes to make sure he told us everything that was going on.'

'And who is this sick bastard?'

'His name's Nigel Grayley.'

'And what's his use?'

'He's third in command at Customs and Excise.'

In the far distance, through the sound of the rain, I could hear the first sirens. It felt like a long time had passed since the first shots had been fired, but in reality I doubted if it was much over three minutes.

'So that's how you found out about where they were taking the accountant?'

He nodded, and I thought I detected shame in his manner. His shoulders were stooped and it looked like a lot of the *joie de vivre* had disappeared, probably forever.

'What was the accountant going to expose about you and your associates?'

'We've got a big illegal immigrant racket going. Have done for years. It was going so fucking well too. We had the infrastructure, the inside contacts. Everything was going fine, no-one was getting hurt, and then that prick decided to blow the whistle.'

'Where are the tapes? The ones you made of this Grayley guy?'

Raymond exhaled slowly. 'You don't want to see them, Dennis. You really don't.'

'I know I don't. But I know people who will.'

'Fucking hell, Dennis, I really wish it hadn't all ended like this.'

'The tapes.'

'There's one in the boot of the Bentley. Down by the spare tyre.'

'What the hell's it doing there?'

'I was going to drop it in a safety deposit box on the way to the airport. I didn't like leaving them all here while I go away, just in case the house burned down.'

The sirens were getting nearer. Now it was my turn to sigh. 'You know, Raymond, this is one of the most horrendous fucking stories I've ever heard.'

'I know, Dennis, I know.' He looked down at his shoes.

I knew it was time to kill him, but even now, for some reason, it seemed difficult.

'And what about Danny? My driver? What happened to him?'

He came at me fast, almost too fast, his bulk moving at an unnerving speed, and he was almost on me by the time I pulled the trigger, the bullet snapping his head back. I fired again, hitting him in the throat, but his forward momentum drove his body into me and knocked me back into the doorframe. I pushed him out of the way and regained my footing, watching as he writhed on the carpet. He rolled round onto his back, making horrendous gurgling noises. He tried to say something, but the only thing that came out of his mouth was blood, huge torrents of it. His head was bleeding severely, and I knew the end was near for him.

I lifted the gun and went to deliver the killing shot, but decided against it. Why let him go quickly? Better that he died with time to consider the terrible wrongs he'd done.

And so, leaving him choking his last breaths, I walked out of the house to the Bentley, stepping over Luke's bullet-ridden corpse as I made my way round to the driver's seat. The keys were still in the ignition and the engine was still running. There wasn't a windscreen, but I felt that for the time being I could live with that.

I put the car into gear and pulled away.

40

The following afternoon, at a hotel in Somerset, I put the tape from Raymond's car into the video recorder in my room, and watched for thirty seconds. It was enough. I have seen many dreadful things in my time. I've been an inner-city copper for close to twenty years so there aren't that many sights that can shock me. But this did.

Molly Hagger was on the tape. She was sitting on a bed in a sparsely furnished room, her hands tied behind her back. She was naked but for a pair of black frilly knickers but she still looked thirteen, maybe even younger, and she was in great distress, sobbing fearfully. A naked man appeared in front of her, side-on to the camera. He was balding, middle-aged, and worryingly thin. I vaguely recognized his face. I think, perhaps, that I'd seen him before on the television. He had a hungry look in his eyes and an angry erection. As I watched he struck Molly round the face and called her a dirty little whore. There was an intense pleasure in his voice. He grabbed her by her curly hair and pulled her towards him, slapping her again. She cried out in pain as he forced her to her knees and thrust himself roughly into her mouth.

I switched off then. There was no point in watching any more. It was too distressing. And I knew, without a doubt, that he had ended up killing little Molly Hagger, and that Raymond had filmed it all in glorious technicolour. The hardest part was realizing that outwardly here was a respectable man who had probably shaken hands with royalty before now; the sort of person who appeared on television to give his weighty opinion on events in the world of Customs and Excise. The sort of man who underneath the façade is a foul, deceitful monster who can keep that fact hidden from almost everyone who knows him.

An hour later, I posted the tape along with a detailed report on what I believed had gone on to DS Asif Malik. As promised, I also posted a briefer version of the report, careful to take out any mention of Nigel Grayley so as not to prejudice any future trial, to Roy Shelley at the *North London Echo*. In neither report did I mention my own part in the affair, although I had little doubt that that would become common knowledge soon enough.

An hour after that, I paid my bill and continued my drive westwards in the rental car I'd hired in the name of Mr Marcus Baxter, a travelling salesman from Swindon.

Epilogue

I approach the Philippine Airlines desk with a smile, and get a
smile in return from the Oriental girl. She's older than her
colleagues, somewhere in her thirties, and I expect she's the one
in charge. She greets me happily as if it really is genuinely good
to see me, and asks me the usual questions about whether it was
me who packed my suitcases or not, and all the rest of it. I
answer everything correctly, and we have a quick banter about
what the Philippines are like at this time of year. 'I've never been
there, you know,' I say, and she tells me that I won't be disappointed. 'No,' I reply, thinking that it's been years since I sat
on a palm-fringed beach, 'I know I won't.' She briefly checks my
ticket, sees that it's all in order, and flashes me another smile as
the cases begin their journey along the conveyor belt.

'Have an enjoyable trip, Señor Baxter.'

'Thanks very much. I will.'

I move away from the desk and head towards passport control
and my new life. I'm not nervous. There's no need to be. Three
months have passed since that night at Raymond Keen's house
and, in a land of constantly changing images and an ever-shrinking

attention span, I am already yesterday's man. I look different, too. I wear a full beard now and glasses, and my face looks fatter. I've put on weight elsewhere too, mainly round the waist, the result of country cooking and quitting the cigarettes. You wouldn't recognize me from the photos they showed in the papers. No-one would.

And I feel better too, like a new man; a man who's put the past behind him. There are regrets, of course. That Carla went to her death soon after I'd called her a liar is something that will stay with me for a long time. But, in the end, the past is the past, and I'm happy to say that. I have achieved more as an individual than I ever achieved as a police officer. Thanks to evidence found on Raymond's premises and my reports to Malik and Shelley, Mehmet Illan and at least half a dozen of his associates are behind bars awaiting trial for their involvement in one of the largest people-smuggling operations in British history. Nigel Grayley, a married father of four, will never go on trial for his crimes, however. Four days after his arrest he slashed his wrists with a smuggled razor blade and bled to death in his cell. An inquiry is now under way to ascertain how he got hold of the blade, but no-one's shedding any tears, and the tabloids celebrated the news, which was fair enough. The world is a better place without him.

The remains of Molly Hagger and the other girls have not been found. Most people accept that the secret of their whereabouts died with Raymond, but there are others, myself included, who think that maybe Illan could shed some light on the mystery. But he isn't talking, and neither is anyone else who might know. In the end, you can't really blame them. No-one wants to be associated with that particular crime. Predictably, Danny never did make it to Jamaica. A week after Raymond's death his body was discovered with gunshot wounds in the boot of a stolen car in the Heathrow Airport long-stay car park after a security guard had detected a particularly repulsive stench coming from it. I was sad but not surprised when I read about it in the papers.

One piece of good news that has come out of all this, though, is that Anne Taylor is alive and well. I'd mentioned in my report that she'd gone missing too, even though Kover had denied abducting her, but a few days later she turned up in one piece, having gone on a jaunt to Southend with another, older girl in search of a new market for their services. She's still heading down a rocky road, one that could yet put her in an early grave, but at least for the moment she continues to breathe the same air as you and I.

Mark Wells had the murder charges against him dropped and has begun legal proceedings against the Metropolitan Police for wrongful arrest, demanding an estimated two hundred thousand pounds in compensation. However, his case has not been helped by the fact that less than a month after his release he was re-arrested after being secretly filmed trying to sell crack cocaine and underage girls to an undercover police officer. He's been in custody ever since.

And so, through all this, there's only one participant who hasn't been brought to justice. One Dennis Milne, multiple murderer. I was specifically and publicly named as a suspect in the Traveller's Rest killings two days after the discovery of Raymond's corpse, and though there's been what police describe as a major manhunt, I've so far managed to evade capture. I suspect now that I'll evade it for ever. I've got enough money for now and I've got a friend in the Philippines for whom I can do some work when funds finally begin to run low. I know I'll always be able to rely on old Tomboy.

Do I deserve to escape? I've thought about that a lot these past months. I've done great wrong, there can be no doubt about that, and if I could be put in the same position again knowing even half of what I know now, there's no way I would have pulled the trigger on that cold, wet night and sent three innocent men to their graves. But you can't change the sins of the past, you can only work to limit those of the future, and try to carry out deeds that help to make the world a slightly better place. In that, I think I have been at least partially successful. Would the world be a better place without me in it? On balance, I think probably not. But then I would say that, wouldn't I?

And to those who may one day sit in judgement? What would I say to them?

Just two words.

Forgive me.

The Murder Exchange
SIMON KERNICK

 St. Martin's Minotaur ⚇ New York

For Amy.
But not just yet.

Although virtually all the places where the events of this book take place exist, some of the residential street names are intentionally fictional.

Now

There is no feeling in the world more hopeless, more desperate, more frightening, than when you are standing looking at the end of a gun that's held steadily and calmly by someone you know is going to kill you. And impotent, too. It's an impotent feeling realizing that nothing you do or say, no pleading, no begging, nothing, is going to change the dead angle of that weapon, or prevent the bullet from leaving it and entering your body, ripping up your insides, and ending every experience, every thought, every dream you've ever had. You think about people you care about, places you've been to that you liked, and you know you're never going to see any of them again. Your guts churn, the nerves in your lower back jangle so wildly that you think you're going to soil yourself, your legs feel like they're going to go from under you like those newborn calves you sometimes see on the telly. And your eyes. You know that your eyes betray your sense of complete and utter defeat.

You are a dead man, and you know it.

And then two things happened.

Tuesday, nineteen days ago

Iversson

To tell you the truth, I knew Roy Fowler was trouble the minute I laid eyes on the bastard. His eyes were too close together for a start, and the eyebrows joined up werewolf-style which, according to a book I once read, is always a bad sign. I didn't like the nose either, or the fake tan, but I wouldn't have let that stand in the way of business. If I was that fussy, I'd be broke. But there was something in the way he walked that put me on my guard, with his eyes carefully registering everyone in the room, like he half-expected one of them to jump up at any minute and put a richly deserved bullet in his back. He might have tried to hide it by dressing in a smart, well-cut suit and putting an easy smile on his face as soon as he saw me, but I could tell you this straight away: Roy Fowler was one of the world's guilty.

I stood up as he approached and we shook hands. His grip was tight but a real moist one, and I had to stop myself from wiping my hand down my shirt once I'd pulled it away.

'Mr Iversson . . .'

'Mr Fowler. Take a seat.'

He plonked himself down on the stool opposite me and took another look round. He didn't seem entirely comfortable. 'Are you sure it's all right to talk here?'

'Someone once told me that this branch of Pizza Hut is the best place to hold a lunchtime meeting if you don't want to be overheard. It's because it's all you can eat.'

He raised a hairy eyebrow. 'So?'

'So, apparently it only attracts women with lots of kids, and people who live for their food. The women have to keep chasing after the kids and the rest of them are far too busy concentrating on what's in front of them to listen to anyone else's conversation. You're meant to be able to spot someone who doesn't fit in a mile off.'

He had another quick look round and pretty much got confirmation of what I'd said. There couldn't have been more than a dozen people in the place, spread out amongst the formica tables and booths, all of them single and at least five stone too hefty, except for one harassed young mum with bad hair who was there with her three shrieking pre-teen delinquents.

'I can't see how they can make any money,' said Fowler distastefully, wiping his brow. The day was hot and close and he was definitely overdressed.

'You ever heard of a poor fast-food chain? Course they make money. It's just tomato ketchup and dough. Maybe a bit of cheese and some cheap meat to decorate. I bet the bloke who owns the franchise drives a Porsche and smokes Cuban cigars.'

'You reckon?'

I nodded. 'Definitely. His name's Marco.'

The waitress, a pasty-faced teenager who looked like she sampled the products a little too regularly herself, sidled over and asked for his order. I'd already eaten before I got there (none of that all-you-can-eat crap for me) and was nursing my second Becks. 'Just a Coke,' he told her, without bothering to look up.

She went off and he removed his jacket. A bead of sweat dribbled down the side of his face.

'So, what can I do for you?' I asked, getting to the point.

Fowler sighed and gave me a hawkish look. I thought that he probably wouldn't have been too bad looking if it hadn't been for the eyes. 'I need some security. I was recommended to speak to you about it.'

'So you said on the phone. Who's been doing my advertising for me, then?'

He paused for a moment while the waitress returned with his drink. He waited until she'd gone before he spoke. 'Johnny Hexham. You used to go to school with him, didn't you?'

'Yeah, that's right.' Johnny had been a good friend of mine once. A nice bloke and popular with the ladies, but not the most honest of Johns. He'd probably want something for the recommendation. Whether he got it or not depended on what came next. 'What sort of security are you after?'

Fowler continued to stare at me intensely, like he thought his gaze somehow made the person being stared at want to trust him. It didn't. If he'd have told me I had two legs, I'd have looked down to check. 'I have a meeting that I need to attend in a couple of nights' time. The people I'm meeting with are not what I'd describe as trustworthy. I've got a feeling that if I turn up on my own, then they might consider that a sign of weakness and take advantage. I'd rather have some back-up.'

'What did Johnny Hexham say about me?'

'He said that you fronted a reliable outfit and that you knew what you were doing. Those are the two things I'm most interested in.'

'That's good. I hope he also said that I like to play things straight. That I'm not interested in getting involved in loads of shit that's going to get me put inside for years on end. I make a good living, Mr Fowler. It's not fantastic, sometimes it can even be boring, and a lot of the people we guard make more money in a day than I see in a month, sometimes even a year, but it's still a good living, and I don't want to trade it in for a room with bars on the windows. Know what I mean?'

'I understand all that. And I'm not asking you to do anything that you wouldn't normally consider doing. This is just one night's work, one meeting, and all I want is to have people behind me that I can rely on if things turn a bit tasty.'

'Are they likely to?'

He shook his head. 'No. It's in the interests of the people I'm meeting as much as mine to make this thing work.'

'And this meeting . . . what exactly is it about?'

'You ask a lot of questions, Mr Iversson.'

'That's why I'm still here. I make it a point to know as much as possible about what I might be getting involved in.'

'Fair enough. I've got something they want, and they've got something I want. It's an exchange.'

'That doesn't help me much. I need to know what you're exchanging.'

'Why?'

'Because for all I know you could be carrying twenty kilos of coke and they could be undercover coppers. I once had a mate who was asked to deliver a package to an address in Regent's Park. He never knew what was in it. Two hundred quid for half an hour's work, no questions asked. He was hardly going to say no, was he? When he turned up at the house, the bloke answering the door was from Vice Squad and he was nicked. Turns out he was carrying a load of porn mags where the models were no older than those kids over there. So you see why I want to be careful.'

'If I tell you, I don't want it going any further. Not even to whoever you bring with you, if you decide to take the job.'

I told him it wouldn't and he turned and looked over his shoulder, just to make sure no-one was listening. No-one was, and he turned back to me. 'I told you on the phone I owned a nightclub, right? Well, a couple of months back, I got an approach to buy it from some, er, businessmen. I wasn't that interested, not for the amount they wanted to pay, so I said no. They upped the offer but I still wasn't that sure. You know, I've owned the place close to ten years and it's always made me a good living. I'm the same as you, I'm not rich, but I'm doing OK. As it happens, I thought they could still up the offer, so I held out for more, thinking that I wasn't so worried either way.'

He paused for a moment to take a gulp from his drink.

'Then things started to happen. The club started getting unsavoury elements coming in, loudmouths looking for trouble. There were fights breaking out, furnishings getting smashed, staff threatened, all that sort of shit. Then some of my doormen stopped turning up for work, saying they'd found jobs elsewhere. It didn't take me long to find out that these buyers were behind it, and that they were people who it wasn't worth messing with. A few days ago they came back and asked if I'd like to reconsider their original offer.' He shrugged his shoulders. 'Well, what was I meant to do? I liked the place, still do, but there's no point in clinging on to the past. Especially when the future's getting ready to kick you right in the bollocks. It just wasn't worth the aggravation. So I said I'd accept the second offer but not the original.'

I managed a smile. Put in the same position, I'd have done the same thing. You never want to let them know they're winning. 'What did they say?'

'They might have been lowlifes but they were still businessmen.

I think they thought they'd won some sort of victory by making me change my mind, and that was good enough for them.'

'And is it a good price, what they're offering?'

'It's not bad. I could have done worse.'

'So what's the problem? Where do I come in?'

'We both want a straight exchange on neutral ground. Basically, the deeds for the money. They don't want lawyers involved and they don't want the taxman seeing any of it. They just want a straight no-hassle swap. And I'm going to get payment in cash, no questions asked. Then I just walk away. Why I need you's pretty obvious. These people might be businessmen but they're not, shall we say, averse to using physical means to get what they want. Without the law involved, I've got no guarantees that they won't just make me sign over everything for nothing. With you there, I've got a lot more chance they'll play it fair.'

'We don't usually deal with a few hours' work here and there. The stuff we do's more long term.'

'This is an important deal to me. I'll make it worth your while.' Fowler took another gulp of his drink while I waited to hear how much 'worth your while' meant. 'As I said, I want three men. One of them's going to have to be you. Johnny said I should insist on you.'

'Oh yeah?'

'Yeah. He said you could keep a cool head.' I didn't say anything so he continued. 'Five grand. In cash. That's what I'll pay for you and two of your best people to come along with me.'

'That's a lot of money.'

'It's a lot less than I'll be getting out of this deal. I look at it as a worthwhile investment. One other thing . . .'

'What?'

'I need at least one of the people with me, preferably you, to be carrying.'

I tightened the grip on my glass. 'I don't want to get involved in anything like that, Mr Fowler.'

Fowler leant forward and I caught a whiff of his breath. It was a nasty combination of sweet and sour, like air freshener in a Gents' toilet. 'Look, I know what you're saying but I'm dealing with dangerous people here and if one of them does something stupid, like pulls a gun, I don't want it to mean the end of my retirement fund. I know your background so I know it's not something you can't handle, and it's because of that that I'm paying big money.'

'Like I told you, I'm not into doing things that are likely to get me put away, and playing around with firearms is not conducive to a free and happy life on the outside.'

'You offer protection, right? You and your employees guard people who feel threatened. Right?' I nodded, since he was pretty much on the ball there. 'Well, I feel threatened, and I want you to guard me for a period of time of what? – no more than a couple of hours tops, and for that I'm going to be paying very serious money. Now I know it's a risky assignment but it would be for what's on offer. If I wanted security to go to a council meeting to protect me in case I got waylaid by angry voters then it would be worth a lot less, but it isn't.' He paused to finish his drink. 'But you know as well as I do that there's virtually no chance anyone's going to pull anything. It's just not worth it.'

'There are a lot of nutters about these days.'

Fowler began to look frustrated. 'I need an answer. Do you want the work or not?'

The thing about life is there's always pressure to make quick decisions. Most of the time people tend just to follow their instincts and get by as well as they can. When they don't follow their instincts, they tend to make mistakes. Often big ones. And it's usually to do with money.

'Make it six,' I told him, 'and I'll do it.'

And that, of course, was my mistake.

My job's a straightforward one. I run an organization that provides security in the form of bodyguards to various minor celebrities, and the occasional dodgy businessman with something to hide, and I've done it for the last five years. Funnily enough, it tends to be a pretty uneventful business and none of our people have ever been injured in the line of duty, which I suppose says as much about our clientele as it does about us, and which is just the way I like it. I've had my days of excitement and adrenalin. They were fun enough while they lasted but I'm past all that now.

I had reservations about this particular job at the time, but in the end I reckoned that, like most businessmen, Fowler's buyers weren't going to do anything to mess up the deal. If they were getting the club at a decent price, which they probably were, then that ought to be enough for them. I know you should never forget how stupid and greedy people can be, but my feeling was that when these blokes saw that their seller had turned up with back-up, they'd be foolish to want a confrontation. I was a bit concerned about the talk of guns but, to be honest with you, I didn't think they'd resort to that. Again, you had to ask yourself, what would be the point? There's a lot of gunplay about in London these days but most of the real psychos tend to be the kids, and they don't go round buying nightclubs.

After Fowler had gone, I tried Johnny Hexham's number, wanting to know if there was any information he could give me about the nightclub owner and the situation at his place, but he wasn't answering, so I put in a call to my partner, Joe Riggs, on the office number.

'Tiger Solutions.'

I cringed like I always did when I heard that name. Tiger Solutions. I should never have let him talk me into that one. Joe reckoned it made the punters think they were dealing with a tough outfit; I thought it made us sound like a fucking wildlife charity.

'Joe, it's Max.'

'Max. How'd it go with Fowler?'

I told him what the deal was, and the amount of money on offer. Joe whistled through his teeth. 'That's a lot of cash. It's getting close to half of what we pulled in in the whole of last month. And in readies, too. What's the catch?'

'The buyers are the type who could turn nasty. And this Fowler, there's definitely something dodgy about him.'

Joe laughed. 'He's a nightclub owner, what do you expect? They're all dodgy, but no worse than some of the people we have to protect. Anyway, let's not turn down anything this lucrative.'

Like I said, money was always the key. You never want to say no to it. I didn't mention anything about Fowler demanding that I carry a gun on the night. There was no point. It would just complicate matters. As it happened, I wasn't even sure I was going to bother bringing one along anyway, particularly as I had no intention of using it in defence of Fowler's pension fund. If they pulled shooters, my hands were going up faster than a porn star's knob, it was as simple as that.

I told Joe there was no fear of me pulling out, not for six grand. 'I'd just like to know a little bit more about him, and the place he owns, that's all. I wouldn't mind finding out why these people want it so much.'

'You can make a lot of money in that line of business, you know that. The youth like to have a good time.'

'Yeah, maybe. So, are you going to come with me on this one, then?'

'When is it?'

'Thursday night.'

'This Thursday?'

'Yeah.'

'Ah shit, I can't, Max. I'm looking after Terri.'

Terri Dennett was a singer, and not a particularly good one at that, with a drugs problem and an ego that was a lot bigger than her talent. Whenever she attended record company events or awards ceremonies she had to be accompanied by a minder who had the dual task of making sure the paparazzi never got too close to her – not that they usually tried too hard – and preventing her from sneaking off and taking too many drugs, and consequently making a fool of herself. Tiger Solutions had the contract for looking after her and she insisted on Joe being the one who escorted her on her various outings. He had the right level of seniority, and the patience to be able to put up with her. I didn't. I'd taken her once and it had all ended in tears. She'd managed to blag some coke while in the Ladies, vacuumed it up her nose in one go, and got into a slanging match with some talentless sixteen-year-old from one of those real shite boybands that make Westlife look like Pink Floyd. He'd told her she couldn't sing for shit – which was true, she couldn't – but coming from him it was an insult of the most heinous kind. I'd pulled her away before she could rip him to shreds and the bitch had turned on me, opening fire with a severe knee to the bollocks, and then adding insult to injury by tipping a glass of expensive white wine on my head while I was doubled over in agony. I don't think she'll ever know how close she came to death that night. It took an immense amount of willpower to stop myself from putting my hands around her throat and squeezing with all my strength until she was dead, but somehow I managed it, opting instead to pick her up, sling her over my shoulders, and walk right out of there, much to the joy of the paparazzi, who for once showed a real interest in filming her being removed kicking and screaming. When we got outside I'd dumped her on the pavement and walked off.

Needless to say, she hadn't asked for me again.

'You know, Joe, you've got an excuse for everything. What's she got to go to this time?'

'Some fucking hoohah where they all tell each other what talented artists they are, even though they don't mean a word of it. A barrel of laughs it won't be. You know, if there was any other way I'd do it.'

'Sure you would. Anyway, who do you think I should take? I want a couple of decent people for this sort of thing.'

Tiger, like most security companies, didn't have any operatives on the payroll. Most of those we hired out tended to be free-lancers, although we were very careful about who we used and tended to stick, wherever possible, to people we'd worked with before. We ran through a few names together and eventually decided on a shortlist of three: two we particularly wanted, and one reserve. All of them had worked with Tiger on and off for at least three years, and all were of a calibre that they could be relied upon should things suddenly decide to go tits up.

'When's he going to get us the money?' asked Joe. 'For this sort of thing, we're going to need it in advance. I don't want him running out on us.'

'It's sorted. I'm picking it up with him. I'll count it on the spot, then drop it round at the office and put it in the safe before we head out to the meet.'

'Good move. So, where's it taking place?'

'Good question. I haven't got a clue.'

'Well, if it's too far, don't forget to charge him for petrol.'

Which was Joe all over. He'd call himself careful; everyone else preferred the word tight. I laughed and hung up.

Thursday, seventeen days ago

Iversson

There were three of us in the car. Me in the front passenger seat, Eric driving, and Tony in the back. You always feel a bit nervous when the people you're dealing with are unknown and likely to be unpredictable, but at least I had reliable back-up.

Like everyone we used, they were ex-military. Eric was an old associate of mine, a big beefy bloke in his early fifties. He was a Taffy who'd done fifteen years in the Welsh Borderers, and he'd been an occasional employee of ours since day one. You didn't mess about with Eric. Not only did he have a face like Frankenstein's monster, he had the body, too, with fists like sledgehammers. He was a calm bloke, not easily given to temper, and a real old-fashioned gentleman with the ladies, but if you fucked him about, you paid a high price. Once, a few years back, he'd been doing some debt-collecting work for a couple of Albanians. When he'd turned up at the flat where he was going to pick up the money, he'd been greeted by the debtor and two of his mates, all armed with pickaxe handles. According to reliable accounts, the three of them launched a full-frontal assault, weapons flailing. It was a big mistake. Eric hit the debtor so hard, the bloke's head flew back and knocked out one of the others. The third swung his pickaxe handle at Eric's head, only to have Eric grab it with one hand and break his jaw with the other, like something out of a Bruce Lee film. Enter the Welsh dragon, and all that. The whole thing took about four seconds, and immediately became local legend.

Tony was just as useful, but a lot different. Late twenties, good-looking in a public-schoolish way, he was an ex-marine who'd also worked with us on and off since the early days. He was only a little guy, no more than five nine and skinny, but he was one of the fittest, fastest people I'd ever met. I liked him, too. He had what you might call a dry wit, and he delivered his lines with all the urgency of Roger Moore's James Bond, like he might fall asleep before the end of the sentence. But there was something about him, something in the way he carried himself, that told anyone who was interested that, for all his laid-back attitude, he was not to be messed with. He was reputed to have shot an IRA gunman in Belfast in the early nineties before the first ceasefire, finishing him off when he could have taken him alive. It was something he neither confirmed nor denied, but you could believe that he'd done it. He was that sort of bloke.

I gave them a brief rundown of my meeting with Fowler, and what I'd found out since, which wasn't a lot, to be honest. Joe and I had both asked around to see if anyone knew anything about Roy Fowler and the Arcadia, but the only person who had any information at all was Charlie White, another ex-soldier who did occasional doorwork for clubs north of the river, and all he could tell me was that he'd heard it had a drug problem.

'Surprise fucking surprise,' said Eric. 'They've all got a drugs problem. So, do you think there's going to be trouble?' He didn't sound like the prospect bothered him too much.

I gave him one of the most confident looks I could muster. 'Not when they see us, there won't be.'

'Famous last words,' said Tony, in that enigmatic way of his. But then, he'd never been the sort to look on the bright side.

We were picking up Fowler from a pub in Farringdon Street, not far from the Underground station. It was a busy late summer evening and darkness was beginning to settle on the lively streets of Clerkenwell as they filled up with revellers. Traffic was still bad even at this time, and I jumped out of the car fifty yards short of the pick-up point, leaving it idling in a typical urban snarl-up.

The place was crowded with students and the younger end of the office-worker crowd so Fowler, with his bad-news fake tan and middle-aged side parting, stood out like a sore thumb. He was sat at a poky little table in the corner, just in front of the Ladies, nursing a Red Bull and looking like someone had just caught him fucking an under-age girl. He was nervous – nervous and shifty – and even from some distance away I could make out the sheen of sweat on his forehead.

As I walked towards him through a gaggle of scantily clad young ladies with loud voices, I saw he had two briefcases on his lap, one of which hopefully contained six grand in readies. You'd have thought the other contained a bomb, given the expression on his face.

'Mr Fowler. Are you ready?'

Fowler saw me for the first time and cracked a relieved smile. 'As ready as I'll ever be. Come on then, let's go.' He got to his feet unsteadily, trying to hold both briefcases in one hand. It didn't work and he dropped one. Quick as a flash, he bent down and picked it up. 'This one's yours,' he said, passing it to me in a way that was almost designed to attract attention. I took it as casually as possible, and, with him following, turned and walked back outside.

The car pulled up just as we stepped onto the pavement and I ushered Fowler into the back with Tony before jumping in the front.

'Do me a favour, Mr Fowler,' I said. 'Don't draw attention to us by handing me a briefcase in the middle of a pub. You could have given it to me back in the office.'

'Sorry, I wasn't thinking straight,' he said, clutching the other case close to his chest.

'Is everything all right?'

'Yeah, no problem. I'm just a little nervous, that's all.' He wiped the sweat off his brow with a grubby-looking handkerchief as Eric did a three-point turn in the limited space available and headed back the way we'd come.

'There's no need to worry,' I told him. 'You're in safe company.'

I introduced him to the other two. Eric just grunted an acknowledgement. He wasn't one to get over-friendly with punters, particularly when they were greasy-looking nightclub owners. Tony gave Fowler one of his half-smiles and put out a hand which was shaken just a little bit too vigorously.

The offices of Tiger Solutions were a set of rooms above a tatty-looking mobile phone shop near Highbury Corner. Eric pulled the car up in the bus lane directly outside and he and Tony waited while Fowler and I went upstairs to count the six grand.

'Have you got the gun?' he asked me as I put the money in the safe. It was all there, in fifties and twenties.

I looked at him closely. He was watching me, moving his weight from foot to foot, a man with far too much on his mind. 'Yeah, I've got it,' I said, making no move to show it to him.

'I want to see it. I want to see that you've got it.' His voice was almost a whine, like some spoilt kid.

This bastard was beginning to give me a bad feeling. Still, anything to shut him up. I reached under the back of my jacket and pulled the Glock 17 from the waistband of my jeans. I held it out in the palm of my hand for him to see, thinking to myself that it really was a fine piece of craftsmanship, and light as a feather, too. Say what you like about the Germans, but they do do all the important things right. Cars, football teams, porn (if you forgive the haircuts) and firearms.

He stepped over and looked cautiously down at it, as if he half-expected it to jump up and bite him. 'It does work, doesn't it?'

'Do you know something I don't?'

'What do you mean?'

'I mean, why are you so interested in whether it works or not? Do you think I'm going to have to fire it or something, because if you do, then I'm not sure I want to be coming along with you. My life and the lives of the other two men down there are worth a lot more than six grand. Do you know what I mean?'

'I wouldn't be going along myself if I thought anything was going to happen, but just in case something does, I want to be certain that we've got some sort of back-up.'

'It works,' I said, 'but if I have to use it, I'll be one unhappy man. And if I'm unhappy, so will you be. I promise you that.'

I opened the door, then waited while he went out, before switching off the lights and following him.

'Left here,' said Fowler.

Eric turned the wheel and the car pulled into the entrance of a deserted-looking business park surrounded by high mesh fencing. An unmanned barrier blocked our path.

'Pull up to the keypad and punch in the code. It's C234.'

Eric didn't say anything but did as he was told, and the barrier went up. The car moved inside, and carried on down to a T-junction. The single-storey building up ahead had a neon red sign identifying it as Canley Electronics.

'Stay here for a moment,' said Fowler, and jumped out of the car before any of us had a chance to ask him where he was going. As we watched, he crossed the road and walked up to a short, tatty-looking hedge in front of Canley Electronics. He stopped and made a great show of looking left and then right, then bent down and pushed the briefcase underneath the hedge so that it was out of sight.

'What's he doing?' demanded Eric. 'I thought you said they were meant to be the deeds to his club.'

I shrugged. 'That's what I thought.'

Eric shook his head, looking troubled for the first time. 'I'm not sure about this, Max. This just doesn't look right. What with all this meeting up in the back end of nowhere . . .'

'Perhaps he's just being careful,' said Tony, calm as always. 'Maybe he wants to see that they've got the money first.'

'Maybe,' I mused, not feeling too convinced either. 'We've just got to keep our wits about us, that's all. Obviously these blokes are dodgier than we thought.'

'Christ, I'm getting too old for this shit. I'm a granddad, for fuck's sake.'

'The key to warding off old age is mental and physical exertion,' said Tony. 'My granddad did nothing but watch telly when he retired, and he went completely senile in five years. Ended up thinking that he was going out with Carol Vorderman, poor sod.'

'I don't know,' I said. 'I quite like her.'

'He used to send her flowers and everything. My mum and dad

had to put him away in a home in the end. Lack of stimulation, that's what they said it was. Think on that one, Eric. There's a moral in there somewhere.'

'Fuck off,' said Eric, giving him a dirty look. Not that there was any real malice in it. He and Tony knew each other pretty well and, as far as I knew, they got on, too. That was one of the other reasons they'd been mine and Joe's first two choices for this job.

The conversation stilled as Fowler returned to the car and got back in. 'OK, turn left and keep going until the end of the road.'

'Tell me something, Mr Fowler,' I said, as the Range Rover swung left and moved slowly through the business park, crawling over the frequent speed bumps. 'How come you chose a venue like this? There must be getting on for two million buildings in this city. Surely one of them's got to be better than round here.'

'We want some privacy, that's all.'

'Christ almighty,' growled Eric. 'If you'd wanted privacy you could have come round my gaff. This is fucking ridiculous.'

'We're nearly there,' said Fowler irritably. He sat back in his seat and sighed, wiping his brow for the hundredth time that night. He looked about as comfortable as a case of piles.

Tony asked him if he was OK.

He nodded. 'Yeah, yeah, I'm fine.' He didn't sound it.

'If things look like they're going to get a bit tasty, we'll just pull out,' said Tony, pulling a pack of cigarettes out of his shirt pocket and offering Fowler one. The clubowner accepted and thanked him as he lit it. 'All part of the service,' said Tony, leaning forward and dangling the pack between me and Eric. Eric took one. I told him I'd given up.

'Oh yeah? How long's that been, then?'

'Too fucking long.'

We came to another T-junction and Fowler told Eric to turn right. We were coming to the other end of the estate now and, beyond the buildings stretched out in front of us, I could make out the fence, and what looked like wasteground behind. It was eerily silent here, a lonely oasis in the middle of the city. The sort of place where the killers in kids' nightmares lurk.

'I think it's here, up ahead,' said Fowler.

Looming up on our right-hand side, about fifty yards in front and partially obscured by trees, was a large whitebrick warehouse, bigger than the buildings on either side of it. It was set back a few yards from the road behind a forecourt where there was room to park at least a dozen cars, and its delivery doors were open. The forecourt was empty but a light appeared to be on inside, the only light I'd seen in a building on the whole estate.

I felt the hairs prickle on the back of my neck like it was being stroked by a poltergeist. Something was wrong with this whole thing. Very wrong. I pushed back in my seat, feeling the comforting closeness of the Glock rubbing against the small of my back, confident that if I had to use it then at least I knew it would fire.

'This is it, the one with the light on. That's where we're meeting.'

'What time's it set for again?' I asked.

'Ten thirty.'

I looked at my watch. Ten past. 'Better early than late, I suppose.'

Eric slowed the car and turned into the forecourt, watching for any signs of activity.

But there were none. No movement, no voices, no nothing. The place was as deserted as a cemetery.

Eric brought the Range Rover to a halt outside the delivery doors.

'Well, someone's been here tonight,' I said.

'It doesn't look like they're here now,' said Eric, peering inside.

There was a growing tension in the car. You could almost smell it.

'You definitely got the time right?' I said.

'Course I did,' snapped Fowler, who looked the most nervous of any of us by a long chalk. 'It's still early, remember?' He leant forward in his seat and wiped his forehead with a handkerchief. His left leg was shaking uncontrollably and, for some reason, I found myself enjoying his discomfort.

'Maybe we should drive in there and take a look around,' said Tony, also leaning forward. 'What do you think, Max? We could take up positions so we're ready when they get here.'

It seemed as good an idea as any. 'Yeah, let's do that. It can't do any harm.' Which was a statement I was to remember for the rest of my days.

Eric touched the accelerator and we drove in through the gap in the doors.

The place was about twenty yards deep by ten yards wide, and empty aside from a row of ancient-looking oil drums which stood a few feet in front of a door in the far right-hand corner. Above the door was a long balcony that stretched the width of the room and overlooked the front of the car. A number of unmarked boxes were positioned along it, some of them stacked two or three high. I looked up at them for any sign of activity, but everything was still. As still as the grave, as my grandma used to say before she was lowered into her own.

The Range Rover stopped in the middle of the floor. Eric put it into neutral and pulled up the handbrake. He too looked up at the boxes. 'Perfect place for an ambush,' he said quietly, almost to himself. 'Saw something like this back in Ulster.'

'Look, this is just a fucking meeting,' said Fowler impatiently. 'Nothing more. All right?'

'It was while we were based out of Londonderry. The RUC got a call from some woman, said she'd been raped out by this disused old factory. This was in the old days, way back at the beginning of the seventies, before they'd got wise to the way the provos worked. The Officials were still around then and they tended to play it more by the book. Anyway, they despatched a car with three RUC men in it to pick her up, and an ambulance as well. Just in case. She'd made the call from a phone box outside the factory gates, but when the car got there, they saw her wandering about inside the grounds, you know, all distraught and that.'

The car fell silent. All you could hear was Fowler's heavy breathing in the back.

'So they drove in through the gates and went down to pick her up. She saw them, started crying hysterically, and ran off into the building, like she couldn't come to terms with getting near any men so soon after what'd happened. The RUC car stopped in front of it and the coppers, all blokes, went to get out. None of them drew their guns, they didn't want to unnerve her, and I don't think the poor bastards ever suspected a thing.

'They never even got their feet on the ground. A couple of provo gunmen stuck their Armalites out of the windows on the second floor, right above the car, and started shooting on fully automatic. The driver was killed outright.'

'What about the one in the front seat passenger side?' I asked.

'If I remember rightly, he died later in hospital.'

'Great. That's a real fucking help, that is.'

'Fucking hell, Eric,' snorted Tony. 'Make us all feel better, why don't you?'

'I wouldn't worry too much, Tone. Or you,' Eric added,

meaning Fowler. 'The one in the back survived. Got hit in the neck but the bullet passed straight through. Didn't touch a single one of his main cables. Far as I know the bloke's still alive.'

'Stop joking around, and keep your wits about you,' hissed Fowler. 'That's what I'm paying you for.'

Eric's face clouded over. He didn't like taking shit from anyone, even paying customers. 'You know, Max, I'm beginning to think this job's worth a lot more than what I'm getting for it.'

'Life's an underpaid occupation, Eric,' I told him. 'Everyone knows that.' I looked at my watch again. 10.14. 'I'm going to take a look around.'

Fowler leant forward abruptly. 'I don't think that's a good idea, Mr Iversson. It's best we stick together and wait for them to come.'

'I won't go far. I just want to check things out.'

'Look, I insist . . .'

I stepped out of the car, ignoring his pleas. I'm pretty good with the punters usually, to tell you the truth, but it wasn't as if I was going to get any repeat business from this prick, plus I already had the money, so basically there was no need to play along with him. Particularly when it was so obvious that there was a lot more to this meeting than he was letting on. Fucking people around was a game two could play.

I stretched my legs, then walked casually towards the door in the far corner, keeping one eye on the boxes overhead. Eric's story had given me the spooks a lot more than I'd ordinarily like to admit. It seemed to have done the same to him too because he stepped out of the car and leant back against the bonnet, lighting another cigarette and watching the boxes like a hawk.

I reached the door and tried it. Locked. So, who the hell had come here and switched the lights on? And where were they now? I turned back towards the car.

Eric looked across at me. 'Nothing?'

I shook my head. 'Locked.' I walked across to the open doors and stepped outside into the warm breeze. Over on the horizon the distant lights of the West End glowed pink. The road was quiet and I listened hard for any sound of a car coming through the estate, but there was nothing bar the distant rumble of traffic. Maybe they just liked to be fashionably late.

It was 10.16 and I was edgy. I decided to go back and question Fowler in a little more detail about exactly what was in that briefcase of his, the one he'd been so reluctant to bring into the warehouse.

I turned round.

In the car, Roy Fowler was still fretting as he waited to get every-thing over and done with. Ten more minutes, he kept telling himself. Just ten more minutes, and he'd be a rich man.

Tony gave him a reassuring pat on the shoulder. 'Look, Mr Fowler, calm down. It's going to be OK.'

Fowler exhaled heavily and turned to Tony. His face was taut with tension. 'I'm all right. I just wish they'd get here, that's all.'

'I wouldn't worry about that,' said Tony encouragingly. 'They're already here.' He motioned towards the front doors where Iversson stood with his back to them.

Fowler wriggled round in his seat and looked out of the rear window. 'Where?'

'Here,' said Tony, and pushed the silencer hard against Fowler's head, just in front of his ear.

Before Fowler even had a chance to react, Tony pulled the trigger. Fowler let out a sharp sigh and the passenger window behind him cracked as the bullet passed through it. He slumped in the seat, and rolled round so he was facing his killer, allowing Tony to press the weapon against his forehead and give him one more, just for good measure.

The front driver's door opened and Eric, having heard the noise of breaking glass, shoved his head in, completely unaware of what had just happened. He spotted Fowler immediately, dead in his seat, blood dripping down his face in thin rivulets and onto his sweat-stained shirt.

'What the fuck's going on?' he demanded.

'I shot him,' said Tony, pulling the gun up from his side and aiming it at his colleague's face. Eric's eyes widened and his body tensed as he tried to come to terms with the sight in front of him.

'Tony, don't do—'

Tony fired twice, both bullets striking Eric in the face. The big man staggered backwards, and Tony leant forward to fire two more shots into his upper body. His legs buckled and went from under him, and he fell heavily to the ground, moaning and clutching wildly at his face and chest.

Tony, meanwhile, threw open the car door and came out looking for the man who until two minutes ago had been his boss.

I was still in the process of turning round as Roy Fowler died. It took a couple of seconds to take in the muffled noises and the movement in the back of the Range Rover, by which time Eric was turning round, still holding onto his cigarette, and hurriedly pulling open the door. I took a step forward as Eric said something to Tony, then a series of popping sounds came from inside the car and Eric's head snapped back and he lost his footing, stumbling like a drunk man.

I knew immediately that he'd been shot, but still not by whom. It didn't make sense. I stopped dead in my tracks, confused by the sudden turn of events, and fumbled in the back of my waistband for the gun.

At the same time, Tony stepped almost casually out of the car, gun in hand, and turned towards me. He raised the weapon, that eerie little half-smile flickering across his face, and prepared to fire. For some reason, the first thought that crossed my mind was how fucking annoying that look was. It made the bastard appear really cocky, which was something I'd never noticed before. The second thought I had was that I'd always liked Tony.

Then my military training took over and I hit the deck, rolling over and pulling out the Glock. The silencer spat twice as Tony came forward, closing in for the kill, and bullets hissed quietly through the air, ricocheting up from the concrete, feet from where I was rolling.

Tony came round the back of the Range Rover, taking aim again, but this time it was his turn for a shock. Without warning, I stopped rolling and leapt to my feet, locating and flicking off the safety in what was close to a reflex action. His face froze in disbelief like he couldn't believe I'd be so cheeky as to pull a gun on him, and then I was firing, the bullets exploding round the enclosed space of the warehouse in an angry cluster of noise. Tony pulled the trigger too, and I felt a bullet whistle past my left ear, but time was moving so fast that I didn't even think about it, just kept firing, two-handed, concentrating on keeping the weapon level, emptying the magazine.

Tony stumbled back as he was hit in the shoulder of his gun arm. A second round struck him in the throat, then a third in the face, knocking him sideways. The next thing I knew, he was falling to the floor, the gun flying out of his grip and clattering out of reach. Immediately, he tried to lift himself up, his face registering another look of disbelief as he realized he was dying. Blood so dark it was almost black poured from the wounds on his face and throat, turning his white polo shirt a deepening horror-film colour. He held the position with his head a foot above the floor for about three seconds, then fell backwards with a thud, choking heavily.

I walked over to him, still gripping the Glock hard. He rolled himself into a ball, coughing and retching as his mouth filled with blood. Well, one thing was for sure: I wasn't going to get any answers out of him now. Once in Africa, a long time back, I'd seen a man take a bullet in the throat. It had taken him close to ten minutes to die, choking and gasping on his own blood. There was nothing that could have been done. As soon as the bullet had struck him the outcome was inevitable. It was inevitable now, but I didn't think I could just let it happen. Like I said, I'd always liked Tony.

I ejected the magazine and checked the bullets. There were three left. Pushing it back in, I leant down, chambered a round, and pulled the trigger, blowing Tony's brains across the dirty floor. The body juddered a couple of times, then lay still.

I stopped for a moment, looking about the warehouse and listening for any suspicious sounds. Nothing, bar the faint sound of light breathing coming from Eric. I walked over to him, holstered the gun, and knelt down. He was lying on his back, his hands laid across his chest in full funeral style. His face was twisted and bloody with the entry wounds of Tony's bullets clearly visible. One was just below his right eye, the other on his lower left cheek, an inch above the jawline. A dark red pool was forming on the floor beneath his head and his eyes were shut. I felt his neck for a pulse. There was something there but it was very faint; and even as I held my finger on it, it faded away until it was gone altogether.

Eric. He'd been a good man. Reliable, professional, all the things you wanted in business. Not someone you could take liberties with, not someone who was afraid of using force when it was necessary, but nevertheless someone whose heart was in the right place. The poor sod had even bought me a bottle of whisky the previous Christmas, which might have been a small gesture but was the sort I appreciated. It made me feel guilty that I'd only intended to pay him three hundred quid for the night's work. It didn't seem a lot to die for.

I stood up, wondering what the fuck had gone wrong and how we could have been betrayed so completely. Eric had three kids, all grown up, and four grandkids too. But he was also long since divorced. This meant that it was unlikely anyone close to him would know where he was that night. I was in a difficult position. If I went to the law and told them what had happened, I'd be leaving myself open to all kinds of questions, particularly regarding the shooting of Tony, and the unlicensed firearm I'd been carrying. I could end up going down for years if my story wasn't believed, and to be honest, who would believe it? The alternatives, it has to be said, were almost as bad. Drive out of there in a damaged vehicle registered in my own name and leave behind three bodies in the hope that no-one would ever connect them to me. Or hide the bodies somewhere and deprive Eric of a proper burial. That was, of course, on the basis that they remained hidden.

It was at times like this that I needed a cigarette. It wouldn't have done a blind bit of good but somehow smoking had always helped me think straight. I tried to fathom out what Tony's plan had been. Kill us all and get rid of the corpses, I assumed. Then what? Joe knew that he'd been there with us so he could hardly just walk around as if nothing had happened. Perhaps he'd had plans to disappear. But that still didn't help to supply any sort of motive.

One thing, however, was certain. This wasn't something he could have put together on his own, and whoever else was involved might well be in the vicinity. I decided that by hanging around I was putting myself in needless danger.

I went round to the rear passenger side of the Range Rover and opened the door. Fowler's crumpled body tumbled out, landing in an ungainly heap on the floor. He was very definitely dead, and if he hadn't been, I'd have killed the bastard myself. Whatever else might have been a mystery, I was pretty damned sure that Fowler had been the architect of his own demise. A slimy bastard like that was always going to make enemies.

I thought about moving the body somewhere less conspicuous, but without gloves it wasn't an option. I was just going to have to leave all three of them there and front it out. It was the only thing I could do, at least for the moment. Maybe Joe would have some ideas.

The damage to the car was superficial: two small holes in the window, surrounded by spider-web cracks. I could knock the whole thing out and replace it easily enough. Fowler had bled inside a little bit but not as badly as might have been expected.

I shut the door, went round switching off all the lights, then walked back round to the driver's side. The keys were still in the ignition so I got in and backed out of the warehouse, before dragging the two doors shut and hoping above hope that no-one opened them again for a long, long time.

Now there was only one thing left to do. I jumped back in the car and drove slowly down the road, following the route we'd come in on, until I got to the bush in front of Canley Electronics where Fowler had hidden the briefcase. I stopped the car and, leaving the engine running, jumped out. This was one mystery I could at least solve. I paused for a moment and listened. Still no sound, bar the continued hum of city traffic and the odd call of a night bird. High in the sky a three-quarter moon stared impassively down, unmoved by the events below.

I jogged up to the bush and knelt down where Fowler had been only minutes earlier, then reached into the foliage and felt about, knowing that I was in the right place because I'd been careful to watch him earlier.

My hand touched something solid. A handle. Bingo. I pulled it out, feeling an irrational excitement. I had to know what was so important that men I knew, men I liked, had had to die for it. I stood up, located the two catches on either side of the handle, and went to press them.

Which was when I heard the sound: a scrape of a shoe on gravel behind one of the two parked cars in front of the Canley Electronics building, only ten yards away. I thought I saw something move. I looked more closely, feeling myself tense. And then I saw him, a man in dark clothing and a baseball cap, face obscured by a scarf, moving about in the shadows. Those were the only details I can remember. I was too busy looking at the rifle nestled against his shoulder, the rifle that was now pointing straight at my head.

There was a hiss as a bullet flew above me, almost parting my hair, and struck something behind with a metallic clang. Immediately, I ducked down behind the hedge and ran, crouching, round to the driver's side of the car as more rounds spat through the air. As I pulled open the door, I chucked the briefcase into the passenger seat, accidentally biting my tongue as a bullet passed right through the car and out the open driver's-side window before ricocheting off the wing mirror. I ripped the Glock out of my waistband and cracked off my last two shots at him as he came round the front of the hedge and into view.

I was sure they'd both missed their target but they forced him to dive behind the bush and temporarily out of sight. Without waiting for him to reappear, I jumped into the car, rammed it into gear, and drove out of there as fast as I could, not bothering to look round or stop when I came to the barrier. I hit it full-on, broke it in two, and carried on going.

I reckon I'd only gone a matter of a few hundred yards when the intense curiosity I was feeling got the better of me. Even though I could hear the sound of sirens closing in in the distance, even though I knew I was taking a huge and needless risk, I couldn't resist pulling over and picking up the briefcase. Once again, I located the catches and this time got the opportunity to press them. They both clicked satisfyingly and the case came open.

I stared for maybe three, four seconds, feeling confused, unable to fully comprehend what I was seeing.

Because, you see, after all that, the fucking thing was empty.

Friday, sixteen days ago

Gallan

The murder of Shaun Matthews, thirty-one, of the Priory Green Estate in Islington was an odd one from the start. Matthews had enemies, there was no doubt about that. Three months before his death he'd been threatened by two men he'd thrown out of the Arcadia nightclub in Holloway where he worked as chief door-man. One of the two, later identified as twenty-eight-year-old Carl Voen, had claimed that he was going to come back and blow Matthews's head off. This might not have been taken seriously had it not been for the fact that Voen had a previous conviction for possession of a firearm and two further con-victions for grievous bodily harm. He was, by most accounts, a man with a short fuse. He was also, unfortunately, a man with a watertight alibi for the time of death. For at least twelve hours either side of the point at which Matthews had shuffled off his mortal coil, he'd been in custody undergoing questioning about an armed robbery, with the questioning being carried out by two of the detectives who were now investigating the murder.

Shaun Matthews was also a drug dealer. According to anecdotal evidence collated by investigating officers, he supplied Ecstasy, cocaine and, on at least one occasion, heroin to Arcadia clubgoers (apparently in collusion with the club's management), as well as to individuals visiting his flat. According to more than one source, he had also earned himself something of a reputation for selling below-par products, particularly when operating off the premises. There was a story doing the rounds that one unlucky punter had challenged Matthews about an especially poor batch of cannabis he'd sold him only to have Matthews dangle him by the ankle from the third-floor balcony of his flat while simultaneously slashing his buttocks with a Stanley knife. The punter had needed more than forty stitches on his behind and he, too, had left the hospital muttering words of dark revenge against the man who'd made it so difficult for him to sit down in comfort for months to come.

Nothing about any of this was odd, of course. There are plenty of criminals out there who fail to recognize or abide by even the most rudimentary facets of capitalism, and insist on riding roughshod over their customers and making enemies as casually as old ladies make cups of tea. Sometimes, inevitably, they end up dead, and usually the people doing the killing are those they've wronged, but in Matthews's case there appeared to be more to matters than initially met the eye.

For a start, it had taken two days to conclude that he'd been murdered. Matthews was what a tabloid report might describe as a 'strapping' young man: six feet two, sixteen stone of mainly muscle, very fit (at least superficially) as a result of his daily visits to the gym, and no history of medical problems. Therefore when he was found dead in his bed one morning by police officers who'd been called by a colleague from the Arcadia who was concerned that he hadn't turned up at work two evenings running, it came as something of a shock to all concerned. Not, perhaps, that he was dead but more that there didn't appear to be any obvious cause. There were no external injuries and no sign of any kind of a struggle. Matthews was lying on his back, with the covers half off him, and his head tilted to one side. The expression on his face was what the first officer on the scene had described as restful. Not fearful, angry, or even shocked. Just restful. His arms were stretched out to his sides with the fists lightly clenched, and he was naked. It looked like death by natural causes, or possibly some sort of drugs overdose.

Matthews's body was taken away for a post-mortem, and this was when things got interesting. For all his strength and build, in actual fact he probably didn't have long to live. He had a serious heart condition, thought to have been brought on by an addiction to steroids. There were traces of nandralone in his blood, as well as cocaine and alcohol, and injection marks on his left arm. Initially, the pathologist thought that he'd had a heart attack, but unfortunately such a diagnosis didn't explain the strange internal injuries Matthews had suffered. There'd been extensive internal haemorrhaging as well as a cloudy swelling in the cells of a number of organs, particularly the kidneys. Somewhat baffled, the pathologist had carried out further tests. These showed significant traces of an extremely potent neurotoxin that would have resulted in these injuries and were, almost certainly, the cause of death. And this was the thing. The poisons department at Guy's Hospital were called in and quickly identified the neurotoxin as elipadae, or cobra, venom.

Snake poison. Hardly the work of your average lowlife thug, the type Shaun Matthews specialized in upsetting. Which left what? The neighbours all agreed that Matthews received a fair number of visitors which, given his alleged trade, wasn't particularly surprising, and it was felt that one of them was the likely perpetrator. Where your average small-time drugs buyer was likely to have got hold of cobra venom, however, was anyone's guess.

The case was an odd one, and as far as I was concerned odd equalled interesting, and interesting equalled challenging, which these days can be something of a rarity. Never underestimate the stupidity of criminals. Most of them'll make every effort imaginable to get caught. In the last murder investigation I'd been involved in, ten weeks earlier, the murderer, a seventeen-year-old carjacker named Rudi, had stabbed an unfortunate BMW owner to death when he'd had the gall to try to prevent his car being taken. Rudi had been arrested three days afterwards when a passing patrol car had spotted the vehicle parked outside his mum's flat. Further investigation had unearthed Rudi's prints all over the interior, as well as those of two of his mates. The knife he'd used, still complete with somewhat telltale bloodstains, had turned up under his bed hidden in a PlayStation box. I reckon the paperwork took up more time than the detective work. Sherlock Holmes wouldn't even have bothered getting out of bed, and who could blame him?

But this was different. A poisoning opened up all sorts of possibilities. It suggested interesting motives. It suggested intelligence, or at least creativity, on the part of the poisoner, but also an incredible naivety. Poisoning was, in general, a pretty foolish method of committing murder. It was too easily traceable these days which meant its one great advantage – that it could make the victim's death look like an accident – no longer held true. Having said this, however, the case was now six days old (or at least the murder was) and had yet to throw up any real clues of note, or anything that pointed to one particular person.

It was a fine sunny morning, the fifth day of what passes for an English heatwave, and DC Dave Berrin was driving as we pulled into the walled car park at the rear of the Arcadia night-club, an imposing post-war structure on the Upper Holloway Road which dominated the corner on which it stood, and parked in a bay marked STAFF ONLY.

Not surprisingly, the club was closed at this time in the morning, but we were expected and walked right in through the double doors at the front. The interior was dark and spacious with tables facing down on to the dance floor on three sides. At the opposite end of the room was a long bar lined with stools. A woman stood on the serving side of it with a pen in her hand, looking down at some papers in front of her. She appeared to be the only person in the place. She looked up when she heard our footfalls on the wooden floor.

'Sorry, we're closed,' she shouted out, going back to her papers. 'We open at twelve for lunch.'

'We're police officers,' I said loudly, crossing the dance floor with Berrin in tow. 'Here to see Mr Fowler.'

'He's not here,' she shouted back.

'He should be. He's expecting us. We've got an eleven o'clock meeting.'

'Well, he's not here.'

I strode up the steps to the bar and stopped in front of her. She carried on making notes on the papers on the bar. 'Perhaps, then, you can tell us where he is.'

She looked up with a faintly bored expression on her face. 'I don't know. He should have been here more than an hour ago.'

This one had an attitude, all right. I gave her a quick once-over. Early thirties, slim with well-defined features, a nose that was maybe a little too sharp, and a vaguely Mediterranean appearance, particularly the olive-coloured eyes. She was definitely attractive – very attractive – but in a hard, don't-mess-with-me kind of way, with the cynical confidence of someone who's not afraid of a fight. If we'd been Nazi stormtroopers, we wouldn't have intimidated her. My ex-wife's all-time favourite film is *Gone with the Wind* and I think that says something about her (though I'm not quite sure what). This girl looked like hers was *Scarface*.

'Is he likely to be at home?' I asked her.

'I told you, I don't know where he is.'

I sighed ostentatiously. 'But I presume you've got his home phone number?' She nodded. 'Well, I'd appreciate it if you'd phone him then and tell him we're here.'

'Look, I'm very busy.' She motioned to the notes in front of her.

'So are we, Miss . . . ?'

'Toms. Elaine Toms. I talked to a couple of your officers the other day.'

'Well, we're very busy too and it would be greatly appreciated if you could phone Mr Fowler and see if he's at home for us. It won't take a minute.'

My tone was even but firm, the kind that says I'm going to keep going until I get some co-operation. It always works in the end, but you'd be amazed how many people take a long time getting the message.

Without a word she turned and walked over to a telephone pinned to the wall in the corner, and dialled a number. I was a bit pissed off because I'd been preparing for this interview for close to a day now. We'd talked to Fowler once but only briefly to ascertain his position within the nightclub, what his relationship was with the deceased, and whether he could throw any light on what had happened. He'd come across as very keen to appear as helpful and as friendly as possible, but hadn't actually managed to tell us a great deal. Predictably, he'd denied knowing anything about Matthews's involvement in drug dealing. He'd claimed that as Arcadia's owner he didn't tolerate drug use on the premises but was aware that it did occur. 'I'm looking at ways to combat it,' he'd said, and had talked about installing cameras in the toilets. 'That's where most of it goes on, I'm sure,' he'd added – a fairly logical assumption. Neither Berrin nor I had found the interview very helpful, mainly because there was something not quite authentic about Fowler's answers, and since then it had come to light that he had a conviction for conspiracy to supply Class A drugs in the late 1980s and that one of his co-conspirators at the time had been Terry Holtz, the late brother of a notorious local crime figure. He'd also been done for driving under the influence of cannabis a couple of years back, and the club had been raided on two separate occasions by the Drugs Squad in an effort to take out suspected dealers, the last time eighteen months ago, although it had to be said that on neither occasion was any contraband found. More promisingly, there was also a rumour doing the rounds that, although Fowler's name was on the deeds of the club, he wasn't what you'd call the real owner. That man, it was claimed, was one Stefan Holtz, the same local crime figure whose brother Fowler had once been involved with.

The feeling in the station's CID was that the motive for this murder was almost certainly drug-related and that it might possibly be something to do with a disagreement between Fowler and Matthews. Since Fowler apparently owned the club, and was almost certainly lying when he said he didn't tolerate drugs on the premises, and Matthews appeared to have been the chief dealer, it was probably down to an argument about something mundane like the split of profits. All this was conjecture, of course, but DCI Knox, the head of the investigation, specialized in conjecture. Me, though, I wasn't so sure, not least because I didn't think Fowler would have used an obscure poison to rid himself of a troublesome business partner. But I did think there were plenty of questions he could provide an answer for, particularly regarding the possible involvement of the Holtzes, and I was keen to hear them.

But it seemed I was going to have to wait a little longer.

'He's not there,' said Elaine Toms, coming back to the papers on the bar. 'Either that or he's not answering.'

'Have you got his address?' She nodded, and wrote it down on a piece of paper. I took it, thanking her, and put it in my pocket. It was local. 'And what's your position here, Miss Toms?'

'I told you, I've already been interviewed about the murder.'

'Well, we're talking to you again. I'd just like to refresh myself of your account.'

'It was a DI I talked to.'

'DI Capper. Yes, I know. Now, if you'll answer the questions.'

'Have you got any ID?'

She was trying to be difficult but I wasn't going to argue about it, so I took out my warrant card and showed it to her, as did Berrin. She inspected them both carefully, paying particular attention to mine. 'It's not a very good photo of you,' she told me.

'With me, the camera always lies,' I said. 'Now, your position?'

'I manage the place.'

'And how long have you been here for?'

'Just over a year. I joined last July.'

'You knew Shaun Matthews pretty well, then?'

She sighed theatrically. 'Yeah, I knew Shaun Matthews pretty well. You know, I've said all this before.'

'Humour me. I presume you knew he dealt drugs?'

'Are you asking me or telling me?'

'I'm asking you.'

She shrugged. 'I heard that he did some dealing here and there and that he might even have done some in this place, but I never saw him do any and I never saw anyone else take any stuff either. Occasionally you get someone off their face, but if they get like that we don't serve them and we chuck them out. They're certainly not sold the stuff in here. I only heard Shaun was meant to be this big-time dealer after he died.'

'You're sticking to the party line, then? That Arcadia's pretty much drug free and that you don't go in for that sort of thing here.'

She glared at me. 'We don't. Now, if you've finished . . .'

'Does Stefan Holtz own this place?'

'Who?'

'Stefan Holtz. You must have heard of him.' She shook her head. 'He's a well-known local businessman, to use the term very loosely.'

'Look, as far as I'm concerned, Roy Fowler owns this place. That's who hired me and that's who pays me.'

'Are you sure the name Stefan Holtz means nothing to you?' asked Berrin.

'Oh, it speaks,' she said with a smirk.

Berrin looked slightly embarrassed. 'Just answer the question,' he persisted, trying not to be intimidated by her, but not making a particularly good job of it.

She slowly turned her head, faced him down, took a breath, then spoke. 'Yes, I'm sure.' She turned back to me. 'I don't know a Stefan Holtz.'

'Mr Fowler was going to get us a list of casual door staff who've worked here over the past six months,' I continued, 'but so far we haven't received it.'

'Oh dear,' she said with a cheeky half-smile.

'You're the manager,' said Berrin. 'Can you provide us with that information?'

46

The smile disappeared rapidly. 'I haven't got time. You'll need to speak to Mr Fowler about it.'

'We would do if he was here,' I said, thinking that this was one of the great problems with policework. That most of the time you were constantly trying to get blood out of a stone. 'Just tell us the name of the company who supplies the doormen, then,' I added, not wanting to waste any more time with Elaine Toms, 'and we'll contact them.'

She paused, and the reason she paused was simple. If there were any dodgy ownership issues, then they would spread to the company who supplied the doormen because with nightclubs that's how things work. She wouldn't want to give out the information but I knew she couldn't lie about it either, in case Fowler had already given us the name and I was just testing her.

'It's an outfit called Elite A,' she said eventually. Berrin wrote the name down. 'But I don't know how much they'll be able to tell you. I don't think they're too hot on the paperwork front.'

'What makes you say that?'

'You know what these security firms are like. They use freelancers.'

'Did Shaun Matthews come via Elite A?'

'I think so, originally, but it was before my time so I couldn't say for sure. The papers said something about him being poisoned.'

'That's what we believe.'

She shook her head as if she couldn't comprehend such an end for him. 'What's the world coming to, eh?'

'To the same place it's always been, Miss Toms. Full of not very nice people doing not very nice things to each other.' I resisted adding that with Shaun Matthews's demise there was at least one fewer of them. 'If you hear from Mr Fowler, please ask him to get in touch with us immediately.'

She took the card I gave her with my number on it. 'So, have you got any suspects?'

'We're working on a number of leads,' I answered, using the stock detective's line which was basically a euphemism for 'No', and she obviously recognized it for what it was because she turned away with another of those half-smiles. The discussion was over.

When we were back in the car, Berrin turned to me with an expression of concern. 'I don't think I did too well in there,' he said. 'You handled it a lot better than me.'

Berrin's young, he's a graduate, and, like most of us, he's still got a lot to learn. Unlike most of us, he recognizes it, and it means he's not as confident as he could be. He'd only been promoted out of uniform three months earlier, and apart from Rudi, the casual killer and carjacker, this was his first murder case. It was also the first time we'd worked together.

I shrugged. 'I've been in the game a lot longer, which makes it a lot easier to handle people like her. Remember, you're the one who's the boss. With the cocky ones it can be easy to forget.'

He nodded thoughtfully. At that moment, he reminded me of a contestant from that TV programme *Faking It*. One month to turn a good-looking Home Counties college boy into a Met detective. He was working hard to master the ropes, to make a good impression, but he didn't look a natural.

He turned to me, the concern replaced by determined zeal, the kind you sometimes see on the faces of door-to-door missionaries. 'I let her get me on the wrong foot. That was the problem. I didn't do enough to make her show me respect. It won't happen again.'

'I know it won't,' I said, patting him on the shoulder. 'You work with me, you'll be Dirty Harry in no time.'

He pulled out of the parking space. 'Yeah, right.'

Roy Fowler lived in a modern, showy-looking development complex near Finsbury Park. It's what these days they like to call a gated community, although there usually tends to be very little community-wise about them. We were stopped at the main gates by a uniformed doorman who was well past retirement age and looked like he'd have trouble stopping a runaway skateboard let alone a shadowy intruder. We showed him our credentials and were waved into the car park in front of the five six-storey buildings that were arranged in a semi-circle around the well-kept, if rather dull, communal gardens. Fowler lived in apartment number 12 which was in the second building on the left.

But if he wasn't at work, he wasn't at home either. We buzzed on his intercom for several minutes but didn't get an answer. I phoned the Arcadia and double-checked the address with Elaine Toms. It was the right one. Fowler still hadn't turned up at the club either, a fact that was beginning to irritate me and her.

We sat in the car and waited for ten minutes without result, then decided to make our way back to the station. It had been an unproductive morning and Berrin was beginning to look depressed, as if it had only just dawned on him that life in CID was a lot less interesting than it looked on the telly.

It was as we were coming out of Fowler's complex that I saw it. A dark blue Range Rover driving by just in front of us. It only passed our field of vision for a couple of seconds at most but I noticed straight away that it had holes in the paintwork and industrial taping over two of the windows. It kept going and I memorized the number plate as Berrin pulled out, heading the other way.

'Did you see that car?' I asked him.

Berrin is not the most observant man in the world. 'What car?' was his reply.

I thought about it for a few seconds. Who'd be daft enough to be driving around in a bullet-ridden Range Rover in broad daylight? But those holes didn't look like they'd been made by anything else – what else could have made them? – and, as I've said before, you should never underestimate the stupidity of criminals. It was probably wasting someone's time but I took my mobile from my pocket and phoned the station to report a suspicious vehicle, giving its location and possible route.

'Do you want to turn round and go after it?' said Berrin, looking like his depression was lifting.

'It's probably nothing. Let's leave it for the uniforms. I need to get something to eat.'

'What do you think? Do you reckon he's flown the coop?'

The loud, confident voice belonged to DCI Knox, the big boss. No question of him ever losing control of an interview. Berrin and I were sat in his office, on the other side of his imposing desk, explaining the position regarding the lack of intelligence as to Roy Fowler's whereabouts.

'We don't know,' said Berrin. 'He was certainly aware that we were meant to interview him this morning.'

'It seems odd, though,' I said. 'Him disappearing off so soon. It's like an admission of guilt, but, if we're honest, we haven't really got anything on him.'

Knox nodded in his sage-like way. 'True. But then where is he?'

It was a good question. 'Maybe he had more pressing engagements and thought we could wait,' I said eventually.

Knox snorted. 'Well, he's wrong if he thinks that. We'll put out an alert. Any patrol that sees him, they can pick him up and bring him in for questioning. I don't like the way these small-time villains think they're royalty these days.'

We both nodded in general agreement. It was always good to agree with Knox, always fatal to pick holes in his pronouncements. Unlike Berrin, he was not one of life's listeners, whatever he liked to claim. 'My door's always open' was one of his favourite mantras, which might have been true literally, but that was about it.

'What about the list of bouncers? I don't suppose we've got that then, have we?'

I shook my head. 'No. We spoke to the manager, a Miss Toms, and she told us that a company called Elite A supplied all the casual door staff they used.'

'I wonder if she's involved in the drugs scene at the Arcadia,' mused Knox.

'Has she got a record?'

He shook his head. 'I don't think so, but that doesn't mean anything, does it? There was definitely dealing going on down there and it's almost certain that it originated on the door. So the manager's probably in on it. You'll need to check up on this Elite A. I don't suppose whoever runs them's whiter than white.' Out of the corner of my eye, I saw Berrin nodding in agreement. Cheeky sod. A politician already. 'Now,' continued Knox, 'we've talked to three of the other doormen at Arcadia who all worked there on a permanent basis, so we only really need to catch up with the temporaries who've been there the last six months, although that could be quite a few. They're a busy club. I'll leave you two to do that. Try to get to talk to them all by Monday p.m. at the latest. We need to tie up all the loose ends on this.'

'And these other doormen haven't told us anything useful?'

'No. They all knew Shaun Matthews to varying degrees but none said they'd ever seen him selling drugs of any description and, of course, they all denied selling any themselves. When confronted by witness statements testifying to his extra-curricular activities, they all expressed varying degrees of surprise.'

'Perhaps we should offer some sort of reward,' I suggested. 'That might persuade them to give us some information we could use.'

'It's a possibility if we still don't get anywhere, but budgets are tight and I'm not sure I'd feel right doling out much-needed money to solve the murder of a violent drug dealer.' Once again, I caught Berrin nodding.

'It might get us a result.'

'We'll have to see. We've got pretty much our whole allocation resting on the Robert Jones case. If we have to pay out on that then we're not going to be able to offer a reward on anything until 2010.'

I baulked at the mention of Robert Jones. Always did. It was one of the few cases that had truly disturbed me in all my time in the Met. Robert was a thirteen-year-old schoolboy who'd disappeared while doing his morning paper round six months earlier. His body had been found a few days afterwards buried in a shallow grave in woodland out in Essex. He'd been stabbed three times in the chest and his clothing had been tampered with, indicating some sort of sexual assault. I'd had to break the news of the discovery to the parents, along with the WPC who'd been their liaison officer. They'd been a pleasant, ordinary middle-class couple who'd only let Robert do the round because he'd been keen to save up enough money to buy a new bike. I'd watched, unable to do anything to help, as they'd crumbled in front of me, while the WPC had comforted his little sister when she'd appeared in the doorway, too young to understand what was going on. Robert had been their only son, his family's pride and joy. What had got me the most was the total and utter injustice of it all. A young boy from a good home, never been in trouble – unlike so many of the little bastards we had to deal with – seeking to better himself, only to be struck down in the space of a few moments by someone who probably had no idea of the terrible damage he was inflicting. It was such a waste and, six months on, we were no nearer bringing the killer to justice, even though a reward of twenty-five thousand pounds had been offered for information leading to a conviction: fifteen thousand from the police and ten thousand from a local businessman. Unlike Robert Jones, his killer had had all the luck.

'What about the poisoning angle?' I asked. 'Any more news on that?'

Knox furrowed his brow into deep, craggy lines. 'Well, it's coming along,' he said without a huge amount of conviction. 'WDC Boyd's been liaising with the poisons department at Guy's and doctors from the Home Office about this substance and its possible source, as you know, but I'm not sure how much help it is. I mean, it's not as if you can pop into the pharmacy, pick some of this stuff up, and sign the Poisons Register. It's cobra venom, for God's sake.'

'So there's no place you could get it in this country?'

Knox shook his head. 'Not officially, no. As far as anyone seems to know, the only place you can find it is in the mouth, or whatever, of the cobra. And as far as I'm aware, none of them lives within five thousand miles of here. You'll have to talk to Boyd about all that, though. She's now our resident toxins expert. The thing is, I don't know how much help either she or anyone else can be. We haven't got a clue where you actually get it from in a useable format, where this particular batch may have originated, or anything like that. All we know is that somehow someone came into possession of enough of the stuff to kill three people, and somehow got the opportunity to inject the whole lot into the left arm of a sixteen-stone bouncer without him noticing, or getting any sort of opportunity to seek medical help.'

DC Berrin exhaled slowly and thoughtfully. 'It's a mystery,' he said. A statement of the obvious if ever there was one, but which pretty much summed things up.

Iversson

The lunchtime traffic was heavy and I was paranoid. Not surprising when you're driving at speeds a two-legged dog could muster in a car that looks like it's been used in an Arnie Schwarzenegger film, even down to the bloodstains on the back seat, and you know that most of the bullets wedged in the exterior were meant for you. But what choice did I have? The Range Rover was registered in my name and I needed to stash it somewhere where it was not going to receive undue attention. I was therefore on my way now to the abode of one Gary Tyler, a bloke who did occasional work for us, and who had the invaluable asset of a lock-up over in Silvertown that I could use for storage purposes until I worked out what to do. I looked at my watch. It was five to one. What a twenty-four hours.

There'd been no news on the shootings the previous night. Not a dickie bird. Whoever had organized our little warehouse reception – and some bastard most definitely had – was as efficient as he was ruthless. Three bodies left behind in an industrial estate in the heart of north London amid a load of gunfire, and not a peep about it in the press or on the TV, and I'd checked enough times that day. When I'd spoken to my partner Joe Riggs on the blower earlier, he'd been shocked (although not half as shocked as I'd been when one of our most reliable employees had started taking potshots at me), and it was only when he'd asked me whether I'd managed to pick up the money in advance that I knew the tight bastard was all right. In the end, we'd decided not to say anything about Eric's death. It was unfair to the family, no-one was denying that, and it was a decision that could easily come back to haunt us, but what was the alternative? At least by keeping stum, we'd hopefully avoid a lot of unwanted attention.

But it was Tony's role in the whole thing we found the hardest to understand. I suppose we both thought we'd known him pretty well. He didn't work for us so much these days, less and less over the past couple of years, but that didn't mean a thing. He was still someone we thought we could depend on, and right up until the previous night he'd never let us down once. So what had made him suddenly turn a gun on me and Eric, as well as a man he'd never even met before, just like that? This was the big question.

We'd left it that I would see what I could dig up on Fowler while Joe would do the same with Tony, and we'd meet up the following day. In the meantime, I needed to be rid of this motor, and Fowler's briefcase, which was still on the front seat.

The lights up ahead turned red and I came to a halt in the nearside lane, the third car back. In front of me was a black BMW with tinted windows blasting out a thumping bass so powerful that it was making me shake in my seat. When I'd been a kid, punk had been the big thing, and my mum had constantly droned on about how the music sounded terrible and you couldn't understand a word the singers were shouting, and I'd thought what the fuck did she know? Now I knew it was a generational thing. This stuff, this garage shite that had suddenly become all the rage, it was a pile of dung, to be honest with you. There weren't even any tunes as such, just some bloke bragging about how hard he was, and how much the ladies rated him. Kids these days – they've got no taste.

I saw the flashing lights in the rear-view mirror and cursed, because I knew straight away that I was trapped. The lane next to me was full of traffic and the lights were still red. The cop car put its hazards on and two uniforms got out, donning their caps. I was just going to have to front it.

They came round either side of the Range Rover and the one nearest me tapped on the driver's-side window.

'Afternoon, officer,' I said as jauntily as possible.

'Can you turn your engine off, sir, please?' he asked, giving me the standard copper's-in-control, I'll-know-if-you're-guilty-don't-try-to-hide-it gaze. He was about twenty-five and not particularly big. Rosy cheeks, too. About as menacing as Tony Blair.

The lights were still red, and on a main road as well. I couldn't believe it. No wonder London had traffic problems. That was the fucking mayor for you. A coma victim could have done a better job. Seeing as I had no choice, I switched off. The other copper, who was even younger, looked to be inspecting the bullet holes on the other side.

'How can I help you, officer?'

'Can I just take these for a moment?' he asked, leaning in the window and removing the keys from the ignition.

'What's the problem? I'm in a bit of a hurry, to tell you the truth.'

He gave the interior a bit of a nose and spotted the two dark stains on the back seat where Fowler had bled. I'd given them a clean-up earlier that morning, but they still looked a bit suspicious. I'd never been much cop at domestic chores.

'There appear to be bullet holes in your vehicle, sir,' he said, totally deadpan, like he was telling me I had toothpaste round my mouth.

'I live on a rough estate, officer.'

The other one now opened the back passenger door and began

inspecting the stains more closely. 'What happened here?' he asked. 'This looks a lot like blood.'

'It's red wine,' I told him. 'I spilled it in there yesterday. It's a right bastard to get rid of.'

'Would you mind stepping out of the car, sir,' said the first one, opening the door for me.

'No problem,' I said wearily, and got out.

Still holding the handle, he shut it behind me at just the moment I delivered a ferocious uppercut that sent him flying. He landed on his back, absolutely sparko, narrowly missing the traffic in the next lane, and his cap rolled off, only to be immediately crushed by a passing minibus full of pensioners.

'Oi!' shouted his partner, going for his extendable baton.

There was too much traffic to cross the road before he caught up with me so I ran round the front of the Range Rover, mounted the pavement, and charged him before he had a chance to actually extend the baton. I punched him full in the face, knocking him off balance, then got my leg round his and tripped him up. He went down, his nose bleeding badly, and I ran back round to retrieve my keys.

But cars were stopping all over the place now to watch the drama unfolding and the lights had gone red again. A well-built workman was getting out of his van and glaring at me, looking worryingly like he was about to carry out a citizen's arrest. Then, from up the street, I heard the sound of a siren. It meant a quick decision.

Run for it.

So that's what I did, and as I tore off at a rate of knots in the opposite direction to the siren, past the surprised expressions of passing civilians, it struck me then that however bad I thought my predicament was ten minutes ago, it was now a hundred times worse.

*

If anyone ever wanted to kill Johnny Hexham, he would not be a difficult man to find. Every lunchtime between one and two, as regular as clockwork, he was in the Forked Tail public house, a mangy dive off Upper Street, gossiping with his lowlife cronies and plotting his next poxy moneymaking scheme. Sometimes he'd be there earlier, sometimes he wouldn't leave until the early hours of the following morning, but without fail, he was always in residence for that one hour. I got there at ten to two, and waited in the doorway of a boarded-up shop across the street, trying to look inconspicuous. As it was a Friday, I guessed that the lazy little shit would be in for an all-dayer, but, like the creature of habit he was, I thought he'd probably whip out for a few minutes to place some bets on the horses, having picked up some tips from the Paddy barman. I didn't much want to approach Johnny in the bar where there were too many people with big ears, but I would if I had to. Things were not going well for me and I wanted some answers quick.

And bang, like an assassin's dream, there he was, coming out of the door, already filling out one of the betting slips he always carried with him. I looked at my watch – one minute past two – and crossed the street, coming up behind him.

'Johnny Hexham. Long time no see.' And it was, too. Getting close to six months.

He swung round and clocked me straight away. He didn't look too pleased but worked hard to hide it. 'All right, Max,' he said, coming to a halt. 'How's it going, mate?'

I walked up and took him casually by the arm. The grip was light but firm enough to let him know I wasn't fucking around. 'Not good, Johnny. Not good. There are a few questions I need answers to fairly urgently, and I think you might be able to help.'

'What's the Bobby, then?'

'Eh?'

'The Bobby Moore, score.'

'It's about a certain Mr Fowler.'

'Fuck,' he said. 'I knew he'd be trouble.'

'You don't know the half of it.' I let go of his arm and we walked down in the direction of Chapel Market.

Johnny looked at me nervously. We might have been old schoolmates but he was switched on enough to notice that that wasn't going to count for much in this conversation. I am a man of compassion but, to be honest, you don't want to get on the wrong side of me.

'What happened, then?' he asked.

'You put this bloke, Fowler, on to me. Why?'

'There was nothing bad about it, honest. I just thought the two of you could do some business. He needed some security—'

'How do you know him?' I had to remember not to use the word 'did'.

'I don't really. It was Elaine who put me on to him. Elaine Toms.'

'Jesus. Is she still around?'

Elaine had been in the same year as us in school, way back when Duran Duran were the kings of the rock world and furry pixie boots were all the rage. She'd always been the girl the boys liked because, without exception, she fucked on the first date, the first date only ever meant buying her one drink, and she was nice to look at. Which you've got to admit is something of a rare and joyous combination. Not that I'd ever managed to get her in the sack. There'd always been too much of a queue in front of me. And I'd been a bit of a skinny runt in school, too. Like decent wine, I'd matured with age. I hadn't clapped eyes on Elaine in getting close to fifteen years, probably longer, and briefly wondered what she looked like now.

'Yeah, Elaine's still around. She's the manager of Fowler's club.'

'The Arcadia.'

'That's the one. I still see her now and again because I drink down there sometimes. Not often, like, cos it's a bit too young for me, all these kids jumping about, out of it on all sorts, but it's worth a Captain Cook. Anyway, she told me that Fowler was having trouble with some people and he needed protection. She asked me if I knew of anyone who might be able to assist and so, you know, I thought about it for a couple of minutes, then your name popped up. I know you're into all that shit. I thought you could do with the business.' He turned and gave me his trademark boyish smile, the one I knew had got Elaine Toms into bed on more than one occasion back in the old days. Johnny Hexham, the loveable rogue.

But it didn't work. Not today. 'It was a bad move, Johnny.'

He looked worried. 'Why? What happened?'

We turned into Chapel Market and made our way down the middle between the two lines of stalls. As usual, it was noisy and crowded. I decided against giving him the whole story. Johnny was no grass and probably wouldn't go to the law if his balls went missing, but it was best to err on the side of caution.

'I almost got killed. That's what happened. These people Fowler had trouble with, they weren't messing about.'

'Blimey, Max, I'm sorry. I didn't mean to get you in the Barry. I thought it was routine stuff.'

'Who are these people? And what's the trouble he's been having, exactly?'

'I don't know. Honest. It was something to do with the club. That's all I was told.' He exhaled dramatically. 'Fuck, this is bad news. What's happened to Fowler?'

I glared at him. 'Forget Fowler. And forget you ever put him in contact with me. OK?'

Johnny's head went up and down like a nodding dog. 'Yeah, yeah. Of course. No problem. Consider it done.'

I took his arm again, this time squeezing harder. He turned to protest but I stared him down. 'Are you sure you're telling me the truth, Johnny? You know nothing about that club that might help to explain why people are getting all trigger happy with Fowler?'

'No . . .'

'Because if I find out you do know something, anything at all, then I'm going to hunt you down and I'm going to kill you. Understand?' Harsh words, but definitely necessary under the circumstances.

'Fuck it, Max, I'm telling the truth. I know there's some dealing goes on down there, charlie and all that, but that's about it.'

They say the eyes are the windows to the soul. I slowed right down and stared straight into his. But the windows were dirty and I couldn't tell whether he was bullshitting or not.

'That's all I know, I swear to you. Look, Max, I'm sorry. I really am. I was just trying to help.'

I let go of his arm, and managed a brief smile, though God knows what there was to smile about. 'Well, it's a brand of help I can do without in the future. And remember, say nothing about seeing me to anyone. OK? Including Elaine Toms.'

'No problem. My lips are sealed.' He gave me a concerned look. A mate to a mate. 'Everything's all right, though, isn't it, Max?'

'Oh yeah,' I told him, turning away. 'Tickety-fucking-boo. See you around, Johnny.'

Gallan

I didn't have to work that night but with my home life being as non-existent as it was, I decided to stay late in the incident room and catch up on paperwork. Berrin wasn't so keen and took off bang on five-thirty, something I duly noted. There was an all-units out on the car I'd spotted with the bullet holes in it. Two of the station's uniforms had stopped it and there'd been an altercation with the driver, who'd fled the scene on foot, having assaulted and injured both officers. Suspected bloodstains had been found in the vehicle, which was registered in the name of Max Iversson, an ex-soldier with no previous record, who matched witness descriptions of the driver. Thankfully, it was nothing to do with me any more, but I was pleased that my observance had paid off, even if the uniforms who'd done the stopping and who were now off sick probably weren't.

It was ten to nine when I left the station. I went to a cheap Italian off Upper Street I occasionally frequent and had a bowl of pasta and some garlic bread, washed down with a couple of welcome bottles of Peroni now that I was off duty. I suppose you could say it was a lonely way to spend a Friday evening, and you'd be right, it was, but I was beginning to get used to it. This time barely a year ago, it had all been a lot different. I'd been a DI at another station south of the river, heading up through the ranks in the direction of the DCI slot, with three commendations under my belt. Crime down there was bad, the hours were tough . . . Paradise it wasn't. But it wasn't a bad life and, unlike a lot of my colleagues, I still had a stable domestic situation. A wife of fifteen years, an eleven-year-old daughter, a decent house in an area where the weekly mugging tallies were still in single figures . . .

Then, on the night they brought in Troy Farrow, it all changed.

Troy Farrow was a seventeen-year-old street robber who specialized in making victims of schoolkids my daughter's age, relieving them of their mobile phones and pocket money, and old ladies, who he liked to pick off on pension day, sometimes breaking a few frail bones in the process. He had nine convictions altogether but had only spent a total of three months inside, so the law didn't exactly have him shaking in his Nike trainers. He was shouting and cursing and threatening all sorts as the arresting officers booked him in for what was likely to be his tenth conviction: the violent removal of a mobile phone from the ear of a young secretary foolish enough to have been walking down a busy street early evening without keeping her wits about her. Unfortunately for him, the street was under surveillance by officers in plain clothes and he was caught within minutes. I was detailed to interview him, along with a DC, because we were interested in getting information from him regarding the near gang rape of an eleven-year-old by a group who'd also robbed her of her mobile and the bag of sweets she was carrying. We didn't think Farrow had been involved – it wasn't his style to molest his victims, and the suspects had been described as being aged between twelve and fourteen – but we were pretty sure he would know who was. There wasn't much that went on in Farrow's estate, crime-wise, that he wasn't aware of, and kids like that would almost certainly have bragged about what they'd done.

Farrow calmed down as he was taken down to the interview room by two of the arresting officers, with me and the DC following a few yards behind. What happened next is still something of a mystery. As Farrow and the arresting officers turned and entered the room, he turned and said something to one of them that I didn't quite catch but which I was told later went along the lines of 'You pussies can't do nothing with me'. The officer had then made a fatal mistake. He'd let his frustration with the legal system and the cocky criminals who frequented it get the better of him, and had apparently called Farrow 'a black bastard', causing a further, much more violent struggle to ensue. We'd hurried into the interview room at just the moment when one of the officers slammed Farrow's head into the wall. Not hard enough to knock him out, but enough to open a nasty cut across his forehead. 'Assault! Assault!' he'd screamed. 'They're killing me! Get me a fucking brief! Now!' The two arresting officers had let go, and we'd helped Farrow, who was handcuffed behind his back, into one of the chairs. 'Get my brief,' he'd said, all calm now, blood oozing out of the wound. 'I want to make a formal complaint. I ain't saying another word until I've seen my brief.' And he didn't. Not a word.

The formal complaint made, all four of us who'd been in the interview room were later questioned by representatives of the Police Complaints Authority, and all of us stuck to the same story: that Troy Farrow had stumbled during the struggle and had accidentally knocked his head against the wall. The arresting officer who Farrow claimed had racially abused him denied the charge but did admit calling him a bastard, and I couldn't comment on this because I hadn't heard the exchange. I know that a lot of people would think it was wrong for me not to say what I saw but at the time I thought no lasting harm had been done. Farrow was patched up by the station's doctor and needed two stitches, and anyway, it was no more than he deserved. Plus, I didn't want to be the whistleblower. The police get enough flak as it is, and sometimes when you're a copper it does feel like the whole world's against you, so you don't want to be putting the knife into your own side. In the end, I was never going to be the one who ruined a colleague's career (which is what I would have done) over one second's stupidity and hotheadedness. I just couldn't justify it to myself.

And, at first, it looked like we might have got away with it. I don't think the people from the PCA believed us but it was our word against that of a known criminal, and we weren't budging, so eventually they had little choice but to conclude that the incident was accidental, and that Farrow had misheard what the arresting officer had said.

But that wasn't the end of it. A couple of months later the second arresting uniform, the one who hadn't pushed Farrow's head into the wall, admitted what had happened to a bloke in his local pub after one beer too many, only to find out afterwards that the bloke was a local investigative journalist, doing an exposé of racism in the Force. With the conversation recorded, the story appeared two days later in the local paper, and the case was suddenly reopened. I found the local media and even *London Tonight* parked on my doorstep, asking me if I was a liar and a racist. I might occasionally be the one, but I'm definitely not the other. The whole thing was a nightmare and, although my boss, DCI Renham, a guy I'd worked for for getting close to five years, fought to keep me in my position, the tide of attention was overwhelming, and in the end, with the story refusing to go away, the Brass were forced to act. Both arresting officers lost their jobs; the DC, with me, was put back in uniform; and I was demoted to DC.

It was a shameful episode, the whole thing, and for a long time I found it difficult to come to terms with. You see, in my eyes, I hadn't done a lot wrong. I'd made a mistake but I thought the punishment far outweighed the crime. I took it out on my wife, made life difficult for her, and maybe things between us hadn't been quite as strong as I'd thought, because three months later, after one argument too many, we separated. It turned out she'd been having an affair. I suppose this would have been understandable were it not for the fact that the other man happened to be the intrepid journalist who'd broken the story in the first place. The cheeky bastard had gone round to interview her about what effect the story was having on her and the family, and clearly it was having quite a big one because somehow, not long afterwards, maybe even that day, they'd ended up in the sack.

What do you do in that sort of situation? What can you do? Nothing except pick yourself up, dust yourself down, and remember that what goes around comes around. There is justice in this world, it's just that sometimes it takes a long time before it bothers to show itself. I had no choice but to cling to that fact as I gathered up my possessions, put in for a transfer, and headed north of the river for the first time in my career, ending up at probably the most controversial station in the entire Met, a place still haunted by the betrayal of one of its most senior detectives.

DS Dennis Milne was without doubt Britain's most corrupt police officer: a valued and long-standing member of CID by day, a hired killer with God knows how many corpses to his credit by night. His shadow still hung over the station like a noxious cloud, even though it had been close to two years since his grim secret had been uncovered and he'd disappeared into thin air. It didn't matter. Time would be a slow healer here, and there were a number in CID, including DCI Knox, who'd be forever tainted by their long association with the station's most infamous son. Mud sticks, and maybe that was why I'd settled in so easily there.

Since my arrival, I'd rented myself a half-decent flat in Tufnell Park, and had managed to pull myself back up to the rank of detective sergeant. A far cry from the old days, and I was still waiting for justice (my ex and the journalist were now shacked up together and my daughter even claimed that she quite liked him), but things could always have been worse. I still had a job and, against all the odds, I still got something out of it.

I left the restaurant at five past ten and headed round the corner to the Roving Wolf, a pub used by the station's CID, to see if there was anyone in there. It was busy, but I spotted a couple of DCs I knew vaguely standing near the bar and joined them for a couple of pints. They were both interested in how the Matthews case was going but I couldn't tell them a lot. Slowly was the word that about best described it. Conversation drifted on to other things and I left them at eleven, wandering down onto Upper Street in search of that elusive late-night creature, the black cab.

Upper Street was buzzing as usual, its constant stream of pavement cafés and trendy bistros bustling with custom as people of all ages, and pretty much every race under the sun, took advantage of the balmy evening. Strains of jazz, mamba, flamenco and half a dozen other musical styles drifted out of the open doors and windows of a dozen different establishments, giving the place a pleasant, continental feel. It almost felt like being on holiday and, for one who'd travelled up Upper Street a few times back in the 1980s, the transformation was incredible. Once a barren, dark place of nasty drinking hovels and little else where only the adventurous and the foolish came after dark, it had now become Islington's version of Paris's Left Bank. If you weren't careful, you might even forget to watch your back.

Incredibly, I managed to hail a cab near Islington Green after only five minutes, which had to be some sort of record for that time of night. I thought about heading home but for some reason I wasn't that tired. Instead, I asked the driver to take me to the Arcadia nightclub. He gave me a funny look in the mirror but did as he was told and we made our way in silence up to the Highbury Corner roundabout, and then left onto the less continental and more menacing Holloway Road. I was hoping to catch Roy Fowler in residence and collar him for a few minutes since I felt confident that if he didn't have anything to hide, he'd return there sooner rather than later. If you're in the nightclub business, you don't trust other people to look after your investment for too long, not if you want anything left at the end of it.

Four hundred yards up the Holloway Road, just past the Liverpool Road turning, the traffic slowed right down as a large group of maybe twenty-five or thirty people standing outside a pub suddenly spilled out into the road. Seconds later there were shouts and the sound of glass smashing, and a group of five of them split off from the rest in what looked like a wild dance. Others ran over to pile in and the whole scrum of them lumbered into the middle of the road, breaking apart and re-forming as half a dozen individual battles were fought, oblivious to the cars driving by. A bottle sailed lazily through the air, bouncing off the roof of the vehicle in front of us before ending up unbroken in the bus lane on the other side of the street.

'Fucking kids,' said the taxi driver in a voice that was half-snarl, half-sigh, as the group, most of whom looked no more than twenty, swirled back towards the pavement. One of them went down, putting up his arms in a vain effort to protect himself as he disappeared beneath a rapid-fire welter of kicks from at least three others. A girl screamed something unintelligible and rushed out of the watching crowd to intervene, wading into the kickers, handbag aloft. The one on the ground, sensing an opportunity, jumped to his feet and got out of the firing line. He was holding his head and bleeding from the nose.

The taxi driver accelerated and we left them behind to their fighting. 'Fucking kids,' he said again. 'They get worse and worse.' I nodded and mumbled something in reply, thinking that that was the thing with London. One minute you were drinking in the ambient atmosphere of a laid-back summer evening, the next you'd stepped unwittingly into an ugly battlezone. I suppose that's why some people like it so much. The variety.

There was a long queue of revellers, mainly under-twenty-fives, snaking back along the street from the entrance to the Arcadia. I got the cab to stop directly outside, paid the driver in full, and tipped him a quid. 'Enjoy yourself,' he said, with a wave, as he drove off. Probably about ten years too late for that, I thought, but you never knew.

I walked to the head of the queue where a group of four male and one female door staff were frisking the waiting punters. One of them turned to me as I approached and gave me the same sort of funny look the cab driver had, like what on earth was a bloke in his mid-thirties in a suit he looked like he'd been wearing all day doing coming to a trendy joint such as this. 'Yeah?' he said, by way of greeting.

I produced my warrant card and thrust it in his face. 'Police. I'm here to see Mr Fowler.' I was getting *déjà vu* now.

He inspected the card, then looked back at me. 'I don't think he's here tonight,' he said.

'Well, Miss Toms'll do,' I said, and walked past him.

There was a line of four further doormen in the foyer just inside the main entrance and I walked past them, showed my warrant card to a very thin young lady with big hair at the desk, and asked her to phone up to Fowler. She reiterated what the doorman had said about him not being in, but I insisted. She let the phone in his office ring for about thirty seconds before telling me he wasn't there. Next she tried Elaine Toms, who apparently was in, but wasn't answering either. I had no great desire to enter the club proper but it didn't look like I was going to have any choice. I thanked her and headed through the door in front of me.

The place was heaving, as befitted a Friday night, with the majority of the youthful crowd packed onto the dance floor. The music was loud, repetitive and boring, the kind my daughter's thankfully too young to like. At the bar at the far end, I noticed a few older people, mainly men in their thirties, and even one or two in their forties, clustered together against the noise. Some of them were wearing suits, though none of them looked like office workers, and I wondered who they were.

My eyes drifted along, then stopped dead. Someone looked familiar. I walked nearer, manoeuvring my way through the crowd until I was only about ten yards away. Now I was absolutely sure. No doubt about it. I'd seen his photograph four hours earlier, after it was faxed over by his old regiment. The man in front of me, drinking a bottle of Becks and looking like he owned the place, was Max Iversson, the fugitive half the station was looking for.

Iversson

There was no way I was queueing to get into Fowler's place. There must have been two hundred people standing there like lemons while they waited for the doormen to give them the sort of attention my ex-missus used to give me when she'd drunk too many white wine spritzers. But who wants it off some bald bloke with no neck? Not me, that was for sure. I thought about heading straight to the front and saying I was mates with Elaine but, to tell you the truth, I didn't really want to draw attention to myself, not now I'd suddenly turned into the Fugitive. So I headed round the back, jumped over the locked gate that led into the staff car park, and scanned the deserted rear of the building for any sign of an entrance. It took all of about three seconds for me to spot a window slightly open on the ground floor, about a foot above head height. It wasn't much of a size but I'm quite a slim lad so I was confident I was going to get in. I hauled myself up with one hand while using the other to flick off the latch and open the window up fully. At the same time, I heard the unmistakable sound of piss hitting urinals and, as I poked my head inside, I saw a row of three blokes staring up at me as they deflated their bladders.

'Evening,' I said with a ready smile, trying hard to wriggle through the gap. 'You couldn't give us a hand, could you?'

The bloke nearest me, a young student type about twenty or so, looked shocked but nodded anyway, re-deposited himself in his trousers, and grabbed hold of my nearest hand, giving it a feeble tug.

'Come on, boy, put some welly into it. You couldn't even give yourself a hard-on with a grip like that.'

He tried again and, after a few grunts and groans of effort, managed to pull me in, with me landing on him a fair bit harder than I think he was expecting. I thanked him as he got unsteadily to his feet and, ignoring the strange looks coming from the other blokes in there, headed out of the door and into the club, recoiling momentarily from the wall of sound that hit me.

I scanned the room for Elaine, not sure I'd even recognize her after all this time, but couldn't see any sign of her. Mind you, I couldn't see a great deal among the buzzing crowd. I took a brief moment to admire a few of the scantily clad young females who seemed to be in abundance, then fought my way to the bar and waited for a space to open up, before ordering myself a beer from one of the harassed-looking bar staff. When it came about two minutes later, it cost me three quid. Three quid for a lousy bottle of Becks. If it was true that people were fighting for ownership of this place then it was no wonder. The money being turned over must have been incredible. I took a sip from the bottle and turned away from the bar, finding myself some space near the dance floor.

Which was when I saw her, walking purposefully in my direction while talking to one of the doormen, a stocky bloke who was striding fast just to keep up with her. I recognized her instantly. She'd changed quite a lot from school, as you'd imagine – I mean, it had been a long time – but it wasn't so much in the look. It was more the poise, the way she carried herself. Back then she'd been attractive, with lovely big brown eyes and a good body, but she'd never really made the best of it, probably because she hadn't really needed to. Now she looked hot, the type of woman most blokes are immediately attracted to because they know without a second's doubt that she'll be a demon between the sheets. She was wearing a black cocktail dress which matched her long curly hair and high-heeled court shoes. I wondered then whether that hound Johnny had slept with her more recently than school. If he had then he'd been a lucky man.

She turned away from the doorman as the two of them reached the bar and our eyes briefly met. Although she was still a few feet away and there were a number of people in between us, I saw an immediate flicker of recognition pass across her face. She stopped for a moment, then looked at me quizzically before approaching.

'Max? Max Iversson?' she shouted above the noise, walking up to me.

I got a glorious scent of musky perfume and warmth as she came up close. I tell you this, I wanted to have this woman before I'd even opened my mouth. She might have started off the chain of events that had almost had me killed but I'd suddenly become a man who was willing to forgive and forget.

'Hello, Elaine,' I said as coolly as I could manage. 'Long time no see. How are you? You look good.' I gave her a smile.

She smiled back. 'I'm well. You?'

'Yeah, not bad, not bad,' I said, my mouth almost in her ear. I was only going to be able to keep up a conversation with this amount of background noise for so long.

'Christ, it's a bit weird running into you like this. The last I heard you was in the army.'

'I did ten years, but I finished a long time back. You know how time flies.'

'Too right. So you're still local, then? I haven't seen you in here before.'

'No, it's a little bit young for me, to be honest. It's my first time.' And my last at these prices, I thought.

'So what brings you in here? On the pull, are you?' She grinned.

'Well, I came to see you, actually.' She looked surprised. 'It's about Johnny Hexham.'

The surprise turned to concern. 'Johnny? What about him? He's all right, isn't he?'

'Oh yeah, he's fine.' That bastard was always fine. 'At least he was when I left him earlier. Look, Elaine, I know it's an odd request, but I need to talk to you fairly urgently and it would be a lot easier if it wasn't here.'

The concern now turned to suspicion. This was a woman with a speedy turn in facial expressions. 'Look, Max, I'm running this place pretty much on my own tonight, so if you've got something to say—'

'I own a company that provides security. A few days ago you asked Johnny to put someone you know in touch with a company like that.'

She clicked. 'Oh shit. And yours was the company?'

'Correct.'

'So where's Roy? I haven't seen him all day. Do you know what's happened to him?'

'That's what I've got to talk to you about. But I don't want to do it in here. Is there any way you can get out and we can go somewhere a little more private? And a bit quieter?'

She thought about it for a moment, then nodded. 'I'll see what I can do. Wait here. I'll be back in a minute.'

I nodded and stayed where I was as she turned and disappeared into the crowd. While she was gone, a kid of no more than eighteen, out of his head on something, walked into one of the pillars that bordered the dance floor and knocked himself out. I watched as people stepped over him like he wasn't there until eventually a couple of his mates turned up and, laughing, dragged him away. Then, a few yards beyond them, I saw a bloke who looked well out of place. Mid to late thirties, scruffy suit, thick black hair; to be honest with you, he looked a lot like Columbo in his early days and, like Columbo, I knew straight off he was a copper. He was talking into a mobile phone and watching me at the same time. Our eyes met and I knew he was on to me, though Christ knows how. It was time once again for quick thinking. If he was in here, there could be more of them out front, making it too risky to go out that way.

I turned and, as casually as possible, headed back in the direction of the toilet, speeding up the moment I'd pushed through a large group of girls out on a hen night.

Gallan

As soon as I saw him, I knew I had to act fast. I didn't have a clue what he was doing there but he didn't look like he fitted in, and he was on his own. All that, however, was by the by. The most important thing was that he stayed put until reinforcements arrived. I pulled the mobile from my jacket pocket and called the station, at the same time moving slowly towards a pillar by the dance floor where I could keep an eye on him without attracting attention. I was bumped by a young bloke pushing past me and I turned and gave him a look, not that he even saw it. He was already ten yards further on. Cheeky little bastard. Dispatch picked up and I informed them loudly of my position and the fact that I was within thirty feet of a wanted man and needed back-up. I needed to repeat myself twice above the noise, and when I looked back towards Iversson I saw that he'd spotted me. He turned and walked away and I followed rapidly, telling Dispatch that he was on the move. 'Get here fast, I don't fancy tackling him on my own. Not after what happened this afternoon.'

Iversson disappeared into the toilet and I broke into as close a run as the crowds would allow, unsure how I was going to handle this. I didn't want to corner an ex-para in an enclosed place and present him with no option but to fight. I'm not as young as I used to be, or as fit, and the reason I'm a detective is that I like to detect rather than get involved with all the physical stuff. Plus, I knew I'd lose. But I wasn't going to let him go either. Not after he'd put two of our uniforms on the sicklist.

I pulled open the door to the toilets four seconds after he'd gone inside, turned left, and headed into the urinals area. There were half a dozen people in the place, all relieving themselves, while at the far end of the room in front of an open window was Iversson. He looked like he was just about to jump up and try to get out through it. Eight yards separated us.

He turned and saw me and I put my hands up to indicate that I wanted things to end peacefully, which I did. 'All right, police. Come along now, Max.' And then, of course, the standard police cliché: 'You're in enough trouble as it is without adding resisting arrest to the charges.' I took a couple of slow steps forward, careful not to agitate him.

Iversson nodded and added his own cliché: 'It's a fair cop, guv,' he said, taking a step towards me. Then, without warning, he grabbed an unlucky punter by the back of his shirt and flung him bodily in my direction. The poor sod was still in the process of taking a leak and I had to jump out of the way to avoid the spray, sliding over in a suspect-looking puddle as I did so. I banged my right knee jarringly hard and the mobile flew out of my hand. Iversson immediately turned, heaved himself up to the window with an agility that made me look even more like a Keystone Kop, and began squeezing himself through.

The bloke he'd pushed at me was first to react. Putting himself away amid a welter of curses, he turned, ran up to the window, and grabbed one of Iversson's flailing legs with both hands. It was a stupid move. The other leg bent, tensed, then lashed out, all in one split-second movement, striking the bloke in the side of the temple and sending him crashing into the communal urinal. His head hit the wall with an angry thud. Iversson's legs then began to disappear like spaghetti being dragged into a giant mouth. Ignoring the mobile phone, I jumped to my feet and ran towards them, managing to grab hold of one of his shoes just as it started to go out of the window. It came off in my hand and I was suddenly left standing looking at a fashionable-looking khaki moccasin while he made good his escape. I heard him land on the other side, then get to his feet and start running, impaired but hardly disabled by the fact that he now only had one item of footwear.

I looked at the semi-conscious bloke moaning on the floor, then at the handful of other punters who stood watching me in slightly amused silence, then finally at my watch.

It was twenty to twelve. Way past my bedtime.

Iversson

I was waiting when she arrived back at her Clerkenwell apartment. I watched her get out of the taxi and pay the driver from across the street, then as he pulled away and she turned towards the entrance, I crossed the road and jogged up behind her.

'Elaine.'

She turned round quickly, saw it was me, and narrowed her eyes. 'Well, well, well. The wanderer returns. What happened back there? You didn't tell me the police were after you.'

I stopped in front of her. 'I couldn't tell you anything in there. It was too bloody loud.'

'You'd better come in,' she said, fishing in her handbag for a key. 'I think we've got a fair bit to talk about, don't you?'

'You can say that again.'

'How did you find out where I lived?' she asked when we were inside her first-floor apartment.

'You're in the phone book,' I told her.

'So are plenty of other people with the name Toms,' she said, leading me through to a nicely furnished lounge with comfy-looking black leather chairs. She slung her jacket over one of the chairs and turned to me, waiting for an answer.

'Not as many as you'd think. I narrowed it down to five, then phoned Johnny Hexham. He said he thought you lived in Clerkenwell and there was only one E. Toms in Clerkenwell. Maybe you should think about being ex-directory.'

'I'll bear it in mind.' She looked down at my dirty sock. 'I won't ask,' she said.

'The police. They don't just want collars any more. They want everything.'

She smiled. 'Do you want a coffee?'

'Yeah, please.'

Five minutes later, when we were sitting in the leather chairs facing each other, she asked me what had happened with Fowler, and how come the police were after me. There was no point holding back, not if I wanted her to open up to me, so I told her everything, bar the bit where I shot Tony, which she didn't really need to know. In the account I gave Tony escaped and I never saw what happened to him.

She sat back in her chair and rubbed her hand across her temple. It was a gesture vaguely similar to one of Fowler's. 'Shit,' she said, which just about summed it up. 'I can't believe it. Dead. Poor old Roy.' Which I thought was a bit rich. Fowler had asked for it, I hadn't.

'What happened after I got out tonight?'

'Two vanloads of Plod turned up, and this detective who was already in there, the one chasing you, he started asking me a load of questions about what you were doing there.'

'What did you tell him?'

'I said I didn't have a clue who he was talking about. He didn't push things.'

'So, who are the people Fowler was having trouble with? I think I owe them after what they've done to me and one of my best employees.'

She leant forward and gave me a cold stare. 'Max, I'm telling you now. Do not get involved. Consider yourself lucky you're still in one piece and leave it at that.'

'Just tell me, Elaine.'

'You don't want to know. Honestly.'

'I'll be the judge of that.'

She paused, then, seeing that I wasn't going to give up, started talking. 'Roy's been under a lot of pressure lately and he's fallen in with some of the wrong people. He was getting into debt with the club.'

'How did he manage that with those prices? I'd have thought he'd be a millionaire.'

'He's a big spender and he's got a nasty coke habit that's been eating away at his finances. Anyway, he started borrowing money from people he should have kept well away from, and it didn't take long for them to start calling for their money back. And that's when he really fucked up. He allowed them to start dictating to him how he should do business. They wanted to sell their drugs in Arcadia with Roy overseeing things.'

'From what I hear the club's always had a drugs problem.'

'There's always been some dealing there, yeah, but not as much as some people seem to think. The place got raided a couple of times before I joined but that was a long time back and they never found nothing. But this was different. This was organized dealing.'

'When did it start?'

'I don't know exactly. At the time Roy didn't say anything to me about it. He was done in the past for importing gear, back in the eighties, and he was inside for four years, so it wasn't something he wanted to repeat. The dealing was all very underhand and if you'd come in there any night, like you did tonight, you wouldn't have seen it going on.' I nodded. That was true enough, although plenty of people had been off their faces. 'But there was stuff in there and if you'd asked the right people you'd have got coke, E, whatever you wanted. There's a few who do the deals, mainly the doormen, and they've never got much on them at any one time, so even if you were an undercover copper, you could only do them for possession. They never deal in big quantities. Roy kept the bulk of the stuff hidden in the place but I never knew where.

'Anyway, a week or two back, Roy starts acting really strange. Turning up late, shutting himself in his office, not getting involved in the running of the business. I asked him what was wrong but he just brushed me off. Then a few days back our chief doorman dropped dead, and it turns out he was poisoned.'

'Poisoned? I'd forgotten you killed people like that.'

'That's what the law said. And when Roy heard about it, it really set him off. He was jittery enough before, but after that he was all over the place, like he was next or something. But still he didn't want to talk about it.

'Then one night after we'd shut, I found him in his office, drunk or coked up or something. I told him he was going to have to tell me what was wrong, that he couldn't carry on like he was, and that's when I think he realized he was going to have to say something to someone. So he told me. He told me all about the dealing, how it was organized, what was going on. He sounded really gutted, like he didn't want to be involved.' Lying bastard, I thought, but didn't say anything. 'But the thing was, that wasn't the worst of it. He was skimming them. These associates of his. Taking more than his cut of the profits. A lot more.'

'How the hell did he think he was going to get away with that?'

She shook her head. 'He told me he was using the money to invest in something – and he wouldn't tell me what that something was – that would double or triple the cash he put in. Then, with that other cash he'd made from it, he'd pay these people what he owed them and get them out of his hair for ever.'

'Except it didn't work.'

'No. The investment never came through and they found out about the skimming before Roy made his cash. On the night I talked to him in his office, he'd been told by them that they knew what he'd been doing and that they wanted the money back with a hundred per cent interest, or they wanted the club. Roy was scared shitless. He didn't have the readies and he didn't want to give up the club. It would have left him with nothing. He'd asked them for an extension on the debt so that he could get himself sorted out, but they weren't interested. They're not the sort of people who specialize in being helpful.'

'I bet they're not.'

'When he talked to me he said they'd given him three days to come up with one or the other. The club or the money. He told me that even if he handed over the deeds to Arcadia, he still reckoned there was no guarantee they wouldn't break his legs for fucking them about. Or even kill him. He said that if he was going to go and see them, then he wanted back-up, but didn't know where he was going to get it from. He didn't know who out of the door staff would stand up for him and wasn't going to count on any of them. So he asked me if I knew of anyone independent, some security company who could be relied upon to provide him with a decent escort.'

'Why did he ask you?'

She shrugged. 'I don't think he knew where else to turn. We've worked together a while and I think he trusted me.'

I finished my coffee and put it on the glass coffee table next to me. 'And you said you'd see what you could do?'

She took a pack of cigarettes out of her handbag and offered me one. It had been a month since I'd quit but for the last few hours I'd known it was never going to last. The way things were going, living to a ripe old age with healthy lungs was the least of my concerns.

'Cheers,' I said, and took one.

She lit it for me with a thin black lighter, then lit her own and sat back in her seat, crossing her shapely legs and blowing smoke towards the ceiling. The dress rode up provocatively and I tried hard, but without much success, to ignore it. 'What choice did I have?' she asked. 'I didn't want to get involved, course I didn't, but he's been good to me since I've been working for him, and the least I could do was try to help out. So I spoke to Johnny and he spoke to Roy and it sounds like he put Roy in touch with you. I'm sorry about what happened but, you know, I had no idea it would end like this.'

'Forget it. It wasn't your fault. But I've got to be honest with you, there's a serious ring of bullshit about what he was telling you.'

'Look, I—'

'Yeah, I know, I know. You're telling me the truth.'

'I am.'

'I'm sure you are, but there's got to be a lot more to it than that. If Fowler was carrying the deeds to the club in the case he took to that meeting, then why kill him before he's signed them over? And, in fact, why kill him at all? Particularly when he's got people with him. There's a lot of unanswered questions.' I was silent for a moment. 'But at least there's one you can answer.'

'I've told you, Max. Don't get involved. It's not worth it.' She stared me down as she spoke, in the way my mum used to do. The expression said: Don't argue. I thought she'd have probably made a good Miss Whiplash, and a lot of judges and politicians would have paid good money to be dominated by someone as good-looking as her, but I really wasn't in the mood to be told what to do.

'I want to know who killed my friend, Elaine. And who tried to kill me.'

'Why? It won't help you. I promise you, there's nothing you can do.'

'Just tell me.'

She stared straight at me. 'The Holtzes.'

That stopped me dead.

'You know who they are, don't you?'

'Yeah, I know the Holtzes.'

Everyone who was anyone in that part of town knew the Holtzes, or who they were anyway. Led by their reclusive founder, Stefan, who was now on the wrong end of middle age, they were one of north London's premier crime families, rulers of a criminal empire that was worth tens of millions. And evil bastards, too. Word had it that they'd been involved in dozens of murders as they'd fought to stay at the top, but even after years of police attention, they remained intact. If anyone could have staged what had happened the previous night, it was the Holtzes.

Elaine sighed. 'So, now you see why I said don't get involved.'

'Jesus,' I said, as reality sank in. 'No wonder I almost got killed.'

'I didn't mean to make you a part of it,' she said defensively. 'I didn't know it would be you, and I honestly didn't think that they'd stoop to killing him, or your friend.'

'It's the Holtzes, for Christ's sake. They're capable of anything.'

She shook her head wearily. 'Fuck, what a mess. What the hell am I going to do now?'

'Keep quiet about it. That's the best thing. If they find out you knew too much about what was going on, well . . .' I tailed off, knowing I'd made my point. 'Anyway, I'm the one who's got things to worry about. Not only am I on the run through no fault of my own, I'm a witness, too. I saw two men die. The law are going to be very interested in getting me to talk. The Holtzes are going to be very interested in making sure I don't.'

'But you couldn't pin anything on them, could you? It was your friend, Tony, who did the actual shooting, so he's the only one who could actually get in any trouble.'

'Maybe, maybe not. The thing is, they might not see it like that. Especially if the coppers manage to trace the blood on the back seat of my car back to Fowler. If that gets public then I'm going to be on the Holtzes' hitlist, aren't I? As well as everyone else's.'

We didn't speak for a few moments. She sat there, watching me now, puffing on her cigarette. It was difficult to tell what she was thinking behind the dark eyes.

'I feel partly responsible for what happened,' she said eventually. I didn't bother telling her that she was partly responsible. At that moment I needed all the friends I could get. 'You can stay here for a couple of days if you want, until things die down.'

'Thanks,' I said, 'I appreciate it.'

'Do you want a drink? A proper one?'

'Yeah, I think I need one. What have you got?'

'Most things. What do you want?'

'A brandy, please. And a beer, too, if that's all right.' I thought that I might as well take advantage of the hospitality on offer, not sure how long it was going to be lasting. She didn't look like she'd taken offence and smiled as she got up and kicked off her shoes. Her toenails were painted a bright red, which they always say is a sign of passion. I began to stop thinking about my current woes and instead concentrated on more immediate possibilities.

She went into the kitchen to make up the drinks and I took my shoe off and casually followed her in. 'You're looking really good, you know,' I said, thinking that I was going to have to buy a book on chat-up lines or at least put more thought into them. The thing is, I've always been a man who preferred the more direct approach. If I thought I was in with a chance – and to be honest with you, I reckoned Elaine owed me one – I tended to go straight in for the kill.

'Thanks,' she said, pouring the brandies. 'You're not looking so bad yourself. You seem to have improved with age.' She gave me a quick once-over, like she was checking out a dress. 'You've bulked out as well. It suits you. You were always a bit too skinny in school.'

Cheeky mare.

I took the brandy with one hand and moved the other round towards her shapely rear, thinking that I was taking a bit of a risk here, since she didn't seem like the sort of person who'd suffer unwanted attentions in silence, and if she kicked me out I really was bolloxed because I had pretty much nowhere else to go. But as the hand made contact, and I gave the left cheek a gentle stroke, she shot me a look that said that after all the fucking mishaps of the day – and by God there'd been a few – I'd finally struck gold. Our lips met Mills and Boon style and her fingers crept up my inner thigh.

Not everything had changed since school, then.

Saturday, fifteen days ago

Gallan

'Do you ever stop work, Sarge?' asked Berrin, nursing his black coffee. 'Turning up at the Arcadia on your tod at half eleven at night, getting involved in a scuffle, and then coming to work next morning. That's the sort of thing you're meant to do when you're like eighteen, isn't it?'

'I was trying to recapture the fading spirit of youth. I won't be trying again for a while.'

'So, did you get anything else from Elaine Toms?'

'Nothing of any use. She said she hadn't heard a word from Fowler, and she claimed she didn't know who Max Iversson was.'

'Do you believe her?'

I shrugged. 'I don't know. I didn't see him with her so she could be telling the truth. There just seemed something a bit coincidental about it.'

It was nine o'clock on Saturday morning and Berrin and I were the only people in the Matthews incident room. I hadn't left the club until quarter to one and I was tired. However, I didn't look as bad as Berrin, who was carrying a mean hangover, and whose breath smelled of long-dead fish. About the only thing he'd got remotely enthusiastic about in the ten minutes since we'd got in was the altercation I'd had with Iversson. He'd found it particularly amusing that the ex-para had chucked someone at me while they'd still been taking a leak. 'Simple but very effective, I should think,' was how he'd summed it up. Fair enough, I suppose. He was right.

It was day six of the heatwave and day seven of the Matthews murder inquiry, and we had plenty to keep us busy. Knox, who wasn't coming in until later, had dropped on my desk a note with a photograph of a hard-looking blonde with Myra Hindley's haircut and the same sort of amiable, light-up-the-world expression. The note identified her as Jean Tanner, a former call-girl, two of whose partial prints had been recovered from Matthews's flat, one of them on a coffee mug, suggesting she'd been more than simply a passing punter after some gear. Knox had supplied us with the address, somewhere up in Finchley, and had instructed us to go round, take a statement from her and find out what she'd been up to there. Like a lot of the work on a murder investigation it was routine stuff, but something that had to be done. He signed off by telling us to continue trying to track down Fowler, whose prints had also been found on a number of items in Matthews's flat, even though he'd claimed the two had never socialized.

Before we collared Ms Tanner, we drove over to the Priory Green estate to show her photo to Matthews's neighbours and see if she was the blonde woman identified by two of them as having gone to his flat more than once in the past few weeks. This, at least, would give us something to throw at her if, for some reason, she proved uncooperative.

The estate itself, a medium-rise collection of red- and greybrick buildings just north of the NatWest building on Pentonville Road, was leafy, quiet and relatively well kept. A few years earlier it had received a large cheque from the National Lottery's Heritage Fund to spruce things up, and there was still a lot of building work going on. So far the money looked to have been pretty well spent, which isn't always the case with construction projects. Priory Green had none of the menace of so many of London's sixties- and seventies-designed council estates, those graffiti-stained fortresses with their mazes of darkened walkways so beloved of muggers everywhere, that for a copper always feel like enemy territory. Bad things might have gone on here, but they were done in quite a pleasant setting.

Things got off to a good start as well. Both the witnesses – a young black woman with a very fat baby and several other yowling kids in the background, and an elderly man who insisted on haranguing us about the estate's supposed litter problem – were in residence and able to confirm that they'd seen the woman in the photo going either in or out of the flat on several occasions, though not in the past couple of weeks. The elderly man thought he might have seen her three times, but he couldn't be sure. While we were there we knocked on a few other doors to see if we could jog some memories but, where anyone bothered to answer, we were given the kind of welcome usually reserved for Jehovah's Witnesses, and no-one could provide any help.

I wasn't sure how much use it was finding out that Jean Tanner, ex or current prostitute, had visited the flat of a known drug dealer on more than one occasion, even if he had supplied her with coffee, but at least it was something. However, our good fortune, if good fortune it could be called, didn't last very long. On the way to Jean's place there was an accident on the Caledonian Road that held us up for getting close to half an hour in steadily increasing heat. Then Berrin, who was in charge of navigation on the basis that I didn't trust him behind the wheel in the state he was in, got us lost in the backstreets of East Finchley. By the time we finally tracked down the address – a flat in an ultra-modern, heavily alarmed four-storey block that sat like an eyesore between the Georgian townhouses on either side of it – it was almost half eleven. And, after all that, she wasn't in.

We had six more addresses to visit that day, all of them door-men who had worked at one time or another in the past six months at Arcadia. The list had been supplied by the proprietor of Elite A, a Mr Warren Case, himself a one-time doorman. We'd interviewed Case, who could fairly be described as a man of many sovereign rings, the previous afternoon at his home, an untidy third-floor flat in Barnsbury which also doubled as Elite A's offices. Case had shown us Elite A's certificate of incorpor-ation and VAT registration, both with his name on it, and had provided us with a list containing nine names. Two of them had already been interviewed during the course of the investi-gation, and another had left the country for Australia more than a month before the murder and was, as far as Case knew, still there. He'd given us the addresses of everyone else and then we'd been on our way. As we'd left, I'd asked him how well he'd known Roy Fowler. 'Well enough to know that he was a slimy cunt,' he'd replied evenly. Which was probably a fair enough description, but made me think that if you've got a man like Case saying that about you, then you've really got problems. Although, of course, at that time I didn't know the half of it.

We hadn't phoned ahead to warn any of the interviewees we were coming, which was not untypical practice in a murder inquiry. It was unlikely that any of them would know anything of real help, but if they did and they didn't want to talk, a surprise visit would help to prevent them making up a convenient story. However, it also meant that, like Jean Tanner, they might not be there when we called, particularly on a hot summer's day like this one, and not surprisingly the first two on the list weren't, while the third was just going out as we arrived. He'd only worked with Matthews on a handful of occasions, and claimed he couldn't really recall too much about him. 'He was a bit of a wanker, I remember that much,' he told us, which wasn't exactly news. Him and Fowler must have been a right pair of cards.

By the time we left him it was gone one o'clock and food called. We stopped at a Greek-owned sandwich place off the Finchley Road, and ate in relative silence, both feeling worn down by the drudgery of detective work.

'You know, don't get me wrong, Sarge,' said Berrin between mouthfuls of turkey, salad and mayo baguette, 'but I thought that there'd be more excitement to murder investigations. I don't mean that it should be fun or anything, but it just seems to be the same sort of monotony that you always get.'

I chewed thoughtfully on my ham and pickle sandwich. It was quite tasty except for the fact there was too much fat on the ham. 'Dave, if it was really like it was on *The Sweeney*, no-one would ever leave, would they?'

'I know. I just wish it felt like we were getting somewhere, that's all.'

He had a point, and at that moment I felt the same way. It would have been a good day to sit out in the garden with a decent book, catching a bit of sun and letting the world drift idly by. Or maybe even to take my daughter out somewhere, making the most of the fact that she was still young enough not to look at me with a teenager's wincing embarrassment. But I'd learnt long ago that you don't do policework for the laughs or the job satisfaction. You do it for the desire to put away criminals, which basically is an end in itself. I could see, though, that Berrin, who was still new enough to think there was a lot more to it than that, was flagging and needed a bit of an interest injection.

'This Jean Tanner's got herself a nice pad,' I said, taking a sip from my mineral water and wishing it was beer. 'How much do you reckon it's worth?'

'Just the location's got to be worth a fair bit. The thing is, we don't know what her actual place is like.'

'Well, say it's a one-bedroom flat. It's a nice area of Finchley, it's still got to be worth – shit, I'm no estate agent, help me out here.'

'Two hundred grand. Maybe more.'

'And it's probably bigger than one bedroom. I don't reckon we'd be looking much short of two fifty. That's a lot of money for a prostitute, the type who hangs about with a lowlife like Shaun Matthews. Particularly if she's got a drugs habit.'

'So what are you saying?'

And this was where the interest went out of the injection. 'I don't know,' I said. 'It just seems odd.'

The fourth address was on a residential road of run-down white-brick terraces, less than half a mile away from Highbury stadium. The traffic was appalling on the way there, mainly due to the fact that Arsenal were playing at home, and it was half two and about ninety degrees when we finally parked up almost directly outside the lower ground-floor flat of Craig McBride. According to Case, McBride had worked for Elite A for the best part of a year in a freelance capacity and was still used by them at fairly regular intervals. He was twenty-seven years old and had prior convictions for ABH, threatening behaviour, theft, and possession of Class A and B drugs, a fact that had been discovered when we'd run his name through the computer. It wasn't strictly legal any more for someone with his record to be employed as a doorman, unless he'd somehow convinced the council that he was a reformed character, which I doubted. But I knew it happened, and for the moment it wasn't worth taking the matter up with Warren Case.

A set of greasy steps led down to McBride's abode. The front door was shabby, the once-white paint peeling off in strips to reveal dull-coloured wood beneath, while an ancient-looking hanging basket containing nothing but dry earth and a cluster of weeds hung limply from one of the outside walls. There was a small dirty window to the right of the door. I wondered briefly whether it had ever been cleaned. It didn't look like it. Straightening my tie, I peered through it and immediately my spirits lifted. Eureka. Just what we needed.

Within a Western country's somewhat limited means of coercion, there's no surer way of getting someone to talk than to give them the alternative of criminal charges, and it looked like Craig McBride was indulging in an activity that left him very much exposed to the latter. Even through the stains on the window, I could clearly make him out sitting on a sofa in his front room behind a coffee table on which a plate piled with white powder was sat. Next to the plate was a large tub of baking soda, and next to that were small transparent plastic wraps, each containing more of the powder. Sherlock that I was, I hazarded a guess that the contents of each one weighed pretty much exactly a gram. McBride himself, dressed only in a pair of shorts, was leaning forward, head down, fiddling with what looked like a small electronic weighing machine. As if confirmation of what he was doing was needed. Criminal mastermind young Craig was not. He might as well have put up a sign on the road saying 'Drugs this way', such was his total and utter recklessness. Never underestimate the stupidity of criminals.

Sometimes it's the only thing that keeps a lot of us going.

I turned to Berrin, put a finger to my lips, and motioned for him to have a look. Berrin peered in, then stepped back, smiling. 'It seems a shame to disturb him,' he whispered. 'He looks so busy. Do you think it's worth knocking on the window?'

I shook my head. 'No, he might make a dash for it, or put up some resistance. Let's spring it on him once we're inside.' I stepped forward and knocked hard on the door.

There was no immediate answer, which was to be expected. He would now be desperately trying to hide the stuff before someone spotted him through the window. I gave him a few seconds, then knocked again. This time, I motioned for Berrin to take a look through the window, knowing that we had to play this right. I wanted McBride to see Berrin but not me (I looked too much like a copper), but I also wanted him to see him after he'd got rid of the stuff. That way he'd probably open the door.

As it turned out, we timed it perfectly. I stood back and watched while Berrin gave him a friendly wave and a smile through the window, like a particularly enthusiastic door-to-door salesman, before receiving a muffled 'Who the fuck are you?' in return. Berrin just kept smiling and moved away from the window.

By the time the front door opened a few seconds later and McBride's head appeared round it, already mouthing abuse, we'd removed our warrant cards and were lifting them for him to see. His eyes widened momentarily and I spoke quickly before he thought about making a dash for it. 'Mr McBride? We're here to ask you a few questions regarding the murder of Shaun Matthews.'

He looked nervous, which was to be expected. 'Who?'

'Shaun Matthews. I believe you worked with him on a number of occasions on the door of the Arcadia nightclub.'

'Oh yeah, yeah, Shaun. That's right.'

'Can we come in?' I said, pushing the door open and stepping confidently over the threshold like I owned the place.

McBride tried to stand his ground, but without a great deal of success. 'Look, it's not a good time right now.'

'It won't take more than a few minutes,' said Berrin, pushing his way in behind me.

'Oi, you can't come barging in like this. Don't you need a warrant?'

I smiled and looked him directly in the eye, an easy feat since we were only inches apart. 'Why? Have you got something to hide, Mr McBride?'

'No, course not.'

'So what's the problem?'

'I'm just going out. Can't you come back later?'

But he spoke this last sentence with defeat on his breath, and I knew we had him.

'We'll be very unhappy if we have to come back later, Mr McBride,' I said, 'and we'll be asking ourselves why you wouldn't let us in, and that might mean we have to investigate you further.'

'All right, all right, you win.' He moved away from the door and led us through the cramped hallway and into the kitchen, well away from the room where he'd been dividing the drugs.

The kitchen was a mess with a big pile of empty plates and cups in the sink. The tops were dirty and there was a vague smell of grease in the stale air. He leant back against one of the tops while we stood in the middle of the floor facing him. 'Ask away,' he said, seemingly a little more confident now. Probably thinking what he was going to tell his friends about this near miss and how stupid the coppers were for not having a clue what he'd been up to when they arrived. I decided to put a pin in his balloon and establish control immediately.

'We'll level with you, Mr McBride. This is a murder investigation, so it's information relating to the murder that we're interested in, nothing else. The fact that you've got a load of white powder hidden somewhere in your sitting room, and that that white powder's very likely a Class A substance, and that possession of such powder with intent to supply is an offence which always ends in a substantial custodial sentence, particularly for someone who already has a lengthy criminal record' – the blood was draining from McBride's face and his body had tensed – 'is not our primary concern. However, if you don't answer our questions truthfully, then we may suddenly become very interested in that white powder and what it represents. Do we make ourselves clear?'

McBride looked like he was weighing his options. The tension in his muscles did not bode well. Even the tattoos on his arms were rippling.

'Now, you could try and make a break for it. You're a big man, you might even make it. But then we'll have the drugs and we'll put out a warrant for your arrest, and you'll get caught, and then you're in a position one hell of a lot worse than if you simply stay here and answer our questions. Do you understand what I'm saying?'

'How do I know you won't charge me anyway, whatever I say?'

'I've just told you why. Now let's do this interview somewhere a bit more comfortable. Your drugs den'll do.' McBride started to say something but I wasn't listening. I turned and walked back towards the front room, with Berrin in tow.

We both sat down on the sofa and motioned for McBride to sit on a chair opposite. He did as he was told, his expression that of a man gutted to have been caught out in such a stupid way.

'All right,' I said. 'How well did you know Shaun Matthews?'

He didn't answer us for a couple of moments as he continued to weigh his options. I looked casually down over the side of the sofa to where the tin of gear, the individual wraps, the baking soda and the scales had been hastily stashed. It seemed to do the trick. 'OK, I suppose.'

Berrin consulted his trusty notebook. 'You worked the door at the Arcadia on sixteen separate occasions in the three months prior to Mr Matthews's death. I expect it's fair to say that he was there on most of those occasions, as he was the chief doorman.'

'Yeah, I knew him quite well. He was all right. Fancied himself a bit, but all right.'

'He was the main dealer in the place, wasn't he?' I said.

'Look, I don't want any of this getting back to me . . .'

Once again, I looked over the side of the sofa at the incriminating evidence. 'I don't really think you've got a lot of choice, Mr McBride. Not unless you don't mind spending the next couple of years behind bars, wondering why you're the only person left who still believes in that outdated concept of honour among thieves.'

'OK, OK, yeah. He was the main dealer in the place. He ran it all on the floor.'

'How did it work?' asked Berrin.

'Basically, all the doormen were dealers. Not big time, mind. But we were allowed to supply.'

'By whom?'

'The management.'

'Roy Fowler, yeah?'

'Yeah, him.'

'Carry on,' I told him.

'We had the monopoly on the place. If anyone else was caught dealing in there, they got a serious kicking. What happened was that it was common knowledge among all the punters that the doormen were the people to go to when you wanted something. You couldn't just keep going up to the entrance and asking for stuff, so if someone wanted to buy something they asked the doormen inside the building, you know, who were patrolling the dance floor and that. They didn't usually carry anything on them, just in case it was undercover coppers, but if they were happy with the buyer, they'd give their order to Fowler or Matthews, or one of the other staff, and they'd go off and get the gear. The doorman doing the selling would pocket the cash and then, at the end of the night, everything would get divvied up. Fowler got eighty per cent of everything you sold, that was the going rate, you got the rest.'

'And was business good?' asked Berrin.

McBride nodded. 'Not bad.'

'How much would you make in a night?'

'A couple of hundred on a good one.'

Berrin whistled through his lips. 'That's a lot of money, especially for the bloke taking the eighty per cent.'

'Did all the doormen get an opportunity to make that much money?'

'Yeah, we took it in turns to walk the club.'

I thought about this for a moment. If McBride was to be believed the club was turning over some serious drugs cash every night. I did the sums in my head. It was more than enough to kill for.

'The Holtzes own the Arcadia, don't they?'

McBride's face experienced a passing shadow of fear. Quick, but noticeable. 'It's Roy Fowler, as far as I know.'

'Who owns Elite A?'

'Warren Case.'

I sighed. 'You're not really helping us very much, Mr McBride. I know that it's Warren Case's name on the company's certificate of incorporation, but I want to know who really owns it. Who takes the profits.'

'I honestly don't know. I just work for them.'

Once again, my eyes drifted towards the drugs. 'What is this stuff? Speed or coke?'

'It's speed.'

'Looks like a fair amount of it.'

'Drugs Squad'll be interested,' mused Berrin.

'Very.'

McBride was sweating. It might have been a hot day but his nerves were unmistakable. He knew he had to talk but the prospect was scaring him. 'Listen, I've told you the truth. I don't know who owns it. A couple of times this geezer would turn up at Elite A and come in and talk to Case, and once I saw him leaving with this big holdall. I heard him say something to Case, you know just joking, saying that he must have done well that week.'

'So it's fair to assume that the holdall contained money?' McBride nodded. 'But I'm a bit confused here. You said Fowler made eighty per cent of the takings and the individual doormen made the other twenty per cent. So where did all these holdalls of cash at Elite come from?'

'From what I've been told, Fowler took the money and checked it, but he didn't keep it all. Most of it went back to Elite.'

'Which means that Elite and Arcadia were very closely linked, wouldn't you say?' McBride gave a very reluctant nod. 'This man you saw at Elite's offices, who was he?'

'Jack Merriweather.'

'Well, well, well.'

Jack Merriweather. Better known, at least behind his back, as Jackie Slap, on account of his shiny Mekon-style bald pate, itself the result of a sudden teenage attack of alopecia. The story went that at the age of sixteen young Jackie had been forced to share a cell in a detention centre with a powerfully built homosexual named Lennie, and such had been the stress of having to fend off Lennie's unwanted advances that he'd lost all his hair. At the time it had made the news, because there was a lot of controversy over the 'short sharp shock' method of teenage incarceration. One wag had suggested renaming it the 'short sharp slap', and for Jackie at least the name had stuck.

Nobody took the piss out of Jack Merriweather any more though. Not now he was a part of Stefan Holtz's crime organization. It also answered at least one question about who really ran things at Arcadia. Merriweather worked directly for Neil Vamen, who was one of Holtz's closest associates, in many ways his eyes and ears in the outside world now that the big boss had become something of a recluse. I'd met Vamen once a few months earlier when we'd interviewed him after his name had come up in connection with a box of twelve Kalashnikov rifles that had been discovered at Gatwick Airport. A short, barrel-bodied individual with thinning hair and striking turquoise eyes, he was good-looking in a thuggish sort of way. And very polite, too, I remember that. Someone in CID had once said that Neil Vamen put the manners back into murder, and, I had to admit, there was definitely something charismatic about him. But, like all these blokes, you had this feeling that if you crossed him you'd pay dearly for it, and he'd been linked to more than one murder, including that of a young female accountant who knew a little too much (nothing ever proved, of course, he was far too canny for that), which to me sort of took a bit of the gloss off the image of Raffles, the gentleman gangster. It fitted with his way of doing things that he used Merriweather to collect the money. The truly successful criminals never get their hands dirty.

'I presume you're aware that Jack Merriweather works for the Holtzes?'

'I've heard that, yeah.'

'So it's probably safe to assume that the Holtzes own Elite A and therefore almost certainly own Arcadia, isn't it?'

'Are you asking me or telling me?' he said, using the same phrase Elaine Toms had used the previous day.

'Don't fuck us about, McBride,' I told him coldly. 'We're only talking in your front room because at the moment we're giving you the benefit of the doubt. However, so far you've told us absolutely nothing that we didn't know already, so you're still looking at a nice long spell in the nick. Now, answer my question unless you want to continue this interview down the station.'

'All right, yeah, I suppose it's safe to assume. I didn't know for sure he owned the place ... both places ... but there were rumours. I don't like to ask too many questions about that sort of thing. You know, I don't want to get on the wrong side of Stefan Holtz.'

I changed tack. 'How well did you know Shaun Matthews? Honestly.'

'I got on all right with him. I knew him a bit, you know.'

'Did you ever socialize with him outside work?'

McBride paused before answering, at the same time breaking eye contact with me. 'A couple of times, yeah,' he said eventually. 'We was both ex-army so I think he thought we had something in common. Most of the other blokes didn't really like him much.'

'Why not?' asked Berrin.

'Well, like I said, he rated himself. Threw his weight about a bit, and he could get nasty if he thought anyone was holding back on money owed to the club.'

'Did he ever upset one particular person more than any of

the others? Enough to give them a motive for killing him?'

'He had a run-in with one geezer, one of the permanent door-men, John Harris. John was getting a blowjob in the bogs from one of the punters when he should have been out on the floor. I don't think it would have mattered – you know, that sort of thing goes on a lot. The birds are attracted to doormen, aren't they?'

'I wouldn't know,' I said, hoping my daughter would never flutter her eyelashes at a lowlife like McBride.

'But the thing was, he did it quite a lot. He was always poking the punters, sometimes two at a time, and the thing was he had, you know, staying power, so he could be at it for fifteen, twenty minutes, sometimes even longer. Which I suppose is why they liked him. Anyway, Shaun had just had enough that night so he went charging into the Gents, kicked open the door, and dragged John out by his dick. John didn't know what had hit him – you know, element of surprise and all that – and he got a fair old slap. Broken nose, couple of black eyes. Nothing serious, but I think it was the humiliation of it. Shaun marched him through the whole club with his trousers still half hanging down, and booted him out the door. Told him to come back when he'd got his sex drive under control.'

'And did he come back?'

'Not after that. Well, you wouldn't, would you? Not after someone's taken those sort of liberties with you.'

'When did this incident take place?' asked Berrin.

McBride shrugged noncommittally. 'A couple of months back. Something like that.'

Berrin and I looked at each other. We hadn't heard about this run-in with John Harris, but then no-one at Arcadia was going out of their way to be of help. Berrin made a note in his notebook. We'd track down the sexually energetic Mr Harris later.

'Did Shaun Matthews ever discuss with you any problems he had with anyone, problems that might have resulted in someone wanting to kill him?'

McBride shook his head. 'I know he dealt a fair bit on the side, and I don't think he had too much in the way of respect for the punters buying off him. He told me a couple of times that he used to mix his gear pretty heavily, but he never seemed to worry too much that anyone'd come back and give him any grief about it. He said he'd just tell them to fuck off if they did. That was the thing with Shaun: he wasn't really scared of no-one. He always thought he was hard enough to get himself out of any shit that came his way. You know what I mean?'

I knew exactly what he meant. Plenty of criminals are like that, too cocky to realize they're walking on quicksand. Matthews was only the latest in a long line of those who found out too late, if they found out at all, that they weren't as invincible as they'd thought. 'We're aware of one particular incident where he dangled a man by the ankles over the balcony of his flat. Do you know anything about that?'

McBride tried without success to stifle a laugh. 'Yeah, I remember him saying something about that one. I think the geezer was a student or something. Shaun sold him some stuff that was meant to be skunk but he'd got it cheap off some Moroccan geezer because it was so shit. Apparently, all it did was give you a sore throat. The bloke tried to get his money back and Shaun demonstrated his refunds policy. I don't think he came back again.'

'Have you got a name for this student?' asked Berrin.

He shook his head. 'No. He just told me the story when we was out one night. I think he said the bloke might have gone to City and Islington, but I couldn't say for sure.'

'Did Matthews ever say anything to you about ripping off the Holtzes?'

McBride gave me a withering look. 'Shaun might have been a bit of a headcase, and a bit of a wanker if you're honest about it, but he wasn't totally fucking stupid. He wouldn't have ripped off people like the Holtzes, and if he had, he wouldn't have said nothing about it. Not to no-one.'

I sat forward in my seat and stared hard at him. I don't like getting withering looks from small-time crooks who've got little but not-so-fresh air between their ears. 'You're still not helping us much, Craig. And you're not giving us any reason to walk out of here and forget that you're sitting on a pile of dope that most assuredly is not for personal consumption. Are you?'

'Look, I don't know who killed him. Honest. You know, what the fuck can I do about that? I can't make it up, can I?'

'Several witnesses reported seeing Matthews with a woman with short blonde hair on a number of occasions. We think they may have been romantically linked. She certainly used to visit him at his flat. We've now identified her as Jean Tanner. Here's a photo of her. Not the most flattering one, but mugshots never are.' I took it out of my pocket and handed it to him. He looked at it quickly, then handed it back, shaking his head. 'I'd like to think, for your sake,' I continued, 'that you can tell me what her relationship was with Mr Matthews.'

McBride made a number of noises suggesting he was thinking hard but they weren't particularly convincing. 'He might have mentioned something once, about some girl he was seeing, but he didn't really say anything about—'

'Craig McBride, I'm arresting you on suspicion of possession of Class A—'

'All right, all right, hold on. Don't be hasty.'

'What do you mean, don't be hasty? I could grow a beard waiting for you to tell me anything.'

'Look, I don't want any of this getting back to me. Seriously.'

'Any of what?'

McBride put his head in his hands, then removed them and exhaled loudly. 'Any of what I'm going to tell you.'

I didn't get too excited. 'We'll treat it as an anonymous source if it's applicable,' I said. 'Now, I suggest you get on with it.'

'Shaun had a girlfriend, a girl he'd been seeing for a few months, and her name was Jean, but I don't know what her second name was. The thing was it was all really hush hush. I'm surprised anyone saw them together. He only told me about it one night after he'd had too much gear and drink. I think he wanted some advice.'

'What do you mean?'

'Well, this girl, and I think it must be the same one, she was sort of already spoken for. She was seeing Shaun on the side.'

'It happens,' I said.

'Not to Neil Vamen it doesn't.'

Once again, Berrin and I looked at each other. This certainly put a new angle on the whole thing. The gentleman gangster. 'You're telling us she was Neil Vamen's girlfriend?'

He nodded. 'That's what Shaun said.'

'Christ,' said Berrin. 'No wonder he wanted it kept quiet. Do you think Vamen found out?'

'I don't know. Honestly.'

'How did Shaun meet her?'

'I heard she used to work as an escort girl for this agency Roy Fowler runs called Heavenly Girls. Maybe that's how he met her.' I raised my eyebrows. This was an interesting one. We hadn't realized that one of Fowler's sidelines was managing a brothel.

Berrin finished writing in his notebook and looked up. 'Neil Vamen's married, isn't he?'

McBride shrugged. 'Yeah, he is, and his missus is a looker too, but you know what blokes are like. Especially ones with money. Everyone knows he plays away from home.'

Berrin looked across at me, waiting to see what came next. It was difficult to know what more we could ask McBride, or whether what he'd told us was enough to get him off the hook.

'One more question,' I said. 'Who did you buy these drugs from?'

McBride sighed, looked pained for all of about one second that he was about to betray someone, then gave us the name of a fairly well-known local dealer. I knew immediately he was lying. The drugs had almost certainly come from somewhere within Stefan Holtz's organization. It was rumoured that Holtz himself strongly disapproved of drugs and, unlike many underworld figures, had never touched them himself. However, his people were responsible for importing one hell of a lot of the cocaine that passed through London every year, so his personal stand clearly didn't prevent him helping to ruin the lives of plenty of other people.

I leant over, picked up the plate of dope and the individual wraps, and stood up. 'If you hear anything, anything at all about the murder of Shaun Matthews, I want to hear about it.' I handed my card to McBride who accepted it with a relieved expression on his face.

'Course I will,' he said. 'Thanks.'

'Where's the toilet in here?' I asked, walking out of the room, with Berrin following.

'It's just on the left. What are you going to do with the gear? I'll give it back, but the thing is I haven't paid for it yet.'

I went up to the dirty-looking bowl and emptied the plate into the water, before chucking down the wraps. I gave it a healthy flush and watched as most of it disappeared.

'Don't take the piss, Mr McBride,' I told the distraught-looking doorman as we left his flat. 'We've done you a major favour here.'

When we were back in the car, Berrin gave me a worried look. 'Was that such a good idea, Sarge? You know, letting him off like that. We could have got a lovely little collar there.'

'And it would have just bogged us down in paperwork, and wouldn't have done anything to hinder the Holtz supply chain. Sometimes you've got to let the small fish go so you can get hold of the big ones. But do me a favour and don't say anything to anyone about it.'

'Course not. Do you think it was worth letting him go like that, though? Did we get enough out of him?'

'We've got other people with motive now, so it's putting us further forward.'

'All we've got to do is find them.'

'That, my friend, is what it's all about.'

Iversson

It was three o'clock in the afternoon when I buzzed Joe up and led him through to the lounge. It was a stinking hot day and all the windows were open. Outside, the traffic rumbled endlessly past.

'Nice place for a hideout,' he said, dropping on the floor a bag containing belongings he'd picked up from my flat. He sat down in one of the leather chairs, and put the four-pack of beers he'd also brought down on the glass coffee table. I went and got a couple of glasses and emptied the contents of two of the cans into them. 'So, where's the girl?'

'She's gone out,' I said, sitting down opposite him. 'She'll be back later.'

'And how long's she going to let you stay here for? I mean, she doesn't even know you, does she?'

'I told you, I went to school with her.'

'But, Max, you're not eighteen. That was a long time ago now. You haven't seen her in, what? Twenty years.'

I took a drink from my beer. 'Not that long.'

'But long enough. You've got to be careful. Time changes people. She might just run to the law.'

'She won't.'

'Well, either way she's going to want you out of here pretty soon, isn't she?'

I nodded, not liking to think about that. After the sexual athletics of the previous night, I was in no hurry to go anywhere. 'I suppose so.'

'So we've got to discuss what you're going to do. The police came round to see me this morning, asking about you. Questions like, what were you doing driving a car riddled with bullets? And why were you so keen to make a break for it when you were stopped for questioning, smacking two coppers in the process? That sort of thing.'

'What did you tell them?'

'What do you think? I didn't tell them anything, just said I'd always thought you were pretty straight, and that I didn't think you were involved in anything untoward.'

'Do you reckon they believed you?'

He shrugged. 'Difficult to tell. I think so, but you never know. It helps that you've never been in trouble before. But they're definitely looking for you, Max, and that's not good.'

'You don't think they followed you here, do you?'

He shook his head. 'No, I was careful. Anyway, at the moment you're probably not a big enough fish to waste that many resources on. I mean, there's still no proof you've actually done anything other than deck a couple of coppers.'

'Fowler bled over the back seat when he died. Not much, and I gave it a fair old scrub afterwards, but one of the coppers spotted the stain when they stopped me. I don't know if they can trace it back to Fowler or not. What do you think?'

He pondered that one for a few moments. 'I doubt it. If they don't know who Fowler is and they haven't got a blood sample of his, then I would have thought you're in the clear.'

I took another drink from my beer. It was going down well. 'What a fuck-up,' I said, shaking my head. 'So did you get anything on that bastard Tony? Anything that might explain what the fuck he thought he was doing?'

'I talked to a few people, other people he'd been doing work with, but no-one seems to have anything bad on him. He did some guarding work for Barry Unwin, looking after wealthy Arabs, and he even had a stint through Barry as a minder for Geri Halliwell, and everyone reckoned he did a fine job. And he'd been with Barry a while, too. More than two years.'

'Well, something happened. Somewhere down the line he met someone who was willing to pay him big money to get involved in some very nasty shit.'

Joe seemed to notice his drink for the first time. He picked it up and took a healthy swig. 'How about you? What did you get?'

I told him what Elaine had told me.

Joe rolled his eyes at the mention of the Holtzes. 'Fucking hell, Max, that's all we need. Let's make sure we stay well clear of it if it's anything to do with them. I don't want to get into a confrontation with people like that.'

I knew he was right, and if a man like him was saying it, then it was best to listen. But the thought of not doing something to retaliate still pissed me off.

'Joe, no offence, but I almost got my head blown off the other night. If I hadn't been carrying, I'd probably be at the bottom of the Thames now. It's sort of affected my viewpoint on all this. We also lost Eric, and no way did he deserve to go like that.'

'I know he didn't, and apart from anything else he's going to be difficult to replace. And his ex-missus called in this morning.'

'Shit.'

'Yeah, my sentiments exactly. He was supposed to be looking after two of their grandkids today, only he hadn't turned up. So she phones, asking me if we've seen him. Luckily she didn't know he was working for us Thursday. I said we hadn't clapped eyes on him since last week.'

'How did she sound?'

'Worried. She said it was totally out of character for him not to turn up, especially for his grandkids.'

'It would have been. He was always our most reliable bloke. I can't remember him ever missing a day. Did she sound like she was going to call in the law?'

'Not yet, but she will do eventually, no question. And that's going to pose a problem because it'll give them a chance to make a link with you. We've just got to hope they don't take it too seriously. I mean, it's not like a kid going missing. This is a sixteen-stone ex-soldier in his fifties. They may just conclude he's fucked off on some military adventure, but the problem is, it's all a little bit coincidental.'

I had to agree with him on that one.

'Anyway, the best thing we can do is forget about everything that's happened and put it down to experience.'

'It doesn't seem right, letting them get away with it.'

'This was a professional operation, Max. Three people dead, but no peep from the press, no sign of any bodies. No nothing. It's like it never happened. Which is exactly the Holtzes' style. Do you remember that jeweller out of Hatton Garden, Jon

Kalinski, the one who did a runner with about a quarter of a million in diamonds? About three years ago?'

'Yeah, I remember reading something about it.'

'Well, I heard he didn't do a runner at all. I heard it was the Holtzes who had a role in that particular disappearance. Apparently he owed Krys Holtz, Stefan's boy, a lot of money, which was part of some scam they were both involved in, and Krys was worried they weren't going to get much of it back. So he paid one of Kalinski's girlfriends to phone him up and invite him round to her pad in Hampstead. When he turned up, Krys and a few of his associates were waiting for him. They took the keys to his safe, found out where every penny he'd stashed was, then killed him. And the girlfriend. Dismembered them both in the bath tub, cleaned everything up so there was no trace they'd even been there, then took the bits out in suitcases in the middle of the night. Then they went down to Kalinski's place of business and cleaned him out of everything he owned, and everything he didn't. Do you know how they got rid of the bits of the corpses?'

'I'm surprised you do.'

'Well, it might be bullshit, I don't know, but it's got a ring of truth to it.'

'Go on.'

'You ever wonder where all those thousands of maggots you get in fishbait come from?'

'No. I can safely say it's never crossed my mind once.'

'Well, they come from maggot farms, places where they breed millions of the bastards in these big stinking rooms. One of the Holtz businesses is a maggot farm out in Essex. They chucked the body parts in there and then let the maggots eat them down to the bones. Then they ground down what was left into dust, and scattered it to the four winds. And that was that. No trace. Gone.'

'If they're so secretive, how come you heard about it?'

'I heard it from a bloke who used to know people attached to them. A while back. I never thought about it too much at the time, not until now.'

'And this bloke, isn't it possible to ask him what all this stuff with Fowler's about?'

Joe managed a humourless smile. 'Not really. The bloke was Tony.'

'Great.'

'The point is, let's just leave it.'

'Don't worry. I think you've convinced me.'

'You're going to need to get out of town for a bit, Max. Probably a couple of months at least. Until everything dies down.' He reached into the pocket of his jeans and produced two thick rolls of notes, which he put down on the table. 'There's six grand there. The money from the job the other night. Use it to rent a place down by the coast or something.'

'I can't take it all, Joe. Three grand of it's yours.'

'And half of Tiger Solutions is yours. Forget it. It's the least I can do. Let's see how things go and then, if you need any more, I'll try and pull some out of the business somehow.'

'Shit, Joe, I don't know what to say.' I leant forward and picked up the money. 'Thanks, mate. Thanks a lot.'

'That's what friends are for, Max. Remember it.'

And I did remember it. Would always remember it. Me and Joe went back a long, long way. We were like that, you know. We'd been in the paras together and, even though Joe had been an officer while I'd never risen above the level of colour sergeant, we'd always been mates in a way that rarely travels across the ranks of the British army. I owed him now – but then, to be honest with you, I'd always owed him. You see, a long time back I'd done something to him that to this day he didn't even know about, but which meant that one way or another I was always in his debt.

Joe was two years older than me, and towards the end of his military career he got married to a German girl he'd met while we were stationed out there. Elsa, her name was; twenty-one, far too good-looking, and with an attitude to sex that you'd have to say was slap bang on the liberal end of liberal. Why she got married, I'll never know. She just wasn't cut out for making do with a one-dick-and-two-ball escort. But the problem with Joe was the same problem you get with a lot of blokes: he was just too smitten to notice. I'd heard stories about her knocking around with other squaddies all through the engagement, but decided it was best to keep quiet about it. In the end, it was none of my business. Joe had made his choice and that was that. I know that might sound a bit harsh, but in my experience no-one ever thanks the bearer of bad news, especially when the bad news is about his missus and her shenanigans.

Then, a few weeks after the wedding, I ran into her in a local bar. She was on her own as well, which was unusual for her. She was quite a looker, was Elsa. We got talking and she told me that she and Joe had had an argument. I didn't mean for anything to happen, you know, but I offered to walk her home and one thing just led to another. We did it in a field full of bored-looking sheep (twice as well) and I knew I should have just left it at that and hoped nothing was ever said, but the thing was, Elsa had a way about her that could really reel a man in. She was addictive, that was the best way to describe her. We started to see each other regularly behind Joe's back, doing it whenever and wherever, including in their marital bed, which I know was a terrible liberty. I felt guilty about it, I really did, and jealous, too, because I knew I wasn't the only one of her lovers. But I just couldn't stop myself. That's my only defence, if you can call it that. I just couldn't help myself.

Then one day, no more than a couple of months after that fateful night in the sheep field, Elsa's partly clothed body was discovered in the grounds of a local high school. Her head had been smashed to a pulp with a blunt instrument. There was a police investigation that initially focused on the army base and its occupants, particularly the husband, but quickly spread into the local community as other lovers came out of the woodwork. After only three days, an arrest was made. A nineteen-year-old local bloke, Dietrich Fenzer, had been seen arguing with her on the night she'd died, not far from where the body was found, and it was known that he was one of her lovers. He also had two prior convictions for crimes of violence. A search of his home revealed the murder weapon, a small lead-filled cosh, and he was promptly charged. Six months later he was convicted and sentenced to twenty years in prison, which I'd always thought was a bit lenient, especially as he'd probably be out in ten.

The whole thing was extremely hard on Joe, as you can imagine, but he held up well considering the humiliation of having your new wife's numerous affairs aired in public. Thankfully for me, the police never did dig deep enough to find out about our little fling, so my friendship with him remained intact. But the reality was that it was the end of Joe's army career. He felt that he couldn't continue to command the respect of his men after what had happened, and he was probably right, especially since half of them had shagged her. Within a few months he'd left the military for good to begin a new career as a security consultant, or, more accurately in those early days, a gun for hire. For me, though, the guilt never completely disappeared, and from then on I always felt that I had a lot to do to make it up to Joe for betraying him in such an underhand way. And here he was doing all this for me. It fair choked me up, to tell you the truth.

'Are you all right, Max?'

I nodded. 'Yeah, yeah. Just dreaming, that's all. All this humidity's sending me into a trance.' I pulled from my pocket a pack of cigarettes Elaine had bought me that morning.

Joe gave me a dirty look. He was like that, always wanting to make sure I stayed on the straight and narrow. 'When did you get back on them?' he asked, not worrying, however, about taking one off me.

'Well, getting shot at by one of my best employees started to break my resolve, but then, after spending most of yesterday running away from various members of the local law enforcement, I thought, fuck it, lung cancer's the least of my worries.'

We both laughed and drained our beers. 'Are you in a hurry,' I asked him, 'or have you got time for another one?' It was rare these days that we sat and socialized, and now I had the feeling that we might not get the chance for a long time to come. It seemed important to make the best of things.

He nodded. 'Yeah, course I've got time.'

So I poured the other two beers and we sat back and smoked and talked about the old days: people we'd known, experiences we'd shared, places we'd served. Only once did things go quiet, when Joe mentioned Elsa and his eyes clouded over as he thought back to what could have been. And I felt guilty again and hurried on to the next subject, maybe just a little bit too quickly.

It was early evening and Elaine had yet to reappear by the time Joe said he had to go, and there was something a bit gloomy about the formal handshake we shared. As if we both knew that for some reason nothing between us was ever going to be the same again.

Sunday, fourteen days ago

Gallan

The station was quiet that morning. The busiest night of the week had come and gone and the cells were slowly being emptied of the drunks, the brawlers, the low-level dealers and anyone else unlucky enough to have had their collar felt. It was another glorious day. The weather woman on the radio had announced chirpily that it was the seventh in a row with more than ten hours of sunshine. Temperatures expected to touch twenty-nine degrees Celsius, eighty-four by the old measurement. No-one would be working who didn't have to, even though crime often went up in heatwaves. Tempers got more frayed, particularly in an over-crowded city; domestic burglary increased as people left their windows open at night. So, too, did rapes, for exactly the same reason. But who wanted to catch criminals on a hot August Sunday?

And that was the thing. I did. I wanted to find out who thought they were clever enough to kill Shaun Matthews and get away with it. I wanted to prove them wrong.

It didn't seem as though too many of the squad shared my wish, or were at least prepared to break their backs over it, and the incident room for the Matthews murder was empty for the second morning in a row when I walked into it at just after half past eight. Berrin was expected in, as was DI Capper, my immediate boss. It didn't surprise me that neither had arrived. Berrin had been particularly reluctant to work that day because he'd had to break a date, and had only had one day off in the previous fourteen, so it was unlikely he was going to make it in before nine. As for Capper, he was never on time if his superiors weren't working. Which was the bloke all over. It was a testimony to his arse-licking skills, and the talent he had for creating a wholly false image of commitment and hard work, that he had reached the level of detective inspector on the back of having absolutely none of the skills required. He was a detective who couldn't detect, a civil servant who didn't like to serve, and a man manager who truly couldn't manage. Every word he ever uttered reeked of insincerity, and his habit of backstabbing colleagues was legendary. He had the luck of the devil, too. His predecessor in the DI's post had been a guy called Karl Welland, by all accounts a good nononsense copper who'd been forced to retire after being diagnosed with terminal cancer, paving the way for Capper to slip into his shoes in the absence of any other suitable candidates. Welland had been dead close to a year now, and Capper continued to thrive in a role he genuinely didn't deserve. Who said life was fair?

There was a message from Knox on my desk, giving me the telephone number of one of the station's former CID men, Asif Malik, now of SO7, Scotland Yard's organized crime unit. Malik had left months before I'd joined, but I knew of him. Everyone knew of him. He'd been the guy who'd worked most closely with Dennis Milne, the part-time hitman. From what I heard, Malik had had nothing to do with any of his former boss's many crimes and was supposedly as straight as a die, but after what had happened he'd found it difficult to remain at the station, and had transferred to SO7 a few months later. Knox hadn't been keen initially to get SO7 involved in the Matthews murder investigation because he didn't want control of the case taken away from him and CID. But when I'd spoken to him the previous afternoon, he'd been interested in the Jean Tanner/Neil Vamen lead and had agreed that someone at SO7, one of whose jobs it was to keep tabs on organized crime figures in London, might at least be able to offer some insights. He'd added on the message (Knox liked his messages) that we were to continue to try to locate Fowler and if necessary widen the search for him, particularly in the light of his continued absence.

I got myself a coffee and tried Malik's mobile. It went straight to message so I left one, explaining who I was and why I was calling, and asking if we could meet up.

After I'd hung up, I reluctantly phoned my ex-wife. The live-in lover, Mr Crusader, answered, sounding like he'd just woken up. 'It's the man whose career you fucked,' I told him evenly. 'I'd like to speak to Cathy, please.' He told me angrily to try phoning later next time as Sunday was their day for lying in. 'Just put her on,' I said. 'It's about Rachel.'

Cathy came on the line sounding equally knackered and I heard Carrier telling her in the background that I'd sworn at him. You had to hand it to the bloke, he was a born whistleblower. There wasn't a tale he wouldn't tell. Cathy told me that she thought we'd got over all the childish namecalling and I apologized, thinking that that would be the easiest tactic, and asked whether I was still having Rachel the following weekend.

'Well, can you fit it in round your work?' she asked, with a hint of sarcasm in her voice. 'The last time you were meant to have her—'

'I know, I know. I'll make sure I've got the time off. I haven't seen her in close to a month. I won't let her down.'

'You promise? I'm not having her looking forward to seeing you and then you dashing her hopes.'

'He can't be allowed to do that again,' said Carrier in the background. 'Just because he's unreliable.'

Not for the first time, I tried to understand what Cathy saw in the bastard. I'd always thought of her as a pretty decent judge of character, someone who knew a creep when she saw one, so it was doubly disheartening to have my view proved so emphatically wrong.

'I promise,' I said wearily. 'I mean it. I'll come and get her Friday evening and bring her back Sunday.'

'Thanks, that'd be nice. Come about six, can you?'

'Sure, six is fine.' I started to say something else but she cut me short, saying she wanted to get back to sleep.

'See you on Friday,' she said, trying to sound pleasant, and hung up, leaving me staring at the phone and thinking that she never used to lie in that late on a Sunday.

'Morning, John. Nice to see you in bright and early.'

I looked up to see Capper come walking in, his suit jacket slung jauntily over one arm, a cheesy smile on his face. There were already sweat stains appearing on the underarms of his faded yellow shirt. It was, I thought, strange how unpleasant people often had unpleasant side-effects to their normal bodily functions. Perhaps it was some sort of divine justice, a punishment from God. I liked to think so.

'Morning, sir.'

'Everything all right?' He motioned towards the phone and I wondered if the bastard had been listening in. Probably.

'Fine. And you?'

'Very well. Had a quiet evening in and an early night for once.

Done me the world of good.' He dropped the jacket at his desk, and walked over to the kettle. 'Do you want a coffee?'

'No thanks. I've just this minute finished one.'

Capper made general small talk as he prepared his coffee and waited for the kettle to boil, and I played the game, sounding interested and occasionally making comments of my own. The thing about Capper was that he was nice to you if he thought you were going to be useful to him and he clearly thought I had potential, that maybe I wasn't going to be stuck under him for ever, which I suppose was one good thing. I think he also thought we got on well and, although I couldn't stand him, it suited me to remain cordial. One thing I'd learnt in the Force was that you never make enemies unless you have to. Pragmatism. That was what it was all about.

Capper grabbed a chair and sat down on the other side of my desk with his coffee. 'How did it go with the doormen yesterday?' he asked, after explaining that his absence from duty the previous day had been down to a 'family matter', whatever that was meant to mean. Capper was a bachelor who looked like the sort of person any right-minded sibling or parent would avoid like greasy dogshit on the pavement. He sat there now with a think-of-me-as-one-of-the-guys smile, showing yellowing teeth, etched firmly on his face.

I gave him a brief rundown, explaining that we hadn't got much that we didn't know already, but mentioning the possible girlfriend lead, as well as John Harris, the doorman who'd fallen out with Matthews.

'Who's chasing Harris?' he asked.

'The DCI gave it to WDC Boyd. She's on it today, apparently.'

He nodded, satisfied. I didn't tell him about the Vamen/SO7 angle. Knox would probably bring it up at the meeting the following day but for the moment it could wait. I didn't want Capper sniffing round and taking hold of leads I'd worked hard to build up myself. 'No sign of Fowler yet, then?' he asked.

'Nothing at all. He might have a connection to this Jean Tanner, though.'

'How's that, then?'

'You know I said she was a prostitute? Apparently she used to work at a brothel which was or is supposedly run by Fowler.'

'Really?'

'A place called Heavenly Girls.'

Capper tried to hide it but I saw immediately that he knew the name, and that for some reason he wanted to keep that knowledge quiet. 'Hmm, that's interesting.' His words tailed off, and we sat in silence for a few moments. 'Where did you hear about this brothel?' he asked eventually.

'From McBride, the one who gave us most of the information.'

'I've never heard of the place,' he said, a little too forcefully. 'Do you reckon he was telling the truth?'

I shrugged, not bothering to mention that we'd effectively blackmailed the information out of him. 'I would have thought so. There'd be no point lying about something like that, would there?'

Capper nodded, acknowledging this fact. 'No, I suppose there wouldn't.'

At that moment, Berrin came in, looking dishevelled but considerably better than he had the previous morning.

'A bit late, Berrin,' said Capper, getting to his feet.

Berrin quickly apologized to both Capper and me in that order, and took a seat. Capper told him bluntly to get his house in order and went back to his own desk. He might have thought that I was potentially useful, but he clearly didn't feel the same way about the younger officer. Plus, Berrin was a graduate, and though he never said as much, Capper didn't like graduates. Berrin looked suitably chastised for a couple of seconds, then pulled a face at Capper's back, before sitting down in the chair he'd just vacated.

As the two of us went over the day's itinerary, I stole an occasional glance at the DI, who was now staring intently at his computer screen. I couldn't help but wonder what he knew about the Heavenly Girls 'brothel and how much of a bearing his knowledge might have on the investigation as a whole.

Roy Fowler wasn't answering any of his numbers; the Arcadia was closed; it was proving impossible to locate any outfit called Heavenly Girls; and the day was getting progressively hotter as Berrin brought the car to a halt about twenty yards short of Jean Tanner's apartment building. According to the Land Registry, she'd bought it in 1998, while it was still being built, and now owned thirty per cent of the equity, while the other seventy belonged to her mortgage lender. According to them, she'd never missed a payment. Obviously Jean was getting quite a lot of money from somewhere, which pointed perhaps to a relationship with a wealthy gangster like Neil Vamen, who was going to have a lot more cash than most of the punters she'd ever been with. The question was whether he cared for her enough to kill a possible love rival like Shaun Matthews.

However, once again she wasn't responding as I pressed the buzzer on the flashy-looking intercom system for the third time.

'What do we do now?' asked Berrin eventually.

'What all coppers have to get used to doing,' I told him. 'Wait.'

'She might have gone away. We could be waiting for days.'

'Look, Dave, I'm not driving back out here again, and I'm not phoning her and giving her advance notice of us turning up just in case she's got something to hide, so, for the moment at least, we're going to stay put.'

'But even if she is Vamen's girlfriend, where does that leave us?' he asked, leaning back against the wall of the porch. 'We don't even know if she was seeing Matthews. And where does Fowler fit into it?'

'I don't know is the short answer,' I said, thinking that he had a point. 'But at least we can hear what she has to say. If Vamen's got something to do with it, and if she thought more of Matthews than he deserved, then maybe she's feeling bad about it, and we may be able to get her to talk.'

Berrin nodded wearily. 'Fair enough. Shall we go and get a cup of tea from somewhere while we wait? I need to rehydrate.'

'Were you out again last night?' I asked him in vaguely disgusted tones. I think I was jealous. He told me he was. Out drinking in the West End with one of the station's more attractive WPCs. He started telling me all about it, but I couldn't handle that, not after a night alone in front of an excruciating edition of *Celebrity Stars in their Eyes*, so, on a whim, I pressed the buzzer below Jean's. Three seconds later a none-too-youthful male voice came on the line. I told him who we were, pointing my warrant card at the camera above our heads, and asked if we could come up.

'Of course,' he said, sounding interested.

We were greeted at the top of the stairs by a very short gentleman in his early seventies who had a very wide head that was far too big for his spindly body, giving him more than a passing resemblance to ET. He had large amounts of fine white hair, tinged with orange bits, and big black heavy-rimmed glasses. A taller lady, about ten years younger, with a tent-like flowery dress on, stood behind him. They both smiled as we approached.

'Good morning,' said the man, as we produced our warrant cards. 'We're the Lackers. Peter and Margaret.' He shook our hands formally with a surprisingly firm grip.

'Would you like a cup of tea?' said Margaret Lacker with an easy smile.

'Yes, thanks, that'd be nice,' I said, wishing there were more people I dealt with like the Lackers. Polite, accommodating, and not totally pissed off to see you.

They led us into their richly decorated apartment and motioned for us to sit down in their lounge, a place that looked more like a drawing room of old. 'So, how can we help you?' asked Peter Lacker, sitting down in a chair opposite. 'I hope there's nothing wrong.'

'Nothing at all,' I said, smiling. 'We're just interested in one of your neighbours, a Miss Jean Tanner. I understand she lives on this floor.'

'That's right. Next door. She's all right, isn't she?'

'I certainly hope so. We need to speak to her in connection with a matter she might have some information on.' Suitably vague, I thought. 'We called yesterday but she wasn't at home and she doesn't appear to be at home now. Do you know if she's gone away anywhere?'

'I don't think so. She was definitely there last night. We heard her.'

'Heard her?'

He looked a bit embarrassed. 'Jean's a good neighbour, don't get me wrong, please, but she does have male visitors and sometimes she can have disagreements with them. There were some loud voices last night.'

'What? Like an argument?'

He nodded.

'How many people were involved?' asked Berrin.

'Just two of them. Jean and someone else. A man. I didn't immediately recognize the voice.'

'She's not in trouble, is she?' asked Mrs Lacker, coming in with a tray containing a china teapot, four puny-sized china cups and a selection of what looked like custard creams.

I smiled reassuringly as she sat down in a chair next to her husband. 'Not at all, but it is important we speak to her. You haven't seen her this morning, then?' They both shook their heads. 'How violent was this argument you heard last night?'

'It wasn't violent as such,' said Mr Lacker. 'It was just quite loud.'

'It didn't last that long either, did it?' added his wife, passing me a cup. 'Jean tends to keep herself to herself. She's not a difficult neighbour at all. Is she, Peter?'

'No, not at all. She's lived here for a long time. Three or four years, I think.'

I asked them how often she received male visitors but they were vague on this. Now and again, said Mr Lacker, adding that he and his wife were sexually liberal and so of course didn't disapprove of such arrangements, which as far as I was concerned was one detail too many. They were also vague on how often Jean had had violent disagreements with said visitors. Mr Lacker backtracked somewhat on his earlier statement and said not very often at all. Mrs Lacker said she couldn't remember the last time before the previous night.

I couldn't help feeling vaguely concerned about what I was hearing. I took a sip from my tea and put the cup down. 'I'd like to try her flat again, if I may,' I said, standing up. Berrin, who was munching on one of the custard creams, followed suit with only limited enthusiasm. It looked like he'd been enjoying his sit-down. 'Can you show me which one it is, Mr Lacker?'

'Of course,' he answered, and led us back out into the hallway. He pointed to a door at the far end. 'That's it.'

I stepped past him with Berrin following and knocked hard on the door. Nothing. I waited a few moments, then tried again. If she was in there, she would definitely be able to hear me. I put my ear against the door and listened to the silence. I tried the handle but it was locked. Then I had an idea. A highly irregular one, but on a day like this I wasn't going to be fussy. 'Have you got a key to Miss Tanner's flat, Mr Lacker?'

'I have,' he said, 'but I'm not sure I should be—'

'I have reason to believe that something might have happened to her,' I told him, 'and I need to see if this is the case or not. To do that, I need access to her flat. You can come in with us if you want to satisfy yourself that we're not doing anything in there that we shouldn't be.'

'Oh dear,' he said. 'I'd better go and get it.'

He turned and went back inside and Berrin looked at me quizzically. 'Don't worry,' I whispered. 'I know what I'm doing.' Which of course were famous last words if ever I'd heard them.

A few seconds later, Mr Lacker emerged with the key in his hand and a worried-looking Mrs Lacker in tow. 'I do hope everything's all right,' she said to me. 'She always seemed such a nice young lady.'

'I'm sure it's nothing,' I said, taking hold of the key, 'but I think it's best to stay on the safe side.' With everyone crowded behind me, I turned the key in the lock and slowly pushed open the door.

The layout was different to the Lackers' place and the door opened directly into a spacious lounge with an open-plan, newish-looking kitchen to the right. A wide-screen plasma TV hung from the wall in front of two expensive-looking leather sofas, and the whole effect was very minimalist but also very tasteful. It also looked very unlived in. There were no dirty cups or dishes and the large glass ashtray on the coffee table in the centre of the room was clean and empty. And no evidence at all of a row.

'Well, she's not short of a few bob,' said Berrin, looking round admiringly at the furnishings, particularly the TV.

'She never said what she did for a living,' said Mrs Lacker, who had come in behind us. Her husband, meanwhile, hung back in the doorway. 'It's very nice, isn't it Peter?'

Peter nodded. 'I expect that kitchen cost a pretty penny,' he said. 'Those are granite worktops in there. They cost a fortune.'

Berrin looked across at me, presumably for guidance as to what to do next, now that we were in the place. The problem was, I wasn't sure. I'd hoped there might be some clues to her whereabouts lying about – not that I was quite sure what – but there was nothing. It looked like the apartment had been cleaned from top to bottom – a slightly worrying sign in itself.

To our left, a short hallway ran down to the rest of the apartment. 'Let's take a look down here,' I said. Berrin looked at me like he wanted to say something but was unable to do so because of the presence of the Lackers. I knew what it would be as well. Something along the lines of 'What the hell are we doing here and what would a defence lawyer have to say about it?' A good point, but I'd worry about that one later.

'I've never been in here before,' said Mrs Lacker, wandering into the kitchen area and looking up at the metallic pots and pans hanging there. 'It's very nice.'

'Don't touch anything, please,' I told her. 'Either of you.'

We started off down the hallway. Mr Lacker meanwhile remained standing in the door, looking around with just a hint of suspicion, as if he too was trying to work out what Jean Tanner did for a living and how she'd managed to accumulate such pricey belongings. It looked like he was jumping to correct conclusions, and was perhaps realizing that he wasn't as sexually liberal as he'd previously thought.

There was a bathroom on our left with the door slightly ajar. I pushed it open with the key while Berrin stepped past. I noticed that two toothbrushes were out on the sink and the lid was off the toothpaste – not that any of that was much use. The shower, however, had been used quite recently, certainly that morning. The curtain was damp and there were still drops of water in the bath tub.

I stepped back out of the bathroom and saw Berrin, who'd put on gloves, opening the door to one of the bedrooms. At the same time he removed another of the Lackers' custard creams from his pocket and began munching it surreptitiously.

I followed him into the bedroom, conscious that Mrs Lacker was coming up behind me, doubtless for more of a nose about. I was just turning round to tell her to stay back when, out of the corner of my eye, I saw Berrin stop in front of an imposing dressing-room cupboard at the end of the double bed, and pull a face. He started to say something but his mouth was full of custard cream and it came out like gibberish. And then, the next second, he was opening the door.

There was an immediate crash as the naked corpse came tumbling stiffly out, arms at its sides, like something out of *The Mummy Returns*. It smacked straight into Berrin, who let out a high-pitched howl, spitting crumbs everywhere, and fell back on the bed with it on top of him. I yelled too, and jumped back as he instinctively shoved it away from him, unfortunately in my direction. It bounced loudly against the corner of the cupboard, then came crashing down by my feet, face upwards, and right in the doorway. Mrs Lacker saw it immediately, let out the biggest scream of the lot, then put her hand on her face and fainted dramatically, hitting her head on the bathroom door as she fell backwards.

'What's going on?' yelled Mr Lacker, running over to his wife.

'Stay back!' I shouted. 'Don't touch anything! This is a murder scene!'

Then I looked across at Berrin, whose hair was now standing on end. His face was as white as a ghost's and he was staring off into space. 'Oh my God,' he kept saying, over and over again.

I looked down at the blank dead eyes gazing up at me, then at the familiar tattoos on the upper and lower arms. A Chinese dragon on the left, a military emblem on the right. 'Shit,' I said as I stared down at the corpse of Craig McBride and wondered why on earth he should be lying dead in the apartment of a woman he was not even meant to know.

I called Capper from the Lackers' apartment, where Mr Lacker was mopping Mrs Lacker's brow with a damp cloth, while Berrin sat bolt upright in his original chair, sipping the tea Mrs Lacker had poured him five minutes and one cuddle from a corpse ago. He didn't look too good, which was hardly surprising.

Capper answered on about the tenth ring and I told him what had happened. 'What the hell was McBride doing in her flat?' he demanded, as if it was somehow my fault.

'I don't know.'

'And there's no sign of her anywhere?'

'Nothing that I can see.'

'Have you touched anything in there?'

'No, we've secured the scene, but you're the first person I've called.'

'Any indication how he died?'

'Well, there was no blood but I didn't really look too closely. Put it this way, he was all right this time yesterday so, whatever it is, I wouldn't think it's natural causes.'

'All right, wait where you are and make sure no-one contaminates the scene. What's the address?'

I gave it to him, said my goodbyes, and put down the phone. I looked over at the Lackers. Mrs Lacker appeared to be coming back to earth. 'It was horrible,' she said as her husband continued to dab her brow. 'Something like that in a respectable neighbourhood like this.'

'I know this is a difficult question, but did you happen to recognize the deceased? Is he someone you've seen here before?'

Mrs Lacker gasped melodramatically as if I'd just asked for her bust measurements. 'I don't know, I didn't see. All I remember was him falling into the doorway and then . . . And then, that's it.' She finished the sentence with another gasp and her head fell back on the seat.

'Mr Lacker,' I said.

He shook his head. 'I didn't see either. I was too busy looking after Margaret.'

'That wasn't what I was going to ask. I know it's not going to be easy but I'd appreciate it if you could come in with me, view the deceased, and let me know whether you've ever seen him here before. It could prove very helpful.'

'What do you think's happened to Jean?' asked Mrs Lacker worriedly.

'I don't know,' I said, thinking that I wouldn't mind an answer to that question as well. 'Mr Lacker?' He nodded and stood up. 'Dave, you stay here and look after Mrs Lacker. OK?'

Berrin nodded, beginning to look slightly healthier now. 'Sure.'

I led Mr Lacker back into Jean's apartment, again reminding him not to touch anything, and walked back through the darkened hallway to where the body lay. Mr Lacker paused a few feet behind me, and put his hand against the wall to steady himself. 'It's so stifling in here, isn't it?' he said, sounding breath-less. 'I don't know how you can do this sort of thing every day, I really don't. I've got nothing but admiration for you.'

'It's not an everyday occurrence, thank goodness,' I told him, thinking that it was a rare day anyone said they were full of admiration for me. 'If it was, I don't think I'd be able to handle it.' And I wasn't sure if I would have been. The longer you're in the job, the more you become hardened to the horrors around you, but the sight of Craig McBride's stiff, lifeless body, sucked dry of personality, of everything, depressed me in a way I find difficult to describe. Particularly as the previous day I'd been holding a conversation with him. It might not have been a very pleasant one, but that was hardly the point. He'd been alive, now he was gone. Permanently.

I stepped out of the way so Mr Lacker could see Craig's face. He looked quickly, then looked away, still standing a few feet back. 'Take your time,' I told him. 'There's no hurry.'

He stayed where he was for a couple of seconds, then steeled himself, took a couple of steps forward, and looked again. 'Yes, I've seen him before,' he said, turning away. 'On two or three occasions.'

'Thank you for that,' I said, leading him back towards the front door.

At that moment, there was a commotion from outside, the front door opened, and a giant of a man about ten years my senior, dressed in an ill-fitting black suit, stepped inside. 'What the hell's going on?' he barked. 'This is a crime scene. Who are you?'

'I'm DS John Gallan,' I said, stopping in front of him. 'And this is Peter Lacker, the neighbour.'

'Well, I'm DI Burley and I'm taking over from here. And you two are contaminating a crime scene. Have you touched anything?'

'No.'

'Well, get out then. SOCO are going to be here in a few minutes and we've got to seal everything off.'

He motioned bluntly towards the door with his head, and we stepped past him into the hall where several uniformed officers were standing. Burley followed us out. After I'd led Mr Lacker back into his own flat, he put a large, hairy hand on my shoulder and half-pushed me over to the top of the stairs. I was going to tell him that as far as I was aware we were on the same side, so he could ease up if he liked on the tough-guy routine, but I never got the chance. He was talking before my lips even parted.

'What were you doing back in there with the neighbour? Seeing if you could fuck up the crime scene as much as possible? Have you forgotten what the procedures are, or did you just never bother to learn them?'

'Did you get out of bed the wrong side or are you always this charming?'

I thought he was going to pick me up then and chuck me down the stairs. I'm not a small bloke – I'm close to six feet tall – but there was no questioning the fact that he could have managed it. His sharp little eyes, by far the daintiest features on his long, heavy-jawed face, blazed angrily. 'That's another thing you obviously haven't learnt then, that a DI's a superior officer to a DS and therefore a DS should speak to a DI with a measure of fucking respect, and address him as sir. And apologize when he fucking forgets that.' His words were spoken in a loud hiss through teeth that looked like they usually spent their time gritted, and whether I liked it or not (and I didn't, I can assure you), what he was saying was correct. I took solace in the fact that a man as rude, angry and clearly stressed as DI Burley was not going to live to a ripe old age, surrounded by loving relatives hanging on to his every word of wisdom.

'I was just doing my job, sir,' I told him, emphasizing the sir. I held his gaze, knowing that the only way a person gets intimidated is if he lets himself. I'd done way too many miles for that to happen.

'Well, you're not doing very fucking well. So, I understand you know who the corpse is, is that right?'

'That's right. His name's Craig McBride. We spoke to him yesterday in connection with a murder.'

'But he doesn't live here?'

'No, the apartment belongs to a Jean Tanner. We came here to see her, but she wasn't here. He was.'

'What were you interested in her for?'

I explained what we knew in short, sullen sentences, giving him more of an overview of the Matthews case than the bastard deserved. As I was finishing, Berrin came over to join us. Burley turned round and saw him. 'What the fuck's wrong with you?' he said. 'You look like you've seen a ghost. Not used to stiffs, then?'

'I'm all right,' said Berrin belligerently.

'Well, I want you both to know that we're taking over this case now. This is our patch and we're investigating it. Thanks very much for alerting us to yet another fucking suspicious death in the division, but we won't be needing any more help from you. So, if you'll excuse us . . .'

'Hold on,' I said, ignoring the murderous glare he shot me. 'We need to speak to Miss Tanner regarding the Shaun Matthews murder case. It's important. Sir.'

'When we locate her, Sergeant, you'll be given the necessary access to question her about your own case, if you follow the procedures. Now, we're very fucking busy so I'd like it if you could be on your way before you mess anything else up. I'll inform your superiors when and if we have her in custody.'

'I'd also like access to the results of the post-mortem on McBride.'

'You'll get the information when we have it,' he said. 'Now, goodbye.' He turned and stalked back towards the open door of Jean's apartment, leaving the two of us standing there like lemons.

Sometimes you genuinely wonder why you bother. When even your own people don't seem to want to help you, then you really are kicking a lead door. I've met plenty of coppers like Burley – far too many, if the truth be told – and, like him, they're generally the older guys with too many years on the Force who've never quite done as well as they think their talents deserve, and who hold a grudge because of it. They're also the ones who are most prone to corruption. I wondered briefly whether there was more to Burley's eagerness to get us off the premises than he was letting on. It also seemed strange that he'd got here so fast. As if he'd been waiting just round the corner.

'Where to now?' asked Berrin with a marked lack of enthusiasm.

I sighed, forcing down the frustration. When one avenue fails, try another one. 'Let's go and see Neil Vamen,' I told him.

'Are you sure this is a good idea, Sarge?' said Berrin. He still looked sick. Sick and nervous.

It was twelve-thirty and we were walking towards the Seven Bells, a pub in Barnsbury which, according to the profile we had on him, was supposedly the Sunday lunchtime haunt of Neil Vamen. The place, no doubt, where he felt most at home among 'his people'. Barnsbury, the traditionally working-class, now partly gentrified district of south Islington that encompasses the area between the Caledonian and Liverpool Roads north of Pentonville, was in many way the spiritual home of the Holtz organization, since it was there that all the senior members had grown up and plotted their first scams together. Most had long since moved out to larger, more ostentatious properties in the suburbs, including Vamen, but he apparently still retained a special affection for the area, not least because his mother still lived there, and he visited regularly.

It probably wasn't a good idea to go and see him. After all, I didn't expect him suddenly to blurt out everything he knew about the death of Shaun Matthews and Craig McBride, as well as the whereabouts of his alleged girlfriend, Jean Tanner. As Berrin had pointed out more than once this morning, he might have known nothing about any of it, but I wasn't so sure. Jean had been linked to him by a man who was now dead. She'd been seeing another man who was also now dead. At least one of those deaths, and almost certainly both, were not from natural causes, and now Jean was missing. I didn't have any particular theory of what Vamen's involvement might be, it was still too early for that, but at least by turning up out of the blue we might be able to rattle him. Particularly if he thought we knew more than we actually did.

'I don't honestly know if it's a good idea or not but I don't see any alternative. I mean, who else is there left to talk to? We've got a murder inquiry where everyone we want to interview is either missing or dead. Have you thought about that? Fowler's nowhere to be seen, McBride talks, then twenty-four hours later he's dead, and now Jean Tanner's disappeared into thin air. At least Vamen's still capable of opening his mouth.'

'I'm not criticizing, Sarge, but don't you think we ought to have checked it out with Capper first?'

'Look, this is just a friendly little chat, following up on a lead. We're just using some initiative, that's all.'

We stopped outside the pub, a small, old-fashioned place with grimy windows and a battered door that fitted in snugly in the quiet, slightly run-down street of terraced housing just off the southern end of the Caledonian Road. The windows were open and we could hear the steady buzz of conversation and the occasional clinking of glasses. It's a sound I usually like because it's welcoming, but I had a feeling the welcome here wasn't going to get much above frosty. We'd both taken off our jackets in deference to the intense midday heat but now put them on again. It was best to be formal.

'I'll do the talking,' I said, thinking that at that moment Berrin looked like a student in a suit at his first job interview. 'You just stand up straight and don't look too queasy.'

'They're not likely to try to rough us up, are they?' he asked, showing a worrying naivety. Sometimes I couldn't help but think that it was only the shortage of detectives in the Met that had put Berrin in plain clothes, and that he'd been promoted above his experience. In the fight against crime, you didn't like to think that the front line was made up of too many men like him.

'He might be a nasty bastard, Dave, but he's still a business-man. He won't want to do anything that brings him unwanted attention. Now, come on.'

I stepped inside with Berrin following. The interior was deceptively large and seemed to go back a long way, as is often the way with London pubs. It was split into two bars, the right-hand one near enough empty except for a handful of old geezers in caps smoking pipes and generally not taking too much notice of one another. Two of them were playing cribbage and they were the only ones who looked up as we arrived.

The other bar, in contrast, was a lot younger and a fair bit livelier, although it was still early so nowhere near crowded. A jukebox played one of the numerous covers of the Righteous Brothers' 'Unchained Melody' and three or four groups of people – mainly men, but some women – milled about in a way that suggested they all knew one another. Most of them were in their thirties and forties, and at the far end of the bar, closely watched by Jack Merriweather and two powerfully built bodyguards, stood Neil Vamen. He was talking to another of the groups – two middle-aged men and their younger, pneumatic blonde partners – who were hanging on to his every word. Vamen was smiling broadly and I got the feeling he was telling a joke.

That all stopped as soon as we stepped inside. In fact, everything stopped, bar the music, the singer continuing to warble boringly while the whole bar gave us what I can only describe as the evil eye. I suppose we just looked like coppers. The barman studiously ignored us and for a couple of seconds I simply stood there, thinking that it might actually have been a big mistake coming here.

Confidence. It's all about confidence. You can command the respect of anyone, even a room full of gangsters, if you walk like you know the walk. So, trying to ignore the fact that I was sweating, I ambled casually through the crowd, Berrin behind me, and stopped when I reached Neil Vamen. His bodyguards tensed but made no move. Jackie Slap's lip curled in an expression of distaste, as if the very presence of police officers caused him to experience an allergic reaction, which it probably did. Vamen, meanwhile, eyed me with a mixture of mild contempt and idle curiosity, his turquoise eyes twinkling playfully. I could almost feel the stares of every other person in the place on my back, and I hoped Berrin didn't do anything stupid, like faint.

'Hello, Mr Vamen. My name's DS Gallan and this is DC Berrin.' I produced my warrant card and saw out of the corner of my eye Berrin produce his. 'I believe we've met before.'

Vamen made a casual gesture. 'I don't remember.'

'We'd like a word with you in private, if we may.'

'No.'

And that was that. The word wasn't delivered rudely but there was a finality about it I really should have expected. Behind me, I heard one of the pneumatic blondes snigger.

'Any particular reason why not?'

He smiled. 'Because I've got nothing to say to you.'

It's difficult when you rely on the authority that comes with your position to coerce people into doing things, and then come up against someone who has no fear of it or you. Particularly when they're on their home territory and you're a long way from yours.

'If you don't talk to me, I might have to conclude that you've got something to hide,' I told him, meeting his gaze.

That made him laugh. 'Your lot have been concluding that for the past twenty years.' Further laughter reverberated around the bar, and someone shouted, 'You tell him, Neil.'

'Ain't you got nothing better to do?' sneered the Slap. He was wearing a black New York Yankees baseball cap to cover up what he hadn't got. I ignored him. At that point, I didn't have to be told that I was losing this one.

'Fine. We'll talk here, then. Your girlfriend, Jean Tanner. We found a man dead in her apartment and we want to know where she is. Any ideas?'

Vamen's face hardened and his eyes lost their playfulness. For two, maybe three seconds the silence was deafening. When he spoke next, his voice was calm and slow, but dripping with menace. 'I don't know what you're fucking talking about, or where you're getting your information from, but I'm telling you this: it's bollocks. Now, you want to discuss anything with me, you go through my lawyer. His name's Melvyn Carroll. You might have heard of him.' I had. The Holtz family brief. As crooked as a busted rib. 'Otherwise, unless you're arresting me – which you're not, are you?' He paused for a moment to let me answer.

'Not at the moment.'

'Well, then, unless you're arresting me, you can fuck off out of here and leave me alone. And if you don't, DS Gallan . . . is that right? Gall-an?'

'Gallon of what?' some wag called out.

'That's right, John Gallan,' I said, determined to hold my own.

'And what's your name again, sonny?' He aimed the full force of his personality at Berrin, who was probably now wishing he'd taken the advice of his university careers adviser and joined an insurance company.

'We've already told you who we are,' I said.

'Berrin, wasn't it?' he said, ignoring me and eyeing him closely, like he was probing for signs of weakness, and doubtless unearthing many. 'Well, DS John Gallan and DC Berrin, if you harass me like this again with no good reason, and I can tell you now you do not have a good fucking reason, then my brief will be paying your superior a visit, and he will then be kicking your flimsy little arses for upsetting a well-established local businessman instead of doing what you're paid to do, which is catching fucking criminals, of whom there are plenty a-fucking-bout. Do I make myself clear?'

'That you don't want to co-operate with us? Yes, you do. Crystal.'

He gave me a look like I was something annoying stuck between his teeth, then turned his back. At the same time one of his bodyguards, who was a good four inches taller and probably a foot wider than me, stepped between us and stared blankly down at the top of my head. The other one then joined him, forming a wall that effectively blocked off all contact. Jackie Slap stayed where he was, a nasty grin on his face. I could have tried to push them out of the way, hassle Vamen a bit more, let him know I wasn't fazed, but in the end there was no point. He had the run of me and he knew it. I knew it, too. The important thing now was to find Jean. Then, possibly, we could move forward. For now, the meeting was over and I had to work hard to overcome the sense of impotence I felt in the sure knowledge that Neil Vamen was a criminal and a murderer who'd become rich by ignoring the laws I was supposed to uphold, who could pay my mortgage off a hundred times over, and yet when it came to a confrontation between the two of us, he was the one who held all the cards. Some people say there's no justice in the world. If they say it in front of me, I tell them they're wrong, that the bad almost always get what they deserve in the end, even if the wait's long. But at that moment in time, standing in a room where everyone was revelling in our powerlessness, I didn't really believe it.

'Gentleman gangster, my arse,' I said in Vamen's general direction. I looked up at the wall of flesh in front of me. 'And you need to change your aftershave, mate.' Puerile, but at least it made me feel a bit better. Like I'd salvaged something from the wreckage of this meeting.

Jackie Slap continued to grin, but I resisted addressing him by the name he allegedly hated. It would have reeked too much of desperation. Instead, I turned on my heel and motioned for Berrin to lead us out of there. He bumped into one of the blondes who'd deliberately positioned herself in front of him, and mumbled some sort of apology. She, for her own part, made some snide comment regarding the poor quality of his eyesight, which he ignored. She started to say something to me but I told her not to bother and kept walking, trying hard to ignore the catcalls and victory whoops that accompanied our exit.

On the four-hundred-yard walk back to the car through the terraced backstreets of Barnsbury, we didn't speak once. When we finally reached it, I looked across at Berrin, who still didn't look too good. I couldn't blame him. It had been a shit day all round. 'Are you all right?' I asked him.

'I don't know,' he said, leaning against the bonnet. 'I think I might be coming down with something.'

Berrin wasn't the hardest worker in the world and he'd already had several short bouts of sick leave in the few months he'd been with CID, but this time I wasn't going to begrudge him. 'Come on,' I said. 'I'll take you home.'

He didn't argue.

Two hours later I was still trying hard to keep a lid on my frustration but it wasn't working. The humiliation of the meeting with Vamen, combined with the heat and the knowledge that nothing about the Shaun Matthews case was going right, including the way I was handling it, was serving to sever the last threads of my patience. I just knew that right now my ex-wife would be sat in the garden, the one I'd helped pay for, soaking up some rays alongside the man who had gone out of his way to wreck my life, while my daughter played happily in front of them, maybe even fetching him a nice cool beer to enjoy while he worked out whose balloon he was going to burst next. And the thing was, I could have handled it. I could have handled pretty much anything if I'd thought that by putting in all these extra hours on the job, hours I'd been putting in since I was eighteen years old, I was actually getting somewhere. But it just wasn't happening. For every weak, staggering step forward we took, there always seemed to be a larger, more confident one backwards. And now I had to deal with an idiot like Capper, who seemed incapable of providing the remotest bit of help.

'We need to be involved, sir. We interviewed the dead man yesterday and it was his testimony that led us to the flat today.'

Capper sat back in his chair, trying hard to look like he was sympathetic to my plight. The act didn't work. 'I'll have to talk to the DCI about it, John, and that's going to be tomorrow now. I don't want to bother him at home. Not over this.'

'With due respect, I think it's important. I feel certain that this man's death is linked to that of Shaun Matthews, and therefore—'

Capper raised his arms and waved them from side to side like opposing windscreen wipers, an annoying habit of his indicating silence to the individual being gestured at, in this case me. I forced myself to fall silent. 'John, it's DI Burley's patch, so at the moment it's his investigation. There's nothing I can do about that. We'll certainly be able to liaise with them if there's a consensus that the two cases are linked.'

'Which they've basically got to be.'

Capper nodded noncommittally. 'There's definitely a possibility there.'

'More than a possibility. Two bouncers from the same night-club, whose owner's been missing for days, both murdered within a week of each other.'

'Are we sure McBride's was murder?'

'Definitely. He was OK yesterday. For all we know, it could even be the same poison that killed Matthews.'

'Could be, John, could be. But it's also possible that it's natural causes.'

'How? He was in a cupboard.'

'We've just got to wait and see what the autopsy reveals. What we'll do is discuss what happened at the meeting tomorrow morning and then maybe the DCI'll get on the phone to their nick and see if there's any scope for information sharing. In the meantime, you need to bring all the records up to date. Where's Berrin, by the way?'

'I took him home. He was feeling sick.'

'Again. That's the third time since he's been in CID. What's wrong with him this time?'

'I don't know, summer flu or something. He's been a bit under the weather these past few days,' I lied.

Capper nodded with some scepticism, an annoyingly serene smile on his face. 'Well, let's hope he gets better soon,' he said, sounding like he didn't mean it at all.

'Is that everything, sir?' I asked, starting to get to my feet. I couldn't hack any more of Capper than I had to.

'Not quite, John,' he answered, still wearing the smile. It made him look like a brain-damaged Buddhist. I stopped mid-crouch and waited for him to continue. 'I got a call this afternoon from a Mr Melvyn Carroll. He says that you and DC Berrin were harassing his client, Neil Vamen. What on earth were you doing talking to Vamen?'

'He's a possible suspect in the Matthews case,' I said, sitting back down.

'Let me get this right. A man with a lengthy criminal record, now deceased, suggested that Vamen was the boyfriend of a woman who visited the home of Shaun Matthews, and was possibly, just possibly, Matthews's girlfriend as well, and this makes him a suspect?'

'Yes, it does. He's certainly a possibility, so he was worth talking to.'

'Neil Vamen. I trust you know who he is?'

'Yes, and that's another reason to consider him a suspect. He's got the resources and the ruthlessness to kill Shaun Matthews and Craig McBride.'

'He's also someone who's had years of practice in knowing how to cover his tracks, so he was never going to talk to you. Even if he is involved, which I doubt, because I don't think he's the type to get sentimental about a woman, it's going to be extremely difficult to prove anything.'

'That doesn't mean we shouldn't try.'

'The point is, Vamen's a big fish and it's SO7 and the NCS who are responsible for building prosecution cases against him and his associates. They're not going to take kindly to you throwing your weight about with him. I thought you were meant to be talking to SO7 about the case.'

'I am. I'm waiting for a call back from Asif Malik.'

'Well, go that route, then.'

'Look, I was doing the right thing—'

The arms started swinging from side to side again and once more I forced myself to button it. 'You're a good copper, John,' he said, talking to me like I was an office junior rather than one rank and only a handful of years below him, 'and we're all pleased with your progress here, but don't start to get ahead of yourself. You'll end up causing problems both for yourself and for CID. Understand?'

I sighed, knowing that he was right and that it was a mistake to go to see Vamen, but longing for the moment when I was a DI again and didn't have to report to him. 'Yes, sir,' I said reluctantly.

'In future I don't want you going to see Neil Vamen or any of his associates without speaking to me about it first. OK? I don't want to sound like I'm not supporting you, but I think it's the best way.'

I nodded, but didn't bother responding. The conversation over, I stalked back to my desk and began the torturous task of bringing everything up to date. Only once did Capper interrupt me, to ask if we were still trying to get hold of Fowler. I said that we were but that we were still having no luck.

'He's the one we've got to concentrate on,' he said, nodding his head as if he was agreeing with himself – another of his annoying habits, most likely brought about by the fact that no-one else did. I didn't bother to comment.

At exactly five o'clock, Capper left for the day, telling me helpfully that I shouldn't work too hard. 'You need to unwind sometimes,' he said with another irritating smile. 'That way it won't all get on top of you.'

I didn't bother telling him that it was a little too late for that. Instead, I put my head down and felt glad for the opportunity of some space and quiet.

Paperwork can be a therapeutic process. It's repetitive and it's mundane, but when there's plenty of it to do, the person doing it can sometimes lift himself spiritually from the pile in front of him and reach an almost Zen-like state where the hand simply writes automatically and the brain sails away to calmer, happier waters where there are no interruptions and no will-sapping and pointless confrontations.

I'd reached that point and was probably wearing a serene smile as idiotic as Capper's when the door to the incident room opened and WDC Boyd walked in. Now, I liked Boyd. She was my kind of woman: attractive, amusing, but definitely no push-over. We got on well, too. I think that if it hadn't been for the fact that we worked together, I would have definitely fancied her, and might even have tried my luck – not that I tended to have a great deal of it where love was concerned. She appeared to be a bit worn out and hot, but her short black hair, cut into a cute bob, looked like it had come straight out of a cheesy shampoo ad, and her grey trousersuit was spotless. For a woman who'd been out tramping the dirty, sweating streets of London, she carried herself remarkably well.

It was ten past six. She smiled, looking genuinely pleased to see me. 'Hello, John, you still around?'

'I could ask the same question,' I said, looking up. 'Did you manage to get hold of John Harris?'

'Ah, the elusive Mr Harris, former stud of the Arcadia. I found him all right,' she said, sighing theatrically. 'Eventually.'

'And?'

She wandered over and sat on her desk a few yards away from mine. 'And, I don't think he's our man.'

'Why not?'

'Because he's been in hospital for the past ten days. He was working the door at a place in Clapham on their garage night and he got caught in the crossfire of somebody else's argument.'

'That's south London for you.'

'Too right. It's bandit country down there,' she added, winking at me. 'Anyway, he got shot in the stomach. Apparently the bullet passed straight through him and hit one of the glass collectors inside. That was three days before Matthews was murdered. What a waste of a day. It took me more than four hours to find that out when I could have been sat out in the park sunbathing.'

I almost said that that would be a sight I wouldn't have minded seeing, but settled instead for a clichéd, 'That's the way it goes sometimes, Tina.'

She took off her jacket and turned on her PC. 'How was your day anyway?'

I grunted. 'I think I can safely say it was probably even worse than yours.' I gave her a detailed rundown of all the disasters that had befallen Berrin and me since we'd arrived for work that morning. She laughed when she heard about his slow dance with McBride's corpse but her look had turned to sympathy by the time I'd finished.

'Blimey, John, you don't mess about, do you? Marching in and interrogating Neil Vamen?'

I sighed and shook my head. 'It was a stupid move. You know, I was thinking this morning how naive Berrin was in the way he dealt with people, but I was far more naive than him over this. I really thought I could rattle Vamen, but in the end I've achieved absolutely nothing, except maybe to alert him to the fact that I might know something about what's going on. And he's already made a pre-emptive strike to get me off his back.'

'You did your best,' she said, giving me a supportive smile. 'Which is a lot more than a few of the people round here.'

'Well, it didn't work,' I said, feeling sorry for myself.

'So, what do you think happened? What's your theory on Matthews and McBride?'

I'd thought about that a fair amount that day but had yet to come up with anything concrete. 'I don't know, Tina. If I had to indulge in a bit of conjecture I'd say that Jean Tanner was Neil Vamen's mistress and that she was also seeing Matthews on the side. Vamen found out about what was going on and had Matthews killed.'

'And what about McBride?'

'This is where it starts not to make much sense. From what the neighbours were saying, McBride had visited Jean on a number of occasions, so it makes me think that maybe he was seeing her as well.'

'So she was seeing three of them? She gets around a bit.'

I shrugged. 'Well, that's what it looks like.'

'And you think Vamen found out about McBride as well?'

I spread my arms wide in a gesture of defeat. 'I don't know.'

'Because that all seems a bit coincidental, doesn't it? Him killing off two of his love rivals in the space of a week. All over one woman who's hardly a picture painting, is she?'

'You know what they say,' I said lamely. 'Love's blind.'

'Not that blind.'

146

'I don't think I've ever come across a murder case as complicated as this one. One where nothing seems to really lead
anywhere. Do you know what I mean? There's no logic in any of
it. I mean, what about Fowler? If he's got nothing to do with it,
then where is he?' There followed a long silence. We were a long
way from any answers. 'You know,' I said eventually, 'it's been
such a long day, I can't even be bothered to think about it any
more.'

'Do you want to go for a drink? Finish up here and grab a
beer somewhere?'

I pondered her suggestion for all of one second. The paperwork could wait. 'Why not? I could do with one.'

We wandered round the corner to the Roving Wolf and I
ordered the first round: a pint of Pride for me, a pint of Fosters
for her. That was another thing I liked about Boyd, she didn't
have any airs and graces. She might have been a college girl like
Berrin but she was still one of the lads. The interior of the pub
was quiet at this hour with most of the hardened drinkers and
passing trade sat at tables outside on the street, so we found ourselves a table away from the bright rays of evening sunshine
streaming through the windows and chatted a while, enjoying the
fact that the working day was over and there was nothing and
no-one to pressurize us. She bought the second round and I
realized I was enjoying things just a little too much. She was
good company, and single, too. I couldn't help but think that
maybe I ought to make an exception to the rule I'd placed on
myself never to have an office fling. That had been after an affair
I'd had with another WDC ten years earlier, when Rachel had
been little more than a baby and I'd been getting the married
man's yearning for something new. It had all got very messy. The
WDC had demanded I choose between Cathy and her, and I'd
done the inevitable and chosen Cathy. The atmosphere between

the WDC and me, and in CID as a whole, where everyone knew what had been going on, had been sour for more than a year afterwards until she'd finally asked for a transfer and got it, much to my relief. I might not have been married any more but I still thought it best to keep to the rule, remembering all too well the hassle of having to work with someone you'd pay good money to avoid.

So when Boyd asked if I fancied grabbing a curry somewhere, I was pretty torn. But with the grim memories of the previous night and *Celebrity Stars in their Eyes* still fresh in my mind, I concluded that life was definitely too short to say no. Boyd suggested a curryhouse she liked down near King's Cross station and, while I would have preferred the continental ambience of Upper Street to the dodgier end of the Euston Road, I didn't make a fuss. To be fair to her, I ended up pleased with the choice. The food was good, which I suppose it would have to be given its location, and I found myself relaxing in a way I hadn't in female company for a long time.

As they cleared away the remains of the food, I told her about Capper's reaction to my mention of Heavenly Girls. 'Do you think he's been paying recreational visits down there? He definitely knew the place.'

She pulled a face. 'It wouldn't surprise me. He's the sort you can imagine visiting toms. He's got that perverted look about him, don't you think? Like the sort of bloke you'd find in a peep show. I bet he gets them to spank his arse.'

I laughed. 'That's your boss you're talking about. I hate to think what you say about me.'

'Oh, it's worse. Definitely worse.'

'I bet it is as well. But I can tell you quite categorically that no-one's ever spanked my arse. Even my mum was against corporal punishment.'

148

'There's always a first time,' she said, with a coy smile. The woman was definitely flirting. I wasn't sure whether to be worried or pleased. She took a packet of Silk Cut out of her handbag. 'Do you mind if I smoke?'

'Be my guest.'

I watched as she lit one and took a long, relaxed drag that gave me a fleeting reminder, even years later, of how good a cigarette tastes after a decent meal. 'What you've got to remember,' she said, blowing the smoke out above my head, 'is that if Capper was, or is, a customer down there, then it's possible that he knows Fowler.'

'I was thinking about that earlier, but I don't really go for it. He's too keen for us to find him. He keeps going on about it.'

'Ah,' she said, taking another drag (it's amazing how elegant a woman smoking can look), 'but there's always the possibility that he might have been put in a compromising situation. If someone down there found out he was a copper, then they might have been able to use it against him, and perhaps it's that someone who wants to find Fowler.'

'And who do you think that someone might be?'

She shrugged. 'God knows.'

I shook my head. This was one complication too far. 'No, I think it's more likely he's just a pervert.'

She blew more smoke over my head. 'So do I, but nothing's set in stone, is it? Maybe it'd be worthwhile watching what you say around him.'

I nodded, thinking that it was funny how when you're talking to another copper, even one who's female and attractive, you always end up back on the subject of work. For once, I just wanted to forget about it. I wanted to talk more about her. What she was interested in. What made her tick. What she looked for in a man. And whether she really was flirting.

But the opportunity had passed, and a couple of minutes later she stubbed her cigarette out and said that she ought to be getting back. We split the bill fifty-fifty and headed outside. Night was falling and the lowlifes who inhabit King's Cross after dark were coming out of the cracks in the pavement and looking round for customers and victims. I suggested we share a cab back but she told me she was perfectly capable of getting herself back on the Tube. 'I am a police officer, you know, John,' she said dismissively.

'Don't say that too loudly round here.'

'And don't keep going on.' Her face broke into a smile. 'Look, I had a good time tonight. We'll have to do it again sometime.'

I nodded. 'Definitely.'

We had an awkward moment when we thought about shaking hands, but didn't quite go through with it, and then she said goodbye and headed off towards the Underground, while I looked around for a cab that would take me back to Tufnell Park.

Part of me thought that maybe I should have tried to kiss her, or at least shown that I was interested, but the other part kept telling me that by taking a little pain now I was avoiding a lot more down the line.

Iversson

'So how did you meet your ex-missus, then?' asked Elaine.

It was Sunday morning and we were sitting up in her bed, naked and drinking coffee. The clock on the bedside table said half eleven and her right hand was on my thigh, which made me think she probably wasn't going to kick me out just yet.

'I was a double-glazing salesman.'

Elaine laughed. 'You? Now that I would have liked to see.'

'It was just after I'd left the army. I was pretty shit at it, to be honest with you. I mean, they taught you all these ways to get the customer to sign on the dotted line, get him fired up and interested and all that, but in the end, as far as I could see, all I was doing was shifting windows. You know, people either wanted them or they didn't. Anyway, my ex was a secretary there and for some reason she took a fancy to me.'

'Well, you're not bad, Max.'

'Thanks. You're too kind.'

'I know.'

'So we started going out, one thing led to another, and somehow we ended up getting wed. Christ knows how it happened. I still don't think either of us cared that much about each other – it was just one of those things. Anyway, it didn't last. We went to Majorca on the honeymoon, it rained nearly every day, she went on sex strike after I said something about her mum she took offence to, and it went downhill from there. I think we managed about four months, no more than that. I got sacked from the company and she took it worse than me. I was quite pleased, but with her it was a pride thing. It made her look bad in front of her mates in the office that her husband wasn't good enough to flog double-glazing, and she really let me know it. In the end I just thought, fuck it, we're never going to work it out so I might as well make the break. So one day, while she was at work, I packed up all my stuff, which wasn't a lot, and walked out. I only saw her once after that, and that was in the divorce courts. She got half of everything I owned, which was nothing. I got my freedom back. It was a fair swap, I thought.'

'How did you get into the mercenary game?'

'My partner, Joe, he'd been doing it for a couple of years. He was working for an outfit who were always on the look-out for people with good military backgrounds to send out to all these places. I put a call into him, he put me in touch with his boss, and three days later I was on the plane to Sierra Leone.'

'Where the hell's that?'

'Somewhere you don't ever want to go. A backwater shithole in Africa. And I'll tell you this, you have to see the place to believe it. I was there four months altogether, but I reckon I lost count of the number of mutilated corpses I saw within four days. We were working for the government, or what passed for the government. To be honest, it was just a bunch of young NCOs who'd overthrown the last bloke, and most of them couldn't run a bath, let alone a country. We were meant to be helping the Sierra Leonean army secure the area around the capital city and capture the diamond mines in the interior from the rebels, the RUF.'

'So who were they rebelling against, the RUF?'

That made me chuckle. 'Anyone who wanted to take the diamonds off them. That was about as radical as they got. They might have said it was all about creating freedom and democracy and all that shit but, like most politicians, all they really cared about was lining their own pockets. It's what most of those wars are about. Some people have got the diamonds and the money, some others want it. Instead of sitting round the table and carving up the proceeds, like they do over here, they get the guns out and start shooting.'

'Did you ever kill anyone?' she asked evenly, pulling out a pack of cigarettes and offering me one.

I took one and let her light it for me. 'Would it matter if I had?' I answered, hoping that she wasn't the sort of girl to get offended by her new lover's tales of mayhem and murder.

She shrugged, and looked me in the eye. 'It was your job, wasn't it? That's what you're trained for. No, it wouldn't matter.'

It seemed she wasn't, then.

I leant back on the pillow and took a drag on the cigarette as her fingers drifted across the hairs on my belly. I got the impression she was horny again. This girl had an incredible appetite.

'I shot at a lot of people,' I told her, 'and quite a few of them fell down, but I couldn't ever say for sure that it was me who killed them. There were always other people fighting alongside me. But I suppose, probability wise, I must have taken out a couple. It's not something I'm particularly proud of.'

'But you shouldn't be ashamed either. Sometimes it's just a case of you or them, isn't it?' Out of the corner of my eye, I was conscious of her watching me as she spoke.

'That's right. I don't regret anything I've ever done. I shot at people who were shooting at me. I never killed anyone in cold blood, and I suppose you could argue that one way or another they all deserved it. They were no angels. None of them. Not the RUF, nor any of the others I ran into on my travels.'

'Where else did you go, then?'

'I did six months in the Congo, three months in Colombia, and a few weeks in Liberia.'

'What was it like? Was it fun?'

I shook my head. 'Not really. Most of the time we were boiling alive in the jungle, getting constantly attacked by all kinds of horrible insects and never knowing what kind of tropical disease we might pick up. The most exciting part was when we actually saw some action, but it didn't happen very often.'

'It still sounds better than what a lot of people do to earn their living.'

'It was better than selling double-glazing, I'll give you that, and I suppose it was a bit of an adventure getting the chance to finally use all my training in a real-life situation, but the reality was a lot more boring than the expectation.'

'It always is, Max. Haven't you noticed that yet?'

'I suppose so, but the money wasn't that much good either. Everyone thinks mercenaries earn an arm and a leg, but it's nothing really. Especially when you think how much you've got to risk. Joe felt the same way, so we decided to set up the company.'

'What's it called?'

'It's not my name, honestly. It's his.'

She smiled. 'Go on, what is it?'

'Tiger Solutions.'

Her laughter bounced off the walls of the bedroom. 'What the fuck sort of a name is that?'

'A bad one, but Joe wanted it and I couldn't think of anything better, so I didn't bother to argue.'

'Max, anything's better than Tiger Solutions. What sort of solutions does a tiger offer anyway?'

'I don't know. Fearsome ones?'

She continued laughing and I chucked one of the pillows at her. It bounced off her head and landed on the other side of the room. 'If you ever meet Joe, you have a go at him about it. I swear it had nothing to do with me.'

We were silent for a few moments, and even though I didn't want to have to say it, I knew there was no point putting it off. 'Look, Joe gave me some money so that I could get out of town for a while, enough to keep me going for the foreseeable future. So I can be out of your hair by tomorrow.'

She smiled at me. 'You don't have to go yet, Max. I like the company.'

'I appreciate it, but you've done enough for me already, and we can't carry on like this for ever. I've got to go out and get some fresh air fairly soon otherwise I'll go stir crazy.'

She put her hand on my arm. 'You go when you want, but not before. Not on my account. It's no problem for me, you being here. Honest.'

Well, there was no way I was going to argue. Not with the sort of accommodation I was getting. So I gave her my best smile and said that, OK, maybe I'd stay a couple of days longer. At that moment, the phone rang out in the hall and she jumped off the bed. I watched as she went out the door, her rear waggling seductively. There was a little red devil complete with trident tattooed on the right cheek. He was grinning. So was I.

When she came back a few minutes later, she told me that it had been the club on the phone. 'I've got to work tonight,' she said, getting back on the bed. She lit two more cigarettes and passed one over. You get my drift about the standard of accommodation. Naked women even firing up your smokes for you.

'Again? Haven't they heard of workers' rights down there? You need a night off occasionally. Can't you throw a sickie?' I remembered how bored I'd been the previous night. For some reason, Elaine didn't have Sky, which had severely limited my options. The high point had been *Celebrity Stars in their Eyes*, if you can call some bird who used to be on *EastEnders* massacring my mum's favourite Patsy Kline song a high point. It wasn't an experience I wanted to repeat.

'You know as well as I do that it's a difficult time at the moment, Max. Perhaps in a couple of days.'

'What's going to happen at Arcadia? Now that Fowler's not coming back.'

'It's all pretty much up in the air at the moment, especially as everyone thinks he is coming back, except me, you, and the people who had him killed.'

'Is there any sign of the Holtzes yet?'

'No. I don't think we'll see them for a bit. Not with the police still sniffing around asking questions about the doorman who got poisoned.'

'Well, they're going to start coming out of the woodwork

pretty soon. Blokes like them aren't the sort to be hands-off about a big investment like the Arcadia. So when they do, make sure you watch yourself.'

She sat up and eyed me coolly, like it was me who ought to be watching myself. 'It's nice to know you care, Max, it really is. But you don't need to worry about me. I know what I'm doing.'

Elaine was a feisty lady and definitely not someone to be messed with, but at the same time her words didn't do much to reassure me. I remember the American commander of another mercenary unit in Sierra Leone saying exactly the same thing just before he disappeared into the jungle on a one-man reconnaissance near the diamond fields of Bo.

The next day an RUF patrol ate him.

In the end the weather was too decent to be indoors, especially as I hadn't set foot outside Elaine's apartment for getting on for forty-eight hours. Joe was right: I probably wasn't the Old Bill's top priority. Yes, I'd slapped a couple of them, plus got one inadvertently pissed on, but people do that to them all the time. It's all part of being a copper, getting slapped in the line of duty. It's like soldiers – it's what they join up for. The action and all that shit. Granted, they were probably looking for me, but I didn't think my crime was so heinous that they'd be scrambling the helicopters and plastering up the Wanted: Dead or Alive posters just yet, so that afternoon we went out for a stroll round Clerkenwell, arm in arm like true romantics, taking in the sun and the warmth, enjoying it the way the tourists do.

On the way back to the apartment we stopped at an Italian deli and I bought some ingredients: anchovies, black olives, fresh oregano, canned Italian tomatoes and, most important of all, a six-pack of bottled Peroni. I found some spaghetti in Elaine's food cupboard and, after a bit of exercise of the bedroom variety, cooked us both a pasta dish my ex-wife had taught me to make years back on one of the few occasions we'd been talking. Puttanesca. Whore's spaghetti, the fiery sauce unfaithful Latin wives would make for their husbands because it tasted like it had taken hours to prepare when in reality you could knock it together in twenty minutes, leaving yourself ample time for an afternoon's shagging. Perhaps she'd been trying to tell me something.

Elaine had to be at the club at nine-thirty, and before she went I told her I'd feel happier if she left the place, which I know was a bit cheeky, given the fact I hardly knew her, but to be honest with you I was beginning to think that maybe something could come of this.

'You're a talented woman,' I told her, assuming that she was. 'You know how to run a place. Why don't you look for a job somewhere else?'

She stopped in front of me and gave me a look which said: Don't push your luck, sonny. In the heels of her black court shoes, she was only an inch below me in height. 'I hear what you're saying, Max, and I will leave. But it'll be in my own time. Understand? I'm a big girl now, I can look after myself. Thanks for the concern, but save it for people who really need it.'

Which was telling me.

After she'd gone, I sat demolishing the Peroni and trying desperately to find something decent to watch on the TV, which, not for the first time, turned out to be a fruitless task. I ended up watching a programme about a family of chimpanzees living in the African jungle. It all started off quite nicely as well. The chimps were messing about, grooming one another and generally acting all cute like they do in the zoo, and I was even musing about what a nice, laid-back life it would be being a member of the ape fraternity when all of a sudden everything went a bit mental. A friendly-looking gibbon appeared up in the trees near the chimps' camp, and one of them spotted him. Well, the next second the whole lot of them were howling and shrieking like a bunch of Millwall fans on angel dust, and before I had a chance to even work out what was going on, they were charging after him through the undergrowth, much to the excitement of the breathless narrator.

After a dramatic five-minute chase they cornered him up on one of the branches, and then, to my horror, ripped the poor little sod apart, disembowelling him with their bare hands while he stared mournfully up at them. They then began to eat him alive, as casually as you like, which to my mind was really quite disgusting. Especially as it was on TV when kids could be watching. And to think these beasts are meant to be our closest relatives.

One of the chimps was staring cockily at the camera while he munched on a hefty piece of gibbon offal, and I got a nasty sense of *déjà vu* because he really reminded me of that treacherous toe-rag Tony, sitting up there like he owned the place with what looked suspiciously like a smile on his face.

Maybe the bastard had been reincarnated.

I switched over at this point, having no desire to get into a staring match with a familiar-looking monkey, and cracked open another Peroni. It made me wonder what I'd have been doing that night if I'd never agreed to take on the Fowler contract. Probably sitting alone at home watching something a lot better. Life would have been a lot easier, that was for sure, but then again it would also have been a lot more boring. And sometimes that's worse.

What I didn't know then, though, and what I do now, is that my troubles were only just beginning.

Monday, thirteen days ago

Iversson

I was woken up by a faint sobbing, almost like a kid's. My eyes snapped to attention and surveyed the room. It was dark, but the light from the street shimmered through the window, providing a murky orange glow, and I could make out a figure at the end of the bed. It was Elaine. The clock on the bedside table said 1.25.

I sat up, fumbling for the switch on the bedside lamp. 'Elaine? What's happened?' The light came on and I inhaled sharply, squinting against the brightness. Her make-up had run where she'd been crying and there were the beginnings of a bruise on her right cheek, just below the eye. The low-cut black blouse she was wearing had a tear in it that exposed the top of her bra, and it looked like an attempt had been made to rip it off which hadn't fallen too far short of success.

She looked at me, trying to maintain some sort of dignity, but the effort was too much and she began to cry again. 'Oh, Max . . .'

Confused and worried, I jumped out of the bed and took her in my arms. 'Elaine, what's happened?'

For a while she didn't say anything, just sobbed quietly against my chest, and I let her get it out, not wanting to hurry her. Finally, she lifted her head and turned away. 'Leave it, Max. Please. I'll be OK.' She took her top off with her back to me – the first time she'd done that – and threw it in the corner before unclipping her bra.

'Elaine, tell me, please. You can't just come in like this and not let me know what's up. Has someone hurt you?' I went over and put my hands on her shoulders, rubbing them gently as I tried to relax her. 'Come on, tell me.'

'I can't,' she said, still keeping her back to me. 'I don't want you to do anything stupid.'

It was a bit late for that. The last four days had been one stupid thing after another. But I didn't say this, knowing that patience alone would get it out of her. 'Do you want a drink? A brandy or something?'

She nodded. 'That'd be nice.'

I went through to the kitchen, found a bottle of brandy, and poured her a generous slug. I poured myself a glass of water.

When I returned to the bedroom, she was sitting on the edge of the bed in her dressing gown. She'd stopped crying and appeared to have calmed down a little. 'I'm sorry about that,' she said, and thanked me as I gave her the drink.

I sat down on her dressing-table chair so that we were facing each other. 'There's no need to apologize,' I said quietly, 'but I want to know what's happened. Please.'

'Why? It won't do you any good.'

'I'll be the judge of that.'

She stared at me for a long moment, and I thought then that even upset and humiliated she looked beautiful. And vulnerable.

For all her tough exterior, she bled just the same as anyone else. 'Just tell me, Elaine,' I said again.

She exhaled for what seemed like a long time, then looked up at the ceiling. 'Krys Holtz came to the club tonight.' I felt something strong in the pit of my stomach, unsure whether it was fear or anger, thinking that it was probably both. 'He asked to see me in the office that Roy used to use. When I got in there he started questioning me about the accounts, about how much we were taking, where the money was going, and all that. He seemed to think I knew all about the dealing that went on there. I told him that that side of it was nothing to do with me, and gave him all the paperwork. I didn't like his attitude. He was treating me like some sort of third-class citizen. I'd heard he was a real bastard but I didn't expect him to be quite so fucking out of order. He kept calling me "hired help", and then, when I couldn't tell him what he wanted to know about the dealing, he told me I was a lying bitch. He said that we'd all been cooking the books down there. Roy, me, and Warren Case, the bloke who supplied the doormen.' She was fiddling intently with a ring on her index finger as she spoke, and shaking her head. Finally, she looked me right in the eye. 'You know me, Max, I don't like being insulted, whoever it is doing the insulting. I told him I was telling the truth and if he didn't believe me that was his fucking lookout. Then I told him I was leaving.'

'What happened then?'

'He hit me. The bastard stood up and smacked me right in the face.' She touched her cheek where his fist had connected, and I felt the rage building. 'I couldn't believe it. No man's ever done that to me before, not in my whole life. Then he came over and picked me up by my hair, telling me I was going to have to learn some fucking manners. The whole thing happened so fast I didn't even have time to be scared, so I called him a cowardly cunt and tried to knee him in the balls, but he just stepped out of the way. Then he started slapping me round the face with one hand and half-strangling me with the other, and all the time he kept saying that I was going to have to learn some manners.' She stopped for a moment, and I thought she might lose her composure, but she held on, her voice quiet. 'At one point, I think the dirty bastard must have started getting turned on because he pushed me back onto the desk and I could feel him getting all hard up against me, and he was saying I was a fucking whore and pawing me all over, getting really worked up ... Christ, it was horrible. I tried to fight him, Max, I really did, but he was so fucking strong. I could hardly breathe with his hand round my neck. I thought he was going to kill me.'

I went over and put my arm around her. I felt sick to the gut. It was difficult to believe what I was hearing. I wondered how much worse things could get. 'Did he rape you?' I asked quietly, desperate for the answer to be no.

She shook her head and removed her hands from her face, but still didn't look at me. I felt relief that lasted for all of about two seconds. 'He did other things,' she whispered, her disgusted tone leaving little doubt as to what those things might have been. 'And when he'd finished, he just looked at me like I was nothing and told me to fuck off. Like I was nothing, Max. No-one ... no-one's ever done that to me before.' She shook her head slowly like she was trying to shake the memories out of her head. She looked distant, and I thought then that I didn't want to lose her. To be honest, amid all the frustration and rage in my head, that was when I sort of knew I loved her. A bit hasty, yes, but sometimes these things really do happen.

We held each other for a long time. Five minutes, ten minutes, it was difficult to tell. It could have been longer. Eventually she sighed and took a drink from the glass of brandy.

'I need a cigarette,' she said.

'I'll find you one.' I opened up the drawer of her bedside table and found a pack and a lighter. I lit two and passed one to her.

'Don't do anything, Max. For Christ's sake. I just want to forget about it, that's all. At least now I've left the club. I don't think anyone's going to expect me to work my notice after that.'

'What? You're going to ignore the fact that a piece of shit like Krys Holtz did that to you?' I tried to keep my voice calm, knowing that she could hardly be blamed for wanting to put an incident like that behind her, but it was difficult.

'He's Stefan Holtz's son, for fuck's sake! What can we do?'

I shook my head. 'Fuck that. I keep hearing about these Holtzes and how fucking invincible they are, but let me tell you something, no-one's invincible. I might be on the run but I'm not going to leave London with my tail between my legs. And I'm not going to move one more fucking foot until I get this sorted out.'

'It won't help anything.'

'It'll help me,' I said, and got up and went to get the rest of the brandy from the kitchen. My blood was up; I needed something to get it back down again. I poured myself a glass, then took the bottle back to the bedroom and poured some more for Elaine. 'You know something, I've never met Stefan Holtz or any of his extended family, never done a fucking thing to any of them, but these people seem to be doing everything in their power to fuck up my life.'

'They fuck up a lot of people.'

'There's one way I can get back at them. And get revenge for what happened to you. I can off that arsewipe Krys.'

'Don't be stupid.'

'I'm a trained soldier, Elaine. I'm perfectly capable of doing it. And it'll make me feel one hell of a lot better.'

'Then what happens? You'll be on the run for ever.'

'I'm on the run anyway, so what's the difference? And I'll have got them back, for me and for you. Krys'll be dead, and his dad'll have to live with the fact that he's lost a son. And if I do it right, they'll never know it was me.'

Something in her face hardened. 'He's not going to be that easy to kill, Max. Someone like him's got a lot of enemies. He's got bodyguards.'

I shrugged. The idea of killing bodyguards didn't bother me either. I knew it could be done. I could also see that Elaine was now coming round to the idea. We both sat looking at each other for a few moments, each of us wondering how far we were really going to go.

'I hate that bastard for what he's just done to me,' she said eventually, 'but I don't want to do anything that's going to make things worse for you and for us. Do you know what I mean?'

But the thing was, I'd made up my mind. 'He's going to have to die, Elaine,' I said simply.

She took a drag on her cigarette and eyed me closely through the bluish haze of smoke. Then, for the first time since returning that night, her gloom seemed to lift. 'There's a better way,' she said.

Gallan

Berrin remained off sick on Monday. The flu, or whatever it was, had supposedly got worse. If the truth be told, he'd picked a good day to be absent. It was another stinking hot one and tempers in CID were frayed. Knox chaired the meeting of the Shaun Matthews murder squad, during which the events of the weekend, including the death of the possible witness

McBride, were discussed, but there remained a feeling that everything had ground to a halt on the inquiry, and Knox was preoccupied by other events. A thirteen-year-old girl, just one year older than my daughter, had been dragged onto wasteground in broad daylight by a man in his thirties while walking home from the park, and violently sexually assaulted. The ordeal had lasted as long as half an hour and the attacker had also slashed her arm with a knife or a razor, even though she'd made no move to resist him. This was a particularly nasty type of crime, one that upset the public, and therefore one that upset the Brass. Which meant immediate pressure to get it solved. By nine-thirty that morning, there'd also been two missing persons reports, one of them a teenage schoolgirl, and Knox was being pushed from above to reorganize his resources. This meant cutting the size of the Matthews murder squad. With the case nine days old, and other business piling up all over the place, Knox reduced it to himself, Capper, DC Hunsdon, myself and Berrin (whenever he turned up for work again). However, due to further staff shortages within CID, I was informed that I was also going to have to work the other missing persons case, that of a fifty-three-year-old ex-con and former soldier named Eric Horne, who'd been missing since the previous Thursday.

At this point, the meeting became heated, and I'd pressed, with a lot less diplomacy than I usually exhibit in front of the boss, for far more serious efforts to be made in tracking down Jean Tanner since if she was alive she at least might be able to help. I also brought up the Neil Vamen angle, undeterred by how it had all gone the previous day, and suggested that he too might have had some involvement. 'And surely, if we've got the opportunity, we want to put someone like him behind bars?'

Knox attempted to answer my concerns as thoroughly as possible, explaining that he would speak to his counterpart on the McBride case straight away, and get what details he could, although he added that the hunt for Miss Tanner was not our responsibility since McBride had not died on our patch. We would, said Knox, continue to look at the possibility of Neil Vamen's own possible motives, but he suggested that, with the death of the one person who'd mentioned his name in connection with the case, it was going to be extremely difficult to prove any involvement on his part, if indeed there'd been any. I think I must have pulled a face because Knox shot me one of his trade-mark dirty looks reserved only for people who really pissed him off, but I was past caring. In my opinion, the whole thing was becoming a whitewash. If the Matthews case had been a straight-forward one, like most murders, and hadn't had any connections to the complicated morass of organized crime, then Knox would have been a lot more interested. Instead, he'd clearly decided that it was more hassle than it was worth, that the chances of a con-viction were too negligible to waste time on. These days it was all about performance league tables. Something like this, par-ticularly when the corpse belonged to a lowlife like Shaun Matthews, was always going to be put on the backburner if there were other, easier crimes coming along that could be solved. That was the long and the short of it.

The meeting broke up at ten past ten and Knox, after doling out orders to various individuals and trying to solve a couple of minor grievances, one involving Boyd and Capper and an alleged sexist comment, called me into his office. Neither of us was in the best of moods and the sweltering heat in the office did little to help matters. Knox had two desk fans blasting away but all they did was push the hot air around the confines of the room.

'Look, John, I know you're pissed off because you don't think things are moving as quickly as you'd like on this case, but you know how things are.' I didn't say anything. 'I'm going to speak to DCI Peppard, DI Burley's boss, later this morning to see what information we can get from them. If they pick up Jean Tanner, I'll make sure we get the opportunity to question her about Matthews, and see what she may or may not know. We'll also chase them to find out how McBride died and whether they've got any leads on who may have killed him.'

'DI Burley wasn't exactly helpful, sir.'

'He can be very brash, I admit.'

'He treated me like a criminal. We're meant to be on the same side.'

Knox's face reddened. He had the look of a man who's been given the job of counsellor without actually wanting it. 'It's not like that. Burley's territorial. He doesn't like people, even fellow officers, muscling in on his patch.'

'I was hardly muscling in. I was actually trying to help him.'

'I'm sure you were, it's just that that's not how he interprets it. He's not very good sometimes around younger officers. I think he thinks they're upstarts.' He gave a reassuring and vaguely patronizing smile as he said this – not that I thought there was anything particularly amusing about it. I continued to look at him stony-faced.

Seeing that he didn't seem to be making much of an impression on his disgruntled charge, Knox changed tack. 'Whichever way we look at it, Roy Fowler still remains for me the prime suspect. He of all people had a motive. Now, I'm not letting this inquiry go, no way. What we need to do is to look into Fowler's background much more deeply because he is most definitely the key to all this.' Warming to his theme in a way that had been conspicuously absent in the meeting earlier, he continued, occasionally banging his fist on the desk for emphasis. 'He and Matthews were definitely involved in the drug dealing. It's a lucrative business. I'm sure they fell out about it, and it's very likely that that fall-out somehow led to his death. Why else would Fowler have disappeared? Unless he's got something to hide. He's been gone, what? Three, four days now. Which I would describe as highly irregular. And didn't you and Berrin tell him not to go anywhere during the course of the inquiry?' I told him we had. 'So let's concentrate on him. I want you to review the case notes, go back and talk to his associates, particularly staff members at the Arcadia, and Capper and Hunsdon are going to dig deeper into what he's been up to in the past. What scams he was involved in, particularly this brothel business. This Heavenly Girls. That might give us some ideas. It's time for some lateral thinking.'

'My lateral thinking would be helped a great deal, sir, if I didn't have to worry about a missing persons case as well.'

Knox sighed. 'I know it's not ideal, but you know the problems we've got with manpower. I've got to put bodies on that indecent assault yesterday. The media are already sniffing around. She's a very pretty girl, and, worse than that, her parents are high-band council taxpayers with a lot of clout, so we're going to need a fast result. No-one wants an animal like that running loose, particularly when he's doing everything possible to make his crime as high-profile as possible, so we're going to have to show plenty of faces. I've also got the Drugs Squad breathing down my neck for help on some major surveillance they're running. Operation Swift Strike it's called, though swift it most certainly ain't, and it's likely to take people out of the loop for the next three or four days. You see what I'm saying?'

'Of course I do, sir, and I appreciate the manpower problems. We've always got them. But you're paring back the murder squad to an absolute minimum, and with Berrin off sick, I think I should really be concentrating my efforts on the case.' I resisted the urge to add, 'You see what I'm saying?' I still wanted to make DI again after all, and I'd more than made my point today.

'This is very much a routine one, John, and it shouldn't take you long. The bloke's ex-wife phoned in this morning, says she hasn't heard from him in days, and that he's missed two family functions which is apparently not like him at all.' He gave me the standard look of weary scepticism which greeted any family members' description of someone's actions as being 'not like him at all'. 'But the point is, he's a big bloke, an ex-con and ex-soldier who works as a freelance bodyguard, so he's not likely to have come to much harm. He's probably just gone off somewhere for a few days but I want you to give it a quick once-over. Apparently, he does most of his work for a company called Tiger Solutions.'

I snorted. 'What sort of name is that?'

'A very foolish one. His ex says she's already contacted them and they haven't seen him for a week or two themselves, but I'd like you to speak to them when you've got a moment, and then give the ex a call and tell her what you've found out. If you can do it in the next couple of days it would be a big help.'

I knew there was no point in arguing. 'Sure, I'll do that.'

'Your hard work's appreciated you know, John,' he said, fixing me with one of his managerial looks. 'It all counts in your favour, I want you to know that, and I'm keen for you to make progress here. But do me a favour, eh? DI Capper told me about yesterday with Neil Vamen. Don't go talking to him about anything unless you've got solid evidence implicating him, and you've checked it through with me.' I nodded, and he let it go. 'Now, remember, this missing persons case is very much a side issue, so concentrate on Matthews, and I'll keep you informed of my discussions with DCI Peppard. And let's try looking at it from some new angles. Lateral thinking, that's what we need.'

I got to my feet and said I'd get on to things straight away. Thinking that Knox had probably never had a lateral thought in his whole life.

When I got back to my desk, my mobile was ringing. I didn't recognize the number but picked up anyway. 'Gallan.'

'Hello, Mr Gallan,' said a pleasant, youthful voice I didn't know. 'It's Asif Malik here, SO7.'

'Hello, Asif. Thanks for getting back to me.'

'No problem. What is it I can do for you?'

'I'm involved in a murder inquiry which may have a link with the area you cover, and I wonder if I could pick your brains about it for a few minutes. As you'll appreciate, it's not something I can talk about over the phone. Do you think we could meet up for half an hour? I'll come to you.'

'Can you tell me who it's regarding, just so I know I'm the person you should be talking to?'

For some reason, I felt impelled to whisper into the phone. 'The Holtzes, and particularly Neil Vamen.'

There was a short silence at the other end. Then, 'I'm the right person. How about Wednesday?'

'Fine.'

'I'll meet you at the Soul of Naples restaurant. It's Italian.' Like it'd be anything else. 'That all right for you? It's up near me.'

I laughed. 'I'm usually limited to a sandwich on the run, so anything above that's a bonus.'

'Well, this place is good. I'll be there at midday.'

'Thanks. I appreciate it.'

He gave me the address and some basic directions, then rang off.

For a few seconds, I sat there staring at the mobile, hoping that somewhere among the morass of information Malik and his colleagues had undoubtedly gathered on the Holtzes there'd be something that would stop this case ending up in the growing ranks of the unsolveds.

At that point, however, I was not feeling optimistic.

Iversson

'Kidnapping, Max? It'll never work, and it's too fucking dangerous.'

We were in the lounge of Elaine's apartment, just the two of us, beers in hand. Elaine had gone out to give us the privacy to talk things through.

'It will work, Joe, if we do it properly. Elaine says that—'

'Is this her idea?'

'Course it isn't. It's a product of a lot of thinking I've been doing. Now, all I want you to do is hear me out. If after I've said my piece you still don't want to know, then fair enough, all you have to do is walk out of here and forget we ever had this conversation.'

Joe took a slug from his beer. 'Go on, then,' he said suspiciously.

'Krys Holtz likes to go to a little gentleman's club called Heavenly Girls which is down round here, not far from Farringdon Road. It's a nice townhouse in a posh street, which is mainly offices, and basically it's full of top-drawer and top-price totty. Krys is meant to keep his movements unpredictable to stop any of his many enemies taking potshots at him, but word is that he tends to go to the club several nights a week, and usually most Friday nights if he hasn't pulled anywhere else. And sometimes even if he has.'

'And where's this information coming from?'

'Elaine. She knows some of the girls down there. Apparently Roy Fowler used to manage it as well as the club.' Joe pulled a face but didn't say anything. 'We might have one or two false starts but we should be able to survey the place all right without arousing suspicion.'

'What about you? You're a wanted man.'

'I won't have shaved for a few days, I'll be wearing glasses, and anyway the street's not particularly well lit or well used after dark, so I don't think we'll have a problem there. When Krys arrives all we do is wait for him to go in – apparently he usually travels with a couple of associates – then one of us goes to the door and gains entry.'

'How does the person gain entry in the first place? Presumably they don't let in any Tom, Dick or Harry.'

'Someone'll have to do a dummy run first to get an idea of the place. Whoever does it'll use the name of one of the regulars, say that the bloke's recommended it to him. Then once he's been once, he shouldn't have any problem going back a second time. So when he gets in the second time—'

'If he gets in.'

'He goes upstairs to reception, which is supposedly fairly quiet, and when he's satisfied that everything's all right, he pulls a gun, takes control of the reception area, and gets the receptionist to let the rest of us in. Then, when we're up the stairs, we find out the room where Krys is doing his thing, and grab him.'

'What about the men with him? What'll they be doing all this time?'

'They usually tend to be with their own women. They certainly don't hang about guarding Krys. The beauty of it is that they'll be really easy pickings. Caught with their trousers down, so to speak. We tie them up, disarm them, and then we're out of there. By this time, we've hired a nice little place out in the country on a short let, and we keep him there until the ransom's sorted out.'

'And how the hell are we going to collect the ransom without getting ourselves killed in the process?'

I paused, not sure whether I still needed to convince myself of this bit. 'We get his dad to deliver it.'

'Who? Stefan?' I nodded. 'Max, we're talking about a man who's a virtual recluse. How are you going to get him out running errands?'

'Because Krys is his son. One of his boys is in prison, and now he risks losing another one. From what I hear, they're a close-knit family, and Krys, even though he's meant to be one mean fucking bastard, is also the apple of his mother's eye.'

'Where are you getting all this information from?'

'A lot of it's common knowledge, Joe. You know that. The Holtzes might try to be secretive but everyone knows about them. I think that if we play this right, then we're going to be able to get his old man to come. And, obviously, if we can do that, then the chances of anyone trying to fuck us over are minimal. They won't dare do anything that'll risk hurting the big boss. Then we take the money, give Krys a nice kicking so he knows what it's like to be on the wrong end of a beating for once, and we're out of there.'

'And that's it?'

'That's it. If we make a straight ransom demand of half a million in cash, that'll be enough to make up for the risks we're going to have to take, and give everyone involved the opportunity to take off elsewhere until things either calm down or they don't. Either way there'll be a nice little nest egg, and it's not a sum that people like the Holtzes are going to have any trouble raising. Not with their money. The whole thing'll take a few days and then, bingo, you'll be a whole lot richer than you are today.'

'If we get away with it.'

'It's a risky venture, I know that. I'm asking for your involvement because you're my mate, and you know I've got to do something to sort out this situation. Plus, I think the money outweighs the risks. Think about it. We spent months at a time fighting people who make the Holtzes look like pussycats, and all for five hundred quid a week tax free. This might be dangerous, but it's no more dangerous than anything else we've ever done, and this time we can all take a nice long holiday at the end of it.'

Joe took another slug of the beer. 'Have you spoken to anyone else about this?'

'Apart from Elaine, no.'

'And what does she think, this woman you've known for all of one weekend?'

'I think she'd prefer it if we just got out of London and forgot the whole thing, but now that she knows I'm committed to doing it, she's right behind me.'

'How do you know she's not going to go and blurt the whole thing out to one of her mates?'

'Because she's no fool, Joe. Plus, she owes Krys Holtz after what he did to her last night. She won't let us down.'

Joe sat back in his seat and lit a cigarette, still not back in the habit of offering me one, so I pulled out one of my own. 'The police came to see me again this morning,' he said eventually.

'Oh yeah? How come?'

'Eric's missus. She's reported him missing. This detective came round asking questions. Had we seen him? How long's he worked with us? That sort of thing.'

'Did he mention anything about me?'

'No, it was a different bloke to the ones who came round Saturday. I got the impression that this one didn't know anything about you. God knows why. You'd have thought they'd have co-ordinated things a bit better.'

'That's the Old Bill for you. Do you think he suspects anything?'

He shook his head. 'I don't think so. He sounded like the whole thing was routine, but we really don't need the attention, not with everything else. And you've got to think, they're going to be able to put two and two together eventually, aren't they?'

'That's another reason to go ahead with this. If we've got money in our pockets, big money, we're not going to have to worry about it.'

He sighed. 'I don't think they can prove much anyway, not without a body, but it's a worry. You know, it's amazing how everything can change just like that. This time last week everything was hunky dory. Now look at it.' He sat in silence for a few moments and I watched him closely, knowing that if he didn't bite I might as well forget the whole thing now. 'This sort of operation's going to need at least four people involved, maybe even five,' he said after a while.

'Yeah, I know. I thought we'd use Johnny Hexham as the driver. He's always available for work, and we don't have to tell him what we're doing. Not until it's too late for him to do anything about it anyway. I can even get him to nick the vehicles we'll use for the snatch. Any ideas who else? Anyone we've worked with in the past? I was thinking of ex-squaddies who are looking for a bit of extra cash.'

'Not many are going to want to get involved in something like this. Too many things could go wrong.'

'With half a million to play with, we could make it worth their while.'

'What split are you suggesting?'

'Equal shares for everyone who has to carry a gun, fifty grand for the driver, and thirty to Elaine for her part in setting it up. Does that sound fair?'

Joe nodded. 'Yeah, but we've got to be very careful who else we bring in on this. We don't want to talk to anyone who then turns round and says they're not interested, because that'll compromise everything and probably land me on the same target list you're on.'

'I agree, but I can't think of anyone offhand. A week ago I'd have said Tony. He was the sort of bloke who'd have gone for this.'

'When are you hoping to make the snatch?'

'As soon as we've got everything organized. The place where we're going to hold him, the cars, and obviously the people. It'll be a few days yet, but that's all.'

'And who's doing the organizing?'

'I'll do all that, if you can get the other people. I think you're right, perhaps we should have four gunmen. So, are you going to come in on it?'

Joe finished his beer and sighed. 'All my instincts tell me I'm an idiot for it, and if it was anyone else I'd run a hundred miles in the other direction, but I guess I could do with the money. Yeah, count me in, and give me a couple of days to come up with other possible men. In the meantime, you get things moving. Are you going to use the cash I gave you to cover the costs?'

I nodded. 'Yeah, that should be plenty.' I offered him another beer, thinking I could probably do with the company, but he said he had to go.

After he'd left, I poured myself one anyway and relaxed in my seat. In the end, I'd always known that Joe would be up for it because, like all people who'd worked the mercenary game, he longed for excitement and had been shot at enough times not to worry too much about the danger involved in what even I had to admit was not exactly a foolproof plan. The rewards, though, were not to be sniffed at.

All I had to do now was make sure the basics were in place, and then we'd be ready to go.

Wednesday, eleven days ago

Gallan

When I arrived at the restaurant, Malik – I assumed it was him – was already there, sat at a table at the far end. I could see why he'd picked this place: he was the only customer in it, which didn't bode too well. I don't usually get an opportunity to sample restaurant fare while I'm on duty, so I hoped Malik knew something the rest of the West End's lunchtime trade didn't.

He stood up as I approached and we introduced ourselves and shook hands. He was a young guy, thirty tops, with a friendly smile and the air of someone with a lot of self-confidence. He was dressed in a dark grey suit that looked more expensive than a copper's wage would allow, and a natty-looking red tie. A bit formal for an eighty-degree day with high humidity, but he carried it well. I thought he looked more like an up-and-coming executive than a copper, but there was something genuine about him. A sense that you could trust what he had to say. If he'd been selling, I'd have definitely been in the marketplace, and it's not often I say that.

A waiter appeared almost as soon as I'd sat down and asked if I'd like a drink. I saw that Malik was on orange juice, but since the Met were paying and I had a pack of peppermints in my pocket, I opted for a beer. I'm not a man who has any problem drinking alone.

'So, this case you're working on,' said Malik as my drink arrived. 'What's it all about?'

I gave him a brief rundown of the Matthews inquiry. 'It's going nowhere fast. There's still been no sign of Jean Tanner – it's like she's vanished into thin air – and the preliminary autopsy on Craig McBride showed he died of a heroin overdose, of all things. Again, no signs of a struggle. Other than that, we've got nothing. No new leads, and no joy with any of the old ones. My hunch is that someone from the Holtz organization is definitely involved, because of the way everyone either ends up dead or disappears, but I'm not in a position to do anything about it.'

Malik nodded thoughtfully. 'I'm not sure how much help I can be, John.'

I took another sip from my drink. 'I don't know either, but I'm beginning to run out of options and you never know, you might have something that'll move us forward. Basically, I want as much information as you can give me on the Holtzes and Neil Vamen. I know a little bit, but it's very patchy.'

'Let's order first,' he said. He picked up a menu from the table and handed it to me. 'I particularly recommend the saltimbocca.'

'What the hell's that?'

'Escalopes of veal and parma ham cooked in a marsala sauce and served with veg of the day and sautéed potatoes. Bellissima!'

'It sounds like you're part-owner of the place.' I gave the menu a cursory scan but nothing else leapt out at me. 'OK, I'll go with the escalopes. In honour of my ex-wife.'

'She used to like them, did she?'

I allowed myself a malicious smile. 'No, she was a strict vegetarian.'

'Clearly not an amicable separation.' He laughed.

'Are they ever?'

'Maybe more amicable than that. But who am I to judge?' He waved the waiter over and gave our order. 'Anyway,' he said when the waiter had gone, 'the Holtzes. I've been part of a team that's been investigating them for getting close to eighteen months now, and let me tell you, they are no easy target. It's like trying to penetrate concrete.'

'Why's that?'

'A couple of reasons. One is they've been around as an organization of sorts for getting close to thirty years so they're very well established. The old man Stefan's the lynchpin. He started out as a nasty little thug and amateur boxer who got into debt collecting on behalf of various scumbags before deciding he'd be better off branching out on his own. What differentiated young Stefan from a thousand other lowlifes was that he had a brain, and a very sharp one at that. He was, and is, a very good businessman. I'd say he was wasted in crime but he probably earns ten times more through that than he would do by being legit, and he's expanded majorly over the years. Moved into gambling, counterfeiting, armed robbery for a while, though of course never getting his hands dirty himself. He organized everything but he made sure he only surrounded himself with people he could really trust. That's why in many ways it's always been a family outfit. His two brothers were heavily involved with him in the early days, and then, when they got old enough, his sons got into it as well. They probably never would have been a massive outfit, though, if it hadn't been for drugs.'

I allowed myself a wry chuckle. 'Same old story.'

'Always the same old story. Everyone's made big cash out of

drugs, no doubt about it, but for an outfit like the Holtzes, with an infrastructure and good underworld contacts already in place, the opportunities have been huge. And they've taken them. You know, the word is Stefan Holtz can't stand drugs. Won't let any of his family touch them, although of course they all do. But as an organization they were into them from the outset. Dope, amphetamines, coke particularly, even heroin. Over the years they've forged alliances with numerous other crime organizations both here and abroad and now they're one of the biggest importers in Britain. They also supply a lot of the gear, particularly Ecstasy and coke, to Ibiza for the summer season. So, if your nice middle-class teenage kid goes over and drops a tab or snorts a line, the chances are that some of the profits on that are heading straight back to the Holtzes, and we're not talking about small quantities here. Thousands of people are taking millions of pounds' worth of gear every night between May and October. And that's just one part of their smuggling activities.

'But what sets them apart is their levels of sophistication and the seniority of their contacts in the criminal world. These days they get their cocaine straight out of Cali in Colombia, no middle men at all. And we believe they've set up a major smuggling route through Bosnia and into western Europe, not only for heroin from Pakistan and Afghanistan but also for illegal immigrants, particularly now the Mehmet Illan/Raymond Keen operation's out of business. They even smuggle in ancient artefacts. There's nothing they won't touch. If it makes money, they'll be there. And the sort of money that comes their way is incredible. We don't know exactly how much it is for sure, there are so many front companies and money-laundering operations, and Holtz employs an army of accountants, but we reckon as a group they turn over in excess of forty million sterling per year.'

I whistled through my teeth. 'No wonder they're difficult to penetrate.'

'Exactly. That sort of money buys a lot of loyalty. And, as I've said, they're well enough established that the main players involved are all very well known to one another, so they're not likely to start grassing each other up, especially if there's no obvious benefit to it. A guy from SO10 did get on the periphery of the organization once but they sniffed him out, found out where he lived, and sent a couple of their people round to pay a visit to his wife and baby.'

'Christ,' I said, wondering how I'd have reacted ten years earlier if the same thing had happened to me.

'They didn't hurt them or anything, just made sure he knew that they could if they wanted to. It spooked the guy so badly he left the Force. And that was the closest anyone ever got. Having said all that, we have had some successes against them, as have other branches of the Met, and Tomas, Stefan's oldest son, is currently doing a nine stretch for possession of two kilos of cocaine and twenty-four M-16 rifles.' I raised my eyebrows quizzically. 'Yes, they also smuggle weapons as well, although that was the first evidence we ever had of it, and of course young Tommy denied knowledge of any such enterprise and claimed that, like the gear, they were a plant.' He smiled wearily, the standard copper's reaction to such boring and uninventive lies.

'What about contacts within the Force?' I asked, thinking of that arsehole Burley. 'Have they got any?'

'We've never actually uncovered anyone, but you know as well as I do there are coppers out there susceptible to corruption.' He paused for a moment as if he was waiting for me to make some mention of his old boss, but I kept silent. 'Anecdotal evidence suggests there's quite a few coppers on the Holtz payroll,' he continued, 'and it would stand to reason. But they've been good at keeping it under wraps.'

'You said there were two reasons why they were so hard to penetrate. One's the way they're organized. What's the other?'

Malik gave me a serious look. 'Their ruthlessness. If you cross them, your days really are numbered. Every criminal firm's prone to violence, of course. I suppose you've got to be in that line of business, especially these days with all the competition, but the Holtzes take it one step further. To them, killing's just another way of protecting their investments. If you get in their way, or do anything that might foul up the smooth operation of their moneymaking, then you die. It's as simple as that. We estimate they've been responsible for something like thirty-five killings since 1985 alone. Incredible when you think that most people have never even heard of them. But we've only ever recovered fourteen bodies which could actually be linked to members and associates of the family. Of those fourteen, not one has ever resulted in a conviction. People don't go against the Holtzes because the consequences are simply too grim, and the rewards of staying onside simply too great.'

'You make it sound like an impossible task to bring them to justice.'

'We'll get them in the end,' he said, and he sounded like he truly meant it. I thought it was a pity there weren't more coppers like Malik. 'We'll pursue them to the ends of the earth if we have to, but I'll be honest with you, it won't be easy. In the eighteen months I've been with the team we've not been able to secure anything above minor convictions, and those have only been against the lower-level players, but things are changing. The government are getting very concerned about criminal gangs supposedly running the country so they're putting a lot of resources into the fight to bring them down. We're not the only people involved. MI5 are looking into them too. So are the National Crime Squad, and even Customs & Excise are involved, which is probably the most frightening prospect of all from a criminal's point of view. So they're feeling the squeeze. But I can't see them bursting just yet.'

The food arrived, and Malik was right, I wasn't disappointed. As I ate, I stole occasional glances at him and I had to admit to being impressed by his overall demeanour. Here was a man whose immediate boss and mentor had been uncovered as a cold-blooded killer, an event that had placed Malik under the microscope of the press and had led to unfounded whispers about his own involvement. I knew what it was like to have the media on your back from my own experience, but the Dennis Milne story had been a much bigger one than our squalid little cover-up, yet Malik didn't portray the remotest hint that it had adversely affected him. If anything, it was quite the opposite. From what I'd gathered from talking to people at the station who'd known him in his time there, he'd been a fairly quiet, unassuming guy, nothing like the confident-looking individual sat in front of me now.

'So, Neil Vamen,' I said between mouthfuls. 'I know a few things about him, none of them particularly nice, but I'd like to hear anything you've got.' I decided not to say anything about my visit to him at the Seven Bells, since it didn't exactly place me in a positive light.

He sawed off a large chunk of veal and popped it in his mouth, clearly savouring the taste. 'Sorry about that,' he said when he'd finished chewing. 'Vamen's an interesting one. He joined the family firm at a fairly low level back in the mid-seventies, apparently as an enforcer. He's thought to have committed at least one murder on Stefan Holtz's behalf, in 1978 when he was twenty-one, but he's a cunning bastard, and very shrewd, and he's moved right through the ranks. Of people outside the immediate family, he's easily the closest to Stefan, and acts as his chief adviser, especially now that Stefan's a virtual recluse. I suppose in many ways Vamen's the most dangerous of all of them because he's as intelligent as Holtz, if not more so, and he's still got the drive. The other family members don't cut the mustard in that respect. Stefan's two brothers are both dead: one, Terry, died from a heart attack ten years ago while he was in prison; the other, Kas, got killed in a car crash last year. And of the three sons, Tommy's in the nick, Robbie's not interested, and Krys is too much of a nutter.'

'I've heard about Krys.'

'A real nasty piece of work, and in a way the others aren't. Everyone connected with the Holtzes is violent, some in the extreme, but in the main it's just business. I'm not saying that that justifies it, of course it doesn't, but at least there's a reason behind it. With Krys, it's all about the enjoyment of inflicting pain. He's the sort who likes pulling the legs off spiders – you know the type. In fact, in many ways he's probably their loosest cannon, although such is the fear he inspires in people he's never been convicted of a thing. No-one would ever testify against Krys Holtz.'

'Do you think it's feasible that Neil Vamen could be behind the murder of Shaun Matthews?'

'Be realistic, John. What have you got? The word of a dead man.'

'So, the name Jean Tanner doesn't actually mean anything to you, then?'

He shook his head. 'Not off the top of my head, no.'

I refused to give up. 'I don't see why McBride would have been bullshitting. He said it was well known that Neil Vamen played away from home. Would that be right?'

'Well, it's certainly well known that Vamen has mistresses, but, like everything else in his life, he likes to keep them as secret as possible. We put him under surveillance whenever resources allow, and we've photographed him with a number of women other than his wife, but as far as I'm aware we've only positively identified two, neither of whom goes by the name Jean Tanner. What I'll do, though, is go through what we've got back at HQ and I'll email over the information, including any photos we have of the women.'

'I'm sure that whoever killed Matthews was also responsible for the murder of Craig McBride, although God knows why. To me, that level of organization suggests someone like Neil Vamen.'

'But you haven't got much of a motive.'

'Not yet, no.'

'Whatever did happen, it wouldn't have been Vamen inflicting the fatal dose, although I suppose it's possible he could be behind it. Remember this, though: he doesn't do things that are going to bring attention on himself. In the end, unlike Krys, he's first and foremost a businessman. A nasty one, admittedly, but still some-one who's not going to risk his position by committing rash crimes. And even if he had something to do with it, you're going to have a sod of a time proving it.'

I nodded wearily, having already heard this several times. 'I know, I know. No-one ever said it would be easy.' I stabbed a couple of sautéed potatoes. 'It would be useful if I could find Matthews's boss, Roy Fowler, as well. Do you know anything about the ownership of this club, the Arcadia? I'm hearing that the Holtzes run it, but I've got nothing concrete.'

Malik shook his head. 'Not specifically. The number of front companies they've got is incredible; it has to be when you've constantly got millions of pounds to launder. I'll ask around within the team and see if they've heard anything, but don't hold your breath.'

'So you don't have any informants within their organization, then?'

For the first time during the course of the conversation, Malik appeared cagey. 'I'm afraid that's classified information, John, as you'd appreciate.'

'Well, if you do, I'd take it as a favour if you could ask the questions.'

Malik said he'd see what he could do. 'I'm sorry if I'm not being too much help,' he added with a sheepish smile.

'It's a lunch's worth,' I said, 'and anyway, I came here more in hope than expectation. But if you can get me that info on Vamen's associates and women, I'd appreciate it. It might even be worth buying you coffee for.'

Malik smiled. 'Now that's an offer I'll take you up on.'

I ordered two coffees – a cappuccino for me, a black filter for him – and the conversation drifted on to other things, mainly what life was like back at the station. I told him I didn't think he was missing much: Capper was still a talentless arsehole, Knox was still yearning for a detective superintendent role, the chief super was still an idiot. We had a few laughs about things, and found we got on pretty well, but soon Malik was looking at his watch and saying it was time to go.

We stood up at the same time, me a good four inches taller, and shook hands.

'Good luck with the case, John,' he told me, 'but be careful as well. The Holtzes, and Neil Vamen in particular, are not people to mess about with. If it came to it, they're not afraid to put a bullet in a copper.'

Which is just the sort of uplifting advice you need on a Wednesday afternoon.

*

Wednesday was Berrin's first day back at work after his impromptu bout of summer flu, which was the reason I hadn't allowed him to come on the lunch with Malik, but had instead got him reviewing witness statements. He wasn't going to get a decent meal on the Met when he'd spent the last three days lolling about at home. The bastard looked quite brown, too, which made me suspicious. When I got back to the station that afternoon he was doing an interview with a man who'd been arrested for possession of eight hundred quid's worth of counterfeit currency. Apparently there'd been no other CID available, and such was the quality of the fakes it was thought appropriate that there was plainclothes representation when they were talking to him.

While I waited for him to come out of his interview, I wrote down what I'd picked up in the meeting with Malik. I also checked my emails but he'd yet to send through the information he'd promised me, which wasn't a huge surprise. He was a busy guy and it could wait, particularly since it didn't sound like there was going to be anything earth-shattering contained in it. The Shaun Matthews incident room was eerily quiet again that afternoon, with me the solitary person in it. For some reason, it made me feel sorry for Matthews in a way I doubted he'd ever deserved, but there was something vaguely undignified about the way his death was steadily being forgotten by those charged with finding his killer. As if he simply wasn't important enough.

I picked up the phone and dialled the elusive DI Burley, expecting to get his voicemail as I had on the last two occasions I'd called. He hadn't returned either of those calls. This time, however, I was in luck.

'Burley,' he grunted. Even his telephone manner was obnoxious.

'Hello, sir,' I said, trying hard to sound as polite as possible. 'It's DS Gallan here.'

'You again. What the fuck are you hassling me for now?'

'I wondered if there was any sign of Jean Tanner yet.'

'Listen, I told you the other day, and I've told your DCI since then, that when she turns up we'll let you know.'

'Is there any actual effort being made to find her?' I asked.

'What do you want me to do, run adverts on the front page of *The Times*? Do a door-to-door poster campaign? We're looking all right, but we haven't got unlimited money and manpower, so it's going to take some time.'

'And what sort of progress are you making?'

'A lot more if I didn't keep getting my voicemail clogged up by the likes of you.'

'If you'd let us fucking help in the first place—'

'Don't ever swear at me, Gallan,' he growled, but by this time I was past caring.

'Is someone paying you to drag your feet on this? Is that why you're taking so fucking long about it?'

'You piece of shit. You'll be hearing from me about what you just said.'

I think we both hung up on each other at pretty much the same time, and I was left staring at the phone, wondering what motivated some people to join the police force. In Burley's case, it was probably a desire to mess up people's lives. I hoped he didn't make a formal complaint to Knox, who had no idea I was hassling Burley.

Next, I tried Roy Fowler's numbers, more out of habit than anything else. I knew he wouldn't answer, and he didn't. I then phoned the Arcadia and asked the man who picked up whether they'd heard from him, but they hadn't. It also turned out that Elaine Toms had left, which was vaguely interesting. No-one had a forwarding number for her, and there wasn't one on the murder log, so I was reduced to scanning the phone book until I found it. She wasn't home; a man I assumed was her boyfriend or flatmate answered. I introduced myself and asked if she could call me back. The man on the other end politely asked what it was about and I gave him the usual spiel that it was simply a routine police inquiry. In truth, I wanted to find out why she'd left the club and whether or not there was anything she might want to add to her existing statements. A bit of a straw-clutching exercise, perhaps, but if you don't ask, you don't get.

When Berrin came back from his interview, we discussed any new developments on the case, but there was nothing of note to report. At about five o'clock, Elaine Toms phoned back. She seemed in better spirits and was certainly a lot politer than the last time we'd talked, but that didn't alter the fact that she had nothing further to add to her statement.

Fifteen minutes later I decided to call it a day, and on the way out I bumped into WDC Boyd in the corridor. I hadn't seen her for a couple of days as she'd been transferred to the assault case on the thirteen-year-old girl and was in charge of liaising with the victim. It was a role I reckoned her well suited to. She had the right combination of sensitive and strong.

We both stopped and made small talk for a minute or two. I asked her how she was getting on with the new case and she told me that, like all sexual assaults, it was a difficult one, but particularly so when the victim was so young. 'She's bearing up well, considering,' she told me, 'but it breaks your heart, John.' There was a genuine pain in her eyes as she spoke, and all I could do was tell her that hopefully the girl was young enough to shrug off the trauma of what had happened. I wasn't sure I believed it, though.

'Have you managed to get anywhere further with the poisons lead?' she asked me.

'No, I'm still not sure where else I can go with it.' I'd taken Boyd's notes on what she'd uncovered regarding the venom that had killed Shaun Matthews after she'd left the murder squad. They were very thorough but didn't contain any hidden gems of information. 'You seem to have covered every angle,' I told her.

'I've covered the obvious ones, but I'm sure there's something I've missed and we're missing.'

'Did you ever search for any matches on the Internet?'

'I had a couple of dabbles but as soon as you put in key words, you get hundreds of pieces of information that are totally irrelevant. Sometimes I think the net's overrated as a means of finding out about stuff. And you know what it's like round here. If you start surfing, people think you're just messing about and not working. They're still Luddites in CID.'

'I think I might have a go at home,' I said. 'I bought this PC a while back and I never seem to get the time to use it.'

'Story of our lives,' she said.

I wanted to ask her what she was up to now and whether she had time for a quick drink, and I was just about to open my mouth when Knox appeared round the corner, looking troubled.

'Hello Tina, John.' He stopped and took hold of my arm. 'You'll have to excuse us, Tina, but we've had some movement on the Matthews case. John, I need to speak to you in the incident room. Urgently.'

I said a brief goodbye to Boyd then walked back towards the incident room with Knox. 'What's happened, sir?'

'That stain in the car we stopped the other day. The one you phoned in about.'

'Oh yeah?'

'It was blood. And guess who the blood belonged to?'

'I couldn't tell you, sir.'

'None other than Mr Arcadia himself, Roy Fowler. It matched

the sample we took from him when he was nicked for driving under the influence.'

'Well, well, well.'

He turned and fixed me with a self-important stare. 'I think I know what's happened,' he said.

Capper, Hunsdon and Berrin joined us in Knox's office in the incident room. Capper asked me how it had gone with Malik that afternoon. 'Has he heard anything from Dennis Milne lately?' he asked with a snide smile as he grabbed a chair and sat down.

'Yeah, he got a postcard from him the other day,' I said, smiling back. 'Apparently he's opened a guesthouse in Bourne-mouth. Says he'll do discounts for CID and pensioners.'

Capper didn't look too amused, knowing that his attempt to score a point, however pathetic, had backfired, but he didn't say anything. Hunsdon yawned.

'All right, gents,' said Knox, bringing the meeting to order. 'Important news.' He then explained what had happened for the benefit of Capper, Berrin and Hunsdon, before sitting back, bolt upright, in his chair. There was a moment's silence while the news sank in.

'That puts the cat among the pigeons,' said Capper, exhaling dramatically.

'My theory's this,' said Knox, looking at us each in turn for maximum effect as he spoke. 'Fowler had Matthews killed. He used poison to make it look like an accident but obviously wasn't aware how easy it was for us to find out about it. That's why I don't think it was the work of organized criminals. They would have just shot him. Fowler's motive was drugs. We know that dealing went on at the Arcadia in fairly sizeable quantities, we know that Matthews ran it, and we're almost certain that Fowler organized it. I reckon Matthews was ripping Fowler off, Fowler found out about it, and took revenge.

'But I think Matthews had a business partner. Someone involved with the drugs with him, and that person was Max Iversson. He and Matthews were both ex-soldiers, same regiment in fact, and I think we'll find that the two of them knew each other. Iversson found out about what Fowler had done and decided to take revenge. He may have simply assaulted Fowler, but more likely he's killed him, and is consequently lying low.'

'It certainly sounds plausible,' said Capper, nodding.

I wasn't sure. Given that there was no evidence whatsoever to suggest that Iversson and Matthews knew each other, Knox's theory relied one hell of a lot on suppositions.

'What about McBride?' I asked. 'Where does he fit into it? And what about the Holtzes?'

'I don't know is the short answer,' he said, which at least was honest. 'McBride may well be something completely different. And, as for the Holtzes, I just can't believe that they'd use an obviously traceable and extremely rare poison to get rid of a business rival.'

'Fair enough,' I said, because he had a point. I still didn't go with it particularly, but it was hard to argue with the logic. A poisoning did seem a very odd way for a gangster to operate.

'Anyway, the most important thing is we find Max Iversson and see what he's got to say for himself. His details are going to have to be distributed to other forces, along with that photo of him we've got.' He looked at Hunsdon. 'Paul, you get that sorted out, OK?' Hunsdon nodded. '*Crimewatch* is going out next Wednesday and I want a photo of Iversson on it for the rogues gallery. That ought to get some response. Plus, I'm organizing a search warrant for Fowler's place.' He looked at Capper. 'Phil, you and Paul turn it over and see what you can find. At the same time, start really digging up on Fowler's background, generate some clues. I know he's the key to it.'

Next, Knox turned to Berrin and me. 'John, something's going on down at this Tiger Solutions company, or whatever they're called. It may be coincidence but that missing person, Eric Horne, worked for them and he still hasn't turned up, has he?'

'Not that I'm aware of, sir, no. I spoke to his ex-missus briefly yesterday and he hadn't then. She seems pretty worried.'

'I don't know how we missed the fact that he and Iversson worked for the same outfit. Anyway, you and Dave go back, grill the people there, particularly Iversson's partner, and get some answers. Something very dodgy's been going on, and I want to find out what it is.'

Which were my sentiments exactly. I hoped Knox's theory was right, because if it wasn't we were left with dozens of pieces to a jigsaw that seemed to be getting more complicated with each passing day.

Introducing Krys Holtz

Krys Holtz was a man who knew that a show of weakness, any show of weakness, inevitably destroyed a man's authority. You had to be strong. You had to break the bastard in front of you and shut out every last fucking scream for mercy he made, however loud it was. After all, if a bloke didn't do Krys any wrong, then the bloke had nothing to fear. It was only cunts who took major fucking liberties who found themselves paying the price, and the price was always justified. They could yell and squeal and beg as much as they fucking wanted. They could piss their pants, even shit in them (and some of the bastards did, too), but it was never going to make a blind bit of fucking difference, because if he let the geezer go, gave him a pat on the head and told him not to be naughty again, then they'd be lining up to put one over on him, and that was never going to happen. No fucking way.

'First things first. Admit to me you took that fucking money. Because I know you fucking did so there ain't no fucking point in pretending that you didn't. Is there?'

The 'you' in this instance was Mr Warren Case, proprietor of

Elite A Security and supplier of door staff to the Arcadia nightclub, who was, at that moment in time, tied to a filthy old bed in Krys's cavernous workshop. He was naked and spread-eagled, his hands and feet tightly bound, and very very frightened, which was hardly surprising given the fact that he'd been part of the Holtz organization for getting close to ten years and therefore knew exactly what Krys was like.

'Please, Krys,' he whimpered, 'I didn't do nothing, honest.'

Krys laughed. So did the three other men gathered round the bed: Big Mick, Fitz and Slim Robbie. 'I tell you, boys,' said Krys, shaking his head, 'this cunt's taking me for a fucking fool. Have I got "gullible cunt" written on my fucking forehead or something?'

'No, boss,' said Fitz somewhat unnecessarily.

'Oh God, God . . . Please, please . . .' Case might have been a big man with a reputation to match but his words were spewing out so fast that no-one could really understand what he was saying. Not that anyone was listening. It had gone way too far for that.

'Why don't you torture him, Krys?' suggested Slim Robbie helpfully, looking down at Case's sweating, panic-stricken features.

'Good idea, Rob, I think I might just do that. It'll save us all a lot of time and will, in this case, be particularly fucking enjoyable.'

Case tried to struggle with his bonds but he was too well secured for anything more than the smallest of movements. 'Krys, please, I swear I didn't fucking do anything. Honest. On my kids' lives . . .'

Krys looked mildly put out by this. 'On your kids' lives? That's a mean fucking thing to say, Warren, especially as I know you're as guilty as sin. I can't understand why you don't just come fucking clean and admit it. I mean, we're going to get it out of you sooner or later. Why don't you save us all the trouble?'

But Case continued to protest his innocence in forced, desperate tones, which really peeved Krys. It reminded him of that time with Jon Kalinski. Right up until the bitter end, that bastard had sworn he'd never nicked a penny off Krys, when in reality he'd had him over for close to two hundred grand in cash and diamonds. And for a long time Krys had believed him, too – the smooth-talking cunt – but in the end he'd had the last laugh, making him watch while he'd gone to work on his girlfriend, telling him to be patient, because it would be his turn next. Come to think of it, Kalinski had shat himself as well. Terrible smell it had been. Runny, too. Some people have got no self-respect.

It was time, Krys decided, to drop the Mr Nice Guy act with Case and take more radical measures. He picked up a dirty apron from the chair beside him and made a great show of putting it on, ignoring Case's whines. When that was done, he walked up to his tool rack where a vast array of implements covered almost the entire length of one dank, grimy wall. He stopped, inspected what was on offer for a few moments, then selected his Bosch 3960K battery-operated drill, a fine piece of German workmanship if ever there was one, and vastly superior to the equivalent Black & Decker. It had been a birthday present from his dear old mum and was something he only liked to use on special occasions. Removing it from its handy carry-case, he spent some time selecting a suitable drill bit, opting eventually for a nice thin three mill. After all, he didn't want any accidental fatalities. Not before he'd found out what he wanted to know. After that, he'd have to see.

He fitted the bit and turned the drill on, enjoying the revved-up shriek it made as it shifted between the two gears. He turned it on and off several times in rapid succession, and once again the naked prisoner struggled on the bed, tears of frustration and bowel-churning fear streaming down his face.

'It ain't looking good, is it, Warren? This is Teutonic tool-making at its finest. Vorsprung durch technik, and all that. This cunt goes through concrete like it ain't even there, and with hardly an ounce of pressure. Not like its cheaper, more substan-dard rivals. So, think how easily it'll go through human flesh. Your flesh.' As he spoke, he approached the bed until he was standing right above it, looking down at Case's fear-engraved face.

'Please, Krys, I swear. I have never, never, never fucked you over. I've never skimmed you, I've never taken nothing that wasn't my due. Honest. Please, for my kids' sakes. Don't hurt me.'

'Admit you did it, Warren. That's all you've got to do. Just fucking admit to me that you took my fucking money, and maybe, just maybe, I'll let you go.' He switched the drill on again.

'But Krys, I didn't, I didn't. I promise—'

Krys shoved the drill into his face, ripping a vicious hole right through the cheek. Blood splattered angrily across his features and the dirt-encrusted mattress, and flecks of it splashed onto Krys's apron. He held the drill in there for a few moments while it made a nice mess, careful not to push too hard and damage the tongue, then pulled it out, taking a lump of meat with it. He switched it off, removed the lump, and chucked it back at Case. 'That's yours,' he said evenly.

Case coughed and choked as his mouth filled with blood. He managed to turn his head and spit most of it onto the pillow. Then he sicked up some pinkish fluid.

'Ooh, that's horrible,' said Fitz, attempting to wrinkle his flattened nose.

Krys grinned. 'Fuck that, I'm only just warming up.' He turned to Big Mick and told him to turn the radio up a few notches. 'I think we've got a screamer here.' A couple of seconds later, the sound of 'Take on Me' by veteran eighties rockers a-ha jingled catchily over the airwaves.

Case stopped vomiting and looked towards Krys with wide, pleading eyes. He opened his mouth to say something, perhaps to make a confession, but Krys would not be denied his prize. The cunt had held out, he'd had his chance and refused to take it, and now he was going to pay the price, there was no getting away from that. No fucking way.

He pounced on the bed, half-screaming, half-laughing, and shoved the drill into his prone victim's left knee. There was a moment's stubborn resistance, as he worked to create a decent opening, but then he was into his stride and the bit was coursing through bone like the Nazis through Poland, triumphant in its efficiency. Krys was forced to look away as the debris flew off in every direction, the screams of Case so loud that they all but drowned out the vocals of one-time Norwegian heart-throb Morton Harket, but then old Morton had never had the most forceful of voices.

Finally, the bit was through and cutting into the mattress beneath. Krys pulled it out, a crackle of almost sexual excitement surging from his groin to his neck. He paused for a moment to relish the feeling, then fell upon the other kneecap like a wolf upon freshly killed prey, lost in the noise and the blood.

By the time he'd finished this one, Case had passed out and a-ha had been replaced by trendy American rockers Mercury Rev. Krys thought that he preferred the Norwegians, mainly because the song reminded him of his youth. He was sure he'd once fucked a girl to the sound of 'Take on Me'. Take her on, he fucking had. And won.

'Wake him up,' said Krys, looking down at the blood as it dripped onto the bed. Fitz put some smelling salts under Case's nose. At first they didn't seem to do too much, but then Case started coughing and dribbling, and his eyes opened. 'Oh God,' he managed to say, then shut them again. Krys wiped the drill bit with a handkerchief and noticed that some blood had got onto his jeans, which annoyed him still more. This cunt, Case, hadn't yet paid enough. It was hardly Krys's fault if he was such a fucking nancy boy that he fainted rather than took his punishment.

He walked back round the other side of the bed, switched the drill on again, then shoved it into Case's other cheek, this time pushing hard and twisting it around a bit before retrieval. Case didn't scream at all this time, he just turned his head from side to side, alternately coughing and moaning.

'So, did you nick my money then, Warren?' Nothing. Case didn't even open his eyes. Instead, he vomited again. Krys's face darkened. 'I said, did you nick my drugs?' Then, louder: 'Did you nick my fucking money, you fucking cheap dirty lying cunt? Well, did you? I'm fucking talking to you, you piece of shit, fucking answer me!'

And then the rage came surging up like a wave in a storm and, with his face carved into a terminally unforgiving sneer, Krys Holtz pushed the drill into Case's left eye, at just the moment when the weather girl came on to say that heavy rain was on the way.

Some time afterwards, while they were standing drinking beers and wondering whether to call a doctor for Case or patch what was left of him up themselves, Slim Robbie made an interesting point. 'What if he was telling the truth all along, and he hadn't ripped you off?'

Krys shrugged. 'Fuck it. I never liked the bald cunt anyway.'

Thursday, ten days ago

Gallan

'This is beginning to become worryingly regular,' said Joe Riggs with a slight smile as he led us into Tiger's cramped offices and took us into a back room where the window above the street was wide open and a desk fan tried in vain to disperse the intense heat. Quarter to eleven and it was already excruciatingly hot, the last hurrah of the heatwave before the expected storms came in.

Riggs went out and brought in another chair for Berrin, then sat behind the small, untidy desk facing us. Unlike the other day, he didn't ask if we wanted anything to drink. 'Before last week, I'd never had a visit from the police in my life and, as you're no doubt aware, I've got no criminal record. Now three times in five days.' He didn't sound particularly worried, just mildly curious as to why we'd come again.

'The name of your company and individuals who work for it just keep coming up in our inquiries,' I told him, a smile of my own playing round my lips. It was all very civilized.

Riggs was a powerfully built individual with very muscular,

tattooed arms. He had a thick moustache and a vaguely rural Home Counties accent, and there was no mistaking the fact that he looked like a soldier. Not necessarily an officer, which I knew he'd been, because there were no obvious airs and graces, but definitely a soldier. I suppose women would have found him quite attractive in a rugged sort of way. He looked the outdoor type. He also looked a fairly upfront bloke although, as a copper, I knew that didn't necessarily mean anything.

'So, how can I help you this time?'

'It's about your partner, Mr Iversson.'

'Have you found him yet?'

'I presume that means you haven't heard from him?' put in Berrin.

'You presume right. And I've got no idea where he is either, before you ask. I haven't seen him since last Thursday. He was meant to come in on Friday and he didn't. He called in to say he was feeling under the weather and that was the last I heard from him.'

'You supply security, don't you?' I said. 'Bodyguards for celebrities and business people.'

'That's right, as I mentioned to you when we met on Monday.'

'Do you ever supply doormen?'

He shook his head. 'No.'

'Why not? I'd have thought it was quite a lucrative trade. There are plenty of bars and nightclubs out there, and plenty of trouble.'

'There are specialist companies who do that sort of thing.'

I nodded. 'I've heard.'

'Look, no offence, Mr Gallan, but I'm a busy man. Particularly now that Max has gone AWOL. So, if you could let me know what all this is about, I'd appreciate it.'

'Do you know a Shaun Matthews?' asked Berrin.

He shook his head. 'Never heard of him.'

'How about a Roy Fowler?' I asked, and I thought I caught a tiny glimmer of recognition in his eyes, though I couldn't be a hundred per cent sure.

'No, no-one of that name either.' He sat back and folded his arms. 'I think I'm entitled to know what this is all about, don't you?'

'We found a bloodstain belonging to Mr Fowler in the back of Mr Iversson's car. That's why.'

'Really? Are you sure?' I gave him a look that said of course I'm sure, I'm not sitting here making it up as I go along. 'It's just I've never heard of this bloke, and it doesn't sound at all like Max. I mean, he's a tough guy, I won't deny that, but he's no murderer.'

'How do you know Mr Fowler's been murdered?'

He fixed me with a moderately annoyed expression, the first time in both my meetings with him that he hadn't looked like he was trying to help. 'I don't,' he said firmly. 'I'm guessing. But a substantial bloodstain in the back of a car . . . It doesn't sound promising, does it?'

'But you still don't think Mr Iversson's capable of murder?' said Berrin, looking up from his notebook.

'It's certainly not in character,' he said wearily. 'But then again, it's not in character for him to lash out at police officers either.'

'Has he been acting at all strangely recently?' I asked.

'In what way?'

'In a way that suggested that something might have been bothering him.'

'We're business partners but we don't tend to socialize much outside work these days, and we certainly don't talk like we used to. I'd say that at one time we were good friends, but ironically enough, since we've been in business we've drifted apart. I haven't noticed him acting particularly out of the ordinary lately but I'm not sure I'd have noticed if there had been something bothering him. He's always been quite a cool customer. Someone who's good at keeping his emotions to himself.'

We talked for another ten minutes, Berrin and I trying to squeeze out of him any possible motives Iversson might have had for killing Fowler, but he couldn't, or wouldn't, provide us with any further information. According to Riggs, Iversson was as normal as normal could be, totally above board, not one to get involved in anything dodgy. Or, even worse, to talk about it.

'Have you heard anything from Eric Horne?' I asked eventually.

'Nothing,' he said. 'Not a dickie bird.'

'You don't think he's connected with all this, then?' asked Berrin.

'With all what?' said Riggs. 'I haven't seen Eric in two weeks, maybe even longer. Long before Max went missing. I'm sorry, but I can't help you any more than that.'

I got to my feet and Berrin followed suit. 'Well, thank you for your time, Mr Riggs. If Max Iversson does make contact with you then I'd strongly suggest you advise him to give himself up. Because we're after him, and we're going to get him. And the longer he stays out there on the run, the more we're going to assume he's responsible for Roy Fowler's disappearance, and possibly worse.'

'I will,' he said, leading us to the door. 'I don't want him getting in any more trouble than he's already in.'

When we were back out on the street and walking along the Holloway Road in the direction of Highbury Corner, Berrin said that he wasn't sure about Riggs. 'He reminded me of what

Fowler was like the first time we interviewed him,' he said. 'Very keen to help, but never actually said one thing that we could use.'

'No, I know.'

'Plus, I think he was lying. He was good at it, but I reckon he was definitely giving us the runaround. Especially that bit when he let slip about the murder.'

'Do you think he knows what's happened to Fowler, then?'

He nodded, thinking about it. 'I got the impression he does. What about you?'

'What I'm thinking is that every time we talk to someone about this case we seem to come up against a brick wall, with no-one willing or able to help and not enough evidence to break the thing apart. I think it's time we tried a new approach.'

'What kind of new approach?'

'I'm not sure,' I told him, but I was beginning to get an idea.

Iversson

I was in bed with Elaine when the phone rang. It was five past two in the afternoon and we were taking a short break from one of those sex marathons you sometimes have when you've met a girl you're really into and you've still got the sex drive to do something about it. To be honest with you, it had been like that all week. Great fun, yes, but parts of me were beginning to feel the strain. I was absolutely fucking cream crackered, and still only just past the panting stage from the last bout when Elaine picked up on the fourth ring and handed me the receiver. 'Joe,' she said.

'All right, Joe, where are you calling from?'

'A phone box in Tufnell Park, no trace possible. I've got two interested parties for our arrangement, men I think we can trust.'

'That was quick.'

'I had a good idea where I was going to look.'

'Oh yeah?'

'Yeah. You see plenty of people owe our man big time, which is what happens when you spend your days throwing your weight about and upsetting people.'

'So, who are they?'

'You know I told you about that jeweller, Kalinski, and his business arrangement with our man? The one who ended up at the maggot farm with his girlfriend? His brother Mike's an ex-armed robber and someone with a grudge.'

'Are you sure it's a good idea to use someone we don't know?'

'I've got it from decent sources that he's reliable. Plus, he's greedy. Plus, they chopped up his brother, and they're a close family. That's enough pluses, as far as I can see.'

'Fair enough. Who's the other one?'

'Iain Lewis, remember him?'

'Christ, yeah. I didn't think he was still alive.'

'Alive, well, and short of money.'

Iain Lewis, Tugger to his mates for a reason best not gone into, was a Geordie ex-marine and mercenary who'd served with me and Joe on some of our more exotic overseas tours, and who'd been wounded in Bosnia fighting against Serb forces back in the early nineties. He'd be useful on this sort of job because the potential calibre of the opposition wouldn't faze him.

'Where's he living now?'

'Down in Swansea of all places, but he'll be up here tomorrow. How are you getting on with your end of things? Have you talked to your mate Johnny yet?'

'I saw him last night. He's in already. I've dropped him five hundred in expenses and he's going to sort out the vehicles. He's meant to be calling me back later.'

'But he doesn't know anything about the targets?'

'Not a thing.'

'Good. Have you taken a look at any possible locations for storage?'

'I drove out to Essex yesterday and visited a couple of letting agents.'

'What cover did you use?'

'I said I was a writer looking for a short let somewhere nice and isolated so I could complete my first novel in the peace and tranquillity I needed. It's a thriller apparently.'

I heard Joe sigh down the phone. 'Look, we've got a problem. The police have traced the stain on the seat of your car back to Fowler.'

This was bad news. 'So?' I said all casually, keen not to worry Elaine.

'So now they're really after you, although they still don't have a clue about what's happened. The thing is, if anyone who rents you out a place sees a picture of you anywhere, it could put the whole thing in jeopardy.'

'Don't worry, I wore specs, and I've got a bit of a beard now, so I don't know how easy it'd be to make the connection.'

'It's still too risky, Max. You're not exactly a master of disguise.'

'I thought I looked quite good.'

'I'm sure you did, but I'd better take over on that side from now on. Did they show you any suitable properties?'

'There were two I liked the look of. One'll be empty next week, the other's empty now. Both farmhouses. I said I'd get back to them but I wanted to run the details past you first. See if there was one you preferred.'

'All right, I'll come over and get the stuff off you, and then I'd better do the booking. I'll need some of that money back.'

'No problem. Come over now.' Elaine pulled a face. It looked like she wasn't finished with me yet. Much more of this and I was going to have to find some bromide to stick in her tea.

'I'll be there in an hour,' he said.

'One last thing,' I said, 'before you go. The tools we're going to need for the job . . .'

'I've got enough. Don't worry about that.'

'I'll see you in an hour, then.'

I rang off and forced myself to smile at Elaine. I was trying to take in the news that I was now a suspect for a murder. One more reason, I reckoned, to make sure everything went to plan with the Holtz snatch.

She sat up in the bed and lit a cigarette. 'So, things moving along then, are they?' she asked.

'Everything's going peachy,' I said, but there must have been something in my tone.

'But?'

What is it about women? They can always see through your lies. I gave her a quick rundown of our conversation, mentioning about the police being on to me.

'What are you going to do about it?'

I shrugged. 'Not a lot I can do, really. It's a pain having them on my back, but if I keep my wits about me, then that's all it'll be. Not enough to mess up any of the plans.'

'It's suspicion of murder, Max, not unpaid parking tickets, so they're going to be making an effort to find you.'

I nodded. She was right. 'I'll be careful, don't worry.'

She took a drag on her cigarette and blew the smoke up towards the ceiling. 'What are you going to do when this is all over?'

'I'm going to get out of the country for a while. I know a bloke who puts together perfect-quality fake passports, and I'll have money as well, so I'll be able to survive. Anyway, everything'll die down in a few months. I mean, they haven't got any other evidence against me on the Fowler thing, and they're never going to find the body, not if the Holtzes have done their bit, so it'll end up gathering dust in the unsolveds. I'll just come back in a while and tell them it was nothing to do with me.'

'What about me, though?' she asked.

I thought about that one for a moment. 'Do you want to come with me? We'll both have cash, and there's nothing keeping you here any more.' I might have only known Elaine for a few days but sometimes you can just tell when they're right for you. My mum and dad had got engaged after only two weeks, so whirlwind romances obviously ran in the family. They'd lasted close to five years, too. Not that I fancied getting hitched just yet.

'Do you want me to?' she asked, her expression serious. I knew then that she felt the same way. Sometimes, with her, it had been difficult to tell. She could be a bit distant on occasion, to be honest with you, and it had made me wonder more than once whether I was maybe outstaying my welcome.

I nodded. 'Yeah. I do.'

'Have you got anywhere in mind?'

'As long as it's not Sierra Leone, I don't much care.'

She smiled. 'How about Bermuda? I've always fancied going there.'

I shrugged, thinking that whoever said money didn't buy happiness was badly fucking mistaken. 'Sure, Bermuda it is.'

'Let's have a little celebration, then. Fancy a beer?'

Life doesn't get much better than that, does it? A beautiful naked woman with a devil tattooed on her shapely rear offering to go and get you a nice, cool lager while you lounge idly on her bed.

'Yeah, I'd love one,' I said, getting myself comfortable and lighting a cigarette of my own.

I watched as she breezed out of the bedroom, thinking that this time in a week I'd either be the happiest man on earth, or dead. And if I was dead, none of it was going to matter anyway. High stakes, yes, but then that's what it's all about, isn't it? That's what made it all the more exciting. I remembered a phrase some-one had quoted to me when I was out in Africa. It was something a French general had said to his men back in the nineteenth century when they were defending a town from the British. 'The enemy have vastly superior numbers. They are coming at us from three sides. Soon their encirclement will be complete. Our right flank is collapsing, casualties are high, our forces are in retreat. Situation perfect. Attack.' And that's the thing. Half the joy is facing superior odds and winning. I might have thought I wanted the quiet life, but in the end, like all true soldiers, I longed for that old call to arms. Even better when there was a pot of gold at the end of it that would set me up for ever.

When Elaine returned with the beers, I had a grin on my face the size of China.

Friday, nine days ago

Gallan

I was in court all Friday afternoon giving evidence in the case of a child molester. He'd been accused of abusing young boys at the swimming club he helped run for inner-city kids with limited access to leisure facilities. It was something I'd worked on months before but, as everyone knows, the wheels of justice turn incredibly slowly. The defence barrister gave me as hard a time as possible in the stand, taking full advantage of the fact that forensic evidence was limited and that most of the case against his client rested solely on the words of children, several with learning difficulties, who could easily be lying. But I'm no pushover and I held my ground firmly and with barely concealed contempt for the man in front of me. The defendant already had three previous convictions for exactly this type of offence – not that the jury were aware of that – so, as far as I could see, the defence barrister had to be pretty damned sure the man he was defending was guilty. In which case, he was helping to put a dangerous man back on the street so that he could continue to prey on the kind of people least able to stop him. You can couch it how you want it, spout all this bullshit about everyone being entitled to a proper defence, but it was still wrong. As far as I was concerned, to put the rights of someone who abused children for his own enjoyment above those of the same children to live their lives free from these kinds of assaults was probably the single most perverted aspect of the British justice system, and one of the few things that made me doubt my own role in upholding the law. That well-educated, supposedly respectable men and women were paid sums of money vastly out of proportion to their talent to help keep this situation going, and from the public purse as well, only served to spawn that doubt.

The best way to combat this, however, is to beat them at their own game, and in that particular battle I knew I'd done just that, constantly staring my enemy down and using just the right levels of sarcasm in my answers to make him look foolish in front of the jury. It was a small victory – after all, the lawyer still went home with a nice fat sum of money for his efforts, if you can call them that – but it was a victory nonetheless, and I felt confident that a conviction was on the cards which, ultimately, was the most important thing.

So I was in good cheer when I escaped at just after five (the wheels of justice are not only incredibly slow but also work, with rare exceptions, to office hours) and took the DLR south of the river to pick up my daughter for the weekend. I hadn't seen her in close to a month, so I was looking forward to it, and so it seemed was she, still being of the age where she can appreciate her dad's company. We travelled back by Tube and I took her to the Pizza Express on Upper Street for an evening meal during which I caught up with everything in her life: school, fashion, friends, boyfriends, all that hair-raising stuff that makes you think kids grow up far too fast these days, while at the same time being careful to avoid the topic of her mother and the boyfriend. She mentioned him once, telling me about some clothes he'd bought her, but I changed the subject. I really didn't want to hear about him. In the early days after I'd left, Rachel would ask me when I was going back home, and would say how much she missed me. She'd tell me how much she disliked Carrier and how he could never take my place, and it used to break my heart because I could do nothing about it. Over time, though, she'd complained about him less and less, and, although she always said she missed me, and would always give me an enthusiastic hug whenever we met, she talked less and less about me going back there, as if she'd finally got round to accepting the situation, and Carrier had finally got round to convincing her that he wasn't such a bad bloke after all. Even though the bastard was.

During our meal that evening she talked just like a happy, well-adjusted kid leading a happy, well-adjusted life. It seemed I'd become somewhat surplus to requirements.

We didn't get back to my flat until quarter past nine, and it was gone ten by the time I finally shut the door to the bedroom and left her sleeping. I'd forgotten how tiring kids can be.

I wanted to sit down and veg out in front of the TV but things were still bugging me on the case, and I'd promised myself I'd try a new angle, so I cracked open a beer and booted up my rarely used PC. It was time to see what the Internet had to offer as an investigative tool.

First of all I went through the ritual of checking my emails, which didn't usually take very long as I rarely received any, and immediately saw that there was one from Malik entitled 'Information as requested' which came with a load of attachments. It appeared to have been sent that morning and had been copied to my PC at work.

The first set of attachments comprised photographs, mostly surveillance ones, and short biographies of known or suspected associates of Neil Vamen. There were nine of them in all and they included Jackie Slap Merriweather and several others I recognized. The biographies contained the criminal records of the nine, which encompassed a whole variety of offences with a particular emphasis on ones of violence, and a summary of each of their relationships with Vamen. I blew each photo up to full size and printed them off one by one so they could be shown to the neighbours of Shaun Matthews and Jean Tanner, in the hope that they might be familiar.

The second set of attachments contained details and photographs of three women suspected of being Vamen's mistresses. One of them, as suggested by McBride and missed initially by Malik, was Jean Tanner. According to the records, Vamen had been seen visiting her home in Finchley on a number of occasions. He'd also taken her for a long weekend to his luxury apartment in Tenerife back in March with one of his other mistresses in tow. The report confirmed that she was a prostitute with two previous convictions, but said nothing else of note. Out of curiosity, I looked at the files on the other two mistresses and was vaguely interested to see that both women were very different. The one who'd accompanied Jean and Vamen to Tenerife was a glossy-looking nineteen-year-old former dental nurse, now full-time plaything, while the other was an attractive forty-six-year-old psychotherapist who'd fallen for his charms while she'd been reviewing his progress during his only stint in prison (drugs and weapons offences). They'd apparently been enjoying an on–off relationship for the past twelve years, ever since he'd been released, and I wondered idly if she was pleased with the way he'd come on.

But nothing really stood out, so I sent a quick message back to Malik, thanking him for his help, and moved on to the net proper. I started by finding a search engine and typed in the words 'snake poison', which I thought ought to give me some hits. It did, far too many, most of which were totally irrelevant. I tried different search engines, then narrowed the hunt down, putting in 'venom', 'snake venom', 'elapid venom' and, finally, 'viper venom'. I reeled through the dozens of hits I picked up, switched search engines constantly, and went back over Boyd's notes on the subject, all the time racking my brains for ideas that could actually move me forward.

I'd been at it well over an hour, and was already beginning to agree with Boyd's assertion that the Internet was a hopelessly overhyped means of uncovering information, when something caught my eye. The intro line read: 'Snake Venom part of Mujahidin Arsenal' and referred the reader to what looked like an eastern European media website. I yawned and double-clicked. Outside, I could hear the rain tumbling down, and the ominous rumble of thunder.

The article from which the intro line came had been written in October 1995 and concerned the so-called mujahidin, foreign Islamic fundamentalists who were fighting alongside fellow Muslims in Bosnia Herzegovina. It seemed they had become an integral part of the conflict, being both well organized and well financed, with extensive backing from a number of Gulf states, particularly Saudi Arabia. According to the article, they were also using some interesting weapons in their fight, one of which was snake venom. Vials of venom from the Egyptian viper, or asp, had been used by their spies within the enemy camps to poison senior enemy officers. In one cited instance three Bosnian Croat officers, including a colonel, had had the venom slipped into their food by a female Muslim cook posing as a Croat (an easy thing to do since they were essentially the same ethnic group) and all had died before the plot had been uncovered. The article didn't say what had happened to the cook but stated that the poisons definitely existed and had originated with the mujahidin and, in particular, an Arab officer with the *nom de guerre* Tajab.

At last I had something. It wasn't much, but it was a start. Malik had mentioned Bosnia as a supply route used by the Holtzes to bring both drugs and illegal immigrants into western Europe and, ultimately, Britain, although the connection was a tenuous one. There was a list of related articles on the left-hand side of the screen and I scrolled through them, skim-reading about the role the fundamentalists had played in what was described, quite accurately it seemed, as the bloodiest European conflict since 1945. Ruthless in battle, they were a formidable fighting force, their infamy far outweighing their actual numbers. So much so that, according to one of the articles written in January 1996, the United Nations demanded their removal as part of the 1995 Dayton Peace Agreement between the warring parties. The next article, written later that month, continued in the same vein, this time citing a claim made by the Bosnian Serb leader Radovan Karadzic that mujahidin had attacked Serb positions north-west of Zenica, and that, in separate ceasefire violations, Iranian military advisers and British mercenaries were continuing to train Muslim forces in bases east and south of Sarajevo.

The British connection again. Still tenuous, but there all the same. I made some notes, then left the website and typed in 'mercenaries in Bosnia' in the search-engine box. Plenty of hits came up, as expected, and once again I began the long trawl.

As I looked, I began to wonder whether this man Karadzic was making things up. After all, all wars contain plenty of lies and propaganda. But then I found an article in the *New York*

Times, dated October 1995, which covered the story of foreign involvement in the war, stretching back to its beginnings in early 1992, and contained information about who'd been involved. There'd been the usual suspects: the mujahidin; the occasional middle-class Western boys who'd been so sickened by the atrocities being visited on the Muslims that they'd gone out to try to help; the adventure seekers and nutters who for some reason are always attracted to the world's troublespots; and there'd been a company called Contracts International, based in London, who'd been supplying former British soldiers to help train Muslim forces in a variety of military techniques, including guerrilla warfare. The spokesman for Contracts International was Martin Leppel, a former captain in the Parachute Regiment. In the article, he admitted that some of the firm's employees were in Bosnia but declined to comment any further. The writers stated that no fewer than twenty-one of the company's operatives were there, and that it was almost certain they were being bankrolled by senior members of the Saudi Arabian royal family.

I noted the name of the company and its representative, then checked to see if they had a website. Not surprisingly they didn't, so I did a search on Contracts International and discovered a number of newspaper articles about the company. Founded in 1991 by Leppel, and with a full-time staff estimated at two hundred, they'd been involved in conflicts all over the world, but I concentrated solely on Bosnia. From what I could gather, there was nothing untoward about their activities in the region. You could even say, depending on your point of view I suppose, that they were actually providing a service, since the Muslims were so hopelessly outgunned. But the other warring parties had demanded they leave after the Dayton Accord because their presence was seen as provocative, although there was evidence that some had stayed behind to continue their work in breach of the treaty.

It was getting close to midnight when I opened an article from *Der Spiegel*, dated September 1997, in which the words Contracts International appeared. I was too tired to take in the fact that it was written in German, but something immediately caught my eye. It was a black and white photograph of two men walking towards a camera along what looked like a mountain road. One of the men, the younger of the two, was dressed in military fatigues, the other in a dark suit. They appeared to be talking to each other, and neither was looking at the camera. In fact, it looked as if they were unaware their picture was being taken.

The one on the left, the soldier, looked familiar, but I couldn't work out from where. It wasn't a particularly good shot of him, but I knew I wasn't mistaken. I'd definitely seen the man before.

As for the one in the suit, he was even more familiar. But then he would have been. Not only had Malik supplied me with his photograph: I'd run into him only days earlier.

It was Neil Vamen's man, Jackie Slap Merriweather.

Saturday, eight days ago

Iversson

The rain came down like a tropical monsoon. A month with none and then the whole lot arrives at once, just like London buses. It was difficult to see out of the car window, there was so much of it, but I suppose in a way that was useful. At least no-one would be paying me too much attention as I sat parked across the road from the flash-looking four-storey townhouse where the Heavenly Girls brothel was based.

For the hundredth time that night, I looked at my watch. 1.15 a.m. I'd been there close to two hours now, watching and waiting, seeing how much activity there was, wondering if that pervert Krys Holtz was going to turn up. A steady flow of cabs had been pulling up and spitting out their male passengers, mainly of the suited and booted variety, all looking like they had the cash to pay the sort of prices this place apparently asked. Elaine had told me she'd heard that thirty or so women worked for them but only about ten were there at any one time, in keeping with the intimate atmosphere. I reckoned that those ten were being kept pretty fucking busy if tonight was typical, and there'd probably be as many as twenty-five bodies in there when we hit the place. This meant we were going to have to move extremely fast. With that many people and that many rooms, it would be impossible to secure everyone, so you had to guess that one of them was going to be able to get a call in to the police. The Met were never the speediest bastards in the world, but if the person on the other end of the blower sounded desperate enough, they'd probably pull their finger out. That would mean a five- or six-minute initial reponse time, which didn't give us a lot of leeway.

But things were coming together, and that was the main thing. Johnny Hexham, a man always in pursuit of money, had already stolen the first car, the one I was in now, and was currently hunting down a van to use as transport for Holtz. Joe, acting as a businessman in pursuit of some much-needed recuperation, had made a verbal agreement to hire one of the farmhouses I'd seen on a one-month let, starting the following day, and was scheduled to go down there in a few hours' time to put down the money and pick up the keys. Johnny was on driving standby every night the following week, and the rest of the team were together, although I still hadn't met the jeweller's brother, Kalinski. If all went according to plan, I'd get to give him the once-over the following night when the four of us, minus Johnny, met to discuss the final details.

A black Toyota Land Cruiser pulled up outside Heavenly Girls and stopped, engine rumbling, by the side of the road. A couple of seconds later a big bloke, at least six four, probably more, stepped out. This was Fitz, if Elaine's description was correct. Another bloke, only slightly shorter and with the same build, came out the other side. Big Mick. And then the man himself, Krys Holtz, emerged from the front passenger side and stepped onto the pavement. Krys was a lot shorter than the other two, probably no more than five ten, but again he had the big build. He was no fucking oil painting either, and you could understand why he had to pay for it a fair amount. He dressed well, in an expensive dark suit and leather coat, but his face was all fat and jowly, like someone had lived in it too long, and his haircut – a big black Elvis-style quiff that had gone out of fashion when the King was still below fifteen stone – was all over the shop. He was only meant to be thirty but he looked at least ten years older. I was surprised that the sight of him didn't fill me with rage. Instead, I watched him calmly, knowing that I'd be getting even shortly.

Krys hurried up the steps to the house, flanked by the other two, then the door opened and a very satisfied-looking Tugger Lewis stepped out. Tugger moved aside, avoiding the group, who walked through the space he'd just occupied as if he wasn't there. He made his way over to the car and, after turning round to check that Krys and his men had entered the building, got in the passenger side. I started the engine and pulled away from the kerb. It was 1.25 a.m.

'So, how did it go?'

'Very nice,' said Tugger in his thick Geordie accent. 'The lasses are high quality, I have to say.'

'They ought to be for that sort of price.'

'Aye, I know. Two hundred quid for half an hour. That's about two quid a thrust. It's a shocking price. I was down at a place in Puerto Banus a couple of years back and it cost £38.70 for a girl once the exchange rate was taken into account. And you got forty minutes.'

'See, that's what I'd consider a fair deal. A quid a minute. Not much more expensive than a fairground waltzer.'

'And considerably more exciting.'

'Exactly. So, what's the layout in there like?'

'Reception's on the second floor. There's a lift goes up there. You come straight out into a foyer and you're facing the lass on the desk.'

'Security?'

'Two bouncers in dickie bows. Big lads, mind, but not armed. As far as I saw, it's only them, and they won't be any trouble. There's a bar that's off the foyer and that's where the lasses hang out when they're not otherwise engaged. You can go in there and have a drink with them; if you like one, you go off with her to one of the rooms. I'm not sure how many rooms there are, definitely no more than a dozen. I went up to the next floor and there were six that I counted, all very spacious and comfortable. They use rooms on the fourth floor as well, and I reckon it'll be the same layout. The second floor's just the reception area, and the first and ground floor's accommodation for the staff, I think. Basically, the whole building belongs to them.'

'Well, you know the plan, Tugger. Will it work in that sort of place?'

He appeared to think about it for a moment. 'Aye, I think so, but it's risky, no doubt about it.'

I grinned at him. 'But think of the rewards. Think of how far a hundred grand'll go up your way. You could probably buy a whole street in the north-east for that.'

'Aye, maybe so, but you'll have to move up there too, Max. You can't even get a garden shed round here for that sort of price. Hardly worth risking your neck for.'

'It's only a short piece of work,' I replied, stopping at a red light. It struck me then that Fowler had said pretty much the same thing on the day we'd first met.

But you know what they say. Once bitten, twice ready.

Monday, six days ago

Gallan

My weekend was blissfully quiet. Rachel and I did the tourist thing, stuff we'd never done together when we'd been living in the same house, because at that time I'd never really felt the need. We went to the Tower of London, the London Aquarium, Madame Tussaud's, and even the Houses of Parliament. And when we weren't treading the pavement, we were taking it easy and enjoying each other's company. I cooked curry on the Saturday night and we ate it in front of a video of *The Nutty Professor*. The food was terrible, the film not a lot better, but it didn't matter. It was just a nice way to spend the evening. I let her stay up until quarter to eleven but warned her not to tell her mother. 'Otherwise she won't let you stay with me again.' She winked and gave her nose a conspirator's tap, telling me not to worry, it would be our secret. Girls can be so manipulative.

Manipulative or not, I was a lot sadder than I thought I'd be when I had to take her back on Sunday evening. I promised I'd have her for the weekend again in two weeks' time and she told me that she'd look forward to it. I think, then, I must have done something right, but it was still a lonely journey home.

When I walked into the station on the Monday morning, however, I was feeling more refreshed than I had for a long time. Crime in the area had continued to be fairly stable in the intervening time. A fifteen-year-old Somali refugee had been put in hospital with severe head injuries after being beaten with a baseball bat during a gang fight (three minors had been arrested at the scene and bailed pending further enquiries); a spate of seven muggings had occurred on one estate, one ending in a stabbing, but the two perpetrators, both fresh out of a young offenders' institute, had already been arrested and charged; and a twenty-one-year-old woman had knifed and seriously wounded her common-law husband with a kitchen knife. She too had been arrested, and charged with GBH.

Although harrowing for the victims and their families, particularly the parents of the Somali boy who'd come to Britain seeking sanctuary and who now had to keep vigil at their son's bedside in intensive care, in many ways these crimes were a CID officer's dream because they were all pretty much self-solving. There'd be plenty of paperwork, as there always was when someone was arrested, but other than that the manpower effort would be minimal, and it would make our clear-up rate that much better. All of which meant less pressure from above.

In fact, so confident were the Brass that morning that the chief superintendent, in tandem with Knox, announced that the long-awaited 'Back on the Beat' initiative was going ahead that week. Members of CID, including the DCI, were to spend a night out patrolling with uniformed officers in an effort to regain an understanding of the pressures the uniforms had to endure, and to help, in the words of the chief super, 'to foster a continued and ever deeper spirit of co-operation between these two essential and ultimately symbiotic arms of law enforcement'. These words were uttered with a completely straight face, which told you a lot about the sort of leadership we had. I was pissed off to learn that members of the Matthews murder squad were also being used on this exercise, and I was told later during the squad meeting by Knox that Berrin and I would be going out on Wednesday night. I made a brief complaint about this, but I knew that one way or another I was going to have to be in attendance. The chief super had sanctioned it, therefore Knox would enthusiastically go along with it, as would Capper. My problem, like that of so many other coppers, was that the chain of command above me was made up almost entirely of politicians.

In the meeting that morning, the first ten minutes were taken up with Knox's prime suspect, the elusive Mr Iversson, and his possible victim, the even more elusive Mr Fowler. Of Iversson there remained no sign, although his photo and details had now been distributed to all the relevant security services, so progress was expected in this quarter; but more worryingly, at least for Knox's theory, was the fact that there didn't appear to be anything to link him with Matthews. Capper and Hunsdon had also been digging further into Fowler's background, and had even searched his flat, but it soon became clear, as they detailed what they'd been doing and who they'd been speaking to, that they hadn't found out anything that wasn't known already. Effectively, things hadn't moved on.

Knox then casually dropped a bombshell. Jean Tanner, he said, had turned up safe and well, and had told DI Burley that she and Craig McBride had been experimenting with heroin and that McBride had taken an accidental overdose. 'Apparently she panicked, put him in a cupboard and fled her home, going up north for a few days. She thought everything would die down, which I know was a bit stupid of her, and she got nicked when

225

she arrived back yesterday. She's still in custody. We're still going to need to talk to her, of course, and Burley's given us permission to do that later on today.' He turned to Capper. 'I think it's best if you and Paul do it, Phil,' he said. I opened my mouth to protest but Knox put a hand up to stop me. 'I know you originally turned up the lead, John, but I think you must have rubbed Burley up the wrong way.'

'The Pope would have rubbed him up the wrong way,' I said, thinking that I would have put money on the fact that Burley was somewhere on the Holtz payroll. 'All I did was ask him a few civil questions.'

'I know, I know, but he's a touchy sort. Let's leave it at that, eh?'

We moved on, and now it was my turn to explain the poisons lead. I went through what I'd discovered, trying to ignore the occasional quizzical looks from Capper and Hunsdon, and even Knox, as I detailed the background to the Bosnian conflict and its connections with Britain, and ultimately with organized crime in the form of the Holtzes. 'I've emailed the photograph of Merriweather and this soldier down to Malik, along with the article, and I've asked him if he can find out the identity of the soldier and get someone who can translate it. The words Contracts International appear in the article so I think it's fair to say there's some link between them and the Holtzes. I haven't been able to get anything on the company as yet, but I want to look into it a bit more closely.' No-one said anything for a moment; they all looked like they were thinking. Quite what was anyone's guess. 'Look, I know it's a long shot, but I spent three hours hunting down information on this sort of poison, and the only place I could find where it was used before was in Bosnia. And there's definitely a link between Bosnia and the Holtzes, and also a possible link between the Holtzes and Shaun Matthews.'

'Well, go that route for the moment, John,' said Knox, not sounding too confident that anything would come from it, 'and keep me and Phil posted on what turns up.'

'I'm not sure, guv,' said Capper. 'It looks like it could be another red herring. Maybe it'd be better if John and Dave went to see Jean Tanner, as it was their lead. We've got quite a lot of other things that need doing.'

But Knox wasn't keen on that idea. 'No, it'd be better if you and Paul did it, Phil. Much better.'

Capper nodded, but didn't look too pleased. I wondered again if he really had been a customer at Heavenly Girls, and couldn't help but think how amusing it would be if Jean Tanner had been one of the women whose services he'd used. It would make for an interesting meeting even if it didn't help us too much. I was pretty certain Jean knew a lot more than she was letting on. The thing was, nothing about her story smelled right. No-one had said anything about her being a smack addict, and there'd been absolutely nothing in McBride's demeanour or appearance when we'd questioned him to suggest that he was one either. And if he'd OD'd, why hadn't she? I could have done with questioning her, but instead I'd have to make do with getting hold of interview transcripts and pushing Knox to find out what he could from Burley.

The meeting broke up shortly afterwards and I brought Berrin further up to date with my extra-curricular enquiries as we sat at our desks. He also looked vaguely sceptical and said something about it all sounding 'a bit obscure', but, in the absence of anything else, I was determined to press ahead with what I had. The important thing initially was for us to track down Martin Leppel, the man who could tell us more about Contracts International. I got Berrin to check police records and liaise with Special Branch and the NCIS to see if they had anything on him, while I phoned round journalist contacts to see if any of them could dig up an address.

It didn't take long to strike gold. Roy Shelley, a local scribe who was well known to the station's CID, had taken barely half an hour to come up with the goods. Now a leading reporter on one of the nationals, he told me that Contracts International had been disbanded in 1997 after some financial irregularities and an unwelcome TV investigation into alleged illegal arms shipments to Liberia, but that Leppel was now running an outfit called Secure Consultants from an office in Moorgate. I wrote down the address and telephone number.

'Apparently it deals with much the same thing as Contracts did,' Roy told me. 'Supplying ex-soldiers abroad to provide training for the natives, and also hostage negotiators for kidnappings and the like. It's much smaller than Contracts was, and I think it's probably a lot more above board as well. Leppel got his fingers burnt last time. He hasn't got a record as such, but he came close to it.'

'Any information on what he's like?' I asked. 'Is he a crook?'

Shelley chuckled. 'Now if I answer that, I might be done for slander. How come you want to know anyway?'

'I might have a story for you.'

'A good one?'

'I'm not sure. But I promise if anything comes of it you'll be the first to know.'

'That's what I like to hear. To answer your question, he's not a hundred per cent kosher, but from what I understand he's not an out-and-out villain either. He's like a lot of people, Mr Gallan. Tries to stay on the right side of the law because it's easier that way, but doesn't let it stand in the way of a money-making opportunity.'

I thanked him and, after promising once again to inform him immediately if a story presented itself, rang off.

'All right, Dave, we've got him,' I said, and rang the number Shelley had given me.

It was answered on the third ring by a well-spoken male voice, stating the company's name. I asked to speak to Martin Leppel. 'Speaking,' came the crisp reply.

I introduced myself and explained why I was phoning. 'I'd like to have a chat with you with regard to one of your former employees at Contracts International.'

'Contracts was wound up years ago,' he answered brusquely, clearly not wanting to waste time speaking to the police.

'I'm aware of that, sir, but you may have information that would be of use to us. It'll only take up ten minutes of your time.'

'I don't see why I should help, DS Gallan, since the police have never done anything to help me. Most of the time I'm being harassed by members of Scotland Yard who appear to have bugger all better to do than try to ruin the reputations and live-lihoods of perfectly respectable businessmen.'

I remembered Neil Vamen saying much the same thing. It made me wonder sometimes whether they did in fact actually believe it. 'Any co-operation you give will be favourably viewed, sir, and as I said, it'll only take up a very small amount of your time.'

'What type of investigation is it?'

'Murder.'

'All right. I've got a meeting in the West End this afternoon but I'm free after that. Come to my office at five o'clock and I'll see you then. I presume you know where to come?'

'We do indeed, sir. Thank you very much.'

Leppel grunted something and hung up.

The offices of Secure Consultants were on the sixth floor of a grand-looking City building on a road off London Wall. I rang the bell next to a polished brass plaque with the company name and logo on it and Berrin and I were buzzed through the door without preamble. A lift opposite took us up to the sixth floor where we were met by Martin Leppel, a short but fit-looking individual with an aquiline nose and piercing blue eyes. He was dressed in a short-sleeved shirt and what looked like a regimental tie, and his thin, slightly weathered face was deeply suntanned. He nodded in greeting and we shook hands all round.

He led us through a glass door emblazoned with the company name, then through a small reception area which was unmanned (Leppel explained that his secretary had the day off) and into his spacious office that looked out on to the street. Photographs of various men in military uniforms, including a large one of Leppel in officer's garb holding a regimental sword, adorned the walls. It set off the right image of a man with a very strong army background.

Leppel took a seat behind his imposing and spotless desk and motioned for the two of us to sit in chairs opposite. He didn't offer us a drink. 'So, what can I do for you, gentlemen?' he asked, getting straight to the point.

'We're after some information regarding Contracts International's involvement in the Bosnian conflict.'

'Can I ask why you need this information?'

'We're investigating a murder and it might be that an employee or employees of the company working in Bosnia at that time could throw some light on an area we're still a bit hazy on.'

'Which is?'

'I can't tell you that, sir. Not at this time.'

'Well, I'm afraid I wasn't in Bosnia. I've never been to any of the Yugoslav republics in my life.'

I could tell this wasn't going to be easy. 'But you managed the company, which is why we're here today. Now, as I said to you on the phone, this shouldn't take long.'

'What is it you want to know?'

'How long were Contracts International involved in Bosnia?'

'We got our first contract in October 1993 when it became obvious that the West was going to stand by and watch the Muslim population suffer. It was to train regulars of the Armija BiH.'

'The who?' asked Berrin.

'The Bosnian Muslim army. The contract was successful and we were awarded a number of others. We remained *in situ* until the Dayton Peace Agreement in December 1995.'

'I heard suggestions that some of your operatives on the ground remained after this time.'

'You heard wrong, then,' said Leppel icily. 'There were, aside from our employees, freelancers in the area providing a similar if somewhat inferior service to ours. They were the ones who stayed on after the ceasefire. As soon as Dayton came about, our contracts were terminated and we left.'

'Could you tell me who funded the work your company did in Bosnia?'

'Plenty of people have written that we were funded by all kinds of fanatics, but they're wrong. However, I'm afraid I have always treated my client list, both at Contracts and at Secure Consultants, as confidential, so I'm not going to comment on that.'

I nodded. 'Fair enough. Can you recall how many employees you had in Bosnia in total during the two or so years you were there?'

Leppel thought about it for a moment. It looked like he was making calculations. 'I would say something like forty altogether, though it's possible it could have been more. Bosnia was one of our biggest operations at Contracts.'

'Now I know you weren't there, Mr Leppel, but were you aware that any of your men had contacts with the so-called mujahidin, the Islamic fundamentalist fighters who were also in the region at the time?'

'Yes, I know who they were, but as far as I'm aware, no, none of them did. You must remember that these fundamentalists hated all Westerners, whom they regarded and regard as infidels. Some of them have even been linked to Osama bin Laden, so they would never have socialized with our people, even if they were nominally on the same side. Might I ask where we're going with these questions?'

'We're trying to build up a picture, sir, that's all.' I fished in my jacket pocket for the photo of Merriweather and the soldier. When I'd got it out, I unfolded it, stood up, and showed it to Leppel. 'Do you recognize the man on the left?' I asked.

He nodded slowly without looking at me. 'Yes, I recognize him. His name's Tony Franks.'

The name, like the face, had an immediate ring of familiarity, but still I was unable to pinpoint from where. 'Do you recognize the man standing next to him?'

Again, he nodded. 'His name's Merriweather. I can't remember the first name.'

'Jack,' said Berrin.

'That's right,' he said. 'Jack.'

'This photograph came from an article in *Der Spiegel*.'

'I know.'

'The article was in German, and we're waiting to have it translated. Could you tell me what it was about?'

'It was libellous. I almost sued them over it.'

'What did it say?'

'It suggested that Contracts International consultants, they called them mercenaries, were involved in drug smuggling through Bosnia and into western Europe. They never produced any hard evidence other than that photo yet it helped to ruin the reputation of an organization that employed a lot of people and, whatever anyone likes to think, provided a service that was needed. Ever since that article came out, I've had problems. Scotland Yard were round like a shot, asking all sorts of questions, and our client base simply dried up. That's why I'm perhaps not as co-operative as I might otherwise have been.'

'I understand that, sir, but I can assure you I'm not interested in having a go at your company or you, I'm simply interested in solving this murder.'

Leppel observed me for a few moments as if trying to gauge how genuine I was. I gave him my standard I-won't-piss-you-about look back, thinking that I might just be winning this sanctimonious bastard over. 'As I've said, they never actually named names but said that our consultants were in partnership with organized crime figures in Britain and were using UN aid convoys to transport the contraband into western Europe. But they had no proof, nothing.'

'Do you think, Mr Leppel, in all honesty, that one or two of your employees might have had some contact with these organized crime figures?'

'That photograph was taken close to two years after we ceased operations in Bosnia. Yes, it's clear from the picture that Tony Franks had at least some dealings with them, and others might have done so too, but it was entirely off their own bats. Until that article was written, I knew nothing about it.'

I nodded, trying to work out whether Leppel was telling the truth or not. He was certainly exhibiting the right level of indignation, but it was difficult to say for sure. 'And Tony Franks? Do you know where he is now?'

'The last I heard he was doing some work for a company

called Tiger Solutions run by two of Contracts' ex-employees.'

Tiger Solutions. Things kept coming back to them. 'Can you give me the names of these two ex-employees?' I asked, wanting to get it confirmed.

'Joe Riggs was one of them; the other was Max Iversson.'

'Do you know if they had anything to do with Jack Merriweather or any of his associates?'

'No, as far as I know, they didn't.'

'Have you got a list anywhere of the employees of Contracts who served in Bosnia?'

He sighed. 'I thought you might ask that. I haven't, no.'

'But presumably you could dig up the information?'

He sighed again. 'It means going back over the old accounts for the company, but yes, the information can be dug up, as you put it. Though it would probably take a bit of time.'

'I would greatly appreciate it, sir, if you could provide us with a complete list. It may well be very useful to our inquiry.'

'I'll see what I can come up with.'

I stood up, and Berrin followed suit. 'Thank you very much for that, Mr Leppel,' I said, putting out my hand, 'and for your time.'

Leppel stepped forward and gave it a brief shake. 'You're certainly a lot less difficult to deal with than the last lot who paid me a visit.'

'Glad to hear it.'

'If you do get to speak to Tony, send him my regards, will you?' he said as he led us out to the lifts.

I nodded, and said that I would. 'Did you get on well with him, then?'

'He was good company, and very professional. I like dealing with people like him.'

When we were outside, I looked at my watch. Twenty past

five. The streets of the City of London were beginning to fill with the first wave of smartly dressed workers hurrying like ants in every direction, none looking as if they had a moment to spare.

'Do you think this Tony Franks character could have something to do with Matthews's death, then, Sarge?' asked Berrin as we started walking towards Moorgate Tube.

'He's linked to the Holtzes, albeit fairly indirectly, and he's linked, again indirectly, to the snake poison. It's not a lot to go on, but it's something. Did the name mean anything to you?'

Berrin shook his head. 'No, never heard of him. Does it to you?'

'It does, but I can't think from where.'

'Something's going on at that Tiger Solutions, though, isn't it?'

'The name keeps coming up, that's for sure, and it's not a name you're going to forget. We're going to have to pay another visit to Joe Riggs, but I think maybe we should leave it for a day or two. I'd like to have something to pressure him with, and at the moment we haven't got much.'

'At least now we're beginning to get somewhere, though.' For the first time in a while, he sounded enthused.

When we got to Moorgate Tube it was shut by a security alert, and the traffic had near enough ground to a halt. I called Malik on my mobile but he wasn't answering, so I left a message, asking him to call back urgently. I'd intended to go back to the station, but by the time the two of us had walked up to Old Street it was twenty to six and hardly worth it, so we went our separate ways.

But on the Underground, heading back home, sweating with the commuters, I couldn't get the name Tony Franks out of my mind. It bugged me, so much so that I got off at Highbury and Islington and returned to work, thinking that I'd never be able to relax until I'd satisfied my curiosity.

As usual, the incident room was empty, which suited me just fine. I switched on my PC, got a coffee while it booted up, and logged on to our criminal database. I then typed in: Franks, Anthony.

One match.

I opened the file and a photograph of a good-looking, youngish man with short dark hair and a calm, almost mocking expression appeared. It was the same man in the photograph with Jackie Slap. According to the computer, he'd been arrested in December 1997 on suspicion of the importation of Class A drugs, but released without charge. He had no convictions, and did not appear to have been arrested on any further charges.

I looked at the mugshot for a long time, racking my brains, trying to remember where the hell I knew him from. I'd questioned him about something. Something not that recent, but also not that long ago. It had been a serious crime but Franks had not been a suspect. He'd answered the questions put to him helpfully and with the right level of concern. I remembered I'd found him a likeable character. He'd said he worked in security. He'd once been a bodyguard for Geri Halliwell.

And then it came to me, and I was puzzled because I wasn't sure what the information meant. I'd questioned him at his home, and the reason was that Tony Franks had lived on the very same street on which thirteen-year-old paperboy Robert Jones had last been seen alive on a cold, dark February morning all those months ago.

Iversson

'So you can't tell me nothing about it?' said Johnny, looking at me like he honestly thought I might suddenly change my mind.

'Not at the moment.' I pulled the cap low over my face, then climbed into the passenger side of the red Mercedes van that would be used to transport Krys Holtz the two miles from Heavenly Girls to the lock-up in Finchley Joe had rented the previous day where we'd be changing vehicles. Johnny got in the driver's side and took the car out onto City Road.

'I hope it's nothing that's going to get me in trouble, Max. I like a quiet life, you know.'

'As do I, Johnny, which is something you should have thought about when your recommendation almost got me blown away.'

'Give us a Scooby.'

'A what?'

'A Scooby Doo, clue. Just so I've got some idea. Is it something illegal?'

'I've asked you to steal two vehicles, both of which are going to end up burnt out. What do you think?'

'I think I'm fucking nervous.'

'Don't be.'

'Where are we heading, then?'

'A pick-up in Muswell Hill.' I gave him the address and the main road it was off. 'You know how to get there?'

He nodded. 'Sure.' It was half ten and long dark. The streets were fairly quiet, it being a Monday night, and a light rain was falling. 'So, I might not be needed after tonight, then?'

'Not if all goes according to plan, but don't bet on it. It might take a while.'

We didn't speak for the rest of the journey. Johnny continued to look nervous and uncomfortable but he drove without losing concentration and within fifteen minutes we'd pulled up outside Joe's place, a flat in a slightly worn-out-looking redbrick townhouse. I rang up to him on the mobile and a couple of minutes later Joe, Tugger Lewis and Mike Kalinski came out of the door. Tugger was dressed in a suit while Joe and Kalinski wore similar boiler suits to the ones Johnny and I were wearing, and both were carrying holdalls. Tugger came round to my door while the other two went straight to the back of the van and climbed inside. I stepped out and let him in. 'Johnny, Tugger. Tugger, Johnny. You two are going to be spending some time together. Johnny, do whatever Tugger says.'

'Hold on, Max. I thought—'

'I'm going in the back. Less attention that way.'

I gave Johnny the address of Heavenly Girls, shut the passenger door, and got in the back with Joe and Kalinski. Joe gave a double knock on the interior panel separating the back from the front, and Johnny pulled away from the kerb.

Ten minutes later, the van parked up and I heard Tugger getting out to feed the meter. I looked at my watch. It was five to eleven.

An hour passed, and we sat there in relative silence, occasionally hearing Johnny's muffled voice jabbering on about something in the front, and the odd bored-sounding reply from Tugger. Traffic on the road seemed quiet. Joe had watched the place the previous night and Krys hadn't shown. It was anyone's guess whether he'd come again this evening, but if he did we were prepared.

I watched Kalinski as he sat staring up at the van's ceiling, chainsmoking Rothmans. To be honest, I didn't much like him. He was too flash; a typical robber really. When I'd met him the previous night, he'd been dressed in an immaculately tailored suit, with gold cufflinks on his shirtsleeves and a thick gold Rolex any self-respecting mugger would have killed him for. I don't like people who think they're bigshots, and Kalinski definitely rated himself as one. Joe had told me that he'd claimed to have earned more than a million quid down the years through armed robbery and the investment of the proceeds in dope deals. He might well have done, but I didn't like the way he thought it was worth boasting about. You could tell he thought he was better than us, sort of a cut above us riffraff who had to earn their livings by actually working, though fuck knows why. A thief and a dope peddler. He was hardly royalty, was he?

Still, as Joe had pointed out, he knew how to handle a gun, which meant he was less likely to use it. The last thing we needed was a shootout in the brothel. The whole thing had to be neat and professional. That way, as always, lay the route to success. And if he didn't want to say much, then that was fine by me. Johnny more than made up for his brooding silence.

I sat back in the seat and relaxed, unaffected by the boredom of the wait. I'd learnt how to be patient a long time back. It was one of the first things you got used to in the army.

Another hour passed. Then two. Kalinski shuffled about, stretched, muttered the odd curse, and at one point told us a story about how he'd once been out with a Lady someone or other who had apparently liked nothing better than to have Kalinski dress up in a balaclava, complete with sawn-off shooter, and pound her from behind while calling her a dirty rich whore. Kalinski seemed to think this made him come across like a stud, but I thought that it would be a bit of an insult if some chick I was sleeping with asked me to put a mask over my face, although in Lady whateverhernamewas's case, I could see her point. Kalinski was not what you'd call a handsome sort. He had a face like a frog and pockmarked skin.

Neither I nor Joe reacted much to his story and, seeing that he hadn't impressed us with his sexual forays into the upper classes, he settled back into sullen silence, which was just the way we liked it.

In the front, I heard Johnny say that he needed a mickey bliss, like some annoying fucking kid. Tugger, once he'd deciphered what he was trying to say, told him to piss in an empty bottle of mineral water, but Johnny said fuck that, he would wait. He didn't sound too pleased.

At ten to three I heard a car pull up somewhere across the street and I tensed, stretching, hoping that this was it. But Tugger made no signal. Just another punter looking for an enjoyable end to the evening.

At three o'clock I heard the sound of Johnny finally succumbing to nature's demand as he took a leak into the bottle, continuing for what seemed like an impressively long time.

At five past, I turned to Joe and said that we might as well call it a night. Kalinski grunted something in agreement, and Joe, who'd been half-asleep, nodded. I banged the interior wall four times. Thirty seconds later the engine was on, and Johnny was pulling away from the kerb.

I lit a cigarette and hoped we didn't have to do this for too many more nights. But that, I suppose, is what warfare is all about. Hours, sometimes days, of long waiting, then a few stunning moments of adrenalin and excitement that are gone before you know it, but live on in the memory, etched with pride, for years afterwards.

Tuesday, five days ago

Gallan

I hadn't been down that road since the investigation had wound down all those months ago. It was an attractive tree-lined street of large semi-detached whitewashed villas that meandered north of the Lower Holloway Road past the greenery of Highbury Fields. An oasis of calm in the midst of the bustling city. From where I stood now, looking down the incline in the direction of Clerkenwell, I could see the imposing spire of Union Chapel on Upper Street as it towered upwards above the trees that peppered the bottom of the park in the foreground. So often London's residents and councils liked to tag the word 'village' onto the end of their middle-class ghettoes in a usually futile bid to create the illusion of community and push up the area's property prices, but the description actually seemed to fit here. You could almost be in the middle of rural Gloucestershire. Even the traffic wasn't that bad. It was a place that reeked of money.

Perhaps that was why I felt I should have looked into the background of Tony Franks more. A man who worked in security wasn't the sort who could afford to live on a street like this. As I recalled, a lot of the neighbours had been bankers and lawyers, the sort of people with serious cash. I thought he might have said something about being part-owner of the firm he was employed by but I couldn't remember for sure, and there was nothing in the notes to confirm it. At that time, I hadn't been unduly interested in Tony Franks. He had no criminal record as such, didn't come across like he had anything to hide, and, rightly or wrongly, simply wasn't a suspect. We'd always assumed that Robert had been snatched by a predatory paedophile who'd taken advantage of the dark morning and the quieter residential area to abduct his prey from the street. Robert had been a small boy, four feet eleven, and wouldn't have been able to put up much of a resistance if his attacker was of a reasonable size, and determined.

The weather was fine and sunny that morning, very different from the bitterly cold February mornings when we'd been doing the house-to-house enquiries on this, probably the grimmest case I'd ever worked on. I stood on the spot where Robert had last been seen alive by an accountant for Citibank who was leaving for work. The time then had been five to seven and Robert had been walking past the man's driveway as he'd pulled out in his car. The man had recognized him instantly because Robert wore a distinctive woolly hat with a green fluorescent strip running round it. He'd been doing the round for more than six months, and they often saw each other in the morning. Robert had given him a brief wave and the accountant had waved back. He'd started crying when he'd related this story to the detectives because he had a son of his own the same age. I knew how he felt. There was nothing worse than the taking of a child's life, particularly for a parent. I remembered how grimly determined I'd been to solve the case and bring the perpetrator to justice, and how impotent I'd felt when we'd finally had to scale everything down because the leads had simply not materialized.

It was difficult to believe that a crime so heinous had taken place on what was such a quiet and peaceful street, and for me that's the worst thing about policework, the knowledge that effectively nowhere's safe. In a free country, those with evil in their hearts can roam wherever they want.

I'd wanted to come here alone. I'd told Berrin that this was because it would waste less time. I'd got him hunting down any further information he could find on Contracts International, and chasing Leppel for the list of Bosnian operatives. The real reason, however, was to give me an opportunity to revisit the scene of what I considered one of my most important pieces of unfinished business, and perhaps take a bit more time to reflect on what had happened that cold, dark morning.

The newsagent for whom Robert did his round was situated on Highbury Grove, approximately half a mile north-east of where I now stood. This street, Runmayne Avenue, was about halfway along his route. He would make his way down Runmayne, which was just under a quarter of a mile long, then come back the other way on Fairfield Avenue, the next street down, before returning along the main road back to the newsagent's. I was sure it was on this street that Robert had been snatched. Even at that time in the morning, there were cars and people about. Not that many, but enough to expect that if he'd continued the whole length of it he'd have been seen by someone else. After all, he would hardly have been inconspicuous.

Franks's house was about a hundred yards further along from the spot where Robert had last been seen and wasn't one to which he delivered. Slowly, I started towards it, trying to remember the exact route he would have taken and which houses he delivered to, but without much success. It was too long ago.

Too much time and too many cases had come to pass since then, and already the life of Robert Jones was passing into ancient history. He would always be remembered, of course, by his parents and his sister, but even they would think about him less and less as time wore on, and to everyone else he would simply become a vague memory, a smiling, permanently young face in a photograph that would occasionally inspire a sad and wistful conversation. It was more than a tragedy, it was an injustice. Someone, some day, would have to pay.

Franks's place was the end extension of a huge villa, set back a few yards from the road, that probably housed at least half a dozen professionally spacious flats and which had two grand entrance porticoes along its length. The extension had been built much later than the villa, probably in the sixties, and looked as if it had been attached at a slightly crooked angle. The paintwork was a fading sky blue rather than the white of the rest of the building, making it stand out for the wrong reasons. Apart from that, though, it looked OK. Small, but reasonably well kept. Newish windows had been installed on both floors, and there was a tiny, recently cobbled driveway in front of it with room for two cars at a squeeze. A high stone wall separated it from the main parking area in front of the rest of the villa, as if its occupants didn't want anything to do with their tattier neighbour.

Today, Franks's driveway was empty as I walked up it to the front door. Through the net curtains, I could make out a clean, well-furnished interior but no obvious signs of life. I rang the doorbell but no-one answered, then looked through the letterbox. There was a pile of tacky-looking brochures and various other bits of junk mail on the carpet – at least a week's worth, probably a lot more. It looked like he might have moved out.

I went round to the nearest entrance portico and saw that there were buzzers for three flats on the wall outside. Beneath the buzzers was a sticker saying that the building was protected by CCTV cameras – not that I could see any in evidence. I rang the first two but got no answer, so I tried the third. I needed to ring several times but eventually a moderately annoyed female voice came on the line. 'Yes?' she said in an accusatory voice. I identified myself, and explained that I was here as part of an inquiry. Her voice immediately lost its initial hostility, and she buzzed me in. Hers was the ground-floor flat, and she came out of the door to greet me, clad only in a dressing gown and slippers. She was about thirty with short blonde hair, and nice-looking in a Sloaney sort of way. In a dressing gown as well. Perhaps I was going to have to watch out.

'I'm sorry,' she said. 'I didn't realize you were the police. I thought you were here to sell me something.'

'I'm not sure if that's a compliment or not,' I told her.

She smiled. 'I don't know either. Anyway, please, come in. You'll have to forgive me, I've got a terrible cold. That's why I'm not working.' She sniffed loudly to prove it, then stepped aside to let me in. 'I hope it's nothing about David,' she added, leading me into a spacious, well-furnished lounge.

'David?'

'My husband.'

I took a seat and she sat down on the sofa opposite, her legs tightly pressed together. Somehow, I got the feeling I was safe from any predatory advances. 'No, it's nothing to do with him. It's about your neighbour to the left, a Tony Franks?'

'Oh yes, Tony. Nice-looking guy. Dark hair.' Her tones were clipped and upper-class. This girl had definitely not been educated at the local comprehensive. Mind you, who had round here?

I nodded. 'That sounds like him. This is a photo.' I removed the mugshot from my jacket pocket and briefly showed it to her.

'Oh yes, that's him.' She excused herself while she sneezed into a tissue she'd removed from the pocket of the dressing gown. 'Why? Has he done something wrong?'

'I don't know is the short answer. Possibly.'

'I thought it was funny.'

'What?'

'Well, the way he moved out. It was all quite sudden.'

'When was that?'

'I don't know for certain. I didn't actually see him go. All I know is about a week ago a man turned up in a van and took some stuff away.'

'This man, had you ever seen him there before?'

She shook her head. 'No, I hadn't. On the day he came I was outside putting the rubbish out for the dustmen when I saw him loading it up. I don't normally take too much notice of what the neighbours are up to – I mean, you don't in London, do you?' I nodded, thinking that that was probably the root cause of so much that was wrong with it, and waited while she continued. 'But there are quite a few burglaries around here, as you probably know, so I asked him what he was up to, and he told me he was Tony's brother.'

'Those were his exact words: "I'm Tony's brother"?'

She nodded. 'That's right, so I thought he must have something to do with him. He was friendly enough, too, not at all furtive, as you'd expect a burglar to be.' She paused to blow her nose, once again apologizing. 'He said that Tony was moving out, and he was helping with the removals. There wasn't a lot I could say to that. I asked him if Tony would be coming along later and he said he would. But he never did.'

'You never saw Mr Franks again?'

'No. I haven't seen him for two or three weeks at least.'

I made some calculations. It was sixteen days since Shaun

Matthews's murder. The timing sounded very convenient. Now for the big question. 'Did you take down the registration of the vehicle this gentleman was driving?' I mentally crossed my fingers.

'Yes, I did. I don't like to be a busybody and I know it's none of my business, but I memorized it while I was speaking to him, just in case, and I wrote it down on a piece of paper as soon as I got back in.' She stood up, sniffing loudly. 'Now, what have I done with it? Excuse me for a minute, will you?'

She wandered out of the room and I hoped I was going to get a break. Even if it proved difficult to locate Franks, whoever was moving his stuff had to have some information as to his whereabouts. Somehow I knew I was on the right track. Call it instinct, if you like. It was just a matter of continuing to pursue the scent while at the same time persuading my superiors that it was a worthwhile investment of my time. This would be the hardest part, particularly now that it looked like the area's criminals were beginning to wake up from the previous week's inactivity. An aggravated burglary the previous night in which a pregnant woman had been threatened with a knife by two intruders, who'd threatened to cut her open if she didn't reveal the whereabouts of her valuables, had already caused the chief super yet another serious resources headache. What with the continued clamour over the assault on the young girl, things were getting extremely stretched. Already Knox had hinted that the murder squad was likely to be reduced still further in the next twenty-four hours, so time was of the essence.

'Here it is,' she said, coming back in the room with a piece of paper. 'I wasn't sure whether I'd thrown it away or not, but it was in the drawer.' She handed it to me, and I put it in my top pocket, thanking her.

'Can you describe the man for me, Miss . . .?'

'Deerborne. Mrs Judy Deerborne. I'm not too good at this, but I'll give it a go. He was quite well built. Sort of tough-looking, which was why I wasn't entirely sure about him. About fortyish, maybe a couple of years older, five nine or ten, and I think he was bald, although it wasn't easy to tell, because he was wearing a cap. He also had quite a big head.'

'I disagree with you,' I said, 'I think you are good at it.' I was glad I'd worn the suit I'd been wearing yesterday because it still contained the photograph I'd shown to Martin Leppel. I fished it out now, and handed it to her. 'It wasn't the man on the right, was it? The one in the suit?'

She looked at it closely for a few seconds. In the photo, the Slap had a cap with him but was holding it in his hand rather than wearing it. His bald dome seemed to stand out a mile.

Finally, she looked up. 'You know, I think it is. I can't be a hundred per cent sure – it's not a brilliant photo, is it? But, yes, it looks a great deal like him.'

Interesting. 'You've been here for how long, Mrs Deerborne?'

'My husband and I bought this place ten years ago. I think it cost us about a third of what it would go for now.'

'That seems to be the case for most of London. And how long has Mr Franks been your next-door neighbour?'

'A long time.' She appeared to think about it for a moment. 'Three or four years at least, probably longer. Why? What is it you think he's done?' She sniffed loudly. 'I'm dying to know.' I told her politely that I couldn't divulge that. 'I hope it's nothing to do with what happened to that poor paperboy. The one who got killed.'

I smiled reassuringly. 'No, it's a separate matter entirely. Did Mr Franks live there alone?'

'I saw people come and go occasionally, but as far as I know it was just him in there. He wasn't always there either. He'd be away for a few weeks at a time sometimes.'

'Did he ever tell you what he did for a living? I mean, it's an expensive house.'

'I know he rented it but I don't know how much for. A lot, I suppose. But no, he never said what his job was. He tended to keep himself to himself. He'd talk if you talked to him, and he always said hello, but I don't think I had more than half a dozen conversations with him in all the time he was here, and not one of them lasted more than two or three minutes. Usually they were about the weather or something mundane like that.'

'Do you know who owns the house?'

'Yes, his name's Roddy Lee Potter. He's owned it for years. I know because he's come round here a couple of times, trying to buy our place. I think he owns a few houses in London. It's how he makes his money.'

I asked her if she had a phone number or an address for Mr Lee Potter and, after a bit more hunting around, it turned out she had both. She wrote them down on a sheet of paper and handed it to me. 'I don't know why we bothered keeping his details,' she said. 'It's not as if we'd ever consider selling. We love it round here.'

'I can see why,' I said, getting to my feet. 'It's a nice area.' I put out my hand and she shook it vigorously. 'Thank you very much for your help, Mrs Deerborne. It's most appreciated. If Mr Franks does for some reason turn up, can you call me on this number straight away?' I handed her my card.

'Yes, of course,' she said, leading me back to the front door.

'I hope your cold improves,' I told her as I stepped outside.

'I'm sure it will. They never did catch the man who killed the paperboy, did they?'

'No,' I said. 'We didn't. But one day we will. We always get them in the end.'

*

When I was back out on the street I phoned Berrin and brought him up to date. 'I've got a couple more visits to make,' I told him. 'We'll meet back at the station. Do me a favour, can you check on a car registration for me?' I reeled out the number.

'Do you think you might have something then, Sarge?' he asked.

'I don't know. Possibly. Do me another favour as well, will you? Speak to Capper and Hunsdon. See how the interview went with Jean Tanner.'

When I'd rung off, having given Berrin plenty of things to do for the morning, I suddenly felt guilty. There I was, supposedly teaching the poor kid the ropes of CID, and instead I was dumping all the routine stuff on him and going my own way. I made a conscious decision to be more inclusive in future. But for now, I needed to move fast.

I'd turned my mobile off for the duration of the meeting with Judy Deerborne, a long-standing habit since interruptions always messed up my thought process, and I now saw that I had a message. It was Malik returning my call, and he'd only phoned ten minutes ago. I pressed 5 for callback and waited while the phone rang. Malik was a sod of an individual to get hold of so I had to make the best of the opportunities I had.

He picked up on the fourth ring. 'Hello, John, I've just tried to phone you.'

'I know. You got my message, didn't you, and the emails I sent you?'

'That's right.'

'The guy in fatigues in the photo with Jack Merriweather. We've identified him as a Tony Franks. He's been living at 41F Runmayne Avenue in Highbury Fields for the past few years. Do you know anything about him?'

'Yes, I do,' he said. 'He was suspected of being involved in drug-running for the Holtzes out of eastern Europe, where he'd built up a lot of contacts. He was brought in for questioning and put under surveillance for a while in 1998, mainly because of that article in *Der Spiegel*, but nothing ever came of it. In the end, apart from that photo and two or three other snippets of information, there was no real hard evidence to speak of. Franks has also been seen with Merriweather at least twice in the past few months, but then so have a hundred other people. We've got nothing concrete on him.'

'The address he's been living at doesn't ring a bell, then?'

'Not off the top of my head. I'll have a look for you, but I don't think so.'

I was undeterred. 'It's a decent place in a nice area. The rent must be two grand a month, absolute minimum, probably more. As far as I can tell, this guy Franks's job was as a part-time bodyguard, so someone else must have been paying for it. The question is, why?'

Malik sighed. 'You're right. It does seem an odd set-up, even if he is linked to organized crime.'

'Listen, let me run something by you. It's strange, it might even be outlandish, but it's something that's bugging me.' I looked up and down the quiet street. A brand-new-looking BMW 7-Series drove slowly past in the direction of the Holloway Road. 'And, you know, the more I think about it, the more I think there's something in it.'

'Go on.'

So I told him, and when I'd finished Malik said that I was right, it was outlandish.

'But if there is something in it, think of the possibilities. Think of what it could do to help you against the Holtzes.'

'Talk to the landlord,' said Malik. 'Find out how he gets paid every month and where the money comes from.'

Wednesday, four days ago

Gallan

Roddy Lee Potter lived in a swanky apartment situated on the ground floor of an attractive Georgian townhouse just off Kensington High Street. When I'd finally got him to answer the phone the previous day he'd been in a bar in Soho, sounding extremely drunk. We'd arranged to meet today at midday at Roddy's place, but I'd phoned ahead to make sure he hadn't forgotten our conversation, which he had. He'd wanted to postpone, the hangover in his voice obvious, but I wasn't going to let him off the hook that easily and insisted we keep the time as arranged.

I got there ten minutes early and was buzzed in straight away. The door to the apartment was opened by a large, red-faced gentleman with curly, greyish-black hair who looked like he hadn't been out of bed that long. He was dressed in a crumpled pair of slacks and a short-sleeved shirt.

'Detective Sergeant Gallan, please come in.'

I followed him inside and through to a lavishly furnished but very messy lounge. It looked like the cleaner hadn't been in for a few days. Lee Potter motioned me to a leather armchair and I sat down, wrinkling my nose at the three-quarters-full pub-sized ashtray on the table beside him, the smell reminding me why I'd chosen to give up all those years ago.

'Would you like some coffee?' he asked.

I said I would, and waited while he went to get it. He seemed a genial enough chap, but then I guess you would be pretty genial if you lived an easy, relatively wealthy life from rental income, and had no responsibilities. Was I jealous? What do you think? Of course I was.

When Lee Potter came back with the coffees, he asked how he could be of assistance. 'I hope I'm not in trouble for anything,' he added in a tone that was a little bit too ingratiating, and sat down opposite me.

'No, but it's something you might be able to help with. You've been renting a house out to a Mr Tony Franks?'

He nodded his head. 'That's right. He moved out a couple of weeks ago.'

'How long's he been renting from you?'

'About four years now, something like that.'

'Can I ask how much you charged him in rent?'

Lee Potter looked taken aback. 'Is it strictly necessary to know that? What's it got to do with anything?'

'I'm trying to build up a picture,' I said, 'and this information's an important part of it.'

'Two thousand two hundred a month. I probably could have got more but he was an easy tenant, and they're not all like that, I can tell you.'

'How many properties do you rent out, Mr Lee Potter?'

'Four altogether.'

'I expect they make you a tidy little income, don't they?'

Lee Potter smiled nervously. 'It's not bad. Not bad at all.'

'No, I bet it isn't.' My tone was deliberately suspicious. Lee Potter struck me as a weak character, someone you could push. 'What does Mr Franks do for a living?'

'I believe he owns his own company. I'm not sure what it does, though. As long as he paid the rent on time—'

'. . . Then you didn't ask too many questions. How many times have you met Mr Franks?'

'Er, I don't know. Not many. Two or three times at most.'

'In four years?' I raised my eyebrows.

'There was never any need to see him more than that.'

'He lived there alone, did he?'

Lee Potter nodded, clearly flustered by my rapid-fire questions. 'As far as I know, yes. That's right.'

'Where did the money come from?'

'What do you mean?'

'Did he pay you directly or did it come from someone else?'

'His company paid. They used to send a cheque here every month, and they were always on time. That's why I never bothered too much. Is there something wrong?'

I ignored the question. 'Did he leave a forwarding address when he moved out?'

'No, no he didn't. In fact he never actually came round at all. I got a phone call from his brother saying that he'd gone, and asking what was owed. I was concerned because obviously it was all a bit sudden, so he suggested I go round and check that everything was OK. I did, the house all looked very clean, and then he phoned back a couple of days later, we divvied everything up, and the company sent another cheque for the balance.'

'Did his brother leave a phone number you could reach him on?'

He shook his head. 'No, he didn't. He—'

'So you couldn't actually say for certain that it was his brother?'

'Well, no, but there was no reason to believe otherwise. Why should there have been?'

'The reason I'm asking is that we want to talk to Mr Franks about some very serious matters, and I'm particularly interested in details of any of his associates.'

'As I said, Mr Gallan, I only ever met him a couple of times, and that was alone. He was a model tenant in pretty much every way. He never called me out, never complained, nothing. Just paid his rent and that was it.'

I paused for a moment and took several sips from my coffee before speaking again. 'Was there ever any suspicion on your part that the house was being used for anything other than simply being lived in?'

Lee Potter tried to look like he was thinking hard about the question. It didn't really work. 'No, not really,' he said eventually.

'Are you absolutely sure? It's very important we know about it if there was.'

He sighed. 'I once went round there, I don't know, about a year or so ago, mainly because I hadn't even seen the place for God knows how long, and I was in the area anyway.'

'Go on.'

'It was nothing really, but all the curtains were closed, which I thought was a bit odd as it was the middle of the day, and there were also a couple of cars there. Anyway, I rang on the doorbell a couple of times, but no-one answered.' He paused before continuing. 'Only, I was sure there were people there, because there was a tiny gap in the sitting-room curtains and I was certain I saw the shadow of someone moving around in there. It was probably nothing, almost certainly nothing, but I phoned Mr

Franks up a couple of days later and he made out that he'd been away, which was odd.' He shrugged expansively. 'But that's about it. I can't think of anything else. What do you think was happening there, then?'

'I don't know,' I said, but I had my ideas.

I finished the coffee, got the name of the company that paid Franks's bills from Lee Potter, and then left.

Outside, the sky was darkening and it was already raining, but I hardly noticed as I started off in the direction of the Tube station. I was too busy thinking.

Twelve hours later my thoughts had turned to very different matters. Like why wasn't the chief super traipsing round the rain-drenched midnight streets of Islington if he was so bloody keen to 'foster a continued and ever deeper spirit of co-operation' between those pounding the beat and those who'd hoped it was all behind them? It was ten past twelve and we'd just been called to the ground-floor council maisonette currently occupied by Brian and Katrina Driscoll.

The smell hit me in the face as soon as I followed Berrin and the two uniforms in through the open front door. Shit and BO and stale rubbish. Food that had gone off, trapped stagnant air; the standard, all-pervading odour of decay. A kid of about eight dressed in filthy pyjama bottoms, his ribs sticking out like they were going to burst through the skin, stood watching us im-passively at the bottom of the stairs. It was dark in the hallway but there were lights on further in.

A hysterical wailing came from one of the rooms down the hall. The voice was female. She sounded drunk. 'I can't believe you fucking did that to me, you fucking cunt!'

'Fuck off you old slag or you'll fucking get some more!'

She screamed again. 'Fuck off!'

Then him. 'Do you want some, then? Do you fucking want some?'

There was a sound of glass or crockery breaking and the first uniform, PC Ramsay, called out that it was the police responding to a call. We walked down the hall in a long line to the kitchen, past the boy who continued to stare at us blankly.

'I fucking called you! Look what he did to me!' She came into view, a big, misshapen woman in jeans and a white vest that rode up over her ample belly. A thick trail of blood ran down her face and onto her neck. Its source was a large cut on her forehead where she'd clearly been struck by something. She grabbed hold of Ramsay and pulled him to her like a sexually aggressive bear. 'Look what the cunt did to me! Look!'

The WPC with Ramsay, Farnes, shepherded the victim into the lounge away from her partner, who now appeared, bare-footed, in the kitchen doorway. 'I ain't done fucking nothing,' he said, shaking his head, the words oozing drink. He was tall with a thick head of messy brown hair and an out-of-proportion beer belly. Aged about thirty-five, and dressed in jeans and a checked shirt. We'd been warned he was violent, particularly when drunk. Apparently, the police had been called here plenty of times before.

'Come on now, Brian,' said Ramsay, who seemed to know him. 'I think it's best you come with us.' The words were spoken calmly, almost soothingly. Ramsay was understandably eager to avoid a scene. I was too, since I'd have to get involved if he didn't come quietly.

His response, however, was predictable. 'Fuck off. I'm all right. I didn't touch her. She's fucking lying again.'

Brian came forward, trying to get into the room where his partner was. Ramsay stood in the way and put his hands up to stop him. 'She's made a complaint, Brian. Now we've got to follow up on it. You understand that, don't you?'

'Fuck off. Get out my way.'

'Look, don't make this hard on everyone, Brian. Let's just go nice and quiet now.'

Brian lunged forward and I did my best to grab him in a bearhug from behind while Berrin managed to get him round the neck. Ramsay produced some handcuffs from out of nowhere and the three of us wrestled him towards the front door. Two more recently arrived uniforms came in and helped with what was no easy extraction. Brian cursed and screamed, then fell over, trying to lash out with his arms. I grabbed one, one of the uniforms grabbed another, and Ramsay forced on the cuffs.

'What are you fucking doing to me, you cunts! Leave me alone! Bastards!'

I looked up and saw the kid on the stairs still watching the whole thing, as if it was the most natural thing in the world to see your dad wrestling with a load of police officers. The man reeked of sweat and his hair was greasy. I had my knee in his back and I felt this sudden urge to grab him by the back of his greasy mane and slam his head into the floor.

'I'll fucking kill you, you bastards! You're dead! You know that? Dead!'

We pulled him to his feet and he snorted loudly, filling his mouth with phlegm.

'All right, get rid of that spit,' demanded one of the uniforms in his line of fire. 'Get rid of it now.'

'Come on now, Brian, let's be having you,' continued Ramsay, persisting with his softly-softly approach.

Brian gobbed something thick and horrible onto his carpet, deciding against sending it into one of the arresting officers' faces and risking a charge of assault, and continued with his pointless invective. We got him outside on the pavement and, while one of the uniforms got the doors of the van open, he had a final angry struggle, just to show he wasn't coming quietly, and tried to kick Berrin who dodged out of the way. I grabbed him by the shirt and pulled him back.

'Fuck off, you fucking wanker!' he shouted, and lashed out again with a bare foot, this time in my direction.

I stepped aside, then stepped back and stamped hard on his other foot, grinding the heel of my shoe in. Brian howled in pain and I felt a momentary burst of satisfaction.

'Did you see what he fucking did, the cunt? Did you fucking see?'

I turned away as he was manhandled into the back of the van and cursed myself for losing control. I'd forgotten what these lowlife domestics were like, and how irritating drunks could be. Still, that was no excuse for rising to the bait. As much as anyone, I knew the possible long-term consequences of a two-second loss of control.

'Nice one, Sarge,' said Berrin, giving me a pat on the back.

Another patrol car had arrived now and two more officers went into the house. The van containing the prisoner remained where it was while Ramsay and the other two officers chatted among themselves, ignoring the steady rain that beat down from the night sky.

I didn't say anything. I was pissed off. It struck me as ridiculous that Berrin and I should be sent out on worthless exercises like this that did nothing to bolster morale or understanding, while every effort possible was being made to squeeze the life out of the Matthews murder squad. Capper and Hunsdon had now gone over to the aggravated burglary inquiry involving the pregnant woman, and I'd even had difficulty holding on to Berrin. Knox had lost interest in the case. Particularly now there was no evidence to back up his theory of a Matthews/Iversson partnership. Maybe if the *Crimewatch* mugshot helped to flush out Iversson, things would change, but for the moment Matthews's murder was slipping down the endless list of priorities.

The sound of a baby crying came from inside and I walked back in. The kid on the stairs had gone, and the two officers who'd just arrived were talking in the doorway of the room where WPC Farnes had taken the victim, who was still sobbing and cursing. Since no-one else seemed bothered about the crying baby, I mounted the stairs, wrinkling my nose against the smell, and walked onto the landing. I found a light switch, flicked it on, then went to the door where the crying was coming from.

The smell when I opened it was foul, fetid. I had to work hard to stop myself from gagging as I switched on the lights.

The room was a cramped mess of toys, boxes, tissues, all sorts. It was difficult to make out the floor in places. In the corner was a cot, and in the cot was a baby of no more than six months, naked except for a nappy and crying hysterically. The stench of shit was horrendous, and I saw that a lot of the tissues were stained brown with it.

I walked over to the cot, the smell getting worse with each step, and looked down at the crying infant. He or she had sores round the thighs where the nappy, which looked almost full to bursting, must have been chafing. I wanted to turn round and walk out of there, and I could have done, too – there was nothing to stop me. It wasn't my business if this family, and I used the term loosely, couldn't look after their own. But it wasn't the kid's fault either so, steeling myself against the smell, I leant down and picked it up. My hands immediately felt wet and slimy and I knew without looking that they were covered in shit. Grimacing, I turned the baby over and saw that the nappy had leaked and the stuff was all up the poor little kid's back. No wonder it had been crying, having to lie helpless in its own waste. Nobody had changed this nappy for hours, possibly days.

'Whatchoo doing with her?' came a hostile voice from the doorway.

I turned to see the kid who'd watched us come in standing in the doorway. 'Trying to change her,' I said. 'Find me some wipes or a tissue, will you?' The kid didn't move. 'Look, do as I say. I'm trying to help her.'

As the kid rummaged through the crap on the floor, I laid the baby on her front and removed the nappy, using it to mop up the worst of the stuff that clung to her. I folded it up and put it on the floor, for want of a better place. 'Here y'are,' said the kid, handing me a half-used roll of toilet paper. Not quite what I had in mind, but at least it was clean.

'Thanks,' I said, continuing the grim process. 'Do me a favour, will you? Wet some of these tissues as well, and see if you can find a cloth. If you do get one, put soap and water on it, and bring it in.'

'Is she all right?' asked the kid.

'Yeah, she's fine. I think she was feeling a bit neglected.'

The kid came back a few moments later with a cloth and two wet bundles of tissues. 'Right, see that plastic bag over there?' The kid nodded. 'Put the dirty nappy in it, then bring it back here so I can chuck this stuff in it.' The kid did as he was told, and I thought he'd probably make a good assistant.

When I'd finished making the baby half-presentable, the kid and I hunted round for a clean nappy, finding a bag of them in the corner. 'Have you ever changed your sister before?' I asked him.

'Course I have,' said the kid.

'Good. What's her name?'

'Karen.'

We cleared a place on the floor, then I lifted her out of the cot and put her down gently on her back. 'OK, Karen. Your brother's going to change you now, while I go and sort myself out.'

I found the poky little bathroom and washed my hands thoroughly in the dirty sink. There were a load of hairs clogging up the plughole – hopefully from heads, but it wasn't that easy to tell – and I thought that this woman and her partner deserved absolutely no sympathy whatever. They behaved worse than animals – which was fine if that's how they wanted to live, but to ruin their kids' lives too, that for me was unforgivable.

I went back into the bedroom and helped the kid with the rest of the nappy. Then we both put Karen back into her cot. She was still crying.

'What's your name?' I asked him.

'Dean,' he said.

'I think Karen might be hungry, Dean. You go to bed now, and I'll sort out some feed for her.'

The kid disappeared without a word and I walked wearily back down the stairs, thinking that he didn't really have a chance with parents like that. Neither of them did. The ambulance had arrived for the mother and they were tending her wounds in the lounge while WPC Farnes looked on. The mother was wailing drunkenly and I found it hard not to hate her for her selfishness.

'Your baby needs feeding,' I told her. 'I presume she's on bottled milk.'

There was a commotion outside the front door and Berrin walked inside, talking excitedly to PC Ramsay. He saw me and immediately came over. 'Sarge, we've got an all units out. There's been a shooting.'

'You'd better wait here until social services arrive,' I told Farnes. 'And sort out the baby's feed, can you?' Farnes tried to say something but I wasn't listening. 'Where's this shooting at?'

'Heavenly Girls.'

Iversson

It's true I stood to make a lot of money from the abduction of Krys Holtz, but I'll tell you this, I was going to earn every fucking penny of it.

It was our third night in a row outside Heavenly Girls, and tempers were fraying, particularly mine. It was Johnny Hexham. He was driving me mad. After two nights stuck in the back, I'd finally decided to risk sitting in the front where it was a lot more comfortable. I now had a full beard, and with a cap on and a pair of specs, I looked a lot different than I had two weeks back. In fact the look quite suited me, to tell you the truth. Showed my intellectual side.

But unfortunately there was no escaping Johnny, who'd spent the night constantly trying to weasel information out of me about what we were doing on this street, and coming up with all these theories, some of which veered dangerously close to the truth. Not to mention the complications of his love life, which he insisted on going on and on about even though I wasn't in the least bit fucking interested. Apparently, his ex-girlfriend Delia was pregnant, the result of a flying visit by Johnny to pick up some CDs he'd left there, but she was already shacked up with some seventeen-stone black bloke who thought the baby was his and who was going to have something of a shock come the happy day. Delia wanted to run away with Johnny, who it turned out she still felt something for, and was threatening to tell the boyfriend Johnny had raped her if he didn't. But Johnny, not surprisingly, wanted nothing further to do with her, and was getting worried that any day now he was going to receive a leg-breaking visit from half a dozen of the boyfriend's mates. Also, he had another serious girl now, Amanda, who he'd met at Arcadia some weeks before, and who he was really smitten with.

Matters were further complicated, if you could believe it, by the fact that Amanda was vigorously bisexual and wanted Johnny to share her with her other lover, German student Beatrix.

'The problem is, Beatrix is, like, a full-on Magnus.'

'A what?'

'Magnus Pike, dyke. She wouldn't touch a dick if her life depended on it, so there's no way of, you know, having a bit of fun with both of them together, which would definitely have helped to numb the pain of having to share her. But I don't want to lose Amanda. I don't know what I'd do if she pulled the plug on it. But it's a bit of an odd fucking way to run a relationship, isn't it?'

'You know, Johnny,' I said, taking a swig from my bottle of mineral water, 'you are the only thirty-four-year-old I know who complains that he gets laid too much.'

'It's not like that, Max. Honest. I really love her, but I know what's going to happen. Beatrix is going to make her choose between us.'

'So buy her some flowers or something. Get in there first.'

'No, Max, you don't understand.'

'I know I fucking don't.'

'Amanda says there's something special about girl-on-girl love. It's more gentle than the stuff you get with a bloke, more sort of tender. Do you know what I mean?'

'Not really, Johnny, no. I've never really thought about it, to tell you the truth. I've seen women at it with each other in porno films, though, and they always seem to be enjoying themselves.'

'I tell you, Amanda swears by it. Says it's the only way for her to achieve a multiple orgasm. There's no way she's going to turn down that sort of action, is there? Which means it'll be me who gets the old heave ho. It's making my life a fucking misery, it really is.'

'I'm sure there are millions of blokes out there who really sympathize.'

I turned away and stared out the window in the direction of Heavenly Girls, a hundred yards away down the road. It was raining steadily again, which at least was helpful. We'd been parking on the same stretch of road night after night, so we had to be careful about the amount of attention we attracted. Every wasted night increased the risks, not to mention the stiff-legged, claustrophobic boredom of it, blunting our senses and making reaction times just that little bit slower – something that could prove fatal in this sort of operation.

Johnny continued to rattle on about Amanda, Beatrix, Delia and all his other birds, but I was blanking him totally now. I had enough worries of my own. The waiting around was beginning to lead to the first rumblings of discontent from the others. Kalinski had suggested that snatching him from a place he only visited periodically, and with no obvious advance warning, was tempting fate, which was true I suppose, but there were no other suitable venues. Joe hadn't helped matters either by remarking, after we'd finished a frustrating four-and-a-half-hour stint the previous night during which Kalinski had stunk the place out by shitting in a Tesco carrier bag, that maybe it might be an idea to knock the whole thing on the head. I knew Joe was feeling a bit spooked thanks to his almost daily visits from the Law, but I hoped it was just the frustration talking. If he – or, to be honest, any of us – pulled out then the whole thing was bolloxed and I'd be back to square one. On the run, skint, and with the near rape of my girlfriend unavenged.

I took another swig from the water as Johnny recounted how Beatrix was the dominant partner in the lesbian relationship even though she wasn't good-looking at all, and was, in his opinion, bullying Amanda into dropping him. 'She's got whips and chains and everything,' he explained, shaking his head. 'Apparently, her gaff's like a fucking torture chamber. She's even got a selection of butt plugs. How's Amanda meant to resist?' In the back of the van, I could hear movement as they shuffled about trying to make themselves comfortable.

A Land Cruiser pulled up outside the brothel. It looked familiar. The time was ten to midnight.

'Are you listening, Max, or are you fucking ignoring me?' Johnny whined.

Krys Holtz, Big Mick and Fitz stepped out, and the car did a U-turn and pulled away, driving past us. It looked like the driver was Slim Robbie, and I wondered if he'd be coming back.

'I'm ignoring you, Johnny,' I told him, watching as Krys and his men rang the buzzer, and a couple of seconds later went inside. Johnny hadn't seen them, which suited me fine. If he'd had half an inkling that our job was to kidnap Krys Holtz, he would have been out of the van faster than Wile E. Coyote and running all the way back to Amanda, Delia, even Beatrix and her butt plugs, without stopping.

'I thought you was a mate of mine,' said Johnny, sounding put out, but I hardly heard him. My blood was up, and like a youthful Elvis I was ready to rock and roll.

I banged three times in quick succession on the van's interior panel, then twice slowly, the signal that they'd arrived. Three more bangs came back to acknowledge that the message had been received and understood.

'Sorry, Johnny, but we've got work to do. Start driving.'

Johnny pulled the Mercedes van away from the kerb and drove slowly along the road until he was about fifteen yards past the entrance to Heavenly Girls.

'All right, stop here,' I told him. 'Double park.'

'Can you tell me what's going on now, Max?'

'No.'

I banged on the interior panel twice to let them know we were in position. The back doors opened and I saw Tugger Lewis in the wing mirror as he walked up the steps to the entrance. It was on.

I pressed the stopwatch and watched it as the seconds ticked by, knowing that this was it, the big one. Just like the old days. All my senses fusing together into one single core of absolute concentration. It's life or death, this. Nothing's got higher stakes. You fuck up, you die. Your life ends, just like that. Kaput! You're history. But nothing beats it either. Nothing ever beats the pure adrenalin rush, the intensity, the sheer joy of battle. I bet not even one of Amanda's multiple orgasms comes close.

Thirty seconds. Forty. Johnny said something to me, but I couldn't hear him. His voice was just interference, meaningless. Fifty seconds. Time to go. I banged the interior panel five times in quick succession, put the stopwatch in my pocket, and stepped out of the van. I pressed my mouth against the half-open window. 'Stay here,' I said. 'Do not move.'

I turned away before he could answer and walked towards the front entrance of the brothel, Joe and Kalinski coming up beside me. Joe had a holdall over his shoulder. No-one spoke. As we walked, we took black balaclavas from the pockets of our regulation blue boiler suits, and pulled them over our heads. The rain was coming down in sheets and the street was empty. We didn't look suspicious, we just looked like three normal kidnappers.

Kalinski pressed the buzzer and the door clicked open straight away. So Tugger had the reception area under control. Good. Part one had at least gone to plan. We stepped into the lift, and Joe put the holdall on the floor and took two automatic shotguns with sawn-off barrels out of it, handing one to Kalinski. He then pulled out a dozen spare shells which he stuck in one of the pockets of his boiler suit before replacing the holdall on his shoulder. We didn't want to leave any evidence behind. While he was doing this, I produced the Glock, gave it a quick check, and chambered a round. We were ready.

The lift opened directly into the reception area and the three of us stepped out, weapons at the ready. Tugger was standing there in his suit, balaclava on, in front of a good-looking young receptionist with strawberry blonde hair. She had her hands flat down on the desk in front of her. Tugger was facing her but pointing his gun at two well-built doormen in dickie bows – one white, one black – both of whom had their hands arrow-straight above their heads, their faces suggesting there was no way they were going to be heroes. I couldn't blame them. Being a hero can be a very overrated pastime. And you don't even get paid.

The receptionist's eyes widened when she saw us come striding in and she looked like she was going to scream. Tugger put a finger to his lips. 'Now now, pet, don't go causing a scene. No-one wants to hurt a pretty little thing like you. Just tell us which room Krys Holtz is in.'

I saw the white doorman's eyes widen, like he couldn't believe we'd be messing around with someone like Krys Holtz. Believe it, my friend. Believe it.

'He's in the Lovers Suite on the next floor up,' she stammered, keen to co-operate. 'It's the second door on your left when you come out of the lift.'

'What about the other two with him?'

'I don't know which rooms they'll be in, but they'll be on the same floor. They always stay close together.'

Tugger pulled her to her feet while Joe and me handcuffed the two bouncers under the watchful eye of Kalinski. When they were secured, and Tugger had got hold of the CCTV tape, we shepherded the three of them towards the room to our left. At the same time a potbellied businessman emerged from it on the arm of a stunning-looking oriental girl.

'Ohmigod!' whispered the girl. The businessman simply stood there, looking surprised.

I raised the gun and pushed them back into the room, following them in. Two more men in suits sat in the corner with two equally stunning and scantily clad women, while another girl sat at the bar talking to the lone barman, a baby-faced guy in his early twenties. All eyes went to the door as our unusual-looking convoy entered, but no-one was stupid enough to cry out.

'Ladies and gentlemen,' I said in my best public-speaking voice as we ushered everyone into the far corner of the room, 'you have nothing to fear. We are here to collect a debt from an individual within the building, and are interested in that man only. If you do as you're told and co-operate, no-one will be hurt and we'll be out of your hair within a few minutes.' I motioned to the barman with my gun. 'You, get over in the corner with the rest of them. And you.' The girl sitting at the bar scowled at me but did as she was told, as did the barman.

It was exactly three minutes and fifteen seconds from the moment Tugger had entered the building, and so far things were running smoothly.

Kalinski was tasked with guarding those in the bar, so he stepped forward and stood blankly watching his charges, shotgun pointed towards them, while the rest of us exited and headed up to the next floor, using the stairs behind the reception area. Tugger was leading because he'd gone up that way the other night. When he got to the next floor, he slowly opened the door and looked down the corridor, then turned and gave us the all clear. We followed him in, and Joe took up position by the lift where he could make sure no-one interfered with things.

Tugger and me crept quietly towards the second door on the left.

When we reached the Lovers Suite, Tugger stopped and listened at the door. The rooms were meant to be soundproofed but he could obviously hear something because he motioned for me to have a listen. I put my ear against the wood and immediately caught the noise of some serious humping. The girl was sounding like she was having the time of her life, which, for the money Tugger claimed it cost, was no great surprise. Holtz, meanwhile, was making these horrible grunting noises, sounding like something out of a wildlife documentary.

Tugger turned the handle very slowly and gently eased the door open. When it was six inches ajar the noise of the shagging was amplified several times over, and so far neither of them appeared to notice that they were being interrupted. Tugger used the barrel of his gun to push it open further and, as quietly as possible, we tiptoed inside.

The sight that greeted us was pretty fucking horrible, to say the least. Krys's hairy and surprisingly large arse viewed us like an angry cyclops from its position on the four-poster bed as it pounded up and down, piston-like, while two shapely legs sprouted out like feelers on either side. It was impossible to see the girl's face as it was almost completely enveloped by Krys's furry form. A few locks of blonde hair peeped out over one of his shoulders, and that was about it. I wondered if she could even breathe down there. I looked across at Tugger and he grinned at me beneath the balaclava. I grinned back. I was enjoying this.

The room itself was very flash-looking and worthy of such a high-class establishment. A thick shagpile carpet obscured the sound of our footsteps as Tugger quietly closed the door and we crept up to the bed. Not that it was likely we would have been heard anyway above the noise being made. Krys was grunting like a herd of hungry pigs as he pummelled his way down the home straight, only seconds from the finishing line.

'Aiiieeeee!' he wailed in a final flurry of activity, lifting his head up as he unloaded his milky cargo. 'Oooooffff!'

At that point, two things happened. The girl, her face red and sweaty, courtesy no doubt of being stuck in Krys Holtz's armpit for the previous five minutes, saw me standing over her. Her eyes widened and she went to scream. At the same time Tugger smacked Krys hard on the back of the head with the handle of his gun. Krys let out a surprised gasp and rolled off the girl, moaning faintly.

I stuck the barrel of the Glock against the girl's head and told her not to cry out. 'We're not interested in hurting you, so if you keep quiet and do not say a word, everything will be fine. If you do cry out or raise the alarm at any point in the next ten minutes, then we will kill you. Understand? Nod once for yes.' She nodded frantically. 'Good. Now turn over, put your face into the pillow and be absolutely quiet.'

While I was speaking, Tugger whacked Krys again, just for good measure, before handcuffing his hands behind his back, encountering little resistance from the semi-conscious gangster. The girl did as she was told and I handcuffed her, taking a long second to admire her beautifully rounded rear and ponder the question that has vexed so many observers down the ages: why is the female form so much more attractive than the male? And thinking that maybe Johnny's girlfriend Amanda had got the right idea.

'What the fuck's going on?' moaned Krys while his eyes made a bad job of trying to focus.

'Shut the fuck up!' snapped Tugger, pulling him off the bed by the handcuffs and forcing him to his knees. He gave him a quick smack round the face with the barrel of the gun to establish control. 'Now, get to your feet. Now!'

'Fuck off,' snapped Krys. 'You know who you're fucking dealing with?'

'Course I do, you prick. Now shut it.'

Krys opened his mouth to say something else but I came round the bed, holstering my gun and pulling open a roll of adhesive tape. I bit off a piece and shoved it over his mouth while Tugger held his head still. Krys's face went red with rage and he started struggling wildly so I kicked him hard in the stomach, doubling him over. It was important to break him quickly so we could get out of the place with the minimum of fuss.

Tugger pulled him up by his hair and we manhandled him to the door. When we reached it, I fished out the keys to the girl's handcuffs and chucked them on the bed. No point inconveniencing her any more than was necessary. Krys was struggling again, and in his rage he managed to kick the door, making a little bit too much noise for my liking. So I grabbed him by his bollocks and yanked hard. Twice in quick succession. His eyes bulged and I could almost smell his pain. I put my mouth close to his ear. 'Struggle again and I'll have the fucking things off,' I hissed.

He seemed to get the message, and we pulled him out of the door without further incident. Joe was still standing at the end of the corridor next to the stairs, shotgun in hand. He nodded in acknowledgement as we came towards him. Krys turned to me as we walked and his eyes narrowed, the message in them clear. I stared right back, daring him to try anything.

Then, suddenly, it all went wrong.

A door swung open just behind us and a white-haired geezer of at least sixty came out, saw what was going on, and shouted, 'Oh dear! What on earth's happening?' in tones that made you think he half-expected us to turn round and tell him. However, he decided against waiting around for an answer and immediately jumped back into the room, slamming the door behind him. At this point we were ten feet from the stairs, and fifteen from the lift.

Krys, sensing the possibility of rescue, tried to slow up, dragging his heels along the floor, but I tugged on his nuts again while Tugger pushed the barrel of his gun hard against his face. It seemed to do the trick, and this time he didn't resist as we pushed him right up to the lift entrance. Joe had already called the lift and he pressed the button to open the door. At the same time, out of the corner of my eye, I saw another door open further down the corridor. A second later Big Mick's naked upper half emerged, wielding a handgun that was pointing in our direction.

There was a deafening roar as Joe pushed us aside and pulled the trigger on the shotgun. A huge chunk of skirting and wall disappeared and Mick leapt back out of sight. We immediately pushed Krys into the lift, and I kneed him hard in the groin to minimize any further disruption. He went down to his knees and I turned and pointed the Glock back down the hall. Big Mick appeared again, his body crouched down, and let off a couple of wild shots. Joe and I held our ground and returned fire, sending dust and skirting flying in all directions. Tugger held on to Krys.

Then, without warning, the door opposite the Lovers Suite flew open and Fitz appeared in view with a revolver in hand, firing wildly in our general direction. A bullet whizzed straight past my head and into the lift, narrowly missing Krys. It hit the full-length mirror at the lift's rear, shattering it instantly. Taking advantage of the covering fire, Mick also appeared again, firing off another series of rounds. Joe's shotgun erupted in return, blowing a huge hole in the doorway where Mick's head had just been, while Fitz was forced to retreat as I unloaded a steady burst of gunfire in his direction. I then jumped to one side and disappeared into the stairwell while Joe retreated into the lift as the doors closed.

I dashed down the first flight of stairs until I was in the second floor stairwell. The lift carrying Krys and the others was going all the way to the ground, and from there they were going straight into the back of the Mercedes van. My job now was to make sure Big Mick and Fitz didn't get a chance to balls anything up. I ejected the Glock's magazine and replaced it with a full one, chambering the first round. Above me the door on the next floor up banged open and heavy footfalls came down the stairs. Taking a deep breath, I stepped back so I was leaning against the door that led into the reception area, and raised the gun. Behind me, I could hear people crying out and shouting in the bar, and I hoped Kalinski was calm and ruthless enough to keep a lid on things until it was time for him to go.

Big Mick came crashing into view, dressed only in trousers, almost slipping up in his haste to get down the stairs and intercept the lift before it escaped with his boss. Fitz was right behind him. Mick's eyes momentarily widened when he saw me, but before he could react I pulled the trigger, holding the gun two-handed.

Mick never had a chance. He took a bullet in the gut, then the chest, then the neck, the force of the rounds knocking him back in the direction of the wall. He tottered for a moment, then fell heavily. Fitz dived out of the way, but I kept shooting, my bullets ricocheting off the carpet and taking chunks out of the paintwork. From his position lying on the stairs, and partially covered by his friend, Fitz returned fire, his bullets passing dangerously close. But I stayed calm, adjusted my aim, and hit him in the shoulder and chest as he sat up and tried to get a better shot at me. He fell back down again with hardly a sound, and I turned and charged through the door and into the reception area.

Kalinski was already retreating out of the bar, his weapon trained on the spot where I appeared. I gave him the thumbs up and the two of us went back into the stairwell where the bodies of Fitz and Big Mick lay sprawled above us, their blood mingling as it dribbled onto the carpet. Kalinski paused for a moment to view the men who'd almost certainly helped to murder his brother.

Then, without warning, Fitz sat back up, blood dribbling from the corner of the mouth, and aimed his weapon at us. There followed an excruciatingly long one-second pause, as if we were all just frozen there, and then I pulled the trigger. My first bullet missed but the second ripped the top of his head off, depositing a lump of something nasty on the wall behind. Fitz continued sitting where he was for maybe a couple of seconds, then tipped straight back. I didn't need any more encouragement to get the hell out of there, and turned and charged down the stairs in the direction of the ground floor, Kalinski in hot pursuit.

The van was still double-parked with the engine idling when we got outside. We ran straight for it, pulling the balaclavas from our heads, Kalinski heading for the back, me for the front. In the distance we could hear the first faint sirens.

'What the fuck's going on?' howled Johnny as I jumped inside. 'I saw them shove some naked geezer with an Elvis barnet in the back!'

The back door shut as Kalinski got in, and there were two knocks on the interior panel to tell us they were ready to go.

'Shut the fuck up and drive! Now!'

Johnny took one look at me, saw something in my face he didn't like, and did exactly what he was told.

Gallan

There were already at least a dozen police vehicles and several ambulances double-parked along the street when Ramsay pulled up about fifty yards down from the scene of the shooting. I pulled open the side door of the van and stepped out into the rain. I didn't wait for the others and started walking down in the direction of the brothel, Berrin following behind. The call had said that there'd been a serious shooting incident with several casualties, but it was the location that intrigued me. Heavenly Girls. The brothel Neil Vamen's girlfriend, the woman who had had nothing to say regarding the death of a man in her home, had worked in; the place in which the mysterious disappearing Roy Fowler had an alleged interest. Something was happening, and I desperately wanted to get a handle on what it was.

The front door of the brothel was under police guard, and in the doorway I could see a very concerned-looking DCI Knox with his back to the street, talking to someone. The person came into view as we mounted the steps, and I was pleased to see that it was Asif Malik.

Knox and Malik turned round as we approached them.

'Hello, John,' said Knox grimly. 'Dave,' he added, nodding towards Berrin. 'You both know Asif, don't you?'

'I do, Dave doesn't,' I said. We stepped out of the rain, then did the introductions. 'So, what's happened?' I asked.

'A double murder,' said Knox.

'Off the record,' said Malik, 'they're both associates of Krys Holtz: Danny Fitzgerald and Mick Noble. According to the witnesses here, a number of masked men came in, shot the two of them, and then, from what we can gather, abducted Krys himself.'

'Shit,' was the only reply I could manage.

'Exactly. God only knows what this is going to lead to.'

'We think the Serious Crime Group are going to be taking this case, John,' said Knox, sounding not entirely unrelieved by the prospect, 'but we're going to need some help taking statements. There must be thirty people up there we've got to talk to, quite a few of whom are not going to want to co-operate very much.'

'Sure, no problem. We'll get on to it.'

Knox nodded, and headed up the stairs to the reception area. 'I'd better get up there too,' said Malik.

'Before you do, can I grab a moment?' I asked.

'It'll have to be quick,' he answered. 'This little lot has really complicated things.'

'It will be.' I turned to Berrin. 'I'll meet you up there, Dave.' Berrin looked put out but didn't say anything and did as he was told.

I took Malik by the arm and led him to the far corner of the foyer. 'I spoke to the landlord,' I told him, giving him a brief synopsis of what had been said. 'Something was going on in that house, something very illegal.'

'And you haven't been able to get hold of this Franks guy?'

'Not a word. He's disappeared, just like Roy Fowler, who, for your information, apparently had a share in this place.'

'That's interesting, except it still doesn't prove anything. Whatever was going on in that house won't be going on now, and if there's no evidence of a criminal enterprise taking place, there's not a lot we can do.'

'Does the company name mean anything to you? Dagmar Holdings?'

'John, the Holtzes have God knows how many front companies washing their money. I honestly can't remember them all individually. But I promise I'll look into it for you.'

I could tell that Malik was beginning to think of me as an

irritant, and I could hardly blame him. I might have unearthed a few matters that needed explanation, but in the end I had absolutely nothing concrete, and it was the concrete stuff that any police officer needed.

'You know, Asif, you're always looking for a way into the Holtzes. If what I spoke about to you yesterday ... If that actually happened, think what it could mean. Someone would definitely open his mouth.'

'Ifs and maybes, John. At the moment the most important thing is trying to prevent some sort of gang war breaking out, and that means finding out which madmen decided it would be a good idea to snatch Krys Holtz.'

'Do me one favour.'

'What?'

'I'm going to ask DCI Knox to authorize a full search of Franks's house for any traces that might back up my theory. I'd like to add that I've got your support for it as well. Please. If I can turn something up, I'm sure it'll help your investigations. If I don't, then it's no loss to you.'

Malik thought about it for a moment, then, deciding that it was probably easier to agree than put up with more hassle, said he would. 'But that's the extent of my involvement. Is that clear?'

'As daylight.' I patted him on the shoulder. 'Thanks. I owe you one.'

It was two hours before Berrin and I finished taking statements at Heavenly Girls. A number of the clientele and staff were severely traumatized, including one of the security people, a huge ex-boxer who'd had the misfortune to witness what was left of the two shot men, and who now kept bursting into tears, so it hadn't been an easy task.

The rain had stopped by the time the two of us descended the steps to the street. The van we'd been travelling around in all night remained parked further up and I could make out Ramsay behind the wheel eating a sandwich, lazy bastard.

'Sarge?' said Berrin as we walked along.

I yawned. It was half two in the morning, a long way past my bedtime. 'Yes, Dave?'

'Have you got a problem with me?'

I stopped and looked at him, and realized how difficult I'd made things for him lately. 'Of course I haven't. I'm sorry about the last few days. I've been trying to follow up on a couple of theories I've got, and I suppose I didn't want to share them until they'd come to something.'

'But we're working together on this. I need to know what's happening otherwise I'm not going to be of any use to you at all.'

'No, I understand that.'

'So what was it you were talking to the SO7 bloke about?'

I sighed. 'A theory I'm working on, but a real vague one.' And it was vague, too, but I was sure there was something in it.

Berrin lit a cigarette. 'Well, let's hear it then. You never know, I might even be able to help.'

So I told him. By the time I'd finished talking, it had started to rain again. 'What do you think?' I asked, wondering if I was really any good at man management.

Berrin finished his cigarette and chucked it in the gutter. 'I think I hope it isn't right because if it is then it's a gruesome chain of events. But it wouldn't totally surprise me, you know. I reckon it's got the ring of truth about it.'

'So do I,' I said. 'So do I.'

Thursday, three days ago

Iversson

It was just after nine a.m. and raining hard when I stepped into
a phone box on Seven Sisters Road. I dialled the number of a
restaurant owned by Stefan Holtz. A foreign-sounding gentleman
answered on about the tenth ring. 'L'Espagnol,' he grunted
miserably, which I thought was a bit cheeky. I might have been
a punter looking to book a table, and that sort of tone would
have put me right off.

'Tell Stefan Holtz that the man from Heavenly Girls wants to
get hold of him. He's got a message from Krys. I'm going to call
this number back in fifteen minutes and I want to speak to him
then.'

The guy on the other end didn't speak and I hung up, getting
out of the phone box and walking along the street in the
direction of Camden Road. Fifteen minutes later, I entered
another phone box on York Road and dialled the L'Espagnol
number again. This time it was answered on the first ring by the
same guy as before. 'I've got a number to ring,' he told me

hurriedly. I wrote it down and rang off without further comment, then dialled it.

Four rings later and Stefan Holtz was on the line. 'Where the fuck's my son?' were his first words, delivered in a rough north London rasp that made me think I'd been daft to start smoking again.

'He's unhurt. If you want to see him again it'll cost you half a million quid in cash, used fifties. You've got twenty-four hours to come up with the money otherwise we'll chop his head off, and use his quiff as a bog brush.'

'If you fucking touch him, I'll rip you limb from limb.'

'I'm going to call back tomorrow morning at this time with further instructions.'

'I need more fucking time,' said Holtz, the first signs of desperation in his voice. For all his money and influence, he was powerless in the current situation, and he knew it.

I put the phone down, confident that he'd follow the instructions he'd been set. The two bodies left behind the previous night should have been proof enough of that. I was pissed off that we'd had to kill two men to get what we wanted, particularly since the whole thing had almost gone completely to plan, but it was too late to worry about it now.

I hailed a cab and fifteen minutes later I was back at Elaine's apartment. I used the key she'd given me to let myself in and went up to the bedroom. The curtains were still closed and she was lying in bed, looking good. She opened her eyes and smiled when she saw me.

I grinned back at her. 'We did it.' And then, coming forward towards the bed, 'We fucking did it!' She sat up and we clutched each other tightly. I pushed my face into her neck, revelling in her smell. And do you know what? I almost said I love you, but stopped myself just in time. It wasn't the moment for that yet.

'It's not over yet, hon.'

'No, but the worst part's sorted.'

'I saw on the news that two people got shot,' she said, easing herself away from my grasp. 'What happened?'

'They were Krys's associates. They tried to stop us, we had no choice.'

'Did you know that they've shown your mug on *Crimewatch*?' I shook my head. 'It was on last night. I saw it.'

'How did I look?'

'Fucking ugly, so better than usual. I hope your passport photo looks a lot different.'

'Don't worry. It'll look beautiful.'

'That'll take some work.'

'You know, Miss Toms, you're getting a little bit too disrespectful for my liking.' I removed my shirt and flung it on the floor.

'You need a suntan.'

'You need to be taught a lesson.'

'How's little Krysy doing?'

'Blindfolded and shackled in a cellar, on a diet of bread and water.'

'Good. Kick that bastard for me, will you?' She pulled me towards her.

'I already have,' I said, tugging at my belt.

As I entered her, she asked me if I'd been the one who'd pulled the trigger in Heavenly Girls. I told her I had been.

The sex was fantastic.

Gallan

Knox looked at Berrin and me with a mixture of annoyance and confusion. We were in his office in the Matthews incident room, the last three people on the case, and it was eleven a.m.

'Explain this to me again,' he said, rubbing his eyes. 'We've all had a late night and I know I'm not quite with it this morning, but I'm sure you've just told me that your possible suspect in this inquiry is now tied in with the Jones murder.'

'That's right,' I said, feeling that at this point I had nothing to lose. 'I wouldn't say I'm sure of it, but I've got enough suspicions to warrant a full search of the house, and I believe I can get the owner's permission.'

'How many murders are you trying to solve here?'

'As many as I can.'

Knox sat up in his seat and took a large gulp of coffee. 'If we send SOCO round, what do you think they're going to find?'

'Maybe nothing, but it's got to be worth a shot. The Jones case has ground to a halt, everyone knows that. Even the Essex police found nothing when they reviewed it. So, if we can be seen to be doing something it certainly won't do us any harm.'

'I don't want to raise the hopes of the family. They're good people.'

'I know they are, but look at it like this. Robert Jones disappeared from that street one morning without anyone ever seeing him get taken. Now, that road's quite busy at that time, as we all know, so that was unusual in itself.'

'Not that unusual.'

'If you'll let me finish, sir.' Knox motioned for me to go on. 'I checked the pathologist's notes again yesterday. Robert's clothing had been interfered with but there were no other signs of sexual assault. It was also noted that he was murdered elsewhere before being dumped, and that, because of the lack of signs of a struggle or defensive injuries, he probably died very quickly after being taken. But the most important thing is that there were no signs of him being bound or gagged.'

Knox shrugged. 'We went over this during the investigation. He could have been thrown in the back of a van from where it would have been impossible for him to get out, and driven somewhere isolated where the murderer could finish him off without having to worry about him making a noise.'

I knew this wasn't going to be easy. Knox had been, still was technically, the man leading the inquiry. He was not going to want to have the theory that had underpinned it, that it had been a predatory paedophile who'd killed Robert, taken away from under him. 'That's possible, yes,' I persisted, 'but the thing is, we've never come close to finding the killer, and there's been no other abduction and murder of a young boy anywhere in southeast England since. Or, for that matter, in the year leading up to it.'

'That doesn't necessarily mean anything, John. Robert Black was one of the worst predatory paedophiles of the last twenty years, and he often waited up to three or four years before re-offending.'

'True, but we know, or are pretty certain, that the house on Runmayne Avenue that Tony Franks rented was being used for some sort of illegal purpose linked to one of north London's most dangerous crime families, and it's going to have to have been something pretty lucrative for the Holtzes to shell out that much in rent every month. What if Robert saw something that caught his eye that morning and went to take a closer look?'

'Like what?'

'I don't know,' I admitted, 'but let's say he goes up to the house, takes a look, as any inquisitive thirteen-year-old would, and sees something he shouldn't. He gets spotted, is taken inside the house, and he's then murdered because his killer or killers have no choice but to get rid of him. They then dump his body, making it look like a sex crime in an effort to cover their tracks. Just like they did with Miriam Fox that time. I know it may well not be the likeliest scenario but it's got to be a possibility.'

Knox sighed. 'I understand your desire to get a result on the Jones case, John. I know how much it affected you, all of us, but we're meant to be concentrating on the Matthews investigation.'

'I know, but let's face it, from what we've found out so far, the Holtzes or one or more of their associates had at least something to do with the murder of Matthews. Maybe Iversson's involved there too. And the problem we've got is it's difficult to get anyone to talk, but if somehow we can link members of their organization with what happened to Robert Jones, maybe we can loosen a few tongues and make some headway on both cases. No-one wants to protect child killers.'

'You know how much it costs to get a team to give a house a full once-over?'

'Yes, sir, it's a lot, but we've got a lead. It's not a great one but it's something, and on the Jones case particularly we haven't got any others, and haven't had for months. I know that SO7 are potentially interested in this too,' I added, trying to attach some authority to my request. 'It might give them a route into the Holtzes.'

'Maybe they should pay for the SOCO team, then.'

'It's still our case, sir.'

Knox sat there not saying anything, sipping thoughtfully on his coffee. I knew I'd boxed him into a corner. He could say no and claim there simply wasn't enough in what I was saying, but if he made that decision and then, at some point down the line, it turned out that this had indeed been what had happened to Robert Jones, the buck would stop with him. That was one of the problems with twenty-first-century policing. Such was the power of technology that important evidence could be found years after the event. Although this could mean far more convictions, it also meant that the mistakes of police officers investigating crimes were forever open to exposure. Knox, like the consummate politician he was, decided to play it safe.

'What do you think, Dave?' he asked Berrin.

'I think the sarge is right, sir. It's got to be worth looking into. And it may well help the Matthews case.'

Knox finally nodded. 'All right, we'll go with it.'

Friday, two days ago

Iversson

'Have you got the money ready?'

'I told you, I need more time.'

'So you haven't?'

'Look, you don't know who you're fucking around with here. If you don't let him go, I'll be coming after you, you hear me?'

'I'm not listening. Now, you hear me. We'll start pulling your boy's fingernails out unless you do what we say, when we say it.'

'If you touch one fucking hair on his head—'

'Then what? What will you do exactly?'

'I will kill you. Understand that. I will find you and I will saw your fucking legs off.'

'Nothing'll happen to him if you give us the money we've requested. Why haven't you got it?'

'What guarantee have I got that he's even still alive?'

'There's no point us killing him. He hasn't seen our faces and he doesn't know who we are.'

'You hurt him and I'll hunt you down. There'll be no fucking hiding place.'

'You've said that already. It wasn't frightening the first time. Now, have you got the money or not? Answer me now.'

There was a pause. 'Yeah, I've got the money.'

'Good. Now, listen carefully. At six-thirty p.m. tomorrow, be in the rear car park of the Post House Hotel on the Epping High Road. It's on the southern outskirts of Epping, just before the road crosses the M25. Have your mobile with you, as well as the money. And do not bring anyone else. Do you understand?'

'How do I know you're not going to have a pop at me?'

'All I want's that money. Nothing else. Be at the Post House tomorrow and I'll call you then.'

I thought I was getting good at this as I stepped out of the phone box into the light morning drizzle.

Gallan

After much persuasion, I managed to push the DCI into organizing the SOCO team to start their painstaking work that Friday morning. I watched them arrive from across the street, hoping they would turn up something, however small, that could solve the murder of the thirteen-year-old paperboy.

The previous evening I'd gone round alone to Robert's parents' house to tell them of the new developments and to remind them not to get too optimistic. They'd both nodded in understanding, and had thanked me for my help and my thoughtfulness in keeping them informed. I'd told them I was just doing my job, and Mrs Jones had put her hand on my arm and told me I was doing it well. And I'd thought then that, whatever happened with this lead, I would never stop until I found the person who'd killed their son and brought him to justice. It was why I was a copper. It was my vocation in life. The constant desire to give some sort of justice to people for whom fate had denied it.

I waited there for a long time as the white-overalled SOCO officers strode in and out of 41F Runmayne Avenue with their various paraphernalia. Only when I was satisfied they were taking the job seriously, that they would scour the place until they'd covered every square inch of it, did I finally turn and make my way back to the station.

When I got back to the incident room, Berrin was just coming off the phone. 'That was Martin Leppel,' he said, as I went and got myself a coffee.

'Has he got together that list of people we were after yet?' I knew Berrin had been hassling him about it all week.

He nodded. 'Yeah, he faxed it through about an hour ago. That's what I was phoning him about.'

'Anything interesting on it?' I asked, heading to his desk with the coffee.

'Here, take a look.' He passed over the typewritten list of names and dates and I scanned down it, immediately seeing what had caught his attention.

'Well, well, well. So, Craig McBride was there.'

'Twice. And for a total of nearly eighteen months. Leppel remembers him well. Says he was a right nasty piece of work, but definitely not a drug addict. Apparently some of his colleagues used to take the piss out of him because for all his so-called hardness he was petrified of needles.'

'I knew there was nothing natural about his death. But that arsehole Burley's saying it was a self-administered overdose.'

'Capper told me this morning that all they're charging Jean Tanner with is possession of a Class A drug.'

I sighed. 'I can't see why they don't at least charge her with the illegal disposal of a dead body. At this rate, we'll be lucky if she ends up with a fine.'

'Maybe we should try and talk to her.'

'Maybe.' I sipped my coffee, wishing there was something I could lean on her with. But what did I have that Neil Vamen didn't? There was no way I could put pressure on her and she'd know it. But in spite of everything, I'm an optimist, and that means I don't give up. I was just going to have to think of a way.

'Anyway, good work, Dave. You've done well.'

Berrin shrugged. 'I'm not entirely useless, Sarge. I can do more than just routine enquiries, you know.'

I nodded. 'Yeah, I do know. I'll do a better job of keeping you in the loop in future.' He nodded, acknowledging the fact that I was indirectly apologizing, and I hoped we could leave it at that.

I picked up the phone and tried Malik's number. Amazingly enough, he actually answered, though he informed me he was in a hurry.

'This Krys Holtz thing's turning into a nightmare,' he explained.

'How come?'

'Well, no-one's co-operating, as usual. The family say they don't know what we're talking about and apparently Krys is fine, just not around at the moment, and now suddenly all the staff at the brothel are retracting their statements. Plus, we've got no intelligence on the ground as to who might be behind it.'

'I'm sorry to bother you, Asif, but did you find out anything about this company, Dagmar Holdings?'

'I haven't had time. I'll get something sorted for you by tomorrow, I promise. Have you tried Companies House for any information?'

'Yes, I have. The company exists all right. They sent me pages of stuff but nothing that really tells me very much.'

'I'll see what I can come up with. Can you give me your mobile number again?'

I reeled it out and Malik said his goodbyes, saying he had to go.

I flicked off the phone and stared at the pile of accounts for Dagmar Holdings Ltd in my in-tray. I really needed to give them a closer look. I looked at my watch. Ten to twelve. It could wait until later.

'Do you fancy a drink and a bite to eat?' I asked Berrin.

He nodded and grinned. 'I could do with both.'

'Then let's get out of here,' I said, and we got to our feet, once again leaving the Matthews incident room empty and silent.

Iversson

Tugger Lewis cooked supper that night. Thai fish curry with noodles and stir-fried veg. Very nice. Apparently he'd been working as a trainee chef for the previous six months, and whatever they'd been teaching him seemed to have done the trick because it was one of the best meals I've had in years. It gave me renewed faith in the British education system, to tell you the truth. The only thing spoiling it was Johnny, who'd been moaning pretty much non-stop ever since he'd discovered who the owner of the 'Elvis barnet' was. As I finished my last mouthful, he was just starting up again, like a stuck CD.

'I've got to earn some more out of all this,' he told the rest of us as we sat round the kitchen table. 'That's Krys bark-at-the-fucking-moon Holtz we've got down there, known affectionately as the Barnsbury Torturer, and that's by his mum. The one geezer in the whole of north London you don't want to get on the wrong side of, and I'm part of the team that's kidnapped him. It's all right for you lot. You're all making a decent wedge out of this. I've got to make do with fuck all.'

'That's because you haven't had to do fuck all, Johnny,' I told him. 'All you did was drive the car. We had the hard work.'

'I've had to put my Niagaras on the line, Max, just like everyone else, even though no-one asked me if I wanted to. And I've got to live round this fucking city for the rest of my life, permanently wondering if I'm going to end up making a one-way visit to Krys's workshop.'

'No-one's going to find you out,' said Joe, taking another mouthful.

'I nicked the cars, remember? The coppers could get some sort of lead that puts them on to me and then I'm fucked. I might get nicked for something I didn't even want a part in, and then it'll get back to the Holtzes, which is far worse.'

'You worry too much,' I told him. 'Take the money you're going to get, be pleased with it, and leave it at that. You never know, tomorrow might be your last day on earth. Don't spend it crapping your pants about something that'll probably never happen.'

'It's easy for you to say. You'll have enough so you can fuck off wherever you want.'

'Ah, stop being so fucking gutless.'

It was Kalinski who spoke, his tone contemptuous. He was wearing a black polo-neck sweater with three thick gold chains over it, and his greying hair was slicked back. It made him look like a gangsta version of the Milk Tray man. He'd pushed his plate to one side, having eaten less than half the food he'd been given, and was puffing on a Rothmans.

'You think you know fear?' he said, pointing his cigarette at

Johnny. 'Eh?' Johnny didn't say anything. He looked like he was an expert in it. 'You don't know shit. I'll tell you that now. Fear's when you're standing on the street with no fucking cover and the Filth, them bastards from SO19, are taking potshots at you with sighted rifles, and your best mate, the one you did the job with, is lying dead on the pavement in a pool of blood, inches from your feet, and you know that in two, maybe three fucking seconds you're going to go exactly the same way.' Kalinski stared Johnny down. 'That, boy, is fear.'

'What happened?' asked Johnny, eyes wide.

'You mean, why am I still here? I took a bullet in the gut and one in the leg. I was in hospital for six weeks and the cunts still charged me afterwards. I got fourteen years for armed robbery and attempted murder, because I managed to hit one of their fucking blokes as well. My only regret about the whole thing was that I didn't kill the bastard.'

To be honest with you, I wouldn't get too carried away about Kalinski's role in the gunfight at the OK Corral. From what I'd heard, he'd only ever fired one shot in anger during his long criminal career, and that had been into a sub post office ceiling. And he wasn't exactly Papillon either. According to what Joe had told me, he'd only ever done a couple of short stretches inside, which was another of the reasons we'd hired him. It showed he was careful. Something smelled a little fishy, and it wasn't just Tugger's curry.

Johnny sighed and put his head in his hands. 'What am I fucking doing here?' he said to no-one in particular.

'Being gutless,' snarled Kalinski.

'Give him a break, Mike,' I said. 'The poor sod's had a bad week. His missus is bisexual.'

'What the fuck's wrong with that?' said Tugger. 'Nothing better than a bit of three-in-a-bed experimentation.'

'Not if the third one doesn't want fuck all to do with you.'

Tugger patted him on the back sympathetically. 'Shit, Johnny, is that right? Does her lover not swing to the beat of the phallic drum?'

'Look, fuck off, will you?' said Johnny, brushing off Tugger's hand. He turned and gave me the evil eye. 'That was private what I was telling you, Max.'

'I had a session with a couple of lesbians once,' said Kalinski. 'Porn stars they were, American. Candy and Brandie they was called. Brandie's been in loads of stuff.' He shook his head in awe. 'They knew what they was fucking doing, I can tell you. Could have sucked ballast through a straw, both of them. Did it in a penthouse in the Savoy.'

If Kalinski had been Pinocchio, he'd have had my fucking eye out. This bloke could bullshit for England.

I got up from the table. 'I'd better give Krysy boy something to eat.'

Kalinski glared at me. 'Fuck that, let him starve.'

'I tried him this morning,' said Joe, 'and he told me to fuck off. So I did. We're releasing him Sunday morning. If he wants to lose weight in the meantime, let him. He's had some water so he won't die.'

'He's been here nearly two days and he hasn't touched a thing. I'll just check on him.'

'You just want a chance to give him another kicking,' said Joe, with something close to a smile.

Which was partly true, I did. Krys, like Johnny, had been a pain in the arse from the start. When we'd dragged him out of the van and into the farmhouse on the first night, he'd gone absolutely apeshit, kicking like a donkey and screaming all sorts of uncalled-for insults. Me and Kalinski had been forced to give him the beating of his life, just rewards for past wrongs, Kalinski taking particular pleasure in stamping repeatedly on his bollocks until Joe pulled us both off, fearful we'd kill him. When I'd tried to feed him the following morning, he'd spat in my face and told me I was a dead man, which had been a pretty fucking stupid move on his part and had cost him a broken nose, but he still resisted any effort at co-operation and in those increasingly rare moments when his gag was removed he was full of bluster and threats. In the end, I had no choice but to award him a grudging respect. He was a champion arsehole and about as pleasant as a skidmark, but he was no coward. It made me think, too, that this was a much better way of dealing with him than shooting him outright. This way we broke him down, humiliated him, but we didn't kill him in cold blood. I'm not a bad lad, to be honest with you, and I don't think I'm capable of just executing someone outright without them having a chance to fight back. Plus, this way we made money out of it, so it seemed to me to be a pretty decent sort of revenge all round, really.

'At the moment, Joe, he's the most valuable thing we've got and it's in all our interests to keep him that way. At least if we give him back alive, one day the Holtzes'll forget about what happened. If he turns up dead, we'll have them on our backs for ever.' I picked up a couple of pieces of bread from the kitchen top. 'Look, I'm not exactly giving him the lavish stuff.'

I went out of the room, through the hallway, and over to the door under the stairs that led down to the cellar. I unlocked it, switched on the light, and walked slowly down the wooden steps.

Krys was strapped to a chair which was in turn secured to the bare brick wall. He was wearing a shirt and piss-stained trousers with nothing on his feet. He had a black blindfold round his eyes and masking tape securing his mouth, and his face was covered in bruises. Dried blood had formed a crusty trail running from his nostrils, where I'd delivered the nose-breaking blow, down to his neck. Another badly healed cut wound its way across his fore-head. Basically, he looked a mess.

His head turned as he heard my approach. I stopped and picked up a jug of water, filled a dirty cup, then leant over and pulled the masking tape away from his mouth. Usually this was the cue for a burst of swearing, but instead he just coughed and cleared his throat. 'I think some of my ribs are broken,' he said quietly, 'and I need to change these trousers.'

'If you're looking for sympathy, you've come to the wrong place,' I told him. 'Now, open your mouth, I'm going to feed you some bread.'

Krys did as he was told and I ripped off bite-sized pieces and placed them in his mouth. He chewed hungrily and finished off both slices quickly. 'Have you got any more?'

'That's your lot. Now, I'm going to give you some water.' I put the cup to his mouth and held it there. He gulped it down, drinking about half of it before turning his head away.

I put the cup back down by the jug and thought that I could almost feel sorry for Krys Holtz, tied up and stewing in his own urine. But then I thought of what he'd done to Elaine, and to Kalinski's brother, and that soon put a stop to it. What he was going through now was certainly no less than he deserved, and far more temporary.

'I've got money,' said Krys. 'Plenty of it. If you help me get out of here, I'll make it more than worth your while. How much do you want?'

'Sorry, Krys, no can do.'

'A hundred grand, hundred and fifty. I could get that for you. Honest.' His voice had suddenly taken on a whining quality which didn't improve my opinion of him.

'We're going to be picking up a lot more off your old man tomorrow.'

'He'll kill you, you know.' This time his voice was quiet, but there was an edge to it. He believed what he was saying. 'It doesn't matter where you hide. He'll find you and he'll kill you.' I started to replace the masking tape and Krys's tone immediately changed. 'Please change these trousers. Please.'

I ignored his request and finished what I was doing. Krys struggled violently in the seat for a few moments until his strength deserted him. 'In the morning,' I told him. 'We'll change them in the morning.'

Then, wondering if I really was being too sadistic, I turned and walked back up the steps, switching off the light when I reached the top.

Yesterday

Iversson

I got the call at 6.26 p.m. 'He's here,' growled Kalinski into the phone. 'Just pulled in now. Driving a matt-black Merc.'

'Does it look like he's alone?'

'I can't see anyone else.'

'No-one's pulled in behind him or anything?'

'No-one. He's definitely on his own.'

'All right. I'll talk to you shortly.'

I rang off and pulled the cap down over my head. It was raining hard again, and you had to think the gods were smiling on us as far as the weather was concerned. Usually there were plenty of walkers in Epping Forest, the only serious stretch of woodland this close to London, but tonight I had the feeling that most would be staying away. Tugger and I had taken up position at the edge of the treeline looking down across a slightly inclined grass clearing about a hundred yards long and fifty wide. It led down to more woodland from which Stefan Holtz would emerge, once we guided him to the spot. There was no-one else in the vicinity that we'd seen, and I was confident the transaction could be made without fuss.

Tugger sat on a thick branch, his feet resting on a log, an M-16 in his hands. Purely precautionary, but always worth keeping, just in case. 'He's there, then?'

I nodded. 'Yeah, he's there.' I pressed the button to dial Holtz's mobile and waited while it rang.

He answered with an angry grunt.

'Mr Holtz, I'm glad you made it.'

'Where's my son?'

'He's safe and he's well.'

'How do I know that?'

'Listen to this.'

I flicked on the short tape we'd got Krys to make that morning in exchange for changing his trousers and allowing him to use the toilet in privacy. It was short and to the point: he gave the date and the time, and said that he was OK and was being treated well. He hadn't wanted to add this last bit but I'd suggested that he ought to unless he wanted Kalinski to stamp on his bollocks again. Krys might have been no coward but he was no fool either, and had done what he'd been told.

I switched off the tape. 'Satisfied?'

'He'd fucking better be all right.'

'Don't threaten me, Mr Holtz,' I told him coldly. 'You really haven't got much of a bargaining position. Now, have you got the money?' Holtz grunted that he had. 'Good. Now, when we finish this conversation, drive out of the car park and turn right, crossing the M25.' I then gave him a short set of further instructions, about where he should turn off the main road and how he should proceed from there. 'When you get to the sign that says "No Tipping", stop and park up the car on the bank. That whole journey should take you fifteen minutes. I'll call you then. Let me tell you something else as well, something very important. Do not bring anyone else with you. When you park the car, you're going to be watched. If anyone else is with you, the whole thing's off, and that'll be the last you hear from your boy.'

Holtz started shouting something but I rang off. I wasn't prepared to listen to threats.

'Christ, Max,' said Tugger with a laugh. 'You were almost scaring me then. You'd make a great film villain, I tell you.'

'Alan Rickman's got nothing on me, mate. Anyway, you've got to be harsh, haven't you? I don't want him thinking he's dealing with amateurs.'

I called Kalinski back and told him to be at the rendezvous point at 6.45 sharp, then phoned down to Joe. 'I've made contact,' I told him. 'He's driving a black Merc and he'll be with you in fifteen minutes.'

'No problem,' said Joe. 'If there's anyone else with him, I'll let you know. Otherwise I'll follow him up, then peel off when it's sorted, and meet you at the rendezvous.'

The call ended. Everyone knew what they were doing. Now it was simply a matter of waiting.

'It's a long time since I've used one of these,' said Tugger, stroking the rifle like it was some sort of cuddly toy. It was one Joe had brought back from the Gulf War in '91. 'I think Bosnia was probably the last time, and Christ, that was years back. A good weapon, though. I can see why the Yanks like it.'

'I think I prefer the AK if I was to be given the choice. Less prone to jamming.'

'You know, Max,' he said, loading and unloading the rifle's magazine, 'I do like chefing, and I reckon I could make a lot of money out of it, especially if I can afford to open up my own place.'

'You make a mean Thai fish curry, I'll give you that.'

'Aye, I know, but . . .' He thought about it for a minute, at the same time putting the stock to his shoulder and aiming at an imaginary target among the trees. 'But it can never give you quite the same sort of buzz as a job of violence does. You know what I mean? You don't get that sort of excitement out in the normal world.'

'Yeah,' I said, remembering the mad adrenalin rush I'd had when I'd been standing in the stairwell of Heavenly Girls, ripping holes out of Fitz and Big Mick. 'Maybe you don't.'

At 6.44 my mobile rang. It was Joe, and he was whispering. 'He's here. Looks like he's alone.'

'Thanks.' I rang off, then dialled Holtz's number. It was answered immediately. 'Stand facing the "No Tipping" sign, five feet away from it.'

'How do I know what's five feet?' he demanded angrily.

'Just do it. Now turn ninety degrees to the left and start walking, keeping in a straight line. You'll see the outlines of a path in front of you. Follow it.'

'Where's my son?'

'I told you, he's safe and he's well. Are you on the path?'

'Yeah, I'm on the path. When am I going to see my boy?'

'If the money's all there, you'll see him first thing tomorrow morning. He'll be dropped off somewhere in London, reasonably close to a telephone box.'

'He fucking better be.'

'Keep walking and stop speaking.'

From his vantage point in the undergrowth, Joe watched as Stefan Holtz turned away and began walking up the wooded incline in the direction of Max and Tugger. Holtz had a mobile to his ear and a large holdall slung over his shoulder. Within a minute he'd

disappeared from view, and the forest was silent once again, except
for the steady crackle of rain hitting the trees, and the distant hum
of traffic. No-one else had turned up to follow him and the car he'd
been driving, the Merc, was empty.

He kept listening for a few moments, then, satisfied that Holtz
had come alone, he slipped slowly and carefully out of his hiding
place, crossed the track from which the Merc had appeared,
and started up the path after Holtz, keeping as far back as
possible.

Too late, he heard the noise behind him. The rustle of bushes, the
sound of heavy footfalls on muddy ground, and then the terminal,
gut-wrenching sensation of the hard metal gun barrel being pushed
into the back of his head.

I saw Holtz emerge from the trees at the bottom of the slope,
carrying the holdall. He was about a hundred and fifty yards
away. 'All right, keep walking,' I told him, and switched off the
mobile.

I turned to Tugger. 'Here he comes.' Tugger nodded, and we
both pulled on balaclavas. I checked the Glock, gave Holtz
another thirty seconds to get nearer, then pushed my way out of
the bushes. Fifty yards now separated us.

Holtz saw me but didn't quicken his pace, and we closed in on
each other as casually as a couple of early-evening strollers.
When we were ten feet apart, we both stopped. Holtz looked
pissed off. The rain, which was pouring down now, had flattened
his iron-grey hair and it was running freely down his grizzled,
lined face and onto his khaki raincoat. I'd never seen a picture
of him before (Holtz senior, like all his close cohorts, was very
camera shy), but thought that he looked a lot like Karl Malden,
the veteran actor from seventies cop show *The Streets of San
Francisco*, even down to the bulbous round nose.

'You've made a big fucking mistake doing this to me,' he growled, making no effort to hand over the holdall.

'And you made a big fucking mistake trying to kill me,' I said, unable to resist letting him know who'd done this to him, even though it effectively meant exiling myself for life. Sometimes you just had to show that you hadn't been intimidated.

'I don't even know who the fuck you are behind that poxy mask, so what makes you think I've been trying to have you killed? I'll tell you something, though, you cunt. If I want someone dead, that's how they end up. Dead. No fucker ever escapes from me.'

I thought about lifting my balaclava, but that really would have been stupid. But then it struck me that maybe he didn't know who I was. Maybe I was that insignificant. 'That holdall looks very heavy,' I told him. 'Why don't I take it off your hands?'

Holtz managed the beginnings of a smile for the first time. It wasn't a pleasant sight. 'No, mate, it ain't as easy as that. Before you get this cash, I want to see my son. So, get on the phone to whichever cunt's holding him and get him to drive him down here. Now. Then we'll see if it's worth a trade.'

'I don't want to have to take that bag off you by force, Mr Holtz, but believe me, I will.'

'No you won't, son,' said Holtz, shaking his head. 'No, you fucking won't.'

Tugger had the rifle to his shoulder, the barrel pointing through a gap in a large evergreen bush towards Stefan Holtz. He could see him and Max talking, but Max was making no move to take the holdall. They used to say that Tugger Lewis had a nose for danger, could sense when something bad was going to happen. One time, years back in County Down, five of them had been patrolling in a Land Rover down remote country back roads when they'd seen a car parked in a layby up ahead. Afterwards, he'd said it was just something about the angle it was parked in, slightly skewed with the bonnet pointed towards the road, like someone had abandoned it too quickly, that had caught his attention. But it wasn't that. He'd just felt it, known that something was going to happen. He'd told the driver to stop and turn round even though he'd only been a private and the driver was a lance corporal, and the road had been so narrow that any turn was going to require some serious manoeuvring, but something in his tone – the desperation, the sure-fire knowledge that they were driving straight towards their doom – convinced the driver to do what he said. Ten seconds later, while they were still turning round, the IRA man with the remote control, seeing that his targets were escaping, detonated the bomb in the car's boot. Two of the men in the jeep had been slightly injured, but no-one was complaining. If they'd been driving past it, the impact of the blast would have killed them all.

He had the same feeling now. It had started slowly, about an hour before, but had accelerated markedly when Stefan Holtz had appeared out of the woods below. Something was wrong. There was no escaping the fact. Something was definitely wrong. Max and Holtz were still talking, and Tugger thought he saw Holtz smile, but he might have been imagining things. Was this a set-up? His jaw tightened and his finger stroked the trigger. He was listening now, listening for any sound that was remotely out of place.

The faint rustle of leaves being trampled underfoot, could he hear that? Off to his left, not far away, coming from somewhere in the trees. He listened harder, couldn't tell for sure, thinking, concentrating . . .

Then he swung round ninety degrees, still holding the rifle at shoulder height, and saw the figure creeping through the under-growth, twenty-five feet away, gun in hand.

Reflexively, he pulled the trigger, firing off five shots in rapid successions, the angry bark of the weapon echoing through the undergrowth. Then he hit the deck as bullets came flying back in the opposite direction.

The loud crackle of gunfire startled us both. I clocked the first shots as coming from the M-16, which had to be Tugger's, and then further shots from at least two other weapons. Holtz might have thought he had some cards up his sleeve but he obviously hadn't expected anyone to start shooting. His eyes widened and he swung round to me with a look of suspicion mixed with panic. 'What the fuck's going on?'

These were the last words Stefan Holtz ever spoke. Before I could even open my mouth to answer, his left eye seemed to burst out of his face, and he fell forward, still clutching the holdall. I dived to the ground and pulled out my gun. Suddenly, shooting seemed to be coming from everywhere. I could see a figure armed with a rifle, kneeling down on the other side of the clearing about thirty yards away, partially concealed by the foliage. I knew straight away that he was the one who'd gunned down the gang leader. The shooter fired again, and blood sprayed up from one of Holtz's thighs as the round struck. I scrambled down behind his body, then, using it as cover, leant over and clattered off five rounds from the Glock in the shooter's direction, knowing that my chances of hitting him were slim but wanting to put him under pressure. He fired two shots back, both whizzing close by, then slipped back into the trees.

But now shooting was coming from behind me, and coming close, too. Clumps of mud flew up from the ground only feet from where I was lying. I whirled round and fired three shots in the general direction of their source, unable to see my assailant; then, knowing that I was a sitting duck as long as I stayed where

I was, I jumped up and pulled the holdall from Holtz's dead fingers. I hauled it over my shoulders, surprised at the heavy weight, then started running for the nearest trees, keeping as low as possible. From behind me I heard the rifleman who'd taken out Holtz cracking off shots at my exposed back, and in front of me I could make out the second shooter behind some bushes. He had what looked like a shotgun balanced over a branch and he was steadying himself to fire. I didn't give him a chance. As I charged towards him, I lifted the Glock and pulled the trigger, bang bang bang. It was a battle of nerves and he lost it, jumping out of the way and dropping the weapon.

I zigzagged wildly, teeth clenched in anticipation of a striking bullet, and at the last second half-dived, half-slid into the treeline and out of sight of the shooter behind me. The second gunman, only partly visible through the undergrowth, swung his shotgun round in my direction, pulling the trigger at the same time. The weapon kicked and he took a stumbling step back, the shot passing way over my head. I fired twice in return and at least one of the rounds hit him. I heard him yelp in shock and drop to one knee; then, without even pausing for breath, I jumped up with the holdall and ran in a crouch in the direction of the spot where I'd left Tugger, keeping within the trees. The branches and bushes battered and scratched me as I charged through them, every sense and nerve-ending homed in on my surroundings, knowing we'd been set up and that there were bound to be more of them about. As if to confirm it, an unseen round whistled by a few feet above my head, letting out an angry crack as it struck a thick branch and ricocheted off into the gloom. I couldn't see the shooter and doubted that the shooter could see me.

Without warning, a figure appeared out of the trees in front of me, no more than ten feet away, running and stumbling in my direction. He had a gun in one hand and was holding an injured leg with the other. I didn't recognize him, and that meant he was the enemy. He didn't even see me until the last second, which was a fatal mistake. Without dropping my pace, I raised my weapon, stretched out my arm so the barrel was no more than three feet from its target, and shot him straight through his open mouth. He died with an expression of confused shock on his face and I was already five yards beyond him by the time the body hit the ground. A staccato burst of automatic weapon fire rattled through the trees somewhere off to my right, but it sounded like there was more hope in it than judgement, and I kept running, undeterred, hoping that Tugger was OK and had followed the instructions should things go wrong, which were to head straight back to the place where Kalinski was picking us up from. The last thing I needed now was for him to hold his ground and take a potshot at me as I came over the brow of the hill. Unlike the rest of these blokes, he'd always been a good shot.

But Tugger wasn't there when I passed the spot, and there was no sign of blood or anything else to suggest that he'd taken an injury. So I kept going, charging through the trees down the other side of the hill, feeling that terrible exhilaration danger always brings, even though it was tempered by another, far more worrying thought. What the fuck had happened to Joe?

The back of the van was open and the engine running when I came out of the trees and onto the road. I threw the holdall inside and jumped in after it. Tugger was already inside, but there was no sign of Joe.

'What the fuck happened, Max?' he demanded, still clutching the M-16. 'What the fuck went wrong?'

'I don't know,' I panted between breaths, finding it difficult to think. 'Somehow Holtz fucked us up, but Christ knows how. We had everything planned down to a tee.'

'Do you think they got Joe?'

'I don't know.'

'There were a lot of them. They could easily have taken him out.'

I leant out the back door and looked up towards the trees. Nothing moved up there. I punched Joe's number into the mobile. It rang. Five times, six, seven. No answer. I kept staring at the trees. No sign. No answer. Eight rings, nine. He would have picked up by now if he was all right. The longer we stayed there the more dangerous our predicament became.

'We've got to move, Max. They could be on us any minute. And the Old Bill could have been called by now. That was some fucking gun battle in there.'

Ten rings, eleven, twelve. Still nothing. Tugger was right, I knew he was. But to leave, to desert my mate. It was a big call to make. We'd agreed to meet back at the farmhouse if it became impossible for any one of us to make the rendezvous, but still I was reluctant to make the decision to move.

Thirteen, fourteen.

'Come on, Max, we're soldiers. We can't stop everything because one man's missing, you know that. We're endangering the whole operation by staying here. Come on! Think about it!'

'What the fuck's going on in the back there?' came Kalinski's muffled but frantic voice. 'Let's get out of here!'

Fifteen, sixteen. I cursed, then closed up the back doors, knowing I had no choice. I leant over and banged the panel twice. 'All right, go!'

Kalinski hit the accelerator like he had lead boots on and we were on our way in a screech of tyres.

As we drove, I holstered my gun, wiped sweat from my brow and, with a deep breath, opened the holdall, wondering exactly what was going to be in there.

It was full. Crammed full with tightly packed bundles of used fifty-pound notes. So Holtz had been genuine. Which begged a major fucking question.

Why had they started shooting?

Gallan

I had a takeaway curry that night. Chicken tikka masala, pilau rice, two poppadoms and an accompaniment of sag aloo. I knew I wouldn't finish it all, that's a lot of food, but I thought I'd at least give it a try. What I couldn't eat, I'd have cold tomorrow. I'd also purchased a four-pack of Fosters and rented a video. It might have been a Saturday night and I might have been on my own but I was determined to enjoy myself. The lounge was comfortable, the telly – a twenty-eight-inch Sony widescreen bought on hire purchase – was on, and all the worries of the world had been relegated to beyond my front door.

I was sitting on the sofa in my dressing gown, warming up for the video by watching a Denis Nordern pastiche of out-takes and bloopers on ITV, and was just about to tuck into the food when my mobile rang. It was ten to nine. I thought about leaving it. I was hungry and I was sure it could wait, but habit got the better of me. I've always been the curious type. I put down my food, went over to the kitchen top, and picked it up.

'John? Asif Malik here.' He sounded breathless, and the line wasn't too good.

I walked out of the kitchen with the phone to my ear and back into the lounge. 'Asif, how are you?'

'Not good. I suppose you haven't heard the news, then?'

'What?'

'Stefan Holtz. He's been shot, up in Epping Forest. That's

where I am now. It looks like whoever kidnapped Krys got Stefan out of that fortified house of his, lured him here, and blew him away.'

I was shocked but not sorry. 'So, it looks like some sort of takeover, then?'

'I don't know,' said Malik. 'That's what we think, but there's absolutely no intelligence coming from any quarter that gives us a suggestion as to who's behind it.'

'Will his death make your job any easier?'

Malik managed a humourless laugh. 'I doubt it. Now they'll all be fighting over the scraps. It means we've probably got to end up watching ten big villains instead of one. It never gets easier, John, you know that. Now, before I forget. This Dagmar Holdings—'

'I feel bad hassling you about them when you've got so much else on.'

'Sure you do. To be frank, I don't know how much help I'm going to be. They are a company suspected of links with the Holtzes but no major associate of theirs sits on their board, so it's going to be extremely difficult to connect Dagmar to individuals, unless you can lean on the board members, see what they know.'

'But they won't be inside players?'

'There are three people listed as being on the board. They'll all be known to the Holtzes, but no, as far as we're aware they're not inside players. But they might be worth talking to. I've got their addresses if you want them.'

I went back into the kitchen and grabbed a pen and paper from one of the drawers. 'I do. Thanks.'

Malik read out the name and address of the chairman, then the managing director. When he said the name of the company secretary, I froze. 'Are you sure that's the name?'

'Definitely,' said Malik.

I took the address, thanked him, then rang off. I looked around, then found the statement of accounts on Dagmar Holdings I'd brought home the previous night. Then I checked the surnames and first initials of the board members, listed at the bottom of the first page. Malik was dead right. How the hell had I missed that?

I looked at the address he'd given me. It might lead to nothing but I knew I was going to have to give the place a visit.

I looked at my watch again. Too late now. I'd go in the morning.

Iversson

'Whichever way you want to read it, it was a set-up,' I said, looking at the other three in turn.

We were standing round the kitchen table, all grim-faced, the holdall containing the money open in front of us. There was no sign of Joe. The clock on the wall above the cooker said that it was five to nine. Outside, it was raining even harder than it had been earlier.

'It had to be a set-up. How the fuck did Holtz get all those people to the drop point without some sort of inside knowledge that it was going to be where it was? There were at least three other shooters there, minimum, and probably more, because somehow they managed to take out Joe as well. So someone fucking talked.'

'Not necessarily,' said Tugger. 'They could have put a tracking device on his car, something that helped them locate it.'

'No way. They were on us within minutes of Holtz arriving. If they'd been tracking the car they'd never have had a chance of getting into position in that length of time. I don't care what anyone says, they were already there. And the way Holtz was talking to me, it sounded like he knew his men were in the vicinity. He was way too cocky for a man delivering a ransom.'

'Yeah, but you said yourself he was shocked when the shooting started,' said Tugger. 'I mean, Christ, they shot him, didn't they?'

'But it was you who fired first.'

'There was some fucking bloke creeping up on me with a gun! What the fuck was I supposed to do? Wave to him?'

'Shit,' said Johnny, who was having difficulty keeping his eyes off the money. 'I can't fucking believe this. Do you think they popped him by accident when they were trying to shoot you?'

'Fuck knows,' I said. 'Maybe.' I turned to Kalinski. 'No-one followed him into the car park, right?' He glared at me, then shook his head firmly. 'And you drove out when he left and no-one was following him then?'

'I'm no fucking fool,' he snarled. 'I know what I'm doing. I followed him and there was no other car, and no other people with him. When he turned off the main road, he turned off on his own.'

'Well then, they were already there. There's no other explanation, is there?'

'No-one fucking talked,' said Kalinski firmly.

'Then you're going to have to explain how the shooters got there that fast. So far, you haven't.'

'I don't have to explain nothing.'

'Fuck it, Max,' said Tugger in exasperation. 'It could have happened. Of course it could. It doesn't take a huge great battle plan to arrive, advance up both sides of a clearing so they're flanking their boss, and confront us. And what's the alternative? That one of us was talking to them? Who? It wasn't Joe. Christ knows what's happened to him, but it doesn't look good. It wasn't me. I'd never even heard of Stefan fucking Holtz before last week. And Kalinski here . . . hardly. Holtz's people murdered his brother.' Kalinski grunted in agreement. 'And Johnny. You had to virtually pressgang him to get him involved. If someone talked, that only leaves you.'

'Or your missus,' said Kalinski.

'She didn't know any of the details,' I snapped. I didn't like the way this conversation was going.

'Are you sure?' Tugger sounded suspicious.

'Of course I'm fucking sure. I never told her anything about the drop-off, where it was going to be, how we were going to do it. So leave her out of it.'

'She might have overheard you talking,' said Kalinski accusingly. 'You know what women are like. I had a bird once—'

'No way. No fucking way. You're right up the wrong tree. I was always careful to keep her out of all the planning, and that's the God's honest truth.'

'Well, that doesn't leave us with anyone, does it?' said Tugger.

I stopped and exhaled loudly. Tugger was right, of course, there wasn't really anyone who could have talked, but I still wasn't convinced. Something had happened out there, something that hadn't been planned for either by us or Stefan Holtz, and somebody somewhere knew a lot more than they were letting on. I looked at them each in turn, trying to keep the deep suspicion I felt off my face. They all looked back with various expressions: Kalinski glowering; Johnny nervous; Tugger calm but concerned.

'We may as well finish off the boy downstairs,' said Kalinski. 'He's no use to us or anyone now.'

'No way,' I said. 'This whole thing's been fucked up enough as it is without us adding another reason for the Holtzes or the cops to come after us. He can't recognize anyone, we've got the money, so we keep our side of the bargain. That means we stay the night here, wait to see if Joe turns up, and release Krys and go our separate ways in the morning. Just like we originally planned.'

'Joe ain't going to turn up now,' said Kalinski.

I knew Kalinski was pretty much on the button there, but I didn't need to hear it from him. 'He may, he may not. We don't know. Anyway, we stay here. Now, let's count this fucking money. We'll divvy up each man his due and I'll look after Joe's share.'

'I don't think it should be kept for him,' said Kalinski. 'If he ain't here, he ain't here. We share it out between ourselves. That's the only way.'

'I thought you were only in it for the revenge.'

'Well, I ain't got my fucking revenge, have I? The cunt's still alive and you're saying we should release him tomorrow. Even though he fucked your missus.'

'Watch what you're fucking saying.'

'If it was me, and he'd done that to my missus, I'd have fucking killed him.'

I took a step forward, feeling my temper boiling over. I'm a patient man, but this bastard Kalinski was pushing it big time.

Tugger put his hand out in front of me. 'All right, boys, calm down. Let's all take it easy, have a drink, and talk about it again tomorrow morning. How does that sound? We're not getting nowhere like this.'

'I think I should get a bigger share of the Russell,' said Johnny. 'You say I didn't have to do too much but, what with all this lot, things ain't never going to be the same for me again.'

I turned to him, wanting to re-establish control. 'Bullshit. You've done your bit, and you've done it well, but nothing changes with the death of Holtz. No-one knows who we are and no-one's going to be able to find us. As long as we keep calm and release Krys. I'll hold the money until tomorrow. If Joe still isn't here when we're due to leave, then we'll split his share evenly, but if he is alive, and he comes looking for it, then it's got to be remembered that it's his money, and it's each bloke's lookout if he doesn't want to give it up. Now, let's count this fucking stuff. Then we can divvy up.'

The atmosphere was tense, unpleasant. No-one felt much like talking, or even eating. Beers were cracked open, as per Tugger's suggestion, but there was no celebration even though every man in the room was significantly richer. It was all there, too, every last note. Half a million pounds in fifties, just as Holtz had been instructed, and that settled it for me. There was no way he'd been accidentally shot by one of his men who was trying to put a hole in me. However many times I went over it in my mind, one thing remained certain, and that was that he'd had every intention of paying up.

Before we retired for the night, I took some bread down to Krys and fed it to him without speaking. Eventually he asked me whether his old man had paid the ransom. He didn't sound angry or defiant any more, just tired and uncomfortable. He'd pissed his trousers again but didn't ask for them to be changed.

'Yeah, your dad paid,' I told him.

'Are you going to let me go?' he asked, his voice sounding strangely like a kid.

'You're going to be released tomorrow morning. Then it'll all be over.'

'Thanks,' said Krys.

I didn't say anything as I replaced the gag, thinking once again that I was glad we hadn't killed him. He deserved it, no question, but you couldn't feel too much hate for a person in his state.

As I came out of the cellar and locked it behind me, I looked at my watch. 10.50 p.m. The others had all gone upstairs. I could hear them moving around. Yawning, I picked up the holdall from the kitchen table, checked to see that no-one had tampered with it, and went up to bed, noticing for the first time that it had stopped raining.

Today

Iversson

My eyes snapped open and I listened hard for a second. Nothing. It was dark in the room; the alarm clock by the bed said 2.57. Something had woken me. I was a good sleeper, usually went straight through, couldn't remember the last time my slumber had been interrupted naturally. I could see through the gap in the door that the landing light was on, but that was how I'd left it when I'd come into the bedroom. Maybe someone had got up to go for a leak. I sat up and waited for a few moments. Still nothing. I picked up the Glock from the side of the bed and checked that it was loaded – there was a round in the chamber – then lay back down again, thinking that I was getting paranoid. No great surprise, I suppose, when you're in a house with half a million in cash and three men with less than scrupulous backgrounds.

I shut my eyes and thought of Joe. Joe Riggs, the man who'd been good to me down the years. The man I'd betrayed by sleeping with his missus, and now the man who was almost certainly dead as a direct result of me getting him involved in a dangerous scheme when all he'd wanted to do was run a business in peace.

There was a noise downstairs. Footsteps on the bare floorboards in the hall, faint but distinctly audible. Someone was moving around down there. This time I slid out of bed, pulled on trousers and a shirt, and picked up the gun. I paused and listened again. It had stopped. I decided to investigate, just in case. The holdall was under the bed but I made the decision to leave it where it was. I'd be back in a few moments. To hinder anyone who thought they could sneak in and take it, I removed the light-bulb from the main light and placed it under the pillow.

Slowly, I unlocked the door and opened it as quietly as possible, then stepped outside, straining against the silence. The other doors on the landing were all shut, and nothing moved. Flicking the safety off the gun, I crept over to the stairs. The lights at the bottom were all extinguished, just as I'd left them, but that meant nothing. Someone had definitely been creeping about down there and, whatever the reason was, I was sure there was nothing innocent about it. Could it have been Kalinski deciding to ignore his instructions and to finish off Krys? If he had, he hadn't come back up the stairs again, nobody had. Maybe he'd taken his share and left. But then I would have heard a car start, and I hadn't.

The hairs on the back of my neck pricked up, the second time they'd done that in just over a fortnight. The first had been in the minutes before Tony Franks had started shooting, and sent us all down the rocky road to where we were now.

I took a step onto one of the stairs and it creaked loudly, interrupting the night's silence. I stood still for a moment, resisting the urge to call out the way they always do in horror films, just before they get sliced into salami by the killer. Is anyone there? If someone was, he didn't want to be discovered. Hearing nothing, I took a second step, paused, then continued down the stairs as cautiously as possible.

When I was at the bottom, I concentrated on trying to pick up any sound that might seem out of place. Breathing, the shuffling of feet ... but the dead silence remained. My eyes scanned the gloom, the darkness almost inpenetrable, only thin shafts of half-light coming through the kitchen windows.

I took two rapid steps forward and switched on all the lights to the hall, then turned and started. Because I spotted it immediately.

The cellar door was half an inch ajar. I'd definitely locked it, no question, and I'd also been the last person in there. Which meant one of two things, neither very good. Either he'd escaped, or ...

I stepped forward, and pushed the door wider. It was silent, and the air smelt fetid, as it always did. Krys Holtz had been incarcerated in there for three days. He stank, no question. I put a foot on the cellar steps, took a quick look round to check there was no-one behind me, and switched on the light.

I could see Krys's feet. So he was still there. I moved down the steps, one at a time, trying to make as little noise as possible ...

And froze.

Krys lay back in his seat, still bound and gagged, still wearing the clothes I'd left him in, but very very dead. His throat had been sliced through deeply. The head was hanging back in the seat at such a precarious angle that only the fact that it was lean-ing against the wall prevented it from toppling off altogether. Blood had turned the front of his shirt a deep crimson and it had run down onto the tops of his legs. The blindfold had been removed, too, and his eyes were wide and terrified. The killer, then, had given him advance warning of what he'd intended.

I moved closer to the body and touched the forehead. Still

warm. The flow of blood had stopped and it was coagulating rapidly round the throat region, so it was unlikely he'd been killed in the last few minutes, but it hadn't been hours ago either.

I hurried back up the steps, switched the light off, listened for a few moments to check that no-one was waiting at the top for me, and then stepped out. I walked back into the hallway, then round to the front door. It was locked. I doubled back and checked the back door of the house, which led into the utility room. Also locked. I went back through the hallway and into the kitchen, holding the Glock tightly, and went to check on the kitchen door, the last means of entry into the house.

It was unlocked. I couldn't remember if I'd checked it earlier or not, but thought I had. I'd been security conscious these past few nights, even more so since we'd taken ownership of all that money, but so much had happened that I couldn't recall anything for sure.

I stopped for a moment and thought about it. Who knew we were here? Who wanted Krys Holtz dead? Who would have bothered to remove his blindfold before he killed him? Only someone who had a personal reason for wanting him dead. Kalinski. It had to be Kalinski. I was going to have to wake the others. I turned round.

A shadow suddenly filled the doorway. I started, then brought up the gun instinctively, finger tensing on the trigger.

'What the fuck's going on?'

It was Tugger. I felt myself relaxing. 'Something very fucking bad,' I said, approaching him.

Tugger retreated, and I saw that he too was holding a gun by his side, though where he'd got it from I didn't have a clue. He lifted it so it was pointing in my direction. 'Hold on, stop there. What are you talking about?'

I stopped. 'I think Kalinski's snuffed Krys. I heard some

movement down here; it woke me up. I came down, saw that the cellar door was open, and went to take a look.'

Tugger didn't move. 'Where were you going just now?'

'I was checking the doors to see whether they were locked.'

'And are they?'

'That one isn't,' I said, motioning towards the kitchen door. 'Look, you can put the gun down now, Tugger. I'm not the one who's offed Krys.'

'You put yours down, then.'

I did. 'Look, Tug, how long have we known each other? A long time, right? I'm telling you the truth. If you don't believe me, take a look. Krys is dead and there's no way I'd want to kill him.'

He stepped over to the cellar door, and peered down, switching on the light as he did so. He watched me carefully out of the corner of his eye as he put his foot on the first step. It was funny what a lot of money did to people's personalities.

'I'm going to check on Kalinski,' I said. 'See if he's done a runner.'

At that moment, the sound of a car starting came from out front. Tugger jumped back through the cellar door. 'What the fuck?'

'Go see who it is,' I snapped. 'I'll see if Kalinski's gone.'

Once again, he gave me a suspicious look, then turned and hurried out to the kitchen door. I ran up the stairs, wondering why Johnny hadn't surfaced by now, and tried Kalinski's door. It opened immediately and I knew he'd gone, an assumption that lasted as long as it took me to reach for the light switch and flick it on.

Kalinski lay on his back under the covers of his bed, his eyes open and staring at the beamed ceiling. The pale sheets covering him were stained with blood around the chest area, and he didn't seem to have made any attempt at a struggle. I stepped forward and pulled them back. Three deep knife wounds an inch to the right of his left nipple suggested that death had been instantaneous, the result of stab wounds to the heart. Whoever had killed him had known what he was doing. But then, I already knew that, because he'd left two people dead with hardly a sound. My bedroom was right next door to Kalinski's, and I'd been lying no more than ten feet away from him while the knife was going in. And I hadn't heard a fucking thing. My luck was still holding, but only just. Whoever was trying to kill me – to kill us all – was getting closer and closer.

I thought I heard a shout from outside and it was at that point that I made a decision: something had gone badly wrong and I needed to get out of there with the money, and fast. I flung the sheets back over Kalinski, turned and ran back to my own room, knocking on Johnny's door as I passed but not bothering to wait around for an answer. I wondered whether the Holtzes had the place surrounded and who among us was the one feeding information to the other side.

I pulled on some shoes, grabbed the holdall from under the bed, and went back out onto the landing. Johnny wasn't responding. I knocked again, then opened the door. Even in the gloom, I could see that the bed was empty. What the fuck did that mean? Was Johnny the traitor? All kinds of thoughts were flying through my mind, clouding an issue that was already as murky as a peat bog. But there was no time to stand around and analyse, so I ran down the stairs and pulled open the front door.

The van we'd used for the ransom pick-up was about ten yards away in the middle of the driveway. It was in the exact spot where Kalinski had parked it earlier but the lights were on and the engine was idling. I stepped outside and looked for Tugger, but he was nowhere to be seen. The thick walls of trees on both sides of the driveway were silent and empty, but who knew what or who was behind them.

Clutching the gun in one hand and the holdall in the other, I jogged up to the driver's side of the van, keeping my head down and turning round every so often, just to check I wasn't being followed, and pulled open the door.

Johnny Hexham's body tipped out unceremoniously and I had to jump out of the way to avoid being knocked over.

'For Jesus's sake . . .'

Johnny stared blankly up at me, glassy-eyed and dead, his throat, like Krys's, cut from ear to ear. But this time the wound was fresh and bubbling, the blood still dripping down onto his shirt. Blood dribbled out of the sides of his mouth like something out of a horror film. For a moment I couldn't move, so stunned was I by the turn of events. I'd been set up, and set up beautifully, and I still didn't have a clue why, or by who. Johnny lay dead in front of me, probably murdered only a couple of minutes ago, if that, and his killer was almost certainly still in the vicinity. And where the fuck was Tugger? Had he taken out Krys and been coming after me when I'd turned round and spotted him? But there'd been no blood on his clothes. Still, that didn't mean anything. He could have changed. Could have stood out of the way of the blood's trajectory as it spurted from the wound. And what had he been doing creeping around down there?

I chucked the holdall across the driver's side and onto the passenger seat of the van, then went to jump in.

Which was when I saw the front tyre. A deep slash ran all the way down it. I looked at the back tyre. The same. Set up perfectly, absolutely perfectly. I'd never been in a situation like this, one where I was so alone, so utterly out-thought, facing an enemy I couldn't see, let alone identify, and who seemed to know every step I'd take before I'd even taken it. At that moment in time I was the most frightened I'd ever been in my life, and the most certain that this was a situation I wasn't going to get out of alive.

I stopped for a few moments to compose myself, to calm down so I could take stock of the situation. But Johnny's dead eyes continued to stare up at me like something out of some murderous, madness-inducing dream and I was forced to use every ounce of self-discipline to stop myself from falling into a blind panic.

Then I heard movement over by the side of the house. Turning round, trigger finger tensed, I saw Tugger coming back round. Shoot him, my instincts screamed. Shoot the bastard now! Except he was staggering drunkenly, not seeming to focus on anything. He stumbled, then fell to his knees, eyes making contact with mine, surprise in them, blood dribbling down his chin.

Instinctively, I started to run towards him, and that was when I saw the knife sticking straight out of his back, only an inch of blade still visible, and there was something in his eyes, and his mouth was opening in a desperate effort to speak. It looked like he was trying to warn me of something.

And then I heard footsteps coming round fast from behind the van, and the next thing I knew something smashed hard into my face, knocking me completely off balance. I felt the gun drop from my hand and I fell to my knees, my vision blurring into watery colours. Someone was standing above me and whoever it was had what looked like a sharpened spade in his hand. He hit me again, this time in the side of the head, and I felt my face smack against the concrete drive.

I was still conscious but couldn't seem to move. Vaguely, I heard my assailant walk over and pick up my gun, and I knew that this was it. The end. Strangely the blows seemed to have knocked all the fear out of me as well. My head ached ferociously and I was still having difficulty focusing, but slowly, I rolled over and lifted my head up, wanting to at least take a look at the man who was about to kill me.

'How are you feeling, Max?' asked a smiling Joe Riggs, the shovel in his hands.

Even in my dazed state, I felt the shock surge through me. 'Joe,' I managed to say, through split and bloody lips, 'what the fuck are you doing?'

'Getting payback, Max. Getting payback.'

I spat blood out of my mouth and managed to sit up. I still couldn't believe that it was Joe who'd killed Krys and the others. 'Why? What for? I thought you were dead. I kept your share. I was waiting here for you.'

'I know you were,' he said. 'I was watching. In fact, I was back here before you were.'

My whole world seemed like it was as blurred as my vision. 'Why?' I managed to ask again.

Joe stared down at me grimly. There was no humanity in his eyes, just a quiet intensity. I'd already come round to the fact that I was going to die but couldn't work out whether the bang on the head was causing me to see things or whether it really was true that my friend and business partner was going to be the one doing the killing. 'Why these blokes? Because it's business. They mean nothing to me. Not your friend, Hexham, who's a fucking coward, not Kalinski, not even Tugger Lewis. He was an OK bloke but nothing special, and I remember once he fucked me over in a game of cards. Cheated, and took money off me that wasn't his. I don't forget things like that.'

'But why me, Joe? What did I ever do to you?'

'You killed my wife, Max. You killed my wife.'

'What the fuck are you—?' I never finished the question. I saw Joe raising the spade, the metal gleaming in the moonlight, and threw up my arms to protect my face as it came crashing down on my elbows, blade first, sending a searing pain up them. I fell backwards and lay there, curled up in a ball. 'I don't know what you're talking about, Joe,' I said, my voice muffled by the fact that my arms were still pressed close to my face. 'Honest, I don't.'

'Modern technology, Max. That's your problem. You remember Dietrich Fenzer, the guy who got convicted? Well, he committed suicide six months ago, still protesting his innocence. Said he definitely saw and argued with Elsa that night but that he never killed her. Three weeks ago, I got a call from the German authorities, saying that they were reopening the case. Apparently they'd started to get their own doubts about it, and they looked again at DNA samples taken from Elsa's body at the time, and after further investigation it turned out that they didn't come from Fenzer at all.' He stopped and struck me hard across the back, making me cry out in pain. 'Too late for him, but it got me thinking back. Because you see, at the time, I knew she was having affairs with other men. It upset me, but I could tolerate it because I really fucking loved her. But I remember things she said, things that made me think that maybe one of the men she was having an affair with was you.'

'Joe, I swear—'

The spade came down again, this time on my fingers. I heard several of them break but didn't move them, knowing that to do so would invite a further blow to my exposed head. I clenched my teeth hard against the excruciating pain.

'I always tried to push those thoughts out of my head because you were Max Iversson, my good mate, my fucking drinking buddy.'

'I was. I am.'

'Like fuck you are!' he snarled, smacking me again on the

broken fingers. I wailed with the pain, my eyes watering. I wondered how much more of this I could stand. 'But then the copper who phoned me said they were looking again at the soldiers on the base at the time because they believed that several of them had been having affairs with her, and I got to thinking about how you'd been after the murder, and how jittery you were, and that maybe, just maybe, if they hadn't arrested Fenzer so quick I would have probably ended up suspecting you, even though you were my friend. And then I also thought that if you'd seen her arguing with Fenzer then maybe you could have planted the weapon you used in his house—'

'Please, Joe . . . please. I didn't do it, I swear.'

I felt the edge of the spade cut deep into my thigh as Joe brought it down with all his strength. Instinctively, I grabbed at the wound with one of my battered hands, feeling the blood gurgle out, and Joe lifted the spade high above his head ready to strike. 'Why don't you just admit it, Max? Why don't you just fucking admit it? I know you—'

The gunshot cracked across the still night air and suddenly Joe's expression changed from rage to mild surprise. He stumbled, and the spade fell from his hands, clanking loudly on the concrete. A second shot rang out, and this time he fell forwards, narrowly missing me, and rolled over. Within a couple of seconds he'd stopped moving.

Slowly and painfully, I manoeuvred my body round so I could see who the shooter was. Tugger was holding the gun, a .38 by the looks of things, different to the one he'd been holding when he'd bumped into me in the hallway. He was still lying on the ground, having propped himself up on one elbow to deliver the shots, and he looked close to death. His eyes seemed glazed and the blood was still coming out of his mouth. The knife, too, remained firmly embedded in his back.

Somehow I managed to stagger to my feet, wincing as I used my broken fingers to lift myself up. I limped over to Tugger, still holding my bleeding leg, but he was fading fast.

He rolled onto his side and coughed violently. A thick load of gluey blood and phlegm emerged, winding its way slowly towards the ground. I sat down in front of him, trying to think what I could do to save his life, but knowing it was a lost cause. His eyes tried to focus on me but they couldn't. Finally, he spoke, slowly but emphatically, the effort looking like it might prove too much for him at any time.

'I don't cheat at cards,' was all he said. Then he rolled onto his back and died.

For a long time I watched him, my mind so torn up by what had happened that I found it impossible to think straight and to come to terms with events. Eventually I forced myself to my feet and staggered towards the van, knowing that I had to get that flight to Bermuda if it was the last thing I ever did.

I had difficulty turning the key to let myself into her apartment, but managed it on the third go. It was five past seven in the morning and I looked a mess, probably the worst I'd ever looked. My eyes had been blackened, my lips were split, and I had a long, deep cut across my forehead. Three fingers were broken and the wound in my thigh looked like it might be getting infected. It had been a bastard of a journey to get here, but I'd made it.

The apartment was dark. I didn't call her name, figuring that she was probably asleep. I needed sleep too, more than I'd ever needed it. I was going to have to get myself cleaned up before she saw me, otherwise the poor woman would get the shock of her life, but it was going to have to wait.

I walked down the hall to the bedroom and slowly opened the door. It was dark in there and the curtains were drawn, but I could make out her figure under the sheets. It was the most welcoming sight I thought I'd ever seen. I put the holdall on the floor and removed my jacket and shirt, chucking them down too. When I was naked, I checked my wounds again, and saw that my thigh was still oozing blood. I was going to have to bandage it before getting in beside her.

'Max? Is that you?' Elaine sat up in bed, rubbing her eyes. 'What are you doing here? I thought you were coming back later.'

'Nothing. Don't worry. I'm coming to bed in a moment.'

She switched on the bedroom light and gasped. 'What the fuck's happened to you? Have you been attacked?'

I think I might have managed a grim smile. 'You could say that. Look, don't worry about it. I'm OK, I promise.'

'Christ, come here.' She stepped out of bed, dressed only in a baby doll nightie, and for a moment I felt my troubles fading. It's amazing what female flesh can do for a man. We embraced, and I kissed her on the mouth, ignoring the pain in my lips. 'It's good to have you back,' she whispered, looking up at me, her fingers stroking my inner thigh. In spite of everything that had happened, I began to get a hard on. 'Did you get the money OK?'

I smiled as her fingers drifted across to my balls, and motioned towards the holdall. 'Yeah, I got the money. And I think I've earned it.'

Gallan

I yawned. It was early, far too early for a Sunday, but it was all about surprise. Confront your quarry when they least expect it. However, quarter past seven on a Sunday morning could almost be construed as harassment. I was sure a clever lawyer would see it that way, but I'd worry about that later. I didn't want to waste any time. With all the absentees on the Matthews case, it was good to get the chance to speak to someone who was still actually around.

I crossed the road and walked up to the entrance of the apartment building. An attractive middle-aged lady in jogging gear was coming out. I smiled at her, and she automatically kept the door open for me to walk through. Very careless, particularly in a city like London. I could have been anyone. I didn't complain, though, since it made my job easier. Just smiled and thanked her, and she smiled back.

When I was inside, I started up the stairs.

Iversson

She pulled me towards her, kissing me hard, her tongue slithering and tumbling into my mouth like a three-legged lizard. 'We're rich, baby. Rich beyond our wildest fucking dreams.' She laughed out loud, stroking my cock while I let loose with the old moans of pleasure, beginning to forget all my various aches and pains. Bending down in front of me, she brushed her lips across my nipple, gently nibbling it, before sinking slowly down to her knees in a way that was guaranteed to bring forth a bout of premature ejaculation. I let out a thin gasp like a hamster's squeak as she slowly swallowed me up, all the time gazing up at me with those big brown bedroom eyes.

I smiled down at her, then let my eyes drift around the room as I tried to stop myself from coming, eager to prolong things as long as possible. My battered face stared back at me from the mirror on the opposite wall, grinning stupidly. I focused on it for a moment as Elaine's tongue created sensations I could hardly stand.

And then, as I was beginning to turn away, I saw it. A wicked-looking silencer coming into view. Pointing straight towards the back of my head. I heard the creak of a floorboard behind me and knew immediately that I was one second away from death.

In one single movement I threw myself against the wall, ignoring the pain as Elaine bit me in the shock of my sudden withdrawal, and lashed out with my arm, knocking the gun flying. Its owner, a stocky bloke in a baseball cap, looked momentarily shocked. I took my chance and jumped forward, grabbing him as best I could and headbutting him on the bridge of his nose. The cut on my forehead immediately reopened but the gunman had been hurt. He took a step backwards but quickly recovered himself, delivering a sudden flurry of rabbit punches to my kidneys as he struggled to break my grip.

Every part of my body seemed to be burning with pain, and blood from the head wound was dripping down my forehead and into my eyes. But I knew I couldn't give up. I had to protect us.

Summoning all my strength, I headbutted the gunman again and wrestled him through the bedroom door and out into the hallway, banging him hard against the opposite wall. His cap fell off, revealing a hairless head beneath, and for some reason this seemed to give him a renewed burst of strength, like Samson in reverse. He cursed and managed to push me away, before trying but failing to deliver a punch to my bollocks. I gasped as he got a better shot to my ribs, and took a step back as if hurt, before charging forward, head bowed like a bull, and delivering another ferocious headbutt right to the chin. Something cracked in there and the gunman made a sound half like a cough, half like a scream. Realizing my head was my best weapon, I shoved him back against the wall, then swung round so my back was facing him and delivered a skull-jarring reverse butt. His resistance simply evaporated and he slid down the wall, unconscious.

My head was spinning and my eyes stinging with blood, so much so that I could hardly see. Regaining my balance, I wiped at my face with my forearm, clearing the worst of the obstruction, and tried to focus again.

Which was the moment when the silencer hissed and a searing pain that eclipsed anything I'd yet felt surged through my shoulder, the force of it sending me reeling into the wall.

Gallan

I was just about to knock on the door when I heard a loud commotion from inside and the sound of shouting. I put my head against the wood and listened. It sounded like a fight between two men, and I wondered for a moment if I'd got the wrong place. One of the men howled in pain, and there was a crash as if they'd both just charged into a wall. They were big blokes, I could tell that from the force of the impact, and I decided that discretion was the better part of valour and that it was best just to call for reinforcement.

Then there was a pause in proceedings for a couple of seconds, followed by a faint popping sound, then a cry of pain and a dull thud.

I'd seen enough Hollywood films to know immediately that it was a gunshot from a silencer, and the damage it had done was obvious, even if I couldn't see it. I stepped back from the door and dialled the station on my mobile. The controller answered after four rings. I gave my location and called for back-up.

'I need firearms units as well as an ambulance,' I hissed into the phone. 'Someone in there is definitely armed, and it's the address of a person we need to question with reference to a murder, although I must emphasize that at the moment the person is not, I repeat not, a suspect.'

I switched off the mobile and went back to the door and listened. There were voices coming from inside, one sounding in pain, the other dominant, firm. Ruthless. I knew I should wait for reinforcements. All my training told me there was no point confronting armed suspects in an enclosed space when unarmed, particularly when it was obvious that the suspect had just shot someone. All my instincts agreed. It was a united stand. But at the same time I also knew I couldn't stand there and do nothing while someone was murdered, and from the tone of the conversation in there it sounded like that was exactly what was about to happen. Sometimes, like it or not, you simply have to stick your neck out. The alternative is the eternal knowledge that you could have done something to save a life but chose not to.

I pulled a credit card out of my pocket and, using the method a convicted burglar had once taught me, went to unlock the door.

Iversson

I was sitting back against the wall, shaking as my body went into shock. To my left lay the unconscious gunman. In front of me stood the woman I was in love with, half naked, very beautiful, and pointing a long-barrelled Browning at me, the end of the silencer only a few feet from my face. After everything else, it was a sight my mind really couldn't fathom. It felt like I'd finally cracked and this was the beginning of my short and probably one-way route to the loony-bin.

'Elaine,' I managed to say through teeth that were chattering manically. 'What are you doing?'

She managed a sympathetic smile. 'I'm sorry, Max, I really am. If it's any consolation, it's just business. Nothing else. You're actually not a bad bloke, even if Joe Riggs does say you murdered his missus a few years back; you were just in the wrong place at the wrong time. Now, I didn't want to do this – that was his job.' She motioned towards the unconscious gunman. 'In fact, it was Joe's job, but the thing is, you don't seem to want to die. And now it's left to little old me to do the dirty deed. You know something, Max, I've never shot anyone before, and I've never really wanted to either, particularly someone who was such a good lay, and in my fucking flat as well, but you know what they say, never let emotions stop you from doing your job.'

Still I couldn't get a grip on what was going on. I heard her words, delivered in a slightly weary matter-of-fact tone, saw her standing there pointing a gun at me, but none of it seemed to register. It seemed like maybe I'd fallen asleep, and that any second now I'd wake up in her arms with her stroking my head, telling me it was OK, it was just a bad dream, like my mum used to do when I was a kid.

'Elaine,' I whispered. 'I love you.' And I know it sounds stupid, but I really meant it.

'I know you do, darling,' she said, her finger tensing on the trigger. 'I know you do.'

Gallan

The door lock clicked, and slowly, ever so slowly, I pushed it open.

Peeking my head round, I saw a naked man in the hallway

about three yards away, bruised and bleeding, and apparently suffering from a bullet wound to the shoulder. He looked a mess, and he was shaking badly. Next to him lay another man in casual clothes, not moving, his head turned away. The naked man was staring into a room right in front of him, from which emerged a slender hand and forearm holding a long gun with a silencer attached, aimed at the naked man's head. I couldn't see the actual person holding the gun but I was pretty confident it was Elaine Toms, company secretary of Dagmar Holdings, who owned the flat in which I was now standing.

The naked man whispered something I couldn't quite make out but which sounded a lot like 'Elaine, I love you', and his face suggested he meant what he was saying, which was a bit unfortunate. And I thought I had problems with my love life.

I took a step forward, then another one.

'I know you do, darling,' said Elaine Toms in her slightly grating north London accent. 'I know you do.'

Her finger was tensing on the trigger, I could see it. I took another step forward, frantically calculating what I could possibly do to prevent her from killing him. The naked man's eyes were widening and his mouth was opening, though no words were coming out. He knows, I thought. He knows he's about to die.

'Armed police!' I yelled suddenly. 'Drop your weapon and come out with your hands up. You're surrounded. I repeat, you are surrounded!' My voice was loud and authoritative, probably the most it had ever been. I hoped Elaine Toms didn't recognize it from our earlier meeting.

It seemed she didn't.

'Get back!' she called out, still not showing herself and making no effort to drop the weapon. 'Get back or I'll shoot him! Don't think I'm bullshitting either. If you don't get out of this flat now

I'm going to kill him. Do you understand? And you'll be the one who's fucking responsible.'

The naked man, his face covered in blood, turned his head and looked at me quizzically, presumably wondering where my gun was.

'Drop your weapon, Miss Toms,' I demanded, desperately trying to keep the fear out of my voice. 'You are in enough trouble as it is without adding murder to your crimes. If you drop your weapon, then this will end peacefully. If you don't, then you risk being shot.'

'Retreat now or I kill him. I mean it!'

'Don't do it, Miss Toms. You are surrounded. It won't do any good.'

And then my heart sank as, still pointing the gun at the naked man's head, she stepped out of the room and into the hallway.

For a second she looked confused, then the confusion turned to annoyance. Slowly, the barrel of the gun moved round so it was facing me.

There is no feeling in the world more hopeless, more desperate, more frightening, than when you are standing looking at the end of a gun that's held steadily and calmly by someone you know is going to kill you. And impotent, too. It's an impotent feeling realizing that nothing you do or say, no pleading, no begging, nothing, is going to change the dead angle of that weapon, or prevent the bullet from leaving it and entering your body, ripping up your insides, and ending every experience, every thought, every dream you've ever had. You think about people you care about, places you've been to that you liked, and you know you're never going to see any of them again. Your guts churn, the nerves in your lower back jangle so wildly that you think you're going to soil yourself, your legs feel like they're going to go from under you like those newborn calves you sometimes see on the telly. And your eyes. You know that your eyes betray your sense of complete and utter defeat.

You are a dead man, and you know it.

And then two things happened.

First, Jack Merriweather sat up, rubbing his head and uttering the immortal words, 'What the fuck's going on?'

Second, the naked man kicked out with his right leg and struck Elaine Toms in the calf of her left one, knocking her off balance. She slipped, then fell forward, and the gun went off, the bullet ricocheting off the carpet before flying harmlessly into the ceiling. She landed on her front, gun arm outstretched, but still holding it. As she tried to right herself, I took my chance, running forward and stamping as hard as I could on her wrist. She yelped in pain, but didn't release the gun, so I stamped again, and this time she did. I pulled it up by the barrel, stepped back, resisting the urge to kick her in the face for scaring me senseless, and turned the gun round. Toms massaged her wrist, wailing in pain and accusing me of breaking it, while Merriweather continued to rub at his head and face, smearing the blood over it, still unsure, it seemed, about what was happening. The naked man simply sat where he was, shivering and silent.

'All right,' I said, holding the weapon gingerly, and praying that no-one chose this moment to make a break for it, 'everyone stay where they are.'

'I need a cloth for my face,' said the naked man, and slowly got to his feet. 'Please.'

He stood where he was for a moment, wiping the blood from his eyes. Something about him looked familiar. Very familiar, though the beard made it difficult to tell for sure.

In the distance, I could hear the sirens. 'Just stay where you are for a moment, sir.'

'Please, I need water.' He stumbled forward into the room

from which Elaine Toms had just emerged. At the same time, she started edging along the floor in my direction, eyes watching me like a hawk in search of a weakness.

I pointed the gun directly at her head. 'Do not move,' I told her.

'The man with no clothes,' she said, motioning over her shoulder, 'is Max Iversson. He's wanted for murder.'

Iversson. Shit!

I heard a window opening in the other room, and the sound of someone clambering out. A second later, a noise like a crash came from outside. I stayed put, hoping he wouldn't get far without any clothes, knowing that I had to make sure Toms didn't escape. I cursed myself for not clocking Iversson immediately. It's amazing what some blood and the Grizzly Adams look'll do to a person's face.

Toms looked like she was going to make a break for it. 'You're letting him get away,' she said mockingly.

I smiled at her, holding the gun steady. 'Then I'd better make sure I don't make the same mistake with you.'

She gave me a very unladylike sneer but didn't make any move. At the same time, the sirens seemed to close in from all sides, cars screeching to a halt in front of the building. There was a loud bang as the front door to the building was forced, followed by the sound of heavy footfalls on the stairs.

The cavalry had arrived.

Wednesday, three days later

Gallan

'So, Jack, tell me. Why were you in Elaine Toms's apartment armed with an illegal handgun and silencer?'

Merriweather looked at his solicitor, who gave a slight nod, then back at me. 'No comment,' he said, scratching absent-mindedly at the plaster on his broken nose.

'How do you know Elaine Toms?'

There was a pause. 'No comment.'

'Is it through Dagmar Holdings?' Again, he looked at the solicitor, a bald, pinch-faced individual with outsize glasses and an officious air. This was the infamous Melvyn Carroll. Again, he gave that little nod.

'No comment.'

'What do you know about Dagmar Holdings?'

'No comment.'

I sighed. 'You're not helping us much here, Jack.'

'Or yourself,' added Knox, who was sitting beside me. 'You're facing very serious charges. Charges that carry a substantial prison sentence. We're talking years, Jack, not months. Years. I suggest you think about that next time you get asked a question.'

Merriweather yawned ostentatiously. 'Are you lot going to charge me with anything or are you just going to sit here wasting my time?'

Melvyn Carroll leant forward. He smelt strongly of eau de cologne. 'My client insists he has done nothing wrong, and, as he has informed you repeatedly, has nothing further to say on the matter. I would therefore strongly request that you let him go.'

Knox and I looked at each other, then back at Merriweather. Jackie Slap stared straight ahead at me, his eyes cold. His expression was a simple one. It said: You can't touch me. I held his gaze, looking back at him expressionlessly. The room was silent for several seconds as the two of us stared each other down. Carroll opened his mouth to say something, but it was me who spoke first.

'What do you know about the murder of Robert Jones?' I asked, and something in Merriweather's expression cracked. The composure was restored within the space of a second, but it was too late. I'd caught it. I knew I was on the right track.

He shook his head slowly. 'I don't know nothing about anything like that. Never heard of the bloke.'

'You've never heard of Robert Jones, the paperboy who got murdered six months ago?'

'Oh yeah, yeah, that. I heard about it, but I don't know nothing about it. Why should I?'

'That's a good question,' said Carroll. 'What has the murder of a paperboy got to do with the charges my client is being questioned in connection with?'

'We think Mr Merriweather may be able to throw some light on the child's murder,' said Knox, emphasizing the word 'child'.

'Look, don't try to fit me up with something like that!'

'No need to shout, Jack,' said Knox.

'I'm surprised you thought you hadn't heard of him,' I continued, 'because it was, and is, a very high-profile case, and the last place he was seen alive, before he was so brutally murdered, was Runmayne Avenue where an associate of yours, Tony Franks, has a house—'

'Never heard of him.'

'And where you were seen by witnesses on a number of occasions, including only two weeks ago, when you were emptying out the property and claiming you were Mr Franks's brother.'

'I don't know what you're talking about.'

'And I don't know where this is leading,' Carroll interjected. 'I'm going to have to ask you to desist with this line of questioning. It's completely irrelevant.'

I bent down beside my chair and picked up an evidence bag. I held it in front of Merriweather's face. 'Guess what this is.'

Merriweather squinted. 'I can't see anything.'

'Look closer.' I pointed my finger at something almost intangible in the bag. 'It's a fibre, Jack, or two fibres to be precise. They came from the coat Robert Jones was wearing on the day he died, and guess what? We found them in the house you were emptying the other week. What do you think of that, then?'

'There must be some mistake.' There was no doubting the fear on his face now. Carroll also looked wrong-footed by this unwelcome new development. 'I don't know anything about a dead kid.'

'Are you sure about that, Jack?' asked Knox.

'Course I'm fucking sure.'

'How do you explain it, then?' I asked. 'How they got there.'

'It's nothing to do with me. I didn't live there.'

'Why were you emptying out the place, then?' Knox said.

'Where's Tony Franks, Jack? We can't seem to find him.'

'I don't know a Tony Franks.'

'Why were you emptying out his house, then?'

'I wasn't—'

'We've got a witness who says you were. She even spoke to you.'

'Fuck this, I don't want to answer any more questions.'

'I think my client would like a break in proceedings,' said Carroll.

'We haven't finished yet,' snapped Knox.

'*I've* fucking finished,' said Merriweather, folding his arms and making a great play of looking away.

'Don't you want to have a look at this photo?' I asked, taking it out of my pocket and sliding it along the table towards Merriweather. 'It's the last one ever taken of Robert. Christmas Day lunch last year, six weeks before he died. It's a good one, isn't it?'

Merriweather continued to look away, but I could see that his jaw was quivering.

'I really must protest about these methods. My client has already said he doesn't want to answer any more questions on this matter. I am therefore requesting, in the strongest possible terms, that you terminate this interview.'

'Were you aware, Jack, that a company called Dagmar Holdings paid the rent on Tony Franks's house?'

'I've never heard of Dagmar Holdings.'

'Really?' I said, and Merriweather immediately knew he'd made a mistake. You could see it in his eyes. 'Two cheques from Dagmar Holdings totalling a grand total of nine thousand three hundred and twenty pounds were paid into a bank account belonging to your wife, one in February, another in June. You were also at the home of the company secretary of Dagmar Holdings when we arrested you.'

'With an unlicensed firearm,' added Knox for good measure.

'As your representative, Jack, I advise you to make no further comment at this time.'

'No comment,' said Merriweather.

'One way or another someone's going down for this child murder, Jack,' said Knox. 'We're not going to rest until we find the person responsible.'

'And for some reason, you seem to be lying a lot during the course of this interview.'

'And you're connected very strongly to the house where we believe he died.'

'Where's Tony Franks, Jack?'

'No comment.'

'Did he kill Robert Jones, or did you?'

'What did you kill him for, Jack? Did he see something he shouldn't have done?'

'No comment. I told you! No fucking comment!' He turned to the brief. 'Come on, Melvyn, tell 'em I'm not answering any more fucking questions about stuff I don't know nothing about.'

'You heard my client,' said Carroll. 'He's saying nothing further at this time.'

Knox and I looked at each other and nodded. 'OK,' I said. 'We'll return you to your cells while we continue our enquiries. Before we finish, though, there's one thing I'd also like to show you.' I picked up another evidence bag, again seemingly empty. 'It's one of Robert Jones's hairs, also found at Runmayne Avenue. Amazing what you can discover when you look hard enough, isn't it?'

'Not a very good clean-up job, was it?' said Knox with a sympathetic smile.

Merriweather tried to stare us both down, tried to appear calm and aloof in the face of our threats, but it wasn't working. A single bead of sweat ran down the middle of his forehead and onto the bridge of his broken nose. He was immediately aware of it, and knew we could see it. Knew we knew.

'Interview terminated at twelve forty-five p.m.,' I said, and switched off the tape. I stood up and smiled at Merriweather. 'We'll talk again soon,' I told him.

When the two of us were safely ensconced in Knox's office, along with Berrin, we discussed what we'd gathered from the interview.

'It's still tenuous, John. If he holds out, we're in trouble. He's consistently denying his involvement with the case, and the witness statements and that little bit of forensics are hardly enough to pin him for the murder. At the moment, all he's down for is possession of an illegal firearm, which he's denying. He says it belonged to Iversson. If it carries on like this, he could easily get bail. Is there no way we can get Iversson to talk and let us know what was happening there?'

Iversson had been captured after a short but dramatic chase through the streets of Clerkenwell, but he wasn't co-operating either.

I sighed. 'He's even more of a no-comment merchant than Merriweather. Iversson's linked with the massacre at the farm and the kidnapping of Krys Holtz, so I think he figures he's got nothing to gain by talking, and nothing to lose by staying silent.'

'What about Toms? Can't we prise anything out of her?'

I shook my head. 'She knows a lot more than she's letting on but she's not stupid. Her story's that she was with Merriweather, whom she knows vaguely, when Iversson turned up and tried to rape her. He beat up Merriweather but somehow she managed to get his gun off him and shoot him in the shoulder. She claims

344

it was self-defence and it's a story she's sticking by. Therefore, in the absence of Franks, who we can't find anywhere, our best bet's got to be Merriweather. He knows what's going on, I'm sure of it, and he's got the most to lose by not co-operating.'

'But will he crack?'

'No-one wants to be labelled a child killer,' I said, 'especially a macho gangster type like him, and I don't think he's as much of a hardman as he likes to make out. Yes, in my opinion, he'll crack.'

Ten minutes later, while we were still talking, the phone on Knox's desk rang. He picked it up, listened for twenty seconds, smiled, and told the caller we'd be right down. He looked at me with the sort of expression my wife's lover would pull if he'd just stumbled on a story that would put the prime minister out of a job. 'It looks like you're right, John,' he said, and I think there might even have been some admiration in his voice. 'He wants to talk to us.'

'That's good.'

'Better than good. He wants to do it without his brief present.'

'First things first. I want immunity.'

'You haven't told us anything yet, Jack,' said Knox, lighting his cigarette for him.

'I've got stuff, all right?' he said, looking at us both in turn. 'Stuff that'll put people away, but if I help, I don't want to fuck-ing go down. I'm going to need the works. Immunity, new identity. All that shit. Understand?'

'If what you tell us is the truth,' said Knox, 'and it's a big if, and if you're prepared to testify, then obviously special arrange-ments will be put in place for you. But no decision's going to be made on that until we hear what you have to say.'

There was a long silence while Merriweather thought about

what had just been said. 'You know, I've never done nothing like this before,' he said eventually. 'I'm no grass, I'll tell you that now. If it hadn't been for that fucking kid – that's when it all went wrong.'

'What happened?' I asked, unsure whether I felt excited or depressed that we were so close to the truth.

'I wasn't even there at the time, and that's a fucking promise. I had nothing to do with it. I'd never kill a kid. I mean, I've got three of my own, haven't I? I'm no fucking nonce.'

'Let's start at the beginning, Jack,' said Knox. 'What was the house being used for?'

He took a drag on his cigarette, then answered without looking at us. 'Smuggling. A lot of the smack from eastern Europe went through that gaff. It used to get dropped by the couriers at sites in Kent and then Franks and whoever else he was using would go and pick it up and bring it back to the place for storage. We always reckoned it was the perfect cover because it wasn't the sort of place you'd expect to find gear. You know, it was a nice posh area.'

'And the gear was paid for by Stefan Holtz, right?' I said. 'It was his stuff?'

'It belonged to the organization, yeah.'

'So what's this got to do with Robert Jones?'

'Well, it wasn't just smack that was being smuggled. You see, Tony Franks, me and him both report to Neil Vamen, and there was other sidelines Neil had going that the boss, Stefan, didn't know about, because he wouldn't have approved.'

'What were they?'

'Guns, that was the main one. And not just any guns either. All sorts. Grenade launchers, AK-47s, even anti-fucking-tank missiles. You see, Tony had been a mercenary or something over there, and he got us involved with the drug-smuggling routes through Bosnia. It was his idea to do guns because we had the route set up and the place was chock-a-block with firearms. Well, Stefan never liked that idea, he didn't think we should be putting weapons in the hands of people who could use them against us, but Neil had contacts. Not just here but in Ireland, and he reckoned he could make a serious packet out of it, and there was no need to let the boss know, so that's what we did.

'It worked pretty well, too – so well that Neil began to get this idea that maybe things would be better if he ran the organization rather than Stefan. He used to say that Stefan was too traditional in the way he did business, that he didn't think big enough. A couple of years back he even got us to plant a load of rifles on Tommy Holtz to get him put away. I think Neil's idea was to start taking out the Holtzes one by one. Anyway, things were going nice, Tony's doing most of the work, I'm just checking up on him now and again, and then suddenly I get a call one morning last February from Tony saying he's got a problem. A big problem. I get round there and I can't fucking believe what I see. I still can't fucking believe it. There's this kid, this Robert Jones, and he's laid out on the floor with his paper bag, and he's dead, and Tony's standing over him with this geezer, Shaun Matthews, who used to help him out sometimes, and they're saying what the fuck are we going to do?'

He dragged hard on the cigarette, shaking his head, reliving the scene. 'First things first, I ask them what the fuck's happened, and Tony says that they was unloading some boxes in the front room full of rifles they'd taken delivery of when they heard a noise round the back. Tony goes out to take a look what it is and catches this kid, who's been looking in the window at what they've been doing. Fuck knows what he was up to. Maybe he saw them taking stuff out of the van and got suspicious, and just decided to have a butcher's. It was a stupid thing to do, whatever it was.

'So Tony nabs him and drags him inside, but now they don't know what to do with him. They know they can't let him go because he's bound to tell someone, and then that someone'll tell you lot, and you'll come sniffing round asking questions, and even if they get rid of the stuff and it's their word against the kid, Stefan'll probably find out, and it'll look bad on them. As it happens, I think they just panicked a bit as well, and Matthews, he admitted it was him, took a knife to the kid and killed him. Then they're wondering what to do with the body so they call me. Can I have another fag, please?'

Knox pushed the pack over to him and we watched as he pulled one out with shaking hands, put it to his lips, and lit it. Jackie Slap Merriweather, for all his initial bravado, was carrying a lot of guilt about with him, and had been for six months.

He exhaled loudly. 'So I tells them to get some gloves, not to touch the body unless they're wearing them, and to make it look like a nonce has done it, then get rid of the thing.'

'Did you help in that process?'

He shook his head. 'No. That kid was only a couple of years older than my oldest. I wasn't going to do nothing. It was their problem, not mine. So I left them to it, but not before I'd told them to keep their gobs shut. I didn't want Neil finding out about it.'

'So where's Tony Franks now?' asked Knox.

'Dead,' answered Merriweather.

'What happened?'

'It's a long story and, I have to tell you, it's one I can't hardly believe myself.'

'We're in no hurry, Jack. I think you may as well start talking.'

He exhaled loudly again, then began. 'Well, nothing happened for months. Obviously you lot were looking for the boy's killers but I was pretty sure we – I mean they – were in the clear because it looked like you was searching for a nonce, and I think they'd covered their tracks well enough. Then, a couple of weeks back, it all went wrong. Someone offed Shaun Matthews.'

Knox looked surprised. 'What? You don't know who?'

Merriweather shook his head. 'No. It was no-one from the organization.'

Knox and I looked at each other quizzically. This was an interesting development, and something we'd have to pick up on later.

'Anyway, as well as doing a bit of work with Tony, Matthews also ran the door at this club called Arcadia, as you probably know. Now, Neil owns Arcadia even though his name's not on the deeds, but a bloke called Roy Fowler's the one who's actually been managing it for him. But Fowler was skimming the club, taking money that was meant for Neil, and Matthews was involved as well. So, when Matthews gets topped, Fowler panics, thinks we're on to him, which we were, and thinks we're going to kill him, which we weren't. Not as far as I knew anyway. 'The problem is, though, Fowler's convinced he's a dead man, so he takes evasive measures.'

'What sort of evasive measures?' I asked.

'Blackmail. You see, he's got something up his sleeve he's been keeping as a bargaining chip for just this sort of eventuality. In fact, he's got two things. He's got a tape recording he made of a conversation he had with Matthews, and in this conversation Matthews, who as it happens was pissed, is talking about the weapons scam and how it's run by Vamen, and also what happened with the kid. Just the sort of tape you don't want falling into the hands of Stefan Holtz. But he's got something worse as well. He's got the knife that killed the kid.'

'How the hell did he get hold of that?' demanded Knox.

'I honestly don't know. Maybe Matthews panicked when they

got rid of the body, kept it for a while, then gave it to Fowler to get rid of.' He shrugged. 'I couldn't tell you. But, either way, Fowler decided to hang on to it, just in case it ever proved useful, and so, when Matthews died and he suddenly thought he was next, he sent a message to Neil saying that he had this incriminating stuff and that if we tried to do anything to him he'd make sure Stefan and the Old Bill got to hear about it. He also said he wanted a hundred grand so that he could get out of the country, and if Neil gave him that, then he'd hand over the knife and the tape.

'So Neil, who's none too pleased to find out about the dead kid, arranges to meet up with Fowler to do the exchange. At the same time, he finds out from Elaine Toms, who's like his eyes and ears in Arcadia, that Fowler's going to be getting his security from Tiger Solutions. Well, Tiger's run by a bloke called Joe Riggs, who's a bit of an associate of Neil's, nothing major, but he's had some involvement in the weapons side through Tony. So we set it up that Tony would be on the team taking Fowler to the meet. He'd deal with Fowler, and anyone else who got in the way, and take back the evidence. End of story, end of problem.

'Except it didn't work out like that. Joe's been rumbling on about his partner, Iversson – the naked bloke you nicked – for a long time, and even thinks that Iversson might have offed his missus – that's Joe's missus – years back. So, when it's all set up, Joe makes sure that Iversson's one of the ones escorting Fowler, because he wants Tony to take him out as well. Only problem is, Iversson was a bit tastier than Tony was prepared for, and Tony was the one who got shot.'

'So Iversson didn't have anything to do with the murder of Fowler?'

He looked at me. 'No. He didn't have a clue what was going on. The thing was, though, he was now a fucking complication. He knew what had happened, plus you lot were after him, so things could have got very dodgy if he'd been picked up.

'We were still thinking what to do about him when he turns up at the Arcadia and ends up in the sack with Elaine Toms, who, as it happens, is one of Neil's exes and a girl he's got a real soft spot for. They were going to have Iversson killed round her flat, which was where he was staying after you lot started looking for him, but then Neil has a bit of an idea. A better way of dealing with him. Like I said earlier, Neil's been looking to move in on Stefan for a while, but it was never going to be easy because Stefan didn't move from that fucking house of his, and he's guarded to the hilt. Plus, Neil doesn't want to be seen to do anything that'll make him look disloyal. Far better to get someone else to do it. So he gets Elaine to push Iversson into kidnapping Krys because he knows that's the only way he's going to get Stefan out into the open. Joe helps her set everything up, Krys gets lifted, and when Stefan turns up at the rendezvous with the ransom money, he gets popped by our people. And the beauty of it is that no-one suspects Neil at all.'

'What happened at the farmhouse?' asked Knox. 'We found Riggs's body there, as well as a number of others, including Krys Holtz's.'

Merriweather sighed. 'That was Riggs's fault. He was meant to sort out Krys and Iversson and leave their bodies there so that Iversson would get the blame for everything, but that fucker's got a real knack for staying alive, and it was Riggs who got killed. When Riggs didn't show up to say that it had all been sorted, we had to take our own evasive action. We thought Iversson would head for Elaine's so I went round there, just in case she couldn't handle things, and that's where you found me. She tried to kill him, he attacked her, and I just got in the way.'

'What about Shaun Matthews?' I asked. 'Who killed him if it was no-one from your own organization?'

'Christ knows,' said Merriweather. 'Who the fuck poisons anyone anyway? It's a recipe for getting caught these days, what with all them technological advantages you lot have got.'

'Our information strongly suggests that Matthews's girlfriend of a number of months was also a mistress of Neil Vamen.'

'Who's that, then?'

'Her name's Jean Tanner.'

For the first time in the interview, Merriweather laughed, although there wasn't much humour in it. 'Oh yeah, you were on about her in the Seven Bells the other week, weren't you? Nah, I wouldn't put it quite like that. They went out for a little while – old Neil likes to have a few girlfriends – but it was all over way back.'

'When?'

He shrugged. 'I dunno, four, five months ago? But she was a right weirdo. Used to work in Heavenly Girls, but even the punters stayed a bit clear of her. She was nice looking, and all right when you first met her, but, I dunno, it's difficult to put your finger on, but something about her wasn't quite right, know what I mean? I know old Neil was glad to get rid of her. As it happens, I think she was the first girl he'd ever been with who actually scared him – not that he'd ever admit it, of course.'

'So, what about Craig McBride?' I asked.

'Craigy? They said he died of a smack overdose, didn't they? Not that I ever saw him take any. Always thought he was more of a coke man myself. He died round her place, didn't he?'

'That's right.'

'Well, it wouldn't surprise me if she'd helped him along.'

'Why would she do that?'

'I dunno, maybe he was annoying her or something. The thing is with her, she was the sort you could imagine doing something like that, do you know what I mean? She was dodgy.'

'And it takes one to know one, eh, Jack?' said Knox.

'Whatever.'

We all sat in silence for a while while Merriweather sucked up what was left of his latest cigarette.

'So, do you think she could have killed Matthews, too?' asked Knox eventually.

He shrugged again. 'Fuck knows. That's for you to find out, isn't it?'

Monday, eight days later

Gallan

But we never did find out who poisoned Shaun Matthews.

Five days on, and after much internal discussion, the likeliest scenario suggested that, for whatever reason, Jean Tanner had been the one. The theory, agreed by all the original investigating team, but with absolutely no evidence whatsoever to back it up, was that there had been some sort of relationship between Tanner and Matthews, but it had ended before his death and, for whatever reason, there'd been bad blood between the two of them. Being a girl who liked to throw her favours around, she was also seeing Craig McBride, and had got him to supply her with the poison to get rid of her ex-boyfriend. McBride was the only person we could think of who might have had the means to obtain it, almost certainly when he'd been out in Bosnia. He was also stupid enough to think that he could get away with it by making Matthews's death look like an accident. Jean had undoubtedly thought the same way, and had administered the fatal dose to her unsuspecting ex.

Then, a few days later, we'd paid a visit to McBride and he'd panicked, thinking we were getting too close. He'd gone round to talk to Jean, they'd had an argument, and at that point she'd decided that he was now a liability. Maybe he'd been suggesting she come clean and tell the police, or something like that.

Jean had acted decisively. Somehow, she'd managed to obtain and inject him with a huge quantity of heroin and, unable to get rid of the body, had left to plan her next move, before finally deciding that it was probably best to return and make out that the whole thing had been an accident. Burley, then, had probably not been as corrupt as I'd first thought and, rather than trying to protect her as a favour to Vamen, he was simply being too lazy to do his job properly, and his obnoxiousness was natural rather than artificially created. Fair enough. Hopefully some day, someone in charge would notice it, and he'd suffer as a result.

We'd brought Jean Tanner in for questioning and Berrin and I had kept her in for twenty-four hours while we'd interrogated her. She might have been a weirdo (although I have to say I found her to be pretty level-headed) but she was no fool and, knowing that the police had nothing on her bar theories, had denied everything. She didn't know who'd killed Shaun, she hoped they caught whoever it was, and, as for Craig McBride, that had been a tragic accident that had taught her the dangers of drugs. When I'd pointed out that McBride had had a phobia about needles, her jaw had dropped, her eyes had widened, and she'd simply said, 'Really? How odd.' In the end, we'd had to let her go. Berrin had been pissed off, and was particularly concerned that a woman who might well have committed two murders in the space of a couple of weeks was walking the streets unmolested.

'Let me tell you something,' I'd told him. 'Crime can some- times be a good short-term career move, sometimes it can even be quite a good medium-term one, but I promise you this, it's never a good long-term one. They all get caught in the end. If she is a psycho and she really did kill those two blokes, then somewhere down the line, she'll try it again, and she'll come unstuck. In the meantime, just make sure you don't ever go out with her.'

'Do you think she did it?' Berrin had asked.

'Thinking it and proving it are two very different things. If I can't prove it, then I prefer not to make a judgement. Probably is all I'd say. Probably.'

It was a sunny morning in early September and I was walking down Cleveland Street towards the Middlesex Hospital. My mobile rang. It was Malik.

'John, how are you?' His tone was cheery, which wasn't really a surprise. The object of his last year-and-a-half's work, the Holtz family and their immense criminal enterprise, was finally unravelling. Some might even say it had something to do with my perseverance.

'I'm well, Asif. You?'

'Very good. Look, the reason for my call, it's a thanks, really, for all the work you've done, and to let you know that this morning we arrested Vamen and six of his associates on a whole variety of charges relating to their activities. And Merriweather's continuing to sing like the proverbial canary.'

'I'm glad he's proving useful. It's a pity he's got to get immunity, though.'

'Well, he's not going to get full immunity. There are a couple of charges he's going to be facing, and he might get a nominal spell inside.'

'Not nearly as much as he deserves, though.'

'You know the score, John. Sometimes you've got to swallow your principles when you're dealing with people like that. Whatever happens, he's a marked man for the rest of his life. I'd rather not be in his boots.'

'Any sign of the bodies? Franks and the others?'

'We're still searching that maggot farm but I'm not optimistic. The maggots will have eaten all the flesh and apparently the bones were ground down afterwards. It seems they've done it with a few people.'

'I bet they have. What about the knife in the Robert Jones murder?' Merriweather had told us that Joe Riggs had been at the Fowler murder scene that night, and had retrieved the knife and the tape from Fowler's briefcase while the nightclub owner was being murdered. He had then weighed down the objects in a strongbox, and chucked them in the Thames.

'Nothing yet, but we're still looking.'

'I think that's my only regret in all this,' I said, 'that we didn't get a chance to bring either Franks or Matthews to trial for the killing.'

'In a way it's better this way, isn't it? There wasn't a huge amount of evidence against them. They could easily have got off, and then the family would have been devastated. At least now they know that the people who took their son away have paid a pretty heavy price.'

I wasn't so sure. All we had was Merriweather's word for that. Maybe he'd been more heavily involved than he'd let on, which would have explained why he'd co-operated so quickly when it had become obvious to him that the police were on the scent. If so, he was going to get off scot-free.

Malik asked me if I'd kept the family informed of what had been going on. 'I have as much as possible. I think they realize now that no-one's ever going to go to prison for the murder but, like you say, maybe it's better this way.' Not that I really believed it.

'I'm going to have to buy you lunch sometime soon,' said Malik. 'When things have settled a bit. I'll give you a call, OK?'

'Sure,' I said, doubting if I'd be eating a slap-up meal on SO7 for a while yet. 'That'd be nice.'

We said our goodbyes, and I walked into the hospital entrance.

Iversson

I was sitting up in bed in my hospital room and thinking about how I was going to get out of this situation. It didn't look good. They had two armed coppers guarding me in shifts round the clock. I was obviously a real VIP. Very Important Prisoner, that is. One thing was for sure, I wasn't going to be fighting my way out. Not only was I absolutely fucking exhausted, I also had a minor blood infection, and the wound in my shoulder was making the use of my right arm next to impossible. I was just going to have to front it and hope for the best. I'd thrown the Glock into a wheelie bin in Clerkenwell while I was on the way back to Elaine's apartment on that final, fateful day when the bitch had finally showed her true colours, so at least there was no way that could be used against me. Most of my co-conspirators were dead, and if Elaine and whoever the gunman with her was didn't break (and I had no reason to think they would), I might just be able to scrape through unscathed. I'd been taught anti-interrogation techniques back in my army days so I was reasonably confident I could hold my own, even in my weakened state. As the days had passed and my wounds had slowly healed, so my pecker – battered so badly (quite literally) by my experience with Elaine, and Joe's betrayal – was finally going back up again. I will tell you something about me: I am nothing if not resilient.

I'd almost escaped, too, even after all the shit those bastards had put me through. While Gallan had been occupied by Elaine and the bloke with her, I'd grabbed the holdall with the money, opened up the window, and chucked it onto the roof of a parked Audi before jumping out myself and landing arse-first on the holdall and the roof. Unfortunately, in my haste, and due to my somewhat disorientated state, I'd neglected to put any clothes on and, though I'd made a manful bid for freedom, limping naked along the street with near enough half a million quid on my back, I was always going to look a little bit too conspicuous to be able to melt, commando-like, into my surroundings. I did manage about two hundred yards, though, with half a dozen coppers chasing me Benny Hill-style on foot, before a vicar, of all fucking people, who was cycling to his morning church service, had leapt from his environmentally friendly transport and rugby-tackled me from behind. That was it, then. I'd had enough. With even men of the cloth against me, I knew it was the end of the road.

But since then I'd perked up. You know what they say: it ain't over till it's over. Believe it.

I leant over and picked up the book I was reading: *How to Get Ahead in Business*. You see, I was thinking of opening my own survival school, and after all that had happened there weren't going to be many people better placed to teach survival than me. It was going to have to be from scratch, of course, now that the ransom money from the Holtz job had been lifted by the forces of law and order, but I knew it could be done.

There was a knock on the door and I looked up. It was Gallan again, looking quite spruced up by his standards, a smile on his face.

I tell you, I didn't trust that bastard one inch.

Gallan

'Hello, Max,' I said, entering the room. I stopped at the end of the bed. 'The doctors say you're healing fast. Should be out of here in a few days.'

'That's right, and when I do, I don't want you lot on my back. I've co-operated as much as possible and I'm not saying anything else, apart from I don't know what the fuck you're talking about with all this kidnapping and killing lark. Is that clear?'

I smiled, used to Iversson's clumsy attempts at putting me in my place. 'Clear as a bell.'

'Because I've got bigger fish to fry now.' He showed me the book he was reading. *How to Get Ahead in Business*. Somehow I didn't think Richard Branson would be quaking in his boots. 'I've always been legit, and that's how I intend to stay. I've held up my hands to that assault on those coppers who stopped me, but I was under duress at the time. So, I'm hoping to get bail, and to start again.'

'I don't think that's going to happen, Max.'

Iversson's expression hardened. It wasn't a pretty sight. 'Why the fuck not? I haven't done anything. If it's about that money, I had nothing—'

I held up my hand to quieten him. 'It's nothing to do with the money you were carrying.' Looking surprised, he stopped speaking. 'Max Iversson, I'm here to inform you that you are under arrest at the request of the German federal authorities who wish to question you with regard to the murder on the twenty-sixth of February 1993 of Elsa Kirsten Danziger.'

Iversson looked at me in utter disbelief, then seemed to slump in the bed. 'I don't believe this. You'll be blaming me for John F. fucking Kennedy next.'

He really looked put out, and I might even have been tempted to believe him if I hadn't already heard that the sample of DNA taken from him in the hospital a week earlier had been confirmed as matching that of the killer. He was one of the better liars I'd come across.

I turned slowly and walked away, thinking it was ironic that we would probably never solve the Matthews case, yet its investigation had almost single-handedly provided the clues that had successfully concluded so many others. As I thought about Neil Vamen languishing in a cell of his own design, it also proved my point that crime might have been a viable short-term business opportunity, but as a long-term career it was always the wrong move. And as the technological aids open to the police become more and more advanced, so even the crimes of the short-timers will come back to haunt them. Be sure your past will always find you out, as a preacher might say.

When I got back to the station, I went straight to the Matthews incident room, now the incident room for the investigation into the attempted murder of eighteen-year-old Barry Sevringham, knifed in the neck the previous night in a pub fight in King's Cross. The world was already moving on, as were the criminals, never ones to sit around. Berrin was in there, as was WDC Boyd. Everyone else, I assumed, was out talking to witnesses and possible suspects. They both smiled at me as I walked in, and I thought that Boyd was looking good. She had red lipstick on, and it suited her. I hadn't seen much of her these past couple of weeks and it struck me then that I'd missed her company. Maybe I'd see a bit more of her now we were working on the same case. I hoped so.

'The DCI'd like to see you,' said Berrin, motioning towards the office he'd been using for the Matthews inquiry.

'Do you know what it's about?'

They both said they didn't, but I thought I saw the traces of a smile on Boyd's red lips. I knocked on the door and went in.

'John,' said Knox, who was sitting behind the desk, 'come in and sit down.'

I did as I was told. 'What can I do for you, sir?' I asked.

'Your work's been excellent these past few weeks,' he answered, and waited briefly for the obligatory thanks, which he got, before continuing. 'Thanks in no small part to your efforts, and your persistence in the Matthews inquiry, it looks like we've got a number of results. The north London underworld's in a lot of trouble as a result of the dismantling of the Holtzes, and it's particularly good to be able to close the file on the Robert Jones case, and to give his family some sort of opportunity to move on. I've recommended to the superintendent that you be commended for your work on the Jones case, and I've also got a letter here from SO7 stating how much help your work's been.'

'Thank you, sir. It's always nice to be appreciated.'

'But that's not what I asked you in here for.'

'Oh?'

'I want you to know that I've also recommended that you be considered for a DI post here at the station, and that the recommendation's been accepted.'

I allowed myself a smile. 'That's excellent, sir. Thanks very much. I wasn't aware there was actually a vacancy.'

'Well, an unexpected one's come up on this team,' said Knox. 'DI Capper's asked for a transfer, and he's moving on to another station.'

'Really? I thought he was very happy here.'

Knox didn't say anything for a moment, clearly debating with himself how much it was worth letting on. 'Suffice to say some information came in from an anonymous source that didn't cast him in a very positive light, and it seems that a number of officers in the station are aware of it. He didn't think his position here was tenable and he's moving to another division next week. He's also dropping back down to DS level.'

So, there was justice in this world, and, more importantly, in the Metropolitan Police.

'Between you and me,' he added in a loud whisper, 'it turns out he was something of a regular visitor to Heavenly Girls, which put him in a bit of a compromising position, and we can't afford that. Better to get him out of the way rather than have the embarrassment of him remaining here with everyone knowing about it.'

Somehow I managed to keep the smile off my face. 'It's bad news losing such an experienced officer,' I said worthily, remembering that it's always best to play the game.

I wondered who it was who'd dobbed him in. It was either Jean Tanner or Berrin. Jean had told the two of us when the tape had been off that he'd been a long-standing and not particularly well-liked customer at Heavenly Girls (apparently he had a lot of difficulty getting it up, an unfortunate affliction for which he tended to blame the girls). I suspected that it might have been Berrin. Just a hunch, but it made sense. Jean was too much of a cold-blooded pro. Me, I would have kept the information to myself. You never know when it might have come in useful.

'So, you'll take up the post, then?'

Wild horses wouldn't have stopped me. 'Of course I will, sir. When's it effective from?'

Knox smiled. 'Now,' he said. 'You're in charge of the Barry Sevringham case. Here's what we've got so far.'

Iversson

I never meant to kill her, that's all I can say. I'm going to be pleading not guilty by reason of temporary insanity, or whatever the defence is these days. There was no way I was in the right frame of mind when I bashed her head in that night. I'd been driven mad by her constant shagging of other men, and women, plus the fact that she didn't care one fucking whit that I knew about it. And that Johnny Hexham reckoned he had girlfriend problems! He should have hung round with Elsa for a few days. She went through bodies like an overworked mortician. In the end, it just got too much, I snapped, and the rest is history. It was bad what I did, and I feel terrible about it, but I'm not the only villain in all this. She brought a lot of it on herself. And that Fenzer did smack her around a bit earlier on that night, I saw him do it. I heard that he often hit women, so he got what he deserved as well, didn't he?

Anyway, who the fuck ever said life was fair? Not Max Iversson, that's for sure. Never has been, never will be.

Epilogue

Max Iversson was charged with the kidnapping of Krys Holtz, and is currently in custody awaiting trial. He has also been charged in absentia with the murder of Elsa Danziger, and is the subject of extradition proceedings being brought by the German government.

Neil Vamen was charged with murder, extortion and importation of Class A drugs, and is currently awaiting trial. None of the charges relate to the events covered here.

Jack Merriweather is being held in a segregation unit at Belmarsh Prison, London, where he too faces charges relating to the importation of Class A drugs. He is to be the prosecution's main witness in the trial of Neil Vamen and six of his associates.

Elaine Toms was charged with the attempted murder of Max Iversson but was granted bail and promptly absconded. She is currently at large.

Jean Tanner has a new boyfriend and as yet faces no charges in connection with either the murder of Shaun Matthews or Craig McBride. Police are keeping a close eye on the boyfriend's health.

Asif Malik remains at SO7, where he's concentrating his investigation on several north London crime families who have had something of a bonanza since the collapse of the Holtzes.

And me, well, I'm a DI again, and at least halfway back to the position I was in a year ago.

You see, there is justice in this world. It's just that sometimes it can take a long time to show itself.

Acknowledgements

Briefly, I'd like to thank the following people for their help in getting this book to where it is now: Selina Walker, my editor at Transworld; Amanda Preston, Amelia Cummins, Vanessa Forbes, Luigi Bonomi, and everyone at my agent's, Sheil Land Associates; all those at New Scotland Yard Press Office who've provided invaluable technical assistance with their customary efficiency and courtesy; and last but most definitely not least, my long-suffering wife, Sally, who's always been there to provide encouragement and support. As well as the occasional much-deserved kick up the arse.

I raise my glass to you all.